BOOK STORAGE

BOOKS BY MICHAEL PEARSON

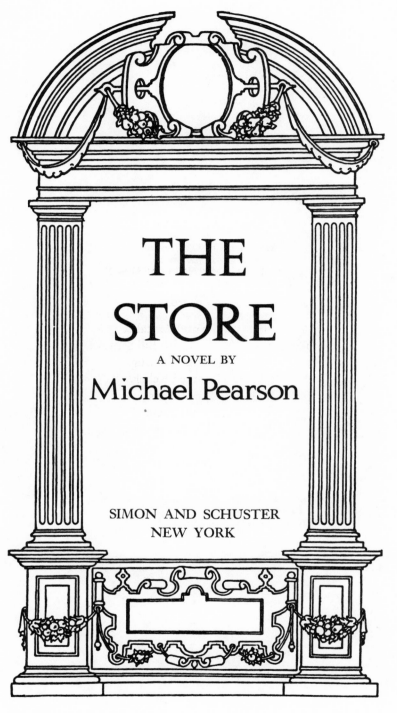

THE
STORE

A NOVEL BY

Michael Pearson

SIMON AND SCHUSTER
NEW YORK

Copyright © 1981 by Michael Pearson
All rights reserved
including the right of reproduction
in whole or in part in any form
Published by Simon and Schuster
A Division of Gulf & Western Corporation
Simon & Schuster Building
Rockefeller Center
1230 Avenue of the Americas
New York, New York 10020
SIMON AND SCHUSTER and colophon
are trademarks of Simon & Schuster
Designed by Edith Fowler
Manufactured in the United States of America

1   2   3   4   5   6   7   8   9   10

Library of Congress Cataloging in Publication Data

Pearson, Michael.
  The store.

  I. Title.
PZ4.P3626St   1980   [PR6066.E218]   823.'914
     80-18266
ISBN 0-671-25114-7

FOR KATIE

Contents

Book One

September 1869

· I ·

As the four-wheeler traveled along Knightsbridge on that sunny Wednesday afternoon, a thought came to Thomas that brought a slow smile to his lips. This journey, he mused, was historic. This short cab drive from the big draper's shop on Ludgate Hill, with the same battered old trunk that his mother had dragged out of the shed on the farm eleven years before, would become famous. His children would describe it to their children, would tell them with wonder how, at a few minutes to five on September 1, 1869, their grandfather had arrived in Sloane Street to found the great house of Kingstons—in a dirty old cab, drawn by a mangy horse, driven by an elderly cabby with a dented hat.

Thomas' ruminations, as he quickly reminded himself, were a fanciful indulgence for a man who had only just collected the keys to his first small rented shop; but his daydreaming was not utterly lacking in realism. He had, after all, selected his site after months of study of different London districts. He had decided his policy—his merchandise, his market, his presentation—only after the most detailed and intricate planning, for which he was well experienced. More than a decade had passed since he had come to London, as a thirteen-year-old, to start his apprenticeship in the drapery trade.

His capital was not large, of course—only seven hundred pounds —but many substantial enterprises had been founded in premises that were just as small—and had thrived in conditions that were far less favorable than the affluent England of today.

The cab passed the stucco facade of the Alexandra Hotel. From its big windows the guests could look across the traffic of Knightsbridge at the wide panorama of Hyde Park, where at that moment, as Thomas could see through the railings, the fashionable in their open carriages were taking part in the usual afternoon parade beside the Row.

It was a scene he had witnessed often enough, and at that moment he was more interested in Wilton Place, which they were approaching on the left. As they went by, he savored the glimpse of the big houses that lined both sides of the crescent beyond it—and the knowledge, gained from hours of walking over the past weeks, of others that were just as impressive in the neighboring squares and streets. For they were the reason he had chosen the district for his venture. Those elegant buildings, which had not existed fifty years ago, were now the homes of the wealthy.

The cabby eased his horse to a walk as they joined the slow-moving congestion of omnibuses, carriages and hansoms caused by the intersection of the Kensington Road and Edinburgh Gate, then turned off into Sloane Street, heading south in the direction of the river, until after a couple of minutes he drew up beside the curb. That was the moment when Thomas' wishful dreaming vanished. For a few seconds he remained seated, his spirits falling as he stared at the shop he had rented—at the dirty windows, at the peeling paint of the fascia, at the chipped gas lanterns. Suddenly he felt ashamed of the surge of optimism he had just experienced. Could these depressing premises ever become the great house of Kingstons?

"Is this where you want, sir?" the cabby asked dubiously, turning from his box.

Thomas roused himself. "Yes," he answered with a sigh. "Yes, this is right."

He stepped from the cab, crossed the pavement and unlocked the shop door. Immediately, he was conscious of the smell of dust—heavy dust, layer upon layer, that had long been undisturbed. The shop had been empty for months, but in the proper hands, so the estate agent had assured Thomas, it could become a thriving establishment. Sloane Street, he said, was improving as an area. It did not have the passing trade of Knightsbridge, of course, which was why the rent was so low, of course; there were not so many people about, of course. But there were *enough* people about, Thomas reminded himself sharply to check his deepening gloom, as he knew for a certain fact. Before finally signing the lease, he had stood outside the shop for hours at different times of day counting the number of ladies who went by its windows.

The cabby helped him carry the big trunk up the stairs to the higher floor where Thomas planned to sleep—and then, pocketing the two shillings and sixpence he gave him, left him standing alone in that desolate emptiness listening to the fading sound of the horse's hooves as they merged with the noise of the street.

Thomas' depression was unfamiliar. He liked to think of himself as a man of firm resolution. The first time he had stood there a few weeks

ago, surrounded by that thick dust, he had found the experience exciting. He could still see the word "Kingstons" that, in a moment of
exuberance, he had written with his finger in the dirt on the top of the
counter. So why was he so strangely unnerved now? Was it because he
was facing reality at last, the need to prove in practice instead of plan
in theory? Well, prove it he would. He had intended to employ some
charring women to clean up the shop, but its appalling state made him
unable to leave it in that condition a moment longer. He ripped off his
coat with a movement that was almost savage and stalked through the
shop into the little scullery at the rear. He found a broom, balded thin
by wear, a bucket and a tattered rag, left by the previous tenant
presumably because they were not worth taking away. Also, strewn
untidily in a corner was a pile of old show cards, mostly advertising
boots, which had evidently been the trade previously conducted in the
shop.

Thomas selected the cleanest of the cards and wrote on the plain
white back the words:

OPENING SHORTLY

THOS. KINGSTON

Fancy goods and lace.
Assistants wanted—Enquire within.

He went into the front of the shop, wiped the dust from a section
of the window, and fixed his notice so that it could be seen from the
street.

Then, filling the bucket from the scullery tap, he started on the
mammoth task he had set himself of cleaning up the shop, wiping the
dirt off the counter and shelving with his damp rag, sprinkling water
on the floor to make it easier to sweep. And as he held the broom he
heard old Clegg's awful rasping voice as if he were standing there
beside him. "Too much dust, mister! God damn your eyes, mister,
that's too much dust! Closer to the floor with that broom, mister, God
damn your eyes, or you'll have the stock disgusting!" Clegg, the heavy-
goods buyer at John Parsons, had dominated his life throughout his
apprenticeship like a malign giant. With his flat hat, like a parson's, and
bloodshot eyes, he had been a constant scourge to David Rawlings, the
other apprentice, and himself—especially after lunch, when he would
come back from the pub, his face flushed, the whiskey strong on his
breath.

Still, Clegg had taught them a lot. He had studied customers for years like a fox outside a chicken run. He understood the psychology of a woman when she walked into a shop. Despite his grossness, he could puff up a roll of muslin in a way that was almost sensual. Often Thomas had seen him sell an item that had been sticking long enough to carry an extra "tinge" commission by presenting it as special—sometimes by wrapping it in tissue paper and keeping it under the counter. "Well, madam, there is this line that actually we've been keeping for another customer but it would appear . . ."

On occasion, in fact, Thomas had watched bemused as he employed the same technique with something she had already seen. "Swap that," Clegg would growl at him quietly, while he took the customer carefully to another part of the shop. And Thomas would wrap up the shawl or the print and take it over to him so that he could deploy the "swap" trick. "Ah, yes," the buyer would say, taking it from him, "there was this really rather fine piece of silk that I 'ad quite forgotten about until suddenly it came to my mind." With delicate care, as though it were so fine that it might disintegrate if he held it too firmly, he would remove it from the tissue—and to Thomas' astonishment, the lady would have no idea that she had already refused it.

Lying had been an inherent part of Clegg's nature. He was always insisting that merchandise came from Paris or Brussels, even when it came from Halifax. "They like to buy things from the Continent," the buyer would say. "It gives them a nice feeling. I like to give ladies nice feelings."

Clegg came from a world of shopkeeping that was changing—a world of false selling, of concentration on the immediate sale. "The bird in the 'and, mister," he would say. "Don't you forget it, mister. It's the bird in the 'and wot counts."

Thomas had learned all that Clegg could teach him, but he planned to establish a very different sort of business. He had witnessed the downfall of a number of shops during his years in the trade—especially during the cotton shortage that resulted from the American Civil War and the slump of '65—and he had studied the reasons for their failure. He was convinced that the most important asset a business could possess was a high reputation, that no great enterprise had ever been founded on the philosophy of a bird in the hand.

For the fifth time in half an hour, Thomas filled the old bucket with clean water from the tap in the scullery and returned, water slopping over the rim, to the shop. It was then that he saw her standing in the doorway.

She was not tall—indeed, she was slight; yet she had stature. She stood almost stiffly upright, her tall bonnet compensating for her lack of height, and the impression she gave was of collected neatness. Everything about her—the way she held her hands, with her arms tucked closely to her sides, the tilt of her head—was precisely positioned, almost as though she had practiced it in front of a mirror. She had small, rather pert features and dark hair that was pinned tightly in curls to the back of her head under her bonnet. Her nose and the upper part of her cheeks were heavily freckled, which no doubt she regretted, though it suited her, but if they were a flaw, nature had compensated her with large, expressive brown eyes.

Thomas, completely taken by surprise, just stared at her for a few seconds, feeling awkward in his shirt sleeves, and it was she who broke the silence. "I was passing . . ." she said. "I saw your notice . . . for assistants"—adding, it seemed almost with difficulty, ". . . sir." She spoke with a degree of deference, as was fitting to a potential employer, but her frank eyes belied the tone.

"You're looking for a position?" Thomas asked, studying her. She was very young. Nineteen perhaps. Probably younger. "Do you have any experience of the trade?"

She knew what he was thinking; knew, too, the effect her answer would have on him. "I've worked for Shoolbreds for two years," she said. "In Fancy Goods until eight months ago. Since then I've been in Drapery."

It was an impressive background, for there was no other shop in London that had the reputation of Shoolbreds of Tottenham Court Road. Suddenly, Thomas realized that he was still holding the bucket. Clumsily, he put it down, slopping water on the floor as he did so. Instinctively, he looked around as though to offer her a chair. "I fear, Miss . . ." He broke off.

"Ramsay," she prompted. "Miss May Ramsay."

"Miss Ramsay. As you can see . . ."

"I'm content to stand," she said, looking around her dubiously. "You plan to do a fancy trade here?"

Thomas nodded. "Ribbons . . . Foreign ribbons in particular . . . Lace too, of course . . . and trimmings and a bit of haberdashery. To start with, that is . . . I believe in doing a small trade well—to provide a sound base on which to build."

"Build?" she queried, conscious of the dirt and dilapidation that surrounded her, and realized at once that her note of doubt had touched a sensitive area in him.

"I don't intend to run an establishment as small as this for the rest of my life," he said, "though you may think this premature . . ."

"I'm sure it's good to be ambitious . . . sir," she answered.

"Indeed I'm ambitious," he insisted. "I've big plans. In fact, from this small shop I intend to create an emporium."

He looked straight at her, defying her to question him, and saw her glance round the room—at the faded blistered paint, at the dirty floor that had not yet been swept, at the broken fittings, at the chipped lanterns standing crooked over the gas mantles—and then back at him, standing there with wet, grimy hands. "An emporium," she repeated without expression. Then, to his embarrassment, she was suddenly gripped by a fit of uncontrollable convulsive laughter. She bent forward, her body shaking with near-hysterical giggling, both hands covering her face.

Thomas watched her unhappily as she fought to compose herself. She was appalled by her lapse. When at last she could speak, she apologized. "I'm sorry . . . it's just that . . ."

"It's hard to imagine?" His tone was gentle, supported by the glimmer of a smile.

She nodded. "Well . . . a bit."

The softness left his face. "If you're going to work for me, Miss Ramsay, you're going to have to be able to imagine. Nothing was ever created without imagining. May I remind you that Shoolbreds was not always a large business."

Her big eyes widened. "You believe you can build an enterprise like Shoolbreds?"

"Better," said Thomas. He was challenging her to laugh again. "And bigger. Far bigger."

"Than Shoolbreds? There's nowhere bigger than Shoolbreds."

"Kingstons will be. The concept'll be bigger, for a start. Do you know, Miss Ramsay, there's an emporium in New York called Stewart's that has more than a hundred departments? . . . A vast range of merchandise all under one roof . . . everything except food. . . . That's where Kingstons'll differ. . . . Eventually, we'll sell food as well."

"In a drapers?"

"In an emporium. We'll sell milk and coal and houses and meat and furnishing materials and clothes and toys for children and . . ."

She stared at him as he spoke, struggling not to laugh again, but the very notion of a draper selling meat seemed utterly ridiculous.

"Miss Ramsay . . ." He spoke gently, patiently, almost as he would to a child. ". . . the world is changing. Only seventy years ago, there were highwaymen just up the road there in Knightsbridge. The journey from Hyde Park to Kensington was so dangerous it could only be safely undertaken in a group under escort. . . . Look at it now. Look at

Belgrave Square and Eaton Place and Wilton Crescent with their grand
houses. Only thirty years ago, the only way you could travel to London from the country was by stagecoach or by carriage or by horse.
Today, you can go by train. Do you realize what this has meant? A
visit to London from Berkshire or Sussex is now a simple affair. . . . For
people who live closer, such as in Hampstead or Streatham, they can
shop in the center of London and be home for tea. . . . Yet most shops
are still run as though all their custom was local. A few are beginning
to wake up, but the process is slow because people are naturally blink-
ered by the past. . . . You yourself find it impossible to believe that
ladies'll buy meat in a shop that sells drapery, but they will, Miss
Ramsay, I promise you. . . . After all, why should they wish to go to
different shops when they can buy all their requirements in one place?
And as for the people who live really far away, such as Yorkshire . . ."

"You plan customers in Yorkshire?" she exclaimed with astonishment. "In Sloane Street?"

"Most certainly," he answered. "We'll send them details of everything our emporium has to offer. They can order all they need by post
and it'll be dispatched to them by return mail . . ." He broke off,
embarrassed by his excitement. "I must apologize," he said. "It's my
favorite subject. My enthusiasm got the better of me."

"Your imaginings?" she queried, and smiled suddenly, and he was
conscious of her brown eyes. She was laughing at him again, this time
more kindly, but it made him feel awkward. He was an employer, even
though he had never employed anyone before. He had not been speaking to her as an employer, he realized, but as another young person,
which was wrong of him. Also, standing there, improperly dressed as
he was, he felt at a disadvantage.

His voice was cooler as he tried to retrieve the initiative. "Miss
Ramsay, may I be permitted to ask why you are contemplating leaving
an establishment such as Shoolbreds?"

"I've left already. . . ." She hesitated before adding, "There was a
difficulty. It became impossible for me to stay."

"Difficulty?"

"Of a personal nature . . . sir."

"You have a reference, of course."

She glanced away, then looked straight back at him. "No," she
said.

It explained why she had responded to the notice in the window
instead, perhaps, of applying to one of the other big shops.

"Then you can give me the name of someone to whom I can apply at Shoolbreds?" persisted Thomas. A reference, after all, was a basic requirement.

"There's no point," she answered. "They wouldn't give you one."

"But surely—" he began.

"I can assure you," she insisted, bold once more, "that I was not dismissed for thieving, if that was in your mind . . . sir."

"That thought never occurred to me," he said, as indeed it had not. "But you must understand I know nothing about you, and—"

"And *I* know nothing about *you*, sir!" Suddenly she was furious, her eyes flashing. "Standing here in this filthy little shop! Nor, now I come to think of it, have you mentioned the wage you had in mind to offer."

"The wage I shall suggest to a suitable applicant," he said carefully, "will be thirty pounds a year—"

"Thirty pounds?" she echoed indignantly.

"And keep, of course. There'll be another lady assistant. You'll share a room upstairs—"

"Indeed I will not," she said angrily. "I'm getting thirty-seven pounds at Shoolbreds and I won't consider a penny less."

"*Were* getting," Thomas reminded her dryly. "I can't afford to pay more—not to start with, at least—and it's a reasonable wage."

"Reasonable?" she said. "It's absurd. Clearly there's no point in wasting your time further, sir, so I'll go . . . and leave you to your imaginings!"

She turned and swept out of the shop with the style that had marked her from the moment he had first seen her.

Suddenly the shop seemed lifeless again, and the lonely gloom Thomas had felt earlier enveloped him once more. Seeking solace again in activity, he thrust the rag into the bucket, squeezed the water from it and began to rub furiously at the grime on the shelving until suddenly he heard her voice once more: "Sir . . ."

He stood up slowly, wondering for a moment if he had imagined it, and turned. She was standing in the doorway. "Would there be a commission on sales?" she asked.

"Of course," he answered.

"Then I'll accept the position."

"But Miss Ramsay," he said, "I haven't yet offered it to you."

"I'd advise you to trust me, sir, as I must trust you. You'll find I work hard and am adequate as a saleslady. I'm experienced in the Fancy trade, with a background that cannot fail to be of value to you in a district such as this. Also I have some ability at bookkeeping, which might be of some additional use. . . . Now, where can I hang this where it won't get too dusty?"

She unbuttoned her mantle, slipped it from her shoulders, and held it out to him. Speechless, he took it from her and, uncertain what else to do, went into the scullery and hung it on a hook behind the door.

When he returned to the shop, she was briskly sweeping the floor.

· 2 ·

It was raining heavily on Sunday when Thomas took time off from the shop to visit the Wilsons. He sat in the front of the omnibus on the journey to Kings Cross, watching the water streaming down the flanks of the three horses that drew it.

His spirits were high, despite the weather, for the last three days had been deeply rewarding. In fact, on reflection, he was amazed how much he had achieved in so short a time. The painters were starting work on Monday. A signwriter had been commissioned to execute the name on the fascia. He had ordered a Kamptulican floor—despite a heated discussion with May Ramsay, who had argued the merits of carpeting with intensity. She was, he was discovering, a lady of strong views on almost everything, but her enthusiasm for the shop, which was almost as great as his own, was encouraging.

He had bought boxes with glazed cloth covers for his stock; ordered a new counter and some shelving from John Hills at New Cut, Lambeth, whose advertisements he had seen on the front page of *The Draper* under the headline "Important to Young Drapers"; and acquired a good supply of price tickets, pins, string and wrapping paper. He had even remembered to buy a tin of Griffiths Glass and Plate Polish, a product with which he was very familiar, since the cleaning of John Parsons' big shop windows had been among the more onerous of the regular duties of David and himself during their apprenticeship.

His most expensive purchase had been a couple of Burrows reflecting window lamps—which, strangely, May Ramsay had thought to be an astonishing extravagance, considering his attitude toward the carpet. But Thomas believed that display was one of the most important aspects of shop management and was always surprised that so many people underestimated its value. "The most vital thing of all," he told her, "is that the merchandise must look marvelous. . . . These lamps'll bring up the colors in the ribbons and lend a sheen to the velvets."

He had been interviewing staff and had taken on another lady assistant, whom he suspected May Ramsay might resent, since she was a lot older than she was—and than Thomas, for that matter; but he needed someone with a thorough experience of the trade. Grace Stewart had been in drapery for twenty years. She was about thirty-five, quite handsome, with dark hair, prematurely streaked with gray. Her husband had deserted her and left her with a child, who was cared for by a friend during business hours.

She was knowledgeable about the merchandise, and Thomas felt that she would appeal to the older customers—which, to his relieved surprise, was exactly the view that May Ramsay expressed, though he did not actually request it.

The final member of the staff was a fourteen-year-old Cockney errand boy named Albert Brown—an urchin, really, with tousled fair hair and a crumpled face, who slept in a tiny room in the attic.

The rain was heavier by the time the omnibus reached Kings Cross, and Thomas ran as fast as he could along York Way to No. 12, Copenhagen Street. When his Uncle Jack opened the door in response to his urgent knocking, he smiled at the sight of his nephew as he stood in the entrance, rain streaming from the brim of his top hat. "You'd better come in and get dry, Thomas," he said.

Thomas hung his sodden coat on the coat stand and followed his uncle across the hall to the parlor, taking pleasure in the familiar sight of his slightly rounded shoulders and the gray hair curling as usual over the back of his collar. For ten years this house had been a second home to him. Whenever he had been able to get away from Parsons, usually on Sunday afternoons like this one, he had always been welcomed by this warm and affectionate couple. Uncle Jack Wilson was a retired printer who had done quite well in business. Aunt Dolly was the sister of Thomas' father, who had died a slow death of consumption when Thomas was twelve, thus creating the need for Thomas to come to London. In the family's new circumstances, when money was so short, there had been too many of them at the farm. It was Uncle Jack who had suggested the apprenticeship. Old John Parsons was a member of his Masonic lodge, and he had offered to say a word to him in Thomas' favor.

Thomas could vividly remember that first evening when he had arrived in London from Quainton. He had stood uncertainly in this hall and smelled kippers cooking. Aunt Dolly had put her arms round him, holding him against the silk of her dress, which had smelled strongly of lavender. Then she had held him away from her, gripping him by the shoulders so that she could have a good look at him, and said, "It's kippers for tea. All boys like kippers, don't they?" And he had grinned happily and answered, "This one does, anyway, Aunt."

He had spent the night there, in a little room under the rafters on the top floor, and had felt that nothing could go wrong. And if it did, he could always run to this womblike haven, with his aunt smelling of lavender, and the soft bed and the whiff of kippers or sausages or bacon and eggs or whatever other delectable teas Aunt Dolly knew that boys liked. After that, of course, he had slept over the shop at John Parsons, and he had discovered, with the help of Mr. Clegg, that quite a lot could go wrong; but Sunday-afternoon teas with the Wilsons had made it all tolerable. Occasionally he had brought David, his fellow apprentice, with him, but usually he had come alone.

When Thomas entered the familiar sitting room, with its paintings of battle scenes on the walls, he was surprised to see Lillian sitting on the sofa—a very different Lillian from the young girl in her teens he had got to know so well. Now, with her blond hair swept back and her fashionable scalloped dress, she had grown beautiful and elegant.

"Hallo, Thomas," she said, amused by his surprise and, in particular, by his uncertainty as to how he should greet her. "I think you should kiss me," she said. "We're cousins more or less."

"Rather less than more," he replied, as he brushed her cheek with his own. Lillian was Uncle Jack's niece and no blood relation to Thomas.

"I'm afraid your Aunt Dolly is not very well," said Uncle Jack, "so Lillian's come down from Buckingham to help run the house until she's better. I think we'll have tea first; then you can go up and see Dolly. I'm sure she's dying to hear how you're getting on with your shop."

Lillian left them for a moment to fetch the tea, since the maid had the afternoon off, and Jack inquired about Thomas' progress. "Are you finding your capital's enough?" he asked. "I mean now that you're actually spending it."

"I think so," Thomas said, "though without your help it would have been quite impossible. It was very good of you, Uncle."

"Nonsense," said Jack, shrugging off the gratitude, waving the pipe he held in one hand. "It'll be a fine investment, I'm sure."

Lillian returned with a tray, all grace and easy movement, and Thomas smiled when he thought what an awkward girl she had been. She guessed what he was thinking. "You've grown up too, you know," she said, pouring the tea. "I'm told you're starting that business of yours at last. For years I've been hearing how Thomas had saved two hundred pounds, then three hundred pounds, then four hundred. . . . I never understood how you did it. Magic, perhaps? Or crime, even?" Her blue eyes, mocking, stirred him, and he looked away.

"I didn't have time to spend much," he said, "not with the hours we had to work. . . . After I'd finished my apprenticeship, it wasn't too hard to save."

"Wasn't it?" queried Uncle Jack, his pipe between his teeth, smoke escaping from his mouth. "You denied yourself absolutely everything—and you know it."

"Not for long . . . only a few years," Thomas said, a note of apology in his tone.

"Everything you did since you were thirteen was calculated, planned for the day you could open your own shop—and that's only a first stage, isn't it? You'll end up rich, won't you, Thomas?"

"Truly?" said Lillian. "Should I be setting my cap at him, Uncle Jack? Could he give me a life of luxury?"

"I hope the business'll grow into something worthwhile," Thomas agreed. "I certainly don't want to be poor. . . . I got a glimpse of that at home after Father died." And for an awful moment he paled as he always did when he thought of his father's death. Those nights when he could hear the endless coughing, knowing there was nothing anyone could do, until eventually he had died in front of him, at the very moment Thomas had taken up a cup of tea his mother had made, and the jaw in that terrible gray face had sagged obscenely open. That was the winter he would never forget in any of its terrible details. His mother always said there were many people worse off than they were. They had the farm, she said. But it was January, and Father had been heavily in debt. Thomas never did discover how she held off the bailiffs until the spring, when things had become a little easier.

After tea, Thomas went upstairs to see his aunt. She was lying back on heaped pillows, wearing a cap of crisp blue muslin—donned, he suspected, in his honor, for Lillian had gone up ahead of him to prepare her. She was looking frail, but her eyes had the usual spark, and she smiled when she saw him. "What sort of ribbons are you going to sell in your shop?" she asked.

"All sorts," he said. "Mostly French."

"What is everyone buying—velvet?"

"Yes—broad velvet ribbons. The ladies of fashion will be tying them in half rosettes or shell bows worn under the ears. At least, that's what they say in Paris. . . . Red—the whole range of red, from pink to plum."

"How strange," she said. "Red is such a violent color."

Suddenly she seemed to sag, and Lillian nodded at him. "You're looking tired, Aunt," Thomas said, "so I'll leave you now and come back again soon."

She smiled. "You can bring me some ribbon," she said. "Red ribbon—to tie up my bonny brown hair." And she closed her eyes.

In the hall, he asked Lillian, "How long has she been like this?"

"About three weeks."

He said goodbye to his uncle, and Lillian came with him to the door. "I'd like to see your shop," she said. "When do you open?"

"The week after next—if all goes well." He leaned forward and kissed the cheek she offered him, put on his hat and coat and strode off along Copenhagen Street, feeling strangely troubled.

On impulse, he took an omnibus to Ludgate Hill, since it was not far from Kings Cross, and went into John Parsons' staff entrance in the hope of finding David Rawlings, though he doubted if he would be there on a Sunday afternoon. But there he was, lying on his bed with a book in his hands.

The rain had stopped, so they took a stroll along the river and went on to the Swan and Crown in the Strand for a drink. They had an easy, pleasant relationship. They had started together at Parsons, endured Mr. Clegg together, helped each other through Saturday nights when fatigue drained away what seemed like the very last reserves of their energy. For the shop was usually open until after midnight, and clearing up after the last customer had left often took an hour or two.

"I hear the shop assistants in Paris are threatening a strike over long hours," remarked Thomas.

"They won't achieve anything," said David, "except the sack."

Thomas glanced at his friend, with his fair hair that drooped over his forehead, and thought how characteristic this attitude was of David. It was a negative response to a cause that they both knew by long experience had much to commend it. The long hours that shops stayed open had many influential critics. But then, Thomas thought, David was a bit negative by nature, a bit prone to unconstructive pessimism—the opposite of Thomas himself, which was probably why they were close friends.

"They may get something out of it," said Thomas. "At least, they'll know they've tried. Some more porter?"

David watched him push his way to the bar through the crowd, a tall, broad-shouldered figure in a frock coat. He always gave the impression of a kind of unreleased strength.

Thomas returned and put the two tankards down on the table. "Well, here's to Kingstons," said David, and drank deeply. "I'll drink to that too," Thomas said with a smile.

"My father asked me the other day if I'd like to have my own business," David said suddenly. "He said he'd help me to set up. I was astonished."

"What did you say?"

"I thanked him and said I'd like to think it over."

"I suppose you want to see how I get on before you chance your arm?" Thomas said, mocking just a little.

"You're cut out for it, Thomas." David spoke seriously. "I'm not sure that I am."

"You'll never know if you don't try." Thomas stood up, drained his tankard. "I must go. I've got a hard day tomorrow."

They walked out of the Swan and Crown into the Strand and shook hands. "Good luck with the shop," said David, and headed east in the direction of Fleet Street. Thomas toyed with the idea of waiting for an omnibus, then changed his mind and, preferring the exercise, strode off toward Piccadilly and Sloane Street.

· 3 ·

Thomas opened his shop to the public on Thursday, September 16, at three minutes to ten—almost an hour and a half late. In truth, the delay was more on the order of two days, because he had planned to start trading on Tuesday, but when it became obvious that this was impracticable, he had accepted the situation with disgruntled reluctance. "What are two days, after all," suggested May Ramsay, "in the existence of a great emporium that'll still be trading in a hundred years?" Thomas had glanced at her quickly, but although he had known she was mocking him, there was no evidence of amusement in those wide brown eyes.

Even with these extra days, they had all had to work immensely hard boxing and pricing the stock in all its varieties—gloves, trimmings, lace, ribbons, feathers, flowers, neck squares, sewing materials and all the other haberdashery items. The preparation of the silk and cotton threads, in the wide range of colors that they would have to maintain as regular lines, had in particular been a great labor. The breaking up of the pound packets of bulk, which is how it was delivered, into skeins that could be sold to the customers took hours.

Grace Stewart was the most adept at working the thread round a yard measure, held upright by two leather loops fixed to the counter, for she had acquired practice over the years, but it was boring work, and May Ramsay took her turn. Even Albert, under some pressure from the two ladies, tried his hand, but made such a mess of it that he was soon relieved of the duty.

Thomas himself was out a great deal during these last days, completing the buying of the merchandise, but he had found time to set up the window displays, which he insisted should be his sole personal responsibility. He had supervised the placing of his precious Burrows reflecting lamps with an agonized concentration, and once he had seen them alight, he had been dissatisfied with their effect and insisted no fewer than three times that the plumber reposition them.

Then Thomas had dressed the windows, draping his ribbons, some of which were two or three inches wide, in long loops from wires fixed out of view above the window glass. He displayed his laces, of which there were more than twenty varieties, in pyramids over a background of rich velvet. He laid out other items of stock with immense care, changing his mind innumerable times, pursuing the subtle aim of presenting enough merchandise to indicate a variety of choice, yet avoiding the temptation to overcrowd the display area.

Late on Wednesday afternoon, after a last visit to the factors, he had returned to the shop in a four-wheeled "growler" crammed with boxes of stock. His eyes bright with excitement, he had hurried inside with a large carton in his arms, dropped it on the counter and ripped off the top. "Look at these, just in from Paris," he said to May Ramsay. "Feel the texture of this double-faced satin." And he drew out a length of ribbon from its roll and draped it gracefully over his hand, as he had seen Clegg do so often. "And how about this? They call it '*grosse faille*'—a corded silk like grogram, but heavier, much more body. The pearl edge sets it off well, doesn't it? You'll sell yards of it."

May responded as she was expected to and praised the quality. Grace Stewart said the ribbons were very fine, though Thomas noticed a certain coolness in her tone. Even Albert, though unasked, expressed himself in favor of the colors.

Then, to the astonishment of the two women, as they unpacked the other boxes that Albert carried in from the "growler," Thomas started to remove from his window some of the stock he had set up with such care earlier that day. In its place he made a special feature of his new purchases, all in different shades of red with slightly shocking color names such as "Sultane" or "Lucifer," ranging the ribbons in long, looped drapes round a showcard worded "New from Paris."

When he was satisfied, he demanded that May immediately stop what she was doing and come out onto the pavement to admire it. "You couldn't pass the window without wanting to buy them, could you?" he asked. "No," she admitted, "you certainly couldn't—at least, not if you were a lady of taste and discrimination."

She found her relationship with Thomas Kingston strange and confusing. Much of the time he treated her as a young equal, even as a partner, sharing with her his enthusiasm. At other moments, however, he would assume the usual role of employer, speaking at times quite sharply—especially if she referred to the way things were done at Shoolbreds, which invariably produced a response of irritation. "Miss Ramsay, this is not Shoolbreds. Shoolbreds is the past—lingering still, but the past. Kingstons is the future."

"But surely something can be gained by studying a house of such established repute," she argued. "Is it by chance that they are prosperous?"

"It's important not to be deflected from our policy," answered Thomas.

They worked on that evening until midnight and were all up the next morning at 5:30. As they sat together sleepily at breakfast round the table in the back room, the dawn was only just beginning to lighten the sky they could see through the window. There was not much talk until suddenly Thomas addressed them. "You've all worked hard," he said, "and I appreciate it. . . . Now I just want to repeat what I've told you about our policy, for this is of extreme importance. . . . Our trade's got a bad name. So in this establishment, there will be no fraudulent selling, no 'puffing,' no bargain cuts in prices of soiled merchandise. We're selling high-quality goods at prices that are competitive and clearly marked. We're going to trade honestly and give sound value. We will never, never press a sale. Is that quite clear? And if our customers wish to leave the shop without making a purchase, they must feel free to do so without the slightest vestige of embarrassment."

He stood up. "Now we must make haste and finish our preparations."

Nearly four hours later, just before they opened, Thomas walked across Sloane Street to indulge himself in a survey of his shop from the far side of the road, taking pleasure in the new paint and the splash of red ribbons in the display and his name on the fascia in bold gold letters. As he recrossed the street, he saw a lady standing hesitantly at the door. "May I invite you to enter the shop, madam?" he said.

"You're open for business, then?" she queried.

"We are indeed—a little late, I fear, since it's our first morning."

She was aged in her forties, unmarried, Thomas surmised, with bright, lively eyes that reminded him of Aunt Dolly. "Then I'm your first customer?" she said, clearly pleased by the notion.

"You are, madam," said Thomas.

"How delightful. I feel I should make a speech or offer a prayer."

"Either would be most welcome, though your good wishes would be sufficient."

He ushered her into the shop, and she looked round with a broad, beaming smile on her face. "It really is most pleasing. I'm sure you'll do well here." She was in search of some bonnet ribbon, and she was lavish in her praise of the stock, especially the new lines from Paris, which she found a little too dear, though they were clearly good value. He was serving her personally when a man entered the shop and spoke to May Ramsay, and Thomas excused himself for a moment, leaving his customer in the care of Grace Stewart.

The visitor's name was Theodore White. He was tall and pale and thin—a man of about forty-five with a bald head and slightly hollow cheeks. "I have the gentlemen's-wear shop just up the road," he said when he had introduced himself. "No doubt you've seen it. We do a small line in drapery as well. I just called this morning to offer you my good wishes. Mind you, I think you'll need them."

"I beg your pardon?" said Thomas, perplexed.

"Perhaps it isn't my place to speak of the matter," the draper went on, "but your windows . . . well . . ." He broke off as though he could not bring himself to continue.

"They're perhaps a little modern," agreed Thomas, who had noted the rather dull shop several doors higher up the terrace of which White was apparently the owner.

"You're a young man," said White, "and I'll give you some advice. The principles of business don't change. They cannot be modern or even old-fashioned, for they are basic."

"Principles, perhaps," answered Thomas, "but methods are a different matter. We live in changing times."

Sadly, Thomas' gloomy visitor wagged his head in dissent. "I think you've been taken in by what you've heard about some of these new American fads, but this is London. Here we know the proper and dignified way to do things, as indeed our customers expect. I have to confess that your attitude does not make me very optimistic."

"Well, I shall do my utmost to convince you, sir," said Thomas. "Now if you'll forgive me . . ." He moved back to the customer whom he had left with Grace Stewart, for he had spotted signs of trouble.

"I'm sorry, madam," Grace was saying firmly as Thomas approached. The lady turned to him. "It's so embarrassing," she said, "I seem to have come out this morning without any money, and I need the ribbon to go out to tea this afternoon, and—"

"Please do not concern yourself, madam," said Thomas. "What is the item, Miss Stewart?"

"Four yards." It was the usual length required for a bonnet, and already she had wrapped it in paper. "I've explained, Mr. Kingston—" she started.

"That's all right," Thomas said quickly, turning back to the lady. "It's a mistake that anyone can make. Please take the goods, madam, and let us have payment the next time you're passing."

The lady sighed with relief. "You're most kind," she said. "I'll come back tomorrow. Would you like my name and address?"

"I would indeed," answered Thomas, "but only so that I can record the identity of our first customer."

Her name was Miss Godfrey, and Thomas escorted her to the door and shook the hand she held out to him with a bow. "Well, au revoir," she said with a smile.

"That's the last you'll see of her, I suspect," Grace Stewart remarked tartly when Thomas returned to the counter. "If I may suggest, Mr. Kingston—"

"When I wish your suggestions," snapped Thomas, "I'll ask for them."

They had quite a busy morning. Several people had obviously just come to look inside the new shop, which had attracted interest in the district. One or two did not buy anything, but several made purchases. At noon, Arthur Stockton, one of the factors, drove up in a gig and stood in the middle of the shop, his legs firmly apart, nodding with approval. He was broad and loud, with a red, jowly face. He wore a checkered waistcoat under his frock coat and, before he had removed it on entering the shop, a topper at a stylish angle. Really he would have looked more in place on a racecourse than in a shop that catered to ladies, but that—as he explained—was his way. People had to take him or leave him. Clearly, however, he liked what he saw. "Seems you know what you're doing, young man," he said expansively. "The stock's good and lively. Quite a few customers. Always like to see activity. Nothing worse than an empty shop. An empty shop's death. Old Mr. Shoolbred would never stand an empty shop. He'd actually stop the customers leaving if they got thin on the ground. Literally. He'd stand between a lady and the door and lock her in conversation—

politics, weather, fashion, children, anything he could think of—until someone else came in to take her place."

Thomas saw May Ramsay smile at the mention of Shoolbreds, and for a moment he thought she was going to comment; but she decided, evidently, not to be provocative in public, for which he was grateful. He did not like Arthur Stockton, but his stock was good; and Thomas was flattered, too, that he should have taken the trouble to call on him in so small a shop.

"You can always rely on me, young man," Stockton went on. "You find yourself in any difficulties, you come and talk to Arthur Stockton. Always glad to help out a friend. I've been in the trade for thirty years, and if I hadn't learnt a wrinkle or two by this time, I'd need to be stupid, wouldn't I? Well, I must be off. Good luck, young man. Good morning, ladies." And before anyone could respond, he was out of the shop and climbing into his gig with an agility that was surprising for a man of his corpulence.

Soon afterward, Lillian arrived by hansom to inspect Thomas' shop. He introduced her to his salesladies and noted a sharpness in May Ramsay's tone as she spoke to her that he had not heard before. Lillian was profuse with admiration for the shop, displayed delight over the Parisian ribbons and insisted she be shown the whole premises. "She's pretty," she remarked about May when they were in the back room, where they took their meals. "I've no doubt she has designs on you."

"Nonsense," said Thomas, "she's just a sales assistant. She's good, though. Works very hard."

It was at that moment that May rushed into the room. "There's a customer just arriving in a carriage, Mr. Kingston."

"A carriage!" he repeated, a delighted smile creasing his face. "That's just what we need. Please excuse me, Lillian."

He hurried into the shop, and sure enough, as he could see through the glass of the front door, there was a brougham with a pair of immaculate grays drawn up outside, and a liveried footman was helping two ladies to step down to the pavement. The first to leave the carriage was a woman of great presence. Aged probably in her mid-thirties, she was elegant and strikingly good-looking, with jet black hair and light blue eyes. She was wearing a long velvet cloak over a pale blue dress, the hem suspended to reveal a yellow underskirt, and a fashionable bonnet, heavily decorated with flowers. Her manner as she spoke to the footman was gracious—as indeed was the way she crossed the pavement smoothly toward Thomas, who was holding the door open for her. She was an important lady who knew she was important. She favored Thomas with a smile as she approached him, and he noticed the pleasing creases that formed at the edge of her eyes. "I haven't seen your shop before," she said to him.

"That isn't surprising, madam," he answered, "since this is our first day in business."

"Really?" she said. "Janet, did you hear that?" She turned back to her companion—a short, plump woman who, in striking contrast to herself, was strangely awkward. Then to Thomas she said, "Your stock must be positively pristine." She moved forward into the shop, looking around her admiringly. "I must say it's delightful . . . isn't it, Janet? Delightful." For a second, Thomas felt her studying him quite openly in a way that he found disconcerting. "You're young to have a shop. Is this your first venture?"

"It is, madam," he answered, "but I'd hoped it wasn't too obvious."

"Oh, please don't think I'm criticizing. Clearly, you have initiative. The country needs young men of initiative."

She sat down carefully on the chair that Thomas held for her in front of the counter. "My attention was caught by the lace in your window as we passed."

"We have a wide stock," Thomas answered. "Please permit me to show it to you. Miss Ramsay . . ."

Already May had begun to lay out some of the lace merchandise on the counter, and their elegant customer soon demonstrated that she was well informed. She spoke with knowledge about Lisle, with its diamond mesh, and Valenciennes, with its hexagon pattern of plaited threads, and Mechlin, with its flaxed yarns twisted to a pillar. "I think I caught a glimpse of something more decorative in the window," she said. "I want it for the bodice for a dress that needs a feature to make it more interesting."

"No doubt what you saw was the Brussels wire ground," said Thomas, indicating to May in which drawer she would find it. It was a silk lace, a little thicker than the others, with an elaborate pattern.

The customer studied it very carefully, holding it with long, slender fingers encased in gloves that reached above her wrists. "The work is certainly beautiful," she said, "and most intricate. It must take great skill."

"The pattern is worked separately and set on with the needle," Thomas explained. "It's not woven into the lace like the others."

"I think it'd be ideal, don't you, Janet?"

"I do," her companion answered. "The detail is quite wemarkable."

She spoke in a little high-pitched voice that seemed out of keeping with her figure. "And what is the price?" asked the first lady.

"Three shillings a yard, madam."

She raised her eyebrows, impressed. "That's not at all unreasonable. I'll have two yards." She stood up, smoothed her dress with her hands. "I shall be sure to tell my friends about you, Mr. . . . is it Mr. Kingston?"

"It is, madam."

"And naturally, you'll see us again."

"We should be most pleased, madam."

And they left the shop, leaving behind them the faint scent of expensive perfume, and stepped into the carriage.

"Well, you certainly made your mark there, Thomas." Lillian had suddenly appeared beside him as he watched the carriage move off.

He smiled. "She's just the sort of customer that can make all the difference to a business like this," he said. "The carriage trade."

"I'm sure she could," answered Lillian, "but be careful, Thomas. She could also be dangerous. Those eyes . . . I wouldn't like to cross her."

During the afternoon, the carriage drew up again in the street outside. The passenger seats were empty this time, but the footman leaped down from the box and came into the shop with a small, beautifully packed parcel tied with ribbon. "With the compliments of Mrs. Fellowes," he said.

It was a box of French bonbons, and inside was a printed visiting card on which Mrs. Fellowes had written the words "To Mr. Kingston —to wish all success to you and your staff—Christine Fellowes."

Thomas was so overwhelmed he could not speak. He just handed the note to May Ramsay, who was almost as moved as he was. "How kind of her," she said. It was a thoughtful gesture which made them all feel more cheerful, though in fact they had no reason to be downcast. Business had been quite good all day. When Thomas finally locked the door at seven o'clock, May counted the takings. "Five pounds four shillings and sevenpence," she reported. "That's rather good, isn't it?"

"I don't think I can complain," replied Thomas. "Not since it's the first day."

She smiled as she wrote the figure in the mauve account book he had bought. "I think I know what's in your mind, Mr. Kingston," she said. "Already you're thinking of the time when it'll be fifty pounds instead of five—or even five hundred. Or is that going too far?"

"No," he answered, "it's not going too far."

The following week, in a grueling scene in the back room of the
shop, Thomas sacked Grace Stewart for pressing a sale. With tears
streaming down her face, she begged him to reconsider his decision;
but he was admant. "I warned you about pressure selling on the day
we opened," he reminded her. "I've warned you twice since then, but I
fear the habit's ingrained."

"But my little girl—"

"I'm sorry, but I've made my decision," he said, and walked out of
the room.

The sacking had the same kind of shock effect within the shop
that an execution must have on prisoners in a jail. Thomas had often
spoken sharply to his staff. He had reprimanded them; he had insisted
on their remaking the counter displays, had criticized the way they
handled certain customers, and had displayed what they thought were
excessive standards about such trivial things as the position of price
tickets—he hated them to be crooked—or a few specks of dust that
had escaped notice on the counter. But they had still been a team,
working for the same objective. The sudden dismissal had introduced a
new realism into their relationship. Thomas, for all the loyalty he had
inspired, had shown that he could behave like any other employer. For
the rest of the day neither May nor Albert said much.

That evening, as May helped Thomas put the shutters over the
windows, she did her best for her colleague and asked him to give her
another chance, but she made no headway. "She was wrong for the
shop," he said. "I knew very early that I'd made a mistake."

"You don't think a little guidance might have—"

"If I had, I wouldn't have dismisssed her," he answered sharply. He
locked the door, pulled down the blind and turned off the lights.
They walked in silence through the darkened shop to the back room.
May lit the oil lamp that stood in the middle of the table, took the
mauve account book from a drawer and laid it open in front of her as
she sat down. "What do you think will happen to her," she asked, "and
the child?"

"She'll take another position," he said, just a little briskly.

"If she can find one."

He sat down at the table beside her, laying a sheaf of invoices
before him. "She has my sympathy too," he said, "but I'm running a
business in a hard and competitive world. If we're to survive, we must
be guided solely by what's in the best interests of the shop. Mrs.

Stewart was not in the best interests of the shop. Now I don't want to discuss it any more."

"Was your generosity to Miss Godfrey in the best interests of the shop?" As soon as she said it, she wished she had not, for Miss Godfrey, their first customer, had not returned to pay for the ribbon, and her remark, therefore, was finely barbed.

"Miss Godfrey may yet return," he responded coldly. "I hope so, for otherwise it'll be a bad omen." Suddenly he turned to her in appeal, and as he did so, the edge of his hand touched hers on the table. "Why are you pleading with me? You know very well I was right to dismiss her."

"I don't, Mr. Kingston. She had qualities. She was experienced . . . she had a good appearance . . ."

"She oversold."

"You could have trained her out of it."

"Never. She'd been doing it too long." Their hands were still touching. Both were conscious of it, but neither sought to move them.

"The decision was mine," he went on. "It's one that I shall have to take again, no doubt. . . . I shall have to dismiss people whom I don't think suitable—or my shop will fail. And Miss Ramsay"—he looked straight at her, pausing for a moment—"my shop's not going to fail."

She looked back at him for a few seconds, and he experienced a sudden violent surge of feeling. For although the challenge was still there in those wide brown eyes flecked with green, their expression was also marked by understanding and loyalty and—to his astonishment—for a very brief heady moment, by overt desire. Their fingers, still touching on the table, seemed to press against each other. She glanced away at last. "No," she said, "I don't think your shop is going to fail." She moved her hand from his in order to steady the account book, and copying from the rough mathematics she had scrawled previously on a slip of paper, she began to write the figures of the day's takings, divided into merchandise sections, in the columns across the page.

Thomas replaced Grace Stewart with a very different type of lady assistant. Emily Lane was forty—a plump, friendly, outgoing woman who was always cheerful. "You can either see life as tragic, which it is, or as comic, which it is," she said to Thomas. "I can't see much point in moaning about the tragic aspect, sir." The customers liked her, and Thomas soon discovered that she was extremely efficient. She knew her stock to the smallest item, and she had the same sort of acute psychological insight that Mr. Clegg had possessed.

Trade during their first few weeks exceeded Thomas' greatest hopes. His policy of competitive prices, good-quality merchandise, lively display techniques, no "puffing," and, of course, no pressure was clearly sound.

Certainly his self-appointed patroness had kept her promise to spread a favorable word about him among her friends. Since that first day, a number of women had arrived in carriages or walked on fine days from Knightsbridge or from their homes in the nearby squares and told him that his establishment had been much commended by Mrs. Fellowes—often adding graciously that they agreed that her judgment had been well founded.

To May, it seemed sometimes that they also appeared to examine Thomas himself with a warmth of interest that approached the outer fringes of ladylike behavior. Indeed, he was as much a part of the advertising as the value of his merchandise on which he set so much store. With his dark, rugged good looks, his shoulders that were broad and muscular for a man so young and his slightly restrained charm, he was strongly attractive to many of his customers. He knew how to talk to a woman of any age, giving her his total attention, deploying his stilted, almost literary style of conversation which was mildly flattering and occasionally touched with wit, so that she could laugh with him; but always he gave the impression that he was keeping something back, that he would have liked to say more had it not been improper to do so—an essential element, of course, in a relationship spanning the vast chasm of class between a tradesman and his customers. All the same, May would sometimes say to herself, none of them—none of these fashionable, often beautiful, always expensively dressed women—ever saw the exuberance in Thomas that she did when the day's business had been exceptionally good or he had bought a line of merchandise for which he had special hopes.

There had been a delicate change in their relationship since their evening discussion about Grace Stewart. For there had been a degree of revelation, though nothing was actually said, that had brought to the forefront of her mind vague feelings of which she had not before been fully aware. Since then, she had been horrified at times to find herself studying his face intently, section by section, as though with a magnifying glass—noting his lips, marked with the tiny indentations that feature any lips, examining his slightly angular nose and remarking the fact that its ridge was really quite sharp. She would detect an area of his chin where the beginning of beard growth indicated that the razor that morning had not cut close enough to the skin. She would be aware suddenly that she was subjecting his sideburns to detailed scrutiny, noting the differing shades of color of the individual hairs—and she would scold herself for being absurd.

In the evenings, when she worked with Thomas in the back room after supper, she would take quite exceptional pleasure in his company. Usually this was enough, but sometimes she would experience an intense desire to run her fingers lightly over his lips; then her imagination would expand the scene, and she would have to fight to stop herself shaking. She knew that he was feeling similar emotions, for at times she would catch him watching her with an intensity that he would hasten to conceal as soon as he realized she was looking at him.

It was easier when Emily Lane and Albert were there, but often they retired early—Emily to read penny romances and Albert to study comics. And they would be left alone with everything unspoken, talking always of the shop—which too had come to form a bond. For it dominated his thinking, and the fact that she shared his hopes for it added a strong extra dimension to their emotions.

She did not want to be in love with him, for she suspected that could only lead to disaster. For he was nowhere near ready for marriage. He was an ambitious young man struggling to build a fledgling business.

Her dilemma had been starkly emphasized one night when he had been out for the evening with his friend David Rawlings and she had encountered him in the passage outside the room she shared with Emily on his way to the upper floor where he slept. For a moment he had hesitated, standing so close to her that she could smell the porter on his breath. Her heart had begun to pound. A fierce ache had gripped her stomach. She was certain he was going to reach out to her and a moment of terror had enveloped her as her wanting him to do so had conflicted with a violent confusing need to reject him. But then he had moved on, whispered, "Good night, Miss Ramsay," and the moment was over. She had gone into her room and closed the door behind her, feeling utterly drained.

In October, only four weeks after Thomas had opened the shop, he decided that his Fancy Goods business was well enough established for him to expand. Rearranging his internal layout, he installed a second counter and a new shelving unit, using space that he had earmarked for it from the moment he had decided to rent the premises, and bought a range of silk and linen dress materials.

He gave detailed instructions to his small staff on the way to sell the new merchandise, drawing heavily on the expertise of Clegg, who had possessed so great a talent for making the most ordinary print look quite exceptional. As was now to be expected, Emily soon proved herself to be the most adept at the technique of transforming material on a roll into the draped form that could enable a customer to visualize easily how it would look upon her body.

Thomas spent hours working on the display of his new stock, setting up the muslins and the silks in long, softly folded sweeps and calling back the plumber to fix another Burrows light to enhance the colors.

His venture into Heavy Goods absorbed one hundred pounds of his slender resources. Some of this he had been able to save from profits, but most had to come from what remained of his starting capital. It was some relief to him, therefore, that sales in his new department—which, of course, conformed with his policy of competitive pricing, sound value and careful display—were good from the first day. Even so, the strong response bothered him a little because it seemed just too easy. "You do worry about some strange things, Mr. Kingston," said May. "I could understand your fussing if the customers were holding back, but just look at the figures."

"True," he agreed, "but narrow margins are dangerous. . . . If our sales dropped in a general trade recession, our profits might not cover our costs."

"I shouldn't worry too much. Women aren't fools—certainly not the women we deal with. They can see value when it's offered to them. I'm sure we'll weather any slump."

He smiled. He always enjoyed it when she spoke keenly like this about the shop. "Let's hope a slump doesn't come too soon," he said, "so we've time to build some reserves."

Later that day, while on his way up Sloane Street to Knightsbridge, Thomas met Theodore White standing on the pavement outside his own shop. As usual, he was free with gloomy advice, this time about Thomas' new department. "Far too early," he predicted. "You're making all the classic errors, young man. You're not giving yourself enough profit for unsold merchandise or for your overheads. But you won't listen, will you?"

"I thank you for your advice, Mr. White," said Thomas. "Good morning, sir." All the same, these meetings with the depressing old draper unsettled him. He had an unpleasant feeling he might be right.

Mrs. Fellowes, meanwhile, was following his progress with flattering care. She usually called once a week with her companion, often displaying enthusiasm for new items of stock that Thomas had bought since her last visit and insisting that Janet confirm her high opinion— which Janet invariably did with the comment that the work or the value or the quality of the material "twuly is wemarkable."

Occasionally Thomas would talk to Mrs. Fellowes about the business and his plans for it. She always asked intelligent questions, and during one visit when he spoke of his concept of the future of the emporium, she appeared deeply impressed.

Sometimes she bought something and sometimes she did not, but he enjoyed her visits because she was always remarking on his flair for business, his distinctive taste and his enterprise, which many young men should envy. Often when she left, May could not help repeating her remarks. "Mr. Kingston," she would say with a serious expression, "I wonder if you'd give me your view of this counter display. You've got such distinctive taste." He would glance at her sharply—then smile a reluctant, sheepish apology.

One morning, after one of her visits, when Thomas accompanied Mrs. Fellowes to her carriage, she said, "Mr. Kingston, there's a gentleman I would like you to meet. I think he might be helpful to you. Would it be possible for you to call on me at five o'clock tomorrow afternoon?"

Thomas was astonished by the invitation. "I should be delighted, madam," he said incredulously.

"Good. I look forward to seeing you then. All right, Henry," she called out to the coachman, "drive on." He whipped up the grays. And Thomas stood on the pavement, feeling slightly dazed, as the carriage clattered away along Sloane Street.

· 5 ·

The next afternoon was cold but bright as Thomas prepared himself for his interview at Mrs. Fellowes' home. He put on his best coat and trousers and, a little reluctantly, yielded to May's insistence that he wear the most expensive octagon cravat in his stock. "Now that you're mixing with the quality," she said, "it's important to dress for the part."

"It wouldn't do to spoil the ship for a ha'p'orth of tar, would it?"

added Emily, who had the same affection for overworn clichés that
Clegg had enjoyed.

So Thomas bowed to the consensus and permitted May to pull and
push his cravat until she was satisfied that its presentation was as good
as she could make it.

"Quite the masher now, Mr. Kingston," said Emily admiringly.
Playing up to them, Thomas put on his hat and tilted it forward at a
rakish angle. "That's the idea," said May, "but maybe not quite so
much." And using both hands, she moved it just a little straighter on
his head. "That's better."

"You really look a toff, Mr. Kingston," said Albert as Thomas left
the shop.

"Thank you, Albert," he said, and strode off down Sloane Street
swinging his stick, feeling the part that May and Emily had been so
insistent he play. The October air was damp and fresh, and Thomas
experienced a heady and unusual self-assurance until the moment he
mounted the steps within the pillared portico of Mrs. Fellowes' house
at 74 Eaton Square. Then, as he looked at the big front door with its
great brass knocker, his confidence began to wane. He would have
liked to pound the knocker on the door with some style, but he now
faced the fact that he was a tradesman, being granted an exceptional
favor. So his knock, when he made it, was a suitable, almost reverential
tap.

The door swung open and the butler stood before him.

"I think Mrs. Fellowes is expecting me," said Thomas.

Instructions had obviously been given to him that Thomas was to
be admitted, for the butler, though making clear he knew he was a
shopkeeper, conducted him up an ornate staircase to a small but luxurious room on the first floor.

Mrs. Fellowes was sitting in a high-backed chair with a tea tray on
a low table beside her. Her companion, whom Thomas had heard
addressed as Janet in the shop, was seated on a small sofa near her.
Opposite them sat a man of about fifty with thick, wavy, immacu-
lately barbered white hair which extended in whiskers down his cheeks
and curved elegantly toward his chin. He had cold gray eyes, a pale
skin that was starting to loosen into folds in his neck and jowls and a
tight, ungenerous mouth.

"Ah, Mr. Kingston," Mrs. Fellowes greeted him expansively, "I'm
so glad you could spare the time from your busy shop. You know Miss
Jones, of course. I'd like you to meet Mr. Ernest Goldsmith, who, as no
doubt you know, is a banker of great repute."

Goldsmith stood up, extended a hand that was limp and pressure-less, sat down again and quite openly studied him. "You appear to have impressed Mrs. Fellowes as a young man with prospects," the banker said at last in a tone that suggested her opinion was clearly unsound.

"She's very kind, sir."

"Do *you* think you have prospects?"

"I hope so."

"That's no answer. Do you or don't you?"

Thomas flushed. "Yes, sir, I do."

"Why?"

The question was so unexpected that for a moment Thomas scarcely knew what to say. "Well, sir, I try to offer a high level of service . . ." His words sounded banal and awkward. ". . . and top-quality merchandise at reasonable prices in a district where I believe there's a market for it. My first weeks of trading have been very satisfactory—though, of course, the support of Mrs. Fellowes has been invaluable."

He looked across the room at her, and she nodded encouragement. "You well deserve it, Mr. Kingston," she said. "Now why don't you sit down? You mustn't allow Mr. Goldsmith to bully you. Ernest, you're positively grilling the young man. Janet, would you kindly take our young draper a cup of tea."

Thomas sat down a trifle uneasily on a small satin-covered chair as Miss Jones carried out her instructions. She smiled encouragement as she handed him the cup, and when she saw him balancing it awkwardly on his knee, she whispered, "I'll bwing you a table, so you don't dwop it"—a thought for which he felt a surge of gratitude toward her.

Goldsmith did not appear to have heard Mrs. Fellowes' suggestion of restraint. He sat back in his chair, delicately stirring his tea with a silver spoon held in slightly podgy fingers that were ornamented with two thick gold rings. "Mrs. Fellowes tells me you favor Continental sources for your goods," he said, "especially Paris. What are you going to do if war breaks out between France and Prussia?"

"I shall have to adjust my buying policy to that situation," answered Thomas, "just as drapers had to do during the civil war in America when cotton was so short because of the Yankee blockade."

Goldsmith gave a short, mocking laugh. "You mean like buying cotton from India? That's what we were asked to do, wasn't it? Just as good as the American cotton, they said, which was absolute nonsense, of course."

"Indian cotton was inferior," Thomas agreed, "just as Macclesfield silk is inferior to Lyon silk, but if there's no French merchandise, then ladies will have no alternative but to buy what is available."

Goldsmith suddenly stopped his idle stirring of his tea, but left the spoon, motionless, in the cup, still holding the end of it. "Isn't that defeatist?" he snapped softly. "How can a man have prospects if he's defeatist? It's a contradiction in terms."

"I don't think so, sir. Shopkeepers have to be realists."

"They also have to think ahead. Why not buy stocks of French ribbon in anticipation of the war? You would then have something that your competitors did not—one of the best recipes for success in business."

Thomas knew the banker was trying to provoke him. "With respect, sir," he said as calmly as he could, "that would be unwise for a fashion product. Our customers' tastes in color, style, even material may be quite different next year. Even if they're not, I do not have the capital to invest in future stock."

"So you're undercapitalized," the banker challenged, continuing once more to stir his tea with a slow, rhythmic movement. "The most common reason why men fail."

"You're twisting my words, sir," insisted Thomas, his voice heightened by growing anger which he knew he must curb. "My resources," he said in a voice that was quieter but still taut, "are adequate for my present situation. I'd like more capital, of course, as would any young businessman."

"Yet already I hear you've opened a new department—dress materials, isn't it?" Goldsmith's tone was sharp again, and once more his teaspoon was motionless in the cup.

"That's true, sir."

"Was that not unwise? You've only been trading a few weeks."

"It was carefully planned, sir. It's proving popular and has brought more customers into the shop, so the Fancy Goods is benefiting too."

"And I suppose," asked Goldsmith, carefully examining his fingernails, "you're going to open more departments in the near future . . . ?" He turned to Mrs. Fellowes before Thomas could reply and remarked, "Christine, I think your young protégé has a taste for overtrading."

Again Thomas had to exercise great effort to control himself. "I plan to incorporate two new ranges of merchandise before Christmas," he said. "Mantles and drapery—light drapery materials, that is. Both are extensions of the existing business."

For a moment there was silence as Goldsmith lifted his cup to his lips. "I hear you believe in the future of emporia," he said at last. "Huge establishments selling a whole range of goods under one roof. Am I correct?"

"Yes, sir. In my opinion, the Great Exhibition in the Crystal Palace, with its many shops, revealed a glimpse of the enormous potential. Also, it seems to me to be the logical trend."

"Logical?" queried his interrogator. "Surely business is best done by men who know their trade. How can anyone be fully knowledgeable about a spectrum of trades that range from drapery and ribbons to . . . meat, was it? I think Mrs. Fellowes said that meat was among your plans . . . and vegetables and fish. I must say it all sounds most bizarre. How can one man be a butcher and . . . well, a milliner and a tailor and . . . and a fishmonger?"

"He can't, sir, but he can employ people who know the individual trades. In America, after all, there are already emporiums—"

"Emporia," Goldsmith corrected dryly.

"Emporia," repeated Thomas, "that offer a vast range of products . . ."

"Oh, dear, oh, me," said Goldsmith with a tired sigh. "America. How can I begin to start correcting your illusions? Mr. Kingston, you cannot compare London to America. Their great shops are merely extensions of the general stores that existed when their cities were very small. Even now most of their business is wholesale, supplying the remote towns and villages of the interior. No, believe me, young man, you've got it all wrong . . . all wrong." He looked away, waving rather effetely with his hand, as though brushing aside a troublesome fly.

Suddenly, Thomas had reached the limit of his tolerance. He knew that he must take a stand, as firmly and politely as possible. "I have *not* got it all wrong, Mr. Goldsmith," he said boldly. "With respect, sir, the trends in London may not be the same as those in America, but I believe that nevertheless they all point to a great future for emporiums—"

"Emporia," Goldsmith corrected again. "I can see you weren't a Latin scholar."

"Emporia," Thomas conceded again, continuing with the enthusiasm that always caught him when he spoke of the future: "The ever-growing size of shops, the expanding transport systems, the increase in wealth. All of these things must, in my view, produce the general store."

"General store's an easier term than emporium, isn't it?" said Goldsmith with a sudden grin. "No troublesome Latin plurals."

Thomas colored, his heart beating. For an awful moment, he had an overwhelming desire to punch Goldsmith in his flabby, laconic face. He turned to his hostess. "Mrs. Fellowes, if you'll excuse me, it's really time I returned to my shop."

He stood up, forcing himself to address the banker who had caused him such distress. "Mr. Goldsmith, it's been a pleasure to meet you, sir."

It was at this moment, when Thomas felt he was retreating from the scene with a few final remnants of dignity, that he failed to notice the small table on which Miss Jones had placed his cup of tea, still full to the brim. He stumbled against it. To his horror, it rocked sideways. He reached out to catch it, but failed. The table fell heavily on its side. The cup and saucer were sent flying and, as they struck the floor, broke into pieces against each other. Tea flowed over the thick, patterned carpet.

Thomas stared aghast at what he had done. "Mrs. Fellowes," he stuttered. "I am so sorry. I don't know how to apologize . . ."

She smiled graciously at him. "Don't give it a thought, Mr. Kingston."

"What, after all," remarked Goldsmith, "is one cup of beautiful Sèvres china and an indelible stain on an irreplaceable Aubusson carpet?"

"I hope you realize," said Mrs. Fellowes, "that Mr. Goldsmith is a great tease. He doesn't mean a half of what he says. The matter's trivial. The servants are always breaking the cups. So please don't uspet yourself. Can you see yourself out?"

Thomas bowed to the ladies and, inclining his head to Goldsmith, was almost out of the room when the banker called after him, "Oh, Mr. Kingston . . ." Thomas stopped and turned, bracing himself for a last taste of sardonic repartee.

"I'm inclined to agree with Mrs. Fellowes," said Goldsmith. "You are, I think, a man of prospects. I predict great success for you. I hope we'll meet again soon."

The shop was busy when he returned, and it was only after the last customer had left that he told his small staff, who were genuinely keen to know what had happened at Mrs. Fellowes', that he had been introduced to an influential banker who had been good enough to express an interest in the shop.

Later that night, however, after Emily and Albert had retired, he admitted to May that the most humiliating part of the interview had been his sense of gratitude for Goldsmith's surprising remark as he had left. "If I'd had a tail I'd have wagged it," said Thomas bitterly. "I appear to be so used to servility that I'm grateful if anyone even utters a kind word. . . . I suppose it was all those years of constant indignity under old Clegg."

"But you *were* an apprentice then," she said.

"I'm not an apprentice now, yet I still didn't dare to stand up to Goldsmith as I should because he's powerful and it would have disturbed Mrs. Fellowes. . . ."

"Well, there are bound to be people it's unwise to offend," May suggested sympathetically. "Mrs. Fellowes is your customer."

"That's just the point. Will there ever come a time when it won't matter if I offend someone, when I won't fear someone, when I can stand up straight and say, 'No one, no matter who they are, is ever going to trample on Thomas Kingston again'?"

May smiled, and her skin looked soft in the gaslight. "Yes," she said. "And then it'll be others who'll fear *you*."

He laughed. "You think I have the makings of an ogre?"

"Doesn't power abuse?"

"Surely it depends on the man."

"Already there are people who fear you, Mr. Kingston . . . Emily Lane . . . Albert . . . You have power—power to dismiss them. . . . Even I fear you a bit."

"You!" He sounded astonished. Instinctively, he reached forward and put his hand over hers. "You've got nothing to fear. You know that. I'd be lost without you."

The touch of his hand caused her heart to beat quicker—and she knew that her situation had suddenly become more dangerous than it had ever been before. "Perhaps," she said quietly, "I have more reason to fear you than they do."

His hand tightened over hers. "May . . ." It was the first time he had ever used her Christian name. "Oh, May . . ." and she was in his arms and he was kissing her. Blindly, she pushed him away. "Please, please stop," she gasped. She stood up and stepped away from the table, breathing heavily. "Mr. Kingston, I didn't want this to happen."

He got to his feet too, but took care not to approach her. "I'm sorry if I upset you," he said, "but it was inevitable. I'm obsessed by you. When I'm not with you I think of you constantly. You know this. I know you know it, just as I know you feel it too."

"You've no grounds to say that."

"I've seen you look at me."

"You've misinterpreted what you think you've seen. You must stop talking like this, Mr. Kingston."

"Thomas. Call me Thomas."

She gave a little shrug of her shoulders that questioned what difference it made what she called him. "It'll spoil everything," she said.

"It won't do that, I promise. I need you far too much—not only as a man, though God knows that's overwhelming, but in the shop. You're an essential part of what I'm building . . . of what *we're* building. You *have* been from the moment you first walked through the front door."

"I've been very happy. That's why I don't want it to change, Mr. Kingston."

"Thomas."

"Not Thomas," she said a little desperately.

"It's better that it's been declared. I believe we should face it."

"No," she said firmly. "When things are declared, they take form. Before that, they're blurred. . . . And what's been declared? I've declared nothing. What have *you* declared?" Her voice was cold and angry. To May herself, it was as though someone else were speaking.

"Don't talk like that, May, not in that tone. Discuss the problem if you like . . . working so close together . . . sharing so much of our lives, yet keeping back so much . . ."

"Again you're assuming things you have absolutely no right to assume."

"I'm not," he said quietly. "You're trembling, May. Why do you think you're trembling? Are you cold? Are you ill?"

"I'm a little angry," she answered tautly, appealing to him suddenly: "Why do you persist?" There was a note of despair in her voice. "I want to forget the incident ever happened."

He moved slowly round the table—choosing the longest way round so that he kept a distance from her. "You're asking too much of me, May," he said softly. "I've been stopping myself for weeks, months . . . Repeatedly, I've told myself that the fact that you worked for me made it impossible. I've accused myself of weakness. At times I've even tried to avoid being close to you, but that wasn't possible in the shop." As he spoke, he moved slowly toward her. "I've lain in bed at nights on the floor above your room and seen you as clearly as if you'd been there with me. . . . I've smelled your skin as vividly as I can smell it now . . . In my fantasy, I've held you in my arms. . . . I've known your lips . . . the contours of your ears . . . the softness of your neck where the small young hairs begin to curl . . ."

He was close to her now, but he did not try to touch her. Later she wondered whether this was the reason she did not move away from him; whether—if he had put his arms round her—she would have pushed him away as she had before. Something in the mood of those few moments kept her still. Slowly, still without touching her, he leaned forward and kissed her very gently on the lips. She did not respond in any way. Unhurriedly, he kissed each corner of her mouth; then her cheek, the side of her forehead, and her ear. His hands remained at his sides, and she stayed motionless, almost as though she were hypnotized. Then he lifted her chin gently with his forefinger and again he kissed her mouth. Suddenly, as though he had struck some key nerve, her lips parted and she clutched him, with her hands at the back of his neck, returning his kiss so hard that her teeth hurt him. The sudden surge of emotion was involuntary. Her body strained to his body. Her tongue sought his tongue. As she clung to him, she felt a need for him that was outside all previous experience. When she felt his hand on her breast, she was incapable of making any move to stop him. His fingers, made clumsy with impatience, were undoing the top button of her bodice when she became aware—slowly, it seemed, almost as in sleep—of the sound of heavy knocking.

"There's someone at the front door," she whispered.

"We'll ignore it," answered Thomas.

"It might be important."

"Nothing can be as important as this."

"The police perhaps . . ." And then she knew instinctively who it was and wished for a moment that she had agreed with Thomas that they should ignore it.

Again the noise of heavy knocking reverberated through the building. Thomas took the oil lamp from the table and went into the shop. She did not follow him immediately, for she needed a few moments to recover her equilibrium. As she did so, she wondered just a little desperately if she would ever be free of Bob, if she would ever be able to enjoy a few weeks of peace in the sure knowledge that he would not suddenly arrive as a symbol of disaster with that terrible boyish grin, leaving a trail of wreckage behind him. Always, his fleeting appearances meant some kind of trouble for her. She would either have to borrow money for him or plead with the police or employers or creditors, or compromise herself as she had been forced to with Turner, the Shoolbreds buyer.

It had been an unchanging pattern for years. Even when he had been a little boy, and she herself had been barely twelve, she had always been trying to persuade schoolmasters or angry parents or magistrates that his offense was a temporary aberration. She had been young to have to take on such a responsibility, but there had been no one else. Their mother had been bedridden for years before she died. Their elder sister had just shrugged her shoulders. Their father had usually been away at work—certainly during the day—and when he was there, he could never comprehend the realities, let alone cope with them.

And every time Bob had promised never to cause her trouble again; but he always did, of course. As he grew older, the trouble just grew bigger. Solemnly he would assure her that he would never come to her for help again. "Get me out of this, Sister May," he would say with the look of youthful appeal that he had used on the magistrates and the schoolmasters, "and you won't see me until I return to repay the money." He called her "Sister May" only at moments such as these. But she did see him again—without the money. To this day she was still repaying Turner after that appalling and humiliating fracas, sending off a postal order once every week.

Composing herself at last, May rebuttoned her bodice, smoothed her dress, touched her hair into order. Then she walked into the shop.

Thomas raised the blind over the glazed section of the shop door and peered out. There was a young man standing in the street looking up at the windows of the upper floors, presumably to see if he could detect a glimpse of light behind a curtain. At that moment, the visitor saw Thomas, illuminated as he was by the oil lamp he was holding, and walked toward the door. Thomas opened it cautiously with the security chain still fixed.

"What do you want?" he said through the narrow opening.

"I am seeking," answered the young man, "a quick word with Miss Ramsay . . . if you will forgive the intrusion." He was a little drunk—just enough to be unsteady on his feet and to have to enunciate his words with concentrated care. He wore a derby hat, tipped to the back of his head, and as he spoke, he grinned.

"At this time of night?" queried Thomas.

"I must beg your pardon," said the visitor, "for the disturbance. . . . Only because it's important . . . very important."

"It's my brother," said May dully, from behind him. "I'm so sorry."

Thomas undid the chain and opened the door. The young man moved forward into the shop but did not remove his hat. "You must be Thos," he said. "Fancy Goods Thos."

Thomas glared at him, and he grinned. "That's what it says up there outside, doesn't it? Thos Kingston, Fancy Goods."

"You promised, Bob," said May. "Last time, you promised, would be the last."

"You're right, Sister May," he agreed. "You're quite right. I promised. But I've good news for you. I'm going away—far across the oceans. You won't see me again for years, and then I'll have made my fortune and will repay all you've done for me." To Thomas he said, "She's always been a good sister. More than a sister. Mother *and* sister."

"Where are you going?" asked May quietly. She knew there would be a price to pay for the joyful prospect he drew, for with Bob there always was.

"Australia," he said. "Ballarat, where the gold is lying around just under the soil—trip over it in the streets. Not, mind you, that I'm going for the gold. No, not Robert. They'll have got the gold under the horse blankets by now. But it's a rich town, Sister May. I'm after the fellows that have got the gold, that work for the fellows that have got the gold. A little shop. That's the idea. With Tom Meaney . . . Remember Tom, Sister May? A carrot-head at school who got into almost as much trouble as me. He's just been there. We're going back together. He's got a bit of money out there to get started. Says if things work out he'll make me a partner."

"When do you leave?" she asked.

"Friday. The *Star of Corunna* from Liverpool. Providing . . . Well, there is just one little problem . . ."

"No, Bob, not this time, I can't—"

"Just the fare. That's all I need. Plus a bit to buy something to eat on the voyage. Ten pounds. That's all."

"Where in the world do you think I can get ten pounds from?"

"I know . . . I know . . . I know." He spread out his hands, palms downward, as though to calm her. "I promised last time. But when Tom suggested it, the opportunity . . . Well, you have to admit it's a good idea . . . and I've got the faintest little suspicion that the notion of your little brother being the other side of the world might not make you entirely distraught. So I said to myself, 'Robert, you made a promise, but you have a problem. So why not put it to her? Sister May will find a way.'"

"Bob," she said, "I don't have the money. This time you'll have to go to somebody else."

"Funny you should say that," he said, and suddenly all the banter was gone and he looked deadly serious. "I thought of discussing it with Turner."

He was threatening her, she realized, despite all she had done for him, gambling that Thomas knew nothing of Turner or of Shoolbreds, that Thomas even cared. Suddenly she felt drained of all energy as the fear arose in her. She did not want Thomas to know about Turner —at least not yet, while the debt was still unpaid—but she was not going to do anything to stop it.

"Then I should discuss it with him," she said firmly.

"Thos," said Bob carefully, "have you met Mr. Turner of Shoolbreds?"

"No," said Thomas, who had absorbed something of the conflict between them, "and I've no wish to hear about him. . . . Miss Ramsay, do you believe this story of your brother going to Australia?"

"Believe?" queried Bob indignantly.

"It's probably true," said May. "I can remember Tom Meaney. It's the kind of thing he'd do."

"In that case, Mr. Ramsay," Thomas went on, "I am prepared to lend you ten pounds against an I.O.U."

May was appalled. She was in almost the same situation as before. "Mr. Kingston," she insisted, "I cannot allow you to do this."

"Please leave this to me, Miss Ramsay," Thomas answered. "It has nothing to do with you. It's entirely between your brother and myself."

"Of course it's to do with me," she said. "You won't get it back. Then the debt will be mine, and I've had enough debts."

"The debt will not be yours," he said. "It'll be your brother's. Mr. Ramsay, I warn you . . . if you're not on that ship when she sails, I personally will ensure that the consequences'll be drastic." He walked into the back room, where he kept the takings, and returned with the ten one-pound notes, a slip of paper and a pen and inkwell. "Sign this bill, please," he said, laying it on a counter. Bob shrugged his shoulders and did as he was asked. Thomas thrust the notes into his hand, strode to the front door and held it open.

Bob smiled and touched his hat. "Bye, Sister May." He looked at Thomas, whose face was rigid with anger. "Thanks, old cock. You never know, you might get it back—when I return with my pockets" —he mimicked the husky voice of a veteran of the California gold rush—"full o' go-old."

Thomas closed the door behind him, locked it and drew down the blind.

"I wish you hadn't done that," said May.

"It hasn't compromised you, if that's what you're thinking," said

Thomas. "I did it for the shop, not for you. . . . You're in no debt in any form. . . . It's vital you believe that—despite what came before."

Warmth for him surged through her. She wanted to run to him and throw her arms round his neck, but she knew instinctively that he did not want her to—not now that he had given money to her brother. "After that distressing scene, you must be very tired," he said softly. "I should go upstairs to bed."

She moved to the door, then turned. "Do you want me to tell you about Mr. Turner?"

"Do you want to tell me?"

She paused. Then she shook her head. "No," she said.

"Then I don't want to hear."

CHAPTER TWO

March 1870

· I ·

A strong March wind was gusting cold and damp as Thomas left the estate agents' office and strode along Piccadilly, his coattails flapping behind him, his head held forward to stop his hat from being blown off. Low gray clouds were moving fast across the London sky. The gaunt leafless trees of Green Park were bending under the force of the weather.

It was an uninviting morning, but Thomas felt a certain stoic need to experience the bite of the elements. So he decided to walk back to the shop by the somewhat circuitous route of Hyde Park.

He had much to think about, for the day was an extremely important one for the enterprise of Thomas Kingston, Draper. In his pocket was the lease he had just signed for a second shop, only three doors away from his first, at a rent of one hundred pounds a year plus rates and liability for repairs. He was, he knew, taking a big risk, for in addition to the new outgoings, the fitting out of the premises and the purchase of stock for his new departments would absorb all his remaining capital including his savings from profits. For a few months, until he could create some more reserves, he would be extremely vulnerable to those unpredictable political or economic events that can so greatly affect small undercapitalized firms. However, as Goldsmith had remarked on an unexpected visit to the shop with Mrs. Fellowes ten days before, "Occasionally, my dear young man, if you don't have major resources, you've got to take risks—that is, if you're going to progress. The alternative, of course, is to forget your emporium and be content with your station as a small shop." He had laughed at the look on Thomas' face and had shaken his head slowly. "No, I didn't think that would appeal to you. Then you must accept it, Mr. Kingston. You're a speculator, a gambler. . . . Get a few good cards in your hand and you'll succeed; have a run of bad luck, then . . ." He shrugged his shoulders.

"So what would you advise, sir?" Thomas had asked.

"Reduce your risks as much as you can. Lay off a few bets if anyone'll accept them. Calculate each move you want to make. Then go for your objective—boldly, without looking back: like taking a big fence out hunting—though I don't suppose you're acquainted with that experience."

"I come from a farming family, sir . . . in Buckinghamshire."

Goldsmith raised his eyebrows in surprise. "Bicester Hunt country, eh?"

"That's correct, sir."

"Then you know what I mean." He picked up his topper and silver-knobbed cane. "Mrs. Fellowes, we shall be late for lunch if we don't go now."

And they had left, as she always left, with style and instructions to the coachman and the clatter of hooves.

Thomas had seen her since. She had shown interest in a line of dress fabrics and had asked him to send them round to Eaton Square. As was normal with important customers, he had taken them himself. On this visit, like previous ones, she had flattered him and asked about his home and his family. "I enjoy our little talks, Mr. Kingston," she had said. "I think we understand each other."

She had held one of the materials up to her body, with the roll on the floor, so that the fabric enclosed her in drapes like a dress. She had leaned slightly back and sideways so that the material clung closer to her—as it would when the dressmaker sewed it; but with her black hair, which she was wearing long that day, and her fine, well-formed figure with its small waist, the movement contained an element that was sensual. "Do you like it?" she had asked him, her eyes bright. "Do you think the pattern suits me?"

"I do, madam. I think it would make up into a most appealing gown."

"You don't think it gives just a shade too much emphasis to the hips?"

"I don't think any pattern could do that, madam," he had replied. He had kept his tone light but flattering.

She had laughed, pleased by his remark. "You always say the right thing, don't you, Mr. Kingston? Certainly it's a pleasing shade of green. I've been told my eyes are green. Would you say my eyes were green, Mr. Kingston?"

She had looked at him boldly, smiling, teasing—a beautiful self-assured woman with eyes that were blue. "I would say, madam, that they were blue, a most pleasing blue, but perhaps in some lights . . ."

. "And under some circumstances?" she had queried lightly. There was now no doubt she was flirting with him—reaching as a woman across the class barrier toward a man who was in trade; and Thomas was in a situation that demanded the greatest delicacy.

"Perhaps, madam," he had replied with a smile that he had hoped possessed a degree of warmth but no commitment.

She had thrown back her head and laughed out loud. "Mr. Kingston, you should have been a diplomat."

She had bought the fabric, but Thomas had left the house in a troubled frame of mind. He was concerned as to how he should respond to her flirtatious comments. If he did so in any but the most circumspect way, she could freeze him with one sentence back into his station as a shopkeeper. On the other hand, if she continued to become more outspoken, would she not expect him to reciprocate? And where, he suddenly found himself wondering, was Mr. Fellowes? In the country; in the colonies; dead?

The following day, Thomas had gone to see Arthur Stockton, the breezy wholesaler who had called at his shop on his first day of trading, and told him about his two meetings with Mrs. Fellowes' banker. Stockton was impressed. "Goldsmith, eh?" he said as he consumed a lamb chop at a pub near his warehouse in the City. "Not as big as Rothschilds or Morgans, but substantial all the same. You could have a useful friend there, Thomas, my boy. . . . Mind you, those bankers'll eat you for dinner if you give them half a chance. . . . Better without them if you can manage it." He wiped his mouth. "So you've decided to take another shop. . . ."

"Well, there's one free quite near me and I'm thinking about it."

"How long have you been open now? Only six months, isn't it? . . . Bloody astounding. Certainly done well, haven't you? Just take your account with me alone. Must be in the hundreds. You've got the touch, all right."

"The problem is," said Thomas, "that I don't know that I can afford another shop yet."

"I know how it is," said Stockton sympathetically: "The better your trade the more capital you need."

"On the other hand," Thomas had continued, "if I wait for a few months, the shop'll probably be rented by someone else."

Stockton nodded, picked his teeth to loosen a piece of meat. "Would a little credit with me help you?" he asked. "You don't take any at present. How about a month?"

Thomas had always paid cash for his goods. He did not really want to borrow money, which Stockton's offer amounted to. The debt to Uncle Jack was liability enough. Certainly, though, it would reduce the risk. "That's very good of you, Mr. Stockton," he had replied.

"Think nothing of it, dear boy. You can always rely on Arthur Stockton."

Thomas crossed Piccadilly and made his way to Hyde Park by way of Shepherds Market. The wind was stronger in the park, for there was less protection, but its icy sting on his face was stimulating. For a few moments, he took off his hat and let his hair fly. There were not many people about—just a few closed carriages and one or two riders in the Row.

Stockton had been right, Thomas mused as he strode over the grass. His first half-year of trading had been "bloody astounding." The selling area of the shop now occupied the whole of the ground floor of the building, meals being taken upstairs. There were four departments, and the staff had been increased by two girl assistants and a man, named Sidney Baines, of whom Thomas had high hopes.

Baines was only about twenty, with his apprenticeship not far behind him, but he was bright and keen and quick. Thomas planned to make him a Senior Assistant—a kind of first step toward the floor-walker employed by most big drapers—in his new shop, where the emphasis would be on clothes rather than fabrics. The biggest department would be dresses.

Thomas intended to move the Mantles Department to the new shop, so that he could extend the drapery, silks and linens in the existing one. And as soon as he had reason to believe that his new acquisition was thriving, he would introduce other sections selling personal attire—millinery, hosiery and gloves.

May had been a great support to him in their months of spectacular progress, discussing his decisions with him, giving her views on applicants for positions, and keeping the books.

He had made no attempt to renew the relations of the night her brother had called. In fact, there had been little opportunity, for the immense amount of extra work that had been created by the expansion of the business had provided little time, while the additions to the staff had given them far less privacy. Six people now sat down for meals, prepared by a parttime cook. One of the small upper back rooms had been turned into an office, but interruption was constant. For Thomas, it was like being head of a large family. In fact, when he led them all to Matins every Sunday at St. Mary's in Pont Street, he felt like a patriarch of twice his age—as he had joked on one occasion to May on the short journey to the church. "I must tell you," she had answered with a smile, "that I don't think of you as a father."

The remark, light and intimate, conformed with the recognition of their feelings that had become evident on the evening of Bob's visit, and Thomas believed that even May now conceded that his confession of that night had provided a release for the explosive tensions that had been growing within both of them. By a kind of tacit consent, they seemed to have agreed to suspend their relationship until some future date when the pressure of work and other factors lessened, and Thomas knew that this was a situation with which, for the moment at least, May was very content.

Their December trading, like that of earlier months, had exceeded Thomas' expectations, and once again he had caused May to laugh with his concern that their success, unmarred by any setbacks, was building a debit balance for which the Lord or the Fates would one day demand payment. Also, the fact that Miss Godfrey, their first customer, had not returned to pay for the few yards of ribbon—and it could now be assumed she never would—still nagged him as a bad omen. "I wouldn't mind so much if she hadn't been the first," he remarked as, just before midnight on Christmas Eve, May was counting the day's takings, which were clearly very big.

"You're so superstitious," she remonstrated.

"I'm a speculator, as Goldsmith pointed out the other day," Thomas answered. "I need luck."

"And you've had it."

"So far."

She had laughed at the serious expression on his face and had quickly finished counting the pile of coins. "Twenty pounds, five and fourpence!" she had announced triumphantly. "*There's* a Christmas present for you!" He had opened a bottle of Madeira to celebrate. Just for a moment he had toyed with the idea of sharing it solely with May. Then he had realized that this would not be fair to the rest of the staff, who had all worked extremely hard. So they had all had a drink together in the room where they ate their meals, and Thomas had had to be content with just one moment when, unnoticed by the others, who were talking together, he was able to hold up his glass to her and say, "Happy Christmas, May." And she had rewarded him with "Happy Christmas . . . Thomas."

On Christmas Day, May had visited her father in Surbiton, and Thomas, who could not spare the time to go home to Quainton, had gone to join Aunt Dolly and Uncle Jack in Copenhagen Street.

It had been a happy occasion, containing no hint of the events that lay ahead. Thomas had arrived with David, whom the Wilsons had also invited on hearing he was not going home for Christmas, and both of them brought gifts, which had been placed under the tree.

Aunt Dolly had been a bit pale and rather quiet, but she seemed to enjoy her presents. Uncle Jack had called a toast to Thomas' business and expressed the hope that it would maintain its exceptional progress. The men had kissed the two women under the mistletoe, Lillian putting her lips to Thomas' mouth and pressing her body against his in a manner that was excessive, to put it mildly, for a Yuletide frolic. Then, almost imperceptibly, she had winked. She enjoyed the notion of herself as a woman who was slightly outrageous.

Uncle Jack had carved the goose, and conversation at the table had been light and easy. After her third glass of claret Lillian had begun to flirt with David, glancing archly at Thomas to ensure that he had noticed.

Dolly had become too tired to stay at table for the whole course of the meal and had retired to bed for a sleep. "I wish she'd get properly well," Uncle Jack had said to Thomas. "She's all right for a few weeks and then seems to revert back again."

At last, Thomas and David had left and walked toward Kings Cross. "Lillian's become very beautiful, hasn't she?" David had remarked.

"Yes," Thomas had agreed, "she has."

"Do you think your uncle would mind if I called on her?"

"I don't suppose so, but *I* might."

David had laughed. "I'm not asking you."

And they had punched each other lightly, as they had when they were boys, and prepared to go off in their different directions. David's omnibus had come first, and he had leaned out from the tailboard as it moved off and shouted, "Happy Eighteen-seventy, Thomas!"

"Same to you!" Thomas had called back, and waved.

Thomas left the park by the Edinburgh Gate and walked down Sloane Street, hoping to avoid Theodore White, though as usual he

failed and had to submit to the usual warning of a dark future because
of his classic errors. But this time, he was disturbed by a sudden premonition that the draper might be right, that by signing the new lease,
with its additional liabilities, he might have endangered his whole enterprise.

Already his wages bill was nearly two hundred pounds a year, and
the extra staff he would need for the second shop would push it well
over two hundred and fifty. His rent and rates were now three hundred pounds. This meant that with the other, smaller outgoings, his
basic overheads would be thirteen to fourteen pounds a week. It was
an enormous sum to be faced with on a regular basis in addition to the
need to plow back a large part of his profits into stock.

The wind seemed chillier than before as he tried to analyze the
reason for his growing anxiety. His overheads had not risen since he
had crossed the park. He had acted with great care, taking heed of
Goldsmith's advice, and calculated his risk. The time, then, had surely
come to be bold. So why were all his instincts warning him of trouble?
He passed the premises he had just acquired, but now they seemed
small and dingy, with little scope for development. Why had his view
of them soured? And then he remembered Goldsmith's parting comment on his recent visit that Thomas would need to get a few good
cards in his hand.

Was there, Thomas thought, as he reached his front door, a joker
in the pack? And then he saw Lillian standing there—a very unusual
Lillian who had taken little trouble with her clothes or her hair, who
had a pale, worried face—and he guessed that she knew the reason for
his strange anxiety.

"At last, Thomas," she said, relieved to see him. "I wondered if
you were ever going to return. I've got to talk to you."

"We'll go to the office," he replied, and led the way up the stairs.

The office was sparsely furnished—just a wooden filing cabinet
and a large table at which were two small seats. There was also one
upholstered chair for visitors, usually wholesalers, and Thomas held
the back of this for her to sit down, then took his place at the table.
For a moment she found it hard to speak. "What's the trouble?"
Thomas asked.

"I fear I've bad news for you," she said. "Aunt Dolly's illness is
now serious. The doctor wants her to go to Paris to see a specialist."

"Paris?" queried Thomas, astonished. "Surely there's a specialist in
London."

"Apparently it's a rare heart complaint. There's only one man in
Europe experienced in treating it, and he's in Paris."

"Is she well enough to travel?"

"I doubt it, but the doctor believes it's a risk that's got to be taken, and Uncle Jack's accepted his advice. Whatever happens, she'll have to spend some time in hospital."

"Poor Aunt Dolly," said Thomas. "Not surprising she wasn't up to much at Christmas."

"The point is," Lillian went on carefully, "it's going to cost a great deal of money. . . ." She paused anxiously, realizing that Thomas still had no suspicion of the reason for her visit. Then she blurted out, "Thomas, Uncle Jack needs the money he lent you for the business."

The shock was so great that for a moment Thomas was speechless. He stared at Lillian, barely comprehending. "I'm so sorry, Thomas," she said quietly. "So's Uncle Jack. He knows how hard it'll be for you."

For a few moments Thomas was silent as he struggled to absorb the facts of the terrible situation that Lillian had suddenly presented to him. Then he asked, "Does he need it *all?*" He spoke with difficulty, a rasp of emotion in his voice. "All three hundred pounds?"

"Most of it."

"How long have I got to raise it?"

"There isn't much time."

"I could probably scrape together fifty pounds now, but three hundred, Lillian . . . It's not possible. I've just taken on a new shop— this morning, literally. Had I known . . ."

"I understand, Thomas. None of us knew."

"Wouldn't fifty pounds be enough as a start?"

She shook her head gently. "I think Uncle Jack wants to be certain that the money's available before she leaves. Paris will be terribly expensive—especially since she may have to stay there several weeks. Then there'll be the hospital costs when she gets back. I'm sure you understand that he wants to do everything possible for her."

Thomas nodded. "I'll raise it as soon as I can," he said. "I don't know how at this moment. At present the money's not in cash—it's in stock, in shelving, counters . . . but there must be someone who'd lend it to me . . ."

"I'll come back tomorrow," she said, "when you've had time to think about it." She stood up, kissed him gently on the cheek. "Don't come down with me. Stay here." And she was gone.

He sat at the table wondering desperately what to do. He began to take stock of his resources and liabilities, writing down the figures on a bit of scrap paper: the cash he had in the safe; the small credit balance in the bank; the stock he had to buy—for the existing shop, not the new one, for already he had decided that despite the drain of the rent, it would be wise to postpone his plans for that. As he sat hunched over his figures, he felt a hand on his shoulder. He did not look up.

"The Fates have sent in a bill at last, May," he said, "for all the luck we've had."

"That wasn't luck; it was judgment."

"Uncle Jack needs his three hundred pounds back . . . urgently. . . . If only I hadn't signed that lease . . ."

"I'm sure that was wise," she said softly. "And when all this worry is over, you'll think so too."

She was calm and confident. She sat down at the other side of the table. "Thomas Kingston, I've watched you running a business for six months and I've not the slightest doubt that you'll overcome this little problem."

"But how, May? I suppose I shall have to borrow it, but I don't really know where to start."

"Nor do I," she said, "but I can think of someone who could tell you."

About four o'clock that afternoon, Thomas turned off from the busy pavements of Throgmorton Street, near the London Stock Exchange, and entered the gloomy quiet of Austin Friars—one of the hundreds of little courtyards of grimy buildings of which the "City" consisted. For a moment, he stood in the middle of the courtyard seeking No. 14, which he had learned was the address of Goldsmith, French & Co., Bankers Since 1787. Under his arm was a brown-paper parcel containing a ledger into which was folded a rough account of his first half-year of trading.

He entered the building and knocked hesitantly on a glass-paneled door marked "Enquiries." A clerk, busy writing figures in a book, said, "Yes?" without looking up, and Thomas asked him if he would inquire whether Mr. Goldsmith could possibly spare him a few minutes.

"I doubt it," the clerk answered, his eyes down, continuing to write. "Mr. Goldsmith never sees anyone without appointment." He looked up at last. "What name is it? Don't you have a card?"

"No," answered Thomas, feeling this was a severe deficiency. "My name is Thomas Kingston."

The clerk told him to wait and went through a door, returning after a while with the information that Mr. Goldsmith was very busy but would see him in a few minutes. It was an unpleasant few minutes of draining confidence. However, when he was at last shown into

Goldsmith's large and comfortable office, the banker greeted him
warmly.

"This is a surprise, Mr. Kingston," he said, shaking Thomas' hand,
"but a most pleasant one. How's trade?"

"Trade's excellent, Mr. Goldsmith," Thomas answered. "In fact,
it's been so good that I signed a lease for a new shop today."

Goldsmith beamed encouragingly. "I admire you, Mr. Kingston.
You're a man of courage. So to what do I owe the pleasure of your
visit?"

Thomas hesitated. "Well, sir . . . I have a problem, which is why
I've taken the liberty of calling on you. . . . I do hope you don't
mind."

"Of course not," the banker assured him with a gesture of mag-
nanimity that no doubt a good lunch had helped to inspire.

"I was hoping you might be good enough to suggest someone I
might go to for assistance in the matter." Briefly, he recounted the
critical situation that had been created by Aunt Dolly's illness.

"So you need three hundred pounds?" said Goldsmith. "Rather
quickly, by the sound of it."

"Yes, sir."

"What's that you've got on your lap—some book of account?"

Clumsily, Thomas undid the parcel and handed the ledger to the
banker. "There's a statement of takings and profits within the front
cover, sir."

Goldsmith studied the figures for a few moments. Then he flipped
through the pages of the ledger. "You certainly got off to a good start,
Mr. Kingston. Of course it's impossible to tell at this stage how realis-
tic your stock figures are—how much is represented by what might be
described as buying errors. Then, if we deduct a salary for yourself,
the profits picture stops being quite so pretty. But even so, you'd seem
to be trading on a sound basis—apart from this little difficulty of
capital. . . ."

He pushed the ledger back across the big desk and stood up,
indicating that the interview was over. Hurriedly Thomas wrapped
the brown paper roughly round the account book and got to his feet.

"Of course, we don't normally deal in figures that are so small,"
said Goldsmith, moving round his desk and conducting Thomas to the
door, "but doubtless you'll need greater support as your business
grows. I suppose I could put it to my partners as a sprat to catch a
mackerel. . . . Our accountants would have to take a closer look at the

figures; but provided they're satisfied, then I'm sure we'll be able to help you."

The deep anxiety that had burdened Thomas since Lillian's visit suddenly lifted, and a wonderful feeling of relief surged through him. He had not considered the possibility that a banker of Goldsmith's eminence would offer to help him personally. All he had hoped was that he might refer him to some trading bank or possibly even to a reputable moneylender, if such a person existed.

"Of course," the banker said as he opened the door of his office, "my partners will probably want us to acquire some degree of ownership in the business in return for our assistance. You'll understand that they're likely to regard the loan as a considerable risk since you've been trading such a short time."

"Ownership?" queried Thomas.

"I'd imagine," Goldsmith went on, "we would suggest that you should form a company that would acquire your business and your leases, and the bank would then take over some of the shares. Our contribution would therefore be in two parts—a loan that would be repayable in due course, on which you would pay interest . . ."

Thomas suddenly felt cold. "What rate of interest would you expect, sir?"

"Oh, I don't know," Goldsmith said expansively. "Five percent, six percent—something like that."

Thomas had expected a figure in the range of two and a half to three percent, which he thought was more usual. "Is that not rather high, sir?"

"It reflects the risk, Mr. Kingston. Naturally, you wouldn't pay interest on that part of our money which went to the acquisition of shares."

"But you would expect an annual dividend on these?"

"Of course. We might agree to waive the dividend for a year or two to give you time to get established. That, after all, is the idea, Mr. Kingston—to invest in your future. As I've told you, I've great confidence in you—and in your concept of an emporium."

To Thomas, Goldsmith's enthusiasm had suddenly become disturbing—especially when, to emphasize his faith in his future, the banker put his arm round his shoulders in a gesture of warm friendship. "What proportion of shares would you propose to purchase, sir?" Thomas asked anxiously.

"Oh, I should think . . ." Goldsmith paused, considering the project. "What would you say to forty percent?"

Thomas stepped back in horrified astonishment. "Forty percent, sir?" he echoed. "You mean I'd only have sixty percent of my own business?"

Goldsmith laughed. "Don't look so shocked, Mr. Kingston. If you're going to expand, you're sure to have to part with some of your ordinary capital. Everyone does. There's a limit to what you can borrow. Also, big loans are a great drain on profits."

Thomas was utterly unconvinced. The moment of joy that had filled him a minute before had vanished. He did not know what he was going to do, but Goldsmith's terms seemed completely unacceptable— at least, until he had explored every other avenue.

The banker watched Thomas' reaction with a smile. "You don't have to decide now, Mr. Kingston. Sleep on it and let me know." He held out his hand—a favor from a man of wealth and influence. It was limp, as it had been the first time Thomas had held it. "I wish you luck," said Goldsmith, and went back into his office, leaving Thomas in the passageway feeling as if he had been supping with the Devil—which perhaps, in a sense, he had.

Thomas left the building and walked into Throgmorton Street, his head low, anxiety tensing his stomach. His determination to reject Goldsmith's offer waned just a little as he strode along the street considering the alternatives. Would it not be better to give away forty percent of his business rather than lose it altogether? After all, was not sixty percent of a thriving establishment, with plenty of capital behind it, better than a hundred percent of nothing? But then, he realized, the cold grasp of the banker would always be there. Perhaps one day he would be telling himself that thirty percent of something was better than a hundred percent of nothing; then twenty percent; then . . . There had to be another way, Thomas thought, of solving the problem.

Arthur Stockton's warehouse lay on the way home, and Thomas decided to call on him and seek his advice. It was a great mistake. Stockton's response was unexpectedly frigid. "I'm rather sorry you told me all this," said the wholesaler. "You'll understand that when I offered you credit the other day you weren't in any trouble. Now, I'm sure you'd agree, it wouldn't be wise of me to extend that facility to you while your situation is, shall we say, precarious."

Thomas could hardly believe what he had heard. He had been counting on Stockton's credit in all his calculations. "You mean," he demanded furiously, "that you're going back on your promise?"

"Not exactly," answered the wholesaler. "Shall we say that I'm postponing it until your situation's clearer—in your own interest as well as mine."

"But the business is sound. Do you think Goldsmith would have offered to invest in it if it wasn't?"

"I'm sure it's sound," agreed Stockton. "I wouldn't have offered you credit myself if I hadn't thought it was sound. But capital's vital. If you're badly undercapitalized, no matter how healthy your business is, you'll go under. An enterprising young man like you is bound to be a bit low on capital because you'll always be expanding, but there's a clear limit, and at this moment you're in grave danger of going beyond it. Mind you . . ." He broke off for a moment, thinking. ". . . I might lend you the money myself."

This was a possibility that had not even occurred to Thomas. Once again he was lifted by a sense of hope—and once more this was to be short-lived.

"It'd be quite useful to me," Stockton went on, "to have an outlet for some of my ranges—especially if something was a bit slow. I could experiment, couldn't I? I mean before I bought in bulk. If I was dubious, you could try out the line for me and see how it went."

For Thomas, Stockton's suggestion represented a danger that was far greater even than Goldsmith's. For it struck at his whole policy and independence in the vital sphere of buying, which to date had been so successful. "Mr. Stockton," he said, "I could only stock my shop with merchandise I believed my customers would want to buy. It couldn't be an outlet, as you put it."

For a moment Stockton pondered what he had said. "In that case, young Thomas, I don't think I can help you." He stood up and walked with him to the front door of the warehouse. "Keep me informed," he said. "I'm sure you'll solve the problem one way or another. Remember—you can always rely on Arthur Stockton."

The wholesaler had used the phrase without thought. It was patter, an element of the Cockney racecourse image he liked to present, but Thomas was infuriated. "Rely on you, Mr. Stockton?" he echoed with disgust. "I *was* relying on you, and you've broken your word."

"Now, that's too harsh, young man . . . you're exaggerating what I said just a little. Now, the fact is—"

But Thomas did not wait to hear. "Good afternoon, Mr. Stockton," he said, and strode off down the street, his anger growing more intense as he walked—against bankers and wholesalers and doctors and even God, who had given him such a heady vision of success only to threaten it with destruction. He was still seething with rage when he arrived at the shop—to be greeted by May, with a broad smile. "Look who's called on you," she said.

And there, sitting on a chair beside one of the counters, was Miss Godfrey—looking a bit frailer, but still characterized by the bright smile that, when he had first seen her on the opening day, had reminded him of Aunt Dolly. "Good afternoon, Mr. Kingston," she said. "I'm sorry to have taken so long to return, but on the very night you last saw me I was carried off to hospital. The doctors only released me today."

Her appearance was so timely that Thomas almost choked with emotion. "Miss Godfrey," he said, "what a pleasure to see you!"

"I've paid what I owe to that young lady over there," she said, indicating May, "but she said that she thought you would like to see me yourself. I hope you didn't think that I had intentionally gone off without paying."

"Good heavens, no," said Thomas. "We had every confidence you'd return—didn't we, Miss Ramsay?"

"We were absolutely positive," answered May, her face expressionless, "as I have already explained to Madam."

Thomas accompanied Miss Godfrey to the door. "We look forward to seeing a lot more of you now that you have recovered," he said.

When Thomas turned back from the door, May said, "I suppose that if her failure to return was a bad omen, her arrival tonight must surely be a good one."

Thomas nodded. "Hopefully," he said. "We certainly need one."

· 2 ·

If Miss Godfrey's return was a good omen, the change of fortune it should have signaled was not evident the next day. One of Thomas' rare letters from his mother arrived by the morning post, bringing news that severely heightened his financial crisis.

"I hate to add to your burdens when I know that you must have all the problems you need with your new business," she had written, unaware of course that these had suddenly become critical, "but we are, I fear, in great trouble here at Quainton. We had thought, as everyone believed, that the Cattle Plague which created such havoc a few years back had finally been defeated. Unhappily, we were wrong. Mr. Jones, the vet, has a theory that it might have been carried by a traveling dog fox, since they often come from a good distance away at this time of year, though goodness knows from where. Whatever the cause, the plain fact is that we have the plague, and as you will remember from the panic of four years ago when they passed the act in Parliament, it means the slaughter of the whole herd."

May came into the office and saw the gray anxiety on his face. "More trouble?" she queried.

He nodded. "Letter from home . . . disaster. Seems to be the pattern of the moment."

"Perhaps you should think of it all as a kind of test. I'm sure you'll meet it—even if you don't yet know how."

He smiled wryly and went on reading. "I don't have to tell you," his mother had continued, "what this tragedy means to us. They are going to pay some compensation, but it will be very small, and even if it was adequate, it would take time to replace the herd and I am not quite sure how we would live in the meanwhile. One possibility is to sell the farm. We have a neighbor who moved into the area about a year ago, a Mr. Cameron, who would like to buy it. He's purchasing a lot of land in the district, but the price he has offered us is very low.

"As you can see, there are decisions to be taken, and although I hate to ask you because I know you are so busy with your shop, we really do need to talk to you. Could you come home just for a few hours? Sunday perhaps? Edward will meet the London train at Aylesbury with the trap in the hope that you can be on it. He thinks it arrives about 11:30. —Your loving mother."

Thomas laid down the letter on the table and without saying anything pushed it across to May so that she could read it. He felt dazed by the scale of this new threat from so unexpected a source—*and* by its timing.

"Of course you must go," May said when she had finished reading the letter. Thomas nodded, and she added softly, "You'll solve this one too."

One of the salesladies came in and said that Miss Lillian Wilson was downstairs, and May left him to see her alone. "It's all coming at once, isn't it?" Lillian commented when he told her about the letter from home.

"I'll find the money for Uncle Jack," said Thomas, "but he'll just have to give me a few days."

She looked at him, soft compassion in her eyes. "I hated giving you the news yesterday," she told him.

"You did it well," Thomas answered, "as well as anyone could. Better, in fact."

"Oh, Thomas!" And she flung herself into his arms. For a moment he just held her and then gently disengaged her. She looked at him appealingly, tears in her eyes. "I'd give anything to be able to help," she said.

"I understand," he said. "Let's hope the day will soon return when we're laughing together again as we did at Christmas. Doesn't Christmas seem a long time ago?"

Edward was waiting for him at Aylesbury Station. Thomas was shocked by how old his brother looked, for he was only three years his senior but he had the appearance of a man in his late thirties. They shook hands warmly, got into the trap, and Edward slapped the reins on the horse's back. "It's good to see you, Thomas," he said. "I only wish the reason for your return was a better one."

"Have you slaughtered the herd?"

Edward nodded. "Yesterday. Most terrible day in my life."

"Any other farms hit yet?"

"Not among the neighbors. There's a rumor about a case at Banbury."

In the distance Thomas could see the outline of the Quainton Hills, which, since their farm lay on their lower slopes, had dominated his childhood. He had known those steep fields, divided by timber fences or blackthorn hedges, in every kind of weather—deep snow, driving rain, bright sunshine. When he was little, he had stood at the top of the ridge, with its view of the whole county and even part of Oxfordshire, and found it hard to stand when the winds were strong. For Thomas, for all his enjoyment of London, the Quainton Hills were home.

"Tell me about this new neighbor," Thomas said. "Did Mother say his name was Cameron?"

"Rich bugger," answered Edward. "Made a heap of money out of factories in the North. He's built himself a mansion at Marston. . . . Got grand ideas for a park and an estate, as though he was the Duke of Devonshire. He's buying all the adjoining farms he can get his hands on. . . . He's not a countryman, of course, but he's trying to be. He's got some beautiful horses, and he makes great play with the hunt. I shouldn't wonder if he's got ambitions to be Master of Foxhounds, but thank God, that's something you can't buy."

"He made you an offer for the farm?"

"I won't even tell you what it was. He's only interested in bargains. He was over again yesterday when he'd heard about our disaster. Thought we might be short of money." Edward gave a short, bitter laugh. "Can't think what gave him that idea. We've had the occasional letter from his lawyers . . ."

"Lawyers?" queried Thomas.

"That's his method if he's after your land. He knows that all small farmers are short of cash, so he makes you spend money in legal costs. He has his lawyers comb the deeds, and then you begin to get letters about rights-of-way, or pasturage, or drainage, or who owns the hedges and who's responsible for what. . . . He hasn't really started on us yet, but he will—because now that he's bought the farms on either side of us, our land juts into his estate like an arrow."

"You mean Arthur Anderson's sold to him?"

"Cameron bought out Arthur's mortgage. That gave him a lot more leverage to apply his usual method with his lawyers. . . . Luckily, we don't have a mortgage, but quite apart from Cameron, I don't think we've got much chance of saving the farm. Even before the plague it was hard, but now . . ." He shrugged his shoulders.

Thomas glanced at his elder brother. He looked tired, and deep lines of worry marked his face. Already, young though he was, his hair was beginning to turn gray. Well, Thomas thought, he had certainly had a lot to worry about just lately. But he had always lacked a tough grain. Even when they were children, Thomas had always known he was the stronger.

Edward turned the trap off the road into the long lane, worn by potholes, that led up to the farm between fields of pasture. And then, in an awful moment, Thomas became conscious of the burned carcasses. He smelled them first—and then, as the high hedge no longer obscured the view of the field, he saw the mounds of charred dead animals, slim wisps of smoke still rising as they smoldered.

Gloom hung in the house like heavy mist. Thomas' mother had obviously had no sleep for nights. "Stop your fussing, Mother," he said as he hugged her. "We'll find a way"—though he still had no notion how, unless it was to accept Goldsmith's hard terms. He shook hands with Brian, his younger brother, and kissed his sisters, Mary and Ellen. All of them looked pale and tired. Even Ellen's young face was marked by an expression of drawn anxiety. The last time he had seen her she had been a child, with breasts barely beginning to form.

"What's this—a wake?" he asked, smiling, and this at least made them try to cover their feeling of hopelessness.

They had chicken stew for lunch, and his mother asked how the shop was doing, and Thomas explained that he had severe temporary difficulties, but apart from these, the prospects were fine. They talked about the problem of the farm, and Thomas said he knew only one thing and that was that they were not going to sell it.

"How can we avoid it?" asked Edward.

"I don't know at this moment," answered Thomas. "But if we start with the certainty that we're not going to sell, then we're only talking about how we're going to hold it. Clearly, you're going to need some money to get started again. . . . What's the smallest number of cattle you can manage with? I mean, first of all to survive, and then to build up a herd that would give you a reasonable milk sale?"

"About ten, I suppose."

"More than that," Brian said. "If half of them are bull calves, it'll take years . . ."

"Of course we'd like more," Edward agreed, "but where's the money coming from?"

"Say I could get you fifty pounds," suggested Thomas. "Just for the time being. Would that be enough to manage? To buy some cows and a heifer or two? Someone'd lend you a bull to serve them, wouldn't they? I'll try to let you have some more money later."

For Thomas, the sudden lightening of the mood at the table was scaring. His mother was smiling. Mary and Ellen were engaged in animated discussion. Brian and Edward began to argue about the expenditure of the fifty pounds. He had given them hope, showed them that possibly there was a way out of their morass—assuming, of course, that he could find the money.

"Tell me a little more about this man Cameron," said Thomas. "Exactly where are the borders of his land?"

"The best way is to show you," answered Edward.

They rode up to the top of the hills, just the two of them. As they cantered onto the higher levels, Thomas thought of the many times he had seen hounds streaking in full cry across that steep grass, with the field riding hard behind them over the big timber fences which it was wise to clear, for the top rails were thick and you were down if you hit them.

Just before they reached the ridge, Edward reined in his horse and they turned and looked down on the view that Thomas had known ever since he was a small child. The village of Quainton, with the church on one edge of it and the windmill on the other, lay below them, smoke rising from the chimneys of the cottages. On either side of the village, spaced at intervals along the base of the hills, were farms—tight little groups of houses and barns and sheds. One of them, the third from Quainton to the east, had been the home of the Kingstons for more than a hundred years.

"Well," said Edward, "if you remember back, our boundary to the south is the road—to the far side of the wood there. The rest of the farm's hidden by the end of the hills. . . . Well, Cameron owns the land to the south and the east. . . . Now let's go over the ridge. . . ."

He heeled his horse and galloped for the top, with Thomas racing after him. "Come on!" Edward shouted, looking back. "What are you dawdling for?"

"You've given me the slow one on purpose!" Thomas yelled back, thinking that for the first time since he had arrived home his brother looked happy.

They rode over the ridge and across a large field that was not steep because it lay along the top of it. The village of Marston, to the north of the hills, came into view below them, and they checked their horses.

"That's Cameron's place," said Edward, "to the right of the village." It was a huge house, with two wings jutting forward from it, and extensive stables and outbuildings at the rear. The brickwork was still a vivid red, since it had not yet had time to weather. A long drive, lined with newly planted young trees, reached from the entrance gates between elegant meadows divided by neat timber fences which enclosed about a dozen horses.

"Our northern border," Edward explained, "is formed by that stream—you fell in it once, you may remember—and that field of young wheat beyond the meadows is our farthest extent. . . . Cameron owns the country beyond it and, of course, to the north. You can see why he'd like our farm . . . it'd tidy up his borders."

Thomas was only half listening. "One of these days, Edward," he said, "we'll have a big house like that, with blood horses behind posts and rails so that we can enjoy the sight of them from inside without even standing up, and seven hundred acres that you can really farm and a model herd that people will come from miles to see."

"Just at present," Edward answered, "I'm more concerned with keeping what we've got."

"You'll keep it. I'll see that you keep it. By God, I'll see that you keep it."

And he wheeled his horse in a tight turn and set off at a gallop up the hill toward home.

Early the next morning, Edward drove him in the trap to Aylesbury to catch the London train. "Thanks for coming, Thomas," he said as he shook his hand.

"It's been good to see you all again," Thomas answered. "I'll let you know as soon as I can about the money." He walked into the station to await the train, feeling strangely confident. What was another fifty pounds? If he could raise three hundred, he could find the rest. Goldsmith would probably provide it, he thought with bitter humor, if he offered his right arm as collateral.

Thomas had, in fact, arrived in London and was on his way from Paddington when, in the shop, May first saw Turner through the display window, standing on the pavement outside. At first she tried to pretend he was somebody else, unwilling to believe that he would call at Thomas' business. Then, as he entered and ambled in his unhurried way across the floor toward her, his face creased in that oily smile she had always loathed, she knew there was no doubt. She recalled vividly the last time she had seen it. "It's all very simple," he had said softly after telling her that Bob had been caught "borrowing" money from the till of the employer to whom Turner had introduced him. "I know Jameson, very, very well. I can arrange things. Let's have dinner and talk about it." She knew he really did have influence with Jameson, because Shoolbreds was the wholesaler's biggest customer.

She had prevaricated. It was difficult that week, she had said. What a pity, he had replied, because the police would have been called before they could have their little discussion. So she had consented and they had gone to one of those restaurants that had private rooms— "cabinets particuliers"—and he had told her that he had saved Bob from the arms of the law at a cost of all of seven pounds.

"I'll pay you back," she had said.

"One way or another." He had smiled.

"I'll pay you eight shillings a week."

"Why bother?" he had asked, putting his hand on her knee.

"Please don't do that, Mr. Turner," she had said sharply.

"Now, that's no way to talk," he had said. "You must be a little more cooperative, you know, if you want us to be friends."

At that moment, he had stopped his languorous approach. He had put one arm round her firmly, and with his other hand he had held her head so that she could not move her lips away as he kissed them. She had struggled and tried to scream, but had been able to do nothing until at last he released her.

"I hope," he said, the gentleness in his voice contrasting with the strength he had used, "that you understand the situation now."

"I understand the situation," she had replied tautly, "but I doubt if you do, Mr. Turner." Unhurriedly, she had taken her glass from the table as though to sip from it—and then flung its contents in his face. Even now, as he walked across Thomas' shop toward her, she could remember the mixture of horror and satisfaction she had felt as she watched him blink away the wine from his eyes and saw it drain down his cheeks to form red stain lines on his white collar.

The next morning he had sacked her without notice, warning her that any references requested from Shoolbreds would ensure that she would never work again. She had repaid the debt—repaid it, what was more, in regular weekly installments without seeking assistance or even giving explanations to Thomas. So why, on this March morning some six months later, was he calling to see her?

"Good morning, Miss Ramsay," he greeted in the oleaginous tone he had always employed to his most favored customers.

"What," demanded May angrily, "could you posssibly want with me now?"

"To do business," he said, as though utterly surprised by her attitude. "I have a wholesale firm now, you know. Didn't Bob tell you?"

"I've never heard such effrontery! Do you seriously think, after what happened, that we'd consider doing business with a blackguard like you?"

A broad smile creased his face, his lips curling back so far that his gums were revealed. "We, Miss Ramsay?" he said softly. "It's like that, is it? Our shop, eh? Well, that's even better, isn't it? Told him about us, have you? Told him how we dined in a private room? I'll wager you haven't. I'll wager it's a dark secret, but don't disturb yourself. Not one word'll escape my lips. The point is that I've got material to offer him that he just can't buy anywhere else—linens, velvets, cottons at prices he'd never believe in a hundred years. In fact, when he hears the details I'm sure he'll—"

"Would you please be good enough, sir," Thomas broke in, "to leave my shop at once." May had been so engrossed by her confrontation with Turner that she had not seen Thomas arrive in the shop, but the surge of relief she felt when she heard his voice was so overwhelming that she felt quite faint.

"You must be Mr. Kingston," said Turner, holding out his hand. "Allow me to introduce myself."

"I'll allow you to do nothing but leave the premises," said Thomas, taking him by the arm firmly and propelling him toward the door.

"You're not being wise, Mr. Kingston. I've got many friends in this trade. I can make things unpleasant for you."

"You already are, sir, by just being here." Without releasing his hold on Turner with one hand, Thomas opened the door with the other. "Please do not return, sir. You're not welcome at Kingstons."

The eviction completed, Thomas crossed the floor back to May. "Are you feeling all right?"

She swallowed hard and nodded. "Do you know who that was?"

"At a guess I'd say it was the famous Mr. Turner."

"Do you want me to explain?"

Thomas shook his head and smiled at her. "Not really."

She smiled gratefully. "How's the situation at home?"

"Not very good, but I'm glad I went. I told them I'd find the money that was needed."

"I'm sure you will, too. Trade's been brisk this morning, if that's any help. And Mrs. Fellowes sent this note for you."

He took the envelope from her and read the small forward-sloping handwriting that was now familiar. "Dear Mr. Kingston, there is something I would like to speak to you about. Could you please call on me at five o'clock this afternoon. Also I am in need of a black velvet mantle, possibly with an interesting trimming, and if you have any in stock that you think might appeal to me, perhaps you could bring them with you."

When Thomas was shown into the small first-floor room where she usually received, she was standing with her back to the door looking out the tall double window at Eaton Square. As he was announced by the butler, she turned, and Thomas, who was always impressed by her, thought she looked even more striking than he had ever seen her. Her hair was arranged in a single plait that rested on the front of one shoulder. She was wearing a simple gray wool dress with a pink silk underskirt that reached to her ankles over neat black button-up boots. "Good afternoon, Mr. Kingston," she greeted him with a warm smile. "How kind of you to come." She noticed the mantles he carried over his arm. "I see you've brought something for me to try on, as I asked. . . . Morton," she said to the butler, "I don't wish to be disturbed."

"Very good, madam," he responded, and withdrew, closing the door behind him.

"Lay those on the chair for a moment," she told Thomas, "and come and sit down." Thomas draped the mantles over the high satin back, wondering as he did so where Miss Jones was. It was the first time he had ever been alone with Mrs. Fellowes. "I'm sure you'd care for a cup of tea," she said, taking up a teapot from a tea tray that had already been set on a small table by the sofa. "I hear you've been away to your family in the country. I trust all is well there."

"Unfortunately not," Thomas answered. "Our herd have had to be destroyed."

"No!" she said with shock.

"Cattle Plague. There was a big epidemic a few years ago. Came in to Hull from Russia, so they said, but everyone thought it'd long been over."

"How terrible for you. . . . Poor Mr. Kingston, you seem to be in a lot of trouble at the moment, but that was why I asked you to come and see me. I want you to stop worrying about the whole matter and get on with directing your business, which I believe has a great future."

Thomas did not understand what she meant. "Oh, don't look so bewildered, Mr. Kingston," she said. "But of course. I haven't explained. How stupid of me. Mr. Goldsmith has told me of your problems—in confidence, of course. Really, he shouldn't have told me at all, but I wheedled it out of him. Well, Mr. Goldsmith, of course, is in a difficult position, as no doubt you realized. He has his bank and his partners to consider. But I, of course, don't have to worry about any considerations such as these. I am, you might say, a free agent, so"— she gave a little shrug of her shoulders and smiled—"you have no more problems."

Thomas was still mystified. "Madam, you must forgive me, but I still don't completely follow."

"You really are a silly sometimes, Mr. Kingston," she said, "if you don't mind my saying so. I shall lend you the money you need. Three hundred pounds, I think, is the figure you told Mr. Goldsmith, though I expect you'll need a bit more now that your family is in such difficulty at the farm."

Mrs. Fellowes' offer completely astonished Thomas. "I . . . I hardly know what to say, madam," he stuttered. In fact, he could not believe it. She was, after all, a woman, and although he began to ask the usual questions that precede acceptance of a loan, he was merely displaying what was now an automatic response. "I . . . I don't know what terms you had in mind, madam, but—"

"Terms?" she queried, looking at him, her eyes wide. "No terms."

"But there must be interest or a consideration of—"

Suddenly she appeared annoyed. "Do I look like a moneylender,

Mr. Kingston?" she asked sharply. "You can repay the money when you can—which I am sure won't be very far off in the future. . . . Mr. Kingston, you're still looking perplexed when the matter is really very simple—and truly only a trifle."

At last the reality of her offer began to dawn on him. "I'm overwhelmed," he said simply. Once again he felt the weight of his anxiety lift from him, but a newly developed instinct had now made him more cautious. "If I appear a little confused by your great generosity, Mrs. Fellowes," he said, "it's because I don't quite understand . . . well, why you're being so kind . . ."

"Why?" she echoed. Again her tone was a little tart. Then she gave a short laugh. "All right," she said, "I'll tell you. From the moment I walked into your shop on the day you opened for trade I realized that you were a young man destined to succeed, that I was witnessing the birth of a big enterprise, and the notion that I could perhaps make some small contribution from the very start was appealing—which is why I've done what little I could to help you."

"I've been most grateful," Thomas interposed, "for your patronage."

"Also, as I've told you before, I enjoy your company, Mr. Kingston. I find you entertaining, and . . . well, I don't know that I can think of the right word to describe my feelings of friendship. I'm in danger of being a little improper. . . . Shall we just say I enjoy talking to you. Now, no one could object to that could they?" She spoke lightly, as she had been speaking since they had sat down together on the sofa—and indeed, as she usually talked, with her stream of sophisticated chatter. But at this moment, as she looked at him, she changed. Her eyes misted in a way that was unmistakably sexual, and Thomas' reaction was immediate in an acute awareness of her body, close to him as she was, her legs only inches from his own. Suddenly he experienced a physical attraction for her that was almost animal in force, that was so strong that he had to fight to prevent himself from reaching and crushing her in his arms—and he was absolutely horrified. With her long plait of black hair curving forward on her soft neck, with her high cheekbones and oval azure eyes, Mrs. Fellowes was without question a lovely woman; but she was a customer, a customer of rank, and even if desires of this power were acceptable when induced by anyone, they certainly had no place in a shopkeeper's relations with his customers.

The tension between them increased sharply. She ran the tip of her tongue over her lips to moisten them, and he found the movement

almost irresistible. His stomach turned. Every muscle in his body was
taut. "Am I wrong," she asked quietly, speaking with evident difficulty, "in believing that the sense of rapport is mutual?" One of her
hands began to tremble, and she quickly covered it with the other.

"I . . . I have the greatest admiration for you, madam," Thomas
stammered.

"That's hardly the same thing as rapport," she said so softly that it
was almost a whisper. With a visible effort, she looked away. "Yet
unless I'm greatly mistaken, I'd swear you enjoyed coming to see
me."

"I most certainly do, madam," he insisted warmly, though he
was, he noticed, addressing her as "madam" more frequently than
normal.

"I'm pleased," she said. "It would have made me unhappy if I'd
misled myself." She stood up, and he knew she had moved because it
was intolerable for her to stay on the sofa. She walked to the window,
her underskirt rustling as she did so. She looked out onto the square,
standing, as she had been when he had entered the room, with one knee
bent slightly, so that her hip line and the tournure that covered it were
slanted in a way that was highly sensual. "I think I know what's in
your mind at this moment," she went on very quietly, without turning
from the window, "but sometimes, don't you think, there are forces . . .
emotions, perhaps . . . between a man and a woman that make any
differences in social standing a little . . . well, unimportant. And the
differences are less than you think. Before I married my late husband, I
was an actress, which is not a profession that is much admired in the
higher social circles." She broke off, and there was a heavy silence, for
Thomas did not know what to answer. To him the difference between
the proprietor of a small shop and a resident of Eaton Square with a
carriage-and-pair was immense, no matter what the backgrounds might
have been. "Mr. Kingston," she said, still with her back to him, "would
you do me a favor?"

"Of course," he replied.

"Would you refrain, just for a few minutes, from calling me
'madam'?"

"If that's your wish."

She turned from the window and looked at him, the strong sexuality still clear in her eyes. He saw her swallow. "Perhaps," she said, "I
should try on the mantles now."

"Very well, m— . . ." He just succeeded in stopping the word
before it emerged.

She smiled—a strange, taut, artificial smile. "You managed it, you see. That was good." She moved toward the fireplace, above which was a big gilt Louis XIV mirror on the wall. "Would you bring one to me—the one you think best."

She stood facing the mirror and watched him in its reflection as he took a mantle from the chair and approached her. Their eyes met in the glass, and he knew that he should look away, that he should attempt to recover some semblance of the relationship that had existed until a few minutes before, but his eyes stayed fixed on hers. He lifted the cloak and draped it over her shoulders. As he did so, she gently raised both her hands to his, holding them against herself above each of her breasts. "Do you think the mantle suits me?" she asked, her gaze intent on his in the mirror.

He barely heard her, his whole conscious mind dominated by the touch of her fingers within his, by the deep urgency in her eyes. "Do you"—she persisted, speaking so quietly that it was almost a whisper—"think it suits me?"

"I . . . I . . ." he began, his voice choked. "I'm finding it hard to think . . ."

She smiled. "I was right, wasn't I?"

He nodded, and very slowly she turned, letting his hands slip from hers as she moved, so that she was facing him. She raised her lips, and very slowly he put his mouth to them. All their movements were strangely unrushed and deliberate, as though they had been rehearsed for a ballet. He put his arms round her waist within the mantle. She lifted her hands to his neck, and the cloak fell from her shoulders. He kissed her with more pressure, and she responded, moving her lips on his mouth, pressing her body against him.

She drew back her head, looking up at him, her eyes shining, and he noticed that their color did seem to be slightly changed, as she had suggested that morning weeks before. "They *are* green," he said, smiling.

"Do you like green eyes?"

In answer, he put his mouth to hers again. "Wait," she whispered, "while I lock the door."

As she turned the key in the lock, the click sounded to Thomas unusually loud. For an instant she stayed with her back against the door, needing perhaps an emotional pause before returning to him. Somehow her hair had become untidy, strands escaping from the plait. Her lips were slightly open and she was short of breath.

"I thank God," she whispered, "that this has happened. . . . Even your problems . . . I'm glad of them too, for they've enabled us to meet alone. . . . I'm so happy I could lift them from you."

The transformation of Thomas' emotions was drastically sudden. Her words, spoken though they were with intense feeling, jarred in him, revealing the reality of his situation, which had become obscured by the strange violence of his need for her, with the brilliant clarity of a flash. He was a young tradesman making love to a wealthy woman customer ten years his senior—a woman who was going to lend him money.

It was an unattractive, unheroic picture. Later, Thomas wondered if it was purely the element of money that had caused his sudden inhibition, that made him decline the opportunity to have this beautiful woman for whom many men would have paid a fortune.

He flared into anger. "It must be pleasant to be rich," he said, his voice suddenly hard, "to think of three hundred pounds as a trifle, to be able to make a crisis as grave as mine disappear at a touch as though you were a magician."

Just for a few moments she was shocked by the change in him. "I've upset you," she said. "What have I done to upset you?" She moved to him swiftly, and he put his arms round her, for he knew he had been ungracious, but he did not kiss her. "Is it so wrong," she asked, "to want to play a part in your life, to take an interest in you?"

"You have already," he said dully. "You've been very kind."

She looked up at him, conscious that his desire for her had gone. "It's the money?" she queried. He nodded, and she released herself from his arms and sat down on the sofa. "You feel you're being bought?"

"You must forgive me. I should never have behaved as I did."

She laughed at his assumption of the blame. The vulnerability she had displayed since he had first kissed her, her exposure of passion, had disappeared. Once more she was the sophisticated woman he had seen stepping down from her carriage on the September morning he had opened his shop. "You silly boy," she said, "how can you feel you're being bought when the money is only a loan?"

"It's not a loan in the real sense."

"It must be repaid. Isn't that a loan?"

"I mean it's not a real business transaction. It's a favor."

"We'll make it a business transaction. We'll have a formal deed . . . lawyers. . . . You can pay interest if it'll make you feel better . . . and if you don't repay it, I promise to sue you and have you flung into jail.

. . . Oh, really, what difference does it make? Money's so unimportant."

"I wish it was as unimportant to me at this moment."

"It will be. You just have temporary difficulties. One day, the thought of being short of three hundred pounds will seem a joke. . . . Now come and sit down for a moment. Your tea must be cold. Would you like me to pour you some more?" She emptied his cup into the slop basin and looked back at him, but he had not moved from the fireplace.

"Oh, dear, you *are* a strange young man. Why don't you think of me as a patroness? I mean a real patroness, like painters and poets and composers often have during the early years of their careers. Do you think *they* think they're being bought? Of course they don't. I've never heard anything so ridiculous in my life. Now come and sit down as I asked—even if you don't want to . . . to please me."

"I think I should go," he said.

"Not yet—sit down for a moment. "Please," she repeated from the sofa.

Thomas shrugged his shoulders. "All right," he said, and sat beside her, a little awkwardly. "You must think me very much a country oaf."

"On the contrary, oafs are simple. You're complex. An oaf would not have stopped himself as you did. But then, an oaf wouldn't have had the opportunity that was given to you."

"I can't express how sorry I feel . . . or how flattered."

She smiled at the compliment, sounding as it did like the sort of remark he made to customers in his shop. "That's more like the Thomas Kingston I know," she said. "Now please look at me." And as he looked into her eyes he felt the pull of her again. "You know, you're making me feel very forward," she said quietly. "You should be pleading with me and I should be retreating when you approach, hiding behind my fan. But here I am saying the things that you should be saying. . . . No!" She put her finger over his lips as he began to remonstrate. "Not a word of explanation. We've had enough of that. I must tell you that I'm not ashamed. Perhaps it's my background. Actresses don't despise their passions as some respectable women do, or even try to conceal them very much . . . and what's happened to *your* passion?" She said if softly, lightly, with a half smile. "Where's that flame that was burning so strongly, that made you kiss me so tenderly, that made me lock the door?"

As Thomas looked at her, desire for her welled up in him again. Sensing it, she leaned toward him. Their lips met, parted, wet. His arms went round her, and she closed her eyes. He held her tightly, kissing her passionately. His hands moved on her body. He felt her breast, firm beneath the material of her dress . . . and for a second time, some reaction in him severed his emotion. The money? The vast social division between them? The fact that she was his customer? May? In all his mental postmortems, he was never really able to isolate the exact reason. Perhaps it was an amalgam of them all. An overpowering instinct ruled that it was wrong. This time, his physical response to the situation came as a sense of suffocation. He released her, his chest heaving, and stood up, gasping for breath. "I'm sorry," he choked, "I can't go on."

"Don't stop now," she said softly, vulnerable again. "Please don't stop now."

"You must forgive me. You are most desirable. You've honored me. But . . ." He broke off. The room was now totally oppressive. He felt as though the walls and ceiling were closing in on him. "I must leave," he insisted.

She stood up and went to him, but he kept his hands by his side and shook his head. "Forgive me."

"Stay . . . please." She touched his cheek with her hand.

"I can't. . . . I apologize, but I just can't." His sensation of claustrophobia, his need to get out of that room, overwhelmed him. His lungs began to hurt as though he were drowning. He pushed her aside, gently but firmly, and moved to the door.

"I don't want you to go," she said. "Please don't go . . . not like this."

"I must," he answered, turning the key in the lock with fumbling hands.

Suddenly she was furious. "I warn you not to leave this room! By heaven, I'll make you regret it if you do!"

He turned back to her. "I've tried to explain, Mrs. Fellowes . . . I can't stay. . . . At this moment I physically can't stay. . . . I'll call on you tomorrow."

"Come back just for a moment." Her voice had lost its anger, but when he shook his head, the harshness was in her tone again. "Where will you get your money now?" She said it with contempt, the woman of power once more.

"I don't know," he said.

"Don't expect Ernest Goldsmith to help, because I'll see he doesn't."

He opened the door. "Please," he heard her say, once more without fury, without power—just appeal.

He closed the door behind him and heard the crash as some china ornament broke against the other side of it. "You oaf!" he heard her yell. "You common, impotent oaf!" He hurried down the stairs, hardly seeing Morton, the butler, who opened the front door for him and handed him his hat and stick as he passed.

When he reached the shop he went straight upstairs to his top-floor bedroom, where he would not be disturbed. He needed to compose himself, to assess his situation, stripped as it now was of the support of Mrs. Fellowes—or, worse, threatened by her malevolence as a woman scorned. He took off his coat, unbuttoned his cravat and sat on his bed in his shirt sleeves, drained by a sense of humiliation and shame, totally mortified by his absurd behavior. At the very best, he had insulted a woman and displayed a naiveté that was unforgivable.

For the hundredth time since he had stumbled away from Eaton Square, he asked himself if he could have not averted such total disaster. Could he not have made some excuse to leave before everything between them had progressed too far? Could he not, for heaven's sake, have taken her as she desired, since he had wanted her so badly? And the problems it would have solved! She would still be his friend. The money would have gone both to the farm and to Uncle Jack. The new shop would have opened on schedule.

And then he knew the reason that lay behind his failure to finish what he had started. The price for accepting her loan would have been enormous. It would not have been just one afternoon of passion that Thomas could perhaps have rationalized with his relationship with May. There would have been other occasions—always at the behest— at the command, even—of his patroness. How could he have retained his self-respect as a man? So there was one thing, he thought wryly, that did come before the interests of the shop, for the shop was an extension of *him*—though in the future, as it assumed, with its expansion, a sovereignty of its own, this was a premise he would question.

Meanwhile, on that evening in March 1870, he was forced to face the bleak facts of his position. For all his dismissal of Goldsmith's offer as unacceptable, he had, he realized, been relying on it as a last solution if all else failed. Now, if Mrs. Fellowes carried out the last threat she had hurled at him as he had left, even that recourse was gone.

It was at this moment, when there no longer seemed any way of overcoming his crisis, that Thomas experienced a moment of desperation that he had never known before in his life. For a few seconds he put his head in his hands. Then, as he began to condemn himself for weakness, which is the first stage of resistance to such black feelings, there was a knock on his door. It surprised him, for people rarely came to his room, apart from the char who cleaned it, and for a moment he did not respond. Only when the knock was repeated did he get up heavily and open the door. May was standing on the landing, holding a small tray on which were a bottle and a glass.

"I thought a brandy might help," she said.

Never before, in all the months she had worked for him, had she climbed the stairs to the floor on which he slept. "Did anyone see you coming up?" he asked apprehensively.

"Concern for my reputation?" she queried. "There are times when other things are more important." She set down the tray on a small table. "I've never seen you as you looked tonight," she said, pouring brandy into the glass. "I don't know what happened at Mrs. Fellowes', but I'm certain of one thing: I've been with you from the first hour you started work in this shop and I'm not going to sit downstairs and let you go through this alone—not at a time when you need me as you've never needed me before." She held out the glass to him. "Thomas, you do realize, I hope, how much I love you."

He took the glass from her, almost as though he had not heard, sipped the brandy and then suddenly flung it aside and grasped her in his arms. "May!" he whispered. "Oh, God, my May!" In his kissing of her there was release, love, passion, exaltation, wild, soaring desire. She clung to him, her body demanding unison. He ripped open her bodice. They overbalanced and collapsed on the bed, but they barely noticed. Their lips were together; somehow the clothing that kept them apart was torn away. As he entered her, she was overwhelmed by a compelling need to consume him, to take him completely into her body. She could not see. She could only hear a roaring in her ears. Her spirit soared higher and higher until the climax and they lay exhausted, satiated, aware of a wonderful sense of peace, his head on her naked breast.

The next day, Thomas' crisis had not changed, of course, but his resolve was strong once more. He considered several new courses of action. He considered writing to Goldsmith, despite Mrs. Fellowes' threat. He toyed with the thought of stomaching his pride and going back to see Arthur Stockton—at least to buy a little time. He even thought of advertising in *The Times*, as he had seen others do, but he suspected that new negotiations would involve too great a delay.

Late in the morning, Mrs. Fellowes' carriage drew up at the door and the footman brought into the shop the mantles Thomas had left behind at Eaton Square. There was a brief note: "I am returning to you your garments. I do not think any of them suit." The cold brevity was a clear indication that any faint hopes he might have had that her resentment had lessened were without foundation.

That evening, as Thomas prepared to close the shop, David Rawlings ambled in with a broad grin on his face. "Hallo, David," said Thomas, warmly shaking the hand of his friend with pleased surprise. "Why are you looking so happy? Had some good news?"

"Possibly. You might think so. Come and have a porter. Can you spare him, Miss Ramsay?" he asked May.

"For about five minutes," she answered with a smile.

They went up Sloane Street to the George II, and David slapped down two pennies on the bar and ordered a couple of tankards. He drank deeply, then said, "You probably know that I've been seeing a bit of Lillian lately." He paused as Thomas frowned in mock censure. "Well, she told me about your crisis with your aunt and the money. I don't know if you've managed to resolve that yet."

"No," Thomas answered, "you certainly couldn't describe the matter as resolved. In fact, David, I'm in one hell of a bloody mess."

"Because," David went on, "a thought occurred to me when I heard about it. Remember my telling you a few months ago that my father had offered to set me up in business?"

Thomas nodded. "Just before I opened—that wet Sunday."

"And I wasn't quite certain if I was cut out for it?"

"Yes—it was nonsense, of course."

"No, it wasn't. I still don't think I'm cut out for it—not on my own, like you; but . . . well, perhaps with a partner it'd be different. . . . Thomas, would you consider taking me in as a partner?—a junior partner, of course."

Thomas just stared at his friend in astonishment. It was a possibility which throughout all his trauma of the past days he had never even considered.

"You don't have to answer yet," said David hastily. "Let me go on. When I heard, I sat down and wrote to my father and said what a good start you'd made. I mentioned the second shop, which Lillian told me about. I even described your belief in the future of emporiums."

"Emporia," corrected Thomas.

"Emporia?" queried David, not understanding.

"No matter . . . go on."

"Well, I had a reply from him today. As you know, he's always been afraid that I wasn't aggressive enough—soft like my mother, he's always said. So he was pleased I'd written. He's agreed to put up three hundred pounds, but he's made one or two conditions."

"I should think he has," said Thomas, still incredulous.

"He says he wants me to have not less than twenty-five-percent ownership in the partnership as an investment and suggests that two hundred of the three hundred pounds should be used to purchase this. The rest to be repayable, but to carry interest meanwhile at the rate of three percent per annum. He would expect me to join you in the business and receive a salary to be negotiated. . . ." He broke off as he saw the expression on the face of his friend. "Thomas, do you feel all right?"

"All right?" repeated Thomas. "All right, you ninny? I feel all right, all right. Landlord!" he called suddenly, turning on his stool. "A bottle of champagne, if you please!"

David grinned. "You mean you accept Father's terms?"

"Of course I accept them!" answered Thomas. "They're generous, and it'd be fine to be working together again. That's why we're going to celebrate. . . ." He broke off as a thought came to him. "Oh, there's one thing I've forgotten."

"What's that?"

"I need more than three hundred, David. I need another fifty."

"It'd carry interest like the rest?"

"Of course."

"Then I'm sure Father would agree."

The pop of the champagne cork sounded to Thomas like a victory salvo fired by a hundred guns. He held up his glass. "Well, here's to Kingston and Rawlings."

"I don't think we should change the name," said David. "Kingstons sounds much better. It's simple and easy to remember. I think the toast should be to Kingstons and its new member of the management."

As they drank, Thomas burst out laughing, choking on champagne as he did so. "I've just had a wonderful thought. What do you think old Clegg would say to this—his two apprentices in business on their own account?"

David grinned. "Let's drink to Clegg. He was a swine, but he taught us a lot."

"To Clegg," said Thomas—adding as though the old buyer could hear him, "you bastard."

They parted at the door of the pub, and Thomas, abandoning his dignity for once, ran back to the shop as excited as a boy. May, like the rest of the staff, was preparing to close up for the night, and he asked her to follow him to the office. He entered the room ahead of her and, with elaborate courtesy, held the back of the visitor's chair for her to sit down. Usually, of course, she took one of the wooden chairs at the table, but now she entered into his game.

"Thank you, Mr. Kingston," she said. "How considerate of you."

He sat down on his usual seat with deliberate care, carefully holding back the tails of his frock coat as he did so to prevent creasing, and leaned forward with his elbows on the table, his hands clasped together. "Tell me, Miss Ramsay," he said, as though interviewing an applicant for a post, "have you ever considered the possibility of matrimony?"

CHAPTER THREE

January 1871

· I ·

Slowly the wave of pain subsided and May opened her eyes. She looked around her, noting as though for the first time the ordinary familiar features of the room: the red flickering flames of the gas fire; the condensation on the glass of the window, through which she could just detect the piled snow on the sill outside; the blue-patterned bowl on the marble washstand, steam rising from the hot water that Lillian, eager to be useful, had just brought in.

The wind moaned, and May thought, What a night to be born! Then she smiled, for she knew that this aspect would appeal to Thomas, with his sense of destiny and taste for drama—a taste that this January evening, with the onset of her labor two weeks early, should have amply satisfied. His eyes had revealed his anxiety as he had sent David rushing off to get the doctor, but he had held her firmly and given her confidence.

"Just like his father," she had joked tautly, "in a rush already." But the strain in her voice had caused him to calm her. "Easy, my love, just relax," he had said.

The midwife, her starched apron rustling, wiped the sweat from May's forehead with a towel. Dr. Henderson's shirt sleeves were rolled up, to reveal muscular arms corded with veins. He smiled encouragement. "Everything's going to be all right, Mrs. Kingston."

Mrs. Kingston. She was still not accustomed to being Mrs. Kingston, even wondering at times when people used the name if they were addressing someone else, though the spring afternoon that Thomas had given her the name remained vivid enough in her mind. "I want to hear bells," he had declared expansively. "I want to hear bells ringing out in joyous celebration!" And ring out they had on that brilliant sunny afternoon, their cascade of sound soaring across the rooftops of Sloane Street and Knightsbridge and the fashionable squares where their customers lived.

It had been a very small wedding, conducted at one of the side altars of St. Mary's, which was why the vicar, accustomed as he was to officiating in his huge church at big fashionable marriages, had suggested that bells might not be entirely appropriate for a ceremony that was perhaps in the nature of a private occasion. "Private?" Thomas had echoed, ignoring the implication that, as a tradesman, he was aspiring beyond the social position in which it had pleased God to place him. "Our wedding's not to be private, sir." And as they walked out of the church and heard the great peals above them in the belfry, she had sensed his pride in the fact that London had been left in no doubt that an event of some importance had just been enacted.

May's father, leaning heavily on two sticks, had come up from Surbiton to give her away. Thomas' mother, his brother Brian and his two sisters had traveled from Quainton, leaving Edward to tend the farm on his own, though this was no hardship, since he was so obsessed with his new cattle he hated to leave them.

After the ceremony they had all gone back to the shop to celebrate in the first-floor staff room, where the table, beautifully decorated by Emily Lane, who had a talent for it, was sagging with food and wine. The salesladies and Sidney Baines, the new salesman, had taken turns to leave the sales floor to share in the festivities. Finally, Uncle Jack—who had come on his own, since Aunt Dolly was still in Paris—had proposed the toast to the happy couple, and Thomas had responded with a short speech, marked with a few "shop" jokes about the merchandise he had just acquired and how well, he was sure they would all agree, it was displayed and how this was one special item of his stock that would never be "tinged." Then May and Thomas had left for Victoria Station by hansom, with everyone waving from the windows, to spend a couple of days in Brighton, which was all the time he could spare.

They had stayed in a pleasant little hotel on the seafront and had taken long, happy walks along the promenade, with Thomas worrying if she was being too strenuous and May assuring him that it was far too soon to worry about things like that—for of course, she knew by then that she was pregnant, and they had even chosen the name for the baby. "We'll call him Ramsay after you," Thomas had said. "Ramsay Edward Thomas Kingston. It's got a good solid ring to it, hasn't it?— suitable for the head of an emporium."

She smiled at his assumption. "Perhaps we shall have a girl."

"No," he said confidently, "you'll bear me a boy, who'll grow up with a brilliant acumen as a man of business."

Those two days were the first time May had ever been with Thomas outside the setting of his business. They induced a heady sense of freedom. She even ventured to speak to him of Lillian, who she sensed was a subject that needed approaching with some care. Since David had joined the firm, Lillian had taken to spending Sundays and some evenings with them—usually in the two rooms over the first shop that May had been preparing to be her first home with Thomas as a married couple.

May's feelings for Lillian were ambivalent. She did not exactly dislike her, and although at first her handsome looks and her self-assurance had caused her some misgivings, she no longer feared her, for Thomas had clearly selected his wife. But she found her uncomfortable. Her determination to be fashionable, her tacit criticism of anyone who did not share this aspiration, her thrusting personality that was motivated, May suspected, by an exceptional ambition hardly created the ideal climate for a relaxed friendship between two women.

May herself could be tart on occasion, though usually with a vein of wit, but Lillian would pounce with a bold frankness that was disarming. The months since May had first met Thomas had been a period of extremely hard work, with little leisure for thought of clothes. She had been surprised, therefore, when Lillian had remarked to her one evening as she was changing in her bedroom, "Don't you ever feel the need for something a little prettier?"

"I wasn't planning to go to a ball," answered May.

"No," conceded Lillian with a smile, "but men do respond to nice clothes, don't they?—especially Thomas. Even when he was twelve, he'd notice if I had a new dress."

The remark suddenly opened a new vista to May. She had never really thought of Thomas as a small boy. "What was he like when he was twelve?"

A smile crossed Lillian's face. "A bit quiet—often laughing, but quiet. Strangely tidy. Not like Edward, who always looked as though he'd been dragged backwards through the cattle sheds. Of course, I didn't go to Quainton often—just a few times with Aunt Dolly when she visited Buckingham. I saw more of him in Copenhagen Street after he came to London. We played cards and Happy Families on wet Sunday afternoons. Occasionally there were outings—the Tower, the Zoo, things like that . . . and a few of the kind of secrets you have at that age—with lots of giggling and dramatics."

"I envy you that," said May simply.

"I would too, if I was marrying him and hadn't known him be-

fore," agreed Lillian. "It's a small bit of him you can never possess."
There was no triumph in the way she said it—nor regret either. "It's
instinctive, I suppose, to want to possess all of a man; but you've got
him, May—most of him: the grown man, not the boy—anyway, for
the . . ." Again she broke off.

"For the time being?" prompted May. "Was that what you were
going to say?"

"Does any woman have any man totally forever? He's going to be
your husband. You should be happy with that."

"Oh, I'm happy with it. There's nothing else I want."

At the time, the conversation had not seemed too barbed. It was
only afterward, when May thought about what she had actually said,
that she realized how undermining Lillian could be if she let her. She
was, however, someone she would have to live with—especially if she
married David.

"I find it hard to see Lillian as David's wife," she said to Thomas as
they walked along the promenade between the Brighton piers into a
strong easterly wind that smelled richly of brine. "He's such an easygoing person."

"You think she needs stronger meat—a husband who'll thrash her,
perhaps?"

"Not quite, but a husband who'll lead, at least."

"Perhaps she'll change him. Perhaps we'll see a new autocratic
David."

May did not answer, but her silence indicated her doubts.

"Let's go back to the hotel," said Thomas suddenly. "I've a violent
urge to assert my rights."

"What—before lunch?" she queried, laughing. "It must be the sea
air that brings out the beast in you."

"*You* bring out the beast in me—if it's the beast. I thought it was
love or adoration or passion. If we don't go back now, I shall disgrace
us both on one of the benches."

She turned suddenly on her heel, her arm in his, bearing him
round with her. "Well, don't dawdle, then," she chided, "or I'll think
it's all talk."

The pain swept through her again and, reaching up with both
hands, May gripped the brass rail of the bedstead as tightly as she could,
trying not to cry out. The contraction eased, but they were coming
more often now, and she waited to be engulfed again in a level of
agony that each time was greater than before. It scorched upward

through her, contorting her body, forcing a muffled scream from her lips.

I'm going to faint, she thought. I mustn't faint—though as the pain lessened she wondered why it would be so bad to faint. Lillian moved to her and took her hand—looking cool and unruffled as usual. What was she doing there? May would have preferred to have Emily with her. Could she not even have a baby without Lillian?

Thomas had been right at Brighton, of course. Lillian *had* tried to change David, but it had taken May some time to suspect the sheer extent of Lillian's intentions. They had married very soon after May and Thomas returned from Brighton, and the occasion was a repeat performance of the earlier wedding, in the same church and with a similar celebration in the staff room over the shop.

Lillian, stimulated by the wine, had been even more outrageous than usual. "Does this make us closer than step-cousins?" she had asked as Thomas had given her a goodwill kiss after the toast to the happy couple.

"A kind of sister-in-law," he had answered with a smile, "by stockholding."

"That doesn't sound very exciting," she said, and held out her other cheek in a demand that he kiss her again. And May noticed that she moved her face at the last moment so that his lips were on the corner of her mouth—which, though she had seen her do it before, struck her as being just a little willful for a wedding day.

May was not really jealous, because Thomas could not have been a more loving husband, and he had always treated Lillian, with her arch flirtation, as something of a clown. But later, in one of those black moments that accompany pregnancy, she had suddenly visualized the power within Kingstons that Lillian would wield if Thomas ever came to view her differently—greater even than if she had become his wife, for she would be in a position to influence both men. May had dismissed the thought at once, but the idea had recurred at times to plague her—especially during the quarrels between the partners in which she sometimes saw signs of Lillian's involvement. For the prospect of being in business with David that had at first made Thomas so enthusiastic had not in practice been as pleasant as the two of them had hoped. They were different kinds of men, with different philosophies, which had not mattered when they were apprentices but was important now they were joint owners of a firm.

From the start David had been astonished by the risks that Thomas took by the hour as he approved the ordering of new stock, for he had never really witnessed bold merchandising in the staid, conservative atmosphere of Parsons.

Emily Lane was now helping with the buying for the women's sections—usually in consultation with May herself—and Thomas was closely involving the new salesman, young Sidney Baines, in the purchasing of the piece goods.

David was sharing Thomas' office, which, during this period, was a scene of constant activity and fast decisions. He would sit, one elbow on his desk, his chin on his hand, a heavy fair lock of hair drooping over his forehead from the right-hand side—though strangely, never from the left—of his center parting.

"How in the world do you know you'll sell them?" he asked Thomas when he heard him instruct Emily to spend thirty pounds on a range of umbrellas.

"I don't," answered Thomas with a grin. "But I think we will. They're decorative and different. So does Miss Lane, and she's got an excellent nose. Oh, take that anxious look off your face, David. This is what the business is about—informed guessing. Guess right often enough and you thrive. Guess wrong too many times and you fail."

There was more risk taking even than usual when David joined the firm because the new shop was being devoted mainly to ladies' clothing that was so far unexplored territory for Kingstons. The Dress Department was to be its bastion, though Thomas had moved the Fancy Goods and the Mantles to trade alongside it, together with new sections for hosiery, gloves and umbrellas. Meanwhile, the original shop was devoted solely to materials—silks, linens, cottons, velvets—in much larger ranges than before.

David's uneasy attitude toward the dangers involved in buying fashion merchandise was not relieved when the second shop had opened at last at the end of May. It was spring, which could not have been a better time, but the sales did not soar away in the pattern of Thomas' previous experience. The first month's trading was profitable, but not very. In long sessions with May and Emily, Thomas searched like a terrier for the reason for this mediocre performance, analyzing the sales in each range of merchandise, section by section. What was moving? What was slow? Why was it slow? Were they investing in the wrong colors or the wrong styles? Was it the whole concept of buying ready-made dresses—instead of material to be passed to dressmakers—that was proving unaccceptable to the customers? Thomas doubted it. Other shops were selling made-up clothes, new though they were, and he was sure the future lay in this area.

David was unable to play any part in these vigorous examinations, and one evening at the end of a hectic session lasting all afternoon when he was alone with Thomas and May in the office, he said sadly, "I don't feel I'm making much contribution."

"You can't pick it all up at once," Thomas countered.

May noticed that the next morning, David began to take a very much closer interest in those aspects of the business which did not require experience of buying. After a few days, he knew exactly what the stock values were in each department. He checked the bank balance every morning, kept a careful note of any debts they had and made a detailed study of the sales trends in each range of merchandise over the past few weeks. When a query came up during their meetings, although Thomas carried all the basic facts of the business in his head, David could often supply precise figures.

"You always were one for looking after the farthings," Thomas joked one evening.

"So would you have been if you'd lived in my home," David answered. His father had been a speculator in commodities, and the family fortunes had seesawed between periods of relative affluence and of extreme poverty, reaching a nadir at one moment in bankruptcy.

"Your father doesn't appear to be exactly hard up now," remarked Thomas.

"He had a stroke of luck," said David. "He came by some vital advance information that enabled him to recover much of what he'd lost."

"That's the sort of luck we need."

David smiled a little wryly. "If you live by luck, you have to accept both good and bad. You can't choose."

"May, I think he's trying to warn us," said Thomas with a grin.

It was a light, good-humored exchange that was to foreshadow their first major quarrel a few days later. The June business in dresses showed an improvement, but not on the scale that Thomas was seeking. "It's not buoyant," he complained to May and Emily on one morning in July. "There's no spirit there."

It was at this moment that young Sidney Baines hurried into the office. "I 'ope it's not the wrong moment to interrupt you, Mr. Kingston," he said, "but they're moving out of the shop next door."

"What?" said Thomas, his eyes bright.

"Miss Simpson saw 'em first—loading a wagon—and only mentioned it casual like about 'alf an 'our later. 'Oly smoke, I said, just wait till Mr. Kingston 'ears."

Thomas had already rushed past him out of the room as Baines went on speaking, but he returned a few minutes later brimming over with excitement. "It's true!" he said. "What's more, I've just seen the managing agent. We can have it for a hundred a year."

David was staring at his partner with disbelief. He had a fair beard, and beneath it his cheeks were a boyish pink that now glowed a shiny red, revealing his agitation. "You're not serious, Thomas," he said.

"Serious?" echoed Thomas. "Of course I'm serious."

"You've been worrying for weeks about your trade in your second shop and here you are considering a third."

"Oh, we'll get the problem of the dresses solved. That's only temporary, but this is an opportunity we just can't miss. The shop's next door. If someone else leases it, years may go by before we get another chance. Also, as you know as well as I do, we're desperate for more space."

This was true. With the growth of the business, the volume of bookkeeping and correspondence was soaring. Every major delivery of merchandise created a crisis, for there was nowhere adequate to unbox it, check it against the invoices, record it in the stock books and attach price tags.

"It's a risk, of course, but sometimes in a growing business you have to take risks," Thomas said.

"Calculated risks perhaps," David agreed, "but not stupid risks. You've given this no thought at all."

"Think of the double frontage," enthused Thomas, "the display space, the extra basement area, the scope for bigger departments."

David sighed angrily. "The dream of your emporium."

"It's not a dream," Thomas shouted at him, suddenly flushed. "It's an inevitable development."

"Thomas . . ." David's tone was calmer, conciliatory. "Can't you see the danger? On top of all the other expenses, it'll be a huge drain. We don't have the money. We just can't afford it."

"We've got to afford it. We'd be mad not to. Somehow we'll find the money."

David shook his head. "That attitude's the way to go bankrupt," he said—pausing for a moment before adding, "as you almost did in March."

He knew at once he had gone too far. All obvious manifestation of Thomas' anger had left him—the high color in his face, the swollen vein in his neck, his raised voice. "If I almost went bankrupt in March," he said in a tone of cold control, "it wasn't due to any unwise business risk, but because of Aunt Dolly—as you well know."

David did, of course, but he still attempted one last appeal.

"You've never seen anyone go bankrupt, Thomas, and I can tell you it's not pleasant. It strips a man of self-respect. I'll never forget the look on my father's face that night when he came home from Carey Street. Thomas, he cried like a child in my mother's arms."

His partner had barely heard. "There are some things you've just got to do," he said. "You can't always explain why, because it's a matter of 'feel.' "

"Feel!" David echoed with disbelief.

"I *know*, David, I positively *know* that we must take that shop."

The next day, Thomas signed the lease of Kingstons' third shop, and once again, the Fates who had seemed to guide his progress during his early months of trading appeared to have returned to his support. Sales of the dresses suddenly leaped and, during the weeks that followed, maintained a steady upward trend.

The quarrel, of course, was a reflection of the conflict that had been growing in the relationship between the two men ever since David had joined the firm—a conflict that May suspected Lillian of fanning. She felt a deep sadness for them both, for the partnership had begun to sour their friendship, and after the third-shop quarrel, it was never to be the same again.

The situation was not helped by the fact that Thomas found in young Sidney Baines a quickness of mind that was in tune with his own. He was lean, with dark hair, a moustache that was rather too ample for a boy who was not yet twenty-one and a bright-eyed, impish humor which appealed to the customers. He was a Cockney boy from the dockland slums of Poplar, and he owed his first apprenticeship in a shop to the head of the local Christian mission, who had detected his potential.

Thomas often spoke of him to May, marveling at the fact that he could have emerged from this background with a flair for dealing with well-bred ladies and a passion for fine materials that had led him, so they discovered, to collecting pieces of cloth which he stuck in an album like stamps.

A few hours before Thomas' quarrel with David, Baines had come into the office to suggest a new way of displaying the silks, and it had caught Thomas's imagination. "Why, that's just capital, Baines," he had said enthusiastically. "Capital. Get on with it right away, and I'll come down and see it later."

"If only I could be as enthusiastic about something David suggested," Thomas said to May that night.

"Perhaps," May answered, "you haven't yet found the proper

outlet for his talents . . . and sometimes I think you overestimate
Baines. He's very exuberant at times, even cheeky. I think on occasion
you should put him in his place." As she said it she wondered suddenly
if she was in fact a little jealous of the enjoyment Thomas clearly
gained from working with him. Was it another case, like Thomas'
childhood, of a part of his life she could not share? "The salesladies are
always complaining of him," she said carefully—conscious that she was
trying to convince herself that others too were critical of Baines.
"They say he can be very lewd. In fact, on one occasion he actually
kissed Miss Simpson in the stockroom."

Thomas just looked at her with the hint of a smile at the corners
of his mouth. "I'll instruct him not to kiss the salesladies in the stockroom," he said.

For a few days after the quarrel, the atmosphere in the office was
very strained. David spoke little, mostly replying to Thomas' questions
with monosyllables—which Thomas saw as childish sulking. May
knew it was far more. On the one occasion when David had tried to
take a stand—on an issue that required no specialist knowledge—
Thomas had overridden him. To David, it had clearly raised the important question as to whether he was a partner or a cipher. May
guessed that it would not be long before Lillian approached Thomas
directly about it—and she did so one afternoon when May was out,
suggesting that they go to the Kingstons' sitting room, out of earshot
of the staff. They had left the door open, so May could hear them
clearly as she climbed the stairs on her return home—moving somewhat slowly, for she had begun to grow heavy with the child. "I just
wondered if you realized," she had heard Lillian say, "the extent of
David's bitterness. He's awfully hurt, Thomas."

"He hasn't exactly been hiding his feelings," Thomas had answered; "but that decision was essential. . . . Lillian, the firm's got to
come before our personal emotions . . . even if it does cause a little
upset sometimes."

"Not so little, Thomas. In fact, what's worrying me is that he may
want to withdraw the money he's invested. . . . He's not an errand boy,
Thomas. You've got to see that."

For a moment, Thomas had been silent. "He can't sell his shares
without my approval," he said at last. "As for the loan . . . well, a lot of
notice'd be needed."

"You're growing harder, aren't you, Thomas? . . . I wasn't asking
you to calculate the figures—just to consider David. He's your friend,
after all . . . or isn't that important any longer?"

"It's important," he had answered after a moment, "but not as important as Kingstons."

"I'd have thought," Lillian had suggested, "that it's important for Kingstons that he stay. . . . Partnerships *can* be broken, even if it does involve a bit of trouble or possibly going to court."

"You're threatening me?" he had queried.

"Not idly, Thomas . . . just warning you of the danger."

Thomas had hesitated. "The trouble is that David's not made for this business—as he guessed at the start. He's too cautious. . . . You've got to be imaginative, Lillian; courageous sometimes . . . even something of a pirate."

"I suppose Baines is a pirate."

"Yes," Thomas had agreed, "he *is* a bit of a pirate."

"Are you wise to trust a pirate?" She had thrown the question away, cutting in before he had time to answer it. "You're missing the point, Thomas." Her words had been soft, gentle. "You've got to make David feel more like a partner or—"

"God knows, Lillian," Thomas had interrupted, his voice raised, "I never stop trying to help him play a bigger part in the business."

"Trying?" she queried. "Then you must try harder . . . that is, if you need his investment, which I suspect you do—for the time being, at least." She had paused, and even May had had to concede that her timing was brilliant. "Oh, Thomas," she had pleaded suddenly, once more the familiar Lillian, a woman talking to a man she found attractive, "surely you realize the importance of this to me. . . . I'd hate it if you two parted company. In fact, I don't know what I'd do."

To May, as she lay there between the pains, those words came back into her mind with the resonant distortion of an echo. She could recall the exact tone of Lillian's voice—soft and sexual over the threat —which had been more disturbing than what she had actually said; which was why May had chosen that moment to enter the room. "Why, Lillian," she had said, "I couldn't help hearing what you said as I came up the stairs. It surprised me. You know very well that David won't want to leave Thomas. He needs him too much—or someone like him." It was the only time she had ever seen Lillian discomposed; but then, she *had* taken her by surprise.

Lillian smiled down at her. "The doctor says it won't be long now." The pain, rushing through her like fire, seemed to consume her again.

"Push down, Mrs. Kingston," said the doctor. "That's it. . . . Now wait. . . . Again, push down. . . . That's good. . . . Once again . . ." He was speaking continuously in a soft burred voice that seemed far away, as though he were in another room. The pain rose to a level she had never known. The room spun as she began to lose consciousness. She heard herself cry out, but she did not faint, staying in a strange state of limbo, knowing the extreme of agony but feeling as though her mind were removed from her body. Then slowly the need to scream became less intense as, with the birth, the pressure eased. She heard the baby cry. "What is it?" she asked.

"A boy, Mrs. Kingston."

She felt a sense of relief because Thomas would not be disappointed, followed by a flare of irritation because he had been so sure, and how dared he be so sure about the product of her body? Then both thoughts were marred suddenly by fear. "Is he all right?" she asked anxiously.

"He's a bit small, being early," the doctor replied, "but he seems a fine little lad."

She closed her eyes, feeling their hands active on her, presumably in preparation for the release of the afterbirth. She felt herself slipping toward sleep, but stayed just this side of it. Dolly would have enjoyed the baby, she thought suddenly. Dear Aunt Dolly. And that terrible day when Aunt Dolly returned from France came vividly into her mind in a series of disconnected images like those of a magic lantern. She remembered that at one moment in the afternoon Thomas had asked her to cross the road with him to view the new premises. The painter was just finishing the fascia across the double frontage of the second and third shops that Thomas had wanted so much. The single word "Kingstons" now stretched across both buildings, followed in smaller lettering by the word "Drapers."

"No longer Fancy Goods Thos," she had said with a smile, recalling her brother Bob's taunt.

"We're drapers now," he had answered. "You've got a respectable husband at last."

They had gone back across the road, with Thomas holding her arm protectively. And there, waiting for them in the shop, was Miss Godfrey with the usual big smile on her face.

"You didn't think I'd miss today of all days, do you?" she had said to Thomas, and then seeing the expression of incomprehension on his face, she had chided, "I do believe you've forgotten it yourself, Mr. Kingston. Today's September the sixteenth. What were you doing this time last year?"

The significance of her visit had suddenly dawned on them both.

"My goodness, Miss Godfrey," he had exclaimed. "It's our anniversary. You're right. We'd quite forgotten. I knew it was the last week of our trading year, but we've been so busy lately that the actual day arrived unnoticed."

They had taken her upstairs for a glass of Madeira. "If I may take the liberty of saying so as an old lady," she had said, "it's important to celebrate your anniversaries. They're your milestones, and if you ignore them, I suspect you'll come to regret it."

"We stand rebuked, Miss Godfrey," Thomas had responded with a smile. "You must come and visit us on this day every year and take a glass of wine—like a godmother, to make sure we keep up to the mark."

"Oh, you must do more than that," she had insisted. "You should make it an occasion for your staff—even hold a ball when you're bigger."

The suggestion had appealed to him—especially the belief in the future of Kingstons that lay behind it. "May," he had said, "I think we should drink to the health of our first customer."

They had raised their glasses. "Your godmother," Miss Godfrey had said, and begun to chuckle. It was then that the telegram had arrived from David to say that Dolly was back and please would they go over to Copenhagen Street as soon as possible.

It was a relief, for the past weeks had been an anxious time. In July, when Dolly, of course, was still in Paris, France had declared war on Prussia. As two armies of the Emperor Napoleon III marched north, half a million of King Wilhelm's troops had advanced south to meet them. A worried Uncle Jack had come to Sloane Street to discuss what he should do about her. Her doctor had written to say she was making satisfactory progress but felt she should stay with him for a few weeks more.

At first, of course, Paris was a long way from the armies; but a few weeks later, on September 2, the sensational news reached London of a big Prussian victory at Sedan. The French had surrendered. The Emperor Napoleon had been captured. The Prussian army was poised to advance on Paris, and there were reports of revolution within the city.

There had been no doubt then. Someone had to cross the Channel at once to bring Dolly home, and Uncle Jack could not go because he had suddenly contracted influenza. The work load for Thomas at that moment had been enormous, and it was with relief that he had accepted David's offer to go in his place.

The three of them had gone to see him off at Victoria. "Don't get guillotined, will you?" said Lillian as she kissed him, referring to the Revolution, though everything was apparently quiet in Paris since the Government of National Defense had been set up. "Good luck," said Thomas. In the cab on the way back to Sloane Street, no one had said much. Despite their jocularity at the station, there was much cause for anxiety.

By the afternoon that Miss Godfrey called, David had been gone for the best part of two weeks and Thomas and May had begun to grow worried, but as soon as they arrived at Copenhagen Street, they saw that their fears had been groundless. Dolly was sitting bolt upright in a chair, looking astonishingly well in view of the long journey she had just endured. "She refused to go to bed until you arrived," Uncle Jack explained.

"I wasn't going to let you celebrate my return without being with you," she had said with that bright, slightly mischievous smile. "Not since I've missed no less than two weddings."

Uncle Jack had sent David out to get some champagne, and they all drank Dolly's health, which was so obviously much improved. But they had hardly sipped from their glasses before David took Thomas aside and said, "I hope you won't be angry, but while I was in Paris I was given the opportunity to buy some lace. I got talking to a man on the train who, when he heard I was in retail, told me there was some fine stuff to be had at a wholesaler's near Les Halles. Everyone's a bit scared there, not knowing what's going to happen, and he wanted to sell up his stock and leave the city. Come and have a look."

May had gone with them both into the hall, where David had left his luggage. Among it was a large parcel, from which he tore the brown paper covering to reveal a bale of the most exquisite Alençon lace Thomas had ever seen. "David!" he said. "That's superb—and now, of all times, with the Prussians closing on Paris. You're positively brilliant. What did you pay for it?"

"About half a crown a yard. Is that too much?"

"It's cheap. With the shortage there'll be from Paris now, it'll be like gold! I hope you bought bales of it." He saw the expression in David's eyes and knew what had happened. "You were offered more?" David nodded. "And you turned it down?"

"It seemed such a lot of money, and I wasn't convinced it was right for us, and there was somebody else in the warehouse, an Englishman, and he was prepared to take the rest. It seemed wiser in view of—"

"No, David!" The exclamation that issued from Thomas' mouth had the quality of a scream of agony. "We could have displayed it as 'Just out of Paris before the Prussians got there.' We still can, of course, but this bale will be gone like a flash. Perhaps, though, we could buy it from this Englishman. He'll take his profit, of course. Do you know his name?"

"Stockton, I think, or was it Stockham? Something like that."

"Arthur Stockton! Oh, no, David, no!" Thomas had covered his face with his hands. Then he had looked up and seen the pained disappointment in his partner's eyes that had replaced the pleasure, inspired by Thomas' initial enthusiasm. "It's not your fault," Thomas had said. "I should have thought about it. There were bound to be bargains in the panic. . . . Trust Stockton. . . . Perhaps he'll sell us some of his purchase. He let me down badly in March, and who knows . . . he might—"

"Thomas!" It had been an anguished cry that had made all three of them turn toward the door into the sitting room. Lillian stood there, her cheeks drained of color. "Aunt Dolly . . ." she said.

The sight of Aunt Dolly had been appalling—her body rigid in the chair, both her hands clutching her throat, her face a strange bluish gray and contorted in agony. There had been no sound, though it was obvious she was trying to cry out.

"Dolly . . . Dolly . . . Oh, no, Dolly . . ." Uncle Jack had put his arms round her awkwardly, for it was not easy in the chair. "Dolly . . . Please, Dolly," he had said.

"Where's the nearest doctor?" May had asked, for everyone had been so shocked by the sudden onset of the attack that no one had taken the obvious action.

"At the end of the road," Lillian had said. "Number twenty-seven." And David had rushed out of the house.

Dolly had seemed to arch her back, turning slowly, reaching out her legs in front of her so that she was, as it were, lying across the chair. Sweat was pouring down her face.

"Dolly . . . Dolly . . ." Uncle Jack had repeated. Suddenly the tension had gone from her and she had become limp. Her hands had fallen away from her neck. "My God," Uncle Jack had said. "Oh, my God." He had bent down and taken her in his arms—awkwardly, because her lifeless body was sprawled across the chair—his face twisted in grief.

The doctor had arrived very soon afterward. "It would have been very quick," he had assured them. They had carried her upstairs and laid her on her bed, and May had brushed her hair, stroking it carefully so that it lay neatly on the pillow beside her.

The midwife brushed her hair. Then, when she had finished, she asked, "Shall I call Mr. Kingston?" May nodded, and as she had expected, Thomas came into the room like a released bull, displaying an exuberant, even boyish delight. "I told you he'd be a son," he said, and tried to scoop the baby up in his arms from the crib so that he could examine him closely, but he was checked by the midwife. "Not just yet, Mr. Kingston. Give him a little time to get used to the world."

"What she means," said May drowsily, "is that it may be a day or two before he can actually take over a department."

Thomas laughed. "He'll make an ideal buyer for the baby clothes when we introduce them," he responded. He bent over the crib, studying his son intently. Then he kissed May. "You're a genius, Mrs. Kingston."

· 2 ·

The jokes, of course, like the baby, were premature. "Early babies are delicate," the doctor warned as Thomas accompanied him downstairs to the front door. "He'll need extra care."

"He's in danger?" queried Thomas anxiously.

"Not exactly—vulnerable's more like it. We lose them more often than babies born at full term."

"We won't lose this one," said Thomas confidently.

"Let's hope not." And the doctor walked off up Sloane Street, carrying his black bag, with the snow swirling round him.

By the end of the first week the baby had lost weight, which worried May, though she had been told that this was normal.

The next week he gained only an ounce; and then, at the end of the third week, he seemed to have turned the corner, putting on nearly half a pound. "I didn't think it could be long before he responded to it," said Thomas with a grin, referring to her milk as he watched her suckle him, though he was more relieved than he revealed.

The arrival of Ramsay, in fact, had made a big difference in Thomas' attitude toward Kingstons. His drive had acquired a new dimension. He would look at the baby in the crib and imagine him as a twenty-year-old youth working alongside him in the emporium.

"Give the little boy a chance," May complained. "He's got his childhood to look forward to first."

David noted an increase in Thomas' sense of urgency which he had always found hard to understand. Why, he demanded once again, was there so great a need for hurry?

"We'll be dead before we know it," Thomas answered, "and there are one or two things I want to do before then."

During the past months the two men had, in fact, been getting on better, following David's lace speculation in Paris. As Thomas had predicted, his purchase of the Alençon had sold within forty-eight hours, and even the extra stock they had bought from Arthur Stockton, though priced higher to cover his profit, had moved out briskly. Artfully, Thomas had sent David down to negotiate the deal with the wholesaler instead of going himself, and Stockton, glad to have an opportunity to reestablish the connection without loss of face, had kept his margin relatively low.

In February, however, the two partners found themselves enmeshed in a series of new conflicts—mainly on small issues that only served to reflect the underlying resentment. One morning, for example, Baines spotted a woman shoplifter, a scourge that had become especially prevalent lately in London's shops. This would not have caused much trouble had not the culprit been a neatly dressed lady in her seventies. At first she had put on a show of great indignation, asserting that she had never been so insulted. But May and Emily, when they searched her, found the goods she had stolen in deep internal pockets of her overcoat.

When Thomas and David were called into the office, where the search had been conducted, they found the old lady slumped in a chair, tears streaming down her face, her hair bedraggled. "Please, Mr. Kingston," she said when she saw him. "I beg you . . . I'll pay for the goods . . . I'll help you catch others . . ."

Thomas looked at her steadily for a few moments as the pleas poured from her. Then he said, "Mr. Baines, fetch the police." She uttered an agonized scream as Thomas turned on his heel and walked out of the office, followed by a highly emotional David. "Thomas," he insisted, "surely we should discuss this."

"What is there to discuss?" asked Thomas. "There's no question of her guilt."

"What'll happen to her?"

"She'll be sent to jail."

"I *am* your *partner*," said David angrily. "I've got a right at least to be consulted."

"About thieves?" queried Thomas. "You want us to let off thieves?"

"She's old, Thomas. Surely we should have some humanity, a little Christian forgiveness in our hearts."

"And get Kingstons a reputation for being lenient with shoplifters?" queried Thomas angrily. "My God, don't you realize what that'd mean? They'd be raiding us every day. They're as fast as lizards. It was only by lucky chance that Baines happened to see her." Suddenly he smiled and put his hand on David's shoulder. "Don't waste your sympathy."

David was not convinced until it emerged that the nice old lady had fourteen previous convictions—and by then they had become locked in another issue that was far more searing. Emily Lane, who ranked immediately below Thomas and David in the hierarchy of staff that now numbered some twenty-two people, had long been urging promotion for Albert Brown, one of the two errand boys. Albert had been the second person that Thomas had employed before opening his first shop and Emily had now taught him to read and write. He was still only sixteen, but Thomas had agreed to give him a trial soon as a salesman when a distraught Emily had appeared in his office with the barely credible news that he had just been caught stealing cash from a customer's reticule.

There was no doubt about the crime. When the customer accused the boy, demanding that he be searched, the two pounds was in his pocket. "Do you deny stealing it?" Baines asked him, and Albert shook his head. "I find it hard to compre'end, Albert," he said. "You're such a keen and 'ardworking youngster. Still, you're Mr. Kingston's business now."

"I'd never have believed it, Albert," said Thomas when he interrogated him in his office. "Have you stolen money before?"

"No, sir. This is the first time ever." Thomas studied him. He had lost the urchin look that had marked him when he had first been employed. The tousled hair was combed neatly, and in his clean apron, Thomas thought he must be quite a good advertisement for Kingstons as he delivered parcels to the customers. Even now, despite his crime, Thomas noted that the boy was not sniveling or pleading to be given another chance.

"Why did you do it?" David asked suddenly.

"I was desperate, sir, but I'm not saying that's any excuse."

"You know we have no choice, don't you, Albert?" said Thomas gently.

"Yes, sir, I do."

"Then you'd better go and get your things."

It was a decision that left Thomas with a great sense of loss all day. In the evening, when he told May about it, she sympathized but agreed that he had had no alternative. The dismissal still left him troubled, largely because the theft seemed so out of character. The following morning, Ramsay had a slight fever and May had no thoughts for anything else, so they did not discuss it again.

"Shall I send for the doctor?" Thomas suggested.

"It's so mild," she said. "It doesn't seem worth troubling him. Babies run fevers very easily. If it gets any worse, we can always send for him then."

An hour later, Thomas and David were going through the morning mail together when Emily came into the room. The Albert affair had disturbed her so much, she explained, that the previous evening after the business had closed, she had gone to the boy's home in Stepney, in the East End of London.

"I know it shouldn't make any difference, Mr. Kingston," she said. "Theft's theft. I just thought you might like to know why he took the money."

"I would indeed," said Thomas, "even though it can't excuse him."

"Of course not. . . . Well, the fact is, Mr. Kingston, Albert's mother has pneumonia, and without her wages there's only his money for food, so the little girls have had nothing to eat for—"

"Little girls?" queried Thomas.

"Albert's sisters. They've been looking after her. One's nine and one's seven."

"Looking after a woman with pneumonia? Has she seen a doctor? Is she going to die?"

"I sent Albert for a doctor as soon as I arrived and stayed while he examined her. He said he didn't know if she'd survive, but without question she was in need of proper nursing, and of course, they don't have the money for that."

Thomas was shocked. The appalling poverty of London was part of their lives, glaringly obvious whenever they moved from the relatively affluent area of Knightsbridge and Sloane Street, but this was the first time he had been confronted with its evils in relation to a person he knew well.

He thought for a moment. Then he said, "I want you to have the day off, Miss Lane. Take the family what food they need. Arrange for a nurse. Ensure that the doctor attends her daily. Give Albert whatever money you think he'll need.

"Naturally," he added, turning to David, "this cost will be charged to me personally."

"It most certainly will not," his partner insisted. "It's a proper charge for the firm."

At that moment, nothing about the issue of Albert divided the two men. Yet, as Thomas mused later, only seconds passed before they were ranged once more in total opposition. It was just as Emily was leaving that Thomas said to her, "I can't help feeling that this puts a slightly different complexion on our decision yesterday."

"Thomas!" David exclaimed. "You're not considering taking him back on the staff?"

"I think we should perhaps consider the provocation the boy faced," Thomas answered. "What would you do if your mother was starving and gravely ill? And Albert's always been loyal. He's developing well. Should we throw him away because he's succumbed to temptation of the most extreme nature?"

David shook his head adamantly, his face suddenly pink with emotion. "Thomas, don't you see? It doesn't matter why he did it. He's still a thief. You can't possibly employ a thief."

"Have you considered what his future will be if we don't? No one'll employ him after he's been sacked for stealing."

"He should have thought of that before." David's face had become strangely wooden. "He's guilty of one of the ten great sins. There must be a penalty, surely."

"Penalty?" queried Thomas, watching his partner carefully. David was a devout man, but Thomas had never before seen him interpret the issues of right and wrong quite so rigidly. "The last twenty-four hours, as he faced a stark future, must have been penalty in the extreme."

"Thomas, he stole."

"Was it not you who was urging me the other day to display a little Christian forgiveness?"

"Only because she was old."

Thomas got up and walked to the window. For a moment, he stood in silence looking down on Sloane Street. The more he thought about it the more he felt it was utterly wrong to punish a young boy so drastically after what they had learned from Emily Lane. Even more important, he did not think it was in the interest of Kingstons.

"God's law on theft is very clear," said David from behind him.

"Why choose the law of Moses instead of the teaching of Christ?" queried Thomas. He turned from the window. "We're taking Albert back," he said.

"Thomas," David began, "I normally concede to you, as you well know, but in this case I insist that—"

Thomas cut him off: "I'm sorry, but as senior partner, I'm going to overrule you."

David stared at him, astounded. "Overrule me?" he repeated. "For an errand boy?"

"For one of the small parts that make up the whole," Thomas answered.

For a terrible moment, Thomas thought that David was going to break down. His whole body became tensed. His arms were rigid at his sides, his fists clenched. "It just shows," he said bitterly, "how important I am to you as your partner." And he rushed out of the office, slamming the door behind him.

After he had gone, Thomas tried to settle down to some work, but the quarrel had upset him and he found it hard to concentrate. He was sharpening a pencil that was hardly blunt when May burst into the room. "Didn't you hear me calling you?" she screamed. She was utterly distraught, with tears streaming down her cheeks. "It's Ramsay! He's dying! Get the doctor!"

· 3 ·

It was fortunate that there was a hansom passing along the street as Thomas ran out the shop door, and that Henderson was in his surgery; for the baby was gravely ill. When he was not vomiting, he lay with a deathly stillness which, at the moment that Thomas hurried into the room with the doctor, had caused May to cry out, "Oh, my God, he's gone!"

"No," said the doctor, moving back one of the tiny eyelids with his big thumb, "he hasn't gone yet." Putting his ear to his stethoscope tube, he listened to the baby's heart, and Thomas stared down at the son he had already visualized as the future head of Kingstons. He was lying motionless in the crib, his face so heavily wrinkled that the eyes and mouth were hollows. The skin of his cheeks had become so dry that the surface was beginning to flake. Surely babies' skins were supposed to be moist. "Why's he so dry?" Thomas asked the doctor.

"It's a symptom of the disease. All the fluid's going from his body." As he spoke, the baby was suddenly convulsed with a retching that shook his little body. White liquid drained from his mouth. Thomas put his arm around May's shoulder as the doctor asked, "You're still breast-feeding, Mrs. Kingston?"

"Of course."

"Does he have any other milk at all?"

May, unable to speak, just shook her head.

"It's strange. The infection is common enough where children are crowded." He shrugged his shoulders. "The ways of God." He snapped his bag closed. "He's got an infection of the intestine," he said. "There's no point in giving him medicine. Don't feed him for a day. Try to get him to take water to replace the fluid he's losing. Keep the fire going well all the time. He must stay warm. But open the window. The room shouldn't be stuffy. I'll return tomorrow." He put out his hand and gently squeezed May's arm. "Be brave, Mrs. Kingston. I'll do my best to save him."

He went downstairs, with Thomas following him. "Is he dying?" asked Thomas. The doctor nodded. "Probably . . . "You never know for sure," he answered. "Mr. Kingston, have you ever heard of the Germ Theory of disease?"

"No," answered Thomas.

"It's controversial. Many doctors think it's nonsense, but much has been discovered over the past twenty years by such scientists as Pasteur, Koch, Lister. Many up-to-date practitioners believe that disease is caused by live organisms, germs, so small the human eye can't see them. They enter the body by being inhaled from the air or by physical contact through the skin. What I believe's happening in your son at this moment is a battle between these hostile germs and his body, which, being so young, isn't as well equipped for defense as it would have become in time. If he succeeds in fighting off the attackers, then he'll live. If he doesn't, then he won't."

"When shall we know?" asked Thomas. "How long do we have?"

"Twenty-four hours. Perhaps forty-eight. Possibly longer, but I doubt it."

"And there's nothing we can do?"

"Well"—the doctor paused, gave a slight shrug to his shoulders—"you could try praying." And again he walked off up the street as he had on the night of Ramsay's birth.

Thomas went back upstairs. Lillian was with May, who was sitting in a chair, pale but composed. She was beyond weeping. "Go and work, Thomas," she said as he bent down and kissed her. "There's nothing for you to do here."

It was a relief for Thomas to leave them, for he was frustrated by his powerlessness to help. He sat at his desk for a moment but found work impossible. Needing action, he went downstairs and, chilled by the dark, damp morning, strode fast up Sloane Street.

He did not recall turning off into Pont Street, but he was already passing St. Mary's when he thought of the doctor's advice to try prayer. He had guessed that the doctor was a skeptic, and he himself had not taken the suggestion seriously at the time. For although Thomas attended church and said his prayers, he was not, in fact, religious. He was superstitious. He had no doubt of the existence of powerful spiritual forces, both benign and malignant, and he assumed that by definition the former included God. Why not, therefore, he asked himself as he stood there outside St. Mary's on that dank February morning, ask Him to intervene? It was not, of course, an act of faith. It was a last resort to something he had not yet put to the test. If he had found himself in this same situation on a native island where savages worshiped the sun, the same reasoning would have led him to imitate their homage.

Thomas entered the vast church by a side door. There was only one gaslight burning in the whole huge building—near the choir stalls, where a warden in a black cassock was busy laying out hymnbooks in preparation for Evensong. Each of his movements sounded inordinately loud. At one moment, he dropped one of the books, and this small noise reverberated between the hard stone walls as though it had weighed a hundredweight.

Thomas stood for a moment in the side aisle, feeling oddly conspicuous even though the warden had not noticed his presence. He moved into a pew, hesitated for a moment, intending to take a place at the side. Then, feeling that this would be inadequate as obeisance, he walked along the pew and knelt at a seat next to the broad center aisle. By placing himself in the middle of that big church immediately before the altar and its gold crucifix and the vast stained-glass window depicting Christ on the Cross, he was in effect prostrating himself before God in the fullest manner possible.

So Thomas prayed for Ramsay's life. He was not very good at sustained prayer, for his attention kept wandering. He opened his eyes and looked at Christ crucified on the glass window, at the features twisted with pain, but he remained unmoved. He closed his eyes again and was mortified to find himself thinking about the piece-goods stock. To force himself to concentrate, he actually spoke words aloud in a whisper in informal prayer: "Please, God, save my son. Help him fight the germs. Please, God." But he still had no sense that his words could be heard. He received more comfort from the solid wood of the pew that he knew had once been part of a great English oak.

Thomas stayed on his knees for over an hour, hoping that the time he was devoting in obeisance would compensate in some way for the shortcomings of his prayer. But he felt no solace, and at last he stood up and left the church.

He walked back to his shops, gripped by an acute sadness. In his depressed state of mind, he hesitated to rejoin May until he had gained enough control of himself to give her strength. The alternative—to go back to his desk—seemed bleak. It was as he was ambling aimlessly along the pavement on the side of Sloane Street opposite his premises that the tenant of the ironmonger's business that divided the Kingston buildings emerged from his shop doorway and beckoned to him. He was a pleasant man in his late fifties, with a bald head and a thick overgrown moustache, named Henry Clark.

"Good day to you, Mr. Kingston," he said when Thomas had crossed the road. "You won't be seeing me for much longer . . . we've decided to settle in Eastbourne. Bit of sea air away from the London fogs. I thought you'd be interested because if you rented this shop, then you'd have a single frontage, wouldn't you?"

"I would indeed," said Thomas. He had, of course, thought of it often, for Clark's shop incorporated with those he already had would give him an undivided block of four buildings. It would be an emporium—only a little emporium, but a foundation that would have the potential for expansion to the big store he had dreamed of for so long. His spirits lightened as excitement at the thought surged through him —only to be marred by the realization, which for a few moments had left him, that the son he had hoped would share it with him was dying in a room above them. It was marred but not extinguished, for with Kingstons he had created an entity that was outside himself and outside his son, that would outlive them both and any other sons he might have. Clark's news, therefore, was of vital importance.

"Can you give me the name of your landlord or his agent?" asked Thomas.

"Of course," Clark answered. "In fact, the freehold changed hands only a few weeks ago. Strangely, the new owner's a lady and she doesn't live far from here."

Thomas knew then—knew that at last the time had come for him to reap the harvest he had sown on that humiliating afternoon last March in Eaton Square. He had not seen her since that day, but clearly she had been watching his progress. When he had acquired the third shop, she had obviously realized the value that at some time the fourth would have for him.

"Her name," said Clark, "is—"

"I can tell you her name, Mr. Clark," Thomas interrupted quietly. "Mrs. Fellowes is her name, and she lives in Eaton Square."

"Good heavens," exclaimed the ironmonger, "how did you know?"

"I'm acquainted with the lady."

"Then there should be no trouble, should there?" said Clark with a bright smile.

"No, Mr. Clark," said Thomas, "there should be no trouble . . . but I won't be absolutely astounded if there is."

·4·

Thomas decided he would not postpone the inevitable confrontation—or, for the time being, face the reality of the doctor's pessimistic prognosis about his son.

On the way to Eaton Square, he considered Mrs. Fellowes' purpose. Was it an act of revenge? Did she plan to install competition? For one wild moment he wondered if it was bait. Was she luring him back to her house for some unpleasant purpose—to have him horse-whipped perhaps?

By the time this last fantastic notion occurred to him, he was actually standing before the big front door of No. 74. As Morton, the butler, swung it open and saw who was in the porch, he was as impassive as ever. "Good morning, Mr. Kingston," he said.

"Is Mrs. Fellowes at home?" asked Thomas.

"If you'll wait in the hall, I'll inquire," answered Morton, in a tone that suggested he would be amazed if she were at home to Mr. Kingston.

However, she was. Morton returned and said she would receive him immediately.

She was in the same little first-floor sitting room in which their drama had been enacted last March. What was more, once again she was alone—sitting on the same small sofa that he recalled so vividly from the previous occasion—and she looked as beautiful as ever, her hair arranged simply, her eyes bright.

"Why, Mr. Kingston," she said with a generous smile, "what a pleasant surprise."

"I hope you'll forgive my calling like this, Mrs. Fellowes."

"Of course," she answered. "I'm delighted to see you. Come and sit down and tell me how you've been getting on." She gestured to the seat beside her on the sofa. As Thomas crossed the room toward her, he was confused. He had not counted on being received with this degree of warmth. He sat down awkwardly, his hands, palms downward, on his thighs.

"I heard you'd married," she went on. "That pretty girl in your shop. I must congratulate you."

"That's kind of you," he said.

"I have to confess," she said, "since we have, after all, shared a degree of intimacy, that when I heard about it I did experience a certain sense of . . . how shall I describe it? Loss? Disappointment? Even a little jealousy, perhaps? Now, there's an admission for you. How many women do you know who'd admit to that? Not that I suppose you've known *that* many women who could discuss so frank and private an emotion with you. But you will, Mr. Kingston. You have a need for women, even if it is a trifle confused at the moment by loyalties and youthful morality. And indeed, women have a need for you. I had a need for you, as you well know. In fact, as I see you sitting there beside me I still have a need for you."

She saw the embarrassment in his eyes and threw her head back laughing, as he had seen her do before. "My immodesty always bothers you, doesn't it?" she said. "But you should be flattered. Most men would be flattered."

"I *am* flattered, Mrs. Fellowes," he answered, a trifle awkwardly.

"I'm just a brazen hussy, you see." She looked at him, her eyes still bright with humor, though this faded as she said softly, "And *you* have a need for *me*, too, don't you? Still, after all that?"

He tried to find a reply, but her boldness had left him without any notion of what to say.

"Don't try so hard," she said. "You don't have to answer. There's no law that says you have to answer. Anyway, it's not necessary. I can sense your emotions. I can feel the stirring in you."

Idly, she reached out her hand and placed it on his knee. "See," she said, "I only have to touch you to turn that stirring into strong desire." And indeed, the response in him was immediate. "And this time," she went on, "there's no problem of money, no question of buying you—"

"Mrs. Fellowes—" he began.

"I know," she broke in, "you're a young husband with a pretty young wife. But despite that, your eyes are on my lips. Already, you can imagine yourself kissing them as you have before. In your mind, your fingers are already exploring . . . well, you know as well as I do where they're exploring."

She was taunting him, exploiting the guilt he felt because of this strange sexual attraction she had for him, and he responded in anger. He stopped her words with his mouth, kissing her violently, biting her open lips, intending to hurt her.

With an effort and a muffled cry, she turned her head to take her mouth from his. "Not so hard," she said, and he paused, glaring down at her, before kissing her viciously again. His hand went to the top of her bodice. "I shouldn't tear it if I were you," she warned, and he saw the glint of triumph, which only increased his rage. He pulled her to him with a roughness that he had never used on a woman before and kissed her hard, ensuring this time that she could not utter a word. As he did so, he forced her back on the cushions of the sofa with his whole weight on her. For a moment, he held her pinioned—then took his mouth from hers and looked down at her as she lay helpless beneath him. For an instant, he too knew triumph, a basic, animal male triumph, but it was only momentary. "That's quite enough of that, Mr. Kingston," she said coldly. "Kindly release me at once."

He did as she asked—immediately—and sat back on the sofa in the same position that he had occupied before she had begun to provoke him. She stood up, flushed. "That was stupid," she said as she straightened her gown and touched her hair. "Very stupid indeed."

"Was it not invited, Mrs. Fellowes?" he asked.

"If anything was invited," she snapped, "it was not to behave like a rude boor. Is that how you treat your wife?"

"The circumstances are a little different."

"And what am I to make of that remark?" she demanded angrily, adding before he could reply, "Oh, this is a silly conversation. We have a lot of silly conversations, don't we, Mr. Kingston? We do a lot of silly things, yet"—she paused and then softly, almost wistfully, she said, "there is a strange kind of magnetism between us, isn't there?"

When she spoke like this, revealing a vulnerable layer beneath that strong personality, it always touched him.

"Would you care for a glass of wine?" she asked formally, and when he accepted, she rang for Morton and asked him to bring it. "By the way, Mr. Kingston," she went on when the butler had closed the door, "you never did tell me the purpose of your visit today. Or was it just a courtesy? Did you happen to be passing and think, I haven't seen that nice Mrs. Fellowes for almost a year. I wonder how she is?"

He knew she was teasing him again, and he toyed for a few seconds with the thought of trying to match her wit, but he was unsure of himself and opted for blunt speaking. "I heard that you'd bought the premises next to mine."

"My goodness," she said, smiling, "you're becoming quite a sleuth, Mr. Kingston. I've only just signed the contract."

"I was a little surprised," said Thomas.

"Really? I can't think why. I've always told you that I had great confidence in your future . . . so when I found it was for sale, I bought it. I'm sure it'll be an excellent investment. So, incidentally, does Ernest Goldsmith. You remember Mr. Goldsmith, of course."

"And what are your plans for it?" he asked.

"Oh, I don't really have any," she replied. "I suppose I could let it again when Mr. Clark leaves." She looked at him with an innocent smile. "Can you think of anyone who might want to rent it?"

"Please, Mrs. Fellowes, you know very well that I want the shop."

"All right," she said, shrugging her shoulders. "I'll let it to *you.*"

Thomas was wary. He knew there would be conditions. "What . . . er . . ." he began.

"What terms?" she queried brightly. "Whenever we meet, we always talk of terms, don't we? Well, this time there *will* be terms. I know you like terms. I'll charge you a rent." She paused, and again he knew she was playing with him. "My rent," she went on, speaking very slowly, "will be . . ." She hesitated once more, like a card player with a good hand as yet unrevealed. ". . . a thousand pounds a year."

Thomas was so astonished that for a moment he could say nothing. At last he repeated incredulously: "A thousand pounds?" Then he laughed. It was an uneasy laugh. "How did you think I was going to respond to that?" he asked.

"I thought you'd think it was a little expensive," she answered.

"Now tell me the rent you really are intending to ask," he said.

"I've told you," she said.

"You're serious, then?" he asked.

"Completely serious," she answered. "Not that it comes easily to me, as you've no doubt guessed. I like to laugh, to treat life as though it's a bit of a game, but sometimes . . . well, one just has to be serious sometimes, doesn't one?"

"But I could almost buy it for a thousand pounds."

"You couldn't, because I wouldn't sell it to you. I wouldn't sell it to anyone." She sat down beside him. "Don't look so worried. It's not the end of the world."

"It's a joke isn't it?" Thomas asked, unable to keep the anxiety from his voice.

She looked at him for a moment as though she sympathized with him—then gave a little shake to her head. "No," she said.

"But that rent is impossible. No one could pay it."

"All right," she said. "I don't mind."

"So what will you do?"

"Do?" she queried. "Why, Mr. Kingston, I shan't do anything."

Once more Thomas did not know what to say. He had a momentary feeling of disorientation, like an animal harassed from different directions so that it does not know which way to turn. After a moment, he asked carefully, "If you won't sell it and you can't let it to anyone at the rent you insist you want, then what is your purpose in buying it?"

She laughed—not very pleasantly, for this time she was laughing at his discomfort. "I shall wait," she said. "You see, I know that as Kingstons grows into your emporium, then the value of my shop will soar."

Thomas was on his feet, flushed with fury. "This is monstrous," he said.

"What's monstrous about it?" she asked. "What greater evidence of faith in your business could you possibly have? What could be more flattering to you?"

"But you could still let it to me. It would rise in value just the same while I paid you rent."

"I've just offered to let it to you."

"At a rent that's quite absurd."

"Well, you may not think it so absurd in a little while. Of course, by then I may think the property's worth a bit more and you may wish you'd accepted my earlier offer."

Thomas moved to the fireplace and, laying his hand on the mantelpiece, stared into the flames. "I'll concede it's clever," he said after a moment, with quiet bitterness. "Two birds with one stone. A valuable purchase and . . ." He broke off and looked at her suddenly. "What would the rent be, Mrs. Fellowes," he demanded harshly, "if we became lovers?"

He saw the anger rise in her eyes at the insult and fade as she controlled it. Suddenly, she laughed. "Oh, dear, what am I going to do with you, Mr. Kingston? All right, let's consider your question. What price would you put on yourself? And how would you assess it? By the hour? By the degree of ecstasy you were able to inspire, like those machines at fairs that you hit with a sledgehammer with the aim of ringing a bell?" She gave a giggle. "A month rent-free if you rang it very loudly? And perish the thought, Mr. Kingston, what if you didn't ring it at all?" She saw how embarrasssed he had become. "All right, I'll stop teasing, but you have to admit you were a little rude."

"For God's sake, I had provocation enough."

"Yes, it must be hard for you. Don't think I don't understand your feelings, Mr. Kingston."

"But you won't rent me the shop?"

"Oh, don't let's go over all that again. The position about that is very clear, and I'm rather glad you think the rent's a little too high . . ."

"A little?" he exclaimed. "It's iniquitous!"

". . . because," she went on as though he had not spoken, "you'll have to come and talk to me about it sometimes, won't you?"

"*Have* to?" he repeated angrily.

"Yes, Mr. Kingston. *Have* to—that is, if you're ever going to acquire the shop. But you'll always be welcome. As I've told you before, I enjoy our meetings."

At that moment, if Mrs. Fellowes had been a man, Thomas would have been tempted to strike her. "I'll never set foot in this house again, I can promise you," he insisted furiously.

"Now, that's an unwise thing to say, because it'll mean sacrificing your pride when you return. Never close the door, Mr. Kingston . . . that's something you should learn about negotiation."

"I don't think there's anything more I want to learn from you, Mrs. Fellowes. . . . If you'll forgive me, I'll leave now."

He walked to the door and flung it open, to find Morton standing there with a tray of wine and glasses in his hand.

"Are you sure you won't stay for a glass of wine, Mr. Kingston?" she asked from behind.

Thomas did not answer. He hesitated, then moved past the butler and went down the stairs.

A few minutes later he was with May—who, under normal circumstances, would have detected his disturbance; but that day her thoughts were totally occupied by her son. "He looks a little better, I think," she said as Thomas stared down at him. "He's taken some water without bringing it up." The baby was lying so still that Thomas wondered if he were dead already. His skin was still marked by arid wrinkles.

In the evening, Thomas toyed with telling May what had happened about Mrs. Fellowes' shop, but the moment never seemed opportune. During the night, Ramsay awoke them with his crying, and

May cradled him in her arms. "Shall I fetch the doctor?" asked Thomas.

She shook her head, smiling, and he realized that she saw the crying as a sign of living. "It's the first time," she said, "for fifteen hours."

In the morning, the baby's eyes were open. When the doctor arrived on his promised call, he examined him, listened to his heart— then stood up with a dour smile on his face. "He's improving. You're fortunate. He's one of few."

When Thomas acccompanied him to the door of the shop, the doctor asked suddenly, "And did you pray for him, Mr. Kingston?"

"Yes," he answered. "I did."

The doctor laughed skeptically and put a hand on his shoulder. "Then God must have been listening, mustn't He?"

He was mocking him, but the question still remained: If he had not gone into St. Mary's the previous afternoon, if he had not spent an hour on his knees, would he still have had a son?

CHAPTER FOUR

February 1875

· I ·

Tuesday, February 2, 1875, was Thomas' thirtieth birthday. He rose at six o'clock as usual and went to the washstand, where the maid had left the jug of hot water. As he began to lather his face in the hard white gaslight, for it was not yet dawn, his feelings were strangely mixed. It was a day for celebration, but he was aware of slight misgivings. No longer was he a young man in his twenties in the early years of his career. The next age milestone would be forty.

He held his blade delicately, with his little finger extended, and started to strip the lather from his skin in slow, methodical swaths. He was wearing side-whiskers now, cut back near his ears and leaving most of his cheeks bare, as was the fashion started by Lord Dundreary, and the navigation of the long, unwieldy razor around the beard demanded skill. When he had finished, he stood for a few moments, studying his thirty-year-old face, now shaven pink and marked with flecks of soap that had escaped the steel, and pondered the evidence of passing time. Lines were appearing—across his forehead, around his eyes, in crescents on either side of his mouth—though they were not yet deep: mere signposts to the future. His hair, he noted with a degree of reassurance, was still thick and as yet unmarked by any hint of gray.

His intense concentration was broken by May's voice behind him. "May I wish my elderly husband many happy returns," she said. She had risen before him and gone downstairs, and he had not heard her come back into the room. He was embarrassed at being caught in so vain an examination of himself, and he turned with a sheepish smile. "I think a man of my position *should* possess a certain maturity, don't you?" he said as he kissed her.

"Without question," she agreed. "To look too youthful now would be quite out of keeping—but you're still the handsomest man in Chelsea. And if you don't hurry, your breakfast'll spoil."

He finished his toilet, dressed and went down the stairs. As he entered the dining room, the children looked expectantly at their mother, and when she nodded approval, they chorused, "Happy birthday, Father." He acknowledged their greeting with a big smile and sat down at the head of the table. While May at the sideboard heaped a plate for him with kidneys, sausages, lamb chops, bacon and eggs, he surveyed his family with a sense of great affection. He was always proud of them, but the day a man reaches thirty is a time to take stock. He looked at his two sons—Ramsay, now aged four, and Harry, born a year later. They were very different, in both character and temperament, which perhaps was why they got on well together. Ramsay, with Thomas' dark hair and May's large brown eyes, was an intensely active child, fascinated by the world around him, a great initiator, with a strong will that often led to tantrums. Even if he had not been the elder, he would still have become the leader of the two, for Harry, though big for his age and almost the same size as his brother, was an easygoing, passive, good-tempered boy, who was always laughing. Both were possessively devoted to Rose, their two-year-old sister, sitting there at the table in a high chair, and she exploited this affection with an undisguised calculation that always amused Thomas. Soon there would be four of them, for May was pregnant again, and Thomas noted that she looked a bit pale. It worried him a little because, although, apart from Ramsay's early arrival, she had experienced no problems carrying the other three children, she had been forced to retire to bed several times during the past few months. However, Dr. Henderson had assured them that provided she did not do too much and rested when she felt tired, there should be no trouble.

They were a happy family, Thomas mused that cold winter morning, and a very lucky one. The business had continued to prosper. Since they had moved three years ago from the rooms over the shop to this little house in Caroline Terrace, just south of the Kings Road, they had occupied a pleasant home that was infused with May's warmth of personality.

As Thomas finished his breakfast, he opened *The Times* to glance at the news of the day, but there had been few events of great note. The Liberal Party was in the throes of electing a new leader following the resignation of Mr. Gladstone—which was hardly of great moment to Thomas, since he voted for the Conservatives, who, after years in opposition, were now solidly in power under that strange genius, Mr. Disraeli. He put down the paper and pondered the significance of the fact that ever since he had been in business, England had been unscathed by the national misfortunes that had seared other nations. While America had endured the panic of 1873, with banks failing throughout the nation, Britain had enjoyed an economy that had grown steadily stronger. When France and Germany had gone to war, the country had merely been a slightly appalled witness. The siege of Paris; the setting up of the Commune, that strange Socialist experiment in rule by the citizens; the burning by the Communards of such great buildings as the Tuileries and the slaughter in the streets of the city that brought the venture to its bloody end had caused anxiety and horror, but no involvement. Even now that relations between France and Prussia were deteriorating again, no enemy army would be at the gates of London. And if war broke out once more, Thomas' main concern would again center on the sources of his Continental merchandise.

It was light by the time Thomas went to work, though some of the street lamps were still burning. In Sloane Street, he walked along the pavement on the side opposite his business because he always liked to view the panorama of his windows before entering. The firm now consisted of seven shops—one block of three buildings, which he had made into a mini-emporium by building an extension at the rear and fitting out selling areas on two floors, and two pairs of shops that were not connected to it or to each other. In the whole frontage, therefore, there were two shops that Kingstons did not possess. One, of course, belonged to Mrs. Fellowes. Thomas had returned to discuss it with her, but made little progress. She had not let it to anyone else, which Thomas wished she would, for almost any tenant would have been better than the sight of it as it was now, left empty—dirty, with soiled windows and a fascia of peeling paint, like a rotting tooth in a healthy mouth, lying between his three smart shops on one side and two on the other.

The occupant of the other shop that was not part of Kingstons was Theodore White, the cadaverous man who had warned him so often in his early months of trading that he was heading for disaster—and still insisted that his prediction would prove to be sound. "Wait until the slump comes," he would say, "and see how you prosper then. You've been very lucky with the economic conditions."

Thomas had at last declared war on White, and as he stood there, looking across Sloane Street on his birthday, he saw his heavy artillery on display in one of his windows. Until now Thomas had not competed with him in his main trade of gentlemen's wear, directing Kingstons' expansion round the twin bases of women's clothing—he now sold shoes, millinery, underclothes, as well as a wide range of dresses—and household items. To the furnishing fabrics he had offered previously, he had now added ironmongery, turnery, crockery, glass and even small articles of furniture.

It was inevitable that sooner or later Kingstons would start selling men's clothes, but when Thomas had first mentioned the possibility to David in October, they had once again been in conflict.

It was a sensitive issue. More than a year before, when Kingstons had acquired shops on either side of White's premises, Thomas had sent David to negotiate with the old draper, suggesting that he either sell his lease or move to one of their new acquisitions on the edge of the Kingston complex. This would have given them a single block of four shops in addition to the three-unit block they already possessed.

Thomas was willing to offer generous terms for either option, but David returned from his first meeting with a flat refusal. "He was shocked," he reported, "and I must say I see his point. He's had that shop for forty years."

"That was why you went to see him. What would make it worth his while?"

"Nothing. He doesn't want to move."

"Did you ask him? Did you make him an offer?"

"He wouldn't discuss it."

At Thomas' urging, David had returned to see him, but made no progress.

A year later, therefore, when Thomas raised the question of starting a Gentlemen's Department, David at once accused him of trying to obtain White's shop by breaking him with cutthroat competition.

"It won't be cutthroat," Thomas answered; "it'll conform with our usual policy—quality at competitive prices. At some stage, we've got to go into the trade," he went on, "and—"

"Got to?" David interjected. "Why have we got to?"

"Because our policy is eventually to sell everything. That's what an emporium is. In time, we're bound to be competing with all the local shops. Now's just the right moment for us to start selling to men. We've taken the women's clothing just about as far as we can for the present. Men's fashions are in a state of considerable change, which makes it an opportune moment for us to enter the trade, and our lady customers will help us promote it by talking to their husbands and their sons."

David was silent for a moment. "You know perfectly well it'll put White out of business."

"Possibly," Thomas agreed, "possibly not. Who knows? David, can't you get it into your head? White and all those little shopkeepers who think as he does are lingering from the past. You can't maintain business attitudes that are forty years old in a world that is changing as fast as ours is. You've got to adapt, which White's not prepared to do. I managed to run a thriving business as a small shopkeeper, and so could White if he was prepared to adjust to the times. And sooner or later this reality's bound to be forced on him—if not by me, by someone else."

"I suppose my vote'd count for nothing, as usual," said David.

Thomas shook his head. "Not if you're going to cast it for the wrong reason; not if you're going to impede our progress."

"Progress!" David echoed with disgust. "Progress! Sometimes I think Kingstons has become a deity to you—literally. Every time you stand and look at the shops from the other side of the street with that expression of pride in your eyes, you're really paying obeisance. When you sit there at your desk, you're a High Priest in a temple. It justifies everything you do. You can crush people with the confident belief that you're acting in a sacred cause."

His voice had acquired a note of hysteria, and he broke off as he saw the expression in his partner's eyes. "Oh, David," said Thomas sadly, "you've really come to hate me, haven't you?"

"Not hate, Thomas."

Thomas shrugged. "We don't share the same aspirations, do we? Should we face up to it and split up?"

David shook his head. "Lillian would never let me—*you* know that. She'd have fought it hard enough before Charles was born, but now it'd be over nothing less than her dead body. Her faith in your emporium has never wavered, and she sees my share as Charles's inheritance."

Thomas nodded, almost in sympathy. Charles had been born the year after Ramsay—the first of the two Rawlings children—and Thomas knew how Lillian worshiped him. "In that case, David," he said, "we're stuck with each other"—suddenly he smiled at his partner—"and speaking personally . . . I'm not sorry."

David glanced at him, surprised and touched by the generosity of the remark. "It's good of you to say that, Thomas."

"You can warn White, of course," Thomas went on, "and make him another offer if you want to . . ."

"I'll have a last try," David said, "but I don't think it'll do any good."

The two partners no longer shared a room, as they had at first. David now devoted himself to the bookkeeping and accounts, which had become extremely complex with the growth of the business, and had accepted Thomas' suggestion, made as a placatory gesture after one of their quarrels, that he become formal secretary of the firm. Working apart from each other, they found that the internal pressures of the partnership were lessened, but they were both acutely aware of the delicacy of the relationship, and each trod the sensitive areas with care. They did, of course, have a background of friendship, eroded though it had become, but their wives had none of this common territory. The passing years had not eased the undercurrent of friction between May and Lillian, who resented the fact that her husband's position in the firm was so secondary to that of Thomas. In what seemed to be an attempt to compensate for this, to emphasize her personality, she gave more rein to her taste for overdressing—at least, what May called overdressing—and the flamboyance of current fashion gave her an opportunity to appear in the shops in gowns that were often more elaborate than those of the customers.

She tended, too, to be more proprietorial on the sales floors than she had been in the past, only too ready to offer the supporting assistance of an owner's wife to the efforts of the staff, which naturally did not endear her to them. She still flirted archly with Thomas, but seemed to May to dwell much more on their childhood than she had in the earlier days.

May tried to control her irritation when Lillian did this, but she was not always successful. "I sometimes think that Lillian has an obsession with her early youth," May remarked to Thomas one day after listening to an elaborate description of a minor incident during a harvest at Quainton when he was about eleven.

He laughed in response. "She does get a little tedious, but you allow her to occupy you far too much. . . . She'd like to be the Queen Bee of Kingstons because that's the sort of person she is. But she's not the Queen Bee—*you* are."

"And you, Thomas," May answered carefully, "underestimate her. . . . Sometime she's going to cause you a lot of trouble—and probably me as well."

It had, perhaps, been inevitable that when the time had come for the two families to leave the accommodation over the shops, Lillian should have made the selection of a home a matter of competition. She had the advantage that the Kingstons left first and acquired the pretty little house in Caroline Terrace, which May adored. When the

Rawlingses too vacated Sloane Street, they moved—with help from David's father—into a slightly better address in Brompton Place, near Knightsbridge.

"I think it's preferable to be nearer the park," Lillian told May. "Easier for the children."

"One day," remarked Thomas on their way home, "I'll buy you a mansion—two mansions: one in London and one in the country. She won't be able to keep up with you then."

"She can't keep up with me now," responded May. "It's not a matter of great concern."

Meanwhile, by Thomas' thirtieth birthday in 1875, Sidney Baines had amply fulfilled his earlier promise and, now aged twenty-five, was working very closely with him in the direction of Kingstons. Emily Lane was responsible fo the Ladies Clothing and Fancy Goods sections in the three-shop block. Baines was in charge of all other departments, split up as they were within the two smaller buildings. It was unfortunate for him that, for different reasons, his progress was deeply resented by almost everyone concerned with the higher levels of the business. In the fragile network of the Kingston-Rawlings association, Lillian saw him as a special threat to David. Emily, of course, regarded him as competition, but it was May's attitude toward the young man that bothered Thomas because, despite her strong loyalty to Emily, he never quite felt that this explained her hostility. "I can understand the others' feelings about Baines," he said to her, "personal jealousies are part of the fabric of a growing business, but I can't see any reason for you to object to him."

"I find him cocky and impudent," she said.

"He's never impudent to you," Thomas insisted. "He always treats you with great respect."

"I'm sure my reaction to him is purely feminine," she responded with brisk sarcasm. Sometimes her antipathy bothered May herself, and she had wondered at times if she blamed him, quite irrationally, because she missed those early days when she had worked alongside Thomas as he did now. "However," she continued, "I suspect you're giving him far too much responsibility for his age."

"He's worth it, I can promise you."

"I wonder if you'd place such dependence on him if he was a woman."

Thomas looked at her with astonishment. She was working on some embroidery, and her stitching was suddenly faster and more irritated. "What an extraordinary thing to say," he said. "Anyone would think I'd stood in Emily's way. I've given her every opportunity. In fact, I'm always surprised she's so sensitive about poor Baines."

"Perhaps she realizes he's sure to be promoted above her in due course because he's a man—despite his youth. Perhaps she doesn't think it's fair—and nor do I."

"He's older than I was when I started the business, and you'd do the firm a service if you'd dissuade Emily from her constant criticism of him."

The next morning, Emily came to see him in his office to make a formal complaint against Baines. "I want you to instruct him to stay out of my departments, Mr. Kingston," she said. "He upsets my salesladies."

Watching her—a flushed, emotional woman in her mid-forties—Thomas could understand her feelings of injustice. She had no husband and was working with great competence in one of the very few professions that were open to a person of her sex.

"Have the ladies complained to you?" asked Thomas gently.

"Not in so many words," she answered. "It's hardly a subject they'd care to discuss. But I'm not blind, Mr. Kingston. I've seen the way they respond to him. . . . And then this morning, Miss Simpson told me she'd decided to leave."

"Because of Baines?"

"She declined to give a reason, but I'm quite convinced it's Baines. He's always pestering her. . . . He really isn't a gentleman, Mr. Kingston, but I suppose it's not surprising when you consider his background."

Thomas too had seen Baines joking with the salesladies, and he doubted from his own observation if the girls objected to him as much as Emily suggested.

"Did you ask Miss Simpson if Baines had been paying her unwelcome attention?" Thomas queried—adding quietly when she hesitated, "Well?"

"Yes. She denied it," Emily conceded reluctantly, "but I don't believe her."

"How does she get on with the other ladies? Has there been a quarrel with any of them recently?"

"Oh, there's often a tiff of one sort or another," she answered. "You know what these young girls are. . . ."

"So Miss Simpson *has* had a quarrel recently," said Thomas, and when she could not deny it, he gave a sigh. "Miss Lane," he said, "Mr. Baines is very helpful to me—as indeed are you—and this bickering has got to stop because it's harmful to the firm. In fact, you've got no real grounds to blame him for Miss Simpson's decision to leave, have you?"

His question was gentle, and although she began by saying, "If you saw the way he . . . ," she broke off and conceded, "Well I've no actual proof . . ."

"Exactly. Miss Lane, I'll see he doesn't bother your ladies anymore if you'll do something in return." He looked at her, then pleaded gently, "Give him a chance, Emily—for my sake and for Kingstons'."

She nodded reluctant agreement, but the hard line to her mouth did not give Thomas much hope of a change of attitude. However, he carried out his side of the bargain. He sent for Baines to attend their morning meeting.

The young man had developed a certain maturity with the responsibility he had been given. He was very neat, his morning coat always newly pressed, his hair, parted in the center, carefully combed. He gave an impression of standing with his weight on his toes, poised, as it were, for service. Invariably, when he appeared in Thomas' office, he was fully prepared, having assessed in advance many of the decisions that would need to be taken.

This morning, however, as he stood in the doorway, holding the usual pile of papers balanced on his arm, he had not foreseen the subject for discussion.

Thomas was standing looking out his office window, as he often did when faced with unpleasant problems. "Close the door," he said with his back to him.

"We all have our weaknesses, Baines," he went on. "I suspect that young ladies are yours."

"Pardon, sir?" Baines queried with surprise.

Thomas turned and faced him. "Now, answer me this: have you had a relationship with Miss Simpson?"

Baines hesitated, his cheeks coloring slightly. "Do I 'ave to answer, Mr. Kingston?" He was trying hard not to drop his aitches, but in moments of stress he tended to revert to his old way of speaking.

"You most certainly do," said Thomas sharply.

He paused. "Yes, sir, I'm afraid I 'ave."

"Have you stopped seeing her recently?'

"Well, you know what young ladies are, Mr. Kingston. . . . She got in a bit of a stew. . . ."

"Answer the question, Baines."

"Yes, sir."

"When? Yesterday? The day before?"

"Yesterday, Mr. Kingston. . . . Why? 'As she complained?'"

Thomas glared at him. "No, she has not," he said. "She's behaved with great integrity. But she's resigned. She's one of the best salesladies we've got, and it's through your stupidity that we're going to lose her."

Baines responded by standing up straighter and holding his elbows pressed into his sides in a military stance. "Now, understand one thing, Baines," Thomas continued. "I want to hear no more of you and the salesladies. No familiarity, no jests. Any female associations you wish to form will be made outside the business if you wish to retain your position in Kingstons. And if I was in your shoes, I'd go out of my way to be polite and helpful to Miss Lane. Now let's get to work. There's much to do."

Thomas had put Baines in charge of plans for the new Gentlemen's section, and they had long meetings every day on progress. Following his policy with the women's merchandise, Thomas intended to aim for the men of fashion, giving great attention, as always, to display. In long sessions with Baines, he hammered out an opening strategy. To begin with, they would sell suits and coats—formal wear such as frock, dress and morning coats; overcoats such as Chesterfields and Ulsters; country clothes, with the new lounge suits that had become popular and, particularly, the new reefer jackets and wide-bottomed trousers. They would support these at first only with ties and scarves and hats—especially "mullers," as the short toppers were called, and the new felt "billycocks." Later, once the section was established, they would encompass the whole range of gentlemen's wear to include shirts and underclothes and hose.

It was the first department in Kingstons that had needed a completely new staff. Three male assistants and a manager, experienced in the trade, had to be employed and schooled in the Kingston philosophy of business, and much of Baines's time was taken up in interviewing suitable candidates for Thomas' final selection.

When Thomas saw his advertisement in *The Times*, headed "Kingstons of Sloane Street have pleasure in announcing the opening of their new department for Gentlemen's wear," it gave him proud pleasure. For it was the statement of an emporium, not of a shop. Kingstons might not yet have reached the adult status of a single building, but it was certainly at the stage of an advanced adolescent.

By that cold February morning in 1875 when he stood looking across Sloane Street at the men's displays in the window, the department had been open for ten days. From the start, it had been busy. As he had hoped, his women customers had taken a great interest in it and were a big source of trade.

Predictably, Theodore White had been greatly put out by Kingstons' competition. Every time he had passed Thomas in the street, the tall, bony draper had cut him dead, striding by him with his bald head held determinedly high, his narrow chin thrust forward. Thomas was surprised, therefore, when a few minutes after arriving in his office that morning, he was told that Mr. White was downstairs and wished to see him.

He had him shown up immediately, and as he entered, Thomas got to his feet, wished him a cordial "Good morning" and invited him to take a seat.

"I can say what I have to say standing up," White retorted. He was in a very emotional state, pale and tensed. "I suppose you think," the visitor challenged, "that you're taking all my custom." He had a seal of lapis lazuli set in gold on the end of his watch chain, and as he spoke, he swung it in a way that indicated his agitation.

"I really hadn't considered it, Mr. White," Thomas answered. "Surely our trades are rather different."

"You can't deceive me, Mr. Kingston. I haven't been in business as long as I have without learning something about men. I haven't had my eyes shut, you know. You're trying to break me, aren't you?" As he snapped out the question, the seal on the end of the watch chain began to whirl at double the speed. "Aren't you?" he repeated when Thomas, astonished by the outburst, was slow to reply.

"Of course I'm not trying to break you, Mr. White," he said.

"You tried to buy me out, didn't you? . . . Well, didn't you?" Again the whirling seal increased speed as Thomas' response was too delayed for his liking.

"Yes," Thomas said, "we made you an offer."

"I told Rawlings I wouldn't sell."

"So I believe," Thomas agreed.

"I still won't sell. I'll never sell, Mr. Kingston, no matter what you do. I've come here to tell you that myself, to remove any doubts you might have. I won't sell. What's more, you've taken none of my trade, so don't think you have. In fact, it's been better than it was before . . . despite your prices, despite your methods. So it's failed, you see. Your little plan's failed, Mr. Kingston."

"Please, Mr. White," Thomas interjected. "I have no little plan."

"It won't work, Mr. Kingston. I'll still be here, I can promise you, when you're a bankrupt, when all this fragile edifice of departments has crashed round your neck like a pack of cards." Abruptly he returned the seal at the end of the chain to his waistcoat pocket and stalked awkwardly from the room, leaving Thomas sitting at his desk somewhat dazed by the scene he had just witnessed.

It was nearly nine o'clock, the time at which every morning Thomas made a tour of his departments. There were now twenty-two of them, including the small ones, and it usually took him the best part of an hour and a half by the time he had criticized or admired the counter displays and discussed the merchandise with the sales assistants.

He got to his feet, put on his hat and went downstairs. He spent a long time in the Gentlemen's section. Then he moved on to the linens, where young Albert Brown, the errand boy who had become so big an issue between him and David, was now, at the age of twenty, a senior assistant. Thomas' autocratic decision on that occasion was one that he had never regretted. As he watched him serving a most demanding customer, Thomas wondered what his situation would have been if his dismissal had not been reversed. Crime, probably, Thomas thought, and not very clever crime, for Albert lacked the necessary cunning for that pursuit.

He moved on to the Ladies' Department in his three-shop block, and as he entered, he saw Lillian standing at one of the counters. "Good morning, Lillian," he said.

"I was hoping I'd meet you," she said, walking with him away from the assistant to whom she had been speaking, so that she would not overhear them. "Thomas, I'm unhappy about you and David. Would it be possible, do you think, for us to have a talk about it? I mean just you and me. Not with David."

"Of course," he answered.

"It's not the easiest of things to arrange," she went on. "I don't want to deceive him, but I couldn't speak my mind openly in front of him. Could we perhaps encounter each other in Knightsbridge one afternoon by chance and you could invite me to take tea with you somewhere?—that is, if you could drag yourself away from the business for half an hour."

Thomas laughed. It was labored planning, but he could understand her problem.

As it turned out, she did not have to engineer a chance meeting. For later that week, May fell ill again. Dr. Henderson prescribed change and rest for her, so she went with the children and Ruby, the maid, to Quainton, where Thomas' mother and sisters could look after her.

In her absence, Thomas would usually dine out or, if he had work to do, cut himself some cold meat from the larder and spend a few hours in his little study at the back of the house. It was on one of these evenings that he was surprised to hear a knocking on the front door and, when he opened it, to find Lillian standing there. "Is it a convenient time fo me to call, Thomas?"

"Of course," he said. "Come in."

"David is out for the evening," she explained, as he took her cloak from her shoulders and laid it on a chair in the hall. "Something to do with St. Mary's. He's become very busy with church affairs during the last few months." As she spoke, she took her bonnet off carefully, looking in a mirror on the wall as she did so. She touched back into place a couple of curls that had become disturbed from her hair, which was arranged in a cascade of plaits and ringlets. "I knew May was away. It seemed a good moment to have our talk—and less conspicuous than meeting in a tearoom."

She walked into the sitting room ahead of him, leaving a whiff of heady perfume suspended in the air behind her. She was wearing a dark green and yellow check dress, with a simple curiass bodice, drawn tight across her belly and hips. Beneath it, the skirts flared to the floor in overlays of braid and chenille fringe below a large satin bow at the back, forming eventually in a short train behind her. Current fashion, revealing of the body as it was, suited Lillian, who, despite her twenty-nine years and the carrying of two children, still had a fine figure.

She sat down, with her hands lightly clasped on her lap, and smiled just a little mischievously as she accepted his offer of a glass of sherry.

"I hope you don't think I've been unwise to come here," she said, "but since I'm now a lady of some maturity and you're a father of three and we're sort of cousins . . ."

"And of course," he said with a smile as he went through the double doors to the dining room to pour sherry from a decanter on the sideboard, "our great ages ensure respectability—as I'm certain anyone who observed you arrive would agree."

"Do you think anyone did observe it?" she asked.

"I doubt it—not on a cold winter's evening with the curtains drawn."

"I must confess," she said, "that I rather like the idea of it mattering whether or not we're observed. I don't recall ever doing anything before that couldn't be observed by the Archbishop of Canterbury.

And how disappointed our observers would be if they knew the innocent reason for my visit."

"Oh, I don't know," he responded. "It's a little outrageous." He
walked back into the sitting room with two glasses and handed one to
her. "You always liked to be a little outrageous, didn't you?"

He put his glass on the mantelpiece and bent down to put a match
to the fire that was laid, but unlit, in the hearth. "You should have let
me know you were coming. I'd have had the fire burning."

"I could have sent you a note, but by whom? It would have
seemed even more like an assignation. You'd never think that a little
half-hour talk about one's husband's career would present such enormous problems."

Thomas watched the flames licking round the kindling and the
coals, then stood up. Standing with his back to the fireplace, he raised
his glass to her in silent toast and sipped the sherry.

She looked round the room with approval. "I must say," she said,
"May has great taste."

"Thank you," Thomas responded, "though I think your home too
is very handsome."

"Are you happy with her, Thomas?" she asked suddenly.

"Good heavens, what a question! But yes, I'm very happy with
her. How about you and David?"

"Oh, we get on well too. He's kind and considerate. The only
thing I wish sometimes is that he was a bit more ambitious. I always
liked that aspect of you. You seemed so determined—so thrusting,
somehow—as though you'd fight your way through any opposition.
It's attractive to a woman, you know. Power, I suppose. Already
you've achieved so much. . . ."

"So much?" he queried with a smile. "I hope we're only at the
beginning. And we've been lucky, as old Mr. White's always telling
me."

"It's not just luck, Thomas. Your progress'll continue. I'm positive
of that, though I don't know why I'm so sure."

"The reason's simple . . . if you want something badly enough,
and devote all your energies to it, you usually get it. I wanted my
emporium."

"I don't think that's an invariable rule," Lillian said quietly. "I
wanted you, but I didn't get you."

He looked at her, unsure whether she was being serious or not. "If
you did, which I doubt, perhaps you didn't want me enough. Oh, you
liked to flirt, to shock a bit, but you weren't very serious. May I fill
your glass?"

"Do you think you should?"

He shrugged, smiled. "I'm going to replenish my own . . . and there's no one here to disapprove."

Her eyes met his. For one instant there was no responding smile in them—just a brief look of agonized longing. Then the cloud was gone from them and they lightened. "Just a half glass, then."

The effect on him of that glance, with its brief moment of revelation, was immediate. As he held the decanter over one of the glasses, his hand shook so badly that he spilled the sherry. He tried to fill the other glass and again the wine slopped over the edge. One second in time had done this to him, a flare in the eyes of a woman lasting no longer than the tick of his watch, a sudden transient flash—a woman, what was more, who had never before inspired in him anything more than amusement.

"We haven't talked about you and David," she said from within the sitting room, and he knew from the slight break in her voice that they were not going to talk about him and David—at least, not yet.

As he entered the room, he found that she had moved from the chair and was standing, as he had been, with her back to the fire. Her cuirass bodice was cut down to a low point at the front, emphasizing the curve of her hips and the near-flat mound of her belly. The careful disarray of her hair was no longer so perfect. Two curls had escaped onto her forehead. A fugitive blond ringlet lay on the side of her neck. He hesitated at the doorway, a glass held in each hand as before. The expression that had fired so fierce a response in him was back in her eyes. No humor. Stark need, but no lightness, no hint of the banter they usually exchanged.

He walked toward her and held out a glass with a hand that trembled. For an instant, she took her eyes from his, glanced down at the glass with its clear signal of his emotion, and gave a little shake with her head. He put both glasses on the mantelpiece, and she moved to him, throwing her arms round his neck, her mouth hungrily seeking his. He put his hands on her hips and, holding them close to her body, slowly raised them to the sides of her breasts. Her lips became more demanding, moving and pressing on his with an urgency that was almost frantic. He slid his fingers under her hair, tracing her neck. She let out a slight whimper and pulled back, looking into his eyes. "Serious?" she queried, referring to the comment he had made a few minutes before. "I'm serious."

He did not speak, just gripped her by the hand and led her upstairs to the bedroom, leaving the door open so that there was light from the gas lamps on the landing. He took her in his arms and kissed her again. He kissed her neck, her throat. He burrowed a way through her hair so that he could put his mouth to her ear. Then he turned her, gently but firmly like a dancing partner, and began to unhook her bodice until it fell from her shoulders to the floor.

Her long corset, as he recognized from his stock, was French, covered in black satin and edged at the top with lace. With trembling fingers, he undid it, eye by eye, and when this too dropped from her, he put his arms forward round her, holding her breasts, soft beneath the silk of her chemise, and gently drew her back to him.

She turned within his embrace and put her mouth to his. With their lips still together, she released her underskirt at the waist and her petticoats and her pantaloons, and, asking him to hold her so that she did not lose her balance, she took off her shoes and stockings. At last she stood in front of him covered only by the finespun fabric of her chemise, looking strangely innocent, except for the desire in her eyes.

The chemise, heavily embroidered at the neck and sleeves, was held at the throat by two fastened buttons. Very slowly, Thomas began to lift it by walking his fingers in the material, gradually revealing her knees; her thighs; her hips; her pelvis, covered as it was by golden hair; her breasts. "My God," he said softly as he looked at her naked body.

"Wait," she whispered, feeling awkward and inelegant. She undid the buttons of the chemise, and he helped her to lift it over her hair.

Once more, he studied her with wonder—then leaned forward and kissed her right breast, with small light kisses, in circular motion. "Lie down," he asked, and began quickly to take off his clothes. She did as he told her and lay on her back on the bed with one knee raised, her mass of blond hair beside her on the pillow. He came to her naked; paused, looking down at her, softly illuminated as she was by the gaslight from the landing. He bent down and ran his fingers along her thigh. "You're ready," he said in a whisper.

She shook her head, half-smiled. "Not quite," she answered. "Come down beside me." For a moment they lay clutching each other, their legs entwined, their lips together. Then their kissing became frenzied. His hands roamed her body, enjoyed her breasts, reached down through the hairs to the soft wetness between her thighs. He moved onto her. "I must have you," he whispered.

"Just one moment," she pleaded. He raised his shoulders, with one hand on the bed on each side of her, arms rigid, and looked down at her. Then she nodded and he was in her.

Afterward, he wondered at what moment it had gone wrong. It should have been the most overwhelming, unifying of two human bodies that it was possible to conceive—a mutual flaring of passion, a spiraling sexual whirlwind. Yet early in their lovemaking, Thomas realized that something was lacking, that the high ecstasy was gone, leaving only the need for release.

Quite consciously, he tried to recapture their emotion, playing her almost like an instrument, striving to find the chord that would summon back their former inspiration. He kissed her constantly—on her lips, her throat, her breast. He held her nipples between light-moving fingers. He altered the manner of his thrusting—at one moment making love to her fast and hard and then reverting to a rhythm of slow, languorous strokes. Sometimes he penetrated deep within her and at others he barely entered her. He changed their positions constantly and at last, almost in desperation, he rolled her on top of him, though he doubted if this would appeal to her, since the idea of male power was so important to her—and he was right, for soon she said she would prefer to be beneath him. At one stage, he sought to kiss her as the French did, but she stopped him, knowing his reason. And when he tried to use his fingers as he would have used his tongue, she moved his hand away.

Several times, he thought with eager hope that she was caught in a rising wave of feeling that would lift her to the summit, but she never approached it, and at last he himself could wait no longer and they lay together in silence, out of breath, sweating, feeling just a little degraded.

For a few moments, Lillian was completely numb, wondering if she would ever feel anything again. Her disappointment was so extreme, so bitter, that she realized with sudden clarity that for years in unacknowledged thoughts she had been preparing herself like a bride for what had just occurred. Her mortification became scarcely bearable. At last, in a dull, lifeless voice, she said, "I feel used, Thomas. Did you feel you were using me?"

He was lying beside her, his head on the pillow, staring at the ceiling. "I wasn't using you," he replied.

"It's like being a prostitute."

"That's too harsh," he had said, and leaning toward her, he kissed her gently on the lips.

"Please don't," she said. She got up and began to dress, and he understood her need to cover herself. She put on her stockings and her underclothes, and in pantaloons, chemise and petticoats, she sat on a

stool before May's little dressing table and looked at herself in the
mirror in the light from the landing. She took up May's brush and
began to brush her hair, using May's comb to twist her ringlets and her
curls into some semblance of order. It was not the ideal hair arrangement for a visit to a lover. "We still haven't talked about you and
David," she said at last.

Thomas gave a short, bitter laugh. "The reason for your visit.
What was it you wanted to say?"

"I'm not sure now's the right moment."

"When's the right moment? Here I am. I'm listening. I even feel
joined to you in a strange way. We've shared the greatest intimacy
two human beings can know. It's made you feel cheap. It's made me
feel inadequate. But we have it in common . . . a secret . . ." He broke
off. "What about David?"

"I want to know what his position is . . . what it will be."

"He owns a substantial share of the business. He's the Secretary of
Kingstons."

"You seem to work more closely with Mr. Baines."

A feeling of total sadness suddenly enveloped him as he watched
her at the mirror, her arms moving gracefully as she tried to arrange
her luxuriant hair. He thought for a moment of the times they had
played cards together on Sunday afternoons in their early teens at
Copenhagen Street, and how surprised and shocked they would have
been if anyone had ever forecast the scene that was now in the last
unhappy stages of enactment. He thought of May, whose spirit was all
round them in that room. They should never have chosen that bed, but
would any other have been better—Ramsay's? Harry's? The maid's?

"Thomas," she reminded him softly, "I asked you about Mr.
Baines."

"Baines shares my ambitions for the firm," he said. "He has the
same vision. As for David . . . well, you know as well as I do that David
doesn't really understand why we can't just stay as we are."

"So what's going to happen to him?"

"Nothing can change his ownership unless he chooses to sell his
share."

"What about his position?"

"It'll stay as it is."

"Until it gets too big for him?" she queried.

"He'll probably grow with the post. He's good at it. Somebody
has to watch the money, see the bills are paid. Otherwise there'd be
chaos. With David there, I don't have to worry about that part."

"You're describing a clerk—a senior clerk, but a clerk."

"Clerks are important, especially senior clerks."

She turned and faced him, still sitting on the stool, and he felt a sudden pain in his groin as he thought how lovely she looked and how strange it was that the response between their bodies had been so minimal. "Tell me straight, Thomas," she said. "Can he ever be a force within Kingstons?"

Thomas shook his head. "You can't make a man into something he's not, Lillian."

"And Charles?" she said. "What about Charles?"

Thomas was surprised by the question. "Charles is a little boy of three."

"Will there be a place for him in Kingstons?"

"Of course. His father's part owner of the firm. I could hardly refuse."

"You have sons of your own."

"I shall also have a big business—if our hopes are fulfilled. We shall need men to direct it—good men—far more than I can supply."

"Is that a promise?" she asked tautly. "Do you promise that you'll give Charles his opportunity?"

"Yes—if he wants it."

"He'll want it, Thomas."

He was touched by the intensity of her answer. He got up from the bed and moved to her. Gently, he kissed her forehead, her cheek, her lips. His hand caressed her shoulder, fell to her breast. At first, sitting immobile, an expression of anxiety on her face, she did not apppear to be conscious of what he was doing. Then she shook her head slightly in rebuke. "That really is a promise about Charles, Thomas?"

"It's a promise, Lillian."

She raised her lips to his, wanting so much to know again some remnant of the feelings they had felt at first; but it was not there, and she began to cry—quietly at first and then in great racking sobs, with her arms tight round his naked body.

· 2 ·

On Friday of that week, Thomas went to Quainton to join May and the children for a few days. He was glad to get away from London. He had not been home for a long time, and he felt a great need for the country, for the sight of the long high hills that overlooked the farm, for the feeling of wind on his face—a need, perhaps, he mocked himself a little ruefully on the train journey, for a refreshening after the scene with Lillian. Not that he really regretted what had occurred. He felt an acute sadness, a sense of loss, but only a little shame, for he saw it as something that nothing could have stopped. Mentally, he had stood up and brushed himself down. In time, he believed, the episode would become a blurred memory.

Edward met the train at Aylesbury with the trap as usual. It was a cold, bright morning, with the remnants of a light frost still lying in the fields beside the road, and the horse stepped out handsomely—a four-year-old gelding, Edward informed him, that he had only just acquired. As Thomas looked at his brother, he recalled the haggard man who had met him during his crisis visit in 1870 and marveled at the change. He had become a little stout, spoke with confidence about the progress of his herd and even shrugged off the appalling harvest of the previous autumn. "By the way," he said at one moment, "hounds are meeting at Quainton tomorrow. Feel like a day's hunting? You could take my mare . . ."

After the previous night, a few hours of fast riding across country was just what Thomas needed. "I can think of nothing I'd like better," he said.

He inquired if the family had heard again from Cameron's lawyers, who had written the previous year disputing the exact position of the hedges on their northern boundary. "Not since that little try-on," Edward answered. "Just testing our mettle, I think."

Edward wheeled the trap into the lane that led up to the farm, and Thomas enjoyed the sight of the sleek, fat cattle that were grazing in the big field where five years before there had been piles of smoldering carcasses. The children had been watching through the window for their arrival, and as Edward reined in to a stop by the house, they ran out the door yelling an excited greeting to their father. He swept them up one by one in great enveloping hugs, finally holding a giggling Rose high above his head, since she was so much lighter than the boys. They were followed by May, smiling affectionately. "Aren't you supposed to be resting with your feet up?" he asked as he put his arms round her.

"I can't lie about all the time. I'm feeling remarkably well."

Thomas embraced his mother and his sisters, all smiling happily. He turned for a moment to survey the land that the Kingston family had farmed for so long and experienced a great sense of well-being—

until it was soured by the sudden invading thought, vivid to the last detail, of Lillian at May's dressing table.

The scene the next day in Quainton Village was as it had always been on the hunting mornings Thomas remembered as a boy. The hounds were waiting on the same part of the green, tongues lolling out as though they were too big for their mouths. Higgins, the huntsman, white-haired now, sat slouched in his saddle, with the same bored expression that would vanish the moment they moved off. It was a sharp morning, though there was a thin sun in a sky of light cloud, and some riders kept their horses moving to prevent them from getting cold. Others sat in groups, drinking port and brandy, handed up to them by barmen from the Royal Oak. All the men wore coats of pink, as they called the scarlet, or gray that was so dark that it looked black. There were more women out than there used to be, Thomas noted— and very stylish they looked in their toppers and wide-mesh veils to contain their hair, and black habits with skirts that reached to their spurs. But then, women were taking part in all sports far more than they had in the past.

Edward had driven May and the children to the meet in the trap, eager to show off his new young gelding. "I can rest in the cart as easily as I can at home," May had assured Thomas when he had anxiously questioned her wisdom. It was the first hunt the children had ever attended, and their eyes were bright with excitement.

"You see that character over there near the inn," Edward remarked at one moment to Thomas, who was sitting his horse beside the trap, ". . . talking to two ladies . . . on a big black . . . Well, that's Cameron."

Thomas studied the man who had seemed such a threat to his family—and was still a potential enemy. He was a handsome, well-built man in his fifties, dark, with a rather somber expression. Thomas was surprised that he was wearing pink, since this could be worn only by invitation, but it showed how entrenched he had become in the area despite his commercial background. He was listening intently to what one of the ladies was saying, tapping his boot idly with his hunting crop. "Some horse, eh?" said Edward admiringly. He was certainly a beautiful animal, standing over seventeen hands, ears forward, eyes intelligent. "Plenty of blood there."

Thomas nodded agreement as he watched the Master, Sir James Harrison, walking his mount slowly across the green toward the hounds, the other riders making way for him. As Master of Foxhounds, he held the most prestigious position that existed in any English rural community. For a moment, he interrupted his stately progress to talk to a young lady. She was in her mid-twenties, with fair hair beneath a topper worn at a slightly rakish angle, and a habit tailored sharply to reveal a narrow waist. Even from a distance, as she sat her horse with the stiff back that a sidesaddle demanded, it was obvious that she was a most striking young woman. "Who's she?" Thomas asked.

"The Master's daughter, Evelyn. . . . Surely you remember her."

"My God!" said Thomas, remembering her as a ten-year-old driving about the village in a dog cart. "She's changed a bit."

May shook her head at him mockingly. "Just remember, Thomas Kingston, you're here to chase foxes."

At a nod from the Master, Higgins took his short brass horn from its place between two of the front buttons of his coat, blew a brief note and led off his hounds—followed by the congestion of horses and riders that constituted the Bicester Hunt.

"Get on him, then. . . . Get on him. . . . Get on him, then. . . . Get him up. . . . Get on . . ." From within the wood, Thomas could hear Higgins' repeated singsong encouragement to his hounds as they drew the cover. Sometimes one of the hounds would start speaking and others nearby would join him. Then the sound would die as they lost the scent in the undergrowth.

It was a good day for smell, though, the cold holding it down, and they found it quickly. The eager yelping of one hound became a chorus as others rushed to join him, the music rising to crescendo in the morning air.

From the lane, where they were all waiting, Thomas watched him go—a big fox, with a rich brown coat. He seemed in no hurry, as foxes rarely do, unless closely pressed. He went through a yew hedge on the far side of the meadow and ran alongside a ditch of another that intersected it.

One of the riders posted as markers let out a "Halloa," the joyous cry of the chase, and galloped his horse to the exact route the fox had taken, to fix for the huntsman the "line" of scent, which is the key to all fox hunting.

Hounds spilled out of the wood, yelping noisily, muzzles to the ground, and raced across the meadow for the hedge, scrambling over it, or burrowing through where the foliage was light. Higgins jumped out of the copse over iron railings, blowing his horn urgently to call on those hounds that were still behind in the cover.

The fox had made for the high ground, and as Thomas galloped up the steep turf, he looked around him, reveling in the panorama; on both sides, men and women were traveling fast, taking the fences as they came to them, in pursuit of the hounds or in the direction in which they thought the fox would lead them.

They ran over the hills, taking the big timber that divided the fields, and raced down toward Marston. Hounds checked for a couple of minutes as they lost the scent, and Higgins cast them wide in search of it. Thomas reined up his mare, panting, with a group of other riders. They were still on high ground, looking down on Cameron's great house which he had first seen five years before. Below them, they saw hounds find the line again and run right-handed. For a few moments, they sat watching them like generals viewing armies in battle.

Several times, Thomas had seen Cameron on his big horse. Now once more he saw him below, galloping for a high post-and-rails with a group of about ten riders, spread out. The black horse overtook the others with ease and cleared the fence in superb style.

"My God, what pace that horse has got," Thomas said, talking partly to himself and partly to the riders waiting with him.

"It's not strange," one of them answered, "considering his stock." Thomas had not seen Evelyn Harrison join the group, and he turned, slightly surprised. "His sire," she went on, "won the Grand National in 'Seventy-one."

"You're obviously well acquainted with the horse, madam," said Thomas.

"My father bred him," she answered, looking at him with eyes that were so deep a blue that they were almost violet. "I don't think I've seen you riding with the hounds before, sir, have I?"

"I'm Thomas Kingston—of the Kingston farm. You knew me when you were a child, but I've lived in London since I was thirteen."

Her attention was suddenly caught by the hounds, which, after checking again, were streaking across the pasture below. "My gracious, they're going fast! We'd better hurry or we'll lose them." And she set off at a gallop down the steep hill, and Thomas noted the easy unison with her horse, each move of the animal reflected like a ripple through her body.

Hounds ran across the flat country below, then crossed the Kingston farm. For a moment the fox took shelter in Edward's barn, but the whippers-in soon routed him out and again he was running for his life, in the direction of the light woods on the east fringe of the village.

Once hounds had gone away out of the first cover, Edward had driven the trap up a lane to one of the farms on the hills from which they could watch the hunting. Patiently, he had explained to the children how foxes always ran in big circles and used the country with amazing skill. Often, he said, they would roll in manure to mask their scent or make for plowed land, which lost the smell fast, rather than turf, which held it. They would float down streams, even clamber up low-branched trees to counter the biggest danger that nature had given them. Old huntsmen, he remarked, even argued that they could hold their scent for brief periods as a man could hold his breath.

Then, when hounds ran on over to the Marston side of the hills and there was no more to be seen, Edward began to drive home to the farm. It was quiet now as the trap progressed along the Quainton Road; the only sounds were the gelding's hooves and the cawing of rooks in a high tree. Then, faintly at first, they heard the voice of approaching hounds in the distance.

There was no warning for what happened, no chance for Edward to leap out of the trap and hold the gelding's head. Suddenly, four riders, screened by the high hedge, jumped into the road through a gap in the foliage. The first horse almost landed on the gelding, its rider shouting, "Sorry, sir" as he rode away fast. Edward had leaned back hard on the reins to check the trap, and perhaps, if there had been only one huntsman, he could have regained control. But the three other horses coming over the hedge in quick succession ended that possibility. The alarmed gelding reared—then bolted. As Edward fought to hold him, the trap began to yaw from side to side. Then one wheel slipped into the ditch. The trap lurched against the hedge, still being dragged along, until the harness broke and the shafts, freed from the horse, swung upward. All five of the occupants were catapulted from their seats. Instinctively, May clutched her arms round her belly as she fell into the road. She felt a sharp stab of pain. For a brief moment, she heard the sound of hounds growing louder—before she lost consciousness.

The fox had run back into the hills, and Thomas knew it must tire soon. They had been going for an hour and a quarter, and he had gained little respite. Foxes often escaped—more often than they died— but on a day such as this, with the scent strong, this fox was almost certainly doomed.

Hounds were going at full cry about three hundred yards ahead of Thomas as he rode fast down a steep field toward a hedge that was too high to clear, except at one narrow point between two young trees that had grown within it. He saw Cameron approaching from the side of the field, having jumped into it from a different direction. They were both converging with other horsemen for the same gap, but Thomas was way ahead. As he put Edward's mare at the jump, he leaned forward with his head low beside her neck because of the branches of one of the trees. He heard Cameron approaching behind him, but assumed he would wait until his way was clear—incorrectly, it turned out. For the black horse hit the mare behind the saddle, thrusting her hard against one of the trees. To Thomas' astonishment, she survived this midair collision and did not even falter on landing, stepping out as her back feet felt the ground and galloping on.

Thomas heard the noise behind him as Cameron's black came down, and after a few seconds, the riderless horse passed him, stirrups flying. Thomas grabbed the reins, and checking his mare, he turned and led the horse back at a trot to Cameron, who was standing by the hedge where he had fallen, collecting himself, retrieving his crop and dented hat.

As Thomas approached, Cameron glared at him. "You confounded lunatic!" he swore at him.

Thomas was astounded by this response to his act of courtesy. "Would you be good enough to repeat that, sir?" he said angrily.

"I said you were a confounded lunatic," Cameron repeated.

"I wanted to be sure," said Thomas. Deliberately, he dropped the reins of the big horse and lashed him hard on the flank with his whip. The horse leaped away, and Thomas rode after him to strike him again so that he did not slow up. Then he reined back and turned. "I hope, sir," he called out to Cameron, "that a walk'll teach you a few manners."

Evelyn Harrison overtook Thomas as he rode on, turning to him as she went by. "That wasn't very kind, Mr. Kingston," she said with a smile.

"Did you hear what he said?" he responded.

"I'm sure he richly deserved it," she answered. Then they heard the long warbling call of the horn which indicated that hounds had killed their fox.

Thomas caught up with them as they went on to draw the next cover and continued hunting until about four o'clock in the afternoon. By the time he rode back into the yard at the farm, muddy and tired but happy, it was already dark. Brian joined him in the stable. "I'll deal with the mare," he said; "you'd better go inside. The doctor's just left."

"Doctor?" queried Thomas.

"The trap turned over. . . . I'm afraid May's lost the child but she's safe herself. The children escaped with a few bruises. . . . Miraculous . . ."

Thomas hurried to the house, where he was met by his mother. "I've given her my room for the moment," she explained. "The doctor says she'll be all right, but . . ."

"Yes?" Thomas demanded impatiently when she hesitated.

"He doubts if she'll be able to bear any more children."

Thomas ran up the stairs to his mother's room. May was lying in the big bed in a white high-necked nightgown. She looked so pale that her complexion was almost gray. He leaned down and kissed her. "Thank God you're all right."

"He was going to be a fine child, Thomas."

"You always bear fine children."

"What if I can't have any more? What if I've done something to myself inside? The doctor didn't sound too sure."

"Then we'll be grateful for the ones we have."

"I hear Ramsay's got a black eye."

"He'll be very proud of it. . . . Now you ought to be sleeping— not fussing about black eyes."

He leaned down again to kiss her, and she put her arms around his neck and clutched him. Then she began to cry very gently—the sort of crying that comes more from a weak physical state than from unhappiness.

· 3 ·

The incident over Cameron's horse was bound to have repercussions, and Edward's prediction that there would be a letter from his lawyers within a week was accurate to the day.

The lawyers declared that they were bringing action against the Kingston family, first to demand pasturage rights over certain fields and second to claim right-of-way across the farm on the basis of an extremely suspect eighteenth-century deed. Pasturage rights were a feature of feudal England and had faded into disuse with the power of the barons, but a court might be persuaded to uphold them. The right-of-way issue was sounder—and more important to Cameron, because his cattle, when grazed in certain of his fields, had to make a detour to return to their sheds.

Clearly, this was a declaration of war, and Thomas was determined that it must be met with full battle array and no signs of weakness. He consulted a leading firm of London lawyers, recommended by Glynn Mills Currie & Company, the store's bankers, and was relieved to learn that he was correct in believing that Cameron had no real case—but in fact he had consulted them more for their prestige value than for their advice.

"Cameron must be made to believe that unlike the other farms he has taken, we've got enough resources to fight him," Thomas wrote to Edward after seeing the lawyers. "He knows a lot about you and the farm, but I doubt if he knows much about me and the store. So I propose to go and see him when I come home to collect May and the children. For this purpose, I'd like you to hire me a carriage in Aylesbury—a good one, in first-rate condition, with a well-turned-out pair."

Edward was waiting for Thomas on the platform when he stepped down from the train on Saturday afternoon of the following week. He grinned as they shook hands. "Your carriage awaits, my Lord," he said.

Thomas was deeply impressed by the victoria that, polished to a high shine, stood waiting in the station yard. Two well-groomed bays stood in harness that was gleaming. The coachman could have been in the service of a duke. "I hope we haven't overdone it," remarked Edward, seeing the reaction on his brother's face.

Thomas laughed. "Impossible with a man like Cameron. If I had an escort of cavalry, I'd take that too."

The next day at noon, when he reckoned that Cameron would just have returned from church, Thomas was driven to Marston Hall. However, his confidence, stimulated as it had been by the soft cushions of the carriage, began to wane somewhat as they passed through the park gates into the long tree-lined approach to the hall. Was it wise, he began to wonder, to confront so powerful a man as Cameron on his home territory? Certainly, by then it was too late to change his tactics.

The carriage came to a halt in front of the huge red brick house, and Thomas stepped down onto the gravel drive, to be met formally by the butler, standing impassively at the head of the entrance steps. When Thomas asked to see Mr. Cameron, the butler said he would inquire if he was available and meanwhile ushered him into a large study, with windows overlooking the front meadows and a whole wall lined with books. At one end of the room was a magnificent desk of polished walnut on which, ranged neatly awaiting attention, were some unopened letters. Thomas' attention was caught by the envelope that lay on the top of the small pile, because the handwriting seemed familiar, but at that moment he could not recall where he had seen it before.

He was left alone in the study for about ten minutes and was, in fact, examining a book from the bookshelves when Cameron entered so quietly that Thomas did not know he was there until he spoke. "You wished to see me, Mr. Kingston?" he said. His voice was rough, marked with a North Country accent.

Thomas turned. "I appreciate your receiving me, Mr. Cameron."

"I doubt if my lawyers would approve, since litigation's pending, but I decided I'd hear what you had to say."

Cameron did not invite him to sit down and stayed standing himself, indicating that he intended the meeting to be short. His dark eyes were cold but probing. His hands were clasped behind his back beneath his frock coat.

"Well?" Cameron queried.

"My lawyers," Thomas began uncertainly, "tell me that you've no grounds for action."

"I'm informed of their view."

There was no surprise; no challenge, even. After a moment, Thomas added, "They are, of course, a firm of some repute "

Cameron gave a slight shrug that again implied agreement with Thomas' statement. "My own advisers are not unknown," he said. Again there was a moment of silence. "If we may come to the reason for your visit, Mr. Kingston . . ."

"I came, Mr. Cameron," Thomas responded, "because I wanted to assure you that we would aggressively defend the case in every court in the country. There'll be no question of our bowing to pressure."

Cameron moved his head in several little nods that seemed impatient, pursed his lips, but said nothing. "On the other hand," Thomas went on, "it seems stupid for neighbors to be in conflict when possibly it is unnecessary."

"You've come to sell me land?"

The question was sudden and harsh, and the abrupt change of tenor from Cameron's cool conduct of the interview so far caught Thomas by surprise. "Indeed no, sir."

"Then what do you mean? You have some other proposal?"

"My family would possibly consider allowing your cattle to cross our land for brief periods of the year . . . when, for example, you were grazing them in the southern end of your estate—as a courtesy, of course. . . ."

Cameron looked at him curiously. "I'm surprised by your simplicity, Mr. Kingston," he said, "since I've heard good reports of your business. . . . You thought I'd agree to such a thing? A courtesy?"

"Surely it's better than conflict," countered Thomas.

"Why? You speak of conflict as though it was a disaster. Mr. Kingston, conflict is part of the human condition. I've lived my life with conflict. I built this house with conflict. I bought those horses out there with conflict. Everything I've acquired has been gained with conflict. So if you think you can persuade me to alter my intentions by threatening me with a little conflict, then you're even more of a madman than I thought the other day when you cut in front of my horse."

"Cut in front of you!" echoed Thomas angrily. "I was there before you."

"It was fortunate for you I didn't break any bones, or your lawyers of repute would have another issue on which to advise you." He turned and walked to the window, his hands still clasped behind his back, and stood looking out over the fields where the horses were grazing. "Do I understand," he asked, speaking with his back to the room, "that I've heard all you wish to put to me?"

"Mr. Cameron," Thomas answered, "I think conflict's wasteful of time, money and resources that can be better used . . . but if you insist on it, you can have it. If we're attacked, by God we'll fight back."

For a moment Cameron did not respond, and when at last he spoke he did so quite softly, without turning from the window. "If you're not off my premises within one minute, Mr. Kingston, I'll have you physically thrown out."

Thomas was so shocked that he could scarcely credit what he had heard. "Thrown out?" he repeated.

"And don't waste any more money on swank carriages or fancy lawyers," Cameron went on. "You can't deceive me. I know your resources to the last penny. If I was to put a figure on your last month's sales, you'd find I'd be within twenty pounds."

He paused, rocking gently forward and backward on the balls of his feet. "The only attribute you'd appear to have is that you're a fighter. . . . I don't like you. I think you're filled with conceit and pride and arrogance, but I've a regard for fighters. . . ." He broke off, took his watch from his pocket and flicked open the gold cover with his thumb. "You have thirty seconds left, Mr. Kingston."

Thomas strode firmly out of the house and climbed into the carriage that Cameron so obviously knew to be hired. He felt a sense of deep frustration, of being outmaneuvered, of being treated like a youth in his teens. And it was then, as the carriage took him down the long driveway, that he remembered where he had seen the writing on the envelope on Cameron's desk. He had not seen it for a long time, but it had summoned him on many occasions to take merchandise to Eaton Square.

In fact Cameron did not proceed with his action—perhaps because his lawyers came to agree with Thomas' own advisers on the prospects of the case—but Thomas could never recall that letter on the walnut desk without a feeling of slight unease.

· 4 ·

During the weeks that followed their return to London from the farm, the weather was exceptionally fine for February, with cold, bright days and the skies often cloudless. It was good for trade, and all departments did well. The new Gentlemen's section benefited in particular, and sales rose every week. Soon Sidney Baines suggested to Thomas that their men's business was well enough established for them to consider extending the range of merchandise as they had planned.

Thomas often encountered White in the street, but the old draper still looked straight through him whenever they met on the pavement, striding by grimly with his chin in the air.

Baines, as Thomas' first lieutenant, was given the same treatment, though he did not accept White's antagonism quite so philosophically as his chief. He was acutely aware not only that White was convinced that the sole purpose of the Kingston competition was to cause his ruin, but that this obsession was growing by the day. Baines would watch him prowling up and down the pavement, staring angrily at the Kingston displays and glowering at any of his own customers he saw emerge from the rival establishment. Once, when Baines opened the doors that formed the back of one of the windows, he found himself staring into White's face, pressed against the glass with such wild, glaring enmity that it brought his sanity into question.

Then, on an afternoon in early March, one of the gentlemen's-wear wholesalers, who had been supplying White's shop for years, told Baines that he too was worried about him. "He hates your Mr. Kingston of course," he said. "In fact, he told me that if I didn't stop dealing with him, he'd close his account with us. Not that this would be any great loss, but I like the old fellow. He keeps repeating, 'He'll be sorry. I'll make him pay for his little plot. You just see if I don't.' "

Baines worried about this conversation all evening, and the next morning he mentioned his concern to Thomas at the end of their daily meeting. "If I may suggest it, Mr. Kingston," he said as he got up to go, "it might be advisable for us to think about some kind of precautions."

"Precautions?" queried Thomas with surprise.

Baines gathered up his papers, patting the side of the pile so that they were neatly aligned. "I know it sounds a bit dramatic, but I mean if 'e does become a little mad—and already 'e's showing signs of it— then isn't there perhaps a danger that he might resort to some act of aggression?'"

"Good heavens!" exclaimed Thomas. "Do you think he might attack me or something?"

"Possibly—or the store: that's more likely. . . . 'E's very 'ostile, Mr. Kingston; I wouldn't put it past him to start breaking the windows . . . or perhaps even cause a fire."

Thomas paled. To any shopkeeper, the very word "fire" was enough to induce a sleepless night, for it was an enormous danger that sooner or later was encountered by most retailers. "You really think that's a possibility?" Thomas asked.

"I do, Mr. Kingston. I'm certain 'e's near to breaking . . ."

"But surely," Thomas said, "he couldn't set fire to our premises without endangering his own."

"I'm not sure 'e'd mind. It might even solve his problem. 'E's doing very badly."

"You mean end it all in one glorious blaze?" Thomas asked incredulously.

Baines shrugged. " 'Oo knows? When a man's sanity goes, anything's possible, ain't it, Mr. Kingston?"

Thomas worried about what Baines had said for the rest of the day. Then he spoke of it to David, who, predictably, was not sympathetic. "You knew what you were doing, Thomas," he said. "This was the price that had to be paid for an emporium, you said. You've taken his livelihood."

As Thomas left the business that night, he saw the old draper, standing behind the glass pane of his front door, glaring at him as he passed along the pavement.

The next morning, the crisis came to a head in a way that even

Baines had not considered. Thomas was in his office going through his mail when David entered. His face was drained of color. "I've had a note from White," he said. "You'd better read it."

In that instant, as Thomas took the letter from his partner, he knew what had happened, and he felt the muscles tauten in his belly. "Dear Mr. Rawlings," he read in a handwriting that was large and unsteady, "I have at last been forced to concede victory to Mr. Kingston, but I feel too old or too sad to move away. I hesitate to involve you, but I have to involve somebody and you have always been kind and considerate to me. I enclose a key to my shop. By morning it will all be over, and at last Mr. Kingston will get my premises that he has coveted for so long. He may think he is acquiring them cheaper than if I had accepted his offer last year, but warn him that he is not, for the price will be the curses of a tormented soul. —Theodore White."

"My God," said Thomas, and looked up at David. "Have you been in there yet?"

David shook his head. "I thought you should come with me."

As they went down the stairs, Thomas had a faint hope that perhaps it was an attempt to scare them or was even a gesture of bravado. But this conjecture was unfounded. They found him in the basement of his shop, hanging from a rope that he had fixed to the top of the wooden steps that led down from the ground floor.

Thomas experienced a violent sensation of rising nausea, and he thought for a moment he was going to be sick, but then the sensation eased, leaving him feeling drained. "I'm sorry, Thomas," said David gently, and touched his arm. Thomas acknowledged his comment with a nod. Then in silence they climbed the steps and left the shop. Thomas waited while his partner relocked the entrance door. "Will you send someone to inform the police?" he asked. David nodded, and they returned to their respective offices. There was little either could say, for it had all been said while White was alive. When the police arrived, David gave them the letter and the key and they dealt with everything.

Thomas was in the Gentlemen's Department when the Managing Agent arrived about three o'clock that afternoon. Thomas did not like him. He was short, fat and ingratiating, and he had a thick moustache that always bore proof that he had not wiped his mouth properly after his last meal. "What a sad business, Mr. Kingston," he said. "Still," he added briskly, "they say every cloud has a silver lining, don't they?" He saw Thomas' look of distaste. "Well, perhaps that wasn't very happily put, but I assumed you'd wish to take the shop, Mr. Kingston,

so I took the liberty of preparing the lease. I'm correct, I take it . . .
you do want the shop, don't you?"

Thomas hesitated—then nodded.

"Then perhaps you'd care to sign the document now."

For once, Thomas did not read a contract before signing it. He
called Baines over to witness his signature and scribbled his name.
"Good day to you, sir," he said to the agent, and walked out. He
strode up Sloane Street without even glancing at his new acquisition as
he passed. He was deeply troubled, and as always when he was in a
state of distress, he headed in the direction of the Park. Then abruptly
he changed his mind and, feeling a need to talk to May, he turned and
cut through Eaton Square to Caroline Terrace.

He found her in the kitchen. "I've heard what happened," she said
quietly. She did not run to him, for she sensed that in his taut emotional state he did not want this, but her eyes were marked with
immense compassion. "I almost came to you," she said, "but then I
thought that if you needed to talk about it, you'd come home. It
wouldn't be easy at the firm. I've sent Ruby out with the children."

"That was thoughtful of you." He pulled out a chair from the
kitchen table and sat down. "It's made me wonder a little, May. . . . If a
man dies, you ought to stop and wonder a little, oughtn't you? Surely
it's possible to create a growing enterprise without causing havoc. . . ."

"Of course it is," she said. "You've no reason to blame yourself.
His mind had gone. . . . You didn't cheat him or anything. . . ."

Thomas looked down at his clasped hands on the table. "No, I
didn't cheat him. . . . Competition's supposed to be healthy, isn't it?—
like natural selection in wildlife." He paused. "May, it's going to happen a lot more. . . . Competition's basic to our whole concept—often
with small men like poor old White."

"And sometimes," she reminded him, "with men who are stronger
and wealthier than you. . . . You won't win all the battles, Thomas.
Sometimes it'll be you who have to retreat, perhaps severely sav-
aged. . . ."

He nodded, considering May's words. Then, as his imagination
was caught by the new potential that was now available to him, he said,
"That shop's going to make a lot of difference to us, May. It'll give us
a five-shop block. We can build at the rear. We can open up the sales
floors. . . . It's going to mean a complete reorganization—not only of
the selling space, but of the stockrooms, dispatch, accounts, delivery—
everything. It'll be an emporium at last, despite Mrs. Fellowes, despite
the division from the other three shops. . . . It'll be what I've dreamed

of for years, what you've dreamed of with me. . . ." He broke off. "It's just a little sad we couldn't gain it without the curses of a dead man."

"An insane dead man," she interjected.

He stood up. "May . . ." He held out his arms, and she rushed into them and clung to him. Suddenly, the reaction to the whole trauma released in him a violent need for her. "I want you, May—this minute."

"We'll go upstairs."

"No—here."

"In the kitchen? Thomas, you can't be serious."

He did not appear to have heard her. "Will the children be back?"

"Not yet, but Thomas—" He stopped her speaking with his mouth, then lifted her so that she was sitting on the table. "Please, Thomas. Not here. It's ridiculous—certainly for people of our age and position. You're making me embarrassed. Please, let's go upstairs . . ."

"Upstairs is too far." He had already raised her skirt above her knees as she was speaking. "No, Thomas. Please, Thomas. This isn't right, Thomas. . . . Our bedroom. Please, our bedroom, Thomas . . . You're hurting a bit . . ." Then she stopped resisting and suddenly hugged him to her with both her arms and her legs, kissing him passionately, only occasionally conscious of the hardness of the table beneath her in the soaring elation that consumed her.

Afterward, as she sat on the table pulling her skirts over her knees, she was overwhelmed by a terrible sense of sadness because that act of love could not have the result which nature had intended.

An hour later, Thomas was back at his desk, sketching alternative layouts for his store, which is what his shop would now be, when he was astonished to be told that Mrs. Rawlings was downstairs, inquiring if he could spare her a moment. They had met only twice since the evening in his home when May was away. Each time, she had been glacial—meticulously polite, but withdrawn and speaking with a tone in which resentment lay only just beneath the surface.

As she was shown in, he stood up and held a chair for her, then returned to his desk. She studied him openly. "I've heard about poor Mr. White," she said. "I called because I thought it might have upset you, but I hear you've already signed a lease for the shop. You don't waste any time, do you, Thomas?"

He looked at her, wondering what the true purpose was of her call. "Did you really come to commiserate, Lillian?" he asked. "Or to gloat? And what would you advise me to do now—stop competing with people? stop expanding the business? For nothing stays in suspense, you know. We shall either go forward or go back. Which would you prefer?"

She gave a little sardonic smile. "You've always been adept at specious argument ," she said carefully.

"Lillian," he said, "in this unhappy business my conscience is quite clear."

"Oh, I don't doubt that," she answered tartly. "I suspect it's a very convenient conscience." There was no resilience in her. The surface was as hard as steel. "And what," she went on, "was the response of your conscience to what happened between us?"

Thomas was astonished by her implication. "Lillian, that suggests I seduced you . . . or even took you against your will . . ."

Another of those strange smiles came to her face—superior, oddly secretive, as though he did not have the necessary understanding to appreciate her question. "Out of the question, of course," she said sarcastically. "Oh, I'm not saying I wasn't mesmerized by you; merely that there's responsibility—more, probably, than you think."

"Responsibility?"

"It's too early to be sure, of course, but there may be a consequence of that night."

Thomas stared at her. "You mean you think there's a child?"

She nodded. "Does that make any difference, Thomas? Does that touch your conscience?"

CHAPTER FIVE

September 1876

· I ·

It was hot in the assembly rooms, and the dancing had made him perspire. He put his finger behind his stud and pulled his collar forward several times in an attempt to provide a little ventilation inside his shirt. May noticed what he was doing and smiled at him, idly fanning herself. For once, wearing a mildly décolleté gown as she was, it was an advantage to be a woman.

"That Roger de Coverley took its toll," he said.

"It's good for them to see you enjoying yourself," she remarked.

"So that they know I'm not an ogre?" he queried.

"Perhaps," she said. "I think this ball's an excellent idea. I shall insist you do it every year."

It was September 16, 1876, the seventh anniversary of the day that Thomas had started the business with her, and they were playing host and hostess to more than two hundred people at the first of the Kingston staff balls. Uncle Jack, who had aged greatly since Dolly's death, was with them at the partners' table. So too were Thomas' mother, his two sisters, Mary and Ellen, and Miss Godfrey, whose annual visits to the shop every September 16 had inspired the whole occasion.

Thomas was happy, for it was an evening celebrating Kingstons' growth, and his role as the head of so large a family appealed to him. The past year had been exceptionally important, for the acquisition under such unhappy circumstances of the eighth shop had propelled the firm into a huge leap forward. In the five-shop block, the whole ground and first floors were now devoted to selling. A small team of carts, elegantly painted in the Kingston colors of dark blue and yellow, delivered parcels to those customers who lived beyond the radius still covered by the errand boys. There was a whole range of new departments, including Saddlery, Furniture, Riding Clothes, even an estate agency for buying and selling houses.

The partnership of Thomas and David had become a private lim-

ited company, and they were no longer the sole participants. Their
bankers had acquired a few shares as one of the conditions of providing finance. Capital, in fact, was a constant problem, as the payment of
the ever-growing stock inventories and escalating building costs could
be provided only partly from profits, though these too were rising
sharply.

It was Sidney Baines who had proposed to Thomas an ingenious
way of easing the burden of their cash problems. Why not open a
banking department, he had suggested, so that their customers could
deposit funds for their shopping needs? Kingstons, he estimated, could
offer interest that was less than the company would have to pay for
commercial loans, yet higher than the customers could obtain from
deposit accounts in their own banks. So Kingstons had gone into banking, too.

It was a clever idea, and Baines had produced it at a moment when
he desperately needed to display the flair that Thomas had always
asserted he possessed. The resentment of his position in Kingstons had
increased with the growth of the business—despite his great efforts to
be friendly with Emily, to display impeccable behavior with the sales-
girls, to provide David with a high-level cooperation and to treat Lillian like the Queen of England.

Occasionally he had talked of it to Thomas. "Sometimes, Mr.
Kingston," he said, "I feel they're all just waiting for me to make a
big mistake."

"Then you must take care not to make one, mustn't you?" said
Thomas with a smile.

But, of course, he had. He had make a mistake of such gigantic
proportions that the opposition could not have asked for anything
more. It happened on a day when Thomas was away on a quick visit to
Quainton. Baines had gone down to see Arthur Stockton, and the
wholesaler, with his breezy, expansive manner, had invited him to
lunch. Baines did not normally drink much, and indeed he could not
recall having taken alcohol to excess while he was with Stockton, but
the fact was that he became very drunk. He left the wholesaler with an
order for some six hundred pounds' worth of merchandise, even
though his purchase discretion without Thomas' approval was limited
to one hundred. Then, when he clambered out of the hansom that had
taken him back to Sloane Street, he had staggered across the sales floor,
making it quite obvious to customers and staff that he was hopelessly
inebriated. On the stairs to his office, he had met Miss Higgins, one of
Emily's salesladies, put his arm round her, demanded a kiss, suggested a

polka and overbalanced with her just at the moment that Emily herself had appeared from her office floor. He had described Lillian as "a cow," and when David had ordered him to go to his room, he had stood up straight, swaying from side to side, and said, "I only take ordersh from Mr. Kingshton."

Thomas heard about the incident that evening when he got home. "You'll have to dismiss him now," said May.

"Perhaps I will," agreed Thomas.

The following morning, he was amazed to encounter Lillian in Sloane Street on his way to work. "It's early for you to be about," he said.

"You've heard about the disgraceful behavior of your Mr. Baines, I presume," she said. "You'll dismiss him, of course."

"I'll consider the matter, Lillian."

On arrival at the store, David was waiting for him in his office. "You have no option, Thomas," he said. Thomas had nodded and waited for the inevitable arrival of Emily to report that Miss Higgins was so upset she was not fit for work that day. Then he sent for Baines.

"I don't understand it, Mr. Kingston," said Baines. "I don't know what came over me. I've never been drunk before in my life."

"You've placed me in a difficult position," Thomas told him. "I don't want to lose you, but I don't see that I've any choice at the moment. The only possible saving grace would seem to be that you were with Arthur Stockton. I don't trust Stockton, Baines—certainly not when he's getting you to place orders of a size that he knows perfectly well to be absurd. I shall cancel that, of course."

Thomas did not dismiss Baines—but he had to resist the greatest pressure he had yet experienced within the firm. At Thomas' suggestion, Baines apologized to both David and Lillian—in person and in writing. He asked Emily humbly for her forgiveness—which she refused to give, though this rightly made her feel ungracious—and expressed his deepest regrets to Miss Higgins, who had in fact treated it all as a bit of a lark. Thomas placated David and Emily, and gave instructions that no orders were to be placed with Arthur Stockton until further notice, though he knew he would have to rescind this in due course, for Stockton's merchandise was first class.

Thomas had his biggest trouble from May. "I just don't understand you," she said. "What is the hold this young man has on you? Anyone would think he was blackmailing you."

"I know Stockton," answered Thomas, "and I need Baines. He's very able, and he gives me a service that I'd find hard to replace."

Finally Thomas sent for him to tell him he had been granted a reprieve, and he was deeply grateful. "I want you to know 'ow much I appreciate your support, Mr. Kingston," he said, and it was then, as he was about to leave the office, that he said, "Oh there was one thing, Mr. Kingston. I've been thinking . . ." And he had suggested his notion that the firm should go into banking—which, as Thomas pointed out to May that night, was such a good idea that the cash gain on a month's trading would pay his salary for at least five years.

By the date of the staff ball, Baines had been helping Thomas develop plans for the most dramatic move that he had made in Kingstons so far. Thomas had decided that the time had come at last to cross the rigid line that had always existed between drapery and food. He planned to offer groceries, vegetables, and most sensational of all, meat and poultry. It would be the first time, so far as he knew, that any drapery store in the world had ever sold "wet goods," and the innovation was crucial to his whole concept of the universal emporium.

The moment was opportune for Kingstons to open a big new department, since Thomas could now allocate adequate space to it, but the real reason for his big decision was his famous "feel." This time, however, he could support it with logic. The meat trade was in the process of revolutionary change, and he devoted a lot of time to studying it, talking to experts at Smithfield, which, since it had been reconstructed eight years before, was now the largest dead-meat market in the world.

Thomas was soon convinced that the prospects for Kingstons in this new trade were huge. "At present," he said enthusiastically to Baines after returning from Smithfield one morning, "all our meat comes from Britain or the Continent. But it won't be long before the huge prairies of America, Australia, Argentina, where they run herds in tens of thousands, will be open to us. The journey's too far in practice for them to ship the animals live, but refrigeration'll transform the trade in carcasses. They haven't quite solved the problems yet, but they're close, Baines—they're close. Already there's a cold store in London Docks. Last year they even managed to bring a sample shipment of chilled beef across the Atlantic from New York. The Queen tasted it and approved. If it's good enough for the Queen, Baines, just think of the effect it'll have on the trade; but how many butchers have had the foresight to make any plans for it? Very few, I'll wager. They're an inefficient lot anyway—those that aren't actually venal. And by the time these new techniques are perfected, we'll be established."

It was a far more dramatic departure from their regular business even than the move into Gentlemen's Wear almost two years before, and for months Baines was making plans, scouring London for the best grocery and meat buyers, employing the supporting staff—who, of course, needed to be experienced in the trade. In long meetings with Baines and the two buyers, Thomas settled the stock lines they would carry, the display methods, the storage, the layout in the large section of the five-shop block that was to be fitted out as Kingston's Food Department.

Thomas had now learned, with the hardened skin formed by White's suicide, that every time he entered a new area of merchandise, he had to face fierce resentment from the existing traders. Even he, however, had not quite assessed the strength that this time would be massed against him.

The leader of the orchestra approached the front of the platform on which the musicians were stationed. "Would you please," he demanded of the company in a loud, rich voice, "take your partners for the galop!" Throughout the hall, men eagerly got up to do as they were asked. Baines, who was sitting at the next table, reserved for senior members of the staff, came over to claim the dance already promised him by Thomas' sister Ellen. They had first met at the wedding of Thomas and May, when they had clearly been taken with each other, and although six years had passed since then, time did not seem to have diminished the attraction—at least, so it seemed, since they had already danced a mazurka, two waltzes, a schottische and a couple of polkas.

Thomas noted May's glance of disapproval as Ellen left the table with him. "Won't you even be magnanimous about him tonight, when we're celebrating? His behavior has been perfect."

"Do you really want him as a brother-in-law?" May snapped.

"Ellen could do much worse."

May abruptly changed the subject. "I think you should dance this galop," she said.

"Don't you think it's a little too energetic?" he asked.

"Do you want them to think of you as staid? I'm sure Lillian would be delighted to be your partner—wouldn't you, Lillian?"

Lillian, who had not heard the exchange between them, leaned forward. "Wouldn't I what?"

"Thomas is being reticent about his position as head of the company. I think he should take part in these rumbustious dances, don't you?"

"But of course," Lillian responded. "I'm sure it's as well to remind the staff he's a human being." She covered the acid in the remark with a broad generous smile. "Am I being invited, then, to take the floor?" she asked.

As he stood facing her, waiting for the music to start, he asked, "And how is James?" The baby had been born in November, ten months before.

"Very well," she answered. "Everyone says he's the image of his father." It was a remark, rich with double meaning, that was typical of the changed and bitter Lillian. And the timing of it was perfect. Before Thomas could respond, the orchestra struck up and they were dancing fast across the room.

After the music had stopped and the dancers had returned to their tables, hot and out of breath, the leader of the orchestra approached the front of the dais and, in his stentorian tones, called for attention, please, since Mr. Sidney Baines wished to address them. Baines took his place on the platform showing obvious signs of nervousness. At twenty-six, he had filled out, had even begun to develop the beginnings of a paunch, across which he wore a silver watch chain, but he had failed to divest himself completely of the traces of the Cockney boy with the bright humor which grated so much on May and those who opposed him. "Ladies and gentlemen," he declared in his quaint accent. "Before we partake of supper there's something that 'as to be said, something that I know you'll all want to be said. . . . This evening is a most important occasion. In fact, it's 'ard to credit that it's only seven years since Mr. and Mrs. Kingston—Miss Ramsay as she was then, of course —opened the little Fancy Goods establishment from which the emporium, of which we are all a part, 'as grown. . . ."

Public speaking did not come easily to Baines, and he paused and swallowed. "I know that Mr. Kingston still views our firm, our company as it is now, of course, as being in its very early stages . . . on the lowest slopes of the mountain, as you might say . . . and some of you may find that 'ard to believe. . . . But I'm not talking about the future. I'm talking about now, and I don't think there's anyone 'ere who'll argue with me when I say that what's been achieved already in Sloane Street is something of a marvel. . . ." He hesitated in response to the murmurs of "Hear, hear" throughout the hall before adding, ". . . I 'ope therefore you'll all agree that tonight we should rekernize this marvel with a toast." He held up his glass. "Ladies and gentlemen, I ask you to join me in drinking the 'ealth of Mr. and Mrs. Kingston . . . and their two partners Mr. and Mrs. Rawlings."

Thomas was deeply moved. As all present raised their glasses, he squeezed May's hand under the table, then got heavily to his feet and walked across the dance floor to the orchestra dais to respond.

He looked round the crowd of people who depended on him for their livelihoods. They were in a happy mood—watching him with smiling, friendly faces. "Ladies and gentlemen," he began, "fellow members of Kingstons, it is with a deep sense of gratitude that, on behalf of my wife and of Mr. and Mrs. Rawlings, I thank you for your good wishes and Mr. Baines for his generous remarks—but most of all, for the loyalty and endeavors that you yourselves have devoted to our emporium.

"Today, in fact, is a significant moment in Kingstons' history. For we are about to start selling food. In particular, we're going to offer our customers meat. . . ."

"You are not!" The voice from the back of the hall was coarse and resonant, spoken, it seemed, by a man with a cavernous chest. "You are not, Mr. Kingston—not if you are wise."

Suddenly he appeared, moving forward unhurriedly from the back of the hall. He was a huge figure of a man, with great broad shoulders, and he wore the blue smock that indicated he was a butcher by trade. He was followed by three others, all burly and also wearing smocks. He sauntered onto the dance floor and waited while his colleagues joined him. They stood there, the four of them, a rank of defiant giants, facing Thomas with grim faces.

"The butchers' trade is for butchers," declared the man who had interrupted Thomas' speech, "not for drapers. . . . So be warned: we'll protect our trade."

Thomas' surprise was replaced by cold anger. "I don't know how you gained access to this private assembly," he declared from the dais, "but I will just say this before I ask for you to be ejected: We *are* butchers. The buyer of our Meat Department has been in the trade, I suspect, as long as you have."

"He's a traitor!"

"That's nonsense, Mr. Butcher. The notion of the emporium is, I realize, new, but I can assure you it's here to stay. You can't stand in the way of progress, Mr. Butcher. . . . Now"—Thomas nodded to the leader of the orchestra—"let's go on dancing!"

From the moment of the interruption the orchestra had been alerted. The baton was already raised so that, on Thomas' request, the orchestra struck up at once into a noisy polka. Baines, realizing exactly what Thomas wanted to defuse the demonstration, leaped to his feet and, grabbing a somewhat surprised Ellen by the hand, led her quickly onto the dance floor. "Sorry to be so insistent, Miss Kingston," he apologized, "but this is a crisis." Soon there were fifty couples swirling round the four butchers, who remained standing in the middle of the floor, angrily uncertain what to do—until at last the lusty intruders filed slowly, rather sheepishly, from the floor.

Thomas' mother and sisters stayed at Caroline Terrace on the night of the staff ball, and the following morning he went to work late so that he could have breakfast with them. "How's the harvest?" he asked. "Is it as bad as Edward feared?"

"Worse," his mother replied. "There's been so much rain through the summer. It's beginning to get serious now. One bad harvest is bad enough, but three in succession! A lot of people in the county are very worried."

Thomas nodded in sympathy. The repercussions of the bad harvests were wide—on food supplies, on prices and consequently on the economy. According to *The Times*, the Cabinet was considering action, but its scope was limited.

Thomas stood up. "It's time for me to go," he said. He kissed them one by one. "It's been good to see you all. Perhaps we can come down for a few days soon—once the autumn season is well under way and I have a bit more time."

Time was something Thomas was going to be short of for some while. He knew, of course, that the butchers' demonstration at the staff ball was only a beginning. During the next few days, their campaign intensified. Letters began to appear in the *Chelsea News*, the newspaper of the district, castigating Thomas for his ruthless methods which drove small traders out of business. In what were obvious references to the suicide of White, several correspondents wrote of the case when the Kingston price cutting had ended in great personal tragedy and hinted that once the opposition of existing shops was cleared away, Thomas' prices would rise. In a long letter to the *Chelsea News* Thomas defended Kingstons' trading methods, insisting that they were scrupulously fair. He offered the public value and service, he wrote, and the success of Kingstons was not due to the exploitation of small shops (for Kingstons too had been a small shop) but because existing traders were not supplying the public with what they wanted.

The *Chelsea News*, realizing the potential of the story, did its best to fan the conflict. It sent a reporter to interview Thomas, who was surprised, when the article appeared, to discover how many local people regarded him with enmity. For the butchers, of course, were not the only tradesmen to be threatened by Thomas' concept of a comprehensive emporium.

Some of the larger London newspapers had begun to take notice of the butchers' campaign, and they too tended to take the side of the small shopkeepers.

At Smithfield Market the campaign against Thomas was more direct, aimed at preventing him from obtaining supplies. The Chelsea and Brompton butchers approached the wholesalers warning that they would all stop buying from any firm that delivered meat to Kingstons.

It was fortunate that Thomas had deliberately chosen in forty-two-year-old Henry Lloyd a meat buyer of both character and reputation, for a lesser man would have bowed to the pressure. But Lloyd, a short, stocky Welshman, had been a butcher since he was twelve and had fought his way to prominence in the roughest of trades, and he soon became as defiant as Thomas. He warned any wholesalers who showed signs of weakening under the campaign, "You refuse one order and you'll never have another from Kingstons—and I can assure you we're going to be a very big customer."

Thomas was wounded by the ferocity of the opposition, but every attack only increased his determination to win the conflict. One morning, the butcher who was orchestrating the local campaign called to see him. "Feelings are running very high," he said. "Change your mind, Mr. Kingston, while there's still time."

"Kindly leave my store," answered Thomas.

It was fraying him, though. He returned home at night tired and often depressed. May provided her usual strength and support. Once, when he felt especially low, he questioned for a moment whether he was right to persist. Was it, perhaps, placing the rest of the business at risk?

"No, Thomas Kingston," she said. "You go on just as you planned —not that you were really considering anything else."

The food department opened for business on Wednesday, October 4. It was a dramatic occasion, highlighted as it was by the butchers' campaign—which now boomeranged in Thomas' favor, for it had provided invaluable publicity.

As he stood with Baines and Lloyd before they opened the doors on the first morning, Thomas experienced great pleasure. Lloyd had fully understood his instructions about the importance of display. The carcasses were beautifully decked out with paper ruffles. Poultry and game—duck, chicken, partridge, pheasant, woodcock, snipe—lay in perfect formation on a marble slab dominated by a boar's head that had been scrupulously cleaned and prepared. The cuts of meat had been arranged in brilliant profusion. There were aitchbones and briskets and ribs of beef. There was sirloin, offered whole, middle-cut or in wing ends. There were haunches of mutton and legs and fries. There were springs of pork and knuckles of veal. There was a big range of chops and cutlets, artistically displayed with parsley and paper decoration. And instead of wearing the usual butcher's blue smocks, the assistants were clad in white coveralls, trimmed at the sleeves with the Kingston colors.

The Grocery section, which had not been subjected to the same virulence, was equally impressive. There was a huge counter of cheeses, including Cheshire and Gloucester and Cheddar and Stilton and Neufchatel and Limburger and Camembert and Roquefort. There were cooked hams from York; sausages from Norfolk and Cambridge and Brunswick and Strasbourg; bacon from Waterford and Wiltshire. There were pies and confectionery, caviar and lampreys, larks and sturgeon, as well as shelves loaded with cocoa, coffee, tea, rice, jams, essences, currants, almonds, potted meats, biscuits, sugar and a whole range of other products in the grocery spectrum.

From the moment that day when the store opened for business, the Food Department was crowded with customers. Most of them, no doubt, came merely to view the battle area after all the furor, but many stayed to buy. The value was good, as it always was in Kingstons, most of the cuts being a penny or two below the prices charged by the local butchers' shops, and the quality of the meat could not be challenged.

Thomas had expected some kind of demonstration from the opposition and, after discussion with Baines, had agreed to the stationing, as inconspicuously as possible, of some stout fellows who, if all else failed, could be relied on to remove any invading butchers from the premises.

However, by eleven thirty, when Thomas returned to the new department from his daily round of the store, nothing untoward had happened. Baines approached him through the crowd of customers, smiling happily. "The business is overwhelming," he said. "Lloyd's beginning to worry whether he's got enough stock to last until evening."

Thomas nodded, but the expression on his face was one of concern. "I can't believe they won't do *something*," he said.

He had barely said it before there was a crash of breaking glass as the shop window was shattered by two bricks, thrown in quick succession. Thomas rushed to the door, to see a gig disappearing at full gallop in the direction of Sloane Square.

It was not the last attack of that first day. Twice during the afternoon, men leaned out of passing hansoms and tossed lighted squibs under the bellies of the horses in the traces of the waiting carriages, making the animals rear up dangerously. One horse, in fact, slipped and came down in the road, disaster being avoided only by swift action by the coachman.

The conflict had now entered a new and aggressive phase, though quite how violent it threatened to become was not made obvious to Thomas until the following morning, when among his letters he found an envelope addressed to him in a crude hand. "Sir," he read, "this is to inform you that we know your home address and are fully aware of the existence of your beautiful wife and three pretty children. So beware."

"Who was that one from?" asked May from the other end of the table. "The writing looked strange."

"No one of interest, my dear," answered Thomas.

He called in at the police station on the way to the store, but was received with a coolness that surprised him. "What do you suggest we do, sir?" asked the officer.

"Do?" queried Thomas. "I suggest, Officer, you take steps to provide me with protection. That's what the police are for, isn't it?"

"If I may be so bold," answered the police officer, "you have invited this resentment."

Thomas was astonished. "Do I understand, Officer, that although I'm acting completely within the laws of Great Britain, you feel no responsibility to protect my property or my family?"

"I didn't quite say that, sir."

"It would seem you have friends among my competitors, so I warn you, Officer, if these assaults persist I shall complain to your superiors, charging you with personal neglect." And Thomas turned in fury and strode out of the station.

Thomas was never quite sure if the horrific incident that occurred later that day was a repercussion of his visit to the police or whether it had long been planned as part of the campaign against him.

May was upstairs at the time. It was soon after lunch—about two thirty. She had given Ruby the afternoon off and was with the three children. The two boys were playing happily together, and May was having a dolls' tea party with Rose, when there was a knocking on the front door.

She went downstairs and opened the door. For a brief moment, she was surprised that there was no one there. Then she saw what was on the doorstep. The horror that welled up within her would normally have induced a scream, but some instinct must have stifled it because of the children upstairs.

For there, in a wide basket, lay three little piglets, blood still oozing from recent incisions across their throats. They had been scrubbed clean so that they had a naked look, their light pink color lending them some resemblance to human babies. There was a note pinned to the basket worded, "Let there be no doubt."

May stepped back from the doorway, her hand over her eyes, conscious of an overwhelming nausea. She leaned unsteadily against the wall. For a moment, she thought she was going to faint, and she sat on the floor so that she would not strike her head against the hall table if she fell. She heard Ramsay call out to her from upstairs, "Who is it, Mama?" His voice made her concentrate, and the sensation of faintness left her. "No one important, Ramsay," she answered. "I'll join you upstairs in a moment."

Unsteadily, she stood up and looked in the mirror on the wall. Her face was drained of color, but gradually her reaction of sick horror was being replaced by anger. How dare they? she thought. How dare they do such a terrible thing?

Half an hour later, responding to a note sent by hansom, Thomas was with her. "You won't give in, will you?" she said. "You must never give in."

"No," he said grimly, "I won't give in."

He took the basket and the three piglets to the police station and placed them on the officer's desk. "I have three children, Officer," he pointed out, "and I'm warning you: if I don't get full protection now for my family and my emporium, by God, Officer, I'll roast you."

The butchers, of course, had gone too far. There was no question that the police had to act. One constable was posted on permanent duty in Caroline Terrace, and two were stationed outside the store. The violence stopped, the emphasis of the butchers' campaign being changed to other techniques of harassment. For example, one of the meat consignments destined for Kingstons was switched by conspirators in Smithfield. When Lloyd, who personally supervised all unloading, saw it coming off the wagon, he realized immediately that beneath a layer of good carcasses, chosen personally by him earlier that day, was bad meat that he would never have approved.

Then the butchers, in their blue smocks, began to appeal direct to Kingstons' customers, standing in the street outside the store bearing placards worded "Don't be deceived: low prices now mean high prices later. Buy silks and satins from drapers, not meat."

The same message was on leaflets that they distributed to passersby, within their own shops and those of other traders they could persuade to support them and finally, to Thomas' fury, on large posters occupying most of the windows in Mrs. Fellowes' vacant shop—literally within the heart of his business. Immediately, he wrote her a letter, ringing with pained betrayal, asking her to give instructions for the removal of the posters. "How," he asked, "can your investment possibly prosper when you take action that is against the interests of Kingstons?"

The answer was a firm refusal to comply with his request. "Sometimes," she wrote, "in your meteoric progress, I think you make a wrong decision or, in this case, try to move too fast. I am entitled to my views, which I would have expressed to you had you sought them. They are similar to those of many people in the district. In fact, it will not surprise you to learn that I feel positively neglected. You have not come near me for a whole year. And since you mention it, yes, I am content with my investment in your emporium."

Thomas did not make any better progress when he called at the police station and demanded that the protesting butchers be removed from the pavement in front of his store. "From the Queen's highway, Mr. Kingston?" queried the officer, with mock surprise that Thomas should make such a suggestion.

Thomas' reaction to the butchers' campaign was fiercely personal, but its effect on the business was completely beneficial. Sales of the Food Department throughout October were phenomenal, outstripping the record of any other new department he had so far opened. There were many problems, of course, that he had to deal with during those early weeks in a new trade—the most important of which was the question of "Cook's perks." It was customary for butchers and grocers to bribe the cooks who ruled the kitchens in the fine houses and greatly influenced the suppliers to the home, either with cash or with free produce. "Perks" were soon demanded from Kingstons, and Baines asked Thomas to rule on the company policy. "We don't bribe, Baines," Thomas insisted. "The cooks' employers'll soon learn that the cost of bribery must be reflected in the prices charged."

The decision caused a temporary curb on sales, for it made enemies among a lot of the cooks, but Thomas discussed his policy personally with the customers themselves, whom he met so often in the other departments, and his views on "perks" soon spread through the district. By the end of the month, Thomas had won the battle with the butchers. The barrier between drapery and food had been successfully breached. Kingstons' Food Department was clearly a permanent feature of the emporium, though the opposition still lingered, flaring in occasional incidents—one of which was horribly macabre.

It happened on Guy Fawkes night, November 5, when both the Kingston and the Rawlings children had been invited, with their parents, to a local fireworks and bonfire party. At around six o'clock in the evening, as arranged, Thomas' office was suddenly invaded by a highly excited Rose and the two boys, accompanied by May and the maid. He still had to sign some letters to be posted that night, so while they waited impatiently, he went on working. After a few minutes David and Lillian came into the room with their two older children, Charles and Eleanor. It was as they entered that Ramsay, who was by the window overlooking Sloane Street, suddenly called out, "Look! There's a procession!"

Everyone except Thomas, who was still at his desk, joined him at the window. May was the first to realize, almost by instinct, the nature of the crowd marching toward the store along Sloane Street. They carried the flaming torches that were often a feature of bonfire-night parades, and at first, even though the street lights were on, all that could be made out clearly was moving flares among many people —and in their midst a wagon on which, perched precariously, was a "guy." There was, however, a mood of threat about the procession, a strange determination in the striding of the marchers, an anger in the shouts and yells that suggested that this was no normal bonfire-night procession. There was none of the high-spirited good humor that was a usual feature of the ritual burning throughout Britain, every November 5, of the man who had attempted to blow up Parliament in 1605.

May was tempted to call the children away from the window, to warn Thomas, even to suggest that they leave for the party now and that he join them later. But already, it was too late to leave. By the time they got downstairs, the procession would be outside the store. So she just had to wait, powerless to move, as one is so often in a nightmare.

She guessed that they were butchers, of course, and soon, as the crowd approached, it was obvious, for all the men in the front ranks were wearing the familiar smocks and carrying cleavers. Soon, too, the words of their cries could be detected: "Down with Kingston! Kingston—enemy of the people! Low prices now—high prices later."

Thomas became conscious of the shouts and, with a puzzled expression on his face, got up from his desk to join May at the window. The procession was close now, and they could see that it was quite big, numbering anything up to a hundred men, most of them in smocks. The local butchers had clearly increased their ranks with sympathizers and men from the trade in other districts. But it was the "guy" in the wagon that was the focus of the attention of the two families watching from the second-floor window, for as it came nearer and could be seen more clearly, it was apparent that it was not wearing the usual cone-shaped hat of the seventeenth-century Guy Fawkes, but a top hat and frock coat of the present time. May watched with growing horror as she realized that the effigy, lurching with the movement of the wagon on a pile of faggots, represented her husband.

As the marchers approached the store, the cries and yells intensified. Soon the demonstrators and their wagon with the effigy of Thomas filled the street beneath the window and the procession came to a halt. They turned and faced the terrace of shops, shouting their slogans, waving their cleavers. "Kingston! Enemy of the people!" they yelled. "Down with Kingston!" Suddenly several men were shouting it together, and it was taken up by the whole mass of men in a huge chant: "Down with Kingston! Down with Kingston! Down with Kingston!"

"Why are they shouting, Father?" asked Ramsay.

"Because they're foolish, misguided men," Thomas answered.

"Do you think they're going to attack the building?" May asked him quietly.

"No," he said firmly, squeezing her hand. "The police'd have to take action if they did."

The men holding the flaming torches were moving in the crowd, so that angry faces were suddenly illuminated for seconds before being lost once more in the mass, and the whole scene suddenly acquired the character of a war dance of a tribe of savages.

David moved closer to him. "What do you think we should do?" he asked. "Leave by the back entrance?"

"I think we're safer here for the moment—at least until we see what's going to happen. I'm certain it's only a demonstration."

The chant from the massed voices grew louder—"Down with Kingston! Down with Kingston!"—and some of the men with torches held them near the face of the effigy so that the sightless mask, obscene in the flickering of the flares, could clearly be made out from within the building. It was crude, but there was a certain likeness to Thomas, wearing the same style of whiskers, and just for a few awful seconds he found himself identifying with the image, imagining himself on the pile of faggots on the wagon.

He never knew how it caught fire. Perhaps a bit of flaming wool escaped from the flares into the faggots—or possibly, in the excitement of the moment, a torch was thrust deliberately among them. Whatever the cause, they were suddenly alight, flames leaping upward. Hurriedly someone loosed the horse from the traces, and the crowd backed away from the wagon, leaving around it an area of open space. The faggots were clearly as dry as tinder, for the fire spread through them quickly, and within seconds the effigy was brilliantly illuminated above a white-and-yellow blaze that was throwing off showers of red sparks. The bottom edge of the frock coat began to smolder first, but long before its thick material was really burning, the top hat, light and combustible, was in flames, and the mask beneath it, as it became distorted by the heat, seemed to grimace with pain.

All the time the chant was continued: "Down with Kingston! Down with Kingston!" Then all four sides of the wagon seemed to catch fire at once, huge sheets of flame suddenly reaching upward, enveloping what was left of the effigy in a kind of last protective rite before the axles burned through and the whole vehicle collapsed. It went on burning, but more slowly, with flames that were subdued, and the effigy could be seen no longer. It was the end of the demonstration. The chanting faded. The angry men began to move on in small groups, the force of their feelings spent, it seemed, with the decreasing strength of the fire.

At that moment, tears began to course slowly down the cheeks of May, who had been standing impassively, displaying no signs of emotion, during the demonstration. She was holding herself stiffly erect, her back straight. "I'm not crying," she said when Thomas put his arm round her shoulder. In fact, her tears were sourced in anger—the same anger that she had felt when she had seen the piglets. But for the children, who had witnessed so fearful a scene, the distress of fury looked no different from any other kind of anguish. Rose too started to weep, followed by Harry. Both of them ran to their mother, clutching her skirt, and Thomas put an arm down to enclose them.

The Rawlings children did not cry, but they felt shocked and uncertain, suddenly insecure, and they too had moved near to their parents. Thomas could see that David was shaken and saddened, stirred by the remnants of their friendship. Then he looked at Lillian. There was no trace of sympathy in her ice-blue eyes. As she stared back at him, the features of her face relaxed very slightly, and for a terrible moment he thought she was going to smile.

Ramsay, aged five and the eldest of the three Kingston children, had not joined his brother and sister beside Thomas and May. He had remained standing completely motionless at the window, staring at the still-burning pile of wood in the street that had just consumed the effigy of his father. It was a scene that would remain in his mind, vivid to the finest detail, until the day he died.

Book Two

CHAPTER SIX

November 1881

· I ·

At seven o'clock on that critical November morning, it was still dark as Thomas stood in his usual place halfway up the stairs that over-looked the back entrance hallway of the five-shop block. Through the open doors, revealed by the glow from the gas lamps inside, he could see the rain splashing the puddles in the cobbles of the mews at the rear of the building as the staff shuffled past the attendance clerks.

As they stood in queues, water dripping from hats and overcoats, the atmosphere was heavy with dank, sleepy gloom, permeated by the warm smell of sodden mackintosh. Little was said—just an occasional query by one of the clerks when he did not recognize a face, followed by a single-word reply as the name was given. All those on the Kingston payroll had to report at this entrance every morning for their names to be ticked off in the huge attendance ledgers before going to their departments.

A nearby clock struck the hour, and after a few moments Thomas took his watch from his waistcoat pocket and kept his eyes fixed on the dial until the hands revealed that the time was two minutes past seven —the two minutes' grace he always permitted. Then, he ordered, "Close the books!" and waited to confront any staff who had not arrived by his deadline.

There were four of them that day, though they came singly. Each emerged in the doorway, flustered, red-faced, out of breath and, be-cause of the rain, bedraggled. The clerks, holding their heavy books clasped in their arms, stood motionless like officials in a courtroom as the late arrivals waited anxiously in heavy silence under Thomas' cold gaze. "Punctuality," he said at last, "is a vital element of the discipline and alertness of mind that we must maintain if, in these hard times, we're to survive. You're to report immediately to Mr. Baines."

Thomas remained on the staircase, his face grim, as they filed by him uneasily on their way to the management office on the second floor. "Miss Higgins!" Thomas said sharply as the last of them passed him. He did not turn, but continued speaking, standing quite still, his back to her. Miss Higgins was the saleslady who had played a role in Baines's drunken episode in '76. She stopped on the stairs above him, her face pale. "This is the third time, isn't it? It mustn't happen again. You understand my meaning?"

"Yes, Mr. Kingston," she said quietly and, shoulders bowed, continued climbing the stairs.

He watched her go sadly. He fully realized how serious to her was his threat, for most shops were still reducing staff and new positions were hard to find. In many cases, too, dismissal meant a loss of accommodation, since a number of employees lived in dormitories in houses in Chelsea rented by Kingstons for the purpose. This was an extension of the practice of sleeping over the shop, but the scale that "living in" had now acquired, with the growth of stores during the prosperous years before the slump, had made it one of the evils of the trade. As a system, it was rooted in the cost and difficulty of traveling to work in fashionable areas, but it also meant that wages could be low. Thomas was uneasy about it, but there was no question of his permitting his staff bill to rise—not until times changed for the better. At least, he thought, Miss Higgins would not be fined, as she would be in many stores.

The last five years had been a period of enormous difficulty for Thomas. Strangely, that first staff ball and the butchers' campaign that followed it had been a turning point, a peak, as it were, in the Kingston fortunes. In that September, his whole concept of a great emporium had seemed almost at the point of realization—only to be shattered by a terrible winter. Even by the time of the ball, though the hay was not yet in the ricks, it was clear that the nation was enduring its third poor harvest in succession. "At least, it can't go on," Edward had said. "There haven't been three bad harvests in a row for thirty years." But it did go on. The black autumns of '77, '78 and '79 had followed with a relentless regularity which had brought down the Disraeli government and thrust the country into the worst depression it had known for more than half a century.

For Thomas, after seven years of continual expansion and ever-rising profits, it had demanded a complete reanalysis of his business techniques. Retrenchment and efficiency had become essential to survival, and he responded to the new conditions with a fierce and ruthless discipline. Sidney Baines in his turn had adjusted to his lead. Once again, they were a unified team who understood every nuance of the issues they were facing. They ruled the store like the captain and first lieutenant of a Royal Naval frigate, rigorous in their demands over such matters as timekeeping, cleanliness, service, display. They controlled the buying in a minute detail, since every penny now had to be spent well, and carefully studied the movement of the merchandise, altering the size of departments to the flow of trade.

Despite the new conditions—in fact, *because* of the new conditions—Thomas' obsession with the Kingston quality became more intense, for his buyers were often tempted to compromise in the struggle to hold profit margins. Sometimes he would insist on a whole line's being returned to the wholesaler if it did not meet his standards, even losing money on occasion. "Our quality is the key to our future," he would mutter. "Without it, there may not be a future."

Strangely, David was as much an outsider in this drive for efficiency as he had ever been before, even though budgeting was his speciality. But it was, of course, the aggressive approach he found hard to share.

After his warning to Miss Higgins, Thomas tried to shrug off the gloom with which that wet November morning enclosed him and embarked immediately on his daily round of the store. In each department the staff were preparing for the day's business, stripping off the dust sheets with which the merchandise displays were covered at night, dusting the counters, tidying the goods in the stock shelves. On some days, at this time, the store was alive with chatter as they worked, but this morning, with the rain beating on the shop windows from dark clouds, the assistants were somnolent, exchanging words only when absolutely necessary. Perhaps, mused Thomas gloomily, thinking of the meeting that lay ahead of him that day, they sensed the threat with which the store was faced.

As Thomas entered each section, the buyer or senior salesman would approach him and tour the department with him, making a note of his criticisms or praise. That morning, the praise was sparse. He was in an angry, demanding mood. He had no fewer than seven displays stripped right down and ordered their complete reconstruction to his precise directions. One arrangement of saucepans in the Hardware Department annoyed him so much that he knocked it to the floor with a sweep of his hand, and the noisy clatter as the pile of pans and lids collapsed echoed throughout the five-shop block. The cacophonous din made him pause and question the angry zest for perfection he was displaying. Was he taking out on the staff his anxieties about the meeting—a kind of release of his tension? Or did he merely want to impress Henry Jones with the appearance of his store, like the captain of a ship who ordered the brass polished before an inspection? Jones, a principal of the company's bankers, had often visited Kingstons—but never before had he written first to warn that the bank loans were now at their limit.

There had, of course, been many discussions between them about the store's problems. Quite apart from the heavy drain of interest on the loans, Thomas was having trouble paying his suppliers. Now he had many debtors, and he understood Jones's distrust of his belief that something, so far undefined, would happen to solve the huge difficulties that Kingstons faced.

In a sense, something had already begun to happen. The long recession was ending at last. Trade had improved, and the harvest had been good. "We've had the best September for years," he had reported happily to Jones.

"I hope it's in time, Thomas," the banker had responded cautiously. "But you've got a lot of leeway to make up. Are you still adamant about taking in more capital?"

"Positive," Thomas insisted. "Our independence is vital."

"It may be forced on you," Jones had warned. Jones was not seeking to increase the bank's ten-percent holding of stock that it had acquired in return for providing loan facilities. "We're not in the high-risk business," he had said. "We're not speculators; but we know people who are, people who might well regard Kingstons as an attractive investment."

"Give me a bit more time, Mr. Jones," Thomas had said.

"All right," he had conceded, "but don't leave here thinking you've got long, because you haven't."

David had not said much that afternoon in the hansom on the way back to the store, but raised the matter the next day—which, as Thomas knew, meant that Lillian had been at him. "Are you sure we shouldn't do what Jones suggested?" David had asked. "He is a banker, after all. He knows about these things."

"He doesn't know about Kingstons," Thomas retorted, "just about figures, which can be very misleading, even to a banker, especially when prospects are changing. New capital means new partners who may not understand the concept of an emporium."

So Thomas had gone on playing for time; but his Fates had not moved to his support in any adequate way. The increase in profits was continuing, even accelerating, but not fast enough to make a serious impact on the heavy backlog of debt that Kingstons had acquired during the long slump—and Henry Jones's note suggested that the moment of decision could not be postponed much longer.

Thomas strode on into the Saddlery Department, which usually gave him pleasure, for he loved the smell and the look of leather. This morning it left him unmoved, and after a brief tour with the buyer he entered the Food Department, which had been the cause of the dramatic events of five years before. For a moment he stood on the tile floor that was lightly brushed with sawdust, watching the assistants laying out the meat they had just brought up from the cold room in the basement. The war with the butchers had long been over, but the enmity had remained, extending far beyond the meat traders, because the publicity had underlined the threat posed to all shops by the emporium concept. Thomas was uneasily conscious that many people in the district would like to see him fail.

Sidney Baines was in the Grocery Department talking to Henry Lloyd, the meat buyer, when he saw Thomas in the entrance. He crossed the floor to him. "I don't suppose we'll break any records today, Mr. Kingston," he said, referring to the bad weather, which always depressed trade. He still called Thomas "Mr. Kingston," both in public and in private, even though he was now his brother-in-law, having married Ellen the previous year. And Thomas had made no effort to encourage a greater familiarity, feeling that it was better to leave a distance between them. Since he was a good deal older than Baines, his relationship with him was in character that of a father-in-law, as though Ellen were his daughter rather than his sister.

The wedding had been celebrated on a bright Sunday afternoon in June in Quainton's seventh-century parish church. May, faced at last with the inevitable, had been reconciled to the match. She had taken part with enthusiasm in discussions about the dresses; responded warmly to the suggestion that Rose, now seven, should be a bridesmaid, joining Thomas' elder sister, Mary, who was Maid of Honor, behind the bride; and had even permitted the groom to kiss her on the cheek after the ceremony.

Considering the aversion that both David and Lillian felt for Sidney Baines, it was inevitable that his marriage to Thomas' sister should deepen the division between the families, but at first this manifested itself only as an extra irritant. Then, four weeks before this wet November morning, the smoldering had blazed into the most important difference that the partners had experienced in all the years of that difficult relationship.

The spark that was to set fire to these combustible elements was struck at the end of one of Thomas' daily meetings with Baines. "If you've a moment, Mr. Kingston," he said as he collected his papers together, "I'd appreciate your advice on a delicate matter. . . ." He hesitated. "I suppose it's no secret that I've got powerful critics among the owners of the business—even enemies . . ."

"I wouldn't have said," Thomas responded, "that they were as powerful as your friends."

"No," Baines conceded, "but it does mean that I'm dependent on your support, Mr. Kingston, which I value greatly, of course, but there are moments—"

"You've been offered another position?" Thomas interrupted gently.

"Swan and Edgar," Baines replied. "General Manager, with a seat on the board after six months. . . . I'd 'ate to leave, of course, especially now I've married Ellen. I'm very 'appy working with you, Mr. Kingston. . . ."

Thomas nodded, sighed. "I don't want you to go, Baines." He paused. "Could you give me a couple of days to think this over? Would they wait that long?"

"Oh, I think so," Baines answered. "They know my position, of course. . . ."

At that time, the limits of the conflict seemed clearly defined. Kingstons would have to give Baines the same terms as he had been offered or he would go; but Thomas knew that David would resent it deeply, because it enshrined in formal title a situation that, in practice if not in theory, already existed—namely, that Baines, not David, occupied the second place in the Kingston hierarchy of command. So Thomas decided to write David a note, which would give him time to think before they discussed it and would, Thomas hoped, make him feel that he was party to the appointment.

He had arranged for the note to be placed on David's desk with his morning mail. He was surprised that by noon there had been no response—but he had been even more surprised when at a quarter past twelve Lillian had swept into his office without even knocking on the door, her face contorted with fury. "How dare you, Thomas?" she demanded. "This is blatant nepotism!"

Thomas looked at her calmly, his elbows on the desk, fingers clasped. At thirty-seven, she was beginning to look drawn and even a trifle sour. She was still handsome, but time and a certain disappointment had begun to leave their marks on her. The bones of her face now seemed a little overprominent; the corners of her mouth had begun to loosen.

"This intrusion into my office is quite extraordinary, Lillian," said Thomas.

"Did you expect me to write requesting an interview?" she demanded. "Nothing'd surprise me after your reneging on your agreement with David."

"What do you mean—reneging?"

"You're promoting your precious Baines, your brother-in-law, over David's head. If that's not reneging, I don't know what is."

"Nonsense, Lillian. I'm proposing that Baines be made a director. That doesn't affect David's position or his stockholding. The time was bound to come when we'd have to appoint directors from the management."

"Thomas, you can't fool me." She leaned forward on the back of one of the visitor's chairs and shook her head at him. "You're not talking to a woman who doesn't know you," she said. "I've seen you grow up from a little boy. I know how your mind works. . . . The Baines proposal is not the simple matter you suggest. It's far more significant, as you're very well aware."

Thomas sat back in his chair. "Aren't you making a little too much of this, Lillian? And surely I should be discussing it with David."

"Oh, no, you shouldn't." She moved to his desk and sat on the corner, looking down at him in a way that was almost provocative. "You'd dominate him as usual, wouldn't you? Persuade him it was a mere formality, nothing important . . . but you can't dominate me, Thomas—not any longer." She got up and walked toward the window with the short steps demanded by her sheath-skirted "handkerchief" dress, so called because it seemed to be made from one square piece of material, but the limitation did not detract from her elegance, Thomas noted.

"All right," he said at last, humoring her, "what do *you* propose we should do about Baines—let him go?"

She swung round. "Yes—let him go!" she retorted.

"I'd have to replace him."

She nodded agreement with a shrug. "Then what would you gain?" he asked. "If the new man was any good, he too in time would have to be promoted."

"I'll take that chance," she said.

"Would you object to Baines if he hadn't married Ellen?"

She began to stroll idly across the room, swinging her umbrella gently on her arm. "Yes," she said after a moment, "though that hasn't helped." She turned toward him suddenly. "Baines is *your* man, Thomas! *You* created him. You can rely on him completely. On the board, with the title of General Manager, he'd give you more power . . . and I don't want you to have more power. It's become too important to you—which is why you keep postponing the inevitable time when you'll be forced to take in partners who'll share it."

Thomas was astonished by her outburst, but suddenly he realized the reasoning behind her thinking. Her influence on Thomas himself was now minimal. David had accepted his own shortcomings as a merchant. New partners, even a replacement for Baines, would give her fresh scope. "You haven't thought this out," he said. "I made you a promise about Charles, but I can only honor it if I have the means. No one else'd be bound by it."

"How do I know *you* would?"

"Lillian, I've never given you any reason to doubt that."

"When you made that promise, you were a different man. Your store was small . . ."

"What's size got to do with a promise? Anyway"—he assumed a brisk tone—"there's no point in discussing it because I don't propose to lose Baines—and in fact, as you well know, there's nothing you can do about it."

Suddenly, there was fury in her eyes again. "You'll find there's much we can do, Thomas. Proceed with your plans for Baines and it'll be the biggest mistake of your life." She leaned on the front of his desk with both hands and looked straight at him. "Think of David not as a partner but as an enemy. Think of David seeking not to support you but to ruin you. Now, there's a hint for you—make sure you heed it!"

For a moment an expression of light mockery came into those azure eyes which had once inspired in him so great a desire for her. Then she turned and walked out of the room.

The rain had not eased as Thomas made his way through the mews to the stable yard, but daylight had come—gray and unwelcoming. The delivery vans, all painted in Kingstons' colors of blue and yellow, were ranged in rows. Some of the company's forty-two horses were looking out from a line of loose-boxes that opened into the yard, but most of them were tethered in stalls within the stables behind.

Butler, the head groom, approached Thomas as he entered the yard and handed him a pair of clean white gloves, as he did whenever the Managing Director visited the stables, and the routine inspection began. Any grime that had not been brushed out of the animals' coats was revealed on the pale suede as Thomas ran his hands over their necks and backs and quarters. It was a repetition of the scenes that had taken place earlier within the store. Most of the horses passed this rigid test, but a few did not, and Butler had to answer the stream of questions as to the reason. Sometimes he tried to provide excuses—"Lain down in the box since 'e was groomed, I suspect, Mr. Kingston" or "I do believe that mare's sweating up, Mr. Kingston. That'd explain it. 'Ope she's not getting the colic again"—but usually he nodded abjectly, saying he would reprimand the groom responsible.

After the inspection, Thomas handed him back the white gloves, now soiled with dirt and equine sweat, and walked back through the store on his way to the Ladies Clothing departments in Emily Lane's three-shop block which he could approach from the front only in Sloane Street.

He had, of course, ignored Lillian's angry threats, and Baines had been formally appointed in a board meeting in the face of David's opposition. Thomas had met her in the store several times since then, but each time she had greeted him warmly. On one occasion, James had been with her. Now aged five, he was a morose, withdrawn little boy with dark, sad eyes—quite unlike Charles, who had developed into an attractive, outgoing youth. "Say 'Good morning, Mr. Kingston,' James," she had prompted. "Good morning, Mr. Kingston," he had repeated dutifully, staring at Thomas without expression. Lillian gave a shrug of pained irritation. "That wasn't very gracious, James," she said, "but I suppose Mr. Kingston will have to be satisfied with it." And giving Thomas a broad smile, she had moved on, holding James firmly by the hand.

Her cordiality had troubled Thomas, because he could not believe that it reflected magnanimous acceptance of defeat over Baines. Yet he was still unable to think of any way she could execute her threat in view of his control of the stock, and this worried him most of all: was there really some course of action open to her that he had not considered?

He was in Haberdashery, talking to Emily, when Sidney Baines entered the shop to tell him that Henry Jones was waiting in his office. Together—since Baines, as a director, would now be included in financial discussions—they walked out the entrance of the Ladies' section of the store onto the pavement on their way to his office. They were about to pass the derelict building that divided the two parts of Kingstons when Thomas suddenly saw Lillian in front of him, standing by a carriage as a lady stepped into it. He could not see her clearly until he was abreast of the carriage—just as it was moving off—but the brief side glimpse then astonished him. "Good morning, Thomas," said Lillian a trifle sweetly.

"Wasn't that Mrs. Fellowes?" he asked incredulously.

"That's right," she replied.

"I didn't know you were acquainted."

"Oh, Christine Fellowes and I are great friends. We met a few months ago on a charity committee and got on from the start."

"She hasn't set foot in the store for more than ten years. Emily's always taken merchandise to her in Eaton Square."

"So she told me. I persuaded her that it was time she paid us a visit—and she was most impressed. That should please you."

"It does, of course," said Thomas and, excusing himself, passed on with Baines into the five-shop block. But it did not please him. As he mounted the stairs to his office, he found the whole prospect of a close friendship between Lillian and Mrs. Fellowes a matter of concern, though he could not quite define why.

When they entered the room, David was already there, waiting with the banker. All four of them knew why Jones had called the meeting, and the first few moments, as Thomas apologized for keeping his visitor, were uneasy. They took their places at a large mahogany table, used for discussions, with Thomas in his usual position at its head, facing the door.

Henry Jones was a man of seventy-two, with a bald head, thick gray whiskers, and a face so lined and rugged that Thomas had once remarked to May that he would have made an ideal subject for the carving of a god on a Red Indian totem pole. He had always been a good friend to Thomas, who had found his experience and counsel of great value to Kingstons. Now, as he sat down, Jones smiled at him, his gray eyes revealing both sympathy and encouragement. "Well, Thomas," he said with his rare informality which, although Thomas was now middle-aged, always made him feel like an inexperienced boy, "I'm afraid my partners are no longer prepared to leave the situation of Kingstons as it is. And to be frank, I myself can't see any way in which you can extricate yourself on your own from your predicament."

"Profits, Mr. Jones," Thomas responded.

"What profits?" asked Jones. "Last year you made three thousand pounds. The year before you made a loss. The year before that . . ." He broke off. "You know as well as I do—"

"We were in slump conditions. This year's going to be different. Already the trade's almost buoyant. October was even better than September—"

"Thomas, come down to earth," the banker interrupted gently. "It's not like you to refuse to face facts. Yet on this issue you seem to be deliberately blind."

"That's because it's crucial," said Thomas. "I must have a free hand, Mr. Jones . . . our whole philosophy depends on it."

"It's an indulgence, Thomas," said the banker, "but there's no reason why you shouldn't have a free hand—for all practical purposes, anyway. . . . Naturally, others'd be entitled to advise you, but who knows—perhaps their counsel could be of value."

Jones smiled at Thomas' dubious expression. "Listen, Thomas . . ." He leaned forward on the table. "You're in a classic situation that I've seen many times before. You've got a good business that, now the economy's improving, I expect to grow. But you've just got too much debt . . . you're undercapitalized. You always have been, but to start with this didn't matter too much. You were successful. You made good profits that compensated for your lack of resources, but your reserves were quite inadequate. So what happened when the bad times came? You didn't have enough assets to tide you over. You're fortunate to have survived when so many others have failed, but you're in great trouble, and if the economy hadn't turned upward when it did, then you'd have crashed. You still may, but I think it can be avoided, provided you're not too stubborn."

Thomas had sat motionless as the banker had talked. He was aware suddenly that his fists, beneath the table, were so tightly clenched that his nails were digging painfully into his palms. "All right, Mr. Jones," he said at last, "what precisely are you proposing we should do?"

"What I've told you before," answered the banker. "Take in some investment capital . . . issue some more equity shares, together with some fixed-interest secured stock, probably in the form of preference. This'll enable you to pay off your bank liabilities and your debts to your suppliers. Kingstons will then be able to go forward on a sound and proper basis."

Thomas nodded thoughtfully. He knew that the gnarled old banker was giving him what he believed to be the best advice, possibly the only advice; but all his instincts urged him to reject it.

The main issue, of course, lay with the equity shares, the common stock, which carried the voting rights and, in consequence, the control of the company. They would appreciate dramatically when Kingstons prospered once more. "You have someone in mind, I believe," Thomas said at last. "A 'speculator,' as you put it last month."

"There are several who'd be interested," said the banker, "but one in particular. In fact, Thomas, I took the liberty of suggesting that he might call here this morning."

"Today?" queried Thomas in alarm. "You mean he's here now?"

"I hope he's waiting outside. I thought it might be helpful to talk over the various possibilities—without committing yourself in any way at this stage, of course."

Thomas was reluctant to be faced in the flesh so quickly with a person whom until now he had regarded as a vague kind of unformed threat. "Isn't this a little premature?" he asked.

"There's no point in wasting valuable time, Thomas," insisted Jones. "You've got to face up to how serious this problem really is. The discussions are bound to take weeks, and during every day that passes your profits are being drained. . . ." He paused. "Now perhaps, with your permission, Mr. Baines would be kind enough to inquire if our visitor has arrived."

As Jones had arranged, his "speculator" was waiting patiently in the outer office, and when he walked through the door, Thomas recognized for the first time the full extent of his crisis. This, he thought in a brief instant of fear, is how a fox must feel when he is cornered.

Ernest Goldsmith advanced toward him across the floor of his office, with hand outstretched and a broad smile on his face. "How pleasant to see you again after all this time, Mr. Kingston."

· 2 ·

Goldsmith had changed surprisingly little in the eleven years since Thomas had first met him. His carefully barbered white hair was still thick, even luxuriant. His hands, with rings on the fingers, were still soft and manicured. Even his body, though doubtless corseted, revealed little sign of the depreciation that might be expected over a decade. He displayed the same affected air of confidence, marked by slightly superior amusement, that he had in the past.

"I have to confess, Mr. Kingston," he said, after the introductions, as he sat down at the end of the table opposite Thomas, "to a certain pleasure at this moment. After all, I was right, was I not? I look at your emporium with all its departments and its hundreds of staff and your delivery vans that one sees in different parts of London and I think of that tiny little shop you had when I first met you, when you faced disaster for a matter of . . . what was it? Three hundred pounds? I hardly think that three hundred pounds would make much impact on

your problems today. So I can congratulate myself on perceiving your
potential at an early stage—like spotting a good colt before he's shown
any form. . . . Well, we must get down to business, I suppose. . . . Mr.
Jones has apprised me of the situation in general terms. Perhaps we
can proceed from there."

Henry Jones took a sheet of paper from a document case beside
his chair. "I have here a statement of the company's position at the
thirty-first of October," he said. "If I have your permission to show
this to Mr. Goldsmith, Thomas, it'll provide him with all the basic
facts he needs to know."

"You appear to have taken charge, Mr. Jones," said Thomas, a
little coldly. "David, do you have any objection?" David shook his
head briefly in a way that was strangely offhand, as though none of
this were really his business.

Jones passed the sheet to Goldsmith. "As you'll see," he said, "the
company has what might be described as excessive debts of some thirty-
five thousand pounds—twenty thousand to the bank, which we're unwilling to leave outstanding indefinitely, and fifteen thousand that is
owed to suppliers beyond the normal thirty-day terms of trading."

Goldsmith studied the figures for a few seconds and laid the paper
on the table. "I should explain, Mr. Kingston, that I am not acting in
this matter for my bank, but for a syndicate of private individuals of
whom I am one. There's no doubt that we're interested in the project,
of course; I've always believed in you. I'm deeply impressed not only
with what you've already achieved in so short a time but also with
your vision of the Kingstons of the future. As a speculative investment, your company has much to offer. . . ." He paused for a moment,
holding his fingertips upright together, and bent his mouth to them
pensively. "The question is whether you'll be prepared to offer it.
Naturally, for investors to risk their money there has to be incentive.
So I'll come straight to the point, Mr. Kingston—a point on which I
know you to be sensitive. I don't think my syndicate could participate
with much less than, say, thirty-five percent of the equity."

"Thirty-five percent!" Thomas echoed with horror. "Why, Mr.
Goldsmith, if you add that to the ten percent that the bank already
holds, that'd leave Rawlings and myself with barely half the voting
stock in the company!"

"Now, Mr. Kingston"—Goldsmith held up both hands in restraint
—"you really must stop behaving like a startled yearling every time
anyone mentions your equity stock. If Kingstons is going to become
the important institution you've always conceived, you're going to

have a constant need for capital. Now, my syndicate will undertake to supply this. As I see it, your business could grow fairly quickly to two or three times its present size. You and your partner would have effective control—but of a much larger organization. . . . Surely that's a fair offer."

Thomas thought for a moment. "You'll understand, Mr. Goldsmith," he said at last, "that I was unaware you were coming here this morning. . . ."

"And these decisions are difficult, I realize," Goldsmith sympathized. "However, you should also know that, in a manner of speaking, I've already invested in your company." He paused, the slight hint of a smile on his lips, and studied his fingernails for a second. "When Mr. Jones spoke of the fifteen thousand pounds you owed to suppliers, he was not stating the up-to-date position. You have no trade debtors, Mr. Kingston—at least, none that are substantial." He looked up. "You just have me."

For a moment, there was silence in the room. It was Henry Jones who broke it. "Am I to understand, Goldsmith, that you've acquired the company's debts?" he asked indignantly. "Surely I should have been told."

"The matter was only concluded last night," Goldsmith answered somewhat airily.

Jones was now sitting stiffly upright, his eyes dark with anger. "I find your action highly embarrassing, Goldsmith. Just before you entered the room, I assured Mr. Kingston that our discussion today was to be entirely exploratory—nothing more."

"Then let us explore, my dear Jones," responded Goldsmith, beaming with good humor. "Let us explore."

For Thomas, it was not Goldsmith's revelation that alarmed him so much as another aspect, even more serious. "I have one question," he said tautly: "How did you know who our creditors were?"

Goldsmith smiled broadly, even nodded his head with approval. "Ah, Mr. Kingston," he replied, "straight to the point . . . a keen, clear mind. Well, I don't think it's any great secret now, is it, Rawlings?"

For a moment, David did not reply. Then, looking at Thomas, he said quietly, "I told him."

Thomas was so astonished that he just stared at his partner in speechless amazement. This was it. This was what had lain behind Lillian's threat that day in his office, behind her friendship with Mrs. Fellowes. This was what explained David's strangely remote behavior at the meeting so far. If Lillian had done this on her own, Thomas would not have been surprised, knowing the resentment she nursed. But that David should have stooped to betrayal—David, with his deep religious convictions, his sense of honor, his basic decency—was something that Thomas found hard to credit.

"We believed it was vital to the company," David went on in a voice that was toneless. "Your attitude to the question of partners was completely intransigent. You were refusing to face facts, placing the company in enormous danger—as Mr. Jones has just pointed out to you. You see, I was not the only one to . . ." In his embarrassment, he was saying too much, overexplaining, and in the face of Thomas' steady gaze, his words tailed off.

"Do you realize what you've done?" Thomas asked. His voice, tightly controlled, was not raised. "Do you know why Mr. Goldsmith has bought the debts?"

"Well, I presume . . ." David began.

"Did you even know he was going to?" Thomas cut in.

"Not exactly. He said he felt that matters could be made a little simpler if he spoke to the creditors."

"It's a lever, you idiot!" snapped Thomas, his anger now showing. "A weapon! If we don't agree to his terms, he'll be in a position to sue . . . and without delay. For fifteen thousand pounds, it'll be well worth the costs."

"Please, Mr. Kingston," Goldsmith interposed, though neither of the two partners appeared to have heard.

"I don't see how it's altered the situation, Thomas," said David. "Our suppliers could have sued just as easily."

"Of course they could, but would they? With the kind of future business we could offer? Not yet, you ninny—not until we were on the point of collapse; not with the price of litigation being what it is; not with the debt spread out through a range of different creditors instead of being concentrated in one pair of powerful hands as it is now. . . ."

"You know, Mr. Kingston," remarked Goldsmith with studied languor, "I do object to your referring to me as a kind of ruthless Cesare Borgia. Have I not always offered you my help, extended to you the hand of friendship?"

Thomas looked at him coldly across the table. "I'd find it more gratifying, Mr. Goldsmith, if you hadn't engaged in underhand dealings with my partner."

"And so would I," interposed Henry Jones.

"Oh, dear," said Goldsmith, "I appear to be under criticism—

quite wrongly, I assure you both. I didn't seek the contact with Rawlings. I was approached through an intermediary—and sworn to
secrecy for reasons of delicacy. And I knew, of course, that nothing
discussed with Rawlings could proceed without the agreement of the
other shareholders."

"And Rawlings has pledged you his support, I presume?" asked
Thomas.

"For what it's worth," Goldsmith answered, "but it means nothing without your approval."

"Not yet," said Thomas. "But if we sold you the equity you've
asked for, his support would give you control, even if Mr. Jones sided
with me."

Goldsmith favored Thomas with an innocent smile. "Mr. Kingston," he said, "may I suggest that you stop looking for a conspiracy
and consider the advantages I'm offering you without being too—"

"You speak of partners," Thomas cut in, "of a syndicate." His
voice was strangely loud. "They'd be *our* partners too, I suppose. In
view of this, am I permitted to know who they are?"

"Of course," answered Goldsmith. "There are six in addition to
myself. One of them you know well—Mrs. Fellowes. Then there's
Smith . . . he's an underwriter at Lloyds . . . and Jackson . . . he's on the
metal market. There's a lawyer with a City practice . . . he's called
Laidler. And Hobson. There's another whom you may possibly know
. . . by the name of Henry Cameron."

"Cameron?" Thomas repeated quite quietly. Suddenly, he felt
cold. "You mean Henry Cameron of Marston in Buckinghamshire?"

"I thought you might know him," Goldsmith answered with a
smile. "It's Bicester country, isn't it?"

For Thomas, the discussion was over—for that day at least. He
had too much to digest. The betrayal of his partner was by itself a
huge shock, but the fact that David was now ranged against him in
unison with almost everyone whom Thomas had ever regarded as an
adversary in a position of immense strength was so overwhelming
that he felt dazed, even disoriented. There must surely be an alternative to this sinister group of partners.

"Perhaps you'd be good enough to give me time to consider your
proposal, Mr. Goldsmith," he said, and stood up, indicating that the
meeting was over. Jones shook hands with him. "Come and see me
tomorrow, Thomas," he suggested. "Good day, Goldsmith," he said
coldly, and walked out of the room.

Goldsmith took up his "muller," as the short toppers were now
called, from Thomas' desk, where he had laid it when he arrived—

together with the same silver-topped cane that he had carried a decade ago. "Goodbye, Mr. Kingston," he said. "I look forward to our association."

"One final question, Mr. Goldsmith," Thomas asked suddenly, just before the banker passed through the door. "If we don't accept your terms, what will you do about the debts you've acquired?"

Goldsmith turned, paused for a couple of seconds and gave a laugh. "But you *will* accept my terms, Mr. Kingston," he said, and strode out of the room.

Baines, who had said nothing throughout the whole meeting, for there was nothing he could say, asked permission to leave, and the two partners were left sitting in silence alone at the table.

After a moment, David said, "I'd like to explain a little more, Thomas."

"There's more?" queried Thomas. "I presumed I had all the relevant information." His voice was not so much cold as colorless.

David paused. "Lillian can be very persuasive, you know."

Thomas nodded. "If you'll forgive me, David, I have much to think about, so I'm going to leave the store for the day."

He took his hat and umbrella from the hatstand and moved toward the door. "Thomas!" said David. Thomas turned and looked back at his partner. David lowered his eyes. "Truly, it wasn't as it seems."

"Perhaps not," answered Thomas, and left the office.

The next morning he awoke with a high fever, and May summoned Dr. Henderson, who, after examining him, announced that he was suffering from influenza. "One of the oldest of known diseases," he said. "Italian word for 'influence' . . . influence of the stars. That's what they believed was the cause. Of course, we know more about it now. Not serious as long as you take care, stay in bed, let your store look after itself for a while. I'll call again in a few days."

May saw the doctor to the front door. "Don't let him be foolish, Mrs. Kingston. Eight thousand people died in Britain in the epidemic of 'forty-eight, so it needs watching even if it's not normally an important disease."

"I don't think he'll be tempted to be foolish, Doctor," May answered. "In fact, a few days away from the store'd suit him, I think."

Thomas was soon worrying about the store—not about Goldsmith so much as the daily direction of it. He was concerned, too, about David and Lillian. "Baines may need support," he said.

"I'll go in your place, then," May suggested.

"You?" It was an astonishing proposal.

"Ruby can look after you and the children. I'll read your post, spend an hour or two at your desk with Baines. Then I'll come home and tell you all about it, bring any letters that are especially important, and you can say what you want done."

So May began to go to the store every day and sat at Thomas' desk for three or four hours. Most of the problems, she found, could be solved quite easily with Baines's helpful suggestions.

After the third day, she said to her brother-in-law, "You know, I'm beginning to understand why my husband thinks so highly of you."

"It's good of you to say so, Mrs. Kingston," Baines replied. "I hope you won't think it impertinent of me, but for my part, I've been most impressed by the speed with which you've grasped the essentials of the business."

She smiled at him. "You couldn't have made a kinder remark, Sidney," she said.

Lillian, of course, was not so kind. When she first heard that May was at Thomas' desk, she went in to see her. "This is a surprise, May," she said.

"Perhaps it's as well sometimes for you to receive surprises, Lillian," May answered, "as well as to give them."

"I'm amazed Thomas is not content to leave the management in the hands of his precious Mr. Baines."

May looked up at her coldly. "Perhaps he thinks it's not quite fair to him . . . since treachery's in the air. . . ."

"Treachery!" Lillian echoed. "You talk of treachery after what Thomas did to David in the Baines affair!"

"There was nothing underhand about the Baines issue," said May, "as I suspect David has realized to his cost. Now, Lillian, I've a lot of work to do, so I'd be glad if you'd excuse me."

Lillian flushed at the curt dismissal. "I'd advise you not to be too superior," she snapped angrily. "Times in this store are about to change."

Thomas' attack of influenza was a severe one. Ten days passed before he was well enough to leave his bed, and even then he felt very weak—as he complained to Henry Jones when he called on him. "It's not surprising," said the banker. "You're not accustomed to lying down for long periods. However, your illness has had one good aspect. It's given me time to talk to one or two more people."

"Speculators?" queried Thomas. "I'm not sure I like the breed."

"I haven't found the right people yet. The two firms I had in mind as an alternative to Goldsmith have just taken on large commitments which they want time to digest. There are others I wouldn't trust. Unfortunately, the recession has rather narrowed the field. Some fingers have been badly burned."

"How long do you think Goldsmith will wait?"

"Until you're back at work," answered Jones. "I don't think he'll do anything too dramatic. It's a delicate balance for him. He wants you as well as your store. That's your ace, as the debts are his."

"You make it sound like whist. May's urging me to go away for a week—to get properly well, as she puts it. She's got the doctor behind her."

"Then you should go, Thomas. After all, you'll be in for a fight when you get back. You'll need all your strength."

Thomas went to Quainton, and to his surprise, he found himself taking the children. "It'll give you a chance to get to know each other," said May. "You hardly ever see them . . . and your mother and Mary'll be able to spoil them without any interference from me. So everyone should be happy."

And everyone was. All three children were able to ride, and they hacked with Thomas on the Quainton Hills, which he had ridden over so often as a youngster. In the evenings, they were at table to share early supper with the family. Thomas had never talked to them so much—or listened. They told him about their lives at school, and he spoke about his boyhood at the farm.

The four of them did a lot of laughing—which started from the moment that Thomas lifted Rose onto a little gray pony called Dumb-Bell at the start of their first ride together. "I hope he won't run away with me," she said anxiously as she arranged her skirts round the pommel of the sidesaddle.

"Impossible," Thomas assured her solemnly. "He's told me he's particularly partial to eight-year-old young ladies with blue eyes."

"*I* didn't hear him," she said with a smile.

"He spoke in a whisper."

"I didn't know you could speak to horses, sir," Harry cut in with a hint of impertinence which, at another time, might have earned him a reprimand from his father. That day, though, Thomas was in a happy mood. "It's a gift that's only given to some people, Harry," he said with mock mystery as he mounted the same chestnut mare that he had hunted on that dramatic day six years before. He looked at his son as he gathered up his reins and smiled. "Who knows—in time perhaps it'll be given to you."

In fact, Harry impressed him. He rode with a very light touch on the reins, controlling the pony mainly with a subtle use of his body and legs. He looked more at ease than his elder brother, and Thomas was glad, for it was good that Harry should excel at something. At ten, Ramsay had developed a competence at almost everything he attempted, whether it was his studies at school or games—both boys had recently tried their hand at the newly fashionable lawn tennis—or even conversation on those occasions in the afternoon when he was expected to speak to his mother's guests after tea. He rode well enough, too, which, coupled with the fact that he was the elder, was the reason he had been given a pony that Edward had warned had something of a temperament. "Make sure he knows who's in charge," he had advised Ramsay, "and he'll be all right."

Edward opened the gate of the yard for them, and they headed for the hills. Thomas glanced at Ramsay as he rode beside him. He now had thick black hair, a broad forehead and dark brown eyes that, when he smiled, lightened to illuminate his face with a slightly mischievous expression that was appealing. That'll be having an impact on the young ladies when he's a bit older, Thomas thought, smiling to himself. It was only when they reached the top of the hills and the wind came under their tails that Ramsay's pony suddenly launched into a series of bucks. Ramsay shouted at him and tightened the reins to lift his head—whereupon he reared up, pawing with his front legs until his rider leaned forward to press him down.

"Well ridden, Ramsay," Thomas congratulated him quietly. "Let's move on slowly so he settles."

But he did not settle. They trotted over the pasture, but the pony began to buck again, fought the bit when Ramsay tightened the reins, and again stood up on his hind legs. "Give him his head, Ramsay," Harry urged.

Ramsay tried to relax his hands a little as his younger brother suggested, only to find himself riding a great corkscrew leap. "Not as much as that, silly," urged Harry.

Again the pony reared—and this time Ramsay almost lost his balance. "Too tight again," said Harry.

"If you're so clever, why don't *you* ride him?" shouted Ramsay angrily.

"All right, get off and I will," retorted his brother. "If I may, sir," he added to Thomas.

Promptly, in challenge, Ramsay slid to the ground and held the sweating pony's bridle as Harry mounted him quietly. "Let's see how *you* manage him, Clever Dick," he said as he clambered onto his brother's roan.

Harry proceeded to handle him with a natural skill that astonished both Thomas and Ramsay. The pony could have been a different animal. At first he moved his head about impatiently, but he was soon calmed. There was no bucking, no rearing. The sweat dried on his coat.

For a while, Ramsay rode in silence, a grim expression on his face. Then at last he remarked carefully to his father, "Harry's calmed him very well, hasn't he?" And Thomas, understanding the importance of young male pride, silently applauded his generosity.

"Dealing with horses is a bit like dealing with people," he said. "You get on well with one and not so well with another."

When they had returned to the farm, Thomas walked to the house from the stables with Harry. "It'd seem, Harry," he said gently, "as if you already have the gift of speaking to horses." And a broad smile of delight creased the face of his younger son. After that, though no one remarked on it, Harry always rode that pony and Ramsay took the roan.

It did not take long for Thomas to decide that he was sufficiently recovered to go hunting, though the piquant fact that hounds were meeting at Marston Hall had some influence on his decision. So too did the teasing of Edward by Mary and his mother about Agnes Cameron, for the first time she was mentioned, his brother had colored up like a young boy.

"Who's Agnes Cameron?" Thomas had asked.

"Cameron's daughter," Edward answered.

"What, *the* Cameron?" he said, adding, when Edward nodded, "I didn't know he had a daughter."

"She only came to live with him a few months ago. Before that she was abroad or in the West Country or something."

"Don't go thinking she's a youngster," Mary cut in. "She's thirty-five if she's a day. She's no beauty, either; but then"—she broke off, looking quizzically at her brother—"nor's Edward."

"These women'll make a romance out of anything," Edward complained. "I've only met the lady twice—at a meeting of the Parish Council and once out riding."

"You've forgotten the hunting," Mary prompted. "I'll wager you've exchanged a few sweet words as you waited at the covers."

"Now, stop it, Mary," their mother insisted.

"Does she have any brothers?" asked Thomas.

His mother saw the direction of his thoughts, with their land adjoining. "Unfortunately," she said, "he's got two sons. In his business up north . . . and speaking of business, Thomas, how is it with your store?"

She had deliberately avoided mentioning it before, sensing that he did not want to speak of it. His crisis had lain in the back of his mind, giving him a sense of vague unease sometimes, but deliberately obscured by pleasanter thoughts. "I've got a few worries, Mother. Trade's improving, though, and that's the important thing."

The next day, he rode with Edward over the hills to the meet at Marston Hall, where the riders were crowded in the courtyard in front of the house, sipping drinks from silver trays carried among them by Cameron's servants.

The brothers had hardly joined the throng, and reached down to take the glasses of port they were offered, before Thomas noticed the intent expression in Edward's eyes as he looked across the congestion of people and horses. Then suddenly he grinned. "Miss Cameron, I presume?" he queried gently, and his brother nodded.

She was walking her horse toward them—a woman in her mid-thirties, a trifle plump, with a face that was marked with large, rather sharply angled bones. But as Edward introduced him to her, Thomas noted that she had a pleasing smile.

"I'm happy to welcome you both to our home," she said, and Thomas was conscious that she was in a position to do so only because they were there as members of the hunt—as was emphasized almost at once. Suddenly Cameron's big black horse was beside him. He turned. "Good morning, Mr. Cameron," he said.

Cameron, glowering, ignored him. "Agnes," he said sharply, "there are other guests as well as Mr. Kingston who require your attention. The Master himself has just remarked that you have not yet spoken together."

Agnes flushed, excused herself with a smile and rode through the crowd toward Sir James Harrison, who was now over eighty but looking remarkably hale.

Cameron stayed beside the brothers for a moment, his expression somber. Thomas guessed that he wanted to say something to Edward, perhaps even order him to stay away from his daughter, but he could not find the words.

Thomas broke the silence. "I'm flattered to learn, sir," he said to him, "that you're considering investing in my store with Mr. Gold-smith."

Cameron flushed, his eyes dark. "I do not discuss business matters on horseback," he growled, and rode away from them.

Higgins, the huntsman, moved off with his hounds along the path-way that bordered the side of the house and, with the pack spead out wide on either side of him, cantered across two fields that lay at the rear of Marston Hall to a small copse he had been ordered to draw.

The members of the hunt, led by the Master, followed and halted in the first of the meadows. So far, to Thomas' surprise, there had been no sign of Evelyn Harrison, the Master's daughter, but now as they waited for hounds to "find," he saw her in the distance, on a chestnut, cantering down the steep slope of the Quainton Hills, taking the fences that lay in her path. She was too far off to recognize, but he knew it was she by the way she rode.

As she approached she eased her horse to a trot, and once again Thomas was struck by her sheer elegance, by the fact that everything, from the tilt of her topper to her stance in the saddle, was perfectly positioned. She was now over thirty, but maturity had enhanced her, the creases of time adding a quality of experience to her face.

She remembered him at once, her eyes lightening with that same expression of slight mockery which had marked them as she had gal-loped by him after the incident with Cameron's horse. "Why, if it isn't the other Mr. Kingston," she said as she rode up. "*You're* a stranger." She reined up beside him, acknowledging Edward and still breathing a little heavily from the exercise of her ride over the hills. "I really thought I'd miss them today. Oh, my gracious, I nearly did—look, he's gone already!" At the far end of the copse, one of the horsemen posted as markers was hollering, with his hat held high. Within seconds, Hig-gins had his hounds on, blowing the fast urgent call on his horn of "Gone away!"—and they broke from the copse going at full cry. Farther back, at the near section of the wood, one of the whippers-in emerged from the trees. "Get on him! Get on him, damn you!" he yelled at some hounds still in the copse, and the cracks of his whip rang out like gunshots.

For about half an hour the hounds went very fast—visible only as lines of moving dots several fields ahead—running up onto the hills and back again before going left-handed toward the Kingston land. Several times Thomas saw her up there at the front with her father, and it seemed to him that day that there was a special exultant joy about her.

She was taking her fences with an unrestrained abandon, at moments even flourishing her whip and letting out what from a distance looked like a cry of excitement.

At last the hounds lost the line and checked by the stream that bordered Edward's fields. While Higgins cast them on both sides of the water, the hunt waited, horses panting and flecked with sweat. Edward rode up to Thomas with Agnes Cameron. "How's the mare going?" he asked.

"Got a bit stronger since I last rode her," Thomas answered. "She's almost pulled my arms off."

"Perhaps *you've* got *weaker*, Mr. Kingston," Agnes teased. Then her smile seemed to freeze. It was as though she had actually felt her father's presence before his sharp "Agnes! A word with you, please!" As she walked her horse away from the two brothers, Thomas remarked lightly, "You know, Edward, I can't help gaining the impression that you're not very popular with Mr. Cameron."

"And whose fault's that?" Edward snapped in a tone that surprised Thomas, for his brother was serious.

Hounds were not held up long by the stream. One of them found the line on the far side and started speaking. Others joined him, muzzles low, and they were off again, running fast. Thomas and Edward jumped the stream together, riding well up near the front of the group led by the Master. They were checked again at a small wood, but hounds had the fox out quickly, and Thomas, with Edward riding close behind, galloped through a narrow clearing in the cover that reached to a very high overgrown hedge.

There were four riders ahead of Thomas, including the Master. Evelyn Harrison was lying fourth, immediately in front of him, and he could detect the tenseness in her body, shoulders thrust forward, as she urged on her chestnut. She took the big hedge well, her horse brushing through the high branches, where a path had already been worn by those who had jumped ahead of her.

Thomas sensed danger early as he approached the fence, and he started to curb the mare, but since he could see no obvious reason for his anxiety he was not very positive, and this was not enough to stop her. She made a dash for the hedge, and he then had no choice but to help her, because he knew she would need every bit of energy she could muster to gain the thrust to lift her to that height.

He was in midair when he saw them below him, victims of an exceptionally big drop, and he knew—in that moment of utter clarity, strangely devoid of fear, which comes at some point in every hunting accident—that there was nothing he could do to stop what must happen now. Evelyn Harrison was sprawled on the ground but moving slightly, clearly stunned or winded. Her horse was scrambling to get to his feet, thrashing a bit as fallen horses do. Instinctively, Thomas prepared himself to go unresisting with the fall. He felt the mare's forelegs crumple beneath him, her head twist, and then there was confusion—of lashing feet, of the sweat-damp hair of horses' coats, of passing ground, of constant forward movement, of sharp pain in his head—and nothing.

He could have been unconscious only for seconds. "Hold hard!" he heard a man's voice shout. "There are people on the ground!" "Cut through the wood," another called out—was it Edward?—"and take the hedge lower down."

He sat up, blood streaming down his face, his head throbbing. "Good gracious," he heard a woman say—was it Agnes?—"it's Lady Banbury!"

He became aware of Edward bending over him, holding a handkerchief over his wound to stem the blood. "Get his stock off," he said. Hands—he did not know whose—untied his stock from his neck and wrapped it like a bandage under his chin to secure Edward's makeshift dressing on his head. His top hat was then thrust on firmly to hold it all in place.

"Do you think you can manage to ride home, Thomas?" Edward asked. "It'll help if you can. I'll come with you. Now see if you can get to your feet. Your head'll hurt a bit as you stand, I expect."

Thomas stood up slowly and unsteadily. The throbbing within his skull increased, lancing sharp jabs of pain, and he swayed, thinking for a moment he was going to faint, but Edward supported him and slowly his mind cleared. It was then that he saw her, lying on the ground near her horse. The chestnut was on his side, his flanks heaving, his tongue lolling out of his mouth. But she was quite still, her face gray, her blond hair spread out untidily on the ground above her. Her stock had been loosened and a hunting coat had been thrown over her like a blanket. Another was serving as a pillow.

"She's not . . ." Thomas began.

"No," said Edward, "but she's unconscious. We're taking her home, since it's the nearest house. We've sent for the doctor. Now see if you can mount."

The mare stood unhurt, her ears pricked as though nothing exceptional had happened. Thomas, declining the offer of a leg up, put his foot in the stirrup and, with a huge effort, heaved himself slowly into the saddle.

Edward mounted too, and they began to walk the horses slowly across the field. Then Thomas caught sight of the six men approaching beside the hedge, carrying a gate, the customary stretcher for hunting accidents. He reined up.

"Shouldn't we wait for her?" he asked.

"I want to get you home before you collapse," Edward answered. "You're badly shocked. She's in the proper hands. They've only got to carry her across two fields to the lane. One of our wagons'll be waiting there soon to take her the rest of the way to the house."

Reluctantly, troubled by the pain in his head, Thomas consented to move on. Halfway down the lane that led to the farm, they met the approaching wagon that Edward had mentioned. "Lady Banbury, is it, sir?" asked one of the two farmhands on the box.

"That's right," Edward answered. "She's badly hurt. You'll have to take her as gently as you can."

The two brothers rode on in silence. "Why did you say she was Lady Banbury?" Thomas asked after a moment.

"Because that's who she is. She married the Earl about five years ago. Didn't you hear? Important lady now. She was prominent before, being the daughter of the Master, but nothing to what she is today. Huge house in Mayfair. Two thousand acres at the family home at Banbury, and Heaven knows how many more in Scotland. Farms. Racehorses. Blood herds. I hear the Earl's got some big position at Court."

When they rode into the yard of the farm their mother came out of the house, worried because she had heard that Thomas had been hurt. "You've a bed ready for her?" asked Thomas before she could say anything.

"Of course," his mother replied, "with a warming pan already in it. How bad is she?"

But Thomas did not hear her, for he had fainted, slumping forward in his saddle—grabbed just in time by Edward's strong arms to prevent him falling to the ground.

The hoarfrost was white on the roofs of the farm buildings as Thomas looked out the window where she had lain for two days, clad in one of his mother's caps and nightgowns, still unconscious. He himself had slept for twenty-four hours, and when he awoke at last, he had dressed and gone to her room to see how she was, suggesting to the nurse that he would keep an eye on her patient for a few minutes if she wished to slip away for a cup of tea.

For a moment, after the nurse had left the room, he had stood beside the bed watching her. Her skin had lost the grayness that had so disturbed him when he had first seen her stretched out beside the hedge. She was very pale, apart from the bruising round one eye and the cheek beneath it, and her features were completely relaxed in tranquillity. Lying there on her back, with her eyes closed and her face framed by the soft lace of the cap, she had looked very young, even pure.

He had crossed to the window, feeling a strange mood of peace, despite the mild but persistent aching in his head. It was not yet four o'clock, but the dusk had started to close in. There was a light on in one of the stables, and Thomas could detect activity within it—the evening feed time, he assumed. Then a farmhand walked across the yard, and the geese by the frozen pond started to cackle.

"You look as though you're back from the wars." It was a sleepy voice, very soft. He turned and saw that her eyes were half open, though she still lay quite still. He smiled at her reference to the bandage round his head. "I suppose you could say I have, Lady Banbury, *and* you—a fray, at least, though there was no enemy."

"Except Charlie . . ." She was hardly audible.

"He wasn't much of an enemy—running for his life."

"Wise Charlie," she whispered, "with the scent strong . . ."

"He escaped, I expect—with you in trouble. . . . How do you feel?"

"Remote. . . . Where am I?"

"In our home—and welcome, I can assure you. Do you remember much?"

"Seeing you at the meet . . . going away fast . . ." Her voice trailed off.

"You came down at the edge of Tendon Wood . . . a big drop. I didn't see you until it was too late."

For a moment she made no effort to speak. Then, after a few moments, she said, "So it was your fault." Her eyes were open and there was a lightness in them, but she did not smile. "Can you see much damage?"

"A little bruising on your cheek that'll soon fade. . . . If I may be permitted to say so, you still look very beautiful."

She made a slight movement with her head in mild rebuke. "You're a flirt, Mr. Kingston," she said, and fell asleep.

She awoke again a few hours later—conveniently, when the doctor was in the house. Her progress pleased him. "If she can stay here for a

few more days, she should be well enough to travel," he said. "And
what, may I ask, are you doing up and dressed, Mr. Kingston?"

"I'm almost completely recovered, Doctor," Thomas answered.

"You think you are, but you're not. You've been concussed. I
trust you won't consider returning to London for the moment."

It was not hard to obey the doctor's instructions, for he found her
soft wit very congenial. He would sit in her room in an armchair
from which he could watch through the window the routine activity
of the farm. Sometimes they would talk and at others they would be
silent. Often she slept for a while, and occasionally he did too. It did
not seem to matter. People came and went—her maid, the nurses, his
mother and sister, the children, his brother—but they seemed remote
to them both. Questions were answered, services accepted, but it was
as though the two of them, joined by the common experience of the
accident, were living on a different level from everyone else. They
never spoke of this, but it was conscious and accepted. For Thomas,
the sense of communication this created was unique. He did not find it
in the least strange when, on one occasion, she fell asleep in mid-
sentence and, on awakening later, just continued as though there had
been no break in what she had been saying. For his part, he found
himself speaking of whatever came into his head with no restraint and
often not much point—what he saw out of the window, mostly: the
conflict of two cock starlings over a female on the barn roof; a new
route to the pond that the file of geese seemed suddenly to favor; the
loading of the milk churns onto the trap.

"Do you mind me meandering on like this?" he asked her at one
point.

"No," she answered lazily. "Meander."

He sat in silence looking at her. She was no longer wearing his
mother's nightgown, for her maid had arrived at the farm with her
own clothes. Now she wore a white negligee of the finest silk, Thomas
having already priced it mentally out of habit, and no cap. She wore
her hair in a long plait, or sometimes two long plaits, that were carefully tended three times a day.

"You don't think," he remarked after a moment, "we should speak
sometimes of matters of greater import?"

"Than the decisions of the geese?" she asked with mock surprise.

"The Irish problem perhaps?" He was not serious, of course.

"Do you think it's of much moment to the geese? The pond, I
suspect, would raise more serious issues. It's only a question of perspective."

"The new books? Has Mr. Henry James drawn a portrait of a lady in his *Portrait of a Lady*—or just a misty impression, as some allege?"

"Who cares about Mr. James?" she asked, adding mischievously, "I didn't know drapers had time to read books."

He laughed. "Reminding me of my station, Lady Banbury? Am I forgetting myself?"

Immediately she was contrite. "I didn't mean that." She saw he was not offended. "I'm sure you knew I didn't mean that," she said with a smile, the anxiety gone.

"All right," he said. "Fashion . . . drapers surely know about fashion. The Smock Dress, say . . . Will those elegant ladies you entertain in Grosvenor Square soon be dressing like peasants?"

She smiled sleepily, appearing to nestle deeper into her pile of pillows. The violet of her eyes seemed to lighten to a high blue. "Tell me about the geese," she said. "Why have they changed their route to the pond? Are they bored? Or is there good reason—some newly discovered place to call, perhaps?"

"Now you're asking me to think," he replied. "Before, I was observing."

"A mistake," she agreed, "no thinking. . . ."

He leaned back heavily in his chair and put his feet up on the windowsill. "Your husband hasn't been to see you since the accident."

"It's a long way," she said. "And affairs of state are onerous, you know. He's written—perhaps a trifle briefly—but wives mustn't be demanding, must they? Is your wife demanding? No, I don't want to know. I just want to go on drifting, like we have been. . . ."

"They've been strange days, haven't they?" he said without looking at her, his attention caught by Edward's cows, which were coming slowly into the yard from the field for milking. "I don't think I've ever before enjoyed silence quite so much."

She turned so that she was lying on her side, her face against the pillow. "We're both in a weak condition," she said. "Perhaps it's the aftermath of shock."

At least half a minute passed before he spoke again. "No barriers . . . Like being in a wide plain with a very soft warm breeze and long grass and a clear sky . . . Peace, I suppose . . . and a strange sense of . . ." He broke off, searching for the word. ". . . of communion. That describes it, but it sounds a bit pretentious."

She moved in the bed, as though trying to settle lower. Her arm was bent, lying on top of the coverlet, her hand by her face, and her eyes suddenly seemed to match the color of a big sapphire ring on her index finger. "I don't think communion's pretentious," she said softly, "but I must stop you speaking of it, mustn't I? We're treading delicate ground."

With an abrupt movement, she turned again onto her back. "Aren't you impatient to get back to your business?"

He shook his head. "No," he said.

"You surprise me." She was speaking briskly. "I hardly think you created your store so fast by spending hours talking to ladies about geese."

"You see geese were important . . . a matter of persepective, you said. . . . " He gave a slight shrug of his shoulders. "For the first time in years, I've known leisure . . . and shared it."

"Please, Mr. Kingston," she said, just a little sharply. "No more of that."

His expression was serious suddenly. "There are other reasons, too . . . difficulties . . . unpleasant decisions that I've been glad to postpone. I can't, of course, for long."

"They're so very serious?" she asked.

"Extreme crisis. . . ." He paused, his eyes on the cattle wandering toward their sheds, and suddenly recalled that sickly smell, of the piles of smoldering carcasses of the herd they had replaced. "There's been crisis before . . . over ten years ago now. . . . I had one small shop and it looked as though I was going to lose it."

"I'm sure you never really believed that. You're far too determined."

"Perhaps I didn't completely," he conceded, "but I could see no way of saving it. . . . If you'd told me then that with the store as big as it is now I could face the same problems again, I wouldn't have believed it."

"Nor do I. How can you lose it?"

"By being forced to give up control. . . . As they say in financial circles, we're the target of a raid."

"A raid?" she queried, but she did not pursue the subject, because at that moment there was the sudden noise outside the window of horses and shouted commands. Looking down into the yard, Thomas saw a coach drawing up. It was in superb condition, with shining harness, liveried servants and a team that were impeccable. One footman ran to the horses' heads. Another opened the carriage door while the visitor stepped down from it. Aged about fifty, he was beautifully dressed, with a tailored frock coat and trousers that were immaculate.

For a moment, he stood surveying the farmhouse with what seemed to Thomas a manner of disdain. Then he passed out of Thomas' vision and entered the house.

"The meandering, Lady Banbury," Thomas remarked, "would seem to be over. I think the Earl is here to take you home."

The telegram from Thomas arrived at Caroline Terrace just as May was leaving for the store. He would be back with the children, he said, late that afternoon. Her reactions to the wire were mixed. She had missed them all badly, but she had enjoyed the hours she had spent every day in Kingstons and was a little sad that the role she had assumed in Thomas' enterprise would now end.

It was snowing lightly, laying a thin white surface on the pavements—enough to warrant an umbrella but not so heavy as to require a cab. And it was fitting weather, for it was only three weeks to Christmas. In fact, one of the duties May had enjoyed the most had been supervising the installation of the Yuletide displays, to which she knew that Thomas would attach great importance, though as usual he had laid down rigid policy concerning them: nothing too dramatic, just small seasonal reminders that did not distract the attention from the merchandise.

She approached the store, as was Thomas' custom, along the pavement on the far side of the street. The lights were already on in the windows, illuminating them with the exceptional brilliance that the Jablochkoff Candles provided. Other stores had now followed Thomas' sensational introduction of electricity three years before, but most were sparing in their use of it. The Kingston windows, therefore, were always among the brightest in London, and even during the slump years when all other costs were pruned right back, Thomas refused to economize on this item. The installation of this amazing new invention had been the cause of yet another quarrel with David, though they had them rarely now. Thomas, acting stubbornly on "feel," had been convinced that electricity would attract a huge amount of new custom, but it had failed in its aim. Trading increased marginally for about six weeks, when people came from other parts of London to view it, then eased back to its previous levels.

As May studied those brilliant windows on that December morning, however, she was sure that Thomas had been right. She believed, too, that he would be pleased with the Christmas displays characterized only by a careful use of holly and tinsel and scarlet background cloth.

She entered the store and mounted the stairs, acknowledging the respectful morning greetings of the staff. They had become accustomed to her now, no longer looking at her a little strangely, as they had at first. On the first floor she met Lillian, who, since their clash in Thomas' office, had greeted her pleasantly whenever they met, as though it had never happened.

"How's Thomas?" she inquired with a smile.

"He's returning today," May answered.

"He's been very unfortunate—influenza *and* a kick on the head. He couldn't have chosen a worse time, either, could he? Or perhaps he thought it a good time."

May looked at her coolly. "What do you mean by that?"

"Well, he *has* been behaving as though he hoped his problems would all just disappear. Very unlike Thomas to be an ostrich. He's usually so positive . . . but then, he's always had reservations about Mr. Goldsmith, hasn't he? I find it hard to understand. He's such a delightful old gentleman. You haven't met him, have you?"

"No," May agreed, "and I think it should be a matter of some shame that you have."

Lillian laughed. "Oh, May, you still don't understand that business, do you? Truly it wasn't as devious as you think."

"It was devious, Lillian," answered May briskly, "and in my view rather worse."

She was in Thomas' office a few moments later, taking off her bonnet and cloak, when Sidney Baines entered the room, carrying under his arm one of the big purchasing ledgers. "Good morning, Mrs. Kingston," he said brightly.

She flashed him a smile. "Good morning, Sidney."

"You know it pains me to say it, Mrs. Kingston," he went on, "but I fear I 'ave to admit I've been very wrong about Mr. 'Udson."

May laughed. "Well, that's handsome of you." She walked to the desk and sat down. "Are you sure?"

"Positive. You and Miss Lane were on the right track. 'E's quite obviously been taking bribes from suppliers—certainly from Mr. Stockton and possibly from one or two others. It'd appear that 'e's been living like the Prince of Wales. I feel quite terrible about it."

May smiled at him warmly. "I don't think you should blame yourself, Sidney."

"I employed 'im—at least, it was on my urging that Mr. Kingston did. I didn't even suspect anything wrong."

"Why should you? It was only by luck that Miss Lane's suspicions were aroused. It's a danger inherent in the trade—like shoplifting."

He nodded a little ruefully. "Even so, Mrs. Kingston, I do feel I made a big error of judgment. I'm so sorry."

"I'm not," said May. "In fact, Sidney, I'm glad."

Baines looked horrified. "Glad?"

"What a coup for us, Sidney! Firstly, it shows that women are not the stupid creatures men would sometimes have them be—though I concede your help was vital."

"I didn't believe you."

"No, but when I asked you to investigate the matter, you weren't halfhearted about it, as a lot of men would have been. Secondly, it'll impress Mr. Kingston that we're not completely helpless when he's away. Incidentally, he'll be in the store tomorrow."

"So 'e'll deal with 'im?"

"I'm sure he'll want to. But he'll insist on proof. Have you got it?"

"Well, I don't know that it's proof exactly. Certainly, 'Udson's been living at a standard well above what his salary could support. Then, if you look at the pattern of his buying, Stockton has a far bigger proportion of his business than he should 'ave. I've analyzed the figures in the ledger 'ere—"

May interrupted gently. "Pull up a chair beside me, Sidney, and let's go over it carefully together. . . ."

As he laid the big ledger on the desk in front of her, May visualized Emily's gratified response when she knew. Since Thomas and the children had been away, she had seen a lot more than usual of Emily. She had leaned heavily on her for advice, as she had on Sidney Baines, and had spent several evenings with her.

It was, in fact, on the day after Thomas left London that Emily had first raised the issue of the silk buyer—and also set in motion the other events that had so colored May's existence. They had been talking in the office about plans for Emily's Christmas displays when suddenly she had said, "I'm a bit concerned about Mr. Hudson. . . . Of course, it's not really my business, but . . . Well, have you seen the gig he drives to work in—and particularly, the horse?"

"No," May answered, a puzzled expression on her face.

"Unless I'm very mistaken, neither was cheap. In fact, the animal looks to me exceptionally well bred. . . . Then it so happens that about three weeks ago I went to the theater with my friend Joan Simpson . . . you know—the housekeeper at the Fawcetts' . . . *The Pirates of Penzance* it was, at the Savoy . . . and who did we see? Why, Hudson, resplendent in white tie and tails, with a very comely young lady, and

Arthur Stockton . . . *he* had a pretty young thing on his arm too. Disgusting, an old man like that. . . . I heard Stockton say they were going on to Romanos . . . Romanos, of all places!"

The significance of what Emily was suggesting at last dawned on May. "You mean it's hardly the life-style that the buyer of even a large department like the silks could afford?" she said.

"Well, of course"—Emily's expression was one of extreme skepticism—"Mr. Hudson may well have been left a fortune by some rich aunt . . . but every buyer gets offered bribes from time to time to favor a supplier, and Arthur Stockton's got quite a way with him." She stood up to leave. "Anyway, it might be worth having a close look at his orders."

May was pensive. She was sitting with her elbows on the desk, turning a pencil slowly between the fingers of both hands. "It's strange that we've never had a case of this since the store started," she said.

"I'm sure we have. The others thought it wiser not to make it obvious, but Hudson's an arrogant young man, likes to show a bit of style . . . ." She opened the door to leave, then stopped. "Oh, by the way, May . . . are you doing anything special on Wednesday evening?"

May shook her head. "I don't think so."

"Well, I know you're not much in favor of the movement for women's rights, but there's a public meeting of the NSWS at the Exeter Hall—that's the National Society for Woman Suffrage. Joan Simpson's employer, Mrs. Fawcett, is one of the speakers. She's married to that MP who's blind . . . remarkable man . . . Well, Joan and I were planning to go. She's a keen suffragist, of course, as everyone is in that household. . . . I just wondered if you'd like to come too."

May hesitated. "It'd be an experience, wouldn't it?" she said. "I'm not sure that Thomas would approve, but then"—she gave a wicked little smile—"he's not here, is he?"

"Oh, I'm so glad," Emily said happily. "Tomorrow I'll bring you a book you might like to read before we go. It's called *The Subjection of Women*, by John Stuart Mill. It's a kind of bible among the suffragists."

May smiled at her enthusiasm. "I hope you don't think you're going to convert me, Emily. Really, I don't feel subjected. . . ."

"We'll see, won't we?" Emily answered, and left the room.

The Exeter Hall was already so crowded when the three of them arrived that there were no seats left, so they had to stand at the side. May had heard much talk of women's rights, had read the occasional article about it in The *Times* and even found herself in angry agreement with many of Mill's arguments in *The Subjection of Women*; but until she entered that packed hall, she had never before been exposed to a large number of ardent women, for whom the gaining of the female vote in Parliament was no academic matter, but a great emotional cause—and of men, too, for outnumbered though they were, she was surprised how many were in the audience.

"Oh, we've a lot of male supporters," said Emily when May commented on it. "They're very important, since they're the people who'll have to get the bill through Parliament. . . . Look, that's Mrs. Fawcett." She indicated the platform. "It seems she's going to open the meeting."

Millicent Fawcett was in her mid-thirties. She was pretty and feminine, but she had a strength of personality that immediately dominated that crowded hall.

"Friends!" she declared after welcoming her audience. "I want to tell you first how I became a suffragist. . . . When I was still a young bride, I overheard two of my friends—women friends, I'd add—talking about an estranged married couple. 'I can't see what she has to complain of,' said one. 'Look how he dresses her!' " Millicent Fawcett paused and repeated slowly, enunciating each word very clearly: "*Look . . . how . . . he . . . dresses . . . her!* . . . Friends, I've been fuming about the degradation of that woman ever since. Was she a chattel? Was she in the same class in her husband's mind as his horse?"

There was a roar from the audience of "Shame!" and for May that first shout by a mass of women was an astonishing experience—inducing a strange mixture of shock and excitement.

"She was a very fortunate lady!" remarked a man standing behind May and her companions. For a moment, May wondered if she had truly heard the comment. She glanced at Emily, who made a backward movement with her head and whispered, "One of the antis. . . . There's an antisuffragist movement too."

May listened, fascinated, as Mrs. Fawcett on the platform analyzed the changes taking place in society, describing the reform bills that were gradually widening the vote to more people throughout the nation—provided they owned property and, of course, were not women. "Let us be clear about our aim," she declared. "It is to obtain the Parliamentary franchise for women as it is, or may be in the future, granted to men."

"Stuff and nonsense!" said a woman standing behind May. The remark was not loud, but it was heard through the applause by several people sitting nearby. Like them, May turned her head to see who had spoken. She was quite young—part of a large group that consisted,

surprisingly, of two or three girls and about a dozen men. May found
their hostile presence discordant and sinister. "They don't do much,"
Emily whispered. "They may shout a bit in a moment. No one takes
any notice."

Mrs. Josephine Butler, celebrated for her campaign against or-
ganizers of prostitution, was the next speaker. She made an impassioned
attack on the double standard of morality, insisting that the time had
come "to end the idea that male vice, because it is wrongly assumed to
be natural and inevitable, must be serviced by women!"

"It's always been natural," said the same man who had spoken
before, "for thousands of years. . . ."

As Mrs. Butler sat down to enthusiastic applause, May heard one
of his colleagues ask, "How long do we wait?"

"Not long now," another replied.

"Are you positive they're not intent on mischief?" May asked
Emily.

"Don't worry," Emily assured her, and nodded toward the platform. "This is Stella Wainwright."

The new speaker was considerably younger than those who had
preceded her. She was about twenty-five, with abundant golden hair
and a defiance in her stance, a forward thrust of her body as though
she were about to throw a javelin, that May found moving. "Friends,"
she declared, "the central belief of our great movement"—her voice
was light, being young, but oddly penetrating—"is that woman is the
co-ordinate, not the *sub*-ordinate, half of mankind. . . ."

"Absolute rubbish!" yelled one of the men standing behind them.
"Man is woman's natural superior!"

Throughout the audience heads turned in the direction of the
interruption, but the girl on the platform continued as though she had
not heard. "There are in this country today," she asserted, "between
four hundred thousand and five hundred thousand women who are
heads of households . . . who, if they were men, would be entitled to
the vote."

"That's the point!" shouted another man behind them. "They're
not men!"

"Is it possible," Stella Wainwright persisted, "to believe that these
women are not capable of a function of which every male householder
is capable?"

"You should be ashamed of yourself!" This time it was a woman's
voice.

"Have you no sense of womanly feeling?" shouted another.

Within seconds, the whole group was yelling at the platform. "You're a disgrace to your sex!" "No women in politics!" "Woman suffrage is indecent!" "Down with woman suffrage!" "It's an affront to nature!" "Woman's place is at home—not Parliament!"

For a few seconds there was a shocked silence in every other part of the hall. Then, from the body of the auditorium, a man shouted, "Get them out!" And hundreds of angry female voices began to chant, "Shame! Shame! Shame!"

Stella Wainwright held up both her arms. "Friends!" she pleaded, trying to reduce the noise so that she could be heard. "Friends, please . . . !" Gradually the din lessened, and it was then that the egg was thrown—with great accuracy. It broke against Stella Wainwright's left shoulder, leaving thick yolk draining down the bodice of her silk dress. And it was only the first of the missiles. Eggs, tomatoes, even potatoes began landing among the people sitting on the platform. Immediately, there was uproar in the hall. One woman began to scream, and almost at once other screams came from different sectors of the audience. Several men started pushing their way through the crowd toward the protesting group. May saw a tomato strike Millicent Fawcett in the face. One of the others near her was hit by a potato and was obviously hurt by it, for she bent forward with her head in her hands.

A group of young men ran up the side aisle toward May and the other two women. One of them grabbed her and started to hustle her backward, while others took hold of Emily and Jean. "Mr. Wainwright!" Joan Simpson insisted indignantly. "What are you doing? You know *me*! Let go of that lady! And tell these men to release us!"

"Oh, it's Miss Simpson," said the young man, recognizing her. "I'm so sorry . . ."

"So you should be," she snapped. "The ones you want are just behind us."

"Come on!" Wainwright shouted to the other men who were with him. "Let's get them, boys!" They pushed their way past the three women, for there was not much space in the aisle. While May and her companions smoothed their ruffled clothes and repositioned their bonnets, battle commenced behind them. It did not last long, for other male suffragists were closing in from different parts of the hall, and the antis were soon seriously outnumbered. They had positioned themselves near an exit, and they retreated in a well-planned withdrawal operation and escaped in waiting vehicles.

"I've never seen anything like this before," said Emily, "at any meeting I've ever attended."

"Nor have I," said Joan Simpson. "It's quite shocking, but in a way it's a good sign. It means our message is getting through."

Wainwright returned with his friends. He had an angry eye that was swelling, and several of the others bore signs of injury, both in the form of torn jackets and in marking on their faces. "I must ask you to accept my most profuse apologies," he said to May. He was a tall man of about twenty-eight, with a full, well-barbered beard and moustache, and kind brown eyes.

Joan Simpson moved close. "This lady whom you manhandled, Mr. Wainwright, is Mrs. Kingston," she said. "You know—of Kingstons, the store."

"In Sloane Street?" he queried, and held out his hand. "Please allow me to introduce myself. I'm Philip Wainwright, the brother of Stella Wainwright, whom you have just heard. Perhaps, to make up for my disgraceful behavior, you'll permit me to take you to her and her colleagues. I know she'll love to meet you."

There followed a few hours that May would never forget. All three of them were invited to go back with the Wainwrights to their home in Phillimore Place in Kensington. Stella had been badly shaken by her experience on the platform, but she had soon regained her composure. "I suppose you can't expect to challenge the very bastion of male prejudice," she said with a rueful smile, "without someone throwing an egg at you."

The Wainwright house was the most liberal, in the literal sense of the word, that May had ever been inside. During the evening, several people, both men and women, called and were given coffee and Madeira cake. Some of them came from the gentle classes, as of course the Wainwrights did themselves, but there were others who would not normally have been permitted to enter the sitting room of that type of home. Joan Simpson, as a housekeeper, was certainly in this category, and May and Emily, being in trade, would usually be welcomed only under the most exceptional circumstances. However, one girl visitor actually earned her living in a factory. All that mattered to the Wainwrights was that anyone who enjoyed their hospitality should be an ardent supporter of the rights of women—and for that matter, the extension of other human rights.

There was no Mr. Wainwright senior, for he had died some ten years before, but May was surprised that Mrs. Wainwright, who appeared on first impression to be a warm and gentle matron in her late fifties, was an avid militant impatient for more aggressive action. "They think they can win with meetings and letters," she told an astonished May, "but they'll learn they can't. They're going to have to fight."

"What would you have them do?" asked May.

"Why, act as revolutionaries, of course. That's what they are, although they like to think they're not—with their gloves and their bonnets. They're going to have to start getting hurt—that is, if they're going to make any impact at all."

Philip Wainwright paid May great attention. He sat at her feet because there were not enough chairs for all the visitors, though he jested that he did this so that she would not feel that as a man he was superior. "I'm not convinced that I don't believe that," she said, "at least in some ways."

"You can't possibly," he answered, "not if you think about it. Is your husband superior to you? Is he wiser, cleverer?" He added with a smile before she could reply, "He certainly can't be as handsome."

"I'll ignore that remark, young man," she said. "He's certainly clever—"

"I said cleverer."

"I'm not sure. . . . But there's no doubt that he's head of our household—and I wouldn't want it otherwise. Is that supposed to be wrong?"

Philip looked at her intently. His swollen eye was now bruised purple. "You know, Mrs. Kingston, I'm positive you're not the *sub*ordinate of him, as Stella put it from the platform, but the *co*ordinate."

She thought for a moment. "To tell you the truth, I've never thought about it. When I first knew him, he was my employer. Building the business has been very hard work. Then there've been the children. Quite frankly, there hasn't been much time to think about my rights as a woman. . . ."

"Then you must start now," he said. "Not your own personal rights within your marriage, for it seems you have a good husband, but those of women generally. . . . Promise me you will."

She laughed. "You're very insistent. I'll consider it. Will that do?"

He shook his head. "Certainly not. How can you doubt the rightness of the cause? Why can't you just say 'yes' with no reservations? Then I can offer myself as your instructor in political theory."

May laughed at his energetic pleading, and in turn, he laughed—and their laughter, fanned like flames by the response between them,

increased until it became helplessly uncontrollable. At last, feeling
slightly ashamed and dabbing the tears from her eyes with a handkerchief, she recovered herself. "I must go," she said. "Thank you for
being so patient with me."

"I've enjoyed every single second, Mrs. Kingston," he replied. "I'll
call you a cab."

Emily left the house with her, and as he handed May into the
hansom, he said, "Please think of what I've said. There's another meeting next week. Mrs. Lane knows where it is. My sister and I'll be there.
Please come." And he stood on the pavement, looking, with his discolored face, a little like a schoolboy after a fight, waving as the cab
moved off.

After studying Hudson's purchasing ledger, which Sidney Baines
had spread out on her desk, May leaned back in her chair. The case
against the buyer was obvious, but pleased though she was that he had
been detected while Thomas was away, she suddenly experienced a
sense of extreme sadness. Thomas had been out of the office for nearly
three weeks, and this short period of her life had been richly textured.
Her time at his desk had given her new insights into the business, which
had grown so much since she had last worked in it, and she had been
fascinated by the world of the suffragists, even though there were
aspects of the movement that disturbed her. For many of its theories
were rooted in the revolutionary thinking that had spawned the new
socialism of which Philip Wainwright was a great adherent. And May
was a conservative person, suspicious of revolutionary change.

She agreed with him that the terrible poverty, the condition of
women, and many other social evils demanded drastic action, but she
did not share his hot faith that the methods he advocated would
achieve a better world. And when he spoke so ardently of such socialist prophets as Karl Marx and Ferdinand Lassalle and Louis Blanc,
she became positively scared. As he had urged, she had attended the
second suffragist meeting, uninterrupted this time, and again gone
back afterward to the Wainwright home—and talked and talked and
talked, mostly to him, but also to Stella and their militant mother.

He had wanted her to visit them again—on this occasion to attend
a planning meeting of the NSWS. "I want to stop you being fright-
ened about the future," he had said, looking at her with a serious
intensity that had nothing to do with politics or women's rights.

"My husband'll be back with the children any day now," she
explained. "My time will be more occupied."

"Bring him with you," he said. "I can't be more generous than that, can I?—though I'll find it hard to see you with him. . . . I'm sure you won't be the same."

She shook her head briefly in reproach, wishing he would not speak so frankly of his feelings. "If I can come to your meeting, I will," she said, "but I think it unlikely." And she had not gone, though it had been hard for her to stay at home that night. All evening she had been restless, unable to settle down to reading a book or even, as she had attempted at one moment, to clearing out a cupboard. She had tried not to think of him, but vivid pictures of him had kept invading her mind—always in the form of his impassioned explanation of some political thought, his eyes alight, his fist thumping his knee. When at last she had gone to bed, she had experienced an unpleasant sensation of drained dissatisfaction, and it was well into the early hours of the morning before she fell asleep.

With an effort, May forced these intrusive thoughts from her mind and concentrated on the ledger in front of her. "You've convinced me completely, Sidney," she said. "I'm sure my husband will be convinced too."

In fact, she did not tell Thomas about Hudson until they were having breakfast on the morning after his return. She had not wanted to tarnish the happy mood of their homecoming, for she knew that Thomas would regard the buyer's action as gross betrayal of his personal trust and it would make him very angry, which it did—so angry that on his arrival at the store, Thomas did not even pause to study the windows, though he had not yet seen the Christmas displays. He barely greeted the staff who wished him good morning, but strode fast through the building to the stables. "Mr. Butler," he ordered, without making any inquiries about the animals in his charge, "bring out Mr. Hudson's horse!"

He stood in the yard as one of the grooms led a gray gelding from within the main stable block. For a few seconds Thomas strode round the animal, studying him grimly, his arms folded. "Now walk him up the yard and trot him back," he commanded.

The groom did as he was told, and the gray stepped out, his ears forward. "He moves well, doesn't he?" Thomas growled to Butler.

"He does indeed, sir. He's a fine horse."

The scene with the buyer did not last long. He had not even closed the door of the office behind him before Thomas snapped, "Have you inherited money recently, Hudson?"

The question both shocked and unnerved the young buyer. He flushed. "I don't wish to be impertinent, Mr. Kingston, but if you'll forgive my saying so—"

"Answer the question, Hudson," Thomas cut in, "and I warn you that if your reply is in the affirmative, then I'll require proof."

Hesitantly, Hudson said that he had received no inheritance.

"Have you found a rich widow then?" snapped Thomas.

"Mr. Kingston, I don't know why you're asking me these personal questions—"

Again Thomas interrupted. "You've been playing the tables in some club perhaps? . . . Had a big win on a horse?"

Clearly, this last suggestion raised a faint hope in the buyer's mind, for he stuttered, "Well, as a matter of fact, I did have a little luck the other day. . . ."

"Where? When? What was the horse's name? How much did you wager?"

As the questions came at him in quick succession, any remaining pretenses were over—and Hudson knew it. He was out of the store within half an hour.

Arthur Stockton, however, did not give Thomas so easy a time when he responded to his request to call and see him. He was a much richer man than he had been when Thomas had first known him—and a good deal fatter. He was in his sixties now, and he had a great wide belly that gave him an air of magisterial authority which was not diminished by the racecourse style of clothes that he still affected. "Oh, Thomas," he said irritably, tapping his foot with his cane, "I can't think why you're making so much of this storm in a teacup. Of course I looked after the boy. It's the custom of the trade."

Thomas had to concentrate hard to retain his perspective, for Arthur Stockton still treated him as an inexperienced young man in vital need of his benevolent counsel. "It's not the custom of the trade in my store," he said in a tone that was sharper than he had intended. "We don't bribe—or accept bribes . . . not from anyone."

"You'll never stop it, Thomas," Stockton responded wearily. "You can try, but you'll fail. Much better accept it."

"I won't accept it," Thomas insisted. He leaned forward with his forearms resting on the desk. "In fact, I've asked you here today because . . . Well, I'm closing your account."

It was an effort for him to get the words out, and for a moment there was silence. At last, the wholesaler began to chuckle—then broke into loud laughter, his belly shaking. "Again, Thomas?" he said.

"You're always closing my account—but you always open it again because you need my stock."

Thomas' expression was grimly serious. The wholesaler was right, but in the past it had never been more than a gesture in writing. "Not this time, Mr. Stockton," he said. "That's why I've asked you to call. This time it's final. . . . I'll get the merchandise somewhere else—even if I have to send someone abroad for it."

Stockton nodded philosophically. "I'm not sure you're being wise, Thomas," he said. "I've helped you. I know you've always felt I let you down on that occasion at the beginning, but you've always had my goodwill, and you've sold a lot of my merchandise. . . ." He paused, surveying Thomas with eyes that were hard and unfriendly. "I wouldn't advise you to lose my goodwill. After all, you're in trouble again, Thomas, aren't you? I guessed as much when your old friend Goldsmith acquired your debt to me, but since then I've heard the rumor several times in the City. . . . He shook his head, his heavy red jowls wobbling. "You need all the goodwill you can get, Thomas . . . certainly mine . . . so I should exercise care."

Thomas stared out his challenge, his eyes angry. "I won't have bribery, Mr. Stockton," he said in a voice that was coldly controlled. "Whatever happens, I won't countenance bribery."

Stockton sighed. "You have a distasteful turn of phrase, Thomas."

"It describes a distasteful practice. . . . Good day to you, Mr. Stockton."

"All right, Thomas," the wholesaler said, getting heavily to his feet. "Have it your way." He walked to the door, opened it and saw who was waiting in the outside office. "You have a visitor, Thomas. . . . The hounds are closing in."

Goldsmith walked briskly into his room and stopped suddenly, with a kind of flourish that caused the skirts of his long frock coat to swish sideways. He beamed, rubbed his hands together slowly as if he were still cold from the December weather outside. "I trust, Mr. Kingston," he said, "that at last you've recovered from your various indispositions."

"It was most unfortunate," said Thomas. "I must apologize. Please take a seat."

"These things happen. Perhaps we should be thankful that your injuries were not more serious. After all, you could have been unconscious for weeks. Hunting people often are." Sitting down, Goldsmith cocked one leg over the other, carefully adjusting the material of his trousers so that there was no creasing. "However," he continued, "no doubt in your sickbed you've had time to consider our proposition."

Thomas hesitated before replying. "Yes," he said at last, "yes, I have, Mr. Goldsmith, but I've not yet had time to consult further with Mr. Jones. I've a meeting with him arranged for Thursday afternoon. May we call on you after that?"

Goldsmith did not smile. Thoughtfully, he turned a ring on one of his fingers. "I'd hoped that at last the delays would be over, but . . . well, all right—we'll leave the matter until Thursday." He paused, the expression in his eyes suddenly hostile. "I trust it can be concluded then, Mr. Kingston," he said. "Otherwise, in the interests of my syndicate, I may find it impossible to resist any longer my lawyer's pressure to . . ." A trace of his usual genial personality reemerged in his manner. ". . . I wish there was some more pleasant way to put this . . ."

"Sue, Mr. Goldsmith?" queried Thomas.

The slight grimace on the banker's face indicated the pain his duty gave him. "I'm glad you understand." He stood up. "Until Thursday, then, Mr. Kingston."

For a few minutes after he left, Thomas sat at his desk thinking. There was no longer any scope for postponement of the issue, no further give in the elastic. He was left with two days. He could gain more time if he allowed Goldsmith to issue the writs; such legal formalities were not easily hurried. But he dismissed the thought, for the suit would then become known and do much harm to the store. Even now, Thomas believed that there must be some alternative, some avenue that he had not yet considered—or rather, that had not yet been revealed to him by those Fates of his who, though he knew them to be unpredictable and even mischievous, he could not believe would abandon him to Goldsmith and Cameron. For this did not conform with his conviction that it was his preordained duty, his destiny, to build Kingstons into a great emporium.

He had been sitting, staring into space, deep in his dark thoughts, for about a quarter of an hour when there was a knock on his door and Sidney Baines entered. "Mr. Kingston," he said, "the Countess of Banbury is downstairs . . . in the Chinaware. She has asked if you could spare her a few moments of your time."

She was seated on a chair against a background of a large display of Crown Derby, dressed in a gown of high yellow silk. Beside her stood a footman, holding some parcels. "I hope I haven't disturbed you at an inconvenient time, Mr. Kingston," she said.

"I'm delighted to welcome you here," he said. "I hope you'll allow me to show you my establishment."

"I should enjoy that—but you must promise me you won't let me buy anything. As you see"—she indicated her footman with a wave of her hand—"I've already indulged myself."

"You can rely on me to restrain you, m'lady," answered Thomas with a grin.

She sent the footman to the carriage, and they walked through the store together. "You have some very fine things here," she remarked, adding lightly, "here in your empire. . . . I don't know why, but I didn't think it would be quite so big."

"You haven't seen it all yet," he said, and led her out of the five-shop block onto the pavement, beside which the carriage, bearing the Banbury crest, was waiting. As they passed Mrs. Fellowes' shop, still as derelict and dirty as ever, on their way to Emily's section, she asked about it. When Thomas explained, she said, "It quite spoils your store. You've offered to acquire it, of course?"

"Countless times. She's adamant in her refusal."

"What extraordinary behavior. Who is this Mrs. Fellowes?"

"She lives in Eaton Square. She's a friend of a banker named Ernest Goldsmith who's trying to acquire an interest in my store. She's wealthy. Once, I believe, she was an actress. That's about all I know."

They walked on into the Fashion section, and she congratulated Emily on the gowns she saw displayed, admired the ribbons, even tried on a pair of gloves. Thomas found that seeing her here in his store was a strange experience. For although she was warm in her behavior toward him, even teasing him gently at moments, he found it hard to relate her completely to the woman with whom he had spent those hours of unison at Quainton. Here, in his emporium, she was without question a countess. Although he had been conscious of her title at Quainton, it had not seemed to matter. Now, in Sloane Street, the term "m'lady" came easily to his lips, though he noticed that she gave a little smile whenever he used it. She moved and behaved like a countess. "You must be very proud of what you've achieved, Mr. Kingston," she said, when at last they were walking toward her carriage, and again it was an accolade from a lady of rank to a successful tradesman.

"I've always had hopes," he answered simply, "that I could create of Kingstons the finest emporium in the world."

"I was convinced when we spoke of it in your mother's home," she responded. "I'm even more certain now I've seen it." He knew she had mentioned Quainton to help palliate his sense of difference from her. "Mr. Kingston," she went on, "would it be possible for you to join us for lunch on Thursday? I do hope it would be."

His reaction was one of surprised pleasure, combined with confusion. He tripped a little over his words as he accepted, then recalled that he was supposed to be meeting Jones and, afterward, Goldsmith. "I do have an appointment in the City at three thirty," he said. "A rather important one."

"I'll ensure you're not late for it. At midday, then?" She stepped into the carriage, waved a gloved hand with a smile as the coachman whipped up his horses.

Thomas stayed on the pavement for a few seconds in a state of amazement. To be asked to lunch in the home of an earl was extraordinary for a tradesman of his position. Times were changing, of course. Even the Prince of Wales had several friends who had been successful in trade or industry, but these were commercial giants, millionaires, owners of racehorses and yachts. Kingstons was now a sizable business, but did not begin to approach these Olympian heights—not yet. The invitation was strange, therefore—and, of course, intriguing.

On Thursday, in fact, Thomas discovered that there were to be only three of them at table—just his hostess and himself and one other guest, who was already in the drawing room of the Banbury home in Grosvenor Square as Thomas was announced by the butler. He was a man of about fifty-five, named Edwards, with steel-rimmed spectacles and a gaunt, spare face. On first impression, Thomas found him unpleasantly grim and austere, but as they were introduced he smiled suddenly and his features assumed an almost childish expression of friendly warmth.

"I have to confess," she said to Thomas, as the butler offered him a glass of sherry on a silver tray, "that I've invited you here to meet Mr. Edwards with a purpose, and since I know you cannot linger too long over luncheon, I suggest we proceed at once to speak of it. . . . Also, I fear I've betrayed a confidence, Mr. Kingston . . . I've told Mr. Edwards something of your business problems."

Edwards emitted a loud chuckle before Thomas could respond. "I'm sure he'll forgive you, Lady Banbury." He was standing in front of the fire, with his hands behind his back. "Perhaps, though, Mr. Kingston's already solved his problems, in which case we can talk of other matters." He looked with an expression of impish inquiry at Thomas, who shook his head. "Unhappily, there's been little change," he said.

"Except possibly," Edwards continued, "if my information is correct, that the matter is more pressing."

Thomas conceded the point with a slight nod. "I find that to be the tendency with unsolved problems."

Edwards laughed, swaying his long thin body gently to and fro in front of the fire. "Nicely put, Mr. Kingston." He paused for a moment. "Well, Mr. Kingston, where shall we start? My role perhaps, Mr. Kingston? My 'raison d'être,' shall we say? Why has her ladyship brought us together? Answer: because she thought that possibly, just possibly, there were interests we might have in common. . . . It's my duty, I should explain, Mr. Kingston, to administer the investments of the Banbury trust and my honor to advise the Earl on his financial affairs. . . . No doubt you now have a glimmering of what was in her ladyship's mind. . . ."

Thomas glanced at her, but deliberately she looked away. He took a sip from his glass. "A glimmering," he agreed cautiously.

"I've visited your establishment, Mr. Kingston," Edwards went on. "I've even given you my custom. I bought a hat—a bowler; a very stylish bowler, I might add. In other words, you have in me a satisfied customer. Presumably you have others, for without them you'd never have progressed with the speed that you've displayed."

He paused, drank a little sherry. "This fino is remarkably good. It's a little extra pleasure attached to visiting you, Lady Banbury. The Earl's cellar is quite outstanding. . . ." He turned back to Thomas. "Well, to come to the point, Mr. Kingston . . . I know your bankers, of course, and I've discussed your situation at length with Mr. Jones— who, I may say, regards you highly. . . . He was good enough to allow me to view the accounts, which, strictly, he shouldn't have done, of course, but he felt that the normal etiquette could perhaps be dispensed with in the cause of urgency. . . . I do hope you won't give him a scolding." He peered over his spectacles at Thomas, whose emotions were mixed. His first thought, of course, was one of growing elation, but he was well experienced in rising hope—and in its destruction. It was at these moments of mortification that Thomas could almost literally see his Fates—vague, hazy dwarflike figures—roaring with laughter at his distress.

He swallowed. "I'm sure Mr. Jones was doing what he thought to be best," he managed to say.

"Oh, he was," agreed Edwards. "And with reason. I've been most impressed, Mr. Kingston. The potential is, I'm convinced, enormous, not only for a great store here in London, but also in other towns in Britain, and perhaps even abroad . . . in short, I've strongly advised his Lordship that the trust should invest thirty-five thousand pounds in your company, Mr. Kingston . . ." He paused, his eyes bright again, for he knew the question in Thomas' mind. ". . . at terms that Mr. Jones believes you'll find acceptable. . . . We shall require fifteen percent of your equity stock, the exact price of the shares to be negotiated, and . . ."

He went on talking for several minutes, describing the details of the offer, but Thomas was no longer concentrating. The essential point was that Edwards' proposal would leave him in control of Kingstons. No matter who was ranged against him—Edwards himself, David, even Jones at the bank—he would still own more than half the stock, which would give him the power to outvote them all.

His spirits surged. He experienced an almost overwhelming impulse—disturbing in a man of early middle age—to leap into the air, to shout "Hallelujah" or some such epithet of ebullient joy. When the butler announced that luncheon was served, his voice seemed to be coming from a great distance. Even those violet eyes, when she smiled at him, so obviously pleased at the outcome of her efforts, had the ethereal quality of a dream.

At lunch, he slowly calmed himself as they spoke of his store, of the future of the trade, of the effect of the craze for sport on women's fashions, and eventually of politics. When the meal came to an end, Edwards excused himself, pleading an appointment that was even earlier than that of Thomas. "Good luck, Mr. Kingston," he said, shaking hands. "I'm sure your business has a great future."

Thomas went with her into the drawing room, and they sat on the huge sofa while a footman placed a coffee tray on an occasional table beside her. When at last they were alone, he said, "I don't know what to say."

"Then don't say anything," she responded. "After all, we're accustomed to silence together . . . you even said you enjoyed it. . . ."

"I want to be able to thank you," he went on, "but I can think of no words that are adequate."

She laughed. "I can assure you that Mr. Edwards wouldn't have advised the investment if he hadn't believed it sound."

"No," he conceded, "but if it hadn't been for you I wouldn't even have met Mr. Edwards."

"Oh, I don't know . . . Your Mr. Jones might have introduced you."

"I doubt if he'd have treated the matter so urgently."

"Now, there I will take the credit," she said. "I did suggest to Mr. Edwards that he should make haste before it was too late. It seemed an opportunity that the trust'd be unwise to miss. . . . Will you take coffee, Mr. Kingston?"

He did not seem to hear her in the turbulence of his emotions. Almost unconscious of what he was doing, he took up one of her hands gently and studied it. On one finger was the sapphire ring he remembered.

"You were wearing that on your last day at Quainton," he said.

"You're observant, Mr. Kingston," she said, but made no attempt to withdraw her hand.

"Sometimes," he went on, with his eyes still focused on her fingers, "I wish you weren't a countess."

"You'd prefer me to be a shop assistant? I don't think *I* would. There are certain advantages to rank. And what does it matter, really? One's still a person."

"A woman . . ." he corrected.

"All right . . . a woman."

"A woman," he went on, "who hasn't been out of my thoughts since I returned to London . . . lying there in white silk, with her hair in plaits and an expression in her eyes that took possession of me, as though I was in a spell . . . I suppose you'll tell me I'm treading a delicate area."

She nodded.

"Are you going to order me to stop in that strict tone you used before?"

"I should, shouldn't I? . . . You're going to be late for your appointment. Drink some coffee before you go."

He lifted her hand to his lips, his eyes on hers. He kissed one finger, paused, then kissed another, paused again, and then another.

She spoke without smiling, with no lightness in her voice. "I seem to have lost my will. . . . It's not just a delicate area . . . it's dangerous. . . . We should go back . . ."

"And talk about geese?" suggested Thomas. He lowered her hand to the sofa, but still retained it in his.

"We weren't talking about geese, were we?" Her voice was very soft, but intense. "Not really. . . . It was a kind of secret language. . . . I've missed talking about geese. . . ." There was something close to pain in her eyes. "I wish I hadn't missed it so much."

He drew her toward him, hesitated for seconds, just savoring the sight of her—the beautiful, strangely colored eyes; the soft line of her cheek; the fullness of her mouth; the pale neck as smooth as that of a young girl—and kissed her gently.

She responded, also gently, parting her lips, taking his face between her open hands so that she was holding his head as though it
were some valuable vase. She pressed his mouth more closely to hers,
moving it sideways, tasting him—then, using the control provided by
the manner in which she was holding him, she eased his lips away very
slowly, so that it was a movement almost of unpeeling, every fraction
of their skin seeming in turn to resist the act of detachment, and
looked once more into his eyes. "Thomas . . ." she said. "Thomas . . ."
And with the same slow gentleness, she brought his mouth back to hers
and began to kiss him harder, a clutching violence suddenly flaring
through her. She fell back against the cushions of the sofa, still holding
him tight, knowing a need for him that had a quality of wildness. Then
she turned her head sideways sharply, wrenching her lips from his.
"Not here, Thomas. . . . You must go . . . you have to go. . . ."

Under the pressure as she pushed him from her, he sat up on the
sofa. "You'll be late for your appointment," she said.

"It doesn't seem to matter," he answered quietly. "When I'm with
you nothing matters . . . nothing else. . . ."

She was breathing heavily, trying to consolidate her control over
her body. "Except your store."

He looked at her, a softness in his eyes. "Except my store . . . but
that's different. . . ."

She stood up, smoothed her gown, touched her hair. Then, after a
few seconds, she pulled the bell for the butler. "Mr. Kingston is just
leaving," she said when he entered. "Please summon a cab."

"Very good, m'lady," he said, and withdrew. Thomas looked at
her. "I wish I had the words to describe what I feel now."

"Go," she said softly. "Please go. . . ."

He moved to her, but she did not present her mouth to him. He
brushed her cheek tenderly with his lips and walked toward the door.

"Thomas," she said suddenly. "There's something else . . . about
your store. . . ." She was finding it very hard to speak, breathing
heavily still "I've seen Mrs. Fellowes . . . about her shop. . . . She tells
me she'll dispose of it . . ."

For a few seconds, in the confusion of his feelings, Thomas could
not absorb the meaning of what she had said. Even when the content
of her words at last began to dawn on him, he found it difficult to
believe he had correctly understood her. "You mean she'll sell?" he
asked incredulously. Evelyn nodded. "But how have you met her?"

"I invited her to call."

"And she agreed to dis . . ." He broke off. "But why?"

"Because I asked her to. . . . I like her, Thomas. She's amusing. It'll be no strain to receive her. . . ." She was speaking fast, the words tumbling out of her, and it was a moment before Thomas realized the incentive she had offered Mrs. Fellowes. "Patronage?" he queried, and laughed.

Suddenly, she looked radiantly happy. "It'll be good for Kingstons to be a single building, won't it?" she said.

"Good?" he queried. "Good? It'll be wonderful! Oh, Eve . . ." He started to move to her, but she held up both her hands in restraint. "You'll be late," she said.

"I can never begin to pay my debt to you," he said.

"Can't you?" she responded. Her face lit up in a quick, sudden smile. "Oh, I think you can."

CHAPTER SEVEN

May 1884

· I ·

Thomas laid down *The Times* on the table and lifted the cup of coffee to his lips. He was finding it hard to concentrate on the paper this morning. Somehow the Mahdi's holy war in the Sudan—and even that morning's news of General Gordon's telegram to Cairo that he felt abandoned in Khartoum—did not occupy him as he felt it should. He was disturbed by a sudden thought: had his own prosperity and success made him selfish and complacent?

He looked at May, at the far end of the long mahogany table. The return of the fashion of the bustle, with its tight front and rear draping, suited her. She had always had a degree of elegance, but now, in her mid-thirties, it had flowered into a dignity and style that gave him great pleasure. And considering her background, which was even more modest than his own, the ease with which she had taken command of this big new house in Cadogan Place, with its pillared entrance and wrought-iron balconies, was remarkable.

For the past year, Ruby, the maid who had been with them in Caroline Terrace, had taken her place in a staff of eight, including a butler, cook and coachman. Admittedly, May had experienced a little initial difficulty with Brandon, the butler, whose previous service with a marchioness had left a deep impression on him. "Like horses," Thomas had warned, "you have to leave servants with no doubts as to who's master." May had acted on his advice with one sharp confrontation, on the evening of which she had reported with a smile, "I think I'm now the master of the situation . . . if it's correct for a lady to be the master of anything."

Thomas transferred his attention from his wife to his children, allowing his eyes to linger on Rose, now eleven. With her pale blue eyes and straw-colored hair hanging down her back, she was beginning to acquire the first signs of womanhood: a certain dignity, like her mother's; a rounding; an expression of contained self-awareness and . . . Was her bodice a little tight? Surely not a bosom already?

She became conscious of his gaze and suddenly smiled at him shyly. He smiled back, in a way he hoped was reassuring, which told her she was pretty, that he was proud.

He glanced at Ramsay—at thirteen nearly a man. His hair was getting thicker as he grew up, and the black shadow on his cheeks was already revealing the beginning of beard growth. Ramsay still gave the impression of collected control, of quiet confidence, that had marked him when he was younger. Unlike Harry . . . Harry, with his high pink complexion and his tousled hair, was always awkward, clumsy— except, strangely, when he mounted a pony, when he would change suddenly and acquire the discipline, the unison with the animal which approached that displayed so brilliantly by Eve.

Thomas noticed then that one of Harry's eyes was discolored. He glanced back at Ramsay. The skin on one side of his face was marked by a red weal that he had not seen at first because the boy's head had been averted.

"Have you two been fighting?" Thomas asked.

"I fear so, sir," Ramsay answered. "At school yesterday . . . We had to help Charles. . . . Some of them had set about him."

"Charles Rawlings? I didn't think you saw much of Charles."

Ramsay hesitated. "Well, I wouldn't say we were friends exactly. . . . Harry sees more of him than I do, of course, being the same age. . . ."

Harry nodded. "He's top of my form . . . but we don't talk much."

Both boys seemed to be strangely embarrassed. "Well?" Thomas probed.

"It was on our way home," Ramsay went on. "They're a rough set. . . . They'd got him on the ground . . ."

"And?"

"Well, he's sort of in the family, isn't he? . . . As we got near them, Harry said, 'That's Charles they've got, isn't it?' And I said, 'Looks like him,' and we both started running forward . . ."

"How many of them were there?" Thomas asked.

"Five, was it?" Ramsay asked Harry.

"Five or six," his brother answered; "six, I think."

"Was he badly hurt?"

"They'd knocked him about a bit, hadn't they, Harry?" Ramsay answered.

Harry agreed dubiously. "His nose was bleeding and his eye was cut . . . but he was still fighting. . . ."

Thomas looked puzzled. "You were outnumbered two to one, then. How did it end?"

"Oh, we won, sir, of course. . . . Harry got the leader in a half-nelson and warned the others that if they didn't clear off he'd break his arm. . . . By then the chap was really yelling his head off. . . . I don't suppose you've ever seen Harry in a fight, have you, sir?"

Thomas glanced at his younger son, who had always been big for his age. "No," he said, "I'm glad to say."

"Well, I wouldn't like to be in a fight against Harry, sir—even though he *is* younger than me. . . ."

Thomas again looked at Harry with some surprise. His brother's picture of him as an invincible pugilist did not conform with his own idea of his son, whom he had always regarded as an easygoing, friendly boy. "Do you get into many fights, Harry?" he asked.

"Oh, no." Ramsay hurried to intervene on his behalf. "Only occasionally . . . when it's absolutely necessary. . . ."

"And you felt it absolutely necessary to help Charles?"

"Well, we couldn't leave him to them, could we?" said Ramsay. "He'd have done the same if it was one of us, though he's not so good with his fists as Harry. . . . He'd never just have left us."

Thomas nodded, glimpsing for the first time an aspect of the relationship between his sons and David's boy that he would never have suspected—a sense of association that transcended the issue of whether they liked each other or not, a bond that, though unlimited by real family ties, was rooted in their joint connection to his store, the cornerstone they all had in common.

"I'm glad you won," Thomas said, trying not to reveal too much pride in his tone. "I'm glad you rescued Charles." He got up from the table. "Take the carriage if you want to," he said to May as he kissed her cheek. "I shan't require it today."

It was a fine morning, and the brief walk to the store was pleasurable. He crossed the road for his usual daily survey of the store's windows. He still experienced a conscious pleasure in the fact that at last Kingstons was a unified building, stretching across nine double-fronted shops. Instinctively, his eyes still sought out the two big windows in its center that had been the cause of offense to him for so long—even though nearly three years had now passed since Mrs. Fellowes had received him to settle the final terms of the sale. "She's beautiful, I have to admit," she had said of Eve with a smile.

"I beg your pardon," he had challenged a little stiffly.

"Now, Mr. Kingston, you mustn't be pompous with *me*," she had admonished. "I've conceded my investment and I'm happy with my profit. But don't try to tell me she's not taken with you—and more. Her whole face lights up when she speaks of you, which is something she's going to have to watch."

"I think you've misunderstood the situation," remarked Thomas.

She had laughed. "Spoken like a real gentleman," she had said, and winked at him broadly like a Cockney comedienne on the halls.

On this May morning, the windows of the shop that had been hers were devoted to a big display of carpets in one section and to boots and shoes in the other. The acquisition had made a tremendous difference to the store. It had enabled Thomas to replan it as a single unit—which, quite apart from permitting his customers access to all departments without going outside, had meant that he could organize his services to the maximum efficiency. Cash now traveled to the countinghouse in metal boxes on overhead wires. He had extended the stables at the rear to accommodate his horses, which now numbered 120. His dispatch department, where goods were parceled and allocated to sections by district for delivery, now occupied most of the basement area and was carefully designed with a system of moving belts and chutes that he believed to be the newest in London.

He had increased his range of merchandise, of course, and his thirty-four selling departments now extended over the whole of the ground and first floors. An enlarged food section included a fish counter, and a wide variety of wines and spirits were available next to the groceries. Jewelry and furs had been installed on the Fashion floor, where dresses, whose initial sluggish progress had caused much concern, had become the biggest single source of trade in the whole store.

A ticket agency, catering for rail travel, the opera and the theater, had been added to the Estate Property Department. Forage for carriage horses was sold along with the saddlery, and a substantial business was done in riding habits for both gentlemen and ladies. But Thomas' latest pride was his restaurant. It was not very big, but it had fast become fashionable—a popular meeting place for his elegant customers, who were served tea and cakes by his waitresses wearing dresses in the Kingston colors of yellow and blue. Soon they would be serving lunch as well, for at last he had overcome the local opposition to his application to the magistrates for a license to serve wines and spirits on the premises—at least, Eve had overcome it. He had not intended to seek her help, but it had slipped out among the various problems he had been discussing with her one day when they were relaxing in their little refuge in Sydney Street. He had actually asked her not to intervene, but she had insisted. "You're such a dummy about this," she had said. "People of power never hesitate to use their power. They think nothing of it—especially over a simple little thing like this."

"Is it such a simple little thing?" he queried.

"I just have to make one remark to the right person," she said. "I don't even have to elaborate. My wish merely has to be known."

"And if the magistrate is stubborn," Thomas mocked, "will he be sent to the Tower?"

She had smiled—it was a little contented, catlike smile—and she had turned over in the bed so that she was lying face downward, using her forearms as a pillow, looking at him with that worldly expression which bore just a hint of aristocratic derision. "You don't understand, do you, my love? The magistrate will want to please. . . . Sometimes the requests are difficult, involving conscience or politics, but when it's easy . . ." Her eyes sparkled a little mischievously. "I mean who can object to Kingstons' customers' taking a glass of wine? Can anyone believe that Sloane Street will be crowded with helpless drunkards— like a Hogarth etching?"

She giggled—again like a girl in her teens. In fact, Thomas often thought that it was this combination in her of near-child and mature woman that had captivated him. Her help had been tremendous, intervening in his life as she had like a fairy godmother. The new capital provided by the Banbury Trust plus the gaining of Mrs. Fellowes' shop, coupled with the buoyant trading conditions, had transformed Kingstons' fortunes. Annual profits had soared, topping seventy thousand pounds a year, and Thomas had become a man of substance. But it was not just gratitude which made him respond to that smooth skin as though it were electrified. It was no sense of debt that made him flare like one of his Jablochkoff candles when she looked at him with those laughing violet eyes.

As he stood surveying his store that day he wondered if he thought of her too much, stirred as in his mind he saw her quite vividly, her arms outstretched to him, the nipples of those small white breasts already erect. He gave a shake to his head in an effort to block out the image, for Thomas liked his life in tidy compartments, and ten to seven in the morning was the time for directing his business.

He crossed the road, walked round the store to the staff entrance and took up his regular post on the stairs to watch his employees arriving for work. Then he went to his office.

Soon after he had sat down at his desk, Sidney Baines entered the room, carrying a bulky parcel.

"Good morning, Mr. Kingston," he said in his usual breezy manner. "I've got the proofs 'ere of the catalogue. Do you want to study them yourself or—"

"I most certainly do, Sidney," Thomas said. "Put them down on the table over there."

He stood and walked to the table while Baines stripped off the brown paper wrapping. This too was a new development for Kingstons, following its establishment as a unified store, for the dispatch section in the basement was now large enough to handle a sizable volume of sales through the post. It would, in fact, be the second issue of *Kingstons' Illustrated Catalogue and Price List*, although the first, the previous year, had been far smaller than the five-hundred-page volume now planned.

It was with some excitement that Thomas took up the top proof sheet, the title page, and read the words "Kingstons of Sloane Street has great pleasure in presenting its spring range of . . ." He was savoring the elaborate display lettering, in a design he had chosen himself, and was about to commend Baines on the layout when one of the clerks from the outer office entered the room and said, "Mr. Kingston, there's a Mr. Robert Ramsay inquiring if you can spare a few minutes to receive him. He says you know him, though it's some years since you last met."

At first Thomas could not recall who he was. Then slowly he realized, with sinking spirits, that his visitor was Bob, May's brother, who had gone to Australia. For a moment he wondered if he could refuse to see him; but he *was* his brother-in-law, and anyway it was better to know what he wanted. So he told the clerk to show him in and indicated to Baines that he should withdraw.

Bob did not display the brashness of their previous meeting. He stood hesitantly, almost apologetically, in the doorway, appearing highly respectable in a morning coat, wing collar and tie. The nearly fifteen years that had passed since their last meeting had left him with thinning hair that was partially gray, a deep tan and a heavily furrowed face. He was in his early thirties, but he looked a good deal older.

Bob glanced round the room appreciatively, nodding as he did so. "Your business has grown since I last saw it." His voice was marked by a slight accent that Thomas presumed was Australian. "You sell a bit more than Fancy Goods now, eh?"

Thomas stood up, his sense of courtesy overcoming his reluctance to rise, and indicated a chair. "How long have you been back from Australia?" he asked.

"Only a few weeks," Bob answered, sitting down awkwardly, his knees together, his weight forward.

"Presumably you haven't been to see May yet. At least, she hasn't mentioned it."

"Sister May," said Bob with a sudden smile. "How is she?"

"She's well."

"I hear you live in a mansion now."

"Hardly that," Thomas replied, "but it's comfortable."

"No," Bob went on, "I haven't called on her yet. I thought I'd wait until I was settled. I've been a problem to her so many times that I didn't want her to think I was round her neck again. . . . Bit of a young rascal, wasn't I? . . . Well, I've got a surprise for you, Mr. Kingston . . . I've come to pay you back the money you lent me."

And it *was* a surprise. Thomas could scarcely credit what he was witnessing as Bob took a wallet from his pocket, withdrew a ten-pound note and laid it on the desk in front of him. "Much appreciated, I can assure you," he said.

Thomas did not believe, of course, that his brother-in-law's action was as straightforward as it seemed. Every instinct told him that the reason Bob had called had nothing to do with the ten pounds.

"How was it in Australia?" he asked.

"Well, I didn't exactly make my fortune," Bob answered, "but I survived. I didn't stay long in Ballarat. That's a rough town, all right, real rough. . . . Sydney . . . that's where I was mostly. . . . Strangely, I ended up in your trade. Not retailing, but drapery. I joined a wholesale house. Not top-quality like you do, but not cheap either . . . middle market, you know."

"And why did you leave?" asked Thomas, adding with a note of hope, "Or are you just back for a spell?"

"Oh, things got difficult," Bob rejoined. "Everything depends on the rain there. Couple of years of drought and the whole economy goes up the spout . . . no trade . . . not anywhere . . . nobody's got any money. . . . Too up-and-down for me."

Thomas laid his clasped hands on the desk in front of him. "And what," he said after a moment, "are you doing now you're back?"

"Well," Bob answered cautiously, "as a matter of fact, I've joined a wholesale firm here . . . been promised a partnership if I do well. . . . Drapery, like I was in before . . . except the product's better . . . high-class, in fact. . . ." He paused, hoping that Thomas would respond, but when he did not do so, he went on, "The kind of quality you've got here in Kingstons. . . ." Once more he hesitated—and again had to continue without any help from Thomas: "In fact, I was hoping you might at least consider some of our stuff . . . only consider, mind you. . . . It's very fine . . . linens, velvets, silks . . . I mean I'm not asking a favor . . . I don't expect you to buy anything if it doesn't measure up. . . . Well, I suppose it wouldn't hurt to have a look at it, would it? . . . So that you can see for yourself, I mean. . . ."

He tailed off, and for a few seconds there was silence. "Don't we deal with your firm already?" Thomas asked at last.

"Apparently not."

"Why's that? Are they new?"

"Oh, they've been in business ten, fifteen years or so . . . something like that."

"Then surely they must have approached us, haven't they?"

Bob looked uncomfortable suddenly, as though he had not thought the discussion would take this course, even though Thomas' questions were surely predictable. "To tell you the truth, I'm not sure," Bob answered.

"If they've been dealing in quality materials for so long," Thomas persisted, "and we're substantial buyers of quality materials . . ."

"You'd expect it, wouldn't you?" Bob agreed, avoiding his eyes.

Very quietly Thomas asked, "Their name?" When Bob did not answer, he repeated his question a little louder: "I asked their name."

"Oh . . ." Bob gave a slight smile, then spoke very fast, slurring the first word. "Turner-and-Woodward's the name," he said.

It was not too fast for Thomas, and he knew it all then—at least, he thought he did. "Turner?" he repeated. "I've met Mr. Turner, haven't I?" Adding, when Bob hesitated, "Wasn't he once a buyer at Shoolbreds?"

"That's correct," said Bob.

"And a great embarrassment to May over a matter concerning yourself?"

"You remember, then . . ."

"And you've been sent here this morning to try your luck?" He shook his head. "Well, I'm sorry, Mr. Ramsay, I'll never deal with Turner. Never."

Bob stood up. "I won't waste any more of your time," he said. "I don't really blame you for taking this attitude. . . . I thought you might. . . . Arthur Stockton was certain you would."

"Stockton?" Thomas queried. "You know Stockton?"

Bob nodded. "He's our biggest competitor . . . a friendly rival, you could say. He told me I didn't stand a chance. . . . Known you for years, he said. Guided your early steps, he said."

"He did, did he?" Thomas rejoined grimly.

"Mind you, I think it's a pity to carry on these hard feelings," Bob went on. "After all, that unpleasant business happened years ago. And now you'd be dealing with me—with the family, so to speak; not with Turner at all. . . . At least, your buyer would. . . . Naturally, I wouldn't expect to deal with you personally . . . I quite realize you're too important now to actually buy goods yourself."

Thomas remained sitting at his desk for a moment. His instinct told him that there was something wrong with this whole interview. Turner must have suspected what his response would be. Bob's approach seemed oversimple. Thomas stood up. "Once bitten, Mr. Ramsay," he said. "I fear you've had a wasted journey." He walked round his desk to the door and held it open.

"Perhaps in due course I can persuade you to see things differently," said Bob.

"You won't," Thomas insisted. "Not that firm. . . . In fact, in view of Turner's behavior to your sister, I'm rather surprised that *you've* joined them."

"Oh, I'm not as fortunate as you," said Bob, and Thomas noted a new tone in his voice. "I can't pick and choose who I deal with . . . not in my position. . . ." He gave a wry little smile. "I hear you've got some very grand friends now. . . . Well, I suppose that's only to be expected, isn't it?—now that you're living in the style you do. . . . Even the Banbury family—unless I'm misinformed, that is—and you can't get much higher up the tree than that, can you? . . . I hear you're very close to her Ladyship, again unless I'm misinformed . . ." He hesitated for a pause so brief that it was barely noticeable. ". . . you and May I mean, of course . . ."

Suddenly, he held out his hand. "Well, goodbye. . . . I hope you change your mind. . . . I know you say you won't, but I'm not giving up hope. . . . Remember me to my sister, won't you?"

He went into the outer office, and Thomas closed the door behind him. For a few seconds he stayed standing with his back against it, thinking of what Bob had said. He suspected now why his brother-in-law had come to see him, and he knew he would return.

· 2 ·

That afternoon, May took the carriage to attend a meeting of the NSWS at the Wainwrights' home in Kensington. She saw a lot of them now, since after she had learned from Emily that Philip had left

London to live in Paris, she had joined the Society. Until then, she had not gone near them.

At first she had tried to persuade herself that there were other reasons why she should sever all contact with this unusual family whom she found so appealing; but on the morning following that restless evening before Thomas returned when she had boycotted the NSWS planning meeting with such difficulty, she had faced the unpalatable truth. She had sat in front of her dressing table and studied herself—her eyes, her lips—as though they were those of another woman and conceded that though she hardly knew him, Philip Wainwright had released in her emotions of a nature she had never experienced before. He had only to look at her with that expression of concern and she would feel an immediate response to him, a sudden ache in her belly, an involuntary movement of muscles, like a flower opening to the sun.

It had taken an enormous effort to admit to herself that the turmoil he was able to provoke in her body was desire—desire of a strength and character that she had always believed to be known only by men. For she did not love Philip. What she felt for him was no yearning of the soul. Somehow he had touched a basic nerve in her that, when she was with him, made her want him with this terrifying and urgent hunger that seemed totally shocking in a woman—especially a woman in her position as a matron, wife and mother.

So she had run for cover and stayed quite still, unmoving, barely breathing, like one of Thomas' foxes when hounds were close, refusing all invitations from the Wainwright household.

The following year, after she had learned that Philip had gone to study political theory in Paris, she had attended another meeting of the NSWS, going alone since it was in the afternoon. Both Stella and Mrs. Wainwright had greeted her with warm enthusiasm, invited her home as usual, and once more she had become captured by the movement—and even played a minor part in it.

At first she had not mentioned this to Thomas, fearing it would displease him, but at last she had been asked to speak from the platform and she knew she could keep it from him no longer. As she had expected, he was angered by her secrecy, though she had never actually lied to him. "I don't understand why you kept it from me," he had said.

"I wasn't sure you'd approve," she had explained.

"That'd seem to be a reason for disclosure—not concealment. And why shouldn't I approve? These Wainwrights are clearly respectable people . . ."

"I didn't mean the Wainwrights—I meant the movement."

"This woman suffrage?" He gave a little smile of condescension. "I find it a little absurd, but . . . well, I can't see any harm in it if it interests you."

"Why's it absurd?" she had snapped.

He had been taken aback by her sudden anger. "Because," he replied calmly, "women aren't suited to politics. . . . It's a dirty business, May. . . . Parliament's no place for a woman."

"You're not being honest, Thomas," she had said. "With yourself, I mean. It's not just Parliament . . . it's anywhere that thinking is required. . . . Why shouldn't a woman be a doctor? or form a political view? or argue a case in court? or even direct a business, as Emily could? Are you suggesting that all women are more stupid than all men?"

Thomas was amazed by her passion. "I'd no idea you felt this strongly about it," he said, "and if it's these Wainwrights who are responsible for the change in you, then perhaps, as you say, I wouldn't approve of them."

However, he had not asked her to abandon either the Wainwrights or the movement. He did not see himself as a paternalist tyrant. He was directing a business that was reflecting the great changes in progress in society—especially those which concerned women. The "New Woman," who played sport; who smoked, even; who read progressive novels, was much spoken of, if she did not yet form a substantial segment of Kingstons' customers. Also, woman suffrage had attracted some sympathy in the press, although the problems related to it were seen as being too formidable for hasty action. In short, a wife who was a member of the NSWS was not entirely unfashionable.

On the platform, May had not displayed the fiery eloquence of Millicent Fawcett or Stella Wainwright, but she had played a role as a secondary speaker, providing a useful contrast to the more dramatic orators. Also, her down-to-earth common sense had been welcomed on the committee, for she had the practical experience, which hardly any of the others had, of earning her own living.

That afternoon, there were a lot more people in the Wainwrights' drawing room than May had expected—both standing in groups and sitting, with teacups and plates balanced on their knees. "Bit of a crowd today," said Mrs. Wainwright as she greeted her, "but there's an excellent reason. Next month Mr. Woodall's going to present an amendment for us to the Representation of the People Act in the House of Commons. . . . Have you met Mr. Woodall?"

"I don't think so," May replied.

"Then I must introduce you at once," she said, leading her to a man of about forty-five, with spectacles and a neatly barbered iron-gray beard, who was sitting on a sofa. "You must tell Mrs. Kingston all about your plans for the debate," she said.

"I expect you're acquainted with the reform legislation that Mr. Gladstone's introducing," he said as the maid brought May a cup of tea and a plate, and offered her a cucumber sandwich.

"The main design, I think," she said. "It's to extend the vote to all householders, isn't it? Male householders, that is."

"That's correct," he agreed—"broadly correct, anyhow. Well, I'm proposing an amendment moving that it should be extended to include all women householders as well. . . . What I want to do in my speech is to eliminate the arguments against the suffrage for women. . . . The usual one, of course, is that women are emotional." He smiled. "As if men were never emotional. . . . Then there's the theory that their place is in the home. . . . There's a further strange argument that the franchise should be denied to them since they cannot serve in the armed forces, though personally I . . ."

But she was no longer hearing him, for she had just caught sight of Philip Wainwright standing in the doorway. His eyes met hers, and he smiled. Immediately, she experienced the sharp contraction deep within her that she now recognized, with all its humiliation, for what it was. Her heart began to thump, and then, to her horror, she realized she was blushing like a young girl. Her hands began to tremble . . . and suddenly she spilled her tea over her dress and, in the confusion that followed, dropped her plate on the floor.

He was beside her immediately, on one knee, retrieving the cup and the saucer and the spoon and the plate and the half-eaten cucumber sandwich. "How good it is to see you here," he said. "I hear you're doing sterling work for the society."

She looked at him in anguish, caught up in a kind of claustrophobic panic, and wished with such desperate fervency that he had not returned that she almost uttered the words aloud. Instead, she swallowed and asked in a light, uncertain voice that did not sound like hers at all, "Will you be in London long?"

"For several weeks," he answered. "I hope I may be permitted to call on you."

She did not reply to his question. "I'm sorry," she said, "you'll have to excuse me. I have a fearful headache suddenly. If you'll forgive me, I think I'll take the carriage home."

· 3 ·

Thomas stood waiting at the window of the bedroom of the small house in Sydney Street. A hansom was moving slowly up the road, and for a few seconds he thought nothing of it. Then it began to seem vaguely familiar. A cab had, in fact, been passing when he himself had arrived at the house a few minutes before. He had not taken much notice of it, but now he wondered if that horse too had not been a chestnut, if that gray-bearded cabby too had not worn a bowler and sat hunched over the reins with so marked a bend in his back.

Now, as he watched it, the hansom came to a halt, but the passenger, if there was one, did not alight. Perhaps, Thomas wondered, he was looking through the window in the rear of the vehicle at something farther back along Sydney Street that Thomas, with his limited vision within the house, could not see. Within seconds, her carriage drew up below him in front of the house. She stepped down onto the pavement, and almost immediately—but not before whoever was interested had been able to obtain a clear view of her—the cab moved off. Thomas heard her knock on the front door, followed by her greeting of Mrs. Deneuve. He opened the door of the bedroom and stood on the landing at the head of the stairs as she climbed them— looking radiant. She leaped the last two steps and ran into his open arms, pressing the side of her face against his chest, whispering, "Thomas . . . oh, Thomas . . ." She did this always. It was as though she needed a few seconds to renew her sense of his presence, to feel the security of his body. Then she raised her mouth to him and he kissed her.

He led her into their sitting room and offered her a glass of wine, which she accepted. They always did this too for a few minutes, the exact period depending on their mood, to get accustomed to each other again—to peel off, as she had once described it, their other lives. For although there were advantages to being a countess, there were certain difficulties that faced a lady of rank who wished one aspect of her life to remain a secret.

Mrs. Deneuve, who owned the house, had provided at least part of the solution. She had been making clothes for Eve for some years, so visits to her house were an established pattern. She was a friendly Parisian woman in her mid-forties with whom Eve, during long fittings, had developed a relationship that, if it was not exactly intimate, had approached the edges of it at times—enough, at any rate, for her to decide, when Thomas came into her life with the problem of where they could be alone together, to seek her help. As Eve had suspected, lovers were not outside Mrs. Deneuve's experience, and though she urged great caution, she was a willing and trustworthy conspirator. She allocated to them two rooms on the first floor in which Eve took tremendous delight, nesting in them, as Thomas teased her, like a bird. At first this took the form of just a few personal furnishings—a lamp, a rug, some cushions. Then as the "refuge" became more important to her, she had felt the need to make it totally hers. She had the rooms completely refurnished, in particular ordering a large new bed with a rich red velvet counterpane. On the wall of the bedroom she hung a large Louis XIV mirror in a gilded frame. She bought paintings that she felt conformed with the mood of their "home," including one by an artist named Pierre-Auguste Renoir of a strange new school of painters in Paris that was mocked by most people, including Thomas, because their pictures portrayed an unclear, fuzzy "impression," which was the description they used themselves. But Eve insisted that Renoir painted women in a way she felt she was—"Am I always as clearly delineated as a deer on a mountain at sunset?" she demanded sharply—and Thomas conceded with good enough grace.

She made him accompany her to have their "photographs" taken in a studio that had just been installed near Piccadilly to offer to the public the services of this remarkable invention and hung the pictures in the most prominent place on the wall of their sitting room. "I know what you're thinking," she had said as they left the studio, "and you shouldn't be. Since we have so little precious time together, you should be thinking of me."

"What am I thinking?" he asked.

"Of establishing a photographic studio in Kingstons, of course," she answered, and he had laughed, because she had been completely correct.

She had spent hours needlepointing their joint initials onto the cushions and began to buy him presents: books, small objets d'art, clothes of a nature that he would not normally have—clothes that conformed with their "escape," which he could wear when they dined together at a small Sheraton table in their sitting room (Mrs. Deneuve was a superb cook) but would be unacceptable in most other situations. Sometimes they were joke clothes—ruffled shirts in outré colors which he would wear open at the neck, elaborate dressing gowns, smoking jackets in high-toned velvets. He responded, of course, and bought her beautiful negligees so that, as she said of one gown, laughing happily, "I feel like Marie Antoinette." But she also had a peasant-girl costume and a courtesan dress of black chiffon, so sheer that it concealed nothing, and once even dressed like a man. They played these games between their lovemakings, often giggling like children. "One of the many things I adore about you," she said once, "is the sense of elation you can induce in me. I feel at this minute as though I could fly."

"You make me sound like a glass of champagne," he teased.

"Oh, more than that," she insisted; "oh, much more than that."

Sometimes, of course, Thomas met her in public—usually at occasions at Grosvenor Square. Once May had gone with him to dinner there, and on another evening they had joined a party to the opera. May had invited them back, though Caroline Terrace had really been too small for this type of entertaining and she had been relieved when Eve had explained that they would be in Scotland on the date in question. May had asked them again when she and Thomas had moved to Cadogan Place, but once more Eve had thought it politic to decline.

More often, Thomas went on his own to Grosvenor Square, normally in the late afternoon when men of affairs, and often the Earl himself, would be present. She invited him partly because she thought it might be useful for him to meet people of influence but mainly because she wanted him to share one small aspect of her life.

However, although Eve adored the "refuge," she rebelled sometimes against the limits of their relationship. Once, in fact, she had refused to make love to him at all. "If divorce was socially acceptable," she had asked, "would you marry me?"

"What a question," he had said. "Why do you ask questions like that?"

"Answer it," she said. "Please . . ."

He knew the reply she wanted, but he could not give it to her. "Eve," he said, "you're with me every waking moment, even sitting beside me as I do my work. . . ."

"Answer the question," she insisted.

"May's been a very good and loyal wife for many years," he said. "She's been a fine mother to my children. Would you have me abandon her without a thought?"

"You mean you wouldn't?"

"Eve—" he began, but she cut him off: "Then what am I doing here? What are *you* doing here?" The question was so filled with pain that it was almost a scream.

Sometimes she could not resist asking him about the intimacies of the bedroom he knew with May, but he would never speak of it. Once a question had slipped from him about her relations with the Earl, and she had rounded on him sharply. "Those are our secret areas, aren't they, Thomas? Those are the parts we cannot share. . . ." Suddenly she had looked haggard, and Thomas had been shocked by the transformation of that lovely face. "No, they're not the only ones," she added bitterly. "There are so many parts we cannot share. It's like a jigsaw that's only half completed, with big gaps all over it."

Today, on this May afternoon, however, there was no hostility in her, no rebellion. She looked at him lovingly as she sipped her wine. Then suddenly a look of anguish came into her eyes. "Thomas," she asked, "what would you do if we had to part?"

For a moment, he wondered if something had happened to make her ask the question—something like Bob Ramsay's strange references to their friendship or an unknown observer in a hansom cab. "Do you know what I'd do?" she said. "I think I'd kill myself."

"No, you wouldn't," he said softly, smiling.

"I was thinking about it yesterday. I suddenly imagined it—the thought of never lying in your arms, of never feeling you within me, occupying me, possessing me, owning me. . . . Kiss me, Thomas. . . ."

He kissed her, but it was not enough. "Let's go next door," she said—"now."

She ran into the bedroom and began to undress with fingers that were so hurried that they made the process even slower. "They should make clothes for lovers," she exclaimed with frustration. "Clothes that can be undone easily. . . . Oh, I can't be bothered. . . . Take me as I am. . . . Tear them off me. . . ."

He laughed and helped her, unhooking her corset, loosening her petticoats and pantaloons. When she found it hard to unbutton her chemise, she asked, "Shall I leave this on?" And he shook his head and undid it for her, lifting it over her head. But when, as she stood there naked, he bent to kiss her, she drew him to the bed. "Please . . ." she said. "At once, Thomas, please . . ." And as she received him, she let out a great sigh and clung to him with desperation. "Thomas," she said, "you mustn't ever stop loving me. I'd die if you ever stopped loving me."

Afterward, she lay with her head on his shoulder, moving her hand slowly all over his body, exploring him. He had never known her in a mood such as this—so demanding, so fearful, so affectionate.

When the carriage returned to collect her they did not hear it, despite the noise it made. Mrs. Deneuve called up the stairs to tell them, and they dressed without saying much, in a mood that was strangely sad. "I hate the partings," she said. "I need to see you. I need the flaring light of being with you. But the partings are terrible." She looked at him suddenly. "I meant it when I spoke of what I'd do if it had to end."

"Don't think about it."

"What would *you* do, Thomas? You never said."

"I don't know."

"You wouldn't kill yourself?"

"No . . . I'd be desperately unhappy, but I wouldn't kill myself."

"Because of your store?"

He smiled at her anxiety. "Because of my store," he said to placate her. "You wouldn't kill yourself either. And I don't know why you're speaking of it, because I won't let it happen."

"You might not have the power to stop it."

"Why are you worrying so much? Has anything happened to . . ." He broke off.

"No," she answered, "I've just had a horrible feeling the last few days . . . anxiety . . . I don't know why . . . a premonition. . . . It made me realize how much I need you."

He put his arms round her, held her very tight and kissed her. "Stop fussing," he said gently.

She looked at him, her eyes anxious. Then she gave a little laugh. "You're right. I'm just being a little foolish." She kissed him again and then, leaving him in the room as she always did, she went downstairs.

From the window, he watched her leave the house. For a second, as she stood on the pavement, she looked up at him, smiled and waved —which, by agreement between them, she rarely did because of the presence of her servants. Then she stepped into the carriage. Thomas watched it move off and noted that the coachman had to swing out to pass the hansom which had returned and was waiting a little way up the road.

Thomas went down the stairs and knocked on the door of Mrs. Deneuve's sitting room. "Have you had any callers recently?" he asked her. "Anyone who struck you as strange?"

She thought for a moment. "Now you come to mention it," she said, "there was a man the other day . . . said he'd come from the gas company to check the pipes. . . . Gas is corrosive, he said . . . eats away at the pipes, makes holes eventually. . . ."

"What did he want exactly?"

"Just to see over the house, examine all the pipes. . . ."

"And you let him?"

Mrs. Deneuve was surprised by his question. "Well . . . yes. Was I wrong to do so?"

"He saw our rooms upstairs?" asked Thomas.

She nodded. "Every room in the house. Why—is there some trouble?"

"I'm not sure, Mrs. Deneuve. I shouldn't let anyone else in . . . not just for the moment."

"As you say, Mr. Kingston," she said.

When he left the house, the cab was still drawn up at the curb, so Thomas hailed it, as though it were on a rank. But the cabby did not appear to have heard him. Thomas started to walk toward it, hoping to catch a glimpse of whoever was inside, if anyone was, but as soon as he approached, it moved off up the street.

Thomas decided to walk back to the store, since he had so much on which to ponder. It was clear that someone had them under observation and had very probably gained access to their rooms—with all their ample evidence of his relationship with Eve. But who was behind it? Could it be the Earl, or even May? It did not seem possible. It was totally unlike her in character, and the Earl had received him most cordially only three days before in Grosvenor Square.

His thoughts centered on Bob Ramsay and his remark about Eve, with its strange innuendo, when he left the office that day. What was his reason for mentioning her? Was he guessing that it was more than an ordinary social contact, or did he have information? If so, who could have alerted him? Who knew? Mrs. Fellowes perhaps, but she was only guessing. Some of Eve's servants possibly, but their positions would depend on their discretion. And none of these, so far as he was aware, had any contact with Bob Ramsay.

Yet Bob knew about the Banburys—knew something, at least. He was close to the unsavory Turner and, it would seem, to Arthur Stockton, who was now an enemy. What about Stockton, then? Stockton placed great store on information, as a route to business opportunities. But how could Stockton know?

Then suddenly Thomas recalled an evening the previous year when, on leaving the Sydney Street house, he had suddenly encountered Hudson, the silk buyer he had dismissed for taking bribes from Stockton. It was one of the few occasions when he had left before Eve, had in fact waved to her as she looked down from the first-floor window. "Good evening, Mr. Kingston," Hudson had said to him. Thomas recalled his surprise at having been addressed. "Good evening, Hudson," he had said, and not wishing to converse with him further in view of the circumstances of his dismissal, he had walked on up the street.

Now, on this spring evening, as Thomas strode down the Kings Road toward Sloane Square, he wished he had talked more to Hudson on that occasion, for he might have learned something at least that could be of value to him now. There was no doubt he would have wondered what Thomas was doing in an area like Sydney Street and would probably have suspected he had a mistress there. Had he seen Eve at the window? Would he have recognized her if he had? On one fact there was little doubt: he would still have been in touch with Stockton, for he would have needed his help in gaining another position.

Thomas' anxiety was not eased when, on reaching the store, he saw that Bob Ramsay was sitting on a chair in the outer office, waiting patiently for his return.

He stood up when he saw Thomas, and his face creased into his usual easy grin. "I'm sorry to bother you again so soon," he began.

Thomas was in no mood to receive his brother-in-law. "My views of Turner haven't changed," he said sharply.

"Oh, I didn't expect them to change," responded Bob, "not like that . . . not without some reason. . . ."

"What reason," Thomas asked, "could possibly affect the issue?"

"That's what I've come to explain." He was idly turning his hat between his hands, slipping the brim through his fingers.

"I haven't time tonight," said Thomas.

"Well, I suppose I could return tomorrow," Bob answered, "but it'd be better tonight. . . . It'll only take a minute."

"I tell you"—Thomas was suddenly angry—"there's nothing that can make me change my mind."

"Oh, I think there is. . . ."

"Nothing," Thomas repeated forcefully. "Nothing."

"Do you want me to explain out here?" asked Bob, looking round slowly at the clerks at their desks. "Or in private?" He flashed Thomas another open smile. "In private'd be better, I think."

Thomas glared at him, then stalked into his room. Bob followed him and closed the door behind him.

· 4 ·

There are days in a person's life that are so important that they can be recalled, even many years later, in the smallest detail—days after which nothing is ever quite the same again. Wednesday, May 28, 1884, was such a day in May's life.

She had known, of course, ever since Thomas had told her that Bob had been to see him, that it was only a question of time before he would call. Even so, she was still unprepared for the moment when Brandon came into her room upstairs and told her that her brother was waiting in the hall. Her stomach lurched with that familiar spasm of fear. But why? she asked herself. Surely nothing he could do could affect her now—not in this big house, not with Thomas so prominent a man of business. But she was not certain. With Bob she could never be certain.

As she entered the drawing room, Bob was standing at the window, surveying the trees that were in bud, some even bearing early blossom, in the gardens of Cadogan Place. He turned as she came in, his face lighting up with pleasure at the sight of her. She knew the expression only too well—knew, too, that he deployed it with the same practiced ease as a professional actor. "Sister May!" he exclaimed, adding with soft wonder, "Just look what's happened to my sister May. Strike me dead if you're not the most elegant woman in London!"

He approached her and kissed her on the cheek. "You've picked up an accent," she said.

"It's those kangaroos," he said with a grin. "Very infectious."

She indicated a chair with her hand, and he sat down carefully, as though fearful of creasing the upholstery. She perched on the edge of a sofa, keeping a distance between them. "Would you take something?" she asked. "Coffee, perhaps?"

"No, thanks," he said. "I haven't long . . . a busy day ahead of me. . . . I was nearby, though . . . thought I'd call and say hallo after all this time, see how you were getting on. . . ."

He looked round the big, luxurious room with pointed approval. "I certainly never thought I'd ever see you in a home as grand as this. The last time we met you were a shop assistant." He gave one of his practiced smiles. "You've deserved it, though. You've been a good wife to Thomas."

They lapsed into silence, which she broke at last: "Thomas tells me you've started work in wholesale."

Bob nodded. "Did he tell you which firm?"

"Yes," she answered. "Yes, he did."

"Go on, say it," he challenged. "How can I work for a man who

attempted to sully my precious sister? What did he do, for heaven's
sake? Took you out to dinner . . ."

She felt her back stiffen instinctively. "You think to dine alone
with a man of such little consequence?" she asked. "He demanded
payment in kind from *me* to protect *you* from the police—then dismissed me without a reference."

He gave a pained shrug. "I didn't like it, May. . . . There wasn't
much choice, was there? It'd have been choky . . . and you did rather
ask for it, didn't you? Pouring wine over him like that . . ."

"He behaved disgustingly. What would you have had me do?"

Bob sighed. "I don't know, May. It's history now, isn't it? . . . He
was obsessed by you—that's what he told me. . . . Never happened to
him with any woman before, he said. . . . Well, when a man gets
obsessed by a woman he often does things he shouldn't. . . . He still
feels badly about it. That's why he's offered me this chance—and it's a
good chance . . . partnership . . . a way to get properly on my feet . . ."

"Provided you can get his merchandise into Kingstons?" said
May coldly. "Is that right?" This interview was a strange experience
for her—different from all her other times with Bob, presumably because her situation had changed so drastically. A great gulf divided
them now. She was a lady of quality, displaying the style that Thomas
commended. He was her wastrel brother.

"Into Kingstons . . . and other stores, of course," Bob agreed. He
too was conscious of the gulf, for he added, "You've got hard, May.
Should be the other way round . . . good fortune should make you
more charitable, especially to your blood relations. . . . I was hoping
you'd help me persuade Thomas . . ."

"He wouldn't listen to me."

"You could make him listen if you wanted to." He was speaking
very quietly, watching her intently. "But then, you don't want to, do
you?"

She hesitated before answering. "No," she said at last. "Not much.
If there's one man in the world I really dislike, it's Turner."

"Can't you forget Turner? It's me I'm asking you to help."

"And then," she went on, "I never interfere in Thomas' business.
. . . He'd resent it. . . . It wouldn't do any good, anyway. In fact, it'd do
the opposite, make him more determined."

Bob sighed heavily and stood up. He moved to the fireplace and,
for a moment, leaning one arm along the mantelpiece, he stared into
the flames. "Oh, May, I didn't want you to know the whole thing, but
I suppose you'll have to. . . ." He was speaking with his back toward

her. "I'm a desperate man, May, and I mean desperate. . . . Did Thomas tell you I went to see him last night?"

"No," she answered. Anxiety was tightening the muscles of her stomach.

"I didn't think he would," Bob said. He turned and leaned backward on the wall of the chimney breast, resting his elbows on the top of the mantelpiece. "You know about her Ladyship, I suppose. . . ."

"I beg your pardon," said May sharply.

"Wives usually know," he said. "They pretend they don't . . . even to themselves sometimes . . . but they know, all right. . . . I mean Lady Banbury, of course." His voice, though still quiet, was suddenly harsh.

"What about Lady Banbury?" asked May. She tried to keep her voice calm, though her heart was beating faster.

"She's Thomas' mistress . . . has been for years . . . and it's no surprise to you, so don't tell me it is."

May glared at her brother. "I think," she said, "you'd better leave."

"The only person who might be surprised," Bob went on as though he had not heard her, "is the Earl. In fact, I happen to know he'd be very shocked . . . worships her, apparently. . . . He'd divorce her, of course. . . ."

Her anger was of a kind she had never felt before—violent but utterly cold, and directed not at Thomas but at her brother, who was so brutally soiling her home, her life, her relationship with her husband.

"Will you please go at once," she insisted. "Or do I have to summon Brandon?"

"Not till we've settled it," he said.

"Settled what?"

"Surely it's obvious, May. Do I have to rub your nose in it? You've got to persuade Thomas—or I'm going to the Earl."

She looked at her brother with astonishment. "The Earl?" she repeated. "You think the Earl would receive you—or if he did, listen to gossip about his wife?"

"It's not gossip, May." He gave a short laugh. "It's fact; evidence, you might say, all sworn properly in affidavits . . . more than enough for his Lordship to bring action for divorce. . . . Every little detail . . ."

"What detail?" she asked. Afterward, she wondered why it became suddenly necessary to her to know so much.

"You don't really want to hear that, May. And what's the point? Just take my word for it and persuade Thomas?"

"What little detail?" she insisted. Her need to be told had become compulsive. A part of her was seeking, even demanding the pain that she knew the revelation would cause her.

"Why distress yourself, May?" he appealed.

"You've already distressed me beyond belief. What more can you do? Now tell me."

He shrugged his shoulders. "All right," he said a little wearily. "They've got rooms in a house in Sydney Street . . . home of a French dressmaker named Madame Deneuve. . . . There's a bed with a red velvet counterpane . . . and photographs of them both. . . . There are cushions with the letters 'T and E' sewn on them. . . . She keeps some clothes in the wardrobe, mostly negligees. Some of them too have her initials embroidered on them—'EB.' . . . Usually they meet in the late afternoon, though sometimes in the evening. On those occasions Madame Deneuve cooks a light meal for them and it's served at a small table, decorated with silver candelabra, in their sitting room. . . . There are books in a bookshelf. One of them is inscribed, 'To Thomas, who has given me life, who has found in me emotions I never knew I had, who has shown me love of a kind I never dreamed existed.' . . . Do you really want me to go on?"

She said nothing. She was sitting stiffly upright staring straight ahead of her. She was not even near tears, for tears are provoked by feelings and she had no feelings. She was devastated by this brutal trampling on her privacy, for it seemed to be *her* privacy even though she had been no part of it. It was a kind of rape, a forced entry into the most intimate area of her. In Bob's relentless description she had suddenly seen a vivid image of Thomas, her husband, with another woman in a setting of red velvet. It was like having an arm blown off, as soldiers must feel when wounded in battle—an enormous sense of shock, but not much pain. The pain came later, as she knew hers would, but meanwhile her mind was concentrated on the danger her brother represented, the threat he posed of scandal, and quite apart from the ruin it would bring, what that scandal would mean: the ugly exposure of her privacy, her rape, to the public gaze. The one thought in her mind that transcended everything else at that moment was that somehow he must be stopped.

Bob was shocked by the effect on her of his words. "Sister May," he said, "I didn't want to . . . I hoped you could have been kept out of it—which you could if only he'd been reasonable. . . ."

"Thomas refused to listen, I suppose." Her voice was metallic, but dull, with no ring in it.

"It wasn't wise of him," Bob went on. "It'll destroy him. . . . Does he seriously want that, May? Do you think all his elegant customers will continue to give their patronage to the subject of a divorce scandal?" He paused. "Do you think he'll still be able to afford this house, May, your servants, your carriage . . . ?"

She looked at him with pity. "And you didn't want to hurt your sister May?"

"I've told you, I'm desperate. I was forced to tell you. . . . Now you've got to use your influence. You've no choice. . . . It's not as though I was asking a lot. . . . It'd all be so easy for him. . . ."

May stood up and walked slowly to the window. For a few seconds she watched a sparrow, sitting on a branch of a tree, chirping at the day. "What exactly do you want?" she asked.

"Just two things," he said, holding up his hands and counting the items off on the fingers of one of them. "One—a lifting of the embargo on Turner and Woodward materials. That's all. So his buyers can stock them if they choose. Two—a loan of a couple of thousand pounds. That's to buy my share of the business, my partnership. Not a gift, but a loan . . . I'll repay it from the proceeds. . . . A couple of thousand to Thomas is nothing. . . . Now, that's not much to ask from a brother-in-law, is it?"

For a few seconds she remained silent, looking at the bird. "And you've done all this . . . just for that?" she said.

"May, I tried a direct approach first, but he wouldn't listen."

"You've trampled through our life like a rogue elephant for so paltry a cause?"

"It seemed the only way. They told me about her Ladyship, of course. Surefire, they said."

"They?" she queried.

"Turner and Stockton."

"How did they know about her?" May asked, her voice toneless. Why had she asked the question? What did it matter how they knew?

"Some buyer Thomas sacked for taking bribes."

"Hudson?" she queried.

"That sounds like the name," he said. "He knows her, used to serve her with silks when he was with Debenhams . . . went to her house sometimes. . . . He's got it in for Thomas, of course. . . . Well, they all have."

"And you too," she said, turning to face him, "though he's never harmed you. As for me, well, I'd have thought, after all I've done for you, that you owed me just a little more than . . . than the prospect of disaster. . . ."

Bob averted his eyes, and she noted that his fists were clenched.

"May, you just have to persuade him. . . . Otherwise . . . well, it's not just me . . ."

"You'll gain nothing from going to the Earl," she said; "nothing from a divorce scandal. . . . The only value to you can lie in the threat—and you've shot that bolt already."

She saw the anger rise in his eyes again. "Listen, May, I'm deadly serious. I'm going to send the Earl the evidence in bits—paper by paper. Not all of them are conclusive . . . after all, Madame Deneuve's been her dressmaker for years . . . but every document's enough to make a husband suspicious. . . . I'll send the most innocuous ones first, so Thomas'll have time to change his mind. . . ."

She stared at him, hating him totally for the first time in her life. "I warn you," she said, "if you go near the Earl—if you send him a single paper—you'll have in me the most determined enemy you've ever imagined. . . . I mean it, Bob. I'll hound you for the rest of your life."

For a moment, he looked at her with no expression on his face. Then he laughed. "Threats, Sister May?" He shook his head in mock rebuke. "Now, Nanny wouldn't like that, would she?" His tone became serious, cold. "I'm not counting on your help any longer, May. In fact, it's soon going to be you who'll need the help if you don't persuade your husband to become more sensible. Good morning to you, May."

He gave an elaborate little bow and walked out of the room.

· 5 ·

Thomas stood in the Furs Department, turning slowly, his eyes absorbing every detail of the rich skins on the rails, of the stock cupboards, of the counter, even of the carpet—and finally of the assistants. One part of him was alert for dust, for untidiness, for poor display, for any sign that his standards were not being maintained; the other side of him was enjoying the luxury, relishing the sight of a customer trying on one of his sable stoles, nestling her cheek into the soft fur on her shoulder as she looked at her reflection in the mirror.

Thomas nodded approvingly to the buyer and moved on into the dresses, acutely conscious of the deep anxiety that now lay just beneath the surface of the pleasure he always gained from his daily round of the store. He had wondered once or twice, since his meeting with May's brother the previous night, whether he had in fact been wise to refuse all discussion on the subject of Eve. At the time, every instinct within him had made him reject blackmail. Even now, when he had had time to think about it, he knew that decision at least was right— especially after Bob had made it clear that both Turner and Stockton were party to the outrageous investigations that had been conducted into his private life in Sydney Street. For the demands from those two rogues would have been endless.

"Out!" Thomas had demanded. "Out of my office at once!" And when Bob had insisted, "You don't understand, Mr. Kingston, your position is—" Thomas had pounded his desk with his fist, shouting, "Out, Mr. Ramsay! Out! If you ever enter this store again, I'll have you thrown into the street!"

It was not his refusal to bow to Bob's pressure that Thomas was now questioning. It was his tactics. Should he not have talked to him; even suggested he would consider the proposition in order to gain time to think?

There was no doubt in Thomas' mind about the reality of the threat. The damage that would be caused by a divorce scandal would be immense. Eve, at present one of the most prominent hostesses in London, would become a social pariah, unwelcome in any home of standing. The impact on Kingstons, with its managing director so tarnished, would be devastating. In fact, Thomas' first reaction as he walked home after his brief and terrible scene with Bob was despair. He could see no way of avoiding disaster. Then, during that long restless night, he had begun to think in more practical terms. What would Ramsay do first? Would he go and see Eve and try to obtain from her the two thousand pounds, even seek her help in persuading Thomas to stock Turner and Woodward merchandise? Would he go to May? Thomas hoped so much he would not go to May.

By his morning round of the store that day, Thomas had not made up his mind on the action he should take. It was the kind of deep crisis to which he often reacted with indecision, with the hope that his Fates would intervene.

He was deep in thought as he walked into the new restaurant— and so preoccupied that he did not at once hear Lillian speak his name as he passed her table. He did stop, though, to survey the room, with its elaborate wall decoration (flying angels in gold on a pink ground) and its clientele of fashionable ladies—his "guests," as he called them. He heard Lillian the second time and turned to find her sitting alone. "Do you have a moment for a cup of coffee, Thomas?" she asked.

"Good morning, Lillian," he said. "I didn't see you." He consulted his pocket watch. "I've five minutes." He sat down and signaled to a waitress to serve him, then smiled at her. "How are you all?"

The bitterness caused by the betrayal of the Rawlingses in the stock battle had eased now. The defeat of Goldsmith, with the help of the Banbury Trust, had left the family in a position that was awkwardly exposed. David had reacted by withdrawing more from the business and now visited his office in the store only once or twice a week. He was still secretary of the company in title, but a young accountant, who had been hired as his assistant, did virtually all the work. David attended board meetings, but seldom contributed much to them, his mind clearly preoccupied with his interest in church affairs.

As always, Lillian had recognized the facts of the new situation and had done her best to repair her relations with Thomas. He had not made the task hard for her, had demanded no apologies—which May had argued angrily was the least he could expect. "There's no point in exacting penance," he had answered. "David's still an important shareholder. All I want is his goodwill—which, of course, means hers." So he had been courteous to her, even occasionally allowing her to make remarks that were close in character to the flirtatious comments that had marked their relationship in years past. Neither was fooled by the other, of course, but their truce made their coexistence more pleasant.

"I hear your boys helped Charles out of a scrape the other day," she said.

"So I understand," Thomas answered.

"It touched him."

"They said he'd have done the same for them."

She thought for a moment. "He probably would. I've often felt it was a pity that they weren't friends—especially since they're going to work together . . . here in the store I mean. . . ." She paused before adding carefully, "Aren't they?"

Thomas laughed, realizing her fear that her own actions might have negated his promise to her. "If he wants it," he said.

"That wasn't why I stopped you, Thomas," she said. "I'm worried about David—about his latest enthusiasm."

"You mean at the church?"

"It's not just the church. . . . You know of the movement against vice in London, against the people who run these . . . well, these establishments?"

"I didn't know David was involved with that."

"It's more than an involvement . . . it's become a passion. . . . He's got very close to Bramwell Booth—you know, of the Salvation Army.

The Booths run homes for these women . . . well, girls, really . . . some of them are very young. . . . In fact, it was a girl of only thirteen who decided Bramwell that he must do it. They found her sitting on the doorstep of his office when they came to work."

"Surely this is a worthy cause," suggested Thomas.

"Oh, it is," she agreed. For a moment she hesitated, looking suddenly drawn. "It's not the cause that's worrying me, it's David's response to the cause. . . . He spends hours in the Army's homes talking to these women," she went on, but the expression on Thomas' face still indicated he did not understand her anxiety. "Don't you see, Thomas? It's not just a question of good works, of charity. . . . He's obsessed. When he comes home he doesn't speak for hours. . . . His eyes shine. . . . I think it excites him in a way it shouldn't, and . . ."

She broke off, leaving Thomas astonished at this new glimpse of his partner. "I don't know what to advise you, Lillian," he said. "Should you perhaps talk to your doctor?"

"Oh, no . . . I wouldn't know how to put it into words. . . . Thomas, this isn't just my personal problem; it concerns you too."

"Me?" queried Thomas with amazement.

"Well, Kingstons. . . . This campaign against vice is growing all the time. There are all sorts of groups involved, as well as the Salvation Army. There's Mrs. Josephine Butler and her association against legalizing prostitution . . . that's got an enormous following. . . . And the Quakers—the Society of Friends . . . and the suffragists and—"

"The suffragists?" queried Thomas, alarmed because of May's association with them. "Are they involved with this?"

"Of course they are. . . . There's going to be a big battle, Thomas, for they're ranged against powerful interests. Only recently they tried to prosecute the owner of one of those places . . . a creature named Mrs. Jeffries, with eminent clients—you know, aristocrats, judges, civil servants. . . . The case failed. . . . There was intervention, I gather, from the Lord Chancellor. . . . But don't think they've accepted defeat. It's merely whetted their appetite. . . ."

Thomas shook his head with concern, but Lillian could see that he still regarded it as an issue that was remote. "Don't you see, Thomas? It's bound to end in scandal. That's what they want, of course, the Booth family and the others . . . a scandal. . . . That's the only way anything's going to be changed."

"You mean David could be involved in that scandal?"

"He's right up there in the front rank. . . ."

"And because he's a director of Kingstons . . . ?"

"Well, there's sure to be publicity, but it's the form it might take that worries me, Thomas. . . . You see, he's not a determined campaigner like they all are. He wouldn't be calculating his openings, planning his moves, assessing results . . . He's personally obsessed. . . . When he stays with these poor girls, he thinks he's exorcising the Devil. . . ."

At last it dawned on Thomas what she was trying to tell him. It was not just a question of publicity of a type that many of his customers would think unsuitable. His store could be made to look ridiculous.

"I'm warning you so that you're prepared," she said. "David might not be mentioned, of course . . . the main attention'll be on the Booths and Mrs. Butler. . . . But it's as well you should know. . . . Now I mustn't keep you any longer." And she smiled at him with an expression of affection in her eyes that had not been present for many years.

·6·

May had never seen Sidney Baines so embarrassed. His face was puce. He stood in her drawing room, his hands clasped in front of him, his fingers flexing against each other in agitation. As he tried to answer her questions, he stuttered.

"Why don't you sit down, as I suggested?" she said.

"I'd rather stand, Mrs. Kingston . . . if you don't mind."

"Then have a glass of brandy."

"No, I think not," he said, then changed his mind. "Well, perhaps . . . a small one . . ."

She went to fetch it herself from the dining room, preferring this to summoning Brandon, because it would take less time; for she was desperately eager to know the reason for his acute anxiety. She was sure it concerned Bob, because after her appalling scene with her brother she had decided to seek Sidney's help—without, of course, giving him any details. "It's best that no one—not even you, Sidney—should know the hold this man has obtained on my husband. It's hard, too, for me to admit that he's my brother. Nevertheless, he's a huge danger to us all, and he's got to be stopped, Sidney. At this moment, I don't know how, but I suspect that, being the kind of blackguard he is, there'll be aspects of his life that wouldn't stand investigation. Turner too is a rogue. Also, Arthur Stockton may be involved—and *you* know Stockton better than I do."

For a few seconds Baines had looked bewildered. Then his face had brightened. "You mean, Mrs. Kingston, if we could find some way of blackmailing *him* . . ."

She had nodded. "It's drastic, I know, but the situation's drastic. Would you be prepared to turn sleuth, Sidney? After all, Turner and Woodward are in the trade. You must be acquainted with people who know them, and I doubt if their reputation is savory. . . ." She paused. The perplexed expression had returned to his face. "It's a lot to ask, I know, Sidney," she pleaded gently, "but you'll have my deepest gratitude."

Suddenly he had smiled. "I'll do my best, Mrs. Kingston," he said, "though I can't promise I'll achieve anything."

Two days had passed since that short delicate interview—long, anxious days that had seemed to last forever. Thomas, of course, was utterly preoccupied, sitting silently in his chair in the evening, his face drawn. During the nights he had slept little, turning over in bed repeatedly, even getting up at one moment and going downstairs to pace up and down the floor of his study. They did not speak of it, of course. She did not even ask the reason for his worry. During those anxious hours, she felt little resentment of him. Later, she had wondered what her response would have been had there been no threat, had she discovered those vivid details by chance, by a carelessly mislaid letter. Would she have vowed to leave home? Would she have attacked him physically in a jealous rage? Would she have been goaded into repeated hysterics? She did not know. As it was, because their whole security was menaced, the impact was reduced. She felt like a woman living in a village under military attack in which issues of marital infidelity might seem less important than the imminent possibilities of death. Also, she felt oddly removed from the situation, as though it was someone else entirely who was involved.

Her impatience, however, was hard for her to contain. By the second day, when she had heard nothing from Baines, it had grown to an extent that was barely controllable. She was, in fact, considering going to the store in the hope she might encounter Sidney alone when Brandon had come in to report that he was waiting in the hall.

She took the glass of brandy into the drawing room and handed it to Baines. "Now have a good sip," she said, "and tell me why you're in such a state." She waited while he gulped the brandy. "Now, then?"

"It's very difficult . . ."

"Well, do you have any news for me?"

He nodded, took another big sip of brandy. "Yes, Mrs. Kingston. . . ."

"Then why don't you tell me what it is?"

He hesitated. "Mrs. Kingston . . . it's highly delicate. . . ."

May was growing angry with frustration. "This has got to stop, Sidney. Now, out with it. Is it to do with stealing . . . fraud . . . some other kind of crime?"

Again he drank—this time a large gulp, which made his high complexion even redder in hue. "It is, Mrs. Kingston . . . but not that sort. . . ."

"What sort, then?"

"I've never spoken of such a subject to a lady, Mrs. Kingston. . . ."

"Are you afraid of shocking me, Sidney? You can't shock me, I promise you, and even if you do it'll be all to the good because whatever you've found out will have greater value. . . . It's to do with women, I presume. Is he procuring? It can't be rape, surely. . . ."

"Not women, Mrs. Kingston. . . ."

"Well, what, then? Sidney, will you please tell me what you know before I strike you?"

He looked into his glass as he went on. "Well, Mrs. Kingston, I fear there are some men whose tastes . . . that is, that sort of taste . . . are not confined to the female sex. . . ."

"You mean . . . you mean boys?" she queried.

He nodded. "More or less . . . that kind of thing. . . ."

Suddenly her spirits rose. "Can you prove that, Sidney?"

He nodded again.

"But that's what we need!" she exclaimed. "It's a criminal act, isn't it? Tell me what happened."

"Well . . ." he began. "Yesterday I was down in the City not far from Whitechapel Lane . . . that's where their offices are, Turner and Woodward. . . . I'd made some inquiries, and as you'd surmised, their reputation's not good. There's even talk of receiving stolen goods. . . . I think I will sit down now, if I may. . . ."

He sat on the edge of a chair, resting his glass on his knee. He was more relaxed now that he had embarked on the story. "Anyway, I thought I'd call on them. I don't know what I thought I'd find. I suppose I 'oped I might get some kind of a clue, some avenue for further investigation. It'd crossed my mind we might employ a detective. . . . It was nearly six o'clock when I got there . . . and as I approached the building where the office is, I saw 'im coming out of the entrance . . . your brother, I mean. I've seen 'im, of course, at the store when 'e's been to see Mr. Kingston. . . ."

Baines took another sip of his brandy. "Well 'e 'ailed a cab . . . so I 'ailed one too and followed 'im. . . . 'E drove to a public house just off the Strand . . . The Crown, it's called, and I 'eard afterwards that it's well known for it—and for artistic people. . . . Well, of course, a lot of them are 'so' too, aren't they?"

"So?" May queried.

"That's what they call it . . . these people . . . 'So.' . . . It was obvious, of course, as soon as I got inside the place . . . the manner in which they talk and be'ave . . . the way they look—elaborate curly 'air . . . clothes in bright colors . . . some of them 'ad cosmetics on their faces . . . You wouldn't believe it, would you?"

"Go on, Sidney," she urged.

"Then we 'ad a stroke of luck, Mrs. Kingston, if that's what you'd call it. . . . Your brother 'ad gone there to meet a young man who was waiting for 'im. . . . At first I didn't recognize 'im. 'E was done up a bit, with 'is long fair 'air on his shoulders. Then I realized I'd worked with 'im . . . in my first job when I was an apprentice before I came to Kingstons. 'E was a bit 'so' even then. . . . Funny name 'e 'ad, too . . . Blackthorn . . . Terence Blackthorn. . . . But the point is, Mrs. Kingston, that while I stood there watching from a distance, they 'ad the most terrible quarrel. Your brother, it'd appear, 'ad broken off the . . . the, er . . . well, whatever it was between them . . . and Blackthorn was creating . . . like a woman almost, 'e was . . . tears . . . bitter reproaches . . . pleading . . . At one moment I thought 'e was going to scratch 'is face. . . . Then your brother just stalked off out of the pub, and Blackthorn collapsed . . . well, not literally—but 'e sat down . . . 'e was in an awful state . . ."

Sidney broke off for a moment and sipped from his glass, a thoughtful expression on his face.

"You said you had proof," May prompted.

"I 'ave, Mrs. Kingston, I 'ave. . . . Well, after your brother left, I went up to Blackthorn and reminded 'im of the old days and offered 'im a strong drink, which 'e certainly needed. . . . 'E was screaming for vengeance, of course, so I offered 'im the opportunity. 'E was desperately short of money, too. . . . That was due to Mr. Ramsay as well. . . . I gave 'im quite a lot—a tenner. . . . I 'ope that was all right. . . ."

"Of course," said May.

"But not until we'd got it all in writing back at 'is room . . . you know what I mean . . . what they did together . . . the criminal acts . . ."

"You mean you've got an affidavit, a legal document?"

"I wouldn't say 'ow legal it was . . . I'm no lawyer, of course . . . but I got 'is landlord to witness 'is signature on it. I'd say it'd be enough for the police to act. . . . Not that you'll take it to them. You

won't 'ave to; it's being able to that matters. . . . That's what I told
Blackthorn, because, of course, 'e could be prosecuted too. . . . But I
wouldn't think your brother'd want to risk prison, would 'e? . . . I told
Blackthorn there'd be another tenner in it later."

Baines took from his pocket a folded sheet of paper and handed it
to her. " 'Ere it is, for what it's worth. . . . I'd prefer you not to read it,
Mrs. Kingston, not since you're a lady. I didn't want there to be any
doubt about the facts, so I made 'im write it down in very plain words
. . . but it'll serve your purpose, I think."

May was overwhelmed. "Sidney," she declared, "you're wonderful. I'll never forget it. I wish I could tell Mr. Kingston what you've
done for him . . . but of course, I can't do that."

"That's all right, Mrs. Kingston. I understand. I'm glad I've been
able to 'elp—I only 'ope it works. Now I'd better be going . . . or Mr.
Kingston'll want to know where I've been."

· 7 ·

A few hours later, May sat at the escritoire in her little writing
room, unable to keep her eyes from the thick, creased envelope containing the affidavits of Thomas' liaison, which Bob Ramsay—following her summons—had just left with her. At first, of course, he
thought that May had sent for him in order to surrender. As Brandon
had shown him into the room, there had been a swagger in the way he
carried himself. His face had borne the usual twisted smile.

She had wasted no time, using the fewest possible words, feeling a
strange contamination in his presence that made even talking to him
distasteful. "Those are your affidavits?" she had asked, referring to the
package he carried under his arm.

"That's right, Sister May," he had said, grinning.

"I'm just going to show you one document," she had gone on
calmly, "which is enough to send you to prison. Then I want you to
go, leaving behind you those affidavits."

"Now, Sister May—" he had begun.

"*LOOK!*" She had rapped out the word loudly, cutting him off in
mid-sentence as she had thrust Blackthorn's statement at him. And he
had looked, the color draining from his cheeks as he read the bare,
obscene description of his couplings with his former lover. "By God,
you're a quiet one!" he had said. "I'd never have believed it. How in
the world did you get this?" She knew his mind was racing, searching

desperately for an avenue of escape—and saw the expression of sudden relief when he thought he had found a straw of hope. "It incriminates him too, doesn't it?" he had declared, his eyes brightening. "He'd go to jail too, wouldn't he?" Already he was smiling again. "Didn't think of that, did he? Always was a bit silly in the head, was Terence . . . always did seem to . . ." His words tailed off as May shrugged, indicating that Blackthorn's predicament was irrelevant to her. The uncertainty returned to his eyes, for he had never seen her like this—coldly, ruthlessly determined. The sister who had retrieved him from all those escapades when he was a youth was now an enemy, implacable, utterly without emotion. "A proper tigress, eh?" he said. "That's what you've become, isn't it, May? . . . Claws out to kill . . . You'd do it, too, wouldn't you? You'd go to the police, even though I am your brother?"

She had just gazed back at him, unblinking. The movement of her head which confirmed the truth of what he said was barely perceptible. For a few seconds neither of them spoke. "Well," he said at last, "I suppose you win, Sister May. . . . You always win." He was still holding the package of affidavits he had brought, and now she held out her hands for it. Almost involuntarily he handed her the big, thick envelope, looking at her once more, his eyes marked by a pleading to her to say one word to him of consolation. It was an expression she remembered from their youth, when he had been upset by her anger, and now it left her untouched. At last he moved to the door and opened it. "Do you want me to close it—or leave it open?" he had asked, hoping to provoke a response from her to a direct question, but she had refused him even that satisfaction, her shoulders moving in one of those slow, effortless shrugs that she had been using instead of words. "Then goodbye, May," he had said, and she had been conscious of the sound of his footsteps as he had walked along the passage and, after a few moments, of the heavy noise of the front door as it was closed behind him.

For a few seconds after he had gone, she stayed completely still at the escritoire, with the package still in her hands. Then she put it down on the desk, reached within it and drew one of the documents half out of the envelope so that she could read the first words at the head of the uppermost page: "Testimony of Lionel Edward Frewin of 34 Tottenham Road, London . . ." She was strongly tempted to read on, knowing the same desire for the pain of revelation that had made her question Bob when he had first told her about Sydney Street, the same need to thrust her hand into the flames. But she resisted it, knowing it could only make harder the forgiveness of Thomas that was vital to the future of her marriage. With an effort of will, she returned the testimony of Lionel Edward Frewin to the confines of the big envelope and closed the flap.

She addressed herself to the next stage of the problem, which was the most difficult of all: how she should approach Evelyn Banbury, for action by her was now necessary. Any meeting between a wife and her husband's mistress must inevitably be marked by overwhelming emotion, but with the removal of the immediate threat to her security, May had experienced a drastic change in her feelings which had both bewildered and humiliated her. The cocoon of numbness which had enclosed her from that terrible early moment of revelation by her brother had suddenly gone. And the resentment that replaced it, flooding into the vacuum like a torrent, had alarmed her with its intensity. At times during the past hours, she had become obsessed by a violent desire to do physical damage to Evelyn Banbury, to dig her nails into those pale smooth cheeks that had lain beside Thomas on the pillow, to strike the mouth that had known his lips. She would stride up and down the room, her fists clenched with frustration.

Often she would experience a confusing reaction of shame at this debasing need for violence and would even feel for her a kind of sympathy, regretting the pain she must cause her, seeing her almost as a sister in the struggle of life which was not so very far removed from the feminine comradeship she felt in the NSWS. Then the hate, with its primeval intensity, would surge through her once more.

Now, as she sat at her desk after Bob's departure, she wondered how, in these circumstances, she could possibly meet the Countess with any degree of dignity. Was it even necessary? Could she not write to her instead?—for she could put in a very few words all that needed to be said.

She took a sheet of notepaper from the rack within the escritoire. "Dear Lady Banbury," she wrote, and stopped, wondering at the absurdity of what she had written. *Dear* Lady Banbury? Social convention could place strange demands. But she could not continue, and she knew then that she would have to endure the ordeal of confronting her. She rang for Brandon, told him to send for the carriage and went to her bedroom to change. She chose a dark red velvet jacket that was heavily braided and a small brimmed hat, not unlike a bowler, decorated with feathers, which she had just bought. She looked at her reflection in the full-length mirror with critical care and decided after several seconds of study that she had achieved her aim: to appear elegant and fashionable without any hint of ostentation. Then she went downstairs.

She was halfway to the ground floor when there was a knock on the front door, and she had barely reached the hall by the time Brandon had opened it to reveal Philip Wainwright standing in the entrance porch. As always, the sight of him was a shock to her. Since the drama of Thomas had occupied her so totally over the past few days, she had not thought so much about Philip. Twice he had called at the house, but both times, since he had been unwise enough to arrive alone, she had refused to receive him. Now, as she reached the foot of the stairs, he was asking Brandon if she was at home when he saw her over the butler's shoulder. "I see I've been more fortunate today," he said to Brandon—then greeted her directly: "Good afternoon, Mrs. Kingston. I do hope it's not too much to ask for a couple of minutes of your time."

Her heart was already beating faster. "I fear I'm just on my way out," she answered, "and rather late for my appointment."

"Then perhaps," he suggested, "you'll permit me to ride with you some of the way to your destination."

She shook her head firmly. "No, Mr. Wainwright," she said, "but if you'd care to come to tea tomorrow afternoon, with your sister, I'd be happy to see you. If she's otherwise engaged, then you may suggest another day. Now you must excuse me."

She walked past him, descended the entrance steps and climbed into the waiting carriage. "Number twenty-two Grosvenor Square," she instructed the footman.

· 8 ·

That evening, at a few minutes before seven o'clock, Eve Banbury stood in the sitting room of the house in Sydney Street and studied the small Sheraton mahogany table that was laid for dinner. She straightened a knife that was marginally out of alignment at a place setting, removed the hint of a finger smudge from one of the hock glasses with a cloth. Then she stood back, surveying the whole table, much as a painter might view the subject for a canvas, wondering if he could improve the composition. Slowly, she walked round it, the mild air displacement of her movement causing the candles to flicker slightly. She pressed one of them tighter in the holder of the candelabrum, then moved forward and altered by a fraction of an inch the position of the decanter of Château Lafite. She noticed that the long brass poker in the fireplace had slipped off its rest beside its matching shovel, and bending down, she returned it to its proper place.

This evening was unique in her experience—possibly the most important of her life. Everything, she was determined, must be perfect. She had devoted the same degree of extreme care to her appearance as she had to the table. She had exasperated her maid as she had arranged her hair with repeated and precise demands, about the exact placing of every curl, every ringlet, every plait, so that she had been sitting at her dressing table in front of the mirror for more than an hour before at last she had conceded that the result was adequate. She had changed her gown no fewer than seven times before finally opting for the slightly décolleté dress of royal blue velvet that she now wore, satisfied at last that the color heightened the violet of her eyes and formed a suitable setting for the blond hair that had been prepared with such effort.

A few hours earlier, in the space of barely fifteen minutes, her existence had been shattered like glass.

She had known, of course, as soon as her butler had announced that Mrs. Kingston was downstairs, that Thomas was the reason for the visit—had, in fact, in a sense been awaiting it. For a moment, she had known panic, had considered telling him to say she was not at home. Then, as she had realized that nothing could be gained by this, that whatever reason had brought Thomas' wife to Grosvenor Square would not disappear because she kept herself ignorant of it, she was beset by a whole range of worries as to how she should receive her. Should she do so in the drawing room? Should she change her gown, call her maid to do her hair, put on jewelry? Finally, she had elected to do nothing, not even bothering to glance in a looking glass to touch her hair into place. What could it matter, after all, by contrast to the menace that her arrival in her home almost certainly signified?

May Kingston herself had looked very pale but composed as she went through the etiquette of thanking Eve for sparing her the time. As she had sat down, she had declined the offer to take tea. "I think I should be as brief as possible for both our sakes," she had said. "I'd hoped to spare us this interview, to write instead, but I couldn't find the words. . . ." She paused, one hand gripping the other on her lap. "I'm at a slight disadvantage, too, since I'm not sure how much you know of our drama of the past week."

"Drama?" queried Eve.

"So he hasn't told you," said May. "I thought he might have kept it from you—at least until he'd decided what to do. . . . Well, I fear *I* can't, because it's necessary that you should know the facts. . . . They're simple enough, but painful . . . for the two of us." She had spoken quietly but smoothly, as though she had rehearsed with care what she was going to say. "This isn't easy for me, as I'm sure you'll understand, so please . . . no explanations or apologies. . . . For my part, I"—she hesitated—"well, I'll try not to reproach you. . . ."

Again she had paused, glanced down at her lap, then looked straight into the violet eyes that had so entranced Thomas. "My husband," she had said, "has been the victim of blackmail . . ."

"Blackmail!" Eve echoed with horror.

". . . because of your . . ." May broke off, searching for the appropriate word. ". . . because of your relationship."

Instinctively, Eve had tried to remonstrate, but May had continued, interrupting her boldly with a slightly louder tone, speaking of Sydney Street and Mrs. Deneuve, and Eve had realized there was no point in attempting protest. The muscles of her belly had stiffened in spasm as she had listened, eyes averted, as Thomas' wife had told her about her brother's threat, about his revelation to May when Thomas had refused to listen, about his plan to send the affidavits to the Earl, about Sidney Baines's discovery which had given May the weapon she needed to meet the danger.

At last, she had finished. "The documents are in my carriage," she had said. "I haven't read them and I'd advise you not to, but you may if you wish."

Eve had shaken her head, the color high in her cheeks from her mortification of May Kingston's knowledge of such an intimate area of her life. "I don't know how you find it possible to sit in the same room with me," she had said at last.

"It is a little hard," May had agreed quietly.

For a moment, Eve had wondered why she had come, for there was no triumph in her attitude and not really any real condemnation. And May, as though perceiving her thought, had answered the unspoken question. "You must realize," she had continued, "that the danger's not past, which is why I've submitted us both to this ordeal. . . . My brother's not the only person who knows the situation between you. I doubt if the affidavits in my carriage are the only copies that have been sworn. Almost certainly Turner'll have a set, and he'd be a far more formidable opponent than my brother."

Eve felt a wave of nausea, and for a few seconds she thought she would have to leave the room. The very notion of explicit details of her intimacy with Thomas being studied by men who meant him harm chilled her to the bone. "Then what is to be done?" she asked softly.

"What we've gained is time," May had explained. "My brother'll

have to tell Turner something of what's happened. He'll have to explain why the scheme has failed; but he won't want to admit the real
reason, of course. He'll have to think up something else that's more
acceptable. So he won't be in any hurry. . . . For one thing, it'll almost
certainly cost him his job. So he'll put it off and postpone the day of
reckoning."

May paused for a few seconds, and Eve, despite her unhappiness,
could not help being impressed by her practicality, by her will. "It'll
come though, won't it?" said Eve. "The day of reckoning I mean . . .
that's when we'll face the threat again."

"By then," May had said carefully, "there'll be nothing to reveal
. . . nothing in Sydney Street for any detective who manages to gain
access to the house to record . . . no relationship between you and my
husband . . ."

Eve had given a sudden shake of her head, in strong dispute, but
May had continued as though she had not noticed it. "All that'll exist is
the present evidence . . . history, allegations of the past—and who's
going to believe a scoundrel like Turner against the denial of a lady of
your rank or even of a man in the position of my husband? . . .
provided, of course, there's nothing to prove."

Eve had looked back at May, her eyes suddenly angry. "Mrs.
Kingston," she had said, "you're assuming too much."

"You've no choice," May had insisted in a voice that was gentle,
even sympathetic.

"Divorce is a possibility," Eve had said quietly. "It'd mean scandal, but it'd be a possibility . . . it's been done. . . ."

"There's no question of it," May had answered. "Where would
you live? In some remote village on the Continent? You couldn't live
in London, could you? Do you seriously think my husband would
consider it? I'm sure you've realized by now that the most important
single thing in his life is his store . . . more important even than
you . . ." She paused for no more than a second. ". . . or me. . . ."

May had stood up. "It must be done quickly, Lady Banbury," she
had said, pausing for a moment before adding, "I have a favor to ask. . . .
You may not wish to grant it, but you'll concede I've done you no
harm, and this can make no difference to you. . . . I'd prefer it if my
husband remained unaware that I know anything of this whole unhappy business."

"You'd have me lie to him, Mrs. Kingston?" Eve asked coldly.

May had nodded. "If necessary," she had agreed. "I said it was a
favor. . . . If we meet again," she had continued, "I hope it'll be under
happier circumstances." And she had left without waiting for the but-

ler to be summoned. Eve had stayed sitting quite still long after she had heard the noise of the departing carriage. Everything in her resisted what May had told her was inevitable. Thomas was vital to her existence. The thought of life without him seemed impossible. Then, through her anger and determination had come the force of simple logic.

She had gone to her bedroom, thrown herself onto the bed and wept and wept and wept. Then she had thought of the example of Thomas' wife, of the courage and strength she must have needed for the interview she had just conducted, and she had resolved what she would do.

She had risen from the bed and crossed to the dressing table. For an instant, she had glanced at her reflection in the mirror—at her swollen eyes, her untidy hair, the tearstains on her cheeks. Then she had scribbled a note to Thomas: "Dearest . . . I have an overwhelming need to see you tonight. My husband is at the Lords. Please, please, can we dine at Sydney Street. I'll be waiting for you there, my love." She had rung for her maid and told her to send a footman with it immediately to the store.

The clock in the church in Sydney Street was striking the hour of seven when Eve heard Mrs. Deneuve open the front door to Thomas. He climbed the stairs, smiling affectionately at Eve as she stood to welcome him on the landing. "You look quite exquisite," he said. "Like a fragile Dresden figurine. I hardly dare to touch you."

"I hope you'll take the risk," she answered, her eyes bright. "I'll try not to break."

He laughed and kissed her gently, then put his arm round her waist and walked with her into the sitting room, halting when he saw the table laid for dinner in the candlelight. "Doesn't that look splendid!" he said. "It moves me greatly. . . ."

"That was the intention," she said, smiling happily. "Would you care for a glass of champagne, Thomas?"

"Champagne? We have something to celebrate?"

"Don't we always have something to celebrate?" she asked.

He laughed again and took her hand. "You sound very happy tonight," he said.

"I can't be with you for two seconds without being happy," she responded. "You transform my existence. . . . Now, isn't that a pretty speech, sir? And isn't it time you opened the bottle, since I haven't brought my butler?"

He kissed her again and moved to the wine cooler, where a bottle of Veuve Clicquot lay tidily beside the hock. "There was an urgency to your note," he said as he removed the wire that contained the cork.

"I had a need to see you," she answered. "I haven't seen you for two days. Does it merit explanation? Did you have to cancel a grand dinner?"

"Not as grand as this one," he replied, and the cork exploded from the bottle. He filled two glasses and took them to her. "I was doing nothing," he said. "Just dining at home."

"So you mustn't be too late."

He looked at her curiously. It was a strange thing for her to say, and she knew the mask had slipped. Until then, she had been congratulating herself on her performance. "So I mustn't be too late," he agreed, a bit firmly, as though correcting her.

She held up her glass. "Here's to us," she said, "to Thomas and Eve, to everything we've known together . . ."

"And to everything we *will* know together," he added.

"Of course," she said, and putting the glass to her lips, she took a long sip, drinking nearly half the contents. She saw his look of concerned surprise. "I wanted no half measures," she said, by way of explanation. "It was a worthy toast, wasn't it? No polite little sips would do justice to that toast, would they? It was a prayer, Thomas. Think of it as that. . . . Tell me you love me. . . ."

"I love you," he said. "You know I do. . . . Why do you ask?"

"I don't know. . . . Because I love *you* so completely, I suppose . . . I needed to hear you say so. . . . You like my gown? You think it suits me?"

"To perfection . . . I've already said so."

"Of course—the Dresden figurine. . . . Can you desire a Dresden figurine? Thomas, I need you to desire me tonight . . . I need you to love me tonight . . . I need you to take me to heights we've never known before. . . ."

"You're in a strange mood, aren't you?" he said, looking at her anxiously. "When have we ever been together when I didn't desire you instantly?"

"That's a pretty speech too. . . . Shall I take off my necklace, my earrings . . . would that make me seem less fragile?"

"Stop it, Eve," he said gently, and put his lips to hers in a long, passionate kiss which lifted them both so powerfully that at last she pressed him away from her. "We mustn't allow ourselves to be too carried away," she said. "Mrs. Deneuve will be serving dinner . . . and I've selected the menu personally. Truite aux Amandes . . . that's a favorite of yours, isn't it? . . . followed by Canard aux Cerises . . . and a

Lafite 'Seventy-five . . . I was advised that it'll be an ideal partner for the duck. Is that correct?"

"It sounds perfect . . . but what have I done to deserve such royal treatment?"

"What have you done?" she queried, her spirits buoyant again. "What a question! You've done nothing. . . . You just *are*, and I'm filled with gratitude that you *are* . . . so we're having a Thomas night. . . . That was what was urgent. I had an urgent need for a Thomas night . . . a kind of thanksgiving, you see. . . . Oh, I don't know, Thomas. . . . Do I appear very foolish?"

He smiled at her. "You're delightful—and I'm deeply flattered. . . . When can we have an Eve night, an Eve thanksgiving?"

She paused before replying, her mood pierced momentarily by the reality of their situation. "When it can be arranged," she answered carefully, adding brightly, "My glass is empty. . . . Truly, Thomas, I wouldn't employ you as a butler. . . ."

He got up, fetched the bottle from the cooler, and filled the glass. "There's something I have to tell you," he said. "Something I hoped I wouldn't have to speak of. . . ."

"Then don't, please," she urged, "for it sounds a little disagreeable . . ."

"I have to," he said. "You have to be warned. . . ."

"I refuse to be warned, Thomas . . . not tonight. . . ."

"It's important, I fear. . . . We have to discuss it. . . ."

"I don't care how important it is . . . I don't want to hear it. No discussions, not tonight, Thomas. . . . Just love tonight, Thomas, just happiness . . ."

And the issue was ended because Mrs. Deneuve knocked on the door and came into the room with a beaming smile on her face and asked if she might serve their dinner.

Throughout the meal, Eve chattered lightly and cleverly, like the experienced hostess she was, but also like the young girl she sometimes seemed to be, her sentences tumbling over one another, her subjects changing abruptly as new thoughts occurred to her. She was breathless and witty—and, as Thomas noted, strangely in charge, leaving him to respond, refusing him the chance to initiate any line of conversation. They laughed a lot, caught together in moments of gaiety, but it was an artificial gaiety, and occasionally it was shadowed by the same note of desperation that had appeared in their talking before dinner.

Twice Thomas tried to speak again of the blackmail threat, but as she had earlier, she declined to listen, insisting that tonight was a special night, a Thomas night, and changed the subject with expert ease.

To Thomas, she had never appeared quite so beautiful, as she looked back at him in the candlelight with those strange eyes, marked by rising desire, by love, by sheer enjoyment. The gentle curve of her soft, pale breasts was enhanced by the heavy square neckline of the deep blue velvet. Diamonds flashed in her ears and at her throat, and he wished, with sudden painful longing, that he had given them to her, that it was possible for him to give her presents of such jewelry which she could wear without exciting questions from her husband.

Afterward they made love, and the element of determined brightness that had emerged at times throughout the evening appeared again, this time in a level of abandonment, in a clear need to lose herself in him, that had a quality of desperation—and of unfulfillment because she could not completely lose herself, could not soar as she so obviously desired without any contact remaining with the earth. There was a restlessness in her loving, repeated requests for altered positions, a clutching of him as though she would be in danger of dying were it not for his strength, and great, shuddering fits of sobbing at her moments of climax.

At last she lay still beside him, on her back, looking at the shadows cast on the ceiling by the gas burners, just holding his hand, fingers thrust home and firm. The church clock struck midnight. "I suppose you ought to go," she said.

"I suppose we both ought to," he replied.

She made a slight negative movement with her head. "He'll be very late tonight. He'll have gone on to Whites—the baccarat table . . . You don't gamble, do you, Thomas?"

"My whole life's a gamble . . . you know that. . . . When I was most exposed you were my gain, my winnings. . . . That was a throw. . . . Not many gamblers make a throw as good as that."

Suddenly she wanted him to go. She wanted him desperately to stay, but she wanted him to go. She wanted him to hold her tightly forever, but she wanted him to go—eager now for the moment she had been dreading all evening, that she had been postponing, to arrive.

"I know you must leave," she said gently, "but tonight I'm going to stay here for a while."

He was surprised, as he had been surprised by her all evening, for she had never done this before. Usually, when they dined together, they departed at the same time.

"I mean it," she said. "Tonight for me there's no need for haste and I love it here. . . . You must dress. . . . I'll lie here and watch you. . . ."

He propped himself on one elbow, looking down at her—then kissed her gently, but with great, slow passion. It roused her, but she did not want to be roused. She wanted the terrible moment of parting to come, the agony she must endure to envelop her—like a person sentenced to death. When there is only an hour left before the execution, time can have no purpose. There must be a yearning for death. "Dress, Thomas," she said.

He rose from the bed and began to do as she suggested. There was an expression on his face of anxiety. When he had put on his shirt and his trousers, he asked, "What's troubling you?"

"Nothing's troubling me," she answered. "I'm very happy."

But he knew she was not. He wondered if Bob Ramsay had approached her. "Has anyone been to see you . . . to speak of us?" he asked.

"No—why should you think they might?"

"Well, that's what I wanted to talk to you about."

"Not again, Thomas!" she said sharply, adding more softly, "Not tonight . . ."

He looked in one of the mirrors while he tied his tie, then shrugged on his coat.

He moved to her and sat on the side of the bed. "I hope you realize how much you mean to me," he said.

She needed to cry, but held back the tears. "I hope I do too," she answered with a smile. He bent down and kissed her, and she put her arms round his neck and clung to him as though she were about to drown. Then she released her hold on him, and after a second he stood up. "I'll call on you tomorrow," he said.

She smiled and nodded. "Good night, Thomas."

He put his fingers to his lips in a light gesture of farewell, and left. Almost immediately, she was out of the bed. "Thomas . . . !" she called desperately. She opened the door, and from the half-landing at the foot of the first downward flight of stairs he looked up at her standing naked in the doorway, her hair down her back. "Come back—just for a second."

He climbed the stairs and took her in his arms. "Will you always love me?" she asked urgently. Again as he looked in her eyes he saw the same expression of desperation. "Of course," he answered, and kissed her.

Once more, she was the one to end the kiss, pushing him gently from her. "I will too," she said. "Goodbye, Thomas."

He went down the stairs, halted at the half-landing to look back at her, smiling with great affection. "Goodbye, Thomas," she repeated.

"Good night, my angel," he said, and went on down the stairs.

She hurried to the window of the bedroom and, shielding her body with the curtain, looked into the street. She could see her carriage waiting, her servants sitting on the box with shoulders hunched. She watched him appear in the road after leaving the house. He looked up at her, smiled and walked on down the street.

For the first time since seven o'clock, there was no longer a need to pretend. It would not matter if she broke down and cried away some of the terrible sense of desolation that now consumed her—but she did not cry. Quite methodically, she dressed and tried to return her hair to some semblance of order. She put on her earrings and her necklace. Even though she was alone, her appearance suddenly seemed important to her, for she felt like a priestess about to perform a rite.

Standing in the middle of the room, she turned slowly, taking in every beloved detail—the gilt mirror, the photographs of Thomas and herself, the cushions decorated with their initials, the china ornaments, each one of which had been bought as a gesture of love. The smell of Thomas still lingered as she stood there, and although she had planned at first to tidy the bed where they had just possessed each other for the last time, it now seemed more intimate, more suitable, to leave it as it was—with the blankets awry, with the pillows crooked and marked with the indentations of their heads.

She went into their sitting room. The plates had been cleared, but the glasses, still containing a little wine, were there on the table, and the decanter, only half empty, lay in its basket. One of the candles had burned itself out, but another, with a little wax remaining, still flickered, though soon it too would be extinguished.

Earlier, she had decided what she would do, but she had not decided how. She surveyed the room, as she had done next door, enjoying the details that had meant so much to her.

As she looked around her, turning slowly as she did so, her attention was caught suddenly by the long brass poker lying neatly in the hearth where she had corrected its position so carefully a few hours before. On impulse, she crossed to the fireplace and, bending down, picked up the poker with a slow movement that contained an element which was almost reverential. It was heavy and cumbersome—so heavy that with one hand she could hold it only pointing downward. She put her other hand to it to provide additional strength and raised it, so that she was supporting it, point upward, like a sword.

Carrying the poker upright in front of her, as though in ceremonial, she walked slowly back into the bedroom. For a few seconds she stood in front of the Louis XIV mirror on the wall. She studied the reflected image of herself—the luxuriant fair hair, the violet eyes that Thomas had commented on so much, the full lips that he had kissed so often, the soft line of her neck, the swelling of her breasts, divided now by the stiff vertical line of the poker. For a few seconds she continued to stare at herself, feeling strangely detached, almost as though she were somebody else. This, she thought, is the woman who loved Thomas Kingston. With one sudden movement, she struck the mirror with the poker, causing the impact in the middle of her forehead, and her reflection was instantly marred by a thousand jagged lines of shattered glass. She hit it again, harder this time, so that several splinters fell out of the frame and she could barely be seen in the crazed surface that remained.

The ceremony was over. There was need now, even a yearning, for destruction. She wielded the poker again and smashed the pictures on the wall, and with one sideswipe she swept the china ornaments from the mantelpiece to become hundreds of scattered remnants on the floor. She hung with her whole weight on the curtains, so that they were wrenched from the rails which supported them and collapsed in big heaps on the floor. She took up an ornamental paper knife from a side table and slashed the cushions on which she had embroidered the initials of both of them with such devoted care, ripping them open so that their contents of down feathers were strewn all over the floor.

Tears were streaming down her cheeks now—strange tears that were part anger, part desperation. Taking the poker in one hand and the knife in the other, she went back into their sitting room. Laying down the knife for a moment, she swung the poker again with both hands, sweeping the glasses and the decanter from the table, striking the paintings on the wall, shattering their frames, so that they fell from their supports. Only one did she leave untouched—the Renoir, of the new Paris school that they had talked about so much. At last she stood in the middle of the room, her breast heaving. She let the poker fall from her hands and once more took up the knife. She approached the Renoir and, for a few seconds, studied those soft feminine women with whom, as she had explained to Thomas, she had felt so much rapport. Carefully she placed the point of the knife high up the canvas and slashed it in half with one savage downward stroke.

Finally, she approached the bookshelf and drew from it the volume that she had given Thomas, its flyleaf inscribed with such emotion. For a last time she read those words—the paean she had written about the discoveries of herself that he had released in her.

The tears were still wet on her cheeks, but there was no sobbing. Then, in a violent movement, she tore out the page and threw the book over her shoulder. With a sudden angry urgency, she grabbed the other books in the shelves one by one and flung them too behind her.

She stood for a few moments surveying the devastation around her, the destruction of her life with Thomas. Then she took up her mantle, which, on her arrival earlier, she had laid over a chair. Throwing it round her shoulders, she held it with one hand at the neck so that it enclosed her and strode out onto the landing.

Mrs. Deneuve was on the stairs, looking up at her anxiously. "I was worried by the noise, your Ladyship," she said.

"Mrs. Deneuve," said Eve, "we shan't be needing the rooms any longer. . . . Please destroy everything, literally everything. . . . You've shown me a kindness and a friendship for which I'm deeply grateful. . . ."

"My Lady . . ." Mrs. Deneuve began.

"Please say nothing more," said Eve. "You know why, I'm sure. . . ."

She went on down the stairs, opened the front door and, standing in the entrance, alerted the footman with a sharp "Smith!" so that he almost fell off the box. He leaped to the pavement, and the Countess of Banbury stepped into her carriage.

It was about four o'clock the following afternoon when one of Eve's footmen was brought to Thomas in the Grocery Department with a note he had been instructed to hand to him in person. Thomas was deep in discussion with Sidney and Lloyd, but asked them to excuse him while he opened the envelope. But when he read the words, he could scarcely believe them. "My love, it must end," she had written. "You know why it must end, for you wished to speak of it last night. I love you with an intensity that at present I don't know how I'm going to bear. I hope that in time the pain will begin to ease at least a little, for otherwise life will not be worth living. But even knowing the agony I do, I would not have missed a second of our time together. Thank you, Thomas. Thank you, my beloved.—Eve."

Thomas tried to keep the emotion from his face. He folded the note and put it in his pocket. "I fear you must excuse me," he said. "I have urgent business." He walked out of the store and hailed a hansom, leaving Sidney and Lloyd wondering what could be so urgent as to cause him to go out into the street without a hat or a stick.

The cab halted before the Banbury home in Grosvenor Square. Thomas leaped up the steps and knocked on the great front door. "Is her Ladyship at home?" he snapped at the butler.

"I fear not, sir," he answered.

"Then I'll wait until she returns," said Thomas.

"I'm afraid that won't be possible, sir."

"You mean she's gone away?" queried Thomas sharply.

"My instructions are, sir, that if you should call, she's not at home."

"I insist on seeing her," said Thomas.

"No, sir," the butler said firmly. For a moment, Thomas thought of shouldering his way past him, but he was a large figure of a man— once a corporal in the Coldstream Guards, he recalled—and anyway, this would be unacceptable behavior. "I'm deeply sorry, sir," said the butler.

Thomas turned and, since the hansom had not yet moved off, Grosvenor Square being a good place to pick up fares, he climbed back into it. "Where to, sir?" asked the cabby.

Thomas had not thought of what he was going to do, or where he wanted to go, but he knew he would not be able to concentrate on work that day. "Thirty-four Cadogan Place," he ordered.

·9·

"But don't you see, Mrs. Kingston," Philip Wainwright insisted, leaning forward, his eyes shining, "the world's on the point of momentous change. . . . You must forgive me, but I get the impression sometimes that you believe that everything will remain the same forever —the Queen on her throne, the Mother of Parliaments at Westminster, the middle class growing ever richer . . ."

"You're getting bombastic," Stella remonstrated from the window, where she was looking out at the gardens of Cadogan Place. "You won't be asked again."

"Of course you'll be invited again," said May, laughing. "You're both most welcome at any time."

"Both!" he echoed with angry disgust. "Can I never speak to you alone?"

"Do you need to be alone to speak of politics?" asked May. "After all, Stella shares many of your views."

"I don't want to speak to you only of politics. At least . . ." He broke off, suddenly diverted by anger at his sister. "And Stella's only concerned with the cause of women and the vote . . . the vote!" he echoed, holding up his hands in appeal to heaven. "Who cares about the vote—for men *or* women? Do men working for slave wages in the mills of Bradford care about the vote? Do the millions living over there in squalor in Stepney or Whitechapel?" He stabbed his finger toward the slums of the East End. "They're living ten in a room . . . their children have no shoes . . . there are open sewers and plagues of rats . . . and you can still be content with things as they are, Mrs. Kingston, so long as your butler serves the tea and the Royal Navy rules the seas!"

"You're to stop this at once!" insisted Stella, stalking across the room toward him like an angry governess. "All you've been able to speak of for days is how you admire Mrs. Kingston, and within minutes of being in her drawing room, you're insulting her."

"Not insulting her!" Philip responded angrily. "Was I insulting you, Mrs. Kingston?" he pleaded. "Please say I wasn't insulting you."

"Whatever you were doing, I wasn't offended," said May.

"I was carried away, I admit," he conceded. "Please forgive me and say I can call on you again . . . you won't bar me from the house?" he added anxiously.

"I've just invited you with your sister any—"

"My sister! My sister!" he echoed. "It was Stella who made me explode. . . . You see, she poses as a great radical, but in fact she's as bourgeois as any woman in Kensington. You only have to show her a Union Jack and she's marching with the best of the imperialists. . . ."

"Not that again!" Stella cried out. "Patriotism's his latest hate," she explained to May.

"Oh, God preserve me!" he exclaimed. "Can you understand now, Mrs. Kingston, why I want to see you alone, when I'm subject to this constant interruption?"

"All right," said Stella. "I'll leave you for a few minutes . . . that is, if you'll permit me, May. . . . I'd like to see your new Stubbs. It's in the dining room, I think. . . . I'll leave both doors open, so that if he molests you . . ." She gave a mocking laugh. "But you're quite safe. He may start off with a tender speech, but he'll be into politics before he's got within yards of any hint of compromise. . . ."

And with a backward wink at May, she left the room. "There," said May to him as though speaking to a child. "You've got what you were asking for."

"And I value it," he said earnestly. "I value every second, because you've never left my thoughts for a moment the whole time I've been away. . . ."

"Now, I'm sure that's an exaggeration. In Paris, of all places, with all those French ladies . . . Do *they* want to change the world too?"

"All of those in our circle," he answered.

"That's a circle of . . ." She hesitated, uncertain of the words she should use. ". . . radicals?"

"More than that. We're revolutionaries . . . socialists . . ."

"And do the French like having a circle of revolutionaries in the heart of their capital?"

"In due course they'll expel us. . . . Revolutionaries get used to moving from city to city. . . . Mrs. Kingston . . . I wish I could convey to you the excitement, the freedom of the cause . . . For it'll come, you know . . . the world revolution. . . . It's inevitable. . . ."

She poured herself another cup of tea, and holding the teapot over his cup, she looked at him questioningly, but he indicated that he wanted no more. "You know," she said, "I don't understand why you wish to see me so much. We've nothing in common—even less now that revolution is so greatly occupying you. . . ."

"That's nothing to do with it, Mrs. Kingston. . . . I can't help my feelings—as you can't help yours. They're very powerful, as you well know. . . . That's why I went to Paris . . . in desperation because you were a married woman . . . but it didn't make any difference. . . . Do you know that at night sometimes I could picture you so vividly that I was sure you must be thinking of me, that we were in some strange way communicating . . ."

"You must stop speaking like this," said May sharply. She was breathing heavily, knowing that terrifying ache in her belly. "Tell me about patriotism," she said desperately. "You condemned Stella for patriotism. . . . Surely patriotism is a noble ideal. . . ."

"Only if you think it's noble to exploit the masses," he answered. "Patriotism's a trick of the capitalists. . . . There are poor everywhere, Mrs. Kingston, but they're divided by the concept of country. . . . Consider those mill workers in Bradford. Who do they have the most in common with—French workers, as exploited as they are, in a factory in Lyon, or a British lord?"

He broke off to allow her to answer, but she was saying nothing now he was back in this safe territory. "Why should the masses fight for 'King and country'?" he scorned. "Believe me, Mrs. Kingston, the workingman *has* no country. . . . That's what Marx and Engels wrote over forty years ago in the *Communist Manifesto*. . . . Have you ever read the *Communist Manifesto?* Have you even heard of the *Communist Manifesto?*"

"No . . . she . . . has . . . not!" May swung round in alarm as she heard Thomas' voice, each word rapped out in outraged challenge. He was standing in the doorway, glowering. "At least," he went on, "I trust she has not."

He was haggard, the lines of his face furrowed deeply by his unhappiness. For the first time, he suddenly looked old. As May watched him, appalled by his sudden return, she heard the anger in his voice and, aware of its cause, knew that whoever had been there in the drawing room would have provoked it—but it was fanned a hundred times by Philip's attack on patriotism, which was an ideal that, like all right-minded people, Thomas held in high regard. But even if Philip had been lauding her Majesty the Queen, Thomas would still have been astounded to find May alone with a young man he did not know.

Philip had got to his feet, his cheeks reddening. Quickly, May tried to take control of the situation. "Why, Thomas," she said, forcing a smile, "what a pleasant surprise to see you home at this hour. May I introduce Mr. Philip Wainwright . . ."

For a few seconds, Thomas said nothing but stood glaring at Philip from the doorway. "I've mentioned my friends the Wainwrights to you, of course," May went on, trying to keep her tone light and natural. "Miss Wainwright's in the dining room at the moment. I told her about your Stubbs, and since she's a great admirer of Stubbs, she insisted on going to look at it at once. . . . Oh, there she is behind you. . . . Stella, you've never met my husband, have you?" Stella had appeared in the doorway and had immediately grasped the essentials of the embarrassment in the drawing room.

"Good afternoon, Mr. Kingston," she said warmly. "What a pleasure to meet you at last . . . I've heard so much about you from your wife. . . ." She held out her hand boldly, and Thomas took it. "I'm glad to meet you too, Miss Wainwright," he responded gruffly, still somewhat confused by the events of this terrible afternoon. "Your brother, however . . ." He turned back to look at Philip. "I'll shake your hand, Mr. Wainwright, since you're in my home, but I must ask you, while you're under my roof, not to express sentiments such as those I heard when I came in." He thrust out his hand, his expression still grim.

"I realize, Mr. Kingston," Philip said, "that socialism, being so new a concept, is a little difficult to accept. . . ."

"It's against nature," Thomas insisted dogmatically.

"With respect, sir, I've never heard it argued that capitalism conformed with nature. . . ."

"Mr. Wainwright," May intervened quickly, "is home for a few weeks from Paris, where he's been studying political theory. . . ."

"I see," Thomas growled, walking to the fireplace and standing with his back toward it, almost in challenge. "I thought your friends the Wainwrights were suffragists," he added. "I didn't know they were socialists, or I'd have taken a very different view of your association."

"Oh, we're not socialists," Stella interjected. "At least, only my brother is. . . . My mother and I are, as you rightly say, supporters of the suffrage for women, as your wife is. . . . In fact, that's the main reason I'm here today. I'm sure May's told you about our bill in the Commons next week . . ."

"What bill?" asked Thomas.

"I think I mentioned it to you," May answered. "The bill to extend the franchise. Mr. Woodall is moving an amendment to include women householders. . . . We've got great hopes for it."

"All of us have been working like demons among the politicians," said Stella, "and we'll be there in force in the public gallery on Wednesday night. . . . I hope you'll be with us, May. . . ."

"I hope so too," she responded. "You wouldn't mind, would you, Thomas, just one evening? I'd love to hear the debate."

Thomas was staring stonily in front of him. "I think your connection with the suffragists had gone far enough."

"Oh, don't say that, Mr. Kingston," Stella interposed brightly. "I'm sure that you yourself don't really oppose the principle of female suffrage."

"The principle perhaps, Miss Wainwright," Thomas answered stiffly. "But my wife's in a delicate position because of her connection with my store. It'd be most harmful if she was to be the subject of press comment provoked by your campaign."

May had never heard Thomas behaving in this manner—pompous and dogmatic, a stubborn expression clouding his face in a scowl—and she was ashamed for him.

"But Mr. Kingston," Stella persisted, "most of the press have been sympathetic to our movement."

Thomas was standing in a rigid stance, his legs apart, his hands clasped behind his back. "Miss Wainwright," he said coldly, "I've considered the question and told you my view."

Stella was suddenly angry. "Does that mean, Mr. Kingston," she demanded, the color high in her cheeks, "that you are forbidding your wife to attend the debate on Wednesday?"

"It does," Thomas answered, rocking slightly on his heels,

"though, with respect, I would suggest that it was a private matter for discussion between her and myself."

"Discussion!" Stella echoed. "There's no question of discussion, Mr. Kingston. You've given your ruling like an absolute monarch!"

"Please, Stella . . ." May interrupted, "I can fight my own battles." She turned to Thomas. "I've never opposed you before, Thomas," she said, "and I know something very unfortunate must have happened to upset you today for you to be home at this hour. Otherwise I'm sure you'd be more receptive to a matter that's most important to me. . . . But I have to tell you that I intend to hear that debate."

"Against my wishes?" queried Thomas, astonished.

"I'd have preferred your agreement . . . I've asked for it . . . but if you won't give it . . . then, yes, I shall go against your wishes."

Defiantly, she met his eyes, noting even in her own high emotion the anger and frustration and pain that was in them. "I hope," he said coldly, "you'll consider the repercussions of what you've just said, for they'll be very grave. Now, since I have some work to attend to, perhaps your guests will permit me to withdraw. . . . Miss Wainwright . . . Mr. Wainwright . . ." He nodded to each of them in turn and walked out of the room.

For a moment there was silence. Then Phillip said, "Well, at last I've met your husband, Mrs. Kingston."

The challenge had been unfortunate. For if Thomas had not been in the state he was, he would never have forbidden her to attend the debate. Yet once he had taken a stance that was so grossly unreasonable, she had been unable meekly to submit, especially in her own mood of bitterness about Eve Banbury, hard though she was trying to control this.

At first, May thought it was this searing confrontation which made the crucial evening in the House of Commons seem something of an anticlimax, but then it dawned on her that this was not due solely to her domestic conflict. Certainly, the occasion was dramatic enough. There they all were, packed tight on the benches of the public gallery, arrayed like troops in the battlefield—even uniformed in the bonnets and gloves that Mrs. Wainwright scorned. All of them had a sense of taking part in a moment of history. Below them in the arena of the chamber were the symbols of the historic British Parliament—the heavy silver mace, lying on the central table before the "Speaker," clad in full wig and seated in the huge wooden chair from which he controlled the assembly.

The debate was well attended, though many of the members on both sides of the House looked uninterested, slouched in their seats, one or two even appearing to be asleep. Mr. Gladstone was attentive, though. He was sitting impassive, arms folded, a grim expression on his granite face—but listening with care.

And there on his feet, stating the case that was so dear to everyone in the NSWS, was their champion, Mr. Woodall. He was doing exactly what he had told May he would do. He was taking the arguments against female suffrage one by one and exposing their absurdities; but strangely, he had made more impression on May sitting on the sofa in the Wainwright home than he was doing now standing in this great Gothic hall where laws were made.

May looked at Stella beside her and, beyond her, at Mrs. Wainwright and Emily and could see that they too were experiencing the same sense of dissatisfaction that she herself was feeling. She glanced at Philip on the other side of her and noted his expression of slightly patronizing derision, which was not strange in a man who believed that Parliament was a historical irrelevance. He sensed her looking at him and smiled at her warmly. Hastily, she averted her eyes.

Mr. Woodall too appeared to sense that the impact he was making on his audience was inadequate, for he suddenly launched into a vigorous spate of rhetoric. "What about Boadicea," he demanded, "or Joan of Arc? Were they not, as soldiers, the equal of men? How can it be argued that women should be disenfranchised on the ground that they do not contribute to the Army and the Navy?" But his effect remained limited, and May found herself wondering if she had been wise to come, if this had truly been worth the confrontation with Thomas at so delicate a moment in their marriage, when the emotions of both of them were so raw.

Thomas had barely spoken to her since the argument, remaining, when they were together, even at the dining table, in remote and pensive silence. At breakfast that morning, she had asked if he would be dining at home, and he had replied shortly, "I should imagine so."

"I'll arrange a good dinner for you," she had said, and he had nodded coldly in response.

She realized that Mr. Woodall had completed his speech while her thoughts were wandering. Unhurriedly, Mr. Gladstone rose to his feet and surveyed the chamber of the Commons—a lion of a man, with his gray whiskers and his firm expression. "Mr. Speaker," he declared, and began to demolish poor Mr. Woodall's plea with the words that the suffragists had heard so often before. He sympathized, recognized the force of his arguments, but the issue of the female vote was a social question of the utmost possible magnitude. . . .

If there had ever been reason for optimism in the comrades of the NSWS, it was gone now with the opposition of the Prime Minister. May turned to Stella and whispered, "I think I had better go home. I'm sorry about Mr. Gladstone." Stella nodded a little wryly. "If at first you don't succeed . . ."¹ she said.

Philip followed her into the aisle. "Don't worry," she said to him, "I'll get a cab. You stay here with your mother and sister."

"I wouldn't hear of it," he said. "I'm sure your husband would be exceedingly angry if I allowed you to go home alone."

They walked together down the winding staircase of stone steps that led from the gallery to the public entrance at street level. While Philip left her to find a hansom, May predicted sadly to herself that this evening would see the collapse of the movement. Years later, she was to remember this moment very clearly as she stood on the pavement of Parliament Square in the light river mist on this cool summer evening. For that debate *was* the effective end of the NSWS and of the dynamic for the cause of women's rights. . . . at least, it was for the best part of twenty years.

"I sense," she said to Philip as they sat in the cab as it headed for St. James's Park, "that you're feeling a little smug that our old British Parliament has done exactly what you expected."

"Not smug," he corrected.

"I'd have preferred the Prime Minister to have attacked us," she went on, "but this patronizing approval, this attitude that there's much to be said for women but we mustn't be too hasty, must we . . . that's hard to combat."

"It's not," said Philip. "It's hard to combat in what you'd describe as a civilized way. . . . Society can only be changed by revolution, in one degree or another."

"I suppose you'd have us manning the barricades. . . ."

"In a manner of speaking," he agreed. "Your cause is small, so they could be small barricades."

"Small?" she queried. "It doesn't seem small."

"Small by contrast to the total change in society that's my cause . . . but you'll still have to fight if you're going to win it. . . . I mean literally. . . . Blood will have to flow. . . ."

"But only a little blood," she mocked, "to equal the size of the cause."

"No," he said, "probably quite a bit. . . ."

He was only saying what she had been thinking most of the evening, but she felt a need to oppose him. "You're speaking like your mother," she said.

"She's right . . ." He paused, and she could sense his eyes on her, although within the cab it was too dark to see until a street lamp they passed provided a little meager illumination. ". . . as you well know, for you agree with her, although you like to argue with me. It's part of the charade you seem to require us to act out. . . ."

"There's no charade," she answered quietly.

"Pretending, then. You select the word you favor. . . . Denying your feelings . . ."

The horse's hooves sounded louder suddenly as they left the expanse of Parliament Square and passed between the confines of the Treasury and the buildings opposite in George Street in the approach to the park.

"How dare you assume such certainty about my feelings?" She said it quietly, without anger. "And even if you were right, has our will no part to play? You cannot always respond to your feelings . . . that'd be barbaric. . . ."

He laughed. "Oh, May," he started. "I can call you May . . . please?"

"I don't suppose it matters what you call me," she replied. "Your mother and sister do. . . . Is it that important?"

"Of course it's important . . . May." He added the name almost shyly, savoring it, and repeated it with a kind of pride, as though he had won a prize. "May . . . May, from the moment I first met you I've known that you weren't just the ordinary bourgeois matron that you might seem to a casual visitor. . . . I've always known that you had spirit, that you had fires burning within you that leave you restless, that you even had a wildness—the kind of wildness a caged falcon must feel when he looks at the sky. . . ."

"That's very poetic," she said, "but absolute nonsense."

"There are depths in you that you haven't yet discovered," he went on, "aspects of your character, certainly of your emotions, that you haven't yet found. . . . You see yourself in a certain role, in a certain setting, but it's the wrong role, the wrong setting. . . . You're worth far more. . . . You'll not believe this now, but in fact you'd love my life in Paris. . . ."

For a few seconds, as they passed one of the park gas lamps, she could see his eyes. He was staring at her with a hot intensity as he spoke, and she had a need for him that was more violent even than she had ever felt before.

She shook her head with a vehemence that he took to be a denial of his words. "You think you wouldn't," he said, speaking now in the darkness, for they had left the lamp behind, "because you've been trained to the values, to the culture you've been raised in. . . . But these are the very values that should be challenged, because, believe me, they don't stand inspection. . . . That's why you'd love Paris. . . . You'd love the stimulation of exploration, of rethinking the old shibboleths that you've grown up with, of planning a new society, stripped of all the terrible evils of this one such as war, poverty, indignity. . . . Have you ever thought—I mean really thought—about the wounded in the Crimea, let alone the dead . . . the gangrene, the amputations, the screams of agony . . . and for what, May, for what? . . . In Paris, May, you'd be shown the prospect of freedom, and it'd excite you as nothing has before. You'd realize that in marriage you're a slave, that the whole structure of British life is rotten—*and* French life and German life and probably even American life. . . . The world, May, is rotten and must change. . . . Come and help me change it, May. Come with me . . . please come with me back to Paris. . . ."

She could not see him in the darkness, but she was experiencing the force of his feelings as though they were sound waves. "Surely," she asked in amazement, "you're not seriously asking me to leave my husband?"

"That's just what I'm doing," he said. "I'm asking you to break your bonds." Again, for a few seconds, she could see him in a park lamp, his eyes seeming to penetrate her almost physically.

"And get a divorce?" she asked. She seemed to be strangely out of breath.

"If you consider it necessary. . . . In Paris, it'd be an irrelevance. . . . In my whole life, May, I've never felt about a woman as I feel for you. . . . Never have I lived in such torture, experienced such vivid images, had an impression of such knowledge of another person. . . ."

"Please!" she gasped. For a moment, she was disoriented, her desire for him in violent conflict with a certainty that his suggestion was impossible. "Thank God we're nearly home," she said, voicing a thought she had not intended to speak aloud. It was an error, too.

"Cabby!" Philip ordered. "Drive round the park!"

"No!" she said sharply in alarm. "We must go home! We must—" But he stopped her from speaking with his mouth, and all the feelings that she had been repressing for so long exploded within her with such force that she feared she was going to faint. She felt a reeling giddiness, a strange blending of violent sensations and images. Through it all she was conscious of the sound of the horse's hooves, coming and going in waves, of the spasmodic glow when they passed the gas lamps. These were contacts with reality for which she was grateful, a defense against the enormity of the emotions, the aching, induced by his lips, by his hands ranging frantically over her body. They gave her back her will, reflected to her the shame of the sheer impropriety of her behavior, especially within the strict confines of a hansom cab.

With a huge effort, she pushed him from her. For a moment she could not speak, as, breathing heavily, she tried to regain her emotional balance. Madness, she thought, must be a bit like this. I must have been near the edge of madness.

"Come away with me now," he said.

"I have children . . ."

"They can come to you in Paris."

"You don't know what you're saying. . . . I have a husband whom I love . . ."

"It's your cage you love."

"Perhaps it's my cage," she agreed. She was breathing more easily, conscious of a general lowering of her intensity of emotion, like the water level dropping in a river lock.

"You cannot have known an experience like this before," he said. "It'd be an impossibility. You could only ever know emotions of this proportion with one person in a lifetime. . . . Every fraction of you must be crying out for my body at this minute, just as every particle of me is screaming with deprivation. . . ."

She said nothing. What could she say? The cab passed out of the park through the Buckingham Gate and traveled past the side of the palace. There were lights glowing behind several of the windows. "I'm never going to see you again," she said quietly.

"I don't believe you," he replied intensely. "May, don't you realize that God intended us for each other . . . God constituted us as a perfect complement . . ."

"God made me ten years older than you," she said stonily, staring in front of her, "and gave me a husband and three children, all of whom deserve my loyalty. . . . Philip . . ." Her tone was softer. "That's the first time I've ever used your name—and the last. . . . I'm never going to allow you in my presence again. . . . Nor your sister or your mother, much though I deeply admire and like them both. . . ."

"You're going to cut us all away from you," he said grimly, "like one slash with a saber."

"If you like."

"You'll bleed a lot of blood. . . ."

"That'll be my penance."

With relief, she saw that they were entering Eaton Square. "I just don't believe you're as strong as you appear," he said. "I shall call on you tomorrow."

"You'll not be admitted. You must accept it," she said in a softer tone. "I'll not see you again."

The cab came to a halt in front of her home. "Goodbye," she said. "I wish you well. No . . ." She put out her hand in restraint. "Please don't kiss me . . . or leave the cab. . . ."

He did not reply, for there was nothing he could say except, like her, "Goodbye," and he would not say that. She stepped down onto the pavement and mounted the entrance steps between the pillars of the house without looking behind her. Brandon had evidently been awaiting her return, for the front door swung back as she reached it and closed behind her.

"Has Mr. Kingston retired?" she asked.

"No, madam," the butler replied, "he's in the drawing room."

He opened the door for her, and for a moment she stood in the entrance of the big room. Thomas was sitting slouched in his big wing chair, a glass of whiskey in his hand, staring intently at the fireplace, where a fire was laid but not lit.

"Thomas," she said from the doorway. He did not reply or even move. She waited for a few seconds, heard the cab moving off in the street outside. Then she walked across the room toward him, conscious in the heavy silence of the rustling of her skirts. "Oh, Thomas," she said quietly. She sat on the arm of his chair and gently put one arm around his shoulders. For a moment she thought he was not going to respond, but then, almost absentmindedly, without changing his position, he lifted one hand to hers.

CHAPTER EIGHT

October 1888

· I ·

Thomas leaned back heavily, one hand resting on his desk, and studied
the boy who stood before him. His clothes were new, the crease sharp
in his trousers, his boots creaking when he moved, the high shine on his
tall starched collar still undulled by soap and water. He had fair hair,
like David, and was slim, even slight, and rather short—being no more
than five feet seven or eight. His features were fine, closely honed, and
he had his mother's blue eyes, which for a moment when he had
entered the room had slightly disconcerted Thomas, remembering the
circumstances of his promise to her.

At the time of that dramatic evening, Charles had been a little boy
of three; now, in 1888, he was sixteen, and Thomas, who had not seen
him recently, liked the look of him. He imparted an impression of lean
intelligence, his answers were firm like his handshake, and although he
was respectful in attitude, there was a boldness in his eyes. "Well,
Charles," Thomas said at last, "I'm going to say to you what I said to
Ramsay on the morning he joined the store. You're privileged. . . . Do
you understand what that means?"

"I think so, sir."

"What does it mean?"

"Well, if I understand you correctly, Mr. Kingston, you're referring to the fact that as the son of one of the shareholders special
opportunities will be open to me . . . and, of course, special responsibilities in consequence."

"That's well answered, Charles," said Thomas approvingly. "Your
father and I served a long apprenticeship in the trade, as no doubt you
know. . . . Well, like Ramsay, you've had a bit more education than
either of us did . . . and Kingstons is a lot bigger than Parsons ever was.
. . . So you're not indentured. . . . You'll be paid a wage of eight
shillings a week. . . . You'll start on the lowest rung of the Kingstons
ladder, so that you get a proper grounding and knowledge of the trade.

. . . At all times, you're to be clean and tidy. You're to be punctual and obey without question the manager in charge of you."

Thomas paused for a few seconds, realizing that he had not in fact said quite the same thing to Charles as he had to Ramsay when he had stood here before him, almost exactly a year ago. "You've got to be able to breathe the business, Ramsay," he had said then to his son. "You've got to develop an instinct, the way a wild animal acquires a sense of danger. If there's something wrong, you've got to know it without actually seeing it. . . . That's why you've got to do everything that anyone does in this store . . . quite apart from the beneficial effect that this'll have on your character. If you've packed the parcels, totted figures in the ledger, checked in the stock, gone out on deliveries, served customers, you'll get to know it . . . really *know* it, I mean . . . not just the trade, important though that is, but the living, pulsating organism that is this store, which is different from any other store, though the outward impression may bear similarities. You'll know it particularly in the future when you come to go out buying, for that's when you'll hear that inner voice that you must foster and cultivate, for it'll tell you that this line is right for Kingstons and that line is wrong, though you may not be able to explain exactly why. . . . You'll make mistakes, of course . . . that's how you learn; you'll overbuy and underbuy . . . you'll order goods you should never have ordered . . . but that's how you'll acquire the instinct that is vital if you're going to take my place at the head of this company and build Kingstons into the large, world-renowned business I know it can become."

"I understand, sir," Ramsay had answered.

Thomas had found his response vaguely unsatisfying, as though he were taking for granted everything he had said. "It won't be easy, Ramsay," he had added. "Don't think it'll be easy. . . ."

"I don't expect that, sir," Ramsay had answered, "but if you believe I've the talent to develop the instinct you describe, then I shall do my utmost to fulfill your trust."

What more could a father ask of his son? Yet Ramsay's answers still left Thomas with the feeling that he was approaching his career in the store, his destiny, with a certain lack of determination or, at least, an overconfidence. However, Thomas certainly had no cause for complaint about his son's performance. In his first year, he had shown exceptional promise. Reports from all the managers he had worked under had been uniformly good, praising the speed with which he had absorbed their instruction and the high level of his competence.

Thomas should have been delighted, but what bothered him was the impression Ramsay gave of effortless ease. For this must surely mean that he could strive harder, could be even better. And how, Thomas worried, would this relaxed attitude be rewarded when he engaged in battle with the Goldsmiths and the Camerons who were certain to challenge him?

Looking now at Charles Rawlings, sensing that he too had much potential, Thomas wondered for a moment to what extent he would compete with Ramsay, even questioned if he could be a danger to him—then dismissed the thought. Kingstons was a Kingston company, for all David's minority stockholding. Ramsay would succeed him at its head, and in turn, Ramsay's son would follow him. Even so, that would give Charles ample scope to achieve prominence in the store—as Thomas had assured his mother. Yet the thought of Lillian gave Thomas a brief moment of unease. He knew her ambition well enough, and he sensed that this young man standing before him had inherited much of the ruthless drive that she possessed.

There was a knock on the door, and Ramsay entered the room. "You sent for me, sir?" he said.

"I did, Ramsay. . . . You're well acquainted with Charles Rawlings, of course. . . ."

Ramsay held out his hand and smiled. "I'm pleased to welcome you to the store, Charles." Thomas was strangely moved by Ramsay's warm greeting. His behavior was correct, acting as he was as a kind of host, as the son of the Managing Director and major shareholder; but he did it well, with grace and no hint of patronage. At seventeen, with his hair cut short with a side parting in the modern style, he had become handsome, and his relaxed manner, which so disturbed Thomas within the business, was without question a desirable quality at the social level.

"I want you to show Charles the store before he starts work," Thomas said. "Take him everywhere, so he gets a complete picture, what we do and how we do it. Then he's to report to Mr. Patterson in Dispatch . . . Patterson's expecting him. To avoid confusion with his father, he'll be addressed as Mr. Charles. . . . Off you both go, then. You have my best wishes, Charles."

"Thank you, sir," Charles responded, and following Ramsay's indication, he went out the door.

For a few seconds, Thomas stayed sitting at his desk. Then he got to his feet and walked over to the window of his office and stood, with his hands in his trouser pockets, looking down at the traffic in Sloane Street. Seeing the two boys—young men now, though it seemed only a short while since they had been small children—had made him pensive, had caused him to ponder the passing of time, the inexorable passage from youth to old age. It was only a short span, really, and now that he was in his forties the rate of movement seemed to be growing faster. He watched a victoria going by in the street below. It was well appointed, with a fine, sleek pair, and for an instant he thought they were wearing the Banbury livery; but almost immediately he realized that he was mistaken, that it was merely similar. It made him think of Eve, though. Four years had passed since that last strange evening with her in Sydney Street—*and* since the perplexing confrontation with May, which, though having no direct connection with it, formed in his memory part of the same turbulent week. He had not seen Eve since, though he had heard of her from time to time from Edwards, who, as custodian of the Banbury shares, was still on the Kingston board.

The abrupt manner in which she had ended their relationship was something he had never been able to understand. He suspected a connection with Bob Ramsay, for May's brother had made no attempt to contact him again after their last abrasive meeting. Occasionally, he had congratulated himself that a strong line such as this was the way to deal with scoundrels like Ramsay, but he knew that it was more likely that Eve had bought him off. Again, though, she had denied any approach when he had asked her—and why should she lie to him?

Once on impulse he had visited Mrs. Deneuve in Sydney Street and asked if he might see their rooms. She had tried to dissuade him, speaking of lodgers, but when he had insisted, he had realized why this sensitive woman had tried to spare him the experience. For they bore no trace of his life with Eve; not even the curtains or wallpaper were the same. In fact, for a moment he wondered if he had dreamed it all.

"Do we not owe you some money, Mrs. Deneuve?" he had asked.

She had shaken her head with a sad smile. "Her Ladyship was most generous," she had replied, which at least proved the reality.

Since then, whenever he had gone hunting at Quainton he had hoped to see her, but although she went out quite often, so he was told, she was never riding with the hounds on the days that he had been there. He would inquire about her sometimes from his brother, but Edward would deliberately limit his replies, with an expression of disapproval of Thomas' interest in her. Edward had changed since his marriage to Agnes Cameron. He had become corpulent and magisterial and a pillar of the church and was often critical of Thomas, whom he clearly suspected of defects of character—all of which struck Thomas as being a little rich considering the circumstances of his union to

Agnes. For one day Edward had just driven over to Marston Hall to ask Cameron for his daughter's hand, which he had known he would refuse, and taken her straight back to the farm in the trap—with a furious Cameron shouting imprecations from the entrance steps of the hall.

Fortunately, their mother had still been alive at the time, so with Mary there as well, Agnes had been well chaperoned during the three weeks while the marriage banns were read.

Cameron had not attended the wedding, at which Thomas had served as best man, but he had chosen the moment when the couple emerged from the church to ride by in the road, looking sternly ahead of him, as though he had no notion of what was happening in the village that day. Since then Agnes had borne him a grandson, but even this event—which she had written to tell him about in a conciliatory letter—had so far failed to pierce the armor of this strange and bitter man.

Thomas had anticipated that the marriage would incite Cameron to renew his earlier campaign of litigation, but he did not do this. It was only when Thomas decided to buy some land at Quainton that they met in competition, which was even fiercer than it might otherwise have been. The acres Thomas wanted lay on the far side of the village from the farm, on the slope of the hills. It bordered the western edges of Cameron's big estate, so it was not solely malice that made him drive the price up to a level that had Edward urging Thomas to concede defeat—though malice, of course, was there. But Thomas had been determined to gain that land whatever the cost, for it was on that high ground that he planned to build the mansion he had visualized on the cold March day so many years before when he had first looked down from the Quainton Hills at Marston Hall.

And Thomas had got his land. "You're going to have to grow golden grass to merit that price, Mr. Kingston," Cameron had sneered as he had stalked out of the sale room before Thomas could reply.

He had never regretted the purchase. He only had to think of those sloping fields and the plans for the big house that his architects had drawn to find himself smiling—as indeed he was when Sidney Baines knocked on his door and entered the room.

It was time for their morning meeting, and Thomas moved back to his desk. "What do you make of young Charles Rawlings . . . after your interview?" Baines asked.

"Well," Thomas said, sitting down heavily, "our friend Goldsmith would describe him as a colt with promise. Personally . . ." He paused for a second. " . . . I'd say he'll make the weight even in heavy going. . . ."

"The ready-to-wear dresses," Ramsay declared a few minutes after the two boys had left the Managing Director's office, "is now the biggest department in the store. That fact, according to my father, is a signpost to the immense future of the trade. A few years ago, no lady would have purchased a gown off the rails. She'd had bought material and had it made up by her dressmaker. Now the sales rise every year. . . . Why do you think that is, Charles?"

"Well, I suppose it's easier . . . and presumably the design's better. . . ."

"Not bad, Charles," Ramsay responded. "Not bad. . . . Ease, Charles. Shopping-under-one-roof, Charles. Better workmanship, Charles. Better design, Charles, as you say . . . for here at Kingstons we can afford the best of talents. . . . What's more, it's happening in every field of merchandise . . . We stand at the dawn of the new golden age of retailing, Charles. That's what Father thinks, anyway. Mind you, he does labor the point a bit. . . ."

They were standing in the dress alterations room, watching the rows of girls busy with their sewing machines, dexterously feeding material to their needles. Ramsay led Charles between two of the lines to a section where the seamstresses were working on white satin and silk wedding gowns. "Have you sewn a hair of your own head into the seam?" Ramsay asked one girl.

"Not yet, sir," she answerd.

"But you're going to, of course, so let's see you do it. . . ." He turned back to Charles, speaking quietly. "It's a rather pleasing custom. . . . No wedding gown leaves this room without this little personal extra. . . . The young ladies believe it'll ensure them a husband too— like the brides they're serving."

Shyly, the girl put her hand to her head, and with a quick movement, withdrew a long strand, which she threaded with nervous fingers into a hand needle. As she started to sew it into the seam of the dress she was working on, Ramsay smiled at her. "I hope it brings you luck," he said. "You deserve a good chappie—a pretty girl like you." She blushed and looked down.

"And what, may I ask, are you doing in here, Mr. Ramsay?"

The voice came from behind him, but he knew who it was. "Obeying my father's orders, Miss Lane." He turned. "You know Mr. Rawlings, of course?" he said. "Mr. Charles, as we're to call him. It's his first day in the store and I'm taking him on a tour."

"That doesn't include disturbing my young ladies," she said.

"I was introducing him to the customs of the trade," Ramsay responded. "Miss Lane," he added to Charles with a grin, "was one of Kingstons' first employees. I've always had a secret suspicion that she's really the head of the store—an *éminence grise*. . . . Even Father's scared of her."

"That's enough of that kind of talk, Mr. Ramsay," she snapped, though it had pleased her. "You'll enjoy the business, I'm sure," she added to Charles.

They moved to the next room, which was the cobblers' repair department. "For every one sales assistant," said Ramsay, "there are six people employed whom the public never see. These are some of them. Others are packing parcels, doing accounts, checking stock, driving vans, baking cakes and Heaven knows what else."

And so the tour continued, with Ramsay explaining the basic facts of each section, adding any especially colorful details. He spoke to Charles with the slightly superior tone of a young man who had attained the great age of seventeen, as compared with sixteen, and to whom the store was now very familiar territory.

He took Charles into the Dispatch Department, explained the design behind the scene of continuing activity—the chutes and pulleys and moving belts that took the parcels to the various points for loading onto the vans—and drew his attention to the manner in which, on his father's insistence, all bows on the string were tied, whether the goods were wrapped down here or upstairs in the departments. For every package from Kingstons bore the same distinctive character. "You'll learn how to tie them fast enough during your time in here," said Ramsay.

He showed Charles the big arrival bays, where the merchandise was delivered from the wholesalers and manufacturers before being checked, recorded and ticketed. Then they went out to the stables, where they found Harry in a somber mood. He had been working in Kingstons for three months and, during the past few weeks, had been subject to the rigorous supervision of Butler, the head groom. That morning on his daily round of the store, his father had found fault with two horses of which Harry was in charge, and when he had learned that they were his son's responsibility, he had given orders that he was to be disciplined.

As a result of this edict, Harry had barely had time to greet Charles before Butler had roared at him, "You get on with your work, Mr. 'Arry! You get that horse really spanking or by God you'll hear from me!" Gruffly the head groom had acknowledged Charles when

Ramsay introduced him before striding off, grumbling under his breath.

"I think," Ramsay explained as they left the stable yard, "that even as little as three months has been enough to make Father despair of Harry's talents as a merchant. That's why he's agreed at last to let him work in the stables. . . . Horses are Harry's passion. Well, I suppose there are worse passions. . . ."

They made their way through the basement stockrooms—a warrenlike area, consisting of room after room crammed with racks and rails of merchandise—until they reached the Fire Office, where Mr. Foster, the fireman, led Charles to a plan of the store displayed on one wall and pointed out the positions of the hydrants on each floor. "Hoses are permanently fixed to them," he explained, "so that they can be operated without delay. . . . And you see those doors marked in red? They're special. . . . Most are heavy oak, which burns slowly, but the key ones are made of iron. . . . If there was a fire, it'd be my first duty to see that they were closed. That'd cut off the draft, of course. . . ."

They moved on to the detectives' room, where Ramsay introduced Charles to Mr. Smith, a huge man with an enormous moustache, which drooped at the ends. "Mr. Smith's the Kingston sleuth . . . if you'll forgive the levity, Mr. Smith. It's his job to catch the shoplifters. . . . They're a problem, aren't they, Mr. Smith?"

"Like a plague of rats," agreed Smith, whose tone indicated that he did not forgive Ramsay's levity, "and fraud . . . and larceny. . . . The big stores present great scope to the criminal fraternity—especially in conspiracies. That's people inside—staff—working 'and-in-glove with people outside. . . . It's very 'ard to track 'em down, because you can't usually detect it by observation, as you can shoplifters. The thieves get given the merchandise openly, all wrapped up as though they was a customer. . . . Conspiracies are my nightmare. . . . Not that we've 'ad one yet . . . but we will. . . ."

"Mr. Smith came to us from Scotland Yard on his retirement from the force," Ramsay explained to Charles when they had left the office. "We're proud of him. . . . Not many stores have their own detective yet, but Father believes he's already saved us hundreds of pounds."

He led the way through the selling floors—through the food, the wines, the furniture, the saddlery, the piece goods, the fashion departments—and the Mourning. "Bereavement is a major source of business," he explained. "You must have been in mourning a few times yourself, but here"—he performed a sweep with his arm to indicate the whole department, where black gowns and other apparel of grief were displayed and the staff spoke in whispers—"they need to be aware of every fine detail of the etiquette . . . that is, if the loved one is to be shown suitable respect. . . . For a widow, for example, there's first mourning, when she is expected to limit herself to full crape, and second mourning, when she may wear the crape in tucks. . . . In first mourning, she may carry a crape parasol, but without trimming. In second mourning, it may have a fringe of lace . . . black lace, of course.

Charles looked round the department with wonder, noting the handkerchiefs with black borders, the widow's caps, the headstones and memorial plates—even, on one small stand, the stationery edged with mourning. "Most of the trade is done by our staff in the customers' homes, of course," Ramsay went on, "since at times of bereavement they're often in no state to visit us here. . . . We organize everything, including the funerals. We offer a wide range . . . from two pounds ten shillings for a child—the crape is then in white, of course—to forty pounds for a lavish affair with airtight coffins and black ostrich plumes on the horses and the hearse. . . . We can also arrange cremation, but it's a new practice, of course, and I understand there's little call for it. . . ."

He ushered him out of that hushed department into a passage. "You see, Charles," he went on with a smile, "our service is comprehensive. Whatever our customers need in life—or in death—Kingstons is ready to supply it. That's the concept of the emporium. . . ."

Charles was deeply impressed with Ramsay's detailed knowledge of the store, and he did not mind his slightly condescending attitude as he lectured him, partly because he knew it was good-natured enough, but mainly because he was finding the tour itself, with its constant revelation of new aspects of the business, tremendously exciting. When Ramsay had spoken, with that slightly mocking undertone, of his father's concept of the emporium and its future, Charles had suddenly known with great certainty that this was an environment in which he could thrive, in which he would succeed—more, in which he *must* succeed.

During the past few months, when the date for him to join Kingstons had drawn closer, he had been hesitant. For as long as he could remember, his mother had spoken of "When you join the store, Charles . . ." During his last few years at school, she had urged him constantly to "get to know the Kingston boys better. After all, one day you'll be directing the store together. . . ." Sometimes she would speak like this in front of his father, and as Charles had grown older and more aware, he had wondered if she did this to annoy him, for the store did not seem to be very important to him. "Charles'll do well in the store," she would say when they were together sometimes. "Very well."

At these moments, his father, with his gray hair and steel spectacles and the gauntness that had come to his face, would give a little nod and agree: "Yes, my dear . . . yes, perhaps . . . I hope so . . ." She would glare at him for his lack of enthusiasm, and Charles would wish he were not present, would wonder if he himself wanted to join the store, which seemed so vital to his mother.

Charles's parents quarreled a lot, and although he had assumed that all parents quarreled, he had been conscious that the store seemed to cause much of the friction—together with his father's work in the church and, in particular, his associated interest in the Salvation Army. At first Charles had not understood his mother's objection to the Army, for although they argued about it in front of him and the other two children, they did not actually speak of it in detail. It was only when the "scandalous campaign," as his mother described it, began appearing in the *Pall Mall Gazette* that he discovered at last, by reading the newspaper himself when no one was looking, of the Army's program to save fallen women from the streets. Charles was only thirteen in 1885 when William Thomas Stead, one of the most famous editors in London, had thrown his resources behind the Salvation Army and launched an attack in open print in the *Gazette* against the prostitution of young girls—the exact meaning of which Charles found out only by badgering one of the housemaids. But his father's involvement with the campaign caused the most serious spate of quarrels between his parents that he had so far experienced. "It's quite shocking," his mother had suddenly declared at breakfast when she read the first of Stead's articles. "Utterly unsuitable as material for a daily newspaper—especially one of this repute."

His father had looked up with a grim expression on his face. "It's not as shocking or as unsuitable as the crimes it exposes," he said.

"And what about its effect on the store?" she had demanded. "You're a director of the store . . . or have you forgotten that in your obsession with these . . . these . . ." She had broken off her sentence because of the presence of the children.

"What has it to do with the store?" he had asked, genuinely puzzled.

"Oh, you're so foolish sometimes," she had exploded, "that I wonder how I've managed to live with you all these years! You don't deny, I suppose, that you've been helping Mr. Stead gather material for his articles, that you've aided Mr. Booth and the Army in their scandalous campaign . . ."

"Of course," he had agreed. "We've all done our best to help. . . . It's a terrible evil that must be stopped. . . ."

"And if your name should be featured in the papers? As a director of Kingstons?"

He had hesitated, and Charles had noted how he had lifted his head slightly higher before answering her, as though in challenge.

"That's extremely unlikely, but would it matter so much?"

"Of course it would!" she had snapped. "It'd do great harm to the store!"

"You mean," he said, "that you think our customers would condone this . . . this slavery? . . . These are mere children, my dear . . . as young as twelve and thirteen. Surely you don't believe our customers—"

"I doubt very much," she had cut in, "that they'd approve the publication of these salacious details in a family newspaper like the *Pall Mall Gazette*. I doubt that they'd approve of a director of the store being involved with such matters."

Charles had seen his father tense and once more bring himself under control. "I find your logic strange," he said. "Mr. Gladstone's interest in these poor creatures is well known."

"You compare yourself to an eminent man like Mr. Gladstone!" she exclaimed.

"If the public condone these interests in the leader of the nation," he answered quietly, "I don't see why they should object to them in the director of a store . . . but if they do, then I have to say to you that there are some things in this world that are even more important than the store . . . and among these is human suffering . . . and appalling sin . . ."

The quarrel between them became more heated as the articles continued. "Oh, my God!" she had exclaimed at one moment. "Is there no limit to what they'll do?" For Stead and Booth, as Charles discovered later, had actually purchased a thirteen-year-old girl for five pounds to prove that a market in virgins existed and shipped her to France to show how easy it was for white slavers to supply the Continental brothels—though this girl, of course, was safe in the hands of the Salvation Army.

The articles had shocked the nation, and they *had* caused the law to be changed. In an act rushed through Parliament, the age of sexual consent for girls had been raised from thirteen to sixteen. Stead and Booth, however, had been put on trial for abduction, since the facts of the human sale—which had made such dramatic reading—had not been quite so clear-cut as they had seemed. Stead, the famous editor, had been jailed for three months.

Charles's father, who had played so limited a role, had not attracted any attention, either in the newspapers or from the police, but his mother had been distraught, believing that his escape from prosecution had been extremely narrow. During these dramatic days, she had spoken to Charles more often of the store, of the importance of a business career, of the fact that the correct place for religion in a person's life was in church on Sundays and at prayer at home.

However, the cause of young prostitutes continued to be the source of violent quarrels long after the Stead case. In fact, the conflict reached a crisis only two weeks before Charles joined the store over a young girl named Betty Smart in whom his father had taken a special interest. He had been in his bedroom late one afternoon when he had heard his father's raised voice: "Woman, don't press me too far. . . . I know my duty to Betty . . . and to these other poor girls . . . and to God!"

"Your duty to Betty!" he had heard his mother taunt. "What you feel for that slut isn't duty. It's nothing but disgusting desire!"

"How dare you!" he had retorted furiously.

"It's not her soul that leads you to her every evening," his mother had goaded. "It's her body! That ecstasy you feel when you kneel beside her in those fervent prayers is not the Glory of God . . . it's common-or-garden lust!"

"Silence, woman!" his father had raged. "Silence or I'll strike you!" And there *had* been silence—for a few seconds. Then, speaking with more control but still loudly, he had said, "You've no understanding of the course of righteousness . . . or of the ways of God. . . ." And Charles had heard a door slam.

A few moments later, his mother had come into his room. He had never seen her look so upset. "I don't know what I'm going to do about your father," she had muttered. "He could have been a force in the world, Charles . . . he could have been a Thomas Kingston . . . and look what he's become. . . ." Suddenly she had looked at him with great intensity and put her arms on his shoulders. "You'll make your mark, Charles. . . . I've great faith in you. . . . You'll make your mark won't you, Charles?"

"I'll do my best, Mama," he had said. He had spoken with as much confidence as he could muster, but it had only increased his apprehension at the prospect of joining the store. At first, his uncertainty had not been eased by his tour with Ramsay, who, friendly though he had been, had left no doubt that as a Kingston, he was a member of the ruling family. Charles had felt outshone by Ramsay's apparent urbanity and easy manner and had reacted with reserve. It was only after they had left the Mourning Department and he had felt that sudden certainty that he was suited to the retail store business that he began to relax.

"French bodies!" Ramsay declared as they walked along a passage. "*Nude* French bodies . . . that's what I'm going to show you now, Charles. . . . I don't suppose you've ever seen a nude French body, have you?"

"Are they very different from English bodies?" inquired Charles carefully, in a tone intended to suggest that English bodies were not outside his experience.

"Some people appear to think so," answered Ramsay. He opened a door. "This is the window dressers' store . . . and those are our lovelies. . . ."

The room was filled with display equipment of various kinds, but along one wall were about a dozen costume stands of a type that Charles had never seen before. Vague, rather unformed parts of torsos —usually just shoulders—were common enough, for the display of hats, jewelry and even furs, but the figures that Ramsay was now showing him with such pride were full-length, each made closely in the shape of a woman's undressed figure. They were ranged modestly facing the wall, with their backs to the two boys. All except one were headless, with strange short wooden handles jutting rather obscenely from the necks. Some were cut off at the knee, suspended by single metal rods that stood in heavy round bases, but one or two had legs and even feet, enclosed in button-up boots.

"Always in the forefront, Charles," declared Ramsay. "That's Kingstons . . . especially in window dressing, for that's my father's hobbyhorse. . . . We were first with electric light; now we're going to lead the field with French bodies. On Monday this bevy of beauties'll be astounding the passersby in Sloane Street."

"How do you know they're French?" asked Charles.

"Says so on them," Ramsay answered. "Look! . . . Excuse me, mam'selle." He apologized and turned the one model that was equipped with both a head and feet so that she faced Charles in all her nudity. "The label's on her stomach," he went on. "See—Sheldons' Lady's French Body Costume Stand Number Six. . . . Father heard that Sheldons had got a first consignment in, and he sent Mathews to Manchester with orders to bring them back immediately if they were good and persuade Sheldons not to sell to any other store for a month. . . . Mathews is the head window dresser. . . . Wonder where she comes from—the girl they made her from, I mean. . . ." He half-turned the model back, so that he could survey her as well. She had a rather crude face, colored with rouge and equipped with stringy red hennaed hair and glass eyes. "Wonder if she's strolling the boulevards at this very moment. . . . Rather fetching bit of jam, don't you think? Of course, her face *is* a little . . . immobile, would you say, Charles? Not the most expressive lady I've ever met. . . ."

"Rather glassy-eyed," responded Charles with a grin.

"Not too supple, either, I wouldn't think," Ramsay added. "She wouldn't exactly make an ideal partner in the Lancers, would she?"

"Certainly not without any clothes on," suggested Charles, and they both burst out laughing, the reserve between them suddenly gone.

Ramsey closed the door of the store, still chuckling. "You know, Charles," he said as they walked along the passage, "you're not a bad chappie at all. . . ."

"Thank you, Ramsay," he answered happily. "If anyone was to ask me, I'd say you were a pretty good sort yourself."

They went into the Gentlemen's Wear Department, which was where Ramsay, in his training in various parts of the store, was currently posted for a few weeks. He introduced Charles to the buyer, Mr. Albert Brown, who, he said, had started in Kingstons as an errand boy, and explained the principle of the stock-control system—how every time the shop assistants made a sale, they wrote out a bill, a copy of which went to the Accounts Department.

One of the assistants approached Ramsay while they were talking and told him a customer was inquiring for him. "Can you look after yourself for a moment, Charles?" he said.

Left on his own, Charles felt a little lost, even conspicuous in his new clothes. He wandered round the department, examining the stock, watching the assistants at work. Then his attention was caught by one young salesman in particular—or rather, by the customer he was serving, an elegant man in his mid-twenties, in a well-cut morning suit and stylish silk topper. He was buying some shirts, and with Ramsay's explanation of the stock-control system fresh in his mind, Charles noted the way the assistant wrote out the bill for three shirts, totted up the total, accepted some money from the customer and dispatched it in the little metal container on the overhead wire to the countinghouse.

While awaiting the change, he laid out a sheet of packing paper, wrapped up the shirts and tied the parcel with string. Charles would have thought nothing of the scene if he had not seen the bill quite clearly. For he was certain that the salesman had put six shirts, not three, as invoiced, in the package—though he did wonder if his imagination had been overstimulated by Mr. Smith's vivid talk of conspiracies. Yet as he looked at the parcel as it lay on the counter, it seemed far too bulky for only three shirts.

The metal cash container arrived back on its overhead wire from the countinghouse. The assistant extracted the change and handed it, together with the parcel, to his elegant customer, who was walking toward the exit from the department as Ramsay returned. The young man seemed in no hurry, as might be expected, even stopping on his way out to examine a display of handkerchiefs. "I may be making a terrible fool of myself," Charles told Ramsay, "but I'll swear that customer over there has six shirts in his parcel against a bill made out for three."

"Then we must stop him," said Ramsay.

"But I may be mistaken."

"It won't matter if you are. I'll be very polite, I can assure you."

Ramsay hurried up to the customer and was extremely courteous, apologizing with a smile for troubling him, but the young man reacted with flushed anger. By now, the attention of Mr. Brown had been caught. He strode across the room toward them and, on learning the cause, insisted firmly that the young man return to the counter and the parcel be unwrapped. And there, indeed, were six shirts.

"Mr. Ramsey," said Brown, ignoring the salesman's pleas of astonishment, "you'll conduct this customer to Mr. Baines. Mr. Charles will accompany you. . . . Tell Mr. Baines I'll be with him directly. So will Mr. Smith. . . ."

There was no question that it was Charles's day. "What a stroke of luck, by golly!" said Ramsay admiringly. "You haven't been in the store more than a few hours and you've exposed the very type of conspiracy that Mr. Smith described." Mr. Baines congratulated him; Mr. Smith praised his talent for keen observation; and, just before seven P.M., the store's closing time, Thomas sent for him. "You've made a fine start, Charles," he said, "as I'll tell your father. . . . It's not just a question of three shirts. . . . What you saw is probably taking place several times a day. In fact, Mr. Smith believes you've given us a lead into something much bigger, involving salesmen in other departments as well—the tip of the iceberg, you could say."

Thomas had also sent for Ramsay, who now entered the office. "I think you should take young Charles out for a celebratory tankard," he said. Then he smiled suddenly, as a thought struck him. "It'd be a happy thought if you gave the George the Second your patronage. That's where his father and I sealed our partnership eighteen years ago." He reached into his pocket. "There's a florin. . . . Don't spend it

all on beer or you won't be fit for work in the morning. . . . Save some
of it for dinner."

"Of course," remarked Ramsay an hour later as they sat at a table
in the crowded bar of the George II, "you and I are in a strange
position, Charlie." Ramsay had started calling him "Charlie" after the
second pint of half-and-half, which was a mixture of porter and ale.
"We're stuck with each other, Charlie. . . . Our dear papas at least had
some choice in the matter. They elected to be partners—sitting in this
very bar. Let's be partners, they said. . . ."

"And that was the end of their friendship, it seems," Charles
ruminated. "A bit sad, isn't it? Before that they were best friends."

"To be expected, I suppose, Charlie . . . apprentices together . . .
sharing everything . . . those awful hours . . . that terrible buyer . . .
There was a lot binding them together."

"You'd think that sharing a business'd do the same, wouldn't you?"

"Not with Father," said Ramsay. "He's got very fixed ideas. Always has had, according to Mother. . . . I don't suppose your poor old
dad had a chance of making much impact on him. Probably gave up
trying after a while. . . ."

"At least we haven't got that problem," said Charles, putting his
tankard to his lips and drinking deeply.

"What problem?"

Charles put the tankard down on the table. "Well, we haven't
been friends exactly, have we? Certainly not close friends. We never
met, did we? I didn't even see much of Harry, and he was in the same
form."

"No," Ramsay said a bit dubiously, and drank some beer. "Strange,
that. . . . Perhaps it was because our parents didn't meet . . . not
outside the store. . . . Perhaps we thought we should keep a distance . . .
sort of instinctively. . . ."

"Perhaps," agreed Charles. "All the same, it should be a help now.
Nothing to confuse the issue like our paters had . . . no conflicts of
loyalty . . ."

"We can see a lot of each other or not," Ramsay agreed, "as we
choose. . . . I wonder how we're going to get on, Charlie. . . . Ten
years' time, say. . . . Will we be at each other's throats? Perhaps I'll
have fixed ideas then, like Father, and you'll have trouble making an
impact. . . ."

Charles's expression was suddenly serious. "I'll make an impact,
Ramsay," he said quietly.

Ramsay glanced at him, noting the determination in his voice. "I believe you will, Charlie."

"I'm not the same sort of person as my father."

"No . . ." Ramsay ruminated a little doubtfully. "I suppose I'm not like my father either." He sipped his beer. "What sort of person are you, then, Charlie?" he asked. "When you're making your impact in ten years' time . . . what kind of impact will it be, Charlie?"

"I don't know exactly," Charles answered. Then he looked straight at Ramsay, an expression on his face that was almost grimly serious. "I'll be running a store," he asserted.

For a moment Ramsay did not respond. Then, eyeing Charles curiously, he said, "Now, that's a strange way of putting it, Charlie. After all, that's the idea, isn't it . . . running a store? I've spent the day showing you what running a store involves, haven't I?—or at least, some aspects of it. That's what we're both being trained for. . . . So what did you mean, Charlie?"

"What I said . . . I'll be running a store."

Ramsay knew what Charles was telling him. He was saying that the relationship of their fathers would not be repeated in their sons. He was saying that Ramsay should not assume that Charles would be content to accept a secondary role in Kingstons, that the position of Crown Prince was incontestable. It was a challenge, and it was early for such a challenge, and Ramsay knew that had it not been for the effect of the beer, Charles would never have made it. But he *had* made it.

For a moment there was silence between them. Then at last Ramsay said coldly, "For a youth of sixteen who's just completed his first day in the trade, that's a bold thing to say." Suddenly he laughed, breaking the tension. "I'll get us both another tankard . . . and then we'll dine."

· 2 ·

That October of 1888 was to be a month they would all remember to the smallest awful detail. It was unusually cold, and the night fogs— the "London particulars," as they were called—had started early. Even as late as noon of the day that David Rawlings' deep concern for fallen women—and especially for Betty Smart—erupted into tragedy, mist still lingered in Sloane Street.

For Thomas there was no warning sense of what lay ahead. In fact, he was in a very good mood. Ever since seven o'clock, Mathews,

the window dresser, and his assistants had been installing new displays
with the revolutionary French body costume stands. By midday,
Thomas had estimated that they would have made enough progress for
him to take a first critical look at them, and he had gone downstairs
with an eager sense of anticipation that had lost none of its edge for
him with the passing years.

When Thomas saw the new windows, he was delighted. Because
of their female shape, the stands made the gowns look superb, the
elaborate pleats and folds falling into the natural lines the designers had
intended in a way that had never been possible with the previous
methods.

Sloane Street was busy that day. Carriages were arriving at the
Kingston entrance and departing. Hansoms and trade vehicles were
rattling past the store over the cobbles. There were many passersby on
the pavement, and Thomas was amused how their attention was suddenly caught by the full-length models that they had never seen before
—especially by the lady with the head of red hennaed hair, now attired
elegantly in a gown of deep green velvet. Farther off, Thomas could
just hear the newsboys in Sloane Square, calling out the headlines of
the first editions of the evening papers: "Ripper strikes again . . .
Double murder . . . New victims for Jack the Ripper . . ."

Following his usual custom, Thomas crossed the street so that he
could study the new displays in a perspective of the whole store
frontage—and saw David walking along the pavement toward him. He
had not seen him for a week or so, and he was a little shocked by his
appearance. David had aged markedly in recent years. Like Thomas
himself, he was forty-three, but he looked a good ten years older. His
hair and beard were now completely gray, and he had lost a great deal
of weight, becoming thin and bony and, in the face, almost emaciated.
He wore outdated clothes, too—the short topper that had been in
fashion ten years before; a double-breasted frock coat that was now
worn by few—and this, coupled with an awkward, almost labored,
way of walking, contributed to the impression he gave of aging.

"Morning," he said rather sharply, without stopping to talk, and
Thomas noted his expression of grim anger as he stalked across the
road.

Thomas stayed for a few minutes looking at the new windows,
then went back into the store to instruct Mathews to make some minor
changes.

That day he had a lot on his mind; but at that moment, for some
reason, the problem of Harry rose to the surface among his various

worries, and he decided on impulse to go back to the stable yard,
where he had been earlier on his round, for a longer talk with Butler.
Harry was not settling into the store at all well. Even in the stables,
where Thomas could not possibly leave a son of his indefinitely despite
Harry's keen interest in horses, his performance was barely adequate.

As Thomas entered the yard, Harry was trying to hitch a big gray
to the traces of one of the vans. The horse was refusing to back up into
position, swinging his quarters away from the vehicle. Harry was attempting to gentle him. "Come on, now," he said, "easy, now." Thomas
remained unobserved, watching his son.

Harry led the horse forward to give himself room to straighten
him up, and once more tried to back him along the shaft. The other
horse of the pair, a bay, already harnessed, was stamping nervously in
response to the antics of his partner. "Back, boy, back," Harry urged
the gray, holding a whip along the open side so that he could tap his
quarters if he tried to swing out as he had before. At that moment the
horse reared up and, as Harry moved sideways to avoid the hooves,
lunged forward away from the traces.

"Lord God, Mr. 'Arry," Butler suddenly roared from the door of
his office. "Ain't you got that 'orse in the traces yet? What 'ave you
been doing for the last ten minutes—going for a ride in the park?"

"This horse isn't sound, Mr. Butler," Harry protested. "As I told
you, he's got a bad sore under his collar."

"I'll decide whether 'e's sound or not, Mr. 'Arry," said Butler,
stalking over to him. "All you 'ave to do is what you're told. . . .
You've been told to 'itch up the 'orse, so 'itch 'im up!"

"Yes, Mr. Butler," Harry responded, and once again he led the
horse forward and began to back him toward the van. And again the
horse began to fight him, lifting his head to try to jerk the reins from
his hands.

"Give me that whip!" roared Butler angrily, "and get out of my
way!" He grabbed the reins from Harry and quickly twisted them so
that they were tight under the bit round the animal's lower jaw. Then
he jabbed him hard in the mouth. "Now get back, you bastard!" he
snarled at the horse, who responded by swinging his quarters as he had
before. Butler lashed his side with the long whip. "I'll teach you, by
God!" he swore. And he lashed him again. The horse swung away
from the pain into position at the traces—but then, as he had before, he
reared.

It was now a contest between horse and man—and the man knew
he had to dominate him. Twisting the whip in his hands, Butler struck

him hard on the head with the heavy handle. "I'll teach you!" he growled. "By God, I'll teach you!"

The blow shocked the horse, and he lurched against the other animal in the pair, his head twitching, tensed for another stroke. "Get that trace hooked to his collar, boy! Go on—don't just stand there! Glory be to God, how many more times?"

Harry rushed to hitch the trace to the horse. "Mr. Butler, please," he insisted when he had harnessed him. "That sore's troubling him . . . the collar's lying right on it. . . ."

"Thank you, Mr. 'Arry," said Butler, "but I've been looking at horses' sores for forty years and when I want your opinion I'll bloody ask for it. . . . That 'orse'll settle now . . . and so that you can learn, you can go out on the van. . . . Rogers!" he ordered the van driver, who had just appeared from the stables. "You'll take Mr. 'Arry with you."

Thomas, who had still been unnoticed by anyone, did not wait to witness any more. It was not the moment to talk to Butler, though he could not complain at the way he had treated Harry. He had given orders that he was in no way to be mollycoddled.

He walked back into the store and strolled through several of the ground-floor departments, his eyes alert. He was approaching the Fancy Goods, which was positioned near the main entrance, when his attention was caught by a young woman at the counter because she was unusual for the store. Her clothes were of too poor a quality for her to be a customer, and she did not bear the look of the servants who were often sent in to make purchases. As he drew near, he heard her ask one of the salesladies where she could find Mr. Rawlings— which, he thought later, should have struck him as stranger than it did. For what reason could such a woman have for seeking David at work? Some instinct, however, must have led him to offer to conduct her to the Management Office, since he was going there himself.

She was a girl of about twenty-five, quite pretty, though very pale. She walked with lowered eyes, and she held her hands clasped in front of her, as though they were enclosed in a muff. As they climbed the stairs and, with the benefit of this elevation, could see quite a large section of the ground floor, Thomas caught a glimpse of Lillian, just emerging from the Groceries. She saw him too, but her smile faded from her face at once when she noticed who was with him. For the first time since he had seen the girl, Thomas experienced a sense of unease. When they reached the offices, he asked her to take a seat in the waiting area and went into David's room, closing the door behind him. "There's a young lady inquiring for you outside," he told his partner.

David was surprised and joined him at the door, where, on opening it, he could see her. "Why, Betty," he exclaimed, "what brings you here?"

"I hope I haven't done wrong coming to your store, Mr. Rawlings," she apologized, "but the matter's very pressing. . . ."

"Then you'd better come in and tell me about it," he said.

Thomas left them and went to his own room. He had barely sat down when his clerk told him that Mrs. Rawlings was outside inquiring if he could spare her five minutes. Rather wearily, for Lillian's visits to his office were usually attended by drama, he told him to show her in.

"Do you realize what that woman was?" she asked without any kind of preliminary greeting as she entered. "The woman you were with?"

"No," said Thomas.

"Is she with David now?"

"That's right."

She sat down on a chair in front of Thomas' desk, her face crimson with anger. "It's disgraceful," she said. "She's one of those women . . . In this store . . . in Kingstons . . . your store, Thomas . . ."

Thomas looked at her sitting there, highly emotional, her breast heaving. "One of what women?" he asked.

"Oh, don't be so dense, Thomas," Lillian snapped. "She's a prostitute. Couldn't you see? Do you often have prostitutes in the store?"

Thomas was still perplexed. "But why . . ." Then the connection dawned on him. "Oh, you mean she's one of the women he's been helping at the Salvation Army."

"Helping?" she echoed angrily. "He's possessed by her. . . . He thinks it's his divine duty to save her soul. . . ." She saw the skeptical expression on Thomas' face. "Thomas, I warn you that unless something's done, it's certain to end in scandal."

"You've said this before, Lillian," said Thomas. "Kingstons would be headlined in newspapers throughout the country, you said. . . . But it wasn't, was it?"

"You missed it by a hair's breadth, Thomas, so don't get complacent."

Thomas sighed. "I really don't know why you get so worked up like this," he said. "His concern for these poor women seems harmless enough. . . ."

"Harmless!" she echoed, her eyes wide. "Do you know what time he got home the night before last? Three o'clock in the morning. *Three* o'clock," she repeated. "What do you think he was doing until three o'clock?"

"Lillian, I'm sure that David of all people was not engaged in anything reprehensible. . . ."

"Do you know what happened in London between one o'clock and two o'clock that night?" she went on. "Two women were murdered in the East End . . . two prostitutes . . . not very far from the Salvation Army home where he spends so much of his time."

Thomas was so astonished by her implication that for a few seconds he could summon no words. "Good grief," he said after a moment, "you can't seriously be suggesting that David . . ." He broke off, for the very thought that David was a murderer was absurd enough, but that Lillian should consider the possibility that he was Jack the Ripper, who had dominated the newspapers recently with a series of macabre East End killings, cast doubts on her sanity. The only possible logic for her ridiculous suspicion, though this was remote in the extreme, was that Jack the Ripper—as he styled himself in provocative notes to the police—selected only prostitutes as his victims. But then, a large number of respectable men—and women—were concerned about street vice in London.

"Lillian," he began in a placatory tone of voice.

"Do you know what time he got home on August thirty-first?" she demanded. "Or on September seventh? Just as late . . . and what do you think happened on those dates during the hours he was away?"

"I suppose those other women were murdered then. . . ."

"Exactly." She uttered the word with knowing emphasis.

"What's more, those crimes were committed at one thirty and one forty-five respectively. . . . Do you realize what that means?"

"That he would have had time to get home by the hour you heard him come in. . . . Lillian . . ." He was talking as though to a child. "This is absurd conjecture. . . . You're obviously in a very distraught state of mind. . . . You should take a holiday . . . get away for a few weeks . . . take Eleanor to the sea. . . ."

"I'm not imagining it, Thomas!" She suddenly pounded his desk in fury at his patronizing tone. "You can't get away from the fact that he was out late on those nights. . . ."

"He's not the only husband in London who stays out late."

"But they don't all have an obsession with prostitutes!"

Thomas let out a big sigh. "Lillian," he said, "the only evidence you've ever given me about David's interest in these women—"

"This woman!" she snapped.

"This woman, then," he conceded, "concerns helping her . . . giving her strength . . ."

"Oh, it sounds so good the way you say it," she said. "Thomas, I tell you it's sexual . . . *and* sinful. . . . It's a burning religious passion, and that can be sexual. . . ." She broke off, noting the concern in his eyes at her fervor. "I can't go on, Thomas. . . . Unless it stops . . . there'll have to be a divorce, or at least a separation."

"Divorce?" Thomas echoed anxiously. "Separation?" He paused for a few seconds. "That *is* a different matter," he said at last.

In David's office, Betty was on her knees, weeping hysterically. "I'm scared, Mr. Rawlings . . . terrified, Mr. Rawlings . . ."

"You must put your faith in God, Betty," he said.

"I ain't got as much faith as all that, Mr. Rawlings. Not when Johnson looks at me and says, 'You talk to 'em and I'll cut your face into a thousand little pieces.' Not when the coppers say to me, 'You better tell us or you'll get nick for the rest of your life. . . . You'll be an old, old 'ag when you come out.' . . . Oh, Mr. Rawlings, I'm so scared. . . . If only 'e 'adn't found me! If only 'e 'adn't been able to trace me . . . But 'e 'as, Mr. Rawlings . . . 'e 'as. . . ." She let out a small scream, and clutching David, she broke into another wave of sobbing.

"Betty, you must cease this. . . ." David moved round his desk and put his arm round her shoulders. "Now dry your tears and I'll tell you what I'll do. . . ."

"*You'll* do?" she said with sudden hope in her voice.

"What I'll do," he repeated. She took his proffered hand and consented to rise from her knees. "I'm going to take you back to the home and tell Mr. Booth of your situation. He'll ensure that you get special protection, and urge the police to post a man on duty in the street so that if Johnson returns, he'll be arrested. . . . Now does that make you feel safer?"

"You'll come there and see me, Mr. Rawlings?" she asked.

"Of course, Betty," he assured her, "just as I always have. . . . We'll get over this together, Betty. . . . Now we'll go and get a hansom cab."

She stood up and straightened her cloak round her shoulders, comforted by the quiet calm of his voice. "Come, my dear," he said, and taking his hat and coat from the coatstand, he opened the door for her.

For a while after the van had left the yard, the gray had settled down, as Mr. Butler had said he would. They did not have far to go, since they were on a local delivery round, working the streets and squares in the vicinity of the store. But then after about half an hour, Harry noticed that the horse was starting to sweat again. During the frequent stops he began to move restlessly, and Harry could sense then that tension was building up in him.

"Do you think we should have a look at that sore under his collar, Mr. Rogers?" he asked the driver. "It may be rubbing raw. Honestly, it's bigger than Mr. Butler thought."

"If I was you, Mr. 'Arry," answered Rogers, halting the van before a house in Chesham Place, "I'd worry about the things it was my job to worry about. Now get going with those parcels for Lady Endlesham."

There was a certain inevitability in the timing of the events of that day which in retrospect imparted the impression of deliberate planning, as though they were all pieces in a chess game in the hands of some grand master.

After Lillian left Thomas' office, she toyed with the idea of throwing open the door of David's room and surprising them, but abandoned the thought as lacking in dignity and decided to do some shopping instead. The cook had told her that she needed some more pans, so first she made her way to the Turnery Department.

At about the same time, Ramsay had appeared in the Dispatch Department in the basement and approached Mr. Patterson, the manager. "Mr. Baines has sent me to fetch Mr. Charles," he said. "The police wish to talk to him . . . about the fraud."

Patterson nodded. "Hope he won't be too long . . . we're busy today. . . . Mr. Charles!" he called out. "You're wanted!"

Charles took off his coverall, put on his morning coat and accompanied Ramsay upstairs. But instead of taking the staff staircase, which would normally have been nearest, they ascended the stairs at the southern end of the building, where Charles had been working in the dispatch area. Because of this, they had to walk through the eight departments on the ground floor that lay on their route—and in particular, the Turnery.

Meanwhile, David had deliberately chosen to leave the store by a side entrance, so that his departure with Betty would be less noticeable than if he took her through the main front doors. He was therefore passing through the same departments, but in the opposite direction, as Ramsay and his son.

Lillian was actually examining a saucepan when David and his protégée entered the Turnery Department, but at that moment, her attention attracted by a sound or even by instinct, she looked up and saw them. She had met Betty once, during a brief visit with David to the Salvation Army home where she lived. Even so, despite the fact that she knew she was in the store, the actual sight of her with her husband was a great shock. A wave of anger swept through her, and she could feel the color rising to her neck.

David too had been surprised to see his wife and had stopped, checking Betty with his hand on her arm. For a moment none of them said anything. Lillian was the first to recover her poise—helped, perhaps, by the fact that her new gown in chocolate brown, designed with the military look that was fashionable that year, gave her a certain extra confidence. She smiled in the slightly sardonic, superior way that was only too familiar to David, replaced the saucepan carefully on the counter beside her and strolled slowly across the short distance of carpet that lay between them with the kind of easy graciousness she might have affected at a garden party.

"Well," she said, almost in a drawl, openly studying Betty in a way that had she been a lady, would have been highly insulting, "so we meet again . . . Betty, isn't it? Or have I made a mistake with the name?"

"Yes, ma'am," Betty answered quietly.

"Oh, good . . . One's becoming so forgetful these days that it's nice to remember something correctly for a change. . . . But what are you both doing here, of all places? . . . It's rather unusual, isn't it? . . . Wouldn't you say it was unusual, David?"

David was glaring at her. "There was something important she had to discuss with me," he said coldly. "Now, if you'll forgive us, we'll be on our way."

Lillian looked at him with an expression on her face of slightly pained sensibility. "Are you in *so* much of a hurry," she asked, "that you don't even have time to observe the normal civilities?" She smiled with elegant sweetness. "Why, I've barely had a chance to exchange two words with poor Betty. . . . You see her often, I know, but I don't have this opportunity. . . . I'd like to talk to Betty. . . . Perhaps you should bring her to tea one day. . . . Would you like to come to tea, my dear?"

"Lillian," said David sharply, understanding every nuance of what his wife was saying, for the whole idea of a woman such as Betty coming to tea was ludicrous. "We have to leave."

Lillian just ignored him, standing directly in front of them so that they could not pass without pushing her out of their way, and addressed herself to the girl. "Is my husband helping you, Betty?" she asked with sincere interest.

"Yes, ma'am," she answered, again very quietly, this time averting her eyes downward.

"*Really* helping you?" persisted Lillian. "Do you feel confident that you've been able to abandon the . . ." She hesitated, searching for a decorous expression. ". . . well, what you were—"

"Lillian," David cut in, knowing his wife's tone, "you're behaving quite disgracefully. Kindly let us pass!"

"Disgracefully!" she echoed with hurt surprise. "What can you mean? I'm concerned about Betty. . . . Is it so unusual for a wife to be concerned about her husband's interests?"

"You must try not to be upset," he said to Betty.

"Upset?" queried Lillian incredulously, as though she could not possibly have heard correctly. "Upset by your wife? How dare you say such a thing!"

"I think you've forgotten where you are," David rebuked her quietly. "You're in the store. You're always saying the store's so important. . . . You're causing great embarrassment. . . . Now please let us pass without any more ado." He was still speaking calmly, but his fury was evident. His eyes had narrowed. A vein in his neck was throbbing.

"Not until you apologize." By now the buyer had begun to watch the scene with great anxiety, and two assistants near him were trying to conceal their fascination at what was taking place between a director and his wife. "I'm astonished you can speak in that way about your wife," Lillian went on. "Especially to a woman . . . a woman such as she has been. . . ." She gestured at Betty with a dismissive wave of her hand. "I think your sense of decency must have completely deserted you, and I . . ." She broke off, for she had just seen Charles standing looking at her with an expression of appalled disbelief on his face. Beside him was Ramsay, also staring at the three of them with astonishment.

"Oh, Charles!" she said, surprised and slightly disconcerted. "I didn't see you, Charles . . . or you, Ramsay. . . . You both walk about very quietly, it seems." She turned back to David. "Well, aren't you going to introduce them? Aren't you going to introduce your son to your friend? That'd be polite, wouldn't it? Surely one should be polite to a lady one is accompanying, even if—"

"Silence!" said David. "I refuse to permit you to speak in that way." Then, with a movement that was slow and courteous, he turned to Betty, who by now was holding back her tears with only the greatest effort. "Miss Smart," he said, "may I please introduce my son Charles . . . and Mr. Ramsay Kingston. . . ."

"Good morning, Miss Smart," responded Charles, quickly taking his cue from his father. "It's a pleasure to meet you." He held out his hand with an open smile.

"How do you do, Miss Smart," said Ramsay.

It was too much for her. Lillian's sarcasm had increased her state of high emotion, but it was within her experience. People like Lillian had often been sarcastic to her before. But it was David's elaborate politeness—and the boys' well-mannered response to her, as though she were a lady—that caused her to lose her emotional balance. She burst into a sudden fit of weeping, holding her hands over her face. Then, pushing her way past them all, she ran toward the side entrance of the store.

"Betty!" David called after her. "Stop! Stop at once!" But since she showed no sign that she had heard him, he hurried after her. By the time he reached the entrance, she was already outside. Through the glass door he saw her hesitate for a second on the pavement of the side street that bordered the store. He flung open the door, his attention totally concentrated on the girl. "Betty!" he called. Again she gave no sign of having heard him, for she darted across the road—and he rushed after her.

As the van progressed toward Sloane Street from Belgrave Square, the gray was sweating badly and overreacting to every movement in the road around him. He was throwing his head, too, and yawing on the bit. Rogers growled at him as he slowed the pair to navigate a side turning.

Harry never learned exactly what it was at that moment that scared the horse, though in the state he was in, not very much was needed. Harry heard the noise, of course, for it was very loud. It could have been the door of a van being slammed, or that of a nearby house, or perhaps something falling over in a local yard. The gray responded to it, leaping forward as though Rogers had lashed him with his whip, and the bay went with him.

They were not galloping, but they were moving fast, and for a few moments Rogers lost control of them. "Whoa! Whoa!" he yelled at them, hauling on the reins and pressing his foot down hard on the brake. "Jesus!" he exclaimed as they approached the store. "We'll be into Sloane Street in a second!"

Harry did his best to help him, taking a hold on the reins just in front of Rogers' hands and leaning back with his whole weight in the hope that their joint effort would stop the horses.

They were, in fact, beginning to slow down as they passed along the side of the Kingston building, though still moving at speed, when a girl suddenly ran out of the store and crossed the street in front of them, almost as the horses were on her.

"Jesus!" Rogers cried out again. Because their attention was caught by the girl, they barely saw the man who was following her. By the time they had brought the van to a halt at last and clambered down from the cab, he was unconscious.

· 3 ·

The funeral took place late on a damp, chill morning that none of them would ever forget. The emotional shock of the circumstances of David's death, and the involvement with the accident in one way or another of so many members of both families, would have been enough by itself to ensure that the burial service would remain branded vividly on all their memories. But, as was soon to be discovered, it was not the only event of note to mark that terrible day, and in the story of Kingstons' emporium, by contrast to that of the Rewlingses, it was not even to be the most significant.

Thomas, of course, did not know this when, a few minutes before noon, he stood with May and his sons and Rose in the seventh pew of St. Mary's, singing the Ninetieth Psalm. He was deeply moved by complex emotions. The church itself had featured prominently in their lives. It was where he and May had married; Lillian and David too; where the children of both families had been christened; where they had all attended Matins on Sundays and services for Easter, Christmas, Whitsun, Lent—all the milestones, as old Miss Godfrey would have put it, in any family's progress. It was where David had rendered so singular a contribution to the religious life of the parish—and where Thomas, on that January day nearly eighteen years before, had tried to pray for the survival of his infant son—who, standing beside him now as a man, was chanting the funeral dirge rather louder than he should.

"... *Thou art God from everlasting and world without end.* ... *Thou turnest man to destruction: Again thou sayest, come again ye children of men* ..." The massed voices of the congregation rose and fell in the monotonous chant. The young trebles of the choir launched into the higher register, their pure young voices filling the vaulted roof of the church with the praise of God. "*For a thousand years in thy sight are but as yesterdays: Seeing that is past as a watch in the night. As soon as thou scatterest them, they are even as a sleep: and fade away suddenly like the grass . . ."*

The coffin, covered with velvet and flowers, lay in the aisle just ahead of Thomas' pew, flanked by the four bearers on either side. Within it, Thomas was conscious, was David's corpse, prepared by the undertaking section of the Kingston Mourning Department. Suddenly he experienced a wave of sadness so overwhelming that tears nearly came to his eyes. He thought of David as a young man, in particular recalling him at twenty-four hanging from the outside stairs of the omnibus after that Christmas lunch in Copenhagen Street in 1869, the occasion when he had been so taken with Lillian, and then a picture of him as he had become came into his mind, haggard and drawn, an old man at forty-three. His life, both in the store and in his marriage, seemed to have been marked by inadequacy; and yet, Thomas realized, St. Mary's was crowded that morning—clear proof, surely, that David had enjoyed many admirers in the church and charitable sector of his life, and much influence, too. No less a personage than Bramwell Booth himself had delivered the address, paying tribute to a noble Christian and extolling his service to a cause for which Booth himself had been prosecuted and for which, in a sense, David Rawlings had died.

". . . So teach us to number our days: So that we may apply our hearts unto wisdom. Turn thee again, O Lord, at the last: and be gracious unto thy servants . . ."

It was a pity, thought Thomas, that Lillian's ambitions had been limited so closely to the store that she had been unable to share David's success in this other area. Rather, she had hated it. In fact, according to Ramsay's account of the scene in the Turnery Department, her distaste —her confrontation of that poor young prostitute—was one of the several elements that had merged to make her a widow.

There was no point in such analyses, for they could not alter the facts—nor Lillian's situation now as she stood with the boys and Eleanor in the front pew, clad in paramatta gown, hood and veil, all covered with crape, and played her prominent role in the Mourning Department's best class of funeral—with a black airtight coffin; an impressive black hearse decorated, like the heads of the black horses that drew it, with black ostrich plumes; and the Kingston mourners who had led the procession on foot, their black hats bound in black silk "weeper end" scarves.

". . . Now this I say, brethren," intoned the vicar, ". . . that flesh and blood cannot inherit the Kingdom of God; neither doth corrup-

tion inherit corruption . . ." As always, Thomas felt a sense of loss, for
the language of the church never affected him to the extent he felt it
should. ". . . then shall be brought to pass the saying that is written,
death is swallowed up in victory. O death, where is thy sting? O grave,
where is thy victory?"

They all followed the coffin to the graveside, where Lillian stood,
flanked on both sides by her children, her head bent forward and
shoulders slightly bowed. She seemed at that moment a very remote,
dramatic figure, faced with her years of statutory mourning for a
husband she did not love. ". . . earth to earth," the vicar declared, as
the coffin was slowly lowered into the ground, "ashes to ashes, dust to
dust in sure and certain hope of the resurrection to eternal life . . ."
Lillian bent down, took a few grains of soil in her black gloved hand,
and threw it onto the coffin in the grave. Eleanor put her hand in
comfort within her mother's arm. Lillian lifted her head, and although
he could not see her clearly because of the veil, Thomas knew she was
looking at him. He nodded sympathy to her and she bent her head
again. His attention was drawn to the twelve-year-old James, who, he
found, was staring at him with anger. They very rarely met, but
whenever they did, James always demonstrated this same antagonism
which, despite himself, Thomas shared—which was strange if Lillian's
insistence on his paternity was accurately founded. ". . . and the fel-
lowship of the Holy Ghost be with us forevermore. Amen."

The crowd round the grave was silent for a few seconds. Then
Lillian turned and walked with her daughter and her sons along the
pathway to a gate in the railings that divided the graveyard from Pont
Street. The Kingstons were not far behind them, among the others
who were following from the grave, and Thomas suddenly noticed a
young woman standing alone on the grass by a tree, about twenty
yards from the path. She was weeping quietly with her head bowed, so
he could not see her clearly. Then, after a few seconds, he realized that
she was the girl he had taken to David's office the day he died.

Lillian saw her too and stopped instantly, staring at the girl. For an
uneasy moment, Thomas feared she was going to denounce her or,
even worse, cross the grass and strike her. For Lillian's back conveyed
all her injured hatred—rigid, even slightly arched, in quality like a cat
tensed to spring. Often Thomas was to wonder what she would in fact
have done had not her attention at this moment, like that of everyone
present, been so dramatically diverted.

"Hi-ya-hi! Hi-ya-hi! Hi-ya-hi!" The hoarse warning yell of half a
dozen male voices which they all heard now over the noise of the
galloping hooves was a sound that echoed every day in the streets of

London. "Hi-ya-hi! Hi-ya-hi! Hi-ya-hi!" The scarlet fire engine came into view through the railings as it raced along Pont Street behind the usual pair of galloping gray horses, steam and smoke belching from its funnel, firemen in brass helmets clinging to the lurching vehicle. "Hi-ya-hi! Hi-ya-hi! Hi-ya-hi!" they roared—but their raucous warning was not enough to clear their way through Pont Street at that moment. For the thoroughfare had been narrowed by carriages, waiting for the funeral service to end, on either side of the street. The limited space that remained in the middle of the road was blocked temporarily by moving traffic. The driver of the engine had to brake hard and, with wheels sliding, haul back on the reins of his excited horses, who were kept permanently ready at the fire station and well fed without exercise, so that they were bounding with energy for the instant gallop to a fire.

They were delayed for only a few seconds, stamping impatiently, the boiler behind them steaming, bits of burning wood from its fire dropping into the road beneath it, while in the distance a second cry of "Hi-ya-hi! Hi-ya-hi!" signaled the approach of another fire vehicle. The holdup was long enough, though, for someone on the pavement to ask where the fire was and, as the engine moved forward suddenly through a gap in the traffic, for the answer to be shouted back of "Kingstons!"

It was one funeral at which Thomas did not pay respects to the widow. He was on the box of his carriage before the fire-service grays were going faster than a trot. Roughly shoving aside his astonished coachman, he grabbed the reins and urged his horses forward, lashing them with the whip until they broke into a canter.

As they careered toward Sloane Street, the fire engine was some fifty yards ahead of them, having now gathered speed. With the firemen roaring their "Hi-ya-hi!" to warn any approaching cross traffic from whom they might be screened by buildings, the driver made no attempt to slow his horses as he took the corner. "Take care, sir!" the coachman shouted to Thomas as they followed close behind it. "You ain't got the weight that 'e's got!" Thomas knew it, but still he made no attempt to check his speed. As his horses went into the turn, he felt the left-hand wheels of the carriage lift from the road. "Lean out, you fool!" he yelled at the coachman, and flung himself against him to lay as much weight as he could on that side of the carriage to hold it down.

He felt the wheels touch ground again as they went into the straight in Sloane Street, but the overswing caused him to hit a brewer's dray, badly scraping the side, and as the horses veered in response to the impact, he grazed a hansom coming in the opposite direction. He made no attempt to stop, for he could see the store now, and horror completely dominated his mind. Thick smoke was billowing from the roof of the building, and flames were licking from two top-floor windows.

Ahead a big crowd already blocked the street, held back by a police cordon. From two directions behind him, Thomas could hear the "Hi-ya-hi!" cries of other fire engines, one of them still far distant.

The crowd parted to allow the fire engine through, then filled the street again behind it. As the carriage drew close, Thomas leaned back hard on the reins, thrust them into the hands of his shocked coachman, and leaped to the ground before the horses had come to a halt. He shouldered his way roughly through the crowd, murmuring almost absentmindedly, "I'm Kingston . . . I'm Kingston . . ." to placate those angered by his shoving, until at last he reached the line of restraining police.

Close to, the heat emanating from the building was immense—so great that he could look at the burning store for only a few seconds before his eyes began to hurt. Smoke was pouring from the ground and top floors. Within, there were glimpses of flame, suddenly revealed among the billowing black clouds. Five hissing fire engines, with men shoveling coal into the boilers, were supplying power to hoses held by firemen, directing jets of water through windows at ground level and from the ladders that reached upward toward the roof.

There was constant and seemingly confused activity—men clambering up and down the ladders; men appearing at windows and shouting information; men running across the street in front of the building, their boots splashing in the water that now lay in the cobbles; men sweating in shirtsleeves as they operated hand pumps; men moving equipment, hauling escapes, unrolling hoses, hurrying unhitched horses from supply carts and wagons.

As Thomas watched, two more fire engines were galloped up from the south. Orders were shouted to them and they took up station, their crews tumbling from them into immediate action.

Dazed, Thomas focused his attention on his display windows, all of which had been blown out by heat or internal pressure. Broken glass was strewn across the street, but the merchandise was still there—all of it sodden with water, much of it soiled by smoke, even scorched. Mathews' careful designs were in chaos. In one window, materials that had been draped in neat folds now lay in mangled heaps. In another, a silk ribbon hanging, twisted, from a single nail above a confused pile of lace and gloves and fallen units was all that remained of a Fancy Goods display. In a third, a display of glass and chinaware lay in fragments on the window bed, except, strangely, for a lone teapot—Royal Doulton, Thomas noted for all his shock—that still stood on a small platform in perfect condition, unmarked even by the heat.

The new body costume stands that had so pleased him when they were installed had all toppled over as though they were victims of a massacre, and most were lying, like prematurely stiff corpses, in disorder across one another. One had tipped sideways against the internal wall of the window and was still supported in apparent rigor mortis at an angle of some forty-five degrees. Another—the model with a head and face—had fallen across a small display table, the weight of the shoulders carrying it forward onto the floor beyond, so that its legs and feet, clad in button-up boots, projected upward immodestly, the skirts of the gown slipped back to the thighs.

Most of the wooden backs of the windows at the north end of the building, which was where Thomas was standing in the crowd, had been smashed, and beyond, within the Grocery and Wine departments, he could see vague movement among the smoke.

The figures of firemen, crouched down, were suddenly illuminated by a spurt of flame and then, within seconds, were blanketed once more by swirling black fog.

There was an explosion, deep inside the stricken store, like the discharge of a heavy-caliber gun. "Wall gone," said one of the policemen in the cordon in front of Thomas. At that moment, he saw a girl, dead or unconscious, being passed out of a second-floor window onto the shoulders of a fireman on a ladder and suddenly realized that she must be one of his staff. It jerked him from his mesmerized state into a consciousness of his responsibilities. "Excuse me, Constable," he said to the policeman in front of him. "Will you let me pass, please? I'm Mr. Kingston."

"My condolences, sir," said the policeman, but Thomas hardly heard him as he went by, splashing his way over the broken glass and hoses toward the escape down which the firemen had brought the girl, but by the time he got there, she had been carried off. "Who's in charge?" Thomas asked a fireman hurrying past him. "Captain Shaw, sir," said the man over his shoulder. "The long 'un over there." He pointed to a small group of three men standing directing operations from the far side of the road.

Thomas knew who Captain Shaw was, for he was famous as the man who had taken over the ill-organized fire services that had been owned by insurance companies and welded them into a highly efficient disciplined force, geared to fight London's fires, which now numbered nearly two thousand every year. He had organized a network of fire stations throughout the metropolis, linked by a telegraphic communications system and manned round the clock by trained men with horses, supplied by Thomas Tilling, who ran most of the London omnibuses—in the traces of which, in fact, the animals were first accustomed to the city traffic. Steam engines had now replaced most of the manual contraptions, though, as Thomas had already seen, these were still used in support roles.

As was well known—for the London public now flocked to witness fires much as, twenty years before, they had attended hangings—Shaw supervised in person the fighting of major blazes, and for all Thomas' shock and despair, he felt a certain minimal reassurance as he turned his back on the burning building and walked across the street to the tall, moustached fire captain. If anyone could save the store from total destruction, he knew that this was the man who could.

"Captain Shaw?" said Thomas as he approached him. "My name's Kingston." Shaw, who wore a brass helmet like his men, gazed back at him with serious, sympathetic eyes. "You must be a sad man at this moment, Mr. Kingston," he said. Then, looking past him, he called out, "Can't you hold it there?" A group of five men had just retreated through one of the display windows. They were repositioning their helmets, which they had been wearing turned round, with the low backs covering their blackened faces to provide more protection. "Not a hope, sir!" an officer with them shouted back. "The furniture's caught and the floor's about to go."

"Try it from the side!" Shaw ordered, as another fire engine was galloped through the space in the crowd. "You can have this engine to help you," he said, shouting at the driver. "Into the side street there!"

Shaw turned back to Thomas. "We've an idea of the pattern now. Every fire's different, of course . . . has its own character. . . . Not that it'll be much consolation to you, I fear."

"Are many people hurt?" Thomas asked.

"A few, I'm told."

"Any dead?"

"About five, I believe . . . so far, that is. . . . That's not many considering the time of day, with customers and staff in the building. . . . I fear your fireman's dead. Brave man . . . cut off closing the fire doors. . . . That's the trouble with this sort of fire. Probably been smoldering away in the basement for half an hour without anyone knowing till it'd got a hold. Then it blew—right up through your staff staircase . . . and when that happens . . ." He shrugged. "Well, those gases with that intense heat'll set light instantly to anything that'll burn. . . . Then your gas pipes melted. . . ."

"Melted?" repeated Thomas with astonishment.

"Mr. Kingston," Shaw explained, "lead melts at six hundred and twelve degrees Fahrenheit. At the core of a large fire, temperatures run well in excess of three thousand degrees. . . . Not that it's only the pipes . . . it's the gas within them. . . . Then your Dress Department— all those flimsy gowns . . . Fire feeds on itself, escalates all the time. . . . What do you think you're doing?" he suddenly shouted at a group of firemen who had suddenly dropped their hose on the ground, where it writhed, snaking and hissing, and were running to the side.

"That wall, sir!" one of them called back, pointing at a huge vertical crack that had suddenly appeared in the front brickwork of the store. "It's going!"

"No, it's not!" said Shaw confidently. "I'll tell you when it's ready to go. You get back to your hose! . . . We're doing our utmost, Mr. Kingston," he went on to Thomas. "There'll be twenty engines here soon . : . that's nearly half the total complement of London . . . and more than a hundred firemen. . . ."

"I'm most grateful," said Thomas quietly, and wandered away.

For Thomas, the next hour bore the disoriented quality of a nightmare consisting of vivid little cameo scenes, unconnected except for the common link of smoke and flame and water and pain and the pungent smell of burning materials—cloth, fur, rubber and all manner of other fabrics—that permeated everything.

He walked slowly round the dying store, watching the firemen working with engines and escapes on every side, pouring into it tens of thousands of gallons of water in what seemed a hopeless effort to curb the force of that army of fires. Thomas shuddered at the roar of fiercely burning flames, winced with the occasional muffled crash in the interior when a wall or a floor collapsed. He saw firemen running out of the building to bathe their scorched skin in carron oil before rushing back, with what seemed inordinate courage, into that blazing structure.

He noted members of his staff, standing in the crowd in groups. When they met his eyes, they did not know how to respond. Some of them smiled in sympathy. Others looked away embarrassed. He encountered some of the buyers and managers. "Sorry, Mr. Kingston . . . Tragedy, Mr. Kingston . . . Disaster, Mr. Kingston . . ." Each time, he nodded acknowledgment and walked on.

He stood and looked at the bodies of the dead, laid out with their faces covered, on the floor of a stable in a nearby mews, and was moved by a huge wave of helpless sadness that turned suddenly to guilt. Was it his fault? Was there something he had not done, some precaution he had not taken?

Sidney Baines reported to him—coatless, with a shirt that was torn and dirty. Red-rimmed eyes peered at Thomas out of a swollen, blackened face. "I've got two wagons ready, with horses harnessed," he said eagerly. "So that we can start collecting stock . . . see what's still salable. . . . I started, but they stopped me."

"Thank you, Sidney."

"I've told the staff that we'll send news to the dormitories . . . I mean about what we want them to do . . . and I've instructed all the buyers and managers I've seen to meet me in Sloane Square at five o'clock for further orders."

"You've done well, Sidney," said Thomas, knowing that his brother-in-law was responding to the crisis in the proper practical way, while he himself was still trying to absorb the various aspects of the disaster.

Thomas found May at the entrance of the house where he had been told they had taken the injured. She was, of course, still in the black gown she had been wearing for the funeral, though it was badly creased and strands of her hair had escaped from her bonnet. "I've been looking for you," she said.

"I'm sorry to have left you like that," he said. "I should have waited for you."

"I understood. . . . You knew I would."

"There was no point in hurrying, it turned out. . . . At the time, I thought there was."

She smiled encouragement at him, grasped his hand. "It's a great disaster," she said, "but you'll overcome it as you always do. . . . Emily's inside . . . in a bad way. . . . She insisted that all her ladies should be taken down the escape before herself. . . . Smoke mainly, but she's got some burns as well. . . . They say smoke's the worst thing."

He went into the house, thanked the lady who owned it for her great assistance. "It was the least I could do, Mr. Kingston," she assured him. "We've sent for the Knights of St. John; they'll get the more serious ones to hospital."

Some of the wounded members of his staff were sitting on chairs in various rooms, but most of them were lying on the floor under blankets. There was a lady who evidently had some first-aid experience acting as a nurse, applying cold poultices and calamine. He hardly recognized Emily, her face was so swollen and inflamed. She found it hard to respond to his "I've heard how brave you were," though she made a valiant effort and he just caught some words: "Service . . . lucky . . . alive . . ."

"I'll stay with her," May said at his elbow. "I'm doing what I can to help here. . . . You've much to do."

He spoke to the others who had been hurt, murmured a few words that he hoped were encouraging, and left the house. He was not far from the stables at the rear of the store, and he now made his way there through the complex of alleys and mews that approach from the rear involved. It was as he neared the turning into the narrow street that adjoined the stable yard that the horses suddenly started to scream. Of all the moments of those awful hours, those shrill screams of terror—seeming completely unreal, since they were unlike any other sound that ever emanated from a horse—were to remain among the most vivid in his mind. He ran to the corner. Then, as he entered the street, he stopped, horrified by the sight that met him. The near part of the stable roof was on fire, yellow flames tinged purple raging through the low-gabled tiles, loud explosions ringing out like gunshots. The narrow road itself was a chaos of men and terrified horses that were being rushed out of the yard by Butler's staff. Some were blind-folded; some were being driven, the grooms whipping them from be-hind, having clearly just released them from the stalls in the cause of speed and survival. Horses were kicking out, rearing up, prancing, biting, jostling, even mounting one another. Men were shouting, the loudest being Butler himself. "To the Square!" he was roaring. "Tether 'em to the railings! Get 'em to the Square, you dolts! Glory be to God, Edwards, what are you doing? Get 'em moving to the Square!" And above it all, dominating all the noise, was the sound of the screaming horses, intensified to Thomas now by the close confines of that little street.

Butler saw Thomas then. "Terrible, Mr. Kingston," he said. "Ter-rible. We've got most of 'em out. It's the ones in the south block we've lost. . . . By God, it was fast. Some dry straw caught . . . flying sparks or something from the main building. . . . 'Ave you seen Mr. 'Arry yet?"

"Mr. Harry?" queried Thomas. "Is he here?"

"Indeed 'e is, Mr. Kingston . . . been doing stout work, what's more. . . . Smith," he shouted suddenly at a groom who was running by with two horses, " 'ave you seen Mr. 'Arry?"

" 'E's just gone back inside, Mr. Butler."

"What?" Butler echoed angrily. "I just gave orders that no one was to go back inside!" But the groom had hurried on past them. "I gave orders that no one was to go back, Mr. Kingston," he insisted defensively. ". . . Mr. Kingston!" Thomas was running toward the entrance of the yard. "Mr. Kingston! Don't you go inside, sir! The roof's about to go!"

Thomas reached the big yard and hesitated for a moment, trying to guess which stable block Harry would have entered. One whole section of the stables was now blazing, and as Thomas stood there, a line of parked vans caught fire, the flames spreading swiftly through the light timber of their superstructure. For a moment Thomas was disoriented by the glare, the roar and crackle of the fire, the high, unreal shrieking of the horses, the swirling acrid fumes.

Then Harry emerged from the black smoke, leading a gray horse which from fear was resisting him, plunging and jerking his head against the halter rope, even though Harry's own shirt was wrapped round his eyes. Harry himself had thrust his hat so hard on his head to protect his own eyes that the brim had broken. To shield his bare neck and chest, he was holding the lapels of his coat with one hand tight across his throat. To Thomas, in the kaleidoscope of that nightmare afternoon, his shirtless son, with his broken topper and grimy face, seemed like some kind of circus clown as he ran past without seeing him, coaxing the horse all the time, his whole concentration fixed on keeping the animal moving to safety.

Thomas hurried after him and heard Butler order a groom to take the horse. "You ought never to 'ave done that, Mr. 'Arry. . . ."

"His coat's scorched off his flank," said Harry as though he had not heard Butler's reprimand, "but I hope it'll heal. . . ."

"You must be off your 'ead taking a risk like that—against my orders, too. . . . 'E's an 'orse—just an 'orse. . . . After what he did to Mr. Rawlings, too . . ."

"*They're* just horses, too, Mr. Butler," said Harry, making a movement of his head toward the burning stables. Then for the first time, he saw Thomas. "Oh," he said, "Father. . . . Have you ever heard such a terrible sound before in your life?"

Thomas put out his hand to touch his son's shoulder in solace. Then he moved on, returning to the front of the building, where the throng in Sloane Street was now much bigger. News of the blaze had spread through London, and people had been arriving by cab and carriage to witness it. Already the trade that fed on crowds had begun to emerge. A coffee stall had been set up on one pavement. Ginger beer and chestnuts were being hawked.

Vehicles were drawn up behind the crowd on both sides of Sloane Street, and it was as Thomas was passing one of the carriages that he was astonished to see Eve sitting within it, watching the burning building with an expression on her face of shocked pain. Some instinct must have told her he was near, for suddenly she looked at him. He opened the door of the carriage. "I didn't want to see you," she said, "just to grieve for you."

"Eve . . ." he began, deeply moved, but she interrupted him: "Don't wait, Thomas. . . . Please go. . . . Please . . ." And he closed the door.

He shouldered his way through the crowd, wondering if in reality he had seen her or whether that brief scene had been a creation of a fevered imagination. He moved through the police cordon and stood on the pavement on the opposite side of the street from the burning store. He caught sight of Ramsay. He was in his shirt sleeves and had just stepped back, heavily out of breath, from one of the manual pumps where he had evidently been taking a turn. He was looking haggard, for all his youth. Almost at once he saw his father and approached him, clearly needing to speak some word of comfort, to make some mention, perhaps, of shared disaster, but clearly he could think of nothing adequate to say. As he had with Harry, Thomas put his hand on his shoulder in acknowledgment of his emotion. "Thank you, Ramsay," he said, as though his son had actually spoken.

Charles Rawlings joined them, also coatless. Thomas was surprised to see him. "Your mother . . ." he began.

"James and Eleanor are caring for her, sir," Charles answered. "I felt my place was here."

Then, as the three of them stood together in the glare of the fire, there was a great roar, like the salvo of a battery of heavy guns, and slowly—at least, the movement seemed to be slow—part of the roof caved in, throwing out, like some giant firework, a huge shower of sparks and tiny burning fragments. Bare flames could be seen reaching upward toward the sky from within the walls of the building.

In that instant Thomas' spirits sank to their lowest point—but within seconds he experienced the reaction. The sense of shock that had induced in him that strange need to nurse and absorb the detail of his disaster, that had left him reeling round the store as though he had been drugged, was suddenly lifted from him. He experienced a surging need for action, for counterattack against these hostile elements which had destroyed his business.

"Boys," he said suddenly, "we've got much to do. . . . We have to start trading again as soon as possible. . . . Charles!" He snapped out the name sharply, and the boy, responding eagerly to Thomas' new tone, answered, "Yes, sir?"

"We need somewhere to work . . . an office . . . headquarters. . . . Now . . . today . . . this afternoon . . . Find us some rooms as near as possible and report back to me when you've made arrangements. . . . Ramsay!"

"Yes, sir!" said his son, his eyes bright as he too noted the change in his father.

"We'll require temporary premises . . . some kind of hall or warehouse . . . anywhere big enough for us to open for trade . . . at least twenty thousand square feet. . . . This is a chance for both of you to show your initiative. . . . Now, where do you think Sidney Baines has got to?"

But the two boys were no longer there to answer him. Thomas saw them hurrying along the pavement, nimbly avoiding Captain Shaw and his officers, before disappearing into the crowd that filled Sloane Street to the south.

·4·

At seven o'clock that evening, Thomas and his managers, with the exception of poor Emily, were sitting at a long table that had been set up in the rooms that Charles had found on the first floor of a public house, just off Sloane Square, named the Kings Arms. Waiting in the street below were some of the dozen hansoms that Thomas had rented for the whole night so that he had ample transport for dispatching messages and instructions.

Some two hours before, Ramsay had opened negotiations for the hire of a hall, used normally for public meetings, in the Kings Road, about a quarter of a mile from the store.

It was just a bare building with a speaker's platform, but it was large enough, with extensive outbuildings at the rear.

The meeting at the Kings Arms—"Our council of war," as Thomas described it without even the glimmer of a smile—consisted of some twenty-five buyers, managers and senior staff. Ramsay and Charles were sitting at the side, available to act as messengers. A number of clerks from the management offices were preparing themselves in the adjoining rooms for the spate of paperwork that would be required during the next few hours. Even May and the fifteen-year-old Rose were present, together with several of the staff from Cadogan Place, to provide light refreshments for what was clearly going to be a long night of very hard work.

"Well, gentlemen," Thomas declared from the head of the table, looking up from a pad on which he had been writing, "may we please

commence. . . . I'm going to read to you the advertisement I'm proposing to place in tomorrow's daily press. . . ." He took up the pad on
which he had been working. "Kingstons of Sloane Street," he read,
"regret to announce that owing to a disastrous fire, they will not be
open for business for three days."

"Three days?" echoed one buyer with astonishment, only to meet
Thomas' cold stare.

"On Friday of this week, October twelfth," he continued, slightly
louder, "they hope to welcome their customers at temporary premises
at Thirty-seven Kings Road, in which, though the surroundings may
not be of the standard to which they have been accustomed in Sloane
Street, they will do their utmost to offer the usual standards of merchandise and service.

"They ask their customers to forgive the inconvenience this may
cause and to assure them that trading will be resumed in Sloane Street
as soon as appropriate arrangements can be made."

Thomas looked up. "Someone was questioning the schedule I have
planned. Mr. Barratt, wasn't it?"

Barratt was the Gentlemen's shoe buyer, and he flushed with discomfort. "It was just that it didn't seem possible to achieve your aim of
three days, Mr. Kingston."

"Why not?" asked Thomas. "It was possible for Barkers after
their fire. It was possible for Shoolbreds after theirs. It's been possible
for Whiteleys more than once. If they can do it, surely we can?"

"Yes, Mr. Kingston," Barratt conceded flatly.

"Mr. Dutton!" Thomas called out, and one of the clerks appeared
in the doorway to the neighboring office. "This advertisement is to be
in all tomorrow's papers in as large a size as they can accommodate.
Please prepare copies of it, together with the appropriate authorities.
Mr. Charles will then take them down to Fleet Street by hansom. . . .

"To continue," Thomas went on. "Firstly, Sloane Street . . . Volunteers are to be sought from the male members of the staff to mount a
twenty-four-hour guard on the store when the firemen leave to prevent looting. Arrangements will be made to barricade the building
tomorrow. . . . In the morning, under the supervision of a fire officer,
all stock will be removed to a warehouse, where each buyer will be
required to decide if any is still in a condition to be sold or jobbed off.
Buyers will provide me with itemized reports that'll be needed by our
insurers. . . .

"Now the Kings Road premises . . . During this evening, Mr.
Baines and I will interview each of you in turn to discuss your space
allocation in the new premises, the shop fittings you'll need, and a

temporary budget for new stock. By the time we see you, I'll want you to have prepared a basic list of stock lines. Orders for these can then go down tonight by hansom to wholesalers at their homes, if the addresses are known, or to their offices so that they'll get them first thing in the morning. . . . You'll be arranging further buying, of course, by personal visits. . . .

"Now staff . . . We'll be considering our requirements for the immediate future, but there's little doubt that some'll have to be laid off, and . . ."

And so the night went on, with Thomas and Sidney engaged in constant meetings with the buyers . . . in making change after change to the rough layout sketch of the Kings Road hall . . . in constructing the pyramid of budgets, merchandise requirements, master lists of shop fittings . . . transport needs . . .

Throughout the evening and early hours of the morning, messages were being dispatched all over London. The clerks were huddled over the tables, their quill pens scratching furiously as they issued formal orders for merchandise and equipment.

Soon after midnight, reports began to come back about the response from those wholesalers who could be found . . . about the staff who had volunteered for guard duty . . . about the newspaper advertisements . . . about shop fittings . . . about the whole spectrum of tiny detail that is encompassed by the installation of a store.

By then a harassed Mr. Butler had come into the Kings Arms to report on one of the most pressing of the many problems: What to do with the horses? He had found temporary stabling by the river—in several different premises—and the horses were on their way there now.

"How many did you lose?" asked Thomas.

"Twenty-seven it seems, sir."

"As many as that?" He was silent for a moment. Then, unable on that hectic evening to spare the time for the luxury of sentiment, he entrusted the head groom with the task of finding enough covered wagons within the next few hours to meet their massive need for moving stock.

All night, Ramsay and Charles were constantly on the move, scarcely having time to sip a hot drink on their return from one errand before they were hurried off on another.

When eventually Thomas put his signature on the last document, the dawn light was already adding illumination to the gas lamps. "It's time we all got some sleep," he said. "We'll meet here again at midday" —though he knew that before then he would have to visit the City to see the insurers at Lloyds and to call on Henry Jones at the bank to arrange for temporary financing.

May was still there in the room, but she had long before sent Rose and the servants back to Cadogan Place. The two boys were still present too, both fast asleep with their heads pillowed on their arms on the table.

Gently, Thomas woke them. "A few hours in bed's what you two need," he said. "You've given me great support, and I'm proud of you. . . . Charles, you must ask your mother to forgive me for keeping you from her so long."

With May and Ramsay, he went downstairs, clambered into one of the hansoms and directed the cabby to Cadogan Place—but when they drew near to Kingstons, he told him to stop and wait. Sloane Street was still blocked off by the police, for fear of the collapse of the front wall.

A few isolated stars still marked the lightening sky as Thomas walked to the store. Firemen were still working in the building, but all but one of the engines had gone. One of the Kingstons staff guards, huddled within a heavy overcoat, greeted him and sympathized as he passed. Thomas acknowledged his condolence and surveyed his emporium—broken and scarred as it was now, with the windows shattered, bare charred timbers being all that remained of much of the roof; untidy piles of blackened bricks that had once been walls; great holes, edged with scorched joist ends, where floors had been; total desolation throughout the space that had housed the ground-floor departments. Smoke was still rising from several parts of the building, but there was no sign of flame.

Thomas stared at the smoldering ruin of which, until the previous day, he had been so proud. For a minute or so, on that cold dawn, he knew again the same shocked horror that he had experienced when he had first seen the burning store. Then gradually a broad smile began to spread across his face.

"Do you know why your father is smiling?" Until that moment, Thomas had not known that May and Ramsay had followed him from the cab.

"I have to admit, Mama," the boy answered, "that I can see little reason for it."

"I know why he's smiling," she said, "but then, I've lived with him for many years. Thomas, tell your son why you are looking happy."

"Because there's cause," he answered, his eyes still fixed on the smoking building. "I was thinking, Ramsay . . . thinking of the great

store that will rise on those ashes. . . . I was thinking of the splendid
pile that won't just be a terrace of separate shops as Kingstons has been
so far, well though it has served us . . . but a superb new building
designed by architects to be the most magnificent emporium in London. . . ."

His son said nothing for a moment, but stood staring, as his father
was, at the ruins of his store. Then he turned to him, a glimmer of
mischief in his eyes. "The most magnificent emporium *in London*,
Father?" he queried, his emphasis combined with a note of wonder.

At first, tired as he was, Thomas missed the subtlety of his son's
question. He thought he was doubting the truth of the vision he had
just described, considering it too bold. Then suddenly he realized what
he meant, and his face creased once more into a big smile. "No, Ramsay," he declared expansively in a loud voice that echoed through those
deserted streets, "not just in London. . . . In the world, Ramsay . . . in
the whole, wide, wide world. . . ."

And suddenly he began to laugh . . . and Ramsay, pleased by the
effect on his father of his mild teasing, began to laugh with him . . . and
May, caught suddenly by the same infection, started to laugh as well.
. . . And their laughter grew, stimulated as each was by the other two,
becoming at last uncontrollable, so that their bodies shook and tears
streamed from their eyes, and they knew a sense of near-hysterical joy
that was a reaction to the most terrible eighteen hours any one of them
had yet endured.

It has to be admitted—and later each recalled the incident with a
degree of shame—that to an observer, the sight of the three of them
convulsed in such unrestrained hilarity in the face of what any sane
person would regard as great tragedy—under the very walls, in fact, of
the devastated store that bore their name—must inevitably have
seemed extremely strange.

And there *were* two observers. One of the firemen, in the execution of his duty, appeared beside the Kingstons staff guard and reacted
with astonishment. "Isn't that Mr. Kingston?" he asked, recalling him
from earlier.

"It is," said the guard, who, like the fireman, was finding the scene
before him hard to credit, "*and* Mrs. Kingston . . . and Master Kingston. . . ."

"Have they gone mad?" asked the fireman. "Has the strain proved
too much?"

The guard nodded—a little anxiously, since his employment suddenly seemed at risk. "It'd seem so," he agreed, ". . . quite mad. . . ."

Book Three

CHAPTER NINE

April 1897

· I ·

As Thomas sat in his usual compartment of the railway carriage, he found it hard to curb his surging anger. Ever since the train had pulled out of Aylesbury Station he had been trying to read *The Times*, but his concentration had been broken constantly by invading thoughts of seething indignation—despite the fact that the news that morning should have held exceptional interest for him, dominated as it was by the official arrangements for the Queen's Diamond Jubilee in June. For months Thomas had been supervising plans for elaborate decoration of the store, special displays and commemorative merchandise. But that morning it all seemed of less moment than the disturbing fact of Ramsay's return from America.

In an effort to calm himself, Thomas had spent a few minutes before his departure for the station strolling among the mares and foals in the peace of the paddocks that lay in front of Quainton Hall, but this had failed totally to relieve his turbulent state of mind.

For the past two months, since Ramsay's final letter, Thomas had succeeded in keeping his resentment of his son's extraordinary behavior in the back of his mind—until the previous evening, when he had faced the fact that the decisions which so far he had been able to postpone would have to be made within a few hours. For Ramsay would then be in London with his wife—his American wife.

"I wonder," May had said, "if you would have objected to the Mansfields if they had been British."

"You think it's because they're Yankees? May, he's defied me. . . . Do you expect me, as his father, to just shrug my shoulders?"

"When you were young," she went on as though he had not spoken, "you greatly admired the Americans—especially A. T. Stewart. . . . You used to speak in glowing terms of his emporium, which you hoped to emulate. . . ."

"Improve on," Thomas had corrected. "Well, I admit I hoped Ramsay'd marry better. . . ."

May had laughed. "Thomas you're speaking as though America was still a colony and you were a royal prince. . . . New York's one of the world's major cities, and Jack Mansfield's a man of means. . . ."

Thomas looked out the carriage window, his body moving with the rhythmic swaying of the train, and thought of the day a year before when Jack Mansfield had lumbered into his life like some amiable elephant. He had sent notice of his appearance in a letter from Brown's Hotel, saying that he was the proprietor of the J. L. Mansfield Store of Fifth Avenue, New York. He was in London, he had said, on a buying trip to Europe and had been so impressed by Kingstons that he would much appreciate the opportunity of meeting Thomas if he could spare a few minutes of his valuable time.

Thomas had found him an engaging man. He was an outsize character, in both build and personality. He was immensely tall and extremely fat, and he had a huge, body-shaking laugh which seemed to threaten the structure of any building he happened to be in when it was provoked—which was fairly often, as he had an acute sense of humor. Since he had brought with him his two sons, who worked in his business, Thomas had at once sent for Ramsay and Charles, and they too had all found each other congenial.

After Jack Mansfield's initial visit, they had met several times, for although his store catered for a different class of trade from Kingstons', the giant New Yorker was a man of intelligence and ideas. Before the three Americans left for Paris, Thomas had asked them home to dinner—and invited Lillian and the younger Rawlingses to make up the party. It was when the ladies had retired from the table that Mansfield, after commending Thomas' port, suggested that he send Ramsay to New York for a few months. "He could work in my store for a while and then perhaps he would care to spend some time in other stores—Marshall Field in Chicago, for example, or Hudson's in Detroit. I'd be happy to make arrangements."

Ramsay had been enthusiastic. Charles had said that he wished he could go with him, but assumed that someone would have to remain to help in the store. James, as usual, had just stared in front of him gloomily as though the matter did not merit his consideration. And Thomas, after some pondering, gave his consent.

On a sunny morning early in May, they had all gone to see Ramsay off at Euston Station on his way to Liverpool, where he was to board the S.S. *Laurentian*. After reaching the United States, Ramsay had sent home regular letters from which it was clear that he enjoyed America—and in particular, his leisure hours with Mansfield's sons and, even more particularly as the weeks went by, the company of Mansfield's twenty-one-year-old daughter, Dora.

Over the months his references to Dora, laced with comment about her beauty, her wit, her nature, her personality, made it fairly obvious that he was much taken with the young lady. May and Thomas had discussed the obvious possibility that he might wish to marry her but had assumed that they would meet her before any definite plans were made. This, however, was not the course that events had taken. In January, Ramsay had written to say that he had proposed to Dora Mansfield—subject, of course, to his father's approval—and she had done him the honor of accepting. Naturally, since her parents lived in America, the Mansfields intended that the wedding would be celebrated in New York—to be precise, in Mansfield's large home in Westchester—and clearly there was a strong argument in favor of its taking place before Ramsay's return from America. Would his father please give his consent? He was confident, he had said, that they would both be deeply impressed by Dora when they met her and would be happy to welcome her as a member of the family.

Thomas had replied firmly that he was sure Dora possessed all the qualities Ramsay had described, but since the decision was of such great importance, he felt that he should return home to discuss it fully with his parents. Also, since they would both appreciate the opportunity of meeting the young lady before matters were settled, why did she not come to England with him—accompanied, hopefully, by her father, if he was contemplating another buying trip or, failing that, by a suitable chaperon?

Ramsay's response had contained all the calculated skill that was typical of him, but Thomas found it singularly negative. It was not practical for Dora to come to London before the marriage, he had written, since Mr. Mansfield could not leave his business and there was no suitable chaperon. For Ramsay to return home alone would take up a lot of time that could be better spent gaining experience which could be of value to Kingstons. Would his father not consider leaving to him the judgment of Dora's suitability to share his life, since, after all, he was now twenty-six? If the wedding could take place as planned, he could return to London in the spring with a settled future —and, hopefully, they would soon provide Thomas with a grandson who, in due course, could step into Ramsay's own shoes as head of the business.

Ignoring May's warning to be cautious, Thomas answered in one paragraph, ordering him to come home as soon as possible.

Ramsay's reply was almost as short. He was extremely distressed that his father would not give his consent, for he intended to proceed with the marriage. He held Thomas in deep respect and great affection and was extremely upset at acting against his wishes, but was convinced that when they both met Dora they would understand his reasons. However, he had ended his letter, if Thomas felt that their association would no longer be practical he would accept with great reluctance that he must resign from the store—an offer which infuriated Thomas, for he knew Ramsay was drawing his fire. Ramsay was now the only son who could follow him in the business, since Thomas had conceded that Harry would never make a merchant and had agreed to his helping his Uncle Edward on the old family farm. There he had enjoyed considerable success training horses, and was currently bringing on a hunter for Thomas that had the prospect of outclassing any other animal in the Bicester field. Harry had recently wedded a girl named Claire, who, though utterly plain, was equally absorbed by his equine interests and had fitted with great ease into that rural household.

So Ramsay had married Dora. Mansfield had written twice, urging Thomas to give his consent, which Thomas had continued to withhold, and sent them both an invitation to the wedding, which they had formally declined. There had been no further communication between father and son until Ramsay's letter, received at the end of the previous week, saying that he and Dora would be arriving in London during the late afternoon of this day, April 19, 1897, on which Thomas was traveling to London by train in so unhappy a state of mind.

The carriage was waiting for Thomas at Paddington Station, as it always was when he came to London from the big house he had built at Quainton, and he instructed the coachman to drive to the store—the new store, of course, that had been constructed on the site of the original premises after the fire and had now been trading for some eight years. Since Thomas had been able to acquire some of the adjoining properties, it was considerably larger in ground-floor area than his previous establishment, and with three and a half floors devoted to selling, it was now one of the biggest of the London emporia.

Thomas had worked very closely with the architects on the designs, and with its terra-cotta facing bricks and its elegant towers, it had equaled all that he had visualized, with Ramsay and May, on that early morning after the blaze. There were now eighty departments, a fashionable restaurant where the Kingston orchestra played at teatime, a delivery service four times a day in central London and once in the suburbs, and a dispatch organization at the main-line stations which ensured that orders received at the store by the first post at six A.M., even for such items as fish, could be in their customers' country homes in time for dinner the same evening.

Electrical lifts connected all floors, and Thomas' latest pride—an escalator consisting of a forty-foot moving belt with handrails—could now convey as many as four thousand people an hour from the street level to the first floor.

The staff of the new store now numbered some four thousand. Turnover was nearly eight hundred thousand pounds per annum, and Thomas' boast that Kingstons sold everything, from medicine to books, from clothes to furniture, from food to toiletries, from pets to stationery, from servants' uniforms to all the needs of horse and horseman, even to special camping kits for officers serving in Africa and India, was now featured prominently in the store's advertisements—which caused one customer, as a practical joke, to order an elephant, confident that Kingstons would be unable to supply it. It was a joke that rebounded on him when the animal was delivered at four o'clock the following afternoon—though Thomas, entering into the spirit of the affair, had charged the customer only with the expense of returning it to the zoo where it had been acquired.

The carriage turned out of the Bayswater Road and entered Hyde Park, where, as always, the sight of people riding bicycles still filled Thomas with a sense of both wonder and surprise. For during the past couple of years, partly because of the ease and comfort provided by pneumatic tires, this activity had become a craze that had made an extraordinary impact on the nation. It had been Charles Rawlings who had suggested the previous year, when bicycling had been first permitted in Hyde Park, that Kingstons open a department solely devoted to the sport. And even though the price of each machine was as high as thirteen pounds, its success had been phenomenal. It had affected other departments too, heralding a fashion for knickerbockers. "Knickerbockers?" Thomas had repeated in shocked astonishment when Emily had first sought his permission to lay down stocks, believing that so dramatic a departure in women's clothing should have his personal consent. "You mean these trouser garments? For ladies? In Kingstons?" Knickerbockers resembled riding breeches, being fastened at the knee, with the lower parts of the leg encased in gaiters.

"Miss Hanson is convinced," Emily replied with a smile, "that the young ladies will all be wearing them for bicycling. In a wind, she tells me, they're more modest than skirts even when the hems are weighted down with shot."

"And are you as convinced as she is?" Thomas demanded.

"Not completely," she conceded, "but there's so much talk of the 'New Woman' these days that I think we should allow her to put her theory to the test."

And it did not stop with knickerbockers. The Ladies Riding Habit Department had to adjust to a new demand—small, as yet, but constantly increasing—from advanced women who preferred riding astride like men to the sidesaddle. Also, motorcars, as they called the new horseless carriages—the "Butter-Colored Beauties"—were starting to influence the fashion departments, now that the law no longer required them to be preceded by a pedestrian with a red flag. The Kingstons buyers had to cope with a new demand for clothes that would keep motorists warm in cold and windy weather.

"Times seem to be changing faster than they did," Thomas had said to Emily when discussing the knickerbockers issue. Emily's face was still scarred from her injuries in the fire, but her appearance had not been too unpleasantly affected. She was getting old now. Soon she would be seventy, and Thomas knew he would have to make the decision she dreaded.

As the carriage progressed down Sloane Street, Thomas ordered the coachman to halt outside a draper's shop called E. M. Hawkins. For a moment, he sat bolt upright glaring at the windows. The establishment had been opened some eighteen months before by Edward Hawkins, who had previously been a Kingstons sales assistant. His business had grown rapidly from a very modest start, and his progress bore obvious similarities to that of Thomas in his very early years. Hawkins had only six departments, but in these he did the same class of trade as Kingstons—but at prices that were consistently less.

Hawkins, a sandy-haired individual of about twenty-seven, had seen him through the glass door and now emerged from his shop with a cheery grin on his face. "Morning, Mr. Kingston," he said.

"Morning," Thomas grunted. "Those Henleys," he said, pointing to some ladies' waterproof capes in one window. "That's an absurd price, Hawkins."

"With respect, Mr. Kingston, our customers don't appear to think so," the young man answered. "We're selling dozens of them."

"Of course you are," Thomas snapped. "You're giving them away . . . but your profit margin's far too low."

"I've always heard that that's how *you* achieved your success, Mr. Kingston," said Hawkins. "I'm doing my best to follow in your footsteps."

"I've always given value," Thomas conceded, "but that doesn't mean being stupid."

"I'll consider what you say, Mr. Kingston," said Hawkins.

Thomas was not certain if the young man was mocking him or not, but he was sure he would not mark up the price of the Henleys, which had been set to make his own seem expensive. "Good day to you," he said coldly, and ordered the coachman to drive on.

As the carriage approached the store, Thomas savored the view of it. The sheer size, dignity and impression of stability it imparted, making it seem more like a national institution than a commercial enterprise, filled him with great pride. This was the heritage that his fool of a son was prepared to barter for a slip of a girl—or said he was, assuming, no doubt, that Thomas would be forced to concede. Well, he would have to learn, would he not? Thomas would not be blackmailed. Thomas had never succumbed to blackmail. The carriage passed the line of the store's windows—high and wide and deep, with the merchandise uncrowded and elegantly displayed beneath careful lighting—and drew up at the imposing entrance. Thomas waited while the attendant opened the door of the carriage for him, then walked into his great emporium.

He had left London for the big home he had built at Quainton on Friday evening, and although the figures of the Saturday trading had been telegraphed to him as usual, he knew that after a day away from the store Baines would have much to discuss with him during their usual morning meeting. He took the lift to the fourth floor and went to his office to await the Deputy Managing Director, who, as always, would immediately be informed of his arrival.

He was, therefore, slightly surprised when, following the expected knock on his door, Charles stood in the entrance. "Good morning, Mr. Kingston," he said. "Mr. Baines has sent a message saying that he has been delayed at a meeting in the City and instructed me to report to you in his place. I have the analysis of the Saturday trading here, and of course, I'm acquainted with the matters he intended to raise with you."

"You'd better sit down, then," said Thomas, gesturing toward a chair. "Is there any news of Mr. Williams?"

"I understand there's not much change in his condition, Mr. Kingston." Williams was Baines's principal assistant, who had been ill now for more than three months. Charles had taken his place temporarily, his usual duties as buyer of the Chinaware being assumed in his absence by his leading salesman.

"I see," Thomas grunted. "Have you heard that Ramsay's returning today?"

"No, sir. . . . The last letter I had was about six weeks ago. He

didn't mention that he'd be coming home so soon. . . . His wife'll be
with him, I presume. . . ."

"I presume so too," commented Thomas dryly. Perhaps, he mused
in his anger at his son, he should encourage Baines to allow Charles to
attend the morning meetings more often. It was a tempting thought,
for it might teach his son a lesson, but Thomas knew he would never
act on it—for Charles occupied an acutely sensitive place in Ramsay's
life.

Lillian's elder son had turned out to be highly talented as a re-
tailer. So, of course, had Ramsay. Furthermore, both of them had fully
recognized each other's ability, and for the nine years since Charles
had joined the store, they had competed with such ruthless intensity
that Thomas had often been astonished that they could possibly remain
friends. They even shared much of their leisure, though this area of
their lives was colored by the same strong rivalry. One of them had
only to show an interest in a young lady for the other to enter the lists
immediately for her affection. There were no rules, either. On one
occasion, so Thomas had heard, Ramsay had tried to blunt Charles's
effect on a pretty girl by hinting that there was insanity in the family.
He was infuriated to learn that Charles had already told her that Ramsay himself was engaged to be married—which at the time, of course,
was untrue—and sympathized with his unhappy fiancée over his ten-
dencies as a philanderer.

The lies and tricks, however, did not seem to affect their enjoyment of each other's company. They were like two boxers who could
pound each other with punches in the ring, yet spend a friendly evening together at the end of the bout.

Thomas was never quite sure to what extent he should intervene.
Their competition, of course, caused each of them to strive to his
utmost. When, for example, he had sent Ramsay to Paris on a purchasing mission, Charles, as buyer of the Chinaware, had asked permission
to go to Copenhagen, where he had been informed there were excellent prospects. Thomas heard later that Charles had found progress
difficult with prices high, but he had been so determined that his visit
be successful that he had not slept for three nights in his efforts,
encompassing almost every town in Denmark and Holland, to pursue
all possible avenues for merchandise.

On the other hand, their contest also had negative aspects. As
buyers, they regarded their weekly trading figures, and the need to
beat last year's sales, as the biggest challenge of all—a challenge into
which their staffs joined them with all the zest of Rugby teams

Thomas soon discovered that toward the end of the week there was a clear danger that customers in the two departments were being pressured to buy, and several times he had to caution them both; but when he learned that on one occasion in mid-season, when their week's figures were close, Charles had actually cut prices on the Saturday to win the advantage, he had sent for him and given him a severe reprimand.

While Ramsay had been away in America, however, Charles had made considerable progress within the store hierarchy. Because Williams' health had proved so much more fragile than had been anticipated, Charles's tenure of his position had extended from weeks to months until, displaying his undoubted flair, he had become a kind of chief of staff to the Deputy Managing Director—and in practice a fairly prominent member of the Kingstons management, even though this had not been formally recognized.

Thomas had always been wary of giving his managers titles, and apart from the buyers, whose merchandise territory had to be defined to avoid confusion, hardly anyone had one. In essence, despite the size of the store, Thomas still directed it as a one-man business, with Sidney Baines assuming his place whenever he was not there. Beneath this twin leadership was a whole stratum of people in charge of various parts of the business—staff, store fittings, store supplies, transport, accounts, catering and the different sections of merchandise—but they were not termed managers, which was, in fact, what they were.

So although Williams, as Baines's assistant, did not sound as though he were very important, he exercised great power in the store in Baines's name, especially in the vital field of merchandise.

For Thomas, Charles's performance only served to increase the problems surrounding Ramsay's return. If Williams' ill health should lead to his resignation, then Thomas would face a highly delicate decision. For he could make no move regarding Charles without considering Ramsay's position, and this was complicated further by the fierce competition between them and now by Ramsay's foolhardy disobedience. Thomas experienced a new wave of anger at his son.

"Thank you, Charles," he said when their meeting was over. "Now it's time for my round of the store. I think you'd better come with me." For Charles, this was an honor. For Thomas it was a gesture against Ramsay, a frustrated punch at the air, of which he was secretly a little ashamed, because in reality he knew that in this conflict he truly had no adequate weapons.

· 2 ·

"I'm deeply disappointed that you've decided to leave the business, Ramsay," said Thomas. It was six o'clock of the same day, and Thomas had prepared the scene for the confrontation with great care, leaving the store early so that he would be working in his study when Ramsay arrived at Cadogan Place with his bride. May, with a shrug of slight despair at what she considered his mishandling of the whole affair, had agreed to tell Ramsay on his arrival that his father wanted to see him immediately.

When Thomas had heard Ramsay's knock, he had not replied, forcing him to knock again. Then, when his son had entered the room, he had continued with the letter he had been writing, leaving Ramsay standing in front of his desk.

Ramsay had waited patiently until his father had put down his pen and looked up at him. Then he had smiled disarmingly, as though there had been no quarrel, and said, "Hallo, Father."

"Did you have a good voyage?" Thomas had asked.

"Uncommonly so," Ramsay had answered. "The sea was relatively calm the whole way over. Neither of us was seasick."

It was then, with the pleasantries dealt with, that Thomas had called his son's bluff, speaking as though Ramsay's offer to resign were in fact a definite decision by him.

Ramsay displayed no surprise—just looked evenly back at his father. "I've made no such decision, sir," he said. "If anyone's made that decision, it can only be you."

"You suggested it would be the natural consequence of your marriage against my wishes," Thomas responded.

"I did my utmost to obtain your approval," said Ramsay.

"Except return to discuss the matter with your mother and myself, as I asked."

"It would have changed nothing, Father. I'd quite made up my mind. I knew I had to marry Dora."

"*Had* to?" queried Thomas incredulously. "Nobody *has* to marry —certainly not without consulting their father."

"But you *were* consulted."

"My views were ignored . . . on a matter that was vital not only to us, as your parents, but to the store. . . . It's a sad business, Ramsay. I had great hopes for you. . . . You were developing well. . . . I was confident that you'd be able to take over when the time came, when I—"

"Father . . ." It was an interruption—not a loud one, for Ramsay's tone was gentle and even affectionate, but it was an interruption never-theless. "Father," Ramsay went on, "don't you think we could stop this? I'm deeply sorry I displeased you. I certainly sought your bless-ing. . . . But the fact is, as we both know, I'm the only son who can follow you in the business. I regard it as a great honor, as a great responsibility, but is there any point in our pretending that—"

"There's Charles!" snapped Thomas, cutting him off in mid-sentence. "Don't you go thinking you're the only candidate. Charles has matured beyond recognition since you've been in America. . . . Why, he's even a member of the management now. . . . Charles could take over from me. . . ."

Ramsay smiled—which was a mistake. "Please, Father," he said, still speaking warmly, "let's be honest with each other. . . . Charles has considerable talents but he has an enormous disadvantage."

"And what may that be?" demanded Thomas.

"He's not your son. . . . His name's not Kingston."

Thomas' reaction was almost as if Ramsay had actually struck him. He winced, moving his head back sharply, and the muscles of his face became rigid. He rose to his feet in fury. "How dare you make that assumption?" he roared. "How dare you have the impudence to presume that you will automatically inherit my store because there's no one else to whom I can entrust it!"

"Father, please," Ramsay began, alarmed by Thomas' reaction, "I don't think you—"

"Let me assure you, sir," raged Thomas, "that I'll vest control of my store in the hands I think best suited to direct it in the future, to foster it and adapt it to the conditions of the day, to guide it through the storms of slump conditions, to fight its adversaries when it's chal-lenged. . . . I'd always hoped that those hands would be those of a Kingston, but don't count on it, sir. . . . The store comes first . . . before my family, before my wishes, before everything. . . . If the best hands, the most competent hands, should belong to Charles Rawlings or to any other man who displays the merit . . . *then so be it!*"

He spat out the last words with a shake of his head that disturbed his thick gray hair. He was trembling with a degree of anger that Ramsay had never seen in him before—his face a high red, a vein in his neck throbbing, his eyes glaring. "You will now leave the room," he said. "Later I will meet your wife."

He did not join the family that evening until barely five minutes before eight o'clock, when they were due to sit down for dinner. He strode briskly down the hall and entered the drawing room with a flourish—then stopped abruptly, his eyes caught by the young girl who was his daughter-in-law.

She was sitting on a sofa on the far side of the fireplace facing the doorway—in the center of a group of Thomas' family, who were ranged round her almost as though they had been posed by a photographer for a picture. Ramsay and Harry, who had been summoned from Quainton by May, were standing behind her, both resplendent in their evening clothes. Rose and Claire, Harry's wife, were on one side of the sofa, while May herself was sitting on the other, on a small straight-backed Chippendale chair. For an instant, as Thomas had entered so suddenly, they all stopped talking and looked at him, almost as though he were an apparition. Then, slowly, Dora stood up. There was an element of humility in the movement. It was an act of respect to her father-in-law, to the head of the family of which, whether he approved of her or not, she was now a member. Thomas noted it, even appreciated it, but in a way that was almost absentminded, for his attention was gripped by the steady, confident expression in her large, very slightly slanted green eyes.

She was not exactly beautiful, for there was a certain lack of proportion in her features—her mouth, for instance, being a little big —but without question she was striking. She had prominent high cheekbones which, in conjunction with her remarkable eyes, gave her a vaguely Oriental look, and auburn red hair that was arranged in a fringe of curls on her forehead. She was tall for a woman, standing almost as high as Ramsay's five feet nine, but she had a tiny waist and pleasing, well-formed breasts, their soft whiteness partly revealed by the neckline of her green silk gown.

"Ah, Thomas," said May, breaking the brief silence. "We were quite giving you up. This is Ramsay's Dora. . . ."

"Good evening, Dora," Thomas responded a little stiffly, and walked to the position he often chose at delicate moments, with his back to the mantelpiece. "I'm glad to hear from Ramsay that you had an enjoyable crossing."

"Oh, we did, Mr. Kingston," she replied with a soft accent that Thomas associated more with those Americans he had met from the South than from New York. "At times the sea was like a pond. I could hardly believe it after all I'd heard about those great Atlantic rollers. . . ." And as she spoke Thomas was conscious of her steady green eyes. He knew, of course, what she was doing. She was willing him to like her, to acknowledge the soundness of Ramsay's choice.

"And how is your father?" Thomas inquired.

"His health is as robust as always," she said with a smile, "but he was a little sad when I last saw him—as he should be, don't you think, Mr. Kingston?"

"Should be?" queried Thomas.

"I'm his only daughter . . . and we've always been close. . . . I'm sure you'd be sad if Rose here was to marry one of my countrymen and live three thousand miles away. . . ."

Thomas nodded. "Yes, I suppose I would. . . . I would indeed. . . ."

"He was also a little sad for another reason," she went on. "He was sorry that our marriage had . . . How did he put it, now? . . . Oh, yes . . . had marred . . . that was the word he used . . . had marred a little the friendship he had enjoyed with you in London."

Thomas was embarrassed by her frankness. "Difficult," he murmured. "It was a difficult business. . . ."

"In fact, Mr. Kingston," she continued, "he entrusted me with the task of bringing with me a little gift for you that he hoped would . . . Now, there, I've gone and forgotten what he said. . . . Ramsay, what was it Papa said?"

"I think, my dear," Ramsay replied formally, as though he had been a husband for years, "it was something to the effect that he hoped the gift would demonstrate his great desire that our two families should not be divided by our marriage, but rather that they should be cemented by it."

"That's it exactly!" Dora exclaimed. "How clever of you, Ramsay. . . . Obviously, I'm not quite myself at the moment . . . which I suppose isn't terribly surprising under the circumstances . . . though now I've had the pleasure of meeting you, Mr. Kingston, I'm sure I don't know why I should be such a silly scaredy-cat. . . . Ramsay, where did I put that gift for your father? I had it with me just now. . . . Oh, there it is. . . ." She pointed to an occasional table and turned toward him in such a way that Thomas' view of the present was blocked by her body. "Now, Ramsay, would you please unwrap the gift and hand it to me. . . . Papa," she said with a side smile at Thomas, "was most insistent as to how this should be done. He said that the way things are done is sometimes more important than the things themselves."

As Ramsay removed the wrapping paper, Thomas eyed his daughter-in-law. He was not fooled by her performance of chattering femininity and judged that she was a very able, determined young lady of considerable character. Ramsay handed her the present, still, of course, shielded from Thomas' sight, and she spun round with a youthful suddenness that, strangely, was not ungraceful. Then, keeping the present as much concealed from Thomas as she could by holding it with both hands against her body, she gave him a broad open smile. "Mr. Kingston," she said a little breathlessly in the tone of an upper-form schoolgirl about to make a public presentation, "this is a gift from my father that he hopes will convince you of his earnest desire for a renewal of your friendship. . . . He sends it to you, as he sends me, with his utmost goodwill."

And with an abrupt movement she thrust her arms forward, holding out both hands together, palms upward, and Thomas found himself looking at the most beautiful silver model of a horse in motion that he had ever seen.

For a few seconds, Thomas was rendered incapable of speech. He stared in wonder at the model, which had obviously been fashioned by a sculptor of genius who had a passion for horses, for every curve and indentation bore the evidence of love. The animal had the fine lines of an Arab and was portrayed with tremendous delicacy and detail at the trot. It was about eight inches long and five inches high and, standing on a base of black marble, was clearly extremely valuable.

As Thomas took the horse from her with trembling fingers, conscious of the combined weight of the solid metal and the marble, tears came to his eyes. "Why, Dora," he managed to say at last, "I hardly know what to say . . . what words would begin to express my feelings. . . . The execution is perfect, and it's uncommonly generous of your father. . . . I shall write to him tonight. . . ." He passed the model to his wife. "May, look . . ." he began—and then, to her astonishment, for it seemed completely unlike him, he suddenly put his arms round Dora and enveloped her in a great hug. After a couple of seconds he released her, feeling self-conscious. "Forgive me, my dear," he said, "but I was quite overcome."

"Oh, please don't apologize, Mr. Kingston," she responded, smiling radiantly. "Papa will be so glad you like it. He knew you had a great affection for horses. . . ."

"No doubt, in due course, I shall come to have a great affection for you too, Dora. . . . Ramsay, you'd appear to have found yourself a most remarkable young wife who'll do you much credit when . . ." The glimmer of a smile that crossed his face was almost undetectable as he changed the word. ". . . if . . . you take my place as head of the company. . . ."

Ramsay had detected it, of course, for he had been watching his father with close and agonized attention. Now he smiled, relief that he had been forgiven mingling with his pleasure at his father's response to Dora. "Thank you, Father," he said, acknowledging the compliment to her.

"Now perhaps you'd ring for Brandon," said Thomas.

But Brandon was already standing at the door. "Dinner'll have to wait for a few minutes, Brandon," said Thomas. "You'd better warn Cook. . . . I'd like you to bring me from the cellar two bottles of Bollinger 'Seventy-six. . . . Dora," he said, turning to her, "it's been my practice all my life . . . on important occasions . . . to drink a toast in champagne. . . . I'd say this was an important occasion, wouldn't you? —a *very* important occasion."

· 3 ·

"Damnation!" exclaimed Thomas. "Oh, damnation! . . . I suppose everyone knows. . . ."

"I fear so," answered Baines. "Mrs. Williams was in the store today. . . . They're moving to Weymouth, I gather . . . the sea air . . ."

"And I suppose Charles has already raised the issue of Williams' succession?"

"Not exactly . . . 'e just said 'e'd 'eard about it and wasn't it a pity, since Mr. Williams was only in 'is prime, being barely forty . . ."

Thomas got up and strode to the window, his hands thrust deep in his pockets. "I'm going to leave things exactly as they are, Sidney, with Charles working with you on a temporary basis. . . . Oh, damnation . . ." He began to stride up and down the room swinging the "Albert" medallion on the end of his watch chain. "Just a few more weeks and the wheels would have been oiled. Now there's not much room for subtlety. . . . Perhaps it's as well . . . get it out in the open . . ." He sighed. "When he asks you about it, Sidney, you're to tell him nothing's settled. . . . Meanwhile"—he stopped walking and faced Baines—"I've decided that the time has come for Ramsay to have some experience of a senior post. I want him to supervise some of the buying under my direction so I can see how he handles it. . . . All the foods, I thought, including the Bakery, Confectionery and Wines and Spirits. . . . Also the Gentlemen's departments, since he's well versed in the merchandise . . . and possibly the Harness and Saddlery, together with Forage and Vehicle Hire . . . What do you think, Sidney?"

Baines knew exactly what Thomas was planning. The buying was still controlled by either Emily or himself with the help of assistants—

among whom, of course, Charles in recent months had been prominent, attending meetings, coping with the day-to-day problems of
budgets or merchandise. Thomas was now clearly proposing to change
this system in a first move of a process that in time would give Ramsay
control of all Kingstons' merchandise—the most crucial aspect of any
store—before, in due course, he was given charge of broader areas of
the management.

Charles, of course, competitive as he was, would be certain to
resent the change—as Baines now remarked to Thomas.

"I expect he will," Thomas agreed, "but I'm not running my store
to suit Charles. And also . . ." He broke off. "Well, Sidney, sooner or
later, he'll have to accept the realities of the situation. . . ."

Again Baines knew what he meant. There was no true basis to the
competition between them. Charles was assured of a prominent future
with Kingstons, but it was Ramsay's destiny to win the race.

For Thomas, the Williams resignation had aggravated other difficulties with his son. Despite his acceptance of Dora and his emotional
response to Mansfield's gift, his resentment at the defiant marriage,
with its undertone of blackmail, still lingered. Also, Ramsay had returned from America brimming over with new merchandising ideas
that he had seen in operation in stores in the United States—particularly in Marshall Field in Chicago, where his father-in-law had arranged for him to work for several weeks, dispatching him with the
words "Watch him like a hawk over a rabbit . . . study him . . . read
him, mark him, learn him, my son. . . . That's the store of the future."

"Him" was a dynamic man named Gordon Selfridge who had
joined the Field organization seventeen years before, when—though it
possessed an emporium of note—the emphasis of the firm lay on
wholesaling. Within three years, Selfridge had been appointed General
Manager of the Marshall Field store and had transformed it into one of
the most important retailers on the American continent by bold and
brilliant promotion.

"Do you know, sir," Ramsay enthused to his father, "in his first
year as General Manager, he raised the advertising budget from five
thousand dollars to twenty-five thousand?"

"And Field allowed him to do it, just like that?" queried Thomas
with surprise.

"It was an immense success, Father. What's more, he used his
advertising not only to sell merchandise, but to express a philosophy
that changed the attitude of the public. He made Field's into an institution that was almost as central to Chicago as City Hall. At the same
time, he traded up, emphasizing quality and service . . ."

"That sounds good sense. . . ."

". . . and installed a 'budget floor' for bargains in the basement. . . ."

"In a quality store?" queried Thomas.

"It worked, sir. . . . Then in the Piece Goods, he did away with shelving and had the rolls of material set up on tables in the center of the department so that customers could examine the stock without the aid of salesmen unrolling it for them. Revenue trebled . . ."

"And you're suggesting we should do that?"

"If it was so successful there, it might be received well here, sir."

Thomas shook his head dubiously. "Chicago's different to London, Ramsay. We've got different standards. . . ." Suddenly he realized he was using to his son the same dismissive phrases that Goldsmith had employed about America all those years ago. I'm getting crusty, he thought. I'm fifty-two and getting crusty. Which was why he was glad when Ramsay's next suggestion seemed more practical.

"Another thing he did," Ramsay went on, "was to establish a special children's section. Instead of merely having girls' costumes and boys' costumes sold separately, as we do, with other merchandise such as hats and shoes in the adult departments, all the children's needs, including toys and games, were centralized in one place. Again, the response was extremely rewarding. . . ."

"That's worth considering," Thomas ruminated.

"It'd lend itself to advertising, wouldn't it?" Ramsay suggested eagerly, seeing he had caught his father's interest.

"Now, don't you go thinking we're going to start squandering money like Selfridge on advertising, because we're not," said Thomas. "Kingstons is a different store to Field's, and London's not Chicago, but . . . Well, I'll consider the Children's Department. . . ." And he looked at his son, whose eyes were alight with enthusiasm, keen for his proposals to find acceptance, and he felt a mixture of pride and sadness. He knew that they had just had the first mild skirmish in an inevitable conflict between father and son, between a new generation impatient for change and an older generation fearful of innovation. By God, Thomas rebuked himself, are you the man who challenged the butchers?

Despite its undertones, the discussion had been amiable enough, but Thomas knew that it had signaled a new pattern in their relations, that Ramsay would now be seeking constantly to place his own personal imprint on the store, and that he himself must learn to permit this flowering while curbing its excesses and, above all, preserving the identity of his store, which could so easily be lost, which he had personally conceived and fostered.

Thomas had, of course, long been conscious that Ramsay's upward progress through the business would be accompanied by problems, and he had not intended to propel him into the higher echelons of management quite so soon. But the resignation of Williams, and Charles's position in the vacuum that this had created, had forced his hand.

Thomas' daily contacts with Dora, too, had been marked by a special significance—as was to be expected since, as a new member of the family, she was trying to establish her place within it. She had much on her side, of course, considering that he was a man who particularly enjoyed the company of women. She was pretty and lively and, by contrast to the scatterbrained performance she had displayed on that first evening, knowledgeable about world affairs and the arts.

Also she flattered him, occasionally outrageously, and cleverly established a certain intimacy with him with the use of the word "Papa," deliberately exaggerating the English pronunciation, with its stress on the second syllable, into "Pahpah."

When she first uttered the word, somewhat uncertainly, everyone had laughed, including Thomas and Dora herself. There had been some consultation of what she should call him, "Father" being the obvious choice, but she had said that if he did not object, she would prefer to address him by the more informal term. Since then, she had found she could use "Pahpah" in a variety of ways, from indicating warm affection, or light but respectful teasing, to actual rebuke, for at times she would challenge him. If anyone was a "New Woman" in that household, it was Dora.

She enjoyed the moral support of May, who had also been a bit of a "New Woman" in her way, and Rose, too, would normally speak up for her when she took a stand on sexual injustice. Rose was twenty-four now—three years Dora's senior—and possessed a serenity, a quiet poise, that was remarkable in so young a woman. She and Dora had warmed to each other immediately—though, as May commented to Thomas a trifle unkindly in private, this was possibly due to the fact that Rose offered no competition to the radiant star that Ramsay had brought home from America. All the same, it was not a one-way trade. Dora had acted as a catalyst in Rose's life, causing her personality to bloom.

Since Dora's arrival in London, the dinners at Cadogan Place had become stimulating occasions. Ramsay had acquired a small house in Brompton Place, only five minutes' walk away, but they were living with Thomas and May until their new home was ready for their occupation. It was during one of these dinners, about a month after her arrival, that Dora suddenly challenged Thomas in a manner that was completely unlike her usual careful and lighthearted forays with him. It started mildly enough when, while discussing another subject, Thomas spoke in passing of the fine children he was certain Dora would bear.

Dora frowned. "Pahpah," she said, drawling the word slightly, "if you'll forgive me, I'm not absolutely convinced that I like to hear you speak of my . . . of my productive potential . . . in quite that way. . . ."

"Oh?" said Thomas, sipping his claret, "and why should that be?"

"Well, it gives me a strange feeling, Pahpah. . . ." Up to this moment, the discussion had followed its usual pattern. Her "Pahpahs" had an element that was almost kittenish, for she knew that a little display of young claws was quite acceptable, even amusing, to Thomas. "It does sound a bit like the farm, doesn't it, don't you think? As though I was one of those broodmares of yours at Quainton Hall?"

"Good gracious," said Thomas, laughing. "Is that where this 'New Woman' business is leading you? Motherhood, Dora, is the noblest role of woman."

"But you could say that about your mares, couldn't you, Pahpah? Surely it's noble for them too."

Thomas put down his glass, a note of irritation appearing in his tone as he said, "Dora, I don't think I follow you. It's a beautiful thing when my mares foal . . . but I don't think there's any comparison with human mothers any more than there is from the fact that you eat food and they eat food. . . . It doesn't indicate you're like a mare."

"I think, Papa," Rose suddenly interposed, "that what Dora meant was that when you talk of bearing children like that, it sounds as though you're counting on her to do so, just as you expect it of your mares."

"And so I am," he said. "Is there anything wrong with that? I'm hoping she's going to provide me with a brilliant grandson. . . . He'll have a great future. . . . By then the store'll be double the size it is today, perhaps even treble. . . ."

"But he may not want it, Pahpah." Dora spoke quietly but with a firmness, and an edge in the tone of her "Pahpah," that made Thomas look at her sharply.

"Of course he'll want it," he said.

"I find it hard to know how you can be so certain," she persisted, but still speaking softly.

May could see that Thomas was growing angry and moved to intervene. "Dora," she said, "don't you think we should speak of something else?"

"Harry didn't want it, did he, Pahpah?" Dora continued as though she had not heard May's caution.

"No," Thomas answered coolly. "Harry didn't want it . . . but that was different because of Ramsay, who, in any case, was the elder. . . ."

"You mean that if I bear a son, Pahpah"—and now the "Pahpah" was cold, and May stepped in again: "Dora, this is a pointless conversation. I insist we change the subject."

"No," Dora persevered. "If I may . . . the principle's most important to me . . . If he doesn't want it, Pahpah, will he be . . ." She broke off, seeking a less emotive word than had come to mind, but failed to find one. ". . . well, *forced*—"

"Forced?" echoed Thomas, deeply offended. "Forced to direct the fortunes of Kingstons?"

"She didn't mean that, Father," said Ramsay. "Dora, tell Father you didn't mean that. . . . Of course the boy'll want it. He'd be mad not to want it."

"But if he doesn't?" persisted Dora, her cheeks flushed, a note of desperation in her voice. "If, like Harry, he doesn't . . . ?"

"Then, in that unlikely event," declared Thomas in controlled anger, speaking very distinctly with the consonants emphasized, "then the question of duty will arise. . . . He'll enjoy immense advantages, considerable wealth, a position of privilege. . . . He'll inherit the benefit of a great heritage that his grandfather created and his father developed. . . . Yes, there'll be duty consequent on that situation—a duty, I'd add, that most young men would give both eyes to assume."

For a moment, as Thomas glared at his daughter-in-law, challenging her to dispute the truth of what he had said, there was a leaden silence at the table. "I can only agree entirely with what Father has said, Dora," Ramsay rebuked her at last, "as would your own father. . . . I'm surprised at you . . . I really am."

She nodded, avoiding his eyes. "I'm sorry," she said, suddenly penitent, in a strange small voice. "I'm sorry if I offended you, Pahpah." And this time the "Pahpah" was affectionate in tone.

"I can't think what came over you, Dora . . ." continued Ramsay, before Thomas could respond, ". . . or why you felt it necessary to press the matter."

"I suppose I thought it relevant," she answered, looking straight in front of her. "I've done my duty too, like the mares . . . what's expected of me. . . . I'm sure, Pahpah, he'll want to run your store . . . *and*'ll do it well. . . ." Tears began to course down her cheeks. "Please excuse me," she said, rising to her feet.

"You're with child!" exclaimed Ramsay, his eyes alight.

"Of course she is, you stupid!" snapped May, hurrying after her out of the room, followed closely by Rose.

Left alone with his son, Thomas shook his head in a silent comment on the female sex that honored the inconsistencies, the frailties, the conflicts, the beauty, the nature that constituted woman—and a great broad smile spread slowly across his face.

·4·

It was a fine occasion, as everyone agreed—the finest, in fact, that had been held at 34 Cadogan Place since Thomas had bought the house some fourteen years before. As he stood with May at the entrance to the rarely used ballroom on the first floor to welcome their one hundred and fourteen guests, the Kingston orchestra played quietly at the end of the room.

There were candles everywhere, even though the house was equipped with electricity, because May believed that their animated illumination was warm and romantic. Under Brandon's vigorous supervision, waiters from the store's General Hire Department, which had also supplied much of the silver, glass and crockery, served champagne kept chilled in ice baths. In the dining room below, ranged on the white linen tablecloths in the flickering light of five-stemmed candelabra, were huge dishes of cold meats—York hams, spiced beef, boned and truffled turkey; brown bread; pistachio ice cream; and Russian gateaux.

The purpose of the evening was to introduce Dora to the people she should know—the more important personalities connected both with the store and with the trade—as well, of course, as the Kingston friends and family. Also, it was a way in which Thomas could in public give his blessing to the marriage that had been celebrated so far away

He had been concerned that the evening might prove too much for Dora, in view of her pregnancy, but was reassured by both May and herself that his fears were groundless. Certainly, standing with Ramsay beside her parents-in-law, she looked quite lovely in a delicate gown of chiffon over yellow silk that made a great impact on the gathering—to the pleasure of Ramsay and Thomas, both of whom regarded her like a prize won in battle.

Lillian was present, of course, with Charles and James and Eleanor —a Lillian who was now in her fifties, with gray hair, a body that had thickened, but a face that still had the same fine bone structure of her youth. Thomas had never discussed the circumstances of David's death with her, delicate as they were, but he knew she must have been relieved to discover that there was no truth in her astonishing suspicion that he had been Jack the Ripper. For the murderer had struck again weeks after poor David had been laid to rest in the graveyard of St. Mary's.

"She's a picture, Thomas," Lillian declared as she surveyed Dora approvingly. "I have to admit you're quite delightful, my dear," she said to Dora herself.

Charles, who followed his mother, looked at Dora with open admiration. "I'm overwhelmed, Mrs. Kingston," he told her—adding, for Ramsay's hearing, "He really doesn't deserve a wife of such quality and beauty. . . ."

"It's rare for you to be right about anything, Charles," Ramsay responded with a grin, "but I have to concede that in this one instance you couldn't be more correct."

The entire household from the farm had come to London for the evening, except for Letty, the eight-year-old daughter of Agnes and Edward—their only child, Agnes having been forty when they married—because she was deemed to be too young for the occasion. And Sidney Baines, of course, was present with Ellen, as well as their two eldest children, a fifteen-year-old boy and a fourteen-year-old girl.

Among the senior-management contingent, Emily Lane was just as proud of Dora as the male members of the Kingston family, since she had dressed her—although this had involved a minor battle, since Dora had favored one of the fashionable London dressmakers for so important an occasion. Neither Thomas nor Ramsay would hear of it, since for Dora to have gone outside the store for her gown would have been deeply resented.

At the last minute, on impulse, Thomas had asked May to invite Mrs. Fellowes, with whom there had been no contact, apart from brief chance meetings in the store, for two decades. She had accepted but arrived a little late, sweeping up the staircase with the presence of a queen. She was about sixty now, but extraordinarily well preserved, with a fine figure and a face that by some magic seemed to have defied at least some of the years that had passed since her dramatic meetings with Thomas in Eaton Square.

Thomas felt a great sense of contentment as he moved among his guests beneath the big crystal chandelier in the center of the ceiling. On the far side of the room he could see May executing her duties as hostess, gently playing her fan as she did so, and he was proud of her. She was gray now too, being in her late forties, but her waist was still small, and she moved with a smooth grace that made it seem as though she were on wheels. Her gown of heliotrope silk suited her well, with its deep décolletage that made Thomas think of the wag who had commented of that year's fashions that they "hung on the shoulders by a miracle."

At one moment, Thomas found Jones and Edwards, the two veterans of the Kingstons board, locked in discussion with Charles and Ramsay. "I was just asking," Jones said to him, "how the plans for the Jubilee were progressing, though I know we shouldn't really be discussing business."

"I was about to describe the display arrangements, Mr. Kingston," said Charles.

"You must be brief," ordered Thomas with a smile. "Then you must go and be polite to the young ladies."

"We're positive that Kingstons'll be the most outstanding store in London, Mr. Jones," said Charles. "We're going to frame the entire building with garlands and electric lights as well as a big crown that'll be placed above the entrance. . . . Then in the windows we're featuring merchandise in groups from the colonies—furs and leather from Canada, tea and tobacco from India, silks from the Orient, cotton from Africa and the Caribbean . . ."

"Four gentlemen talking together!" May interrupted. "Good gracious . . . I don't know what you're thinking of, Thomas Kingston. . . . Mr. Jones, I have someone who wants particularly to meet you."

And she led off the banker through the throng, while Thomas moved on among his guests. Suddenly his attention was caught by Rose, who was speaking to someone who, for a moment, was screened from him by a group of people near her. She looked very pleasing in a gown of eau-de-Nil, with her fair hair gathered high on the back of her head so that the delicate line of her neck was revealed. But it was her unusual vivacity that struck Thomas. Her eyes were shining, and she was talking with greater animation than he had ever seen her display before. An affectionate paternal smile came to his lips, and he

leaned sideways to see who was inducing this rare response in her—
only to experience a shock of astonished disappointment. For of all the
people in that ballroom, of all the eligible young men, the person she
was finding so engrossing . . . was James, Lillian's brooding, morose,
scowling James. But now, as he spoke to Rose, there was a smile on his
face and his eyes were bright. He was using his hands to express a
point, gesticulating eagerly, and suddenly Rose laughed with an unrestrained gaiety. And James too began to laugh, appearing surprisingly
handsome.

"Is that one of your sons, Mr. Kingston?" he was asked suddenly,
and he found Mrs. Fellowes standing beside him.

"Good heavens, no," he answered. "He's Lillian Rawlings' boy.
It's my daughter, though. . . ."

"She's charming . . . quite charming . . . but you know, there's
something about him that reminds me of you when you were young . . .
the same-shaped head perhaps. . . . Gracious, those were the days,
weren't they? When you were a young shopkeeper? I must admit,
though, that I didn't quite foresee this. . . ." She indicated the size of
the ballroom and the gathering. Her eyes were caught again by Rose
and James. "They appear to find each other appealing. . . . That'd be a
suitable match, wouldn't it—a joining of the two families that own
most of the shares in the store?"

"I don't think that'll arise, Mrs. Fellowes," Thomas replied coolly.
"As a matter of fact, they've never appeared to display much mutual
interest," he said.

She laughed again. "Ah, the human passions, Mr. Kingston. . . .
You never can tell, can you?" The wink she gave him was a flicker of
an eyelid. Then she moved away, fanning herself vigorously, leaving
Thomas in a very troubled state of mind.

James, in fact, had been the source of troubled states of mind in
Thomas from the moment he had joined the store. It had become clear
very soon that he appeared to lack not only his brother's talent, but
also his enthusiasm. In striking contrast to the early progress of both
Charles and Ramsay, the reports from the managers of the various
departments he had been placed in for training had been unanimously
poor.

Thomas had sent for him at regular intervals and attempted to
explore the reason for his inadequate performance, but James had just
looked back at him sullenly with those dark eyes. "I'm doing my best,"
he would say.

Thomas had persisted, exposing him to several departments on the
sales floors in the hope that some aspect of the merchandise would

catch his imagination. He had tried him in various service sections of the store—General Hire, Catering, Transport, Dispatch—but with no better success.

Then one day, James himself had requested an interview, and instead of merely responding to Thomas' questions with his toneless answers and slightly superior half-smile, he had sought his advice. "I don't like causing you problems, Mr. Kingston," he had said, "but I don't know what to do about it. . . ."

Thomas had smiled in what he hoped was an encouraging way. "What can I say to you, James?" he said. "You just have to apply yourself. . . . You have to work. . . ."

James had stared back at him with a troubled expression on his face. There was a slight tremble to his lips, and for one awful moment Thomas thought he was going to cry. Then he had said suddenly, "You dislike me, don't you, Mr. Kingston? You always have. . . ."

"Good heavens, James," Thomas had answered, astonished. "Of course I don't dislike you. . . . I want to help you. . . ."

James had smiled, and Thomas had wondered if he felt in some distorted way that he had gained some minor advantage, for there was a greater confidence as he had continued: "Even when I was quite a small boy, Mr. Kingston, I remember you looking at me in a way that . . . well, in a way you never looked at Charles. . . ."

"James, this is nonsense," Thomas had insisted. "I like you well enough . . . and I've taken great pains to find you a position to which you're suited. . . . If only you had some keen interest that we could exploit . . . but you don't appear to have any interests, do you, James?"

James had hesitated. Then he had said, "Oh, yes . . . yes I have, Mr. Kingston. . . ." But suddenly he had looked secretive, as though keeping to himself with great difficulty something of immense importance.

"What is your interest, then, James?" Thomas had asked gently.

"I don't think you'd approve of it, Mr. Kingston. . . . You'd laugh. . . . I'm sorry I bothered you." And before Thomas was able to respond further, James had begun to leave the room. But at the door, he had turned suddenly and said, "Paintings!"

"Paintings?" Thomas had queried.

"Paintings, Mr. Kingston . . . I'm interested in paintings. . . . We don't have a paintings department. . . ."

"No," Thomas had agreed, "we don't."

"Whiteleys have a Paintings Department. . . . It could be a very small one to start with. . . ."

With amazement, Thomas had realized that James was actually

suggesting that he be placed in charge of it—and James had at once noted his reaction. "I said you'd think nothing of it, didn't I?"

"But *I* didn't," Thomas had answered. "What do you know about paintings, James?"

"Well, I've always been interested in art, Mr. Kingston . . . at school especially . . ."

"About the business of selling paintings, I mean," Thomas had said.

James had given a small wry smile. "Not much," he conceded, adding eargerly, "but I could learn, couldn't I, Mr. Kingston?"

For a few seconds, Thomas had stayed silent. "I'll consider your idea of a Paintings Department, James. If I decide in favor, then I'll have to find a buyer experienced in the trade, but there's no reason why you shouldn't help him. . . . Meanwhile, I'm going to put you in Art Needlework. . . . Needlepoint canvases are the nearest things we have at present to paintings. . . . We can see how you get on there."

James had responded with an unusual degree of gratitude and had again just been leaving the room when Thomas had asked suddenly, "What's your opinion of the work of Pierre-Auguste Renoir?"

James had looked puzzled. "Pierre-Auguste . . ." he began to repeat uncertainly.

"Renoir," Thomas had repeated. "Surely you've heard of Renoir if you're interested in painting—or don't you approve of the Impressionists?"

"I'm not quite sure what you mean, Mr. Kingston."

"All right, it doesn't matter," Thomas had said, and as James closed his door, he had felt the gloom envelop him. For he knew now that James's interest in painting was only superficial, unsupported by application or even by any real curiosity. And as his weeks in the Art Needlework Department had gone by, the same pattern had re-emerged. His attention, the buyer reported, was always elsewhere.

Finally, James had ended up as a clerk in the Accounts Department—where, strangely, he had actually proved to have some minor value. And that was where he had remained for the past two years, leading a pedestrian, dull existence that still troubled Thomas when he thought about it, though he rarely saw him except on those social occasions in Cadogan Place when he accompanied his mother. And during these, Thomas would sometimes find James studying him across the table, with that same irritating half-smile on his face.

Now, at this big reception for Dora, Thomas was faced with the unsavory fact that it was this unremarkable, awkward young man—

just possibly his own son, though even Mrs. Fellowes' comment could not change his disbelief in this—who was producing in his beautiful, gentle Rose a reaction of obvious and intense enjoyment. As he watched them, James seemed to sense he was the object of study, for he looked at Thomas suddenly and smiled. It was not his usual furtive half-smile, but contained an element of triumph, even challenge.

Thomas acknowledged him with a cold nod and moved on among his guests. He found the group of five who had come from the farm gathered in conversation, supplemented only by Dora.

"What are you all doing here together?" accused Thomas lightly, knowing that they felt uncomfortable among so many London people.

"I was just about to remonstrate with them myself," said Dora with a smile, "though I wasn't convinced it was my place to. . . . Now, Pahpah, you can give them all a good scolding." And flashing them one of her dazzling smiles, she moved off.

"How is your father?" Thomas asked Agnes.

"Far too energetic for his age," she replied. "He's just given Letty a new pony, and he rides behind her shouting instructions like a cavalry commander."

"It's good that he takes such pleasure in his grandchild," remarked Thomas, glad that he had succeeded as last in ending the feud between the two families. Land, of course, had done it—the deep human need for territory. One day Thomas had just ridden over to Marston Hall, and without giving Cameron a chance to display his usual hostility, he had said: "I've come to talk about land."

"You're offering me land?" Cameron had asked suspiciously.

"Our fields that cut into your estate for your meadows that divide our farm from Quainton Hall."

"Out of the question!" Cameron had snapped, responding by instinct. "My land's bigger. . . . Prime pasture, too . . ."

Thomas had shrugged his shoulders. "Details," he had said. "We can make adjustments with cash. . . . I'll be at the hall if you change your mind." And he had turned and left the house.

Cameron *had* changed his mind, of course, and now the fences of his estate were relatively straight—and the Kingston fields stretched along the lower slopes of the Quainton Hills all the way from the old farm limits on the east of the village to Thomas' big house on the west.

After supper there was dancing, which was much enjoyed by everybody—except at moments, perhaps, by Thomas when he noticed that James had danced no fewer than five waltzes with Rose, that throughout each of them their eyes were fixed on each other's with such concentration that they did not appear to be aware of anyone else in the ballroom.

· 5 ·

Three days later, at the end of a management meeting, Thomas announced Ramsay's appointment as manager of a section of the buyers. "I'm sure I can rely on you all to assist him in the conduct of his new duties," he said. Then, on returning to his office, he sent for Charles.

Thomas knew that the interview would be delicate, but he had not predicted the outcome. Charles entered his office with an unusual hesitancy, like an animal sensing danger. When invited, he sat down carefully.

"I thought we should have a talk, Charles," Thomas began, "because with Mr. Williams' departure and Ramsay's position that I've just announced, I knew you'd be wondering about your own future in the store."

"Yes, Mr. Kingston," Charles answered, a little tautly. "Yes, I have been."

"Well," said Thomas, "in the short term it's hard for me to be precise, because I haven't quite made up my mind on the immediate direction that your talents can best be employed. In the long term, it's simple. . . . You're good at this trade. . . . You've imagination and the right instincts. . . . Ultimately, I've no doubt that you'll be a prominent member of the board, helping Ramsay direct an enterprise that'll be far larger than it is today—perhaps with stores in other cities, even other countries. . . ."

He broke off, watching Charles, whose face was devoid of expression. "I appreciate your confidence, Mr. Kingston," he said coolly. "However, if I may be permitted to ask, how long do you think it might be before you'll be able to decide my . . . I think 'immediate direction' was the phrase you used . . . sir?"

"Oh," answered Thomas, "a few weeks, I should think . . . a month or two at the most. . . ."

Charles hesitated, considering Thomas' reply. Then he said, "I don't wish to be impertinent, Mr. Kingston, but . . . well, I can't help wondering, as I'm sure you'll understand, why you've been able to decide on Ramsay's 'immediate direction' while my own . . . well, again with respect, sir . . . why my own should cause so great a delay."

The question was put with such deference that Thomas could hardly object to it. He leaned forward, his forearms resting on the desk. "I suppose it all seems simple to you, Charles . . . but from where I sit I can assure you it's highly complex. Many factors are involved . . . I need time . . ."

"I see," said Charles. Then he looked straight at Thomas. "With respect, Mr. Kingston, I don't think you're telling me the truth."

Thomas reacted with shocked astonishment to Charles's insolent suggestion that he was lying. "I beg your pardon," he said as though he must have misheard him.

"I mean no offense, sir, and I must ask you to forgive me for being frank, but there are times for plain speaking. . . . I think the truth is that you want to see Ramsay established before deciding my own position."

Thomas curbed his anger. Charles had needed courage to face him out, and he always recognized courage. "Charles," he said, "I've only permitted you the license I have because of your mother *and* because I consider you to have ability, but don't press me too far. . . . The point is—provided you don't become too impudent—that you've a great future with Kingstons."

"But not as great as Ramsay's," suggested Charles, adding quickly, "Oh, I quite understand, Mr. Kingston. Naturally you want Ramsay to take your place as head of the store. . . . Any father would. . . . But you'll appreciate my need to know where I stand, and . . . well, when I find my progress checked to ensure that I don't compete too closely, then I think it's time to consider my position." He stood up, "I'd be glad if you'd accept my resignation, Mr. Kingston. . . . With your permission, I'd like to leave as soon as possible."

The announcement by his clerk that Lillian wished to see him was expected, of course, but Thomas was surprised that she had learned of her son's decision quite so soon after Charles had left his office.

"Thomas," she declared, sweeping into his office, swinging her parasol like a riding whip, "you must persuade Charles to change his mind."

"I hardly think that's a task for me," he replied with a smile at her effrontery, "and I'd advise *you* not to try."

"But it's the family business. . . ." She gave him a sudden anxious glance. "You'd allow him to withdraw his resignation, surely. . . ."

"Of course. . . . He'll go a long way. . . . I wish it was to be to our advantage, but he's made his reasons plain. . . . He's not prepared to play second fiddle."

"Oh, he's being so petty," she snapped. "This absurd feud with Ramsay . . ."

Thomas shook his head in disagreement. "He knows himself. . . . Perhaps all those years of watching his father made the secondary role seem unappealing."

"There's no comparison," she exclaimed, "as you well know."

"I agree. . . . but the break'd have come sooner or later. . . . Better it should be now before he's got bitter, while they're still friends. . . . Has he any idea where he's going to?"

"Only a ridiculous one," she answered. "Young Hawkins up the road . . . he's offered him an equal partnership. . . ."

Thomas was surprised. It was a coup for Hawkins, of course, as his bold offer of an equal share made it obvious that he realized. "Is he going to accept?" asked Thomas.

"He appears to be of a mind to."

"That'll be a mistake," said Thomas. "I should try to talk him out of it."

"He doesn't listen much to me nowadays, Thomas." She sighed and sat back in her chair, her hand resting on the handle of her upright parasol. ". . . I didn't only come to see you about Charles, Thomas. . . . James is a far bigger problem."

"I think he's probably as settled in Accounts as he will be anywhere."

"James and Rose, I mean. . . . You noticed them, surely, the other evening. . . . Well, they've been seeing a lot of each other since then . . . bicycling together in the Park . . ."

"What—alone?"

"You can't exactly be alone in the Park. . . . Thomas, it's serious between them—and quite impossible, of course . . ." She hesitated for a fraction of a second. ". . . Since they have the same father."

Thomas looked at her sharply. "Not that again, Lillian. . . . After all, how could you possibly have known?"

"Because there was no doubt whatever." She saw his look of skepticism and knew she would have to move deeper into a subject she found distasteful. "I'll have to tell you, I suppose. . . . David was . . . was . . . well, not capable at the time . . . for a few months. . . ."

"So he was aware of it too?"

She shook her head and gave a brief sad smile. "Oh, Thomas . . . needs must when the devil drives . . . and when a married woman finds herself in the position that I did . . . Well, it was vital, wasn't it? . . . Oh, heavens, do you have to know every intimate detail? David was a strange, tortured man. . . . There had to be a key to that part of him, and I found it. . . . It wasn't rewarding, I can assure you . . . nothing about James has been very rewarding . . . but it sufficed. . . ."

Thomas stared in front of him for a few seconds, deeply disturbed. "So there really is no question about it?" he said at last.

"None," she said firmly, standing up. "It has to be stopped, Thomas." And she walked out of the room before Thomas had even realized that she had gone.

It was raining heavily when the time came for him to go home, but despite it, Thomas decided to walk. He strode up Sloane Street, the water streaming from the front of his umbrella, still trying to accustom himself to the now undeniable truth that James was his son. It should have changed his attitude. It should have made him feel some warmth toward the boy. But nothing had been altered. Men were all animals, really, he thought savagely. The crust of civilization was wafer thin. They satisfied the needs of passion. Just like the stallions. The stallions did not recognize their sons either. He could still recall that night of James's conception with vivid clarity—the sheer demanding sexuality of her, his own violent need which had seemed to come up like a sudden storm within him. The thrust of the biological dynamic. And James—poor, pathetic, ineffectual James—had been the result of that unsatisfactory coupling. As Lillian had cried in his arms, the nucleus of James had already begun its long metabolic process of growth.

The thought increased his anger as he mounted the entrance steps of his home. He responded shortly to Brandon's greeting as the butler took his coat and hat. "Tell Miss Rose I want to see her immediately," he said, and stalked into his study.

She knew why he had sent for her, of course. As she entered the room, following her timorous knock on his door, her cheeks were glowing. She looked quite beautiful, as women so often do in early love. "You sent for me, Papa," she said.

"Yes, Rose," he said. "Come in and sit down."

She did as she was instructed, moving carefully, giving an impression almost of being on tiptoe, and sat on the edge of the chair. She looked apprehensively at her father behind his desk—at the thick gray hair and whiskers, the lined, still-handsome face that had become rugged with the years, the brown eyes which were marked by an amalgam of expressions—of hurt and anger and sadness and affection and pride.

"Rose," Thomas began, "we don't talk about it much, but you're my only daughter and I hope I don't have to tell you how extremely precious to me you are."

"Of course, Papa." She managed a half-smile. "I'm devoted to you too, Papa."

"Then you'll realize," he went on, "that the last thing in the world I want to do is to cause you unhappiness. . . . I'm deeply concerned to learn you've been meeting with James."

She seemed to straighten her back, thrust her breasts forward, the color higher in her cheeks. "I'm sorry to have caused you distress, Papa."

"Do you care for him?"

She nodded. "I love him very much, Papa. He's coming to see you. . . ."

"I'm sorry to hear that, Rose . . ." His tone was affectionate, but his face was rigid. ". . . Because there's no point. . . . I cannot consent—"

"But Papa!" The cry had a birdlike quality. "Why not?" It was a small voice, nearly a whisper. "Surely you can't object to his family. . . ."

"Rose, my dear . . . you merit a far finer husband than James Rawlings."

"But I love him, Papa. . . . I must marry him, Papa. . . . Please don't forbid it without even talking to him. . . . He'll persuade you, Papa. . . . You don't know him, Papa. . . ."

He shook his head sadly. "I know James very well," he said. "Believe me, Rose, I wouldn't be doing my duty as your father if I permitted this . . . this relationship to continue."

"Please, Papa," she begged, her eyes now filled with tears. "Don't make up your mind completely. . . . Have you spoken to Mama about it?"

"Not yet, but I'm sure she'll agree with me. . . ." He paused sadly. "I've decided that your distress can only be heightened by your remaining in London, so this afternoon I telegraphed your Uncle Edward, asking if you might stay at the farm for the time being."

"No!" she exclaimed. "No, you can't, Papa. . . . I won't go, Papa. . . . Oh, please, Papa!" And all her composure collapsed as she succumbed to a paroxysm of sobbing and ran out of the room.

Later, as they dressed for dinner in their bedroom, May asked Thomas, "Weren't you a little drastic with Rose?"

"You think I should agree to her marrying James?" he asked incredulously as he tied his bow tie in front of a mirror.

"Well, he's not a leper, is he? Has he insanity in the family?"

"He's a complete dolt. . . . He'll never do anything. . . . There's some grave defect in him. . . ."

"It couldn't be that he's just not suited to the store?" she queried, "like Harry . . ."

"I find your question hard to understand," he answered. "Are you seriously urging me to consider him as a son-in-law?"

May hesitated for a second. "I don't know," she said, and even though he was still looking in the mirror, pulling at the bows of his tie, he knew she was watching him closely. "She's twenty-four—no longer as young as she was. . . . His family's socially acceptable. . . ."

"It's not his family I object to. . . . If it was Charles, it'd be quite different. . . ."

"I just wonder," May suggested, "if your view of James merited quite so precipitate a rejection. . . . I'm a little surprised you didn't discuss it with me first. Then I could have prepared her a little. . . . She's desperately unhappy. . . ."

"Perhaps you're right," he said, still adjusting his tie, taking longer than he needed because he did not want to look at her. "I should have got you to talk to her first. . . . That was a mistake. . . . Still, she's young, and their attraction was brief. . . . I hope it won't take her long to get over it."

"Thomas," May asked carefully, "is your opinion of James the only reason for your objection? Or is there something more?"

She was shrewd, he thought. What was more, she seemed to possess some extra sense that enabled her, if not to perceive exactly what was in his mind, to absorb some of the emotions that were associated with it. Certainly this last question of hers, close to target as it was, had to be denied.

With an effort, he turned from the mirror and looked directly at her. "No, May," he said, "there's nothing more."

· 6 ·

Right along the length of Sloane Street, flags were flying from upper windows or mastheads—as they were in every other thoroughfare in London. The shops were decorated with garlands of red-white-and-blue bunting. Royal insignia and representations of the old Queen—lithographs, sketches, even photographs—were prominent features of displays. In some windows, scrolls bore such loyal messages as "God bless her Majesty—Sixty Glorious Years—1837–1897."

As Thomas walked to the store that morning, his spirits were light. It was a fine summer day. Everyone was smiling. The capital, and indeed the country as a whole, was preparing to celebrate the Diamond Jubilee. For the past few days eminent visitors from overseas had been arriving in London—to be greeted by cheers as they drove in their open carriages through the streets.

London was in celebration. There were to be processions and military bands and banquets. On Jubilee Day, the Queen would ride through the streets in her gold coach escorted by the Household Cavalry with their plumed helmets and heavy swords. A line of bonfires would be lit in sequence on hills across the country.

The seventy-six-year-old Victoria, though often criticized for her long years of seclusion after the death of her husband, Albert, was enjoying a tidal wave of popularity—lauded as the Queen-Empress, the head of a great empire of more than three hundred million people, occupying a fifth of the inhabited surface of the globe.

Striding down the street, Thomas was filled with eager anticipation at the prospect of viewing the jubilee decorations and displays that Mathews and his staff had been installing over the weekend—so engrossed, in fact, by these pleasurable thoughts that he hardly glanced at Hawkins' shop on the other side of the road until he was nearly past it. Then he stopped with an abruptness that almost caused someone walking behind to collide with him. For there, in the end window of the shop, was a silk display that was identical, both in execution and in theme ("Silks from the British Orient"), to the plan for one of Kingstons' main windows. Furthermore, the arrangement of the merchandise, even the colors, were precisely as Mathews had planned for the store.

Thomas looked at the adjoining window and, with his anger rising, saw that this too was exactly the same as another of the Kingston displays—this time built round cotton that, though woven in Manchester, was grown in the empire, in British colonies in the Caribbean, India, Ceylon, West Africa—all featured by flags or other motifs indicating each territory.

The other two windows were also devoted to presentations that mirrored those which Mathews had developed for the celebration under the supervision of Baines—and, of course, of Charles before he had resigned to become Hawkins' partner.

Thomas strode across the street to study the displays more closely and, as he did so, saw to his fury that in each one was a show card with the impudent words "Best value in Sloane Street."

The deliberate imitation of the Kingston design plan was both bold and clever and clearly bore the imprint of Charles's mind. For the message he was conveying was that the Hawkins merchandise was the same as that in the big store—at least in those departments which the little business possessed—but at lower prices! And the more Thomas looked at the displays, despite his anger, he could not help being impressed by the daring of it, even by its brilliance. No other man would have done exact copies—and it was the exactness that carried the impact.

From within the shop, Charles saw Thomas and came out—presumably to draw his fire. "Good morning, Mr. Kingston," he said. "I saw you looking at our windows. . . ."

"I'm deeply impressed by their great originality," said Thomas sarcastically. "No one could accuse you, Charles, of thieving ideas, could they?"

"That's the sad aspect about the Jubilee," Charles replied. "It doesn't lend itself to original thought. The themes of empire, patriotism and honor to the Queen, God bless her, are well worn. . . . But like the decorations on Christmas trees, they do the heart good, don't they?" And he gave Thomas a broad grin.

"Don't you dare mock me, Charles," Thomas warned. "As you know, several buyers are pressing me to run you out of business . . . and this sort of audacity"—he gestured at the windows with a sweep of his arm—"could well tempt me to accede to their requests."

He walked on down the street, knowing that his pleasure in the sight of his own windows, his own decorations, would now be greatly diminished.

Thomas' unhappy reactions to the Hawkins displays, however, were small by contrast to Ramsay's fury. He burst into his father's office almost without knocking. "Charles's behavior is quite disgraceful, don't you agree, sir? I presume I have your permission to retaliate?"

"Retaliate?"

"We could break them in a very short time, couldn't we?"

"Break them?" echoed Thomas with astonishment. "Good heavens, Ramsay, how would you propose to do that?"

"Cut our prices to cost, even under cost. . . . That'll force them to remove those show cards. . . . Then we could warn every supplier who deals with them that we'll close his account if he continues to trade with them. . . ."

Thomas looked at his son, standing rigid in front of him, his

fingers actually clenched tight in his anger at the way Charles had
scored off him—for of course, he regarded Charles's action as completely personal. "Don't you think that'd be a little drastic?" asked
Thomas, despite his own mild threat to Charles. "They're a small,
fledgling business . . ."

"They've declared war, sir."

"War?" queried Thomas. "Ramsay, it's like a cutter attacking an
ironclad. . . . Shrug it off. . . . It's unimportant. . . ."

"They may not always be so small. . . ."

"Perhaps not, but they're small now . . . and I can assure you that
our suppliers would greatly resent our telling them who they can trade
with. . . . Anyway, I don't think Charles'll stay with Hawkins long."

Ramsay was surprised. "He wanted his own business, surely,
sir. . . ."

"Yes, but he won't be able to grow as fast as I did, which is what's
in his mind. . . . There were no big stores when I started, and Charles is
suited to big stores. . . . I give him a year before he joins one of our
real competitors. That's when you may have a battle on your hands . . .
a proper battle."

Ramsay managed a rueful smile. "He told me last night I was in
for a surprise. . . ."

"You still see him as much as you did?"

"Oh, yes . . . several times a week. . . . Dora likes him too, I'm glad
to say. . . ."

"But just now you were talking about breaking him," said Thomas.

Ramsay laughed. "I'd break him, Father . . . as he'd break me.
. . . Our fight's to the death—or at least, to acknowledged su-
premacy."

"But you're still friends?" said Thomas, shaking his head.

"Oh, yes—great friends."

Just after Ramsay had left the room, Thomas' clerk told him
that James wished to speak to him, and wearily, because James had
been to see him twice already since Rose had been sent to Quainton, Thomas told him to show him in. "I've only got two minutes,
James," said Thomas as he entered the room, "and I won't entertain discussion of Rose."

"I *must* speak of Rose, sir. I must ask you to reconsider your
decision."

"James, I told you the subject was closed. . . . You are not
marrying Rose."

James had lost weight in the last two weeks, and with his pale cheeks and deep hollows round his eyes, he looked gaunt. "I don't think I can exist without her, Mr. Kingston," he murmured. "I've tried, but—"

"Rubbish, James!" Thomas snapped. "I've never heard any-thing like it. . . . In due course you'll meet someone else . . ."

"Never!" It was a cry of declaration, a vow almost. "If I only understood, Mr. Kingston . . . My father was your partner in business. . . . Is it purely the fact that I'm not very good at the work? . . . If I was to do better, would it change things?"

"I've told you repeatedly," Thomas interrupted, "that I don't consider you a suitable husband for Rose. That's a father's privi-lege. You must accept it, James. . . . Now please leave the room."

James stared at him angrily, his eyes deep in that gaunt, pale face. "I won't accept it, Mr. Kingston," he said. "I'll never accept it."

His eyes widened as he glared across the desk. Then suddenly, he turned on his heel and strode out of the office. Thomas knew that he was tempted to slam the door, but in the last second he curbed himself. The noise as it closed was louder than it should have been, but there was no real defiance in it, no spirit, no challenge.

· 7 ·

It was still August, but the corn was cut, and hounds were out for the first time since the final meet of the last season way back at the end of March. There was no hunting in the summer—because of growing crops, vixens who needed respite to raise their cubs, horses who had to be rested at grass.

Ludgershall was some five miles from Quainton Hall—a good three-quarter-hour hack—and August or not, the dawn air was chill. Edward and the others had ridden over in the darkness from the farm to collect Thomas, with Harry leading the new hunter he had been training for him. Thomas had been ready and waiting. He had mounted quickly and gone on with them through the country lanes, bordered on both sides by blackthorn hedges. None of them had spoken much until the sky began to lighten soon after half past five— the early start being due to the fact that hounds met for cubbing at sunrise.

Then, as the darkness lifted, Thomas was able to take a cautious look at Rose, who was on a small gray that reminded him of Dumb-Bell, the pony she had ridden as an eight-year-old on those happy family rides in 1881 when he was facing the threat of Goldsmith. Since then she had become a skilled horsewoman who enjoyed hunting.

Since her banishment from London, she had offered little to her father in the way of conversation when they met, making no attempt to conceal her resentment. Thomas had not pressed her, saddened that he should be the cause of her unhappiness. James too had not sought any more interviews following their last abrasive meeting in Jubilee Week, but Thomas had seen him in the store sometimes and had been only too aware of the dark animosity in the young man's eyes.

As they neared Ludgershall Green, the top edge of the sun appeared above the wooded hills near Brill Village to the east. Hounds were there already—"The ladies, Mr. Kingston," the huntsman informed Thomas, meaning that he was hunting a pack of bitches that day, "among 'em five couple of good young 'uns." Now that Thomas was a substantial landowner in the Bicester country, he was a prominent member of the hunt—hardly the social equal of the aristocrats or even the top gentry, but accepted as a man of wealth and importance.

They did not dally long on the green, as they did sometimes at the meets when hunting proper started in November, but proceeded at once to a nearby wood. A young dog fox went away fast with hounds close on him.

They ran on well. The cold morning was fine and clear, and there had been a heavy dew, which gave a moist sparkle to the hedges and long grass. Thomas felt a great exhilaration as he rode up near the front of the field, hounds going fast a couple of fields ahead. At that moment, as he heard their excited crying and felt the wind on his face, life seemed good.

The fox was young but already cunning. He ran through a spinney; doubled back; crossed a stream; doubled back again; crossed the Bicester Road, where he lay in a ditch under a hedge while hounds, who had lost him, were cast by the huntsman. Then he was off again, through a field of kale; on by way of a farm, having learned early, it seemed, that pigs' manure was a fine cover for a fox's scent—then out beyond the barns across pasture and over a railway track onto fields where the wheat had been harvested. He did not hold his line, being clever, but circled back, crossing and recrossing the railway, sensing that the high embankment on which the track was embedded offered scope to confuse his pursuers. The track itself retained no scent. At the foot of the tall banks that sloped downward on both sides there was rough ground which, being owned by the railway company, was fenced off from the adjoining fields and afforded the cover of thick bushes and long summer grass.

Because of the fox's tactics, the huntsman and the field stayed on the top of the embankment. They saw him cross the track again, some two hundred yards ahead. Hounds appeared soon after him—but losing the scent, they became uncertain. Some went on down into the rough ground into which he had run. Others stayed on the track—alert but confused.

The hunt followers were now formed in two long lines on either side of the rails, walking forward slowly so as not to crowd the hounds. Ahead of Thomas in one file was the contingent from the farm—Edward, Agnes, Harry, Claire and Rose. This was the situation when the train came in sight.

The railway at that sector of the line was constructed in a very easy curve, which meant that approaching trains could be seen for some way ahead. The sight of it, therefore, was in itself no cause for alarm, except for the fact of those hounds on the track about halfway between the riders and the train—a distance of some four hundred yards in all.

The huntsman saw the danger at once and, accompanied by a whipper-in, started galloping toward his hounds, shouting as he rode and wielding his whip in great cracks that echoed across the country. But this seemed only to confuse the animals more. They appeared startled, looking this way and that, their ears pricked—and stayed where they were.

The train was traveling at some speed, steam streaming from the funnel, when the driver saw the obstructions ahead. He began to blow long warning blasts on his whistle and started braking to check his speed—but a train moving fast across open country between stations takes time to slow down.

With growing dread, Thomas and the rest of the hunt watched as the noise of the approaching train—of many wheels crossing many rail joints, of thrusting pistons, of gushing steam—grew constantly louder. The driver blew his whistle again and again as the distance closed between that huge engine and the two galloping riders in pink coats— and, of course, the hounds, who, worried by the urgency of the hunts- man's yells, were looking at him with concentrated attention but still seemed uncertain what he wanted them to do.

The end was totally predictable. Only seconds passed, though they seemed extended, as though the tragedy were being enacted in slow motion, before the engine, whistle still blowing, brakes scream- ing, drove into the hounds. Two were flung sideways, spinning in the air, to fall dead at the foot of the embankment. Three others were crushed under the weight and edge of turning steel. When at last the

train came to a halt, steam escaping noisily from the engine, it lay
between the two lines of shocked horsemen. The appalled train driver
leaped down from his cab. He was joined by the huntsman and
whipper-in, who pushed their way through the assembled followers,
the pain clear on their faces, and slid quickly from their horses. The
three of them gathered, bending down, to study the grisly evidence of
what had happened.

It was at this moment that a young and high-spirited passenger,
stimulated by the riders on the track but unaware of what had happened, lowered his carriage window. He leaned from it, let out a
joyous, though slightly mocking, "View halloa" and waved his hat—
just, so it happened, in front of Rose's mount. The pony shied, rearing
up and swinging away from the movement which had scared him. If
the ground had been flat, Rose would have been able to bring the
animal under control; but they were, of course, on an embankment,
only a few yards from the edge. In an instant of impotent horror,
Thomas saw exactly what was going to happen. The bound and turn
of the pony took his front legs into suspension over the verge; then he
lost his balance and somersaulted headfirst down the steep bank.

Within a second, Thomas was off his horse and clambering down
after them. As he got near, the pony managed to scramble to his feet,
but held one of his forelegs off the ground, and one glance told
Thomas it was broken. Rose lay at the foot of the bank, in a clump of
nettles—half on her back, with no movement in her twisted body.
Thomas bent over her, hoping for some sign that she was still alive, but
even before he was close enough to be certain, he had guessed what
had happened. She had fallen under the pony as it fell—some half a ton
of horseflesh and bone. Her back was broken. Her ribs, almost certainly, had been driven into her lungs. He stared at his only daughter,
her face drained of color, no sight in her eyes. The shock overwhelmed him, and he vomited.

He felt a hand on his shoulder. "We'll look after her," said Edward gently. "You get off home to May. Agnes'll go with you."

The long slow ride back to the hall had the quality of a terrible
dream. The condolences of the other riders. The noise of the shot as
they killed the pony, clear in the morning air though they were half a
mile away by then. A brief, faint blast of the horn, a suspicion on the
wind of the sound of hounds. One of the local farmers had offered to
fetch a trap, but Thomas had preferred to go on horseback, conscious
through his numbness that he would have to break the news to May.
He needed time to think of what he would say. Agnes said nothing the
whole way, and he was grateful.

Somehow May already knew, though no one had told her. As always, she was all strength. He wished she would weep, but she did not—not even when he put his arms around her, hoping they would give her some consolation. She just buried her head in his shoulder. It was a sharing.

They buried Rose at Quainton Parish Church, and everyone attended to pay respects, for even though she had lived in London all her life, Kingstons had farmed local land for a century and the village regarded her as its own. Cameron was there too, of course, standing at the graveside with Agnes and Edward and young Letty.

Thomas and May needed a few days of solitude. He rode a lot on his new horse, which was brought over to the stables at the hall— always, however, on his own. Sometimes he went for long walks, striding up onto the hills that he knew so well from his boyhood.

Then they went back to London and he resumed his duties as the head of the store. He did not see James until two days after his return, as he toured the building with Sidney on his morning round—and even then he was a distance from him on the far side of two counters. James stared at him in the same resentful way as he had before, though now, Thomas noted, the hostility in his ravaged eyes had deepened. Thomas understood his emotions. He wanted to cross the department to him and offer some kind of solace, since their grief was ground in common. In an odd way, Thomas sensed that James was conscious of this wish in him—and rejected it, wanting to give him none of the relief that this sharing might provide. It was a strange sensation for Thomas—a kind of communication without words—and abruptly he broke it by speaking to Sidney about a counter display.

That afternoon Thomas sent for Ramsay, but when the door opened following the expected knock, he was surprised to see James standing there. "Your clerk was away from his desk," James explained, knowing the query in Thomas' mind, before he took the revolver from his pocket.

In fact, Thomas did not believe it. His mind just failed completely to accept what he saw in front of him. Had a masked stranger burst into his room with a gun leveled, he would have responded at once to the reality, the danger of the situation; but James? James, of all people? James threatening him with a gun? It was impossible.

James sensed his confusion. "It's really happening, Mr. Kingston," he said quietly. "The gun's loaded . . . all six chambers. . . . It's a Colt forty-five. . . ."

"What in the world are you thinking of, James?" asked Thomas, beginning at last to grasp at least some aspects of the incredible situation.

James's face relaxed into his characteristic half-smile, though there was no humor in his eyes. "It's hard for you, isn't it, Mr. Kingston?" he said. "It's hard to accept that I'm going to shoot you. . . ."

"You're going to shoot me?" Thomas repeated. He felt no threat to his life, because he could see James only as a child pointing a toy pistol.

"And then I'm going to shoot myself," said James, "because my life's no longer worth living . . . not without Rose. . . ."

The mention of Rose touched raw emotions that for days Thomas had been trying to clothe; that he had been attempting not so much to muffle—for there was relief, even joy, in the agony of remembrance— as to position in his mind in a way that was practical. For life, for the rest of them, had to resume its pattern. The store had to be directed. Rose was reality, though. Rose gave reason to James's outrageous behavior. "I understand how you feel, James," said Thomas, sympathy in his voice, "but this is very foolish. . . . God knows it's the most dreadful thing that's happened to any of us . . . but this isn't the way to deal with it. . . . Now, give me that gun and sit down. . . . Perhaps it'll help if we talk about it a bit. . . ."

For an instant, Thomas could see that James was tempted by his suggestion. Then his resolve returned. "No," he said, "no . . . you can't talk me round like that. . . . She was the only woman I've ever loved. . . . *Mr. Kingston!*" Suddenly he was shouting. "*I loved her!*" It was a cry against the injustice of the world, of mankind, of God.

"I know," said Thomas, still sympathetic. "I did too . . . So did her brothers . . . and her mother. . . . All of us'll miss her terribly. . . ."

"But you sent her away!" he challenged. "If you hadn't sent her it would never have happened."

"It could have happened anytime, James. . . . She went hunting often. . . ."

"But not then," James insisted, his features twisted in desperation and appeal. "It wouldn't have happened *then*, would it?" Thomas gave a small sad shrug as if to question who were they to understand the ways of God. "Mr. Kingston," James accused, "you killed Rose."

Thomas glared at him. "That's a terrible thing to say to a father," he said, "and completely wrong. . . . Now, you're to stop this absurd behavior—"

"Absurd!" The word, as James cut him off, was marked with both pain and offense at its inadequacy. "You dare call it absurd . . . absurd,

Mr. Kingston?" The revolver moved with his new anger, and Thomas saw the pressure of his hand increase.

"My tragedy's as great as yours, James," Thomas said quietly; "greater in fact, for she was my only daughter. . . . Now stop being a fool and give me that gun. . . ."

"I hope you're prepared," said James, taking a step back, "to answer before God for what you've done. . . ."

Thomas was watching him very carefully. He knew that he had to control his wounded anger and offense at James's outrageous accusation and concentrate his mind completely on what he would now do and say. Clearly, James was in a highly unbalanced mental state and aiming at him a revolver that Thomas had to accept was loaded. But he had not fired. Thomas did not think he would be able to bring himself to fire, but he could not be certain. A wrong move at this critical juncture might possibly provoke him, despite himself, to shoot. Also, Thomas knew that at any second Ramsay would knock and enter, and he had to consider how James would react to the arrival of a third person.

Obviously, Thomas had to persuade him to relinquish the gun, which meant that he must somehow discover a way of dominating him. All his life, Thomas was aware, James had known him as a figure of great power, and he wondered now if this lay at the root of this challenge. Was it a tribute to Rose, a gesture to compensate for his failure to take positive action to gain her, possibly to elope with her? Was he playing David to Goliath? And had he the courage? It was vital for Thomas to know this, and he decided now to put it to the test.

Suddenly he stood up. "James!" he ordered loudly. "Put that gun down on my desk!"

James took one step back. "You don't think I can do it, do you?" he said, and Thomas saw the self-doubt in his eyes. "I promise I can do it, Mr. Kingston. . . ."

"Put down that gun!" shouted Thomas, pounding the desk with his fist.

"*No!*" James shouted back. "No," he added more quietly, "I'm going to do what I came here for. . . ."

Again Thomas saw the movement of his hand on the gun and guessed that it was not a preliminary to firing but a need for the assurance of hard metal. James took another step back, and Thomas noted the sweat on his forehead. He decided to try a different tactic.

He sat down at his desk. "I presume you'll allow me to write a few last words to my wife, James . . . before you carry out the execution?"

"You still don't think I can do it, do you?" said James.

Thomas shrugged. "Who knows? . . . Do *you* know, James?"

"Yes. . . ." Even that one word was full of the need for self-assurance. ". . . Yes, I know . . ."

"In that case . . . I may write the note . . . ?" James was not sure. He was fearing a trick, fearing delay, fearing the danger that any moment someone might enter. "You can hardly refuse me permission to write to my wife, can you?" asked Thomas.

"All right," said James after a pause, "but only three or four lines. . . ."

"Thank you, James," said Thomas. "The notepaper is in my right-hand drawer. . . . I may reach for it . . . ?"

"Why not?" he answered, though he was doubtful.

"There could be a revolver in it, couldn't there, James? . . . It'd be sensible for a man in my position to keep a revolver, wouldn't it?"

"Why are you telling me, then?" asked James suspiciously.

"I thought you should know," answered Thomas. "I'm going to open the drawer now, James. . . ." Thomas was watching him carefully to test his reaction. For a couple of seconds he seemed mesmerized and did not reply. "See, James . . . I'm putting my hand on the handle. . . ."

"Don't you touch it!" James shouted suddenly, moving back another pace.

"You mean you won't let me write a final note to my wife?"

"Not if it means opening the drawer."

"But you wouldn't have known there was a revolver in the drawer if I hadn't told you. . . ." Thomas saw the uncertainty in James's eyes and decided the moment had come to call what he was now sure was a bluff—a bluff of James by James. He leaned back in his chair and laughed at him. "I think you'd better get on with it, James. . . . Go on, shoot me. . . . What part are you going to aim at—the heart or the head?"

Before James could answer, there was the expected knock on the door and Ramsay stood there. "Good God!" he exclaimed.

"Come in, Ramsay," said Thomas, "James is just about to shoot me. . . . Perhaps you'd better tell my clerk. . . ."

"Stay where you are, Ramsay," ordered James in a quiet voice. "And close the door. . . . Go on," he added as Ramsay hesitated, "close the door or I'll kill your father now. . . ."

Ramsay shut the door gently. "Have you gone mad, James?" he asked.

"A little, perhaps," said James, keeping the gun leveled at Thomas but switching his eyes nervously between them. "I've reason enough, for God's sake, haven't I?"

"Reason?" echoed Ramsey. "You mean you blame Father for what happened? You're out of your mind. . . . Here, give me your gun. . . ." He stretched out his hand and began to move toward him.

"Stand back!" snapped James, and Ramsay did so. "Not another step," he warned.

"James is going to shoot *me* first," Thomas told Ramsay; "then he's going to shoot himself. . . . That's right, isn't it, James?"

James stared at him, the fear now obvious in his expression. "Well, go on, James," said Thomas. "Either shoot me or don't shoot me. . . ."

"You don't think I can, do you?" demanded James, and, Thomas noted, the hand holding the gun had begun to tremble. James tried to control it, sweating profusely now. "Do you?" he repeated. "You don't think I can. . . ."

Thomas leaned forward with his elbows on the desk and looked steadily at Lillian's son—at his son. "No, James, I don't," he said. "I don't think you have the courage. . . ."

"I have!" The yell was high-pitched. "I swear I have. . . ."

"Then do it!" said Thomas. "Do it—or hand the gun to Ramsey. . . ." His gaze, as he looked at James, was steady.

"How dare you question my courage?"

"Do it, then," said Thomas.

James's eyes widened suddenly. For a second he stared at Thomas in what seemed a moment of emotional paroxysm. He raised the gun slightly. "You daren't, do you?" said Thomas. The gun moved again, but he did not fire, and Thomas assessed that he was at the peak of his crisis—the moment when he would break.

"Give the gun to Ramsay," said Thomas in a softer tone. For two seconds James stared back at him, holding his gaze, as though he had not heard him. Then he blinked. He made a slight movement toward Ramsay, and Thomas thought he was going to pass him the gun. But he was wrong. The explosion, in the confines of that office, was enormous, producing in all of them an impact of shock, of ringing ears, of floating dust.

Instinctively, Thomas had ducked—though it would have been a useless movement had the bullet not gone wide, for it would have been made too late. At the same moment, Ramsay had leaped at James, knocking him to the floor. The gun spun out of his hand. "Get the gun, Father!" Ramsay called out. "Get the gun!"

Thomas picked it up from the floor, and Ramsay, seeing it in his hand, released James. The door of the office was flung open and Thomas' clerk stood there. "Are you all right, Mr. Kingston?" he asked.

"Yes, thank you," Thomas answered, "surprisingly. . . . There's been a little accident. . . . You may leave us now."

"I had the courage," said James as the door closed. "You said I hadn't the courage . . . but I did, didn't I, Mr. Kingston? . . . I had the courage. . . ."

"You poor, stupid boy," said Thomas, for he still doubted his courage. He suspected he had deliberately shot wide. "Ramsay, I'd like you to take James home, explain to his mother what has happened . . . tell her to call a doctor. . . . Then I'll think of what to do with him. . . ."

"You mean you're not going to summon the police?" demanded Ramsay angrily. "After he tried to kill you?"

"Even if I was of a mind to do that," said Thomas, "do you think it would be wise? Would *you* do it, Ramsay?" Ramsay realized then. It would be reported in the newspapers. "Now do as I ask, please," said Thomas.

Ramsay looked at James and saw there was no resistance left in him. "Come on, James," he said, and led the way out of the room.

Left alone, Thomas experienced a sudden reaction. Because the drama had been so intimately linked to Rose, was almost a defilement of her memory, because James was his son, because there was uninformed hatred and the agony of open wounds, because at times the human condition was tragic and could be oh, so ironic—because of all these things, a wave of emotion suddenly overwhelmed him.

For the first time since Thomas Kingston had been a boy, he broke down, laid his head on his arms on his great big desk—and wept.

CHAPTER TEN

September 1906

· I ·

"May I please inquire, Mr. Chairman, when the board expects to be able to reduce the current level of the company's borrowings?"

The question came as something of a shock to Thomas as he stood on the platform behind the table at which Ramsay, Sidney and the other directors were seated. It was only the second Annual General Meeting of shareholders that had been held since Kingstons had become a public corporation in 1904—the same year it had won the Royal Warrant—and he still found it hard to accustom himself to this yearly ordeal when he was answerable to any stockholder who chose to cross-examine him about his store. His interrogator was a gray-haired man in his fifties—an accountant, Thomas guessed, probably acting for a family trust.

"I have to confess, sir, to some surprise at your question," he replied. "Our policy has always been progressive, has always been to seek constantly to increase our range of service. . . . That's why we're currently building a big new furniture depository at Battersea suitable for large-scale storage; why we've installed a system of cash transmission by pneumatic tubes throughout the store; why we've introduced a cold storage for furs in summer and a safe deposit for our customers' valuables with unpickable and explosive-proof locks. . . . Of course such innovations cost money. . . . Even so, trading as we are at more than two million pounds a year, with profits nearing one hundred and fifty thousand, I'd suggest, sir, that our loan position is relatively modest. . . ."

Thomas caught the eye of May, who was sitting in the body of the room with the family. She nodded approval at his spirited response, and he was just about to resume his seat when another questioner rose to his feet. He was of an unusual type among the persons who had so far attended the Kingstons AGMs. Aged about thirty-five, he was debonair and barbered and wore a suit that was finely tailored. Rather surprisingly, diamonds flashed from a pin in his tie, from his cuff links

and even from a ring on one of his fingers. "Mr. Chairman . . ." he
began in a languorous voice, and paused, a patient smile on his face,
until he had the attention of the meeting, ". . . in view of the critical
tone of the last question, I'd like to pay a tribute to the board and, in
particular, to yourself. . . . How many other enterprises in this country
have increased their profits every single year without fail since 1890—
and by such substantial margins? Very few, I'd venture to say. . . . I
believe, sir, your achievement is outstanding and that we, as your fellow
stockholders, should feel privileged to share with you the ownership of
this great company. . . . Thank you." And he sat down to applause,
leaving Thomas too moved and astonished for a few seconds to find
the appropriate words of gratified response.

Ernest Jones, who had replaced his father on the board as financial
director, stood up and formally moved the adoption of the accounts.
Thomas brought the meeting to an end and joined May and Lillian in
the body of the room among the dispersing crowd. It was then that the
elegant young man who had acted as his champion approached him.
"Mr. Kingston," he drawled with the same self-confident smile, "my
name is Maurice Etherington. . . . I wonder if you'd do me the favor of
a couple of minutes in private."

Thomas had invited Lillian and the family to lunch, but he had
been grateful for Mr. Etherington's support. "If you really mean a
couple of minutes," he said, "since I have duties as a host . . ."

Thomas conducted him to his office and, inviting him to take a
seat, sat down himself at his desk, "Now, Mr. Etherington . . ." he
said.

At close quarters, Thomas could detect the precision that had
gone into his appearance—the meticulous creases in his tie around the
diamond pin, the exact positioning of the rose in his buttonhole, the
carefully waved hair unmarred by a single misplaced strand.

Etherington deftly cocked one leg over the other, displaying the
highly polished toe of a shoe within a fashionable fawn spat, and gave
Thomas a reassuring smile. "As an institution your store is remarkable,
Mr. Kingston," he said, "yet it lacks one element that would enor-
mously enhance its prestige. . . ." He hesitated. ". . . Its chairman does
not possess a title."

"A title, Mr. Etherington?" Thomas echoed in astonishment.

"Please, Mr. Kingston. . . ." Two manicured hands were raised in
restraint. ". . . Allow me two more seconds. . . . I realize, of course, that
a title would mean nothing to you personally . . . but for this exceptional store? The benefit can't be doubted, can it? Of course, I didn't
quite have in mind the peerage—not at first, at least—but a baronet-

cy'd seem suitable, don't you think? . . . Sir Thomas Kingston, Bart. . . .
Better than a knighthood, since your son would then inherit, as in
turn would *his* son. The title'd become part of the presidency of this
great company . . . a kind of symbol . . . a . . . well, I hardly like to
compare it to a crown, but I suppose it can't be denied that it'd have
something of the same kind of aura . . . in a minor key perhaps, a paler
shade, a watercolor as opposed to—"

"Mr. Etherington!" Thomas cut in. "I must interrupt you. . . . I've
never had such an astonishing conversation in my life. . . . Even assuming a title would be advantageous, as you say, there's no point in our
discussing it. . . . It's an accolade, a reward for service to the nation
bestowed by the King. . . ."

"Ah!" Etherington gave a knowing smile. "You're correct, Mr.
Kingston, completely correct. . . . But how does the King decide, and
what *is* service to the nation? In the past, of course, it could be demonstrated by armed retainers or loyalty in other forms . . . but in the
twentieth century, Mr. Kingston? In 1906? I seem to recall, for example, that in the fight against the Boers, Kingstons equipped ten
companies of London volunteers with no less . . . if my memory's
correct . . . than two thousand helmets, a hundred saddles and twelve
hundred sets of mule harness. . . ."

Thomas gave a deprecatory shrug. "It was a small contribution,"
he said.

"Small, as you say," Etherington agreed, "but an indication of a
patriotic spirit, a sense of duty."

"But hardly, Mr. Etherington, service to the nation. . . ."

Again Etherington smiled tolerantly. "Mr. Kingston," he said,
"you underestimate your store. . . . I'd argue that its very existence is a
service to the nation. . . . Men have been honored for far less—men,"
he added pointedly, "recommended by the Prime Minister in the Honors Lists submitted twice a year to the King. . . ."

Thomas stood up. "Well, I appreciate your sentiments, of course,
Mr. Etherington . . . but now you really must excuse me."

Etherington rose from his chair, as before with every movement
smooth and neat, like a dancer. "Consider the matter, Mr. Kingston. . . .
I'd be happy to advise you. . . . I have some knowledge of . . ." He
broke off with a pained smile. ". . . It's hard to define . . . the world of
reward, shall we say . . . ? Of the wheels within wheels . . . ? If you'd
care to discuss it a little more, may I suggest you dine with me next
Tuesday if you're free . . . ? I'd be glad to be your host at the Reform
Club. . . ."

The invitation confused Thomas. He had found the discussion

both unbelievable and distasteful. He completely distrusted Etherington, whom he had dismissed as an obvious charlatan. He was amazed,
therefore, that he could possibly be a member of so eminent a club as
the Reform, which was the bastion of the Liberal Party. Etherington
had noted his hesitation and gave a careless gesture with his hands.
"Don't bother to consult your diary now," he said, "for I know you're
pressed. . . . I'll await you at half past seven. . . . If it's inconvenient,
think nothing of it. . . . I'll dine at the central table. . . . There's always
good company there. . . ."

He shook Thomas' hand, flashed him a frank smile, and walked
out of the room.

As Dora waited with the others in the Directors' dining room for
Thomas to join them, she knew she must contain her growing resentment, for these black moods were familiar. Always they would begin
as a vague sense of malaise and then, feeding on themselves, would
grow into a seething anger that would cause her to explode suddenly
into a furious quarrel with Ramsay or rage at the servants over a
trifle.

There was no mystery about their cause. It was the huge role
played in her life—and of that of the whole family—by the store.
Once, after a quarrel, Ramsay had expressed surprise at her bitterness.
As he had said, she had been brought up in a store family and should be
accustomed to the demands the business placed upon her. But her
father had lacked Thomas' hard central drive and imaginative sense of
purpose. He was a relaxed, leisure-loving character, and Mansfield's
reflected his attitude, being little different from many other houses
throughout America that traded in the middle market.

By contrast, Kingstons was completely distinctive and no longer
had a real competitor in London—no other store that could truly
compare for prestige, for service, for the finest quality of merchandise;
no other store of which customers would say to their friends with the
same pride, "I bought it at Kingstons."

There were other big emporia, of course, but none of their directors would argue the preeminence of Thomas' enormous building,
with the terra-cotta facing bricks, in Sloane Street.

And supreme as it was, it demanded a supreme tribute from the
family—in particular from Dora herself and even more especially, as
would soon be illustrated, from her son. For it happened that Robert
was seven today, and at the end of luncheon he would take part in a
birthday ritual that would underline the connection which linked the

little boy, like an umbilical cord, to the store. This was the ritual annual visit to the vast cornucopia of toys, games, soldiers, and dolls known as Kingstons' Toy Department which Thomas would conduct in person to assist with the difficult decision, in the face of so enormous a range of choice, of his birthday present to his grandson.

No matter how busy he was, Thomas would take the time to execute this ceremony for all his grandchildren on their birthdays, but Robert was in a special category. He was the only son of Ramsay and Dora, though she had also produced three daughters, one of them older. Harry and Claire had a couple of boys in an ever-growing family that also included three girls, but Thomas clearly doubted that the future head of Kingstons would emerge from the carefree, horse-dominated environment of the farm. He saw Robert as the obvious successor to Ramsay, who had fulfilled all his hopes and now, at thirty-five, was both a director and General Manager of the store.

Thomas' attitude toward her son produced in Dora fiercely conflicting emotions. She was proud of Robert's princelike role; but protective of her children, as she had always been, she was also highly jealous of the lien that had been placed so inexorably on his future. "What if he should display a genius for medicine?" she had screamed at Ramsay in one of her black explosions. "Or for the law . . . or for politics?"

"He won't," Ramsay had insisted.

"You mean he can't . . . it won't be allowed. . . . Right through to his old age, his life is plotted. . . ."

Ramsay had looked at her with the cold stare, almost impersonal, that he used to cloak extreme anger. "So's *my* life," he had said. "So's yours. . . . Is it so tragic? You live in this large house with all these servants and your carriage and your 'at homes' and your wardrobes full of elegant clothes."

The argument deflated her, as it always did, with its sheer logic. The rewards were undeniably great. Thomas was a very wealthy man —even wealthier since the company had gone public. The whole family enjoyed an extremely affluent standard of living. There was a price for everything. So far as Dora herself was concerned, that price demanded of her total discipline—where she went, how she traveled, what she wore, whom she entertained. For she was the wife of Ramsay Kingston. When she walked through the store, the eyes of the staff— and there were now five thousand of them—were on her. "Good morning, Mrs. Ramsay. . . . Have you seen the new velvets, Mrs. Ramsay? . . . Can I get you anything, Mrs. Ramsay? . . . Even when she dined out or took tea in a public restaurant, she was aware of the notice she attracted from casual acquaintances. "You know who that is? That's young Mrs. Kingston. . . . *You* know—*the* Kingstons . . ."

And she was an asset to the store. She knew that. She paid her tribute in full. Both Thomas and Ramsay were proud of her. In the nine years since she had married, she had lost her pert coltishness, though she still sometimes called Thomas "Pahpah," and had acquired a certain unhurried elegance. The web of light indentations that living had brought to her face around those green slanting eyes had ripened an appearance that had always been striking. Since she was tall, the long soft lines of current fashion were ideal for her, too—as, indeed, were the wide-brimmed hats which she wore rakishly over her auburn hair with the style of a cavalier.

It was, however, the totality of the tribute that she resented so deeply, the fact that she was permitted so little independent control over her own life—which was why, earlier that morning, she had rebelled. And how she had rebelled! She had called at the little office in Clements Inn that had just been opened by a newly formed organization which called itself the WSPU and offered her services. She had been received by a vivacious woman in her fifties, to whom she had been much drawn, named Stella Wainwright. "Talk about history repeating itself," Miss Wainwright had laughed on hearing her name. "How's May Kingston?"

But history was repeating itself only in the aims of the WSPU—the Women's Social and Political Union—for its methods were very different. The gloves that old Mrs. Wainwright had so despised had at last been taken off. For two decades, as May had predicted in 1884, the dynamic for female suffrage had been dormant. But in January of this year, 1906, the Liberal Party had swept back into power with a huge majority—*and* made it clear that the big social program of reforms it planned did not include votes for women.

So war had been declared once more—this time outright war, directed by the militant WSPU. Its members harangued ministers at political meetings, shouted from the public gallery of the House of Commons, paraded in angry processions through the streets of the cities. They exhorted huge crowds in Hyde Park to action. They fought like cats with all men who sought to deflect them from their aim, whether they were police or stewards. They were arrested, often with bruises and torn clothing, and jailed. The tacit support that the old NSWS had gained for the cause was gone. The new suffragettes, as they had been dubbed in the press—were seen as revolutionaries, as unsexed viragos.

Dora's action, then, in joining the ranks of such belligerent women was an act of open defiance—a positive action that should certainly have released her frustrations. But it appeared to have done the opposite, and as she sipped a glass of sherry while waiting for Thomas, she wondered why. Then she realized. She had become a member of a militant organization, but she could not be militant—at least, only a little militant, as she had explained to Miss Wainwright. She had rebelled against the control of her exercised by the store, but even she would not wish to damage it. She was faced, therefore, with an inevitable conflict—and her resentment grew.

For a few moments she watched Ramsay talking intently to Charles. Both looked smart in their best morning coats and high collars. Both were handsome in their own ways—Ramsay with his dark hair and thick black moustache; Charles with his lean, alert look of a greyhound which he had retained into his thirties, and his fine fair hair which had begun to recede. Their discussion was energetic and animated. Ramsay's dark brown eyes were shining as, it seemed, he tried to persuade his friend of some point of argument. Sometimes, when she looked at him in company, she had to remind herself that he was her husband, the man who had shared her bed for nine years. For he often seemed unfamiliar, as if he were a stranger. Yet their marriage, though uninspired, had not exactly been unhappy. Ramsay was considerate of her, was even an amusing companion, but he had a remoteness—a reluctance to discuss worries or thoughts that were occupying him, often deflecting her questions with a light joke—that still upset her. She was a warm, convivial person, who had been reared in a demonstrative family, and sometimes she felt a sense of great loneliness.

Charles suddenly burst out laughing and shook his head. As he did so, Thomas entered the room, an unusual expression of concern on his face, and Dora felt her anger rise. He was the real cause of her frustration. He was fine-looking, with his thick white hair and craggy face, and he had always been kind to her, always affectionate; but he was the creator of the store, the God behind the God—its custodian, its advocate, its priest.

With an effort she forced a smile and moved across the room toward him. As she drew closer, she heard Ramsay say, "I've been trying to persuade Charles to return to us, Father. . . . I've told him that Kingstons is his natural habitat—like the marshes to wild ducks. . . ."

"That's extraordinarily poetic, my dear," remarked Dora, pleased to be able to cover her discontent with a light pleasantry, "but I'm not sure that Pahpah will fancy his lovely store being compared with anything so unpleasant and damp as marshes. . . ."

"It could perhaps have been better phrased," Thomas agreed. "Old Mr. Lewis proving a trial, then?" he asked Charles.

"Well, Mr. Kingston, he's of the old school—a fine draper, but I don't think he could claim to be progressive, as you just did on the platform. . . . Not, of course, that I wish to appear derogatory of my employer . . ."

"Oh, you're among friends here," said Thomas, "and as Ramsay says, you're welcome to return . . . but I always fancied you were right in your decision. . . . You haven't found the right horse yet, but you will . . . and when you do, we'll have to get the whips out to keep up with you. . . . May, are they ever going to serve luncheon? . . ."

It was a founding-family occasion. Thomas liked to have as much support as possible at the AGMs, so Ellen was present with Sidney Baines and their children—who, of course, were now grown up. Harry, Claire, Agnes and Mary had come from the farm with Letty, who was now seventeen. In all, including the Rawlingses, no fewer than sixteen of them sat down at the table. With the meeting behind him, Thomas was in a cheerful mood, and the spirit was almost that of a Christmas party—at least, it was until, toward the end of the meal, Dora made her remark.

She was sitting halfway up the table between Harry and Sidney— May and Thomas, of course, being seated at either end. There was a momentary lull in the lively conversation when she said lightly to May, "I met a Miss Stella Wainwright today, Mother. . . . She asked to be remembered to you."

A slight flush came to May's cheeks as she asked, "Oh? Where did you see her?" And as she asked the question, which seemed a natural response to Dora's statement, she knew it was a mistake.

"At the office of the WSPU," Dora answered. "She's still active in the movement."

"You mean the movement for votes for women?" asked Thomas from the other end of the table. His voice was not loud, but the tone was hard enough for everyone else at the table to stop all side discussions.

"That's right, Pahpah," she answered, looking straight at him. He made no response for a moment, his eyes focused on his plate, where he was spreading butter on a Huntley's Bath Oliver biscuit. He was particularly fond of Huntley's Bath Olivers. "Miss Wainwright spoke of her brother," Dora went on to May. "She said she thought you'd be interested to know that he'd been in Russia . . . in the Revolution last year . . . St. Petersburg, with a man called Trotsky. . . . She said you might have heard of Trotsky. . . ."

"And what, if I may be so bold as to ask," said Thomas before May could comment, "were you doing at this . . . SPU, did you say? . . ." He waved vaguely with his knife as he tried to recall the initials. ". . . This woman's-vote office . . . ?"

"The WSPU," corrected Dora. "I was joining it, Pahpah."

For a few seconds there was silence. With apparent unconcern, Thomas placed a slice of Stilton on his Bath Oliver, put it into his mouth, chewed for a second and swallowed. He took a sip of claret. Then he said, still quietly, "In that case, Dora, you'll have to resign."

She paused. "No, Pahpah," she said after a moment. "I'm sorry. . . ."

He glanced at her sharply. "I can't permit you to be a member of a political organization of that nature," he said, still speaking calmly. "The old one with which your mother-in-law made a brief acquaintance was bad enough . . . but this one's out of the question."

Dora straightened her back. She could feel the color already in her cheeks. Everyone at the table was watching her. Almost imperceptibly, one of Charles's eyelids flickered a wink at her across the table, and she felt a surge of gratitude. "I'm sorry, Pahpah," she said in a small strained voice, "but I'm not going to resign."

"He's right, Dora," May interposed gently. She found the scene, with its close link to Philip, acutely painful. "You can't possibly be a member of the union. . . . Their behavior is outrageous—*and* useless. . . . They'll never achieve anything with that sort of action. . . . It's offended everybody."

"Mother," Dora asked gently, "what did the other way achieve? That's why Miss Wainwright's become a member."

Ramsay was highly embarrassed, as he always was on the rare occasions when Dora challenged his father. And as usual, he had waited, his face flushed, his head bowed, tensed for the worst to pass, so that he could take control. "I think it'd be better," he said now, "if Dora and I were to discuss this at home in private. . . . I'm sure she'll see why she must resign."

"I won't, Ramsay," she insisted quietly but firmly, "so I shouldn't waste your time."

"She's completely forgotten who she is," Lillian suddenly interposed, entering the discussion for the first time.

"Dora," said Thomas, "what if you're arrested . . . even sent to jail? . . . Have you any notion of the damage that'd do? . . . Can you imagine the headlines in the *Daily Mail*?"

She was glad of his question. "I've already explained to them," she said, "that I have responsibilities, that I can't serve them in the front line as I would like. . . ."

"The whole union could be declared illegal," Thomas declared. "What'd happen then?"

"That'd be disgraceful," she answered stoutly. "This is a country committed to democracy. . . ."

"The union," said Ramsay, "is not using the methods of democracy."

"Only because those methods have failed to make impact at all on the bastion of male prejudice!" Dora retorted.

For May, the quarrel was moving. She vividly recalled the excitement she had felt at that first meeting at the Exeter Hall and heard those female roars of "Shame!" "Dora," she said, "if anyone at this table understands your feelings, I do. . . . I share your ideals. . . . I think it scandalous that women have not been given the vote. But the only way this can be achieved is by persuasion, hard though it is . . . by Parliament, slow though it may be. . . . Already in a few months your union has lost all support for the cause that we won for it. Its members are universally despised. . . ."

"Mother, that's nonsense," Dora declared. "Where do you think all those thousands of women come from to join in the parades? . . . Why, there are sacks of letters every day . . ."

"They're not *most* women, Dora," May insisted. "They're not *most* ordinary respectable women. . . . They're not *most* Kingston customers. . . . That's why you can't possibly be a member of the union."

"Of course she can't!" said Lillian.

"But I *am* one," Dora retorted angrily.

"You can't remain one," May insisted, speaking with a voice that was calm but very firm. "You can't, as Ramsay's wife, as Mrs. Kingston, remain a member of an organization that is despised by ordinary respectable women. . . . There happen to be some things that you cannot do, that *I* cannot do, because of our position. It's bound to do untold harm, not only to yourself, but to Ramsay, to the family, to the—"

"*I* know, Mother," Dora flared, "to the store . . . to the great big store that dominates us all like some huge heathen deity, that looms over our lives like an enormous Inca temple. . . . By God, Pahpah," she exclaimed, turning to Thomas suddenly, "is there no end to the demands of the store? Have I not given you Robert? Have I not presented that little boy to you like a sacrificial lamb on the altar? Is that not enough, for goodness' sake? Can I not even hold an opinion or advance a cause I feel strongly about? Is there nothing that—"

"Dora!" Ramsay's sharp interruption stopped her in mid-sentence. "You're obviously overwrought. . . . Your behavior is appalling. . . . Just look at the way you've upset Father! . . ."

She had indeed. The spirit seemed suddenly to have left him. As he sat at the head of the table, his shoulders were hunched. He was staring in front of him, looking far older suddenly than his sixty-one years, the flesh of his cheeks appearing to sag loose from the bones of his face. He was impotent in the face of Dora's challenge. There was no action he could take to force her to do what he had ordered—and Thomas was a man who had lived by action, by issuing orders. Stripped of his power as he now was, he became confused, and the effect on him, to those who were watching, was deeply distressing.

"Tell Father you'll resign," Ramsay said now. "It's quite impossible. . . . You know it's quite impossible. . . ."

She made a movement of dissent with her head. For all her frustrations, Dora was extremely fond of Thomas and was deeply unhappy about the impact of her rebellion; but she knew she must cling to her decision or she would be lost. "No, Ramsay," she said a bit too loudly, adding in a softer tone, "I'll apologize. . . . Pahpah, I shouldn't have said what I did . . . and I'll do my best to ensure that I'm not in the headlines of the *Daily Mail* . . . but I can't resign."

Thomas looked at her with eyes that were pained and uncomprehending. He was just about to speak when the headwaiter entered the room. "Master Robert is outside, Mr. Kingston," he said. "Should he wait for a few minutes . . . or should he come in?"

Thomas hesitated for a second. "I think he'd better come in, Harris," he said.

"Very good, sir." Harris returned to the door and beckoned. Robert entered, followed by his governess. He was wearing a velveteen sailor's suit, with short trousers that ended just below the knee, and carried a round sailor's hat in his hand. He bore a distinct similarity to Ramsay, with the same dark hair and broad forehead—except for his eyes, which, like Dora's, were green and slightly slanted. After a few paces he stopped, appearing quite self-possessed despite the size of the company. "Good afternoon, Grandpapa," he said.

For a moment, Thomas looked at him kindly, seeing him as Dora had described him in her tantrum. "A sacrificial lamb, Dora? . . ." he queried quietly. ". . . Or a future man of power and influence . . . a man who'll shape his environment, who'll change the world just a little, who'll sit where I sit now as the employer of thousands of staff, except that then there'll be many more, as the supplier to the best homes in London of more than two million pounds a year of quality merchandise, except that then it'll be many millions? . . . That's right, isn't it, boy?" he said to Robert.

"Excuse me, Grandpapa," he answered, not understanding the question.

"In time you're going to sit where I sit, aren't you . . . in my office along the corridor? That's right, isn't it?"

"If you say so, Grandpa . . ." the little boy replied uncertainly.

Thomas smiled suddenly. "Why, we're forgetting our manners, aren't we? . . . It's a very important day, isn't it? . . . Happy birthday, Robert. . . . Come on, everybody, what's the matter with you? Aren't you going to wish the boy a happy birthday? . . ." There was a murmur of greetings round the table, and May blew the little boy a private kiss. "That's a bit better," said Thomas. "Now come and sit down here next to me, Robert. . . . Bring the boy a chair," he ordered a waiter. "Now tell me, young man," he said as Robert sat down gingerly beside him, "have you thought about what it's to be . . . your present? . . . Do you know what you want? . . . Or are you going to wait until we get to the department and allow your inspiration to guide you?"

"Sprashun, Grandpa? . . . What's sprashun? . . ."

Thomas laughed. "A good question, Robert. . . . Inspiration is something you'll use a lot when you're grown up and working here in Kingstons. . . . Inspiration is feel . . . knowing something without always being able to explain why. . . . Inspiration for you today could be walking into that department and then, when you're surrounded by all those hundreds of toys, knowing suddenly exactly what you want."

"But I know what I want, Grandpa . . . I want a train set with a red engine."

Thomas let out a great laugh. "Then you'll *have* a train set, Robert," he said, "*with* a red engine." And he put his arm round the shoulders of his grandson and gave him a warm hug.

· 2 ·

"No," Thomas asserted into the telephone on his desk an hour later, "I will *not* see Mr. Handfield. . . . I've written to Mr. Handfield and told him so." He hung the receiver back on the hook. "That man's becoming a nuisance," he said to Ramsay.

"Are you positive you're wise, Father?" Ramsay had come into Thomas' office only for a moment and did not really want to discuss Handfield because Charles was waiting for him in the outer office, but he believed that his father's attitude toward the trade union was dangerously rigid. Ramsay had exchanged a few words with the union official on a couple of occasions when he had approached him in the store and found him a reasonable man.

"I'll not have any trade unions meddling in my store," Thomas insisted. "There's no need for them here. . . . No one can say I'm not a good employer."

"I can't see what harm there'd be in granting him an interview," said Ramsay.

"Because once I see him, it means we've opened negotiations. That's his only purpose. He wants recognition of his union. . . . Once he gets that, he'll demand the right to negotiate on behalf of the staff."

"On behalf of his members," Ramsay corrected.

Thomas shrugged. "If he gains any rights at all, he'll increase his members very fast. . . . He'll have something to offer them, won't he? . . . At present he's got nothing—and I'm going to see he gets nothing."

Thomas' argument was persuasive, but all Ramsay's instincts told him that it was flawed, that his father was trying to stem a tide that would grow constantly stronger. Every day, trade unions were gaining more power. Even Handfield's organization—the Shop Assistants' Union—was beginning to make itself felt, although it had been in existence only a few years.

"Surely, Father," Ramsay said carefully, "there'd be something to be said for establishing good relations with the Union. . . . You don't have to give way at all."

"Any relations are giving way," snapped Thomas.

"They've had an impact in other stores, causing strikes . . . Edwards of Swansea last year . . . Barratts this year. . . ."

"About conditions of living in . . . about working hours that were too long. . . . Both needed correction. . . . There are many evils in the trade, Ramsay. We can't deny that. But no one can point a finger at us on those grounds—or on our wages . . . so don't be fooled by Handfield. He can't find much wrong with us, but he wants us for our reputation. He could use it to hook other stores. . . . But he's not getting it. . . . Handfield's an enemy and I'll fight him, by God. . . . No concessions whatever, Ramsay . . . get that quite clear. . . . Furthermore, I'll fire anyone I discover's a member of his union."

"Surely that's a bit drastic, Father. . . ."

"No, it's not . . . it's war. . . . One day you'll thank me."

When Ramsay joined Charles outside his father's office a minute
later, he asked him what he thought of the issue. "They'll only use
you," said Charles, "if you try to cooperate with them. . . . Your
father's right. . . . It's sure to be war . . . them or us. . . . No point in
giving ground until you're forced to. . . . You know, it's strange to
walk through the store with you after all this time. . . . It's home, but I
don't belong here any longer."

"Yes, you do," said Ramsay. "That's why I was trying to persuade
you to return. . . . I need you here."

"You just want to win," Charles answered with a smile, "and if I
came back, you would. . . . Oh, so you've got *her* working for you
now, have you?" They were approaching the Haberdashery, and as
Ramsay knew at once, he was speaking of a girl who was serving
across the counter. She was fairly short, with dark brown hair and a
small pretty face that was almost like a doll's except for its vivacity.
But there was a certain quality, in the way she moved and spoke to her
customer, that made her stand out among the other assistants like a
well-bred horse in a field of mules.

Charles nodded to her with a smile of recognition as they passed.
"Fetching, isn't she?" he remarked.

"Very fetching," answered Ramsay with a grin.

"She was with Debenhams before she joined us. Not for long, I
don't think . . . never seems to stay long anywhere. . . . I think she was
apprenticed at Swan and Edgar. . . . But she's an excellent sales. That's
how I know about her."

"I've heard she's a good sales too," said Ramsay casually. But he
was not feeling casual. For the first time he had broken his father's
veto, laid down on the day he joined the store at sixteen, on social
contact with the staff. That evening, after the store was closed, he
would be meeting the young lady—taking her for a drive, in fact, in
the sixty-horsepower Mercedes-Simplex of which he was so proud.
Quite a few people now owned cars—but not many had a Mercedes
that had walked away with the top prizes at the Nice Motor Show and
the Gordon Bennett race from Versailles to Lyon.

Ramsay's attention had first been caught by her a few weeks
before as he was passing through the department. He had watched her
serve a customer and been impressed by her style. "You're new, aren't
you?" he had said, and she had exposed him to that devastating smile
and answered, "That's right, sir—first week."

"You look as though you've made a good start."

After that, he would often stop and exchange the odd word with
her as he was walking through.

"Mr. Evans tells me you're the best sales in the department," Ramsay said to her. "Keep it up."

"Selling's not difficult with this quality of merchandise," she answered.

He shrugged. "Some people are suited to the top end of the trade," he said. "Some aren't. . . . Some people understand fine things."

"You're very encouraging, Mr. Ramsay," she responded.

It was not really what either of them said that had so great an impact on Ramsay so much as the tone of her voice, the expression in her eyes, the sense he felt of communication that went way beyond the words they used. She could have been speaking Chinese, he thought at one moment, and still have had the same effect on him. In fact, though, she surprised and impressed him with her interest in the problems of the trade and management. She knew, for example, that the Home Secretary had set up a committee which, among other matters, was investigating the question of staff living in their employers' premises—something, of course, that could have repercussions on the whole store business.

"How in the world do you know about that?" asked Ramsay.

"Oh, I read the papers," she answered. "Also, I'm concerned. . . . After all, I live in myself."

"Now, that surprises me," said Ramsay. "You don't seem the sort of girl who'd live in."

"My home's in Brighton. . . . Got to live somewhere, haven't I?"

"How do you find the conditions?"

"Nowhere better," she said. "The working hours aren't at all bad, either . . . not like some stores. . . . You've got a fine business, Mr. Ramsay." And an expression came into her eyes that seemed to penetrate the very depths of his belly.

"I often wish that you and I could have a proper talk," said Ramsay. "I mean more than just the occasional couple of moments like this. . . ."

"That'd be pleasant," she agreed with one of her smiles.

After that exchange, with its clear mutual message, there was a subtle difference in their relationship; but she seemed in no hurry for it to develop beyond the present level of casual encounters. Whenever Ramsay was about to suggest a meeting outside the store, she would skillfully steer the subject to other areas or indicate she was engaged before he actually got to the point of invitation—like the time he spoke of a Mozart concert that was being performed the following Tuesday. "I'll be going out Tuesday too," she said. "I always have

supper with my aunt on Tuesdays. . . . Actually," she added, "I'm very
fond of Mozart. . . ." As he realized, she was keeping the goods in the
window, but they were not for sale—not yet, anyway.

Sometimes she was deliberately mischievous. "Mrs. Ramsay was in
this morning," she said, "buying some ribbon. . . . She's a beautiful lady
. . . gracious, too. . . . You're a lucky man, if you don't mind my saying
so." And she laughed at his discomfort.

Once, Ramsay had just left the counter after talking to her to find
his father standing in front of him, an angry expression on his face.
"Who's that assistant you've just been talking to?" he demanded.

"That's Miss Redfield. . . . She's new . . . been working at John
Lewis, according to Charles. . . ."

"You looked a damned sight too friendly with her," Thomas said,
and strode off.

It was the day before the AGM that Ramsay mentioned his
Mercedes-Simplex Tourer. "I've never been in a Mercedes," she said,
and he waited for her to change the subject, as usual, but on this
occasion she did not do so.

"It wouldn't be hard to put that right," he went on carefully, still
suspecting she was going to sidestep him, and added, "Tomorrow
evening, for example. . . ."

He braced himself for her rejection. "As it happens," she said,
"I'm not doing anything tomorrow evening."

"You are," he said with restrained joy. "You're going for a drive
in a Mercedes-Simplex."

He arranged to meet her after the store closed in Hasker Street,
which was about a quarter of a mile from Kingstons. "Better not make
it too close to the store," he said. "You understand. . . ."

"I understand," she replied with a soft smile.

"It's a yellow car," he said.

He drove her to Hampstead, which she also understood, since
even with the side blinds down someone might have recognized them
in Hyde Park, which was, of course, much nearer. "I rather like the
secrecy," she said. "Turns it into an adventure . . . like something out
of Sherlock Holmes. . . ."

They had driven up Knightsbridge and turned into Park Lane.

"How do you like her?" he asked. "She's pretty fast. . . . I'll show
you in a moment. . . ."

"I think she's a magnificent car," she mocked with a smile.

At one moment, as he was looking at her, an overtaking motor cab
behind them honked loudly, and he had to swerve back closer to the
curb. "I don't think you're concentrating," she said.

"Are you surprised? I'm alone with you for the first time. . . . I've never spoken to you before without a counter dividing us. . . . Now there's just a few inches of air. . . ." And he had put his hand on her knee. She displayed no reaction, not even averting her leg at all—just looked straight ahead through the windscreen without expression on her face.

It was only when they approached the congestion of Marble Arch that she said, "Don't you think it'd be safer to use both hands?" There was no reproof in her tone, nor even coldness.

When they had turned north from Oxford Street and the traffic was lighter, he said, "Did you mind me putting my hand on your knee?"

"You mean, did I like it?" she responded a little sharply. "If it'd just been a question of not minding, there wouldn't be any point, would there?"

"Well, did you?" he asked. "Like it, I mean."

"I wouldn't have allowed it if I hadn't, would I?" she answered. "In fact, I wouldn't be here alone with you in this magnificent monster, would I?"

"I suppose not," he said. He looked at her and smiled, and she smiled back with an unusual element of shyness in her expression. He put his hand on her knee again; and gently but firmly she picked it up and put it back on the wheel.

"I thought you said you liked it," he complained.

"One can't always do what one likes when one likes. There has to be discipline, because otherwise you're just drifting. . . . I think there's a lot wrong with the way women pretend, not only to men but to themselves, about their feelings. . . . I try to face mine squarely without shame. They're natural, after all, aren't they? I don't hold with the theory that they're inspired by the Devil—if there's such a being as the Devil . . . but I still have to be in charge of them."

"You're a strange girl," he said. "You've thought it all out, haven't you? . . . Nothing happens to you by chance."

He stopped the car at the pond on the edge of Hampstead Heath, but left the engine running, so that they sat for a moment being shaken by its throbbing. She did not resist when he kissed her. In fact, she responded warmly, with her hand on the back of his neck, but he was aware of her self-control. She was still in charge. "Aren't you going to turn off the motor?" she asked. "I feel as though I've got Saint Vitus's dance. . . ." Then, as he did so, she held up her lips to him again.

As they drove homeward later, he remarked, "I hardly know anything about you . . . not even your first name. . . ."

"Hannah."

"Or why you find it so hard to settle in one store. . . ."

"I get restless."

"Will you be leaving Kingstons?"

"In time."

"But why?"

"I'll tell you one day. . . ." She put her hand over his, which was on her knee.

He asked her about her background, commenting that she seemed educated, and she told him that since her grandfather had gone bankrupt when she was a child, her parents had been poor. "Highly educated, though," she added. "You can still be poor and an intellectual. . . ."

"That's why you're knowledgeable . . . why you read so much. . . ."

"That's why I'm a member of the Labour Party."

"Good heavens!" he exclaimed, laughing, for the Labour Party, which was very small, despite surprising success in the January election, was committed to socialism.

"You'll have to watch out . . . I'm going to change the order of things. . . ."

"I suppose Father and I'll be among the first to be guillotined. . . ."

"Without question. . . . You're exploiters of labor . . . old-fashioned capitalist bosses. . . ."

"I thought you said we ran a fine business."

"So you do . . . by today's standards, but not those of the future. . . . Why, your father won't even talk to Mr. Handfield, will he?"

"So you know Mr. Handfield?"

"Of course I know Mr. Handfield. . . . I'm a member of his union."

"I should keep quiet about that in the store. . . . Father's threatened to sack anyone he finds in the union."

"That'd be very foolish of him . . . and what little I know of him doesn't strike me as being foolish. . . ."

Ramsay was silent for a moment, studying the road ahead of him. "So what are you doing here with a capitalist boss?"

"Well, it could be that I had a devious purpose or it could be that I liked you . . . or it could be both. . . ."

They were getting near Gertrude Street and the row of houses that Kingstons maintained for their staff who lived in. "You'd better

stop before you reach the end of the street," she said, going on to
mimic him: "You understand?"

He laughed and drew up at the curb. "Will you have dinner with
me next week, Hannah?" he asked. "Thursday?"

"Are you wise?" she said. "I may be planning your downfall."

"I'll take the risk."

She looked at him intently for a moment with eyes that were
suddenly serious. "Good," she said, and leaning forward, kissed him
lightly on the lips. "Thank you for the drive."

· 3 ·

As the carriage progressed down St. James's Street, Thomas wondered
again why he was keeping the dinner appointment with Etherington.
The man was patently a trickster, for a check of the company's register had revealed that he had only a handful of shares, purchased just
before the AGM—thus giving him the right to make his laudatory
remarks from the floor. Clearly, he had sought to win favor with
Thomas—and with his diamond cuff links and tie pins, he bore all the
marks of a cad; but Thomas could not deduce his purpose. What did
Etherington hope to gain? There was no doubt, however, that Thomas
was intrigued by the man and, in particular, by his membership in the
Reform.

"Not anyone can join the Reform," he had remarked to May.

"Perhaps not," she agreed.

"And what he said about a title was correct . . . it would give
much prestige to the store."

May shook her head at his self-deception. "Thomas Kingston," she
rebuked, "I never thought I'd see you, of all people, performing these
moral gymnastics. . . . You know as well as I do that you can't touch
pitch without getting your fingers soiled. . . . I'd advise you strongly
not to dine with Mr. Etherington."

May was right, he admitted to himself in the carriage. So why *was*
he dining with him? "I'm just going to listen to what he has to say,"
Thomas said aloud to himself. "I shan't see him again. . . ."

Etherington was waiting for him in the hall of the club in a dinner
jacket that, of course, was beautifully tailored, with the inevitable
diamonds in his cuffs and in the studs of his starched shirt. His face lit
up with pleasure as he saw Thomas mounting the marble steps toward
him, and he went forward, smiling warmly, his hand outstretched.
"I'm so glad you were able to spare the time, Mr. Kingston," he said.

They dined in the huge main dining room at a table by the window that overlooked St. James's Park. Etherington was a good host. He spoke again with enthusiasm about the store, about the achievements of the past, and about the glowing future. He inquired closely about the circumstances surrounding Kingstons' acquisition of the Royal Warrant and, in particular, about Thomas' contacts within the Royal Household.

Thomas enjoyed his dinner. The club food was excellent, the claret exceptional. Etherington himself was surprisingly entertaining, and Thomas found himself laughing often and responding with warmth. In fact, he suddenly realized he was speaking a good deal more freely about his associations with the Palace than he should be.

Etherington noted Thomas' sudden check on himself, and his face crumpled, as though made of india rubber, into his now familiar smile of reassurance. "Don't you worry, Mr. Kingston," he said. "Anything you say is safe with me. These are delicate matters. . . . I'm used to delicate matters—which brings me to those we touched on briefly in our office. . . . I think the main point is this. . . ." He began to draw a design on the tablecloth with his fork. ". . . Honors tend to be granted to men who, quite apart from the service they may have rendered, appear . . . *appear* to be the sort of people on whom honor would sit naturally. . . . They are men of stature, of generosity, of conscience, of philanthropy. . . . They are to be found on public boards, on the councils of artistic foundations, on the bench as lay magistrates. . . . Naturally, they come to know others with similar interests—statesmen, senior civil servants, eminent judges, leading figures in industry . . ."

Silently, Thomas commended his host's skill. He made social climbing sound positively noble.

"I suspect, Mr. Kingston," Etherington continued, "you're like others I've known who've addressed their energies all their lives to building major enterprises. . . . Suddenly, in their fifties, they realize that with competent managers to run their concerns, even sons to share the helm, they could devote some of their time to other areas—areas of national or public interest. . . . They may even see it as their duty . . . but are uncertain how to proceed, since most of the people they know are associated with their own sphere of commerce. . . . and that's where I can sometimes be of assistance, for I've a wide field of acquaintance. . . . Your glass is empty, Mr. Kingston."

He signaled the wine waiter, who hurried over to the table and refilled their glasses from the decanter.

Thomas was silent as he did so, his brows furrowed in thought. "If I understand you correctly, Mr. Etherington," he said, "you're proposing that you should introduce me to some of these acquaintances . . . that I should take a greater interest in public affairs, the arts, deserving charities, and so forth . . . *and*, presumably, make suitable contributions. . . ."

Etherington gave a small hurt smile and made a slight movement of resignation with his shoulders. "Well, there *is* a great need for funds, I have to admit, so in some cases a degree of patronage would be . . . well received. . . ." He paused as Thomas nodded. "Then, of course," he went on, "there is the matter of . . . well, naturally, I don't know what your politics are, Mr. Kingston, but I'm totally convinced that you're a man of this age, that essentially you're a liberal man . . . with a small *L*, of course. . . . You direct a highly progressive business, as you said yourself the other day, and I'm certain that the last thing you would wish to see is a static world, a moribund world, a world in which new ideas cannot develop and flourish. . . ."

Again, Thomas had to applaud his host's adroitness. With the huge majority that the Liberals had won in January, there would for some time to come be a Liberal Prime Minister—and it was, of course, on the recommendation of the Prime Minister that many titles were granted by the King. "So now, I gather," said Thomas with a smile, "you're urging me to join the Liberal Party and, perhaps, the Reform Club. . . ."

"I think it's your natural party. . . . We've just seen one of those rare watersheds that happen occasionally in history. . . . The party's landslide victory heralds a new era, the real start of the twentieth century. . . ."

Thomas knew that had there been a Tory landslide, Etherington would have been a Tory, but his performance and his argument, for all its false plausibility, impressed him. "And I suppose," he said, "I'd be expected to make substantial contributions to the party, too. . . ."

This time, Etherington leaned back and laughed aloud. "You detest humbug, don't you, Mr. Kingston?" he said. "Yes, of course you'd be expected to contribute—and handsomely. . . . Political parties need funds and look favorably on those who give them strong support. . . ."

"I can see that this may well be an expensive evening," said Thomas.

"Perhaps," Etherington agreed with a facile grin, "but a rewarding one, I hope. . . ."

"And if I accept the kind offer of your services . . . ?" Thomas began.

"What do I expect from it personally?" said Etherington. "I'd suggest that we leave that for the present, Mr. Kingston. If in time you find my advice and help is of value, then perhaps we can discuss a fee. . . . Meanwhile, I have a suggestion regarding the rest of the evening that might possibly amuse you. . . . I've been invited to a small celebration by a friend, and I know he'd be glad to welcome you if you cared to accompany me. . . . I suggest it only as light relief. If you'd prefer a game of cards or to continue our conversation . . ."

"I wouldn't consider keeping you from your friend," Thomas responded, "and if you really wish me to accompany you . . . well, just for a few minutes perhaps. . . ."

"I should warn you," Etherington continued, "that my friend lives in artistic circles . . . painters, writers, actors . . . and actresses, of course . . . A little unorthodox, but there are usually one or two people of note. . . ."

To Thomas, at that moment, the proposal was attractive, even though he knew that Etherington would use him if he could. He was a carpetbagger, a man who lived on his wits, on contacts and introductions. In fact, Thomas' response to him was strangely perverse. When May had warned of touching pitch, she had only made him more appealing. What entertained him about Etherington was the very fact that he was *not* a reputable upright citizen, that he could argue that black was white, that he was different from the men whom Thomas met every day.

"It might perhaps give you a glimpse of a London you don't often see," Etherington continued. "But, as I say, if you'd prefer . . ."

"I'd be delighted to meet your friend . . . and the painters and the actors . . ." Thomas laughed. ". . . and even the actresses. . . ."

"Maureece! Maureece!" she shrilled in a mock French accent. "Angela! Eet's Maureece!" Immediately, another girl on the other side of the crowded room looked in their direction and let out an excited little scream. "Why, so eet ees!" she exclaimed in the same false foreign intonation. "Maureece! Our beloved Maureece!" And to Thomas' surprise, both girls began thrusting their way through that exotic throng toward them as they stood in the doorway, both reaching Etherington at almost the same moment. Each girl took possession of one of his arms and, using this like a rope to hoist herself up him, pressed her cheek to his in ecstatic welcome. "Please—that's enough!" he said, though obviously enjoying his reception. "I haven't seen them for a few months, since I've been away in America," he explained to

Thomas, peering at him between their heads. "There!" he said, giving each girl in turn a light kiss. "Now I have someone I want you to meet—and he's a very important gentleman, so you must be on your best behavior. . . ."

It was only then that Thomas realized that they were identical twins—both very pretty, aged about twenty, with somewhat unruly jet black hair, and sparkling, mischievous eyes. "Mr. Kingston," Etherington said, "may I have the pleasure to introduce to you the Misses Jenny and Angela Renner. . . . The only way you can tell them apart, not that you really have to, is by *that*." He pointed to a small birthmark on the right cheek of one of them, who turned her face obligingly. "That's Jenny. . . . Angela hasn't got one. . . ."

"I'm the pure one, you see," Angela said, preening. "Not a blemish. . . ."

"Not on her cheek," Jenny teased with a quick smile, "but she makes up for it with her character. . . ."

"You know, Mr. Kingston," said Angela, with heavy sadness, speaking, like Jenny, in a voice that was no longer marked by mock French, "at times my sister can be brutal. . . ."

"You'll have to forgive them," Etherington said as Jenny made a face at her twin, "but they're on the halls . . . that is, when someone'll employ them, which isn't often. . . ."

"That's not fair!" Jenny complained. "We were working last week. . . . I think he's become mean and sour, don't you, Angela? I've changed my mind . . . I'm not a bit glad to see him back. . . ."

"Nor am I," Angela agreed. "He's developed a bitter streak. . . ."

"Well, it's understandable, of course," said Jenny, "when you consider his disadvantages. . . ."

"Stop it, both of you," said Etherington, with a resigned grin at Thomas. "Mr. Kingston is head of the famous store that bears his name . . . and you're to look after him and make him feel comfortable, because he doesn't know anyone here . . . and see that his glass is filled with champagne . . . and try, my dear twins, *try* to behave in a civilized manner. . . ."

"Is it that great big place in Sloane Street . . . your store?" queried Angela with wonder.

"That's correct," Thomas answered, feeling awkward in the face of this stream of intimate repartee.

"I've never been inside there," said Angela.

"Then you should make a point of paying us a visit," Thomas responded.

He noticed that Jenny was studying him curiously. "You know, Mr. Kingston, I think you're really *rather* splendid," she said, as though examining a rare porcelain objet d'art, even taking a step back to aid her perspective. "Don't you think he's splendid, Angela?"

"Extremely distinguished," Angela agreed.

"No—that makes him sound pompous and superior . . . and I'm sure he's not pompous and superior. . . ." She moved, so that she could view him from another angle. "I think he's just very, very interesting *indeed*. . . . I shall insist he talk to me all night."

"I apologize, Mr. Kingston," Etherington said uneasily, "but I did warn you. . . . Jenny," he rebuked her, "you're being very ill-mannered. . . ."

"Ill-mannered?" she echoed indignantly. "Was I ill-mannered, Angela?"

"Not ill-mannered, Jenny," said her sister.

"How can it be ill-mannered," demanded Jenny, "to say I think Mr. Kingston's splendid and interesting and that I want to spend the whole evening talking to him? That's not ill-mannered . . . that's being nice. . . . You don't think it's ill-mannered, do you, Mr. Kingston?"

Thomas did not know what he thought it was, for he had never met girls who behaved as these two did. "Oh, I . . ." he began, "I . . . well, I . . . You're right . . . I think it's nice. . . ." And she rewarded him with a dazzling smile.

"There you are, Maurice," she said, "Mr. Kingston doesn't think it's ill-mannered either."

"I don't suppose it's occurred to you, Jenny," Etherington insisted, "that Mr. Kingston may not want to spend the whole evening talking to you. . . . He may want to talk to other people, and certainly other people'll want to talk to him—especially when they know who he is. . . ."

"Because he's a very important man," she caroled. "Well, I think he's a very important man too . . . and I think he's splendid and interesting as well, which is more to the point, because important men can often be dull . . . and I don't mind who else he talks to. . . . I'll just stay by him and fill his glass like a slave girl. . . . That's what you told me to do, Maurice. . . . What's the matter with Maurice, Angela? I say I'll do what he's told me to do and still it's wrong. . . ."

"I don't know, Jenny," she answered. "He's behaving very strangely this evening. . . . I think he's trying to impress Mr. Kingston. . . ."

"Angela," Etherington rebuked her in embarrassment, "that's a foolish thing to say...."

"Anyway," said Jenny, "I'm certain *we* impress Mr. Kingston. We impress you, don't we, Mr. Kingston?"

"I ... of course ..." Thomas agreed, a little uncertainly.

"There you are, Maurice. ... We impress Mr. Kingston. ... I think Maurice underrates us, Angela."

"I'm *certain* he underrates us, Jenny," Angela concurred. "That's the trouble with Maurice ... he's no judgment...."

Jenny had begun to giggle. "You know, Mr. Kingston, I really do think you're splendid. ... I mean it, honestly ... I think you're marvelous ... and I can't go on calling you Mr. Kingston. ... It's too ... too ... Oh, I don't know ... it's too something. ... Would you fly into a terrible rage if I asked your first name?"

"Now, Jenny, that really is the limit!" Etherington was very angry with her now. "I'm truly sorry, Mr. Kingston," he apologized again.

"That's all right," said Thomas with an embarrassed smile. "It doesn't matter. ... My Christian name's Thomas," he told Jenny.

Her eyes lit up. "Tom! That's a *perfect* name ... for a *perfect* gentleman. ... Tom ... Oh, I like Tom. ... Don't you like Tom, Angela? Tom's a magnificent name. ... I'd like to call you Tom, Mr. Kingston. Would you mind terribly if I called you Tom?" She caught a glimpse of Etherington's horrified expression. "Maurice, I do hope you're not going to explode. It'd be dreadfully unpleasant. ... Mr. Kingston," she went on, turning back to Thomas, "I *know* we've only just been introduced, but I do so want to call you Tom. ... Please, Tom ..." And she was laughing in a way that banished his earlier suspicion that she was teasing him, laughing in a way that he found most appealing with eyes that were wide and bright, with small, well-curved lips that revealed two even rows of tiny teeth, with soft cheeks dimpled, with an escaped black curl bobbing on her forehead. "... May I please, Tom?" she repeated.

Suddenly, he was laughing too. "If it'd please you to call me Tom," he said, "I can't see any harm in it. ..."

"Good." She clapped her hands once in delight. "Champagne for Tom, then ..." and she turned and burrowed her way through the crowd.

For Thomas, the next hour in that apartment near Piccadilly was amazingly enjoyable. He talked to a journalist from the *Westminster Chronicle* about the menace posed by the expansion of the German

fleet. He spoke to Mr. George Alexander, the theater manager, about
the production problems involved in staging a play. He discussed at
some length the character of *Raffles*, which he had seen with May at
the Comedy Theater, with an ingenue actress who had a small part in
it. He was introduced to a young artist named Augustus John, who
had just returned from Ireland, and asked him his views of Renoir,
since he was the only painter he knew anything about—not that he
knew much about *him*. He conversed with H. G. Wells, the novelist,
who himself had once been indentured in a store, and was so impressed
with his thoughts on how more mechanization could be introduced
into Kingstons that he invited him to lunch. And all the time Jenny
was at his elbow, seeing that his glass was filled, making necessary
introductions, contributing her views, which, if occasionally lacking
depth or perception, were always delivered with charm and brevity, so
nobody minded.

Around eleven P.M. the throng of people began to thin, and
Jenny, having departed momentarily from Thomas' side, returned to
him. "Maurice is taking us to supper," she said. "I do hope you'll come
too, Tom. . . . He says you may want to go home, that you only came
for a few minutes anyway. . . . You don't want to go home, do you,
Tom? I haven't had a chance to talk to you yet because of all these
other people. . . . So you'll come, won't you?" It was a serious plea,
made with those wide brown eyes filled with concern that he might
refuse.

He smiled. "Of course I'll come to supper with you, Jenny . . . if
you're quite sure you want me to. . . ."

She was laughing again, her whole face alight. "I knew you would.
. . . I'd have been desperate if you'd said no. I'd have fainted or
something to make you feel guilty. . . ."

Etherington too expressed pleasure that he had decided to join
them. "I thought we'd go to Princes'," he said while the two girls were
getting their cloaks. "They're a bright young couple, aren't they? As
long as you don't mind their pranking . . . Like a breath of spring."

Since Thomas had sent the carriage home at the start of the evening, they took a couple of passing hansoms to the restaurant. Jenny
went with Thomas, since she appeared to regard him as her personal
property, and in the darkness of the cab he could feel the firmness of
her young thigh against his. She put her hand within his arm and
squeezed it to her as she snuggled up to him. "Oh, I do like you,
Tom," she said.

"I like you too, Jenny," he responded, putting his hand over hers.

"I hope I'm going to see a lot of you, Tom. . . ."

"So do I," he said. "So do I, Jenny. . . ."

· 4 ·

It was about ten thirty the following Tuesday morning that Ramsay was informed that Thomas wished to see him. He put down the stock analysis he was studying and went to Thomas' office, where, to his surprise, there was a visitor he knew. "Ah, Ramsay," said Thomas. "You are, of course, well acquainted with Mr. Gordon Selfridge of Chicago, aren't you?"

"But of course," said Ramsay enthusiastically, advancing with his hand outstretched. "How are you, Mr. Selfridge?" Selfridge stood up to greet him. He was a dapper man of fifty, with steel-rimmed glasses, gray hair brushed close to his head, and a well-trimmed moustache. He looked more as though he came from the professions—a family solicitor, perhaps—than what he was, the man who had made so big an impact on American retailing.

"My son was so impressed by Marshall Field when he got back here that he never stopped talking about your methods," Thomas told him. "He wanted me to introduce a lot of your ideas into Kingstons. . . . Of course, that was some years ago now. . . ."

"And did you, Mr. Kingston?" asked Selfridge. "Introduce any of my ideas?"

"I don't think we did eventually, Ramsay, did we?"

"No, Father . . . you went through the motions of considering some of them . . . but somehow you never acted on any of them."

Selfridge laughed. "It doesn't surprise me . . . but you'll have to think about them soon . . . or something like them. . . ."

"Mr. Selfridge," Thomas explained to Ramsay, "is planning to open his own store in London, and"—he smiled genially at the American—"I've no doubt he intends to teach us our business. . . . I suspect he thinks we're all too stick-in-the-mud. . . ."

"Well, perhaps a little conservative," Selfridge agreed. "I think the British merchant is by nature reluctant to promote his wares. . . . I think he regards it as rather bad taste. . . ."

"So we can look forward to vast advertising budgets?" said Thomas.

"Inevitably—and much more besides. . . . At this moment, I suspect that you doubt you'll have to respond, but you will, Mr. Kingston. . . . Even Kingstons'll have to adapt to the impact of Selfridges."

"Perhaps," Thomas conceded dubiously. "Who knows? Whatever happens, you have our good wishes, Mr. Selfridge."

"Thank you, Mr. Kingston," said Selfridge. "It'll be good to compete with a gentleman. . . . There is, however, one little matter on which I'd appreciate your advice. . . ."

"I'd be pleased," said Thomas.

"Well, you might not be quite so pleased when you hear what it is. . . . As you'll have guessed, I'm taking a preliminary look at the men I might employ in positions of senior management. . . . I'm sad that Mr. Kingston junior here isn't available to me . . . he impressed me a lot in Chicago . . . but I've been thinking of another of your protégés . . . Charles Rawlings. . . . Would you employ him if you were me? In a senior position, of course?"

Thomas laughed. "Ramsay?"

"Without question, Mr. Selfridge," Ramsay answered quickly, a broad pleased smile on his face. "I'm sure he'd be invaluable to you. . . ."

"I should explain, Mr. Selfridge," said Thomas, "that although Ramsay and Charles Rawlings are close friends, there exists between them a strong element of competition. . . ."

"You mean," Selfridge asked Ramsay, a gleam in his eye, "that you welcome the prospect of battle?"

"Something on those lines, Mr. Selfridge," Ramsay agreed, "but my father'll confirm that he's highly talented. . . ."

"Good," said Selfridge. "In that case you'll have your battle."

Thomas stood up. "Now, perhaps, Mr. Selfridge, you'll permit us to conduct you round our store. . . ."

They walked through the Fashion departments, and the Leather Goods, and the Household, and had just stopped briefly in the Ironmongery when Thomas was approached by a man he did not recognize —though Ramsay knew him and, with sagging spirits, feared what would happen now.

"Mr. Kingston," the stranger said to Thomas, "I'm sorry to approach you in public like this, but you've given me no alternative. . . . My name's Handfield. . . ."

Thomas flushed with anger. "I won't speak to you, Mr. Handfield."

"Mr. Kingston, there's something I must discuss with you most urgently. A few minutes of your time might prevent great harm."

"I'll have no contact with any union, Mr. Handfield," said Thomas. "Now, tell me, Mr. Selfridge . . ." He was talking as though the union official were no longer there. ". . . That display of kettles . . .

would you say it was designed to the best advantage of the merchandise ... ?"

· 5 ·

Kettners, with its walls of red brocade and gilded mirrors, was a restaurant that combined elegance with intimacy and was fashionable in a demimondaine kind of way—the type of establishment where a man would tend to take his mistress rather than his wife, or a woman he hoped to make his mistress.

Upstairs were private rooms—"cabinets particuliers"—and Ramsay had been tempted to reserve one of these but had decided that Hannah might consider it premature. Dora had displayed little interest in where he was dining, for there was a big meeting of the WSPU that evening—as she had informed him somewhat boldly—and she had left the house even before he had begun to dress.

Since the Mercedes was too drafty for evening use, he had collected Hannah in a hansom, waiting for her near the end of Gertrude Street, out of view of the Kingston houses. At the restaurant, they had been conducted to a corner table. She was wearing a simple black gown that was inexpensive but well made by a good dressmaker. She looked round the room happily, absorbing the atmosphere of laughter and pretty women and elegant men in their evening clothes, while Ramsay ordered for both of them—hors d'oeuvre and pheasant, with champagne to start with, followed by claret.

"Have you told anyone we've met?" he asked when the head-waiter had left them. "I mean in Gertrude Street. . . ."

"Good heavens, no. . . . They'd be scandalized and think me very silly."

"Why silly?"

"Because they'd say that as soon as you've had your way with me"—she used the phrase mockingly—"you'll throw me away like an empty bottle . . . and I'll lose my job to boot. . . . You're the son of the boss. . . ."

"The capitalist boss . . ."

"The capitalist boss," she agreed.

"It won't be like that, as you well know," said Ramsay, adding, "And am I going to have my way with you?"

"Of course not," she answered, as the wine waiter poured the champagne. "Who wants to be thrown away like an empty bottle?"

She gave him one of those brilliant smiles that always made him feel as though he had been kicked in the belly. "I don't know what my parents'd think," she remarked, "if they knew I was in an expensive place like this drinking champagne with a capitalist . . . *or* Mr. Hand-field, for that matter."

"Would he drum you out of the union?" Ramsay asked.

"No . . . but he'd make sure I knew he disapproved. . . ."

"I hope that won't stop you dining with me again. . . ."

"Who knows?" she answered vaguely, her eyes suddenly intense. "I hope not too. . . ."

"You speak in riddles sometimes. . . . Put me out of my agony . . . say you'll come out with me again. . . ."

She held up her glass and looked at him through the wine with the bubbles rising. "You've gone quite yellow. Do you feel all right? . . . Oh, don't look so worried. . . . I love being with you. I'm here, aren't I? . . . Don't wish your life away. Enjoy *now*, Ramsay, this very moment. . . ."

The waiter started to serve the hors d'oeuvre, making a random selection from the dishes for them as Ramsay instructed. "I hear Mr. Handfield confronted your father in the store the other day," she said as she was served.

"It was an unhappy moment. Father was furious. . . ."

"I'm sorry he's so adamant. . . . It's going to make things much harder."

"Handfield's not approaching him the right way," said Ramsay. "You should urge him not to be so insistent. . . ."

"But that's his duty. . . . If unionists hadn't been insistent, they'd have made no progress."

Ramsay shrugged his shoulders. "Perhaps . . . but it doesn't help with a man like Father. . . . It only hardens his attitude. . . . Since that scene with Handfield, he's started talking about making all newly employed staff sign an agreement not to join the union."

"I should dissuade him from that. It'll cause enormous trouble . . . as it will if he dismisses anyone for being a member. . . . Handfield'd be delighted if he did, of course. . . . Recruitment'd soar. . . ."

"I can't do much with him so far as Handfield's concerned," Ramsay explained. "I've tried . . . but he regards his interference in Kingstons as utterly unwarranted. . . . Hannah, what are we talking about the union for? . . . To blazes with the union!"

"To blazes with capitalist bosses!" she mocked. "To blazes with the store . . . or is that sacrilege?"

When they had finished dinner she said suddenly, "You know what I'd like to do now? I'd like to climb with you into a cab and just drive and drive and drive and watch the moon, if there is one, and the stars, if it's not too cloudy . . ."

"You mean that beneath that stalwart trade unionist, there's a romantic?" he queried, as he signaled the headwaiter to bring the bill.

"All trade unionists are romantics," she answered. "Especially women trade unionists."

They took a motor cab, because one happened to be available, but Ramsay was glad they had, since the passenger compartment was bigger than that of a hansom and sealed off by glass from the driver. For they had no sooner started in the direction of Hampstead than she became a different girl from the one he had known so far. In the Mercedes she had responded to his lovemaking, but mildly, keeping much of herself in reserve. But now, as the cab headed north, she kissed him with a hungry, urgent passion. To his surprise, she drew his hand to her breast and then, a minute later, to his utter astonishment, she lifted her skirts above her knees. "I want you," she whispered urgently. "Oh, Ramsay, I want you . . . now . . . here. . . ."

"Here?" he echoed in amazement, conscious also of the limited space within the cab.

"We can," she insisted. "It won't be that difficult. . . . I need to give myself to you, Ramsay. . . . I have a special reason. . . ."

"But in the restaurant you said—"

"Never listen to what a woman says . . . surely you know that by now. . . ." It was then that he realized that her legs were bare above her stockings, that there was no underclothing to prevent him from doing what she asked. He put his hand on the smooth flesh of her thigh and as he tentatively moved it higher, she opened her legs. "Ramsay . . ." she whispered, "now . . ." The situation was so astonishing that he could not believe what was happening, convinced it must be a hallucination; but the desire that was surging through him was real enough. Leaning back into the corner of the cab, she slipped lower on the seat and raised one knee to make it easier for him. "Take me, Ramsay . . ." she said. And half kneeling on the floor of the cab, half lying on her— later he was never able to recall his exact position—he took her.

As the cab climbed Hampstead High Street, they came to a great, shuddering climax that left them both breathless and shocked—so shocked that when the cabby, taking care not to look through the dividing window as he spoke, inquired where he should go now, Ramsay could find no words to direct him.

It was soon after two o'clock in the morning that the cab at last came to a halt at the end of Gertrude Street. Ramsay got out of the vehicle and helped her to the pavement. "You won't ever forget this evening, will you?" she asked intensely, "no matter what happens?"

"Every tiny detail, every fraction of a second," he answered, "will stay branded on my memory forever."

For a moment, in the moonlight as she looked at him, there seemed to be an expression of alarm in her eyes. "Good night, Ramsay," she said, and walked away from him down the street. He told the cabby to take him home to Montpelier Square and sat back on the seat, still overwhelmed by a sense of her presence, trying to regain some small part of his emotional balance.

As the cab entered the Square, he saw that the lights were still on behind the curtains of their sitting room—which was odd, for surely Dora would have gone to bed by this hour. The front door was opened for him before he reached it. "Why are you still up, Jones?" he asked the butler. "I told you not to bother. . . ."

"Your father's been awaiting your return, sir."

"At this hour? Is Mrs. Kingston with him?"

"Mrs. Kingston hasn't returned yet, sir. . . . I believe your father has some knowledge of the matter."

Ramsay ran up the stairs to the first floor. As he entered the sitting room, Thomas was standing, his forearm resting on the mantelpiece, staring into the fire. "Father," Ramsay exclaimed, "what are you doing here?"

"You don't know about Dora, then?" Thomas demanded, glaring at him with controlled fury. "She's been arrested. . . . They were making trouble in the lobby of the House of Commons. . . . Ramsay, your wife's in a cell at Cannon Street Police Station."

"My God!" said Ramsay. "I'd better go there at once."

"That's one thing you must not do," said Thomas. "There's just a chance that we can avoid scandal. . . . She got a message to me by one of her colleagues who avoided arrest. . . . She's given a false name, called herself Dora Smith. . . . If she pleads guilty when she goes up before the magistrate, there'll probably be a fine as an alternative to jail. If it's paid promptly, she'll be released and no one'll be any the wiser. . . . Most of them apparently opt for jail, because they want to be martyrs. . . . I've asked Sidney to attend court, since his name's not Kingston. He'll pay the fine, of course. . . ."

Ramsay sat down on the arm of a chair, his head bowed. "I'm sorry, Father," he said after a moment.

"It's got to stop, Ramsay. . . . I warned her . . . we all warned her. . . . She wouldn't be in the front line, she said, didn't she? . . . Well, if this isn't the front line, I don't damned well know what is. . . ."

· 6 ·

As Dora sat in the cell below Cannon Street Police Station during those cold predawn hours that morning, she tried to trace the events that had led to her arrest. For she had not intended it—unlike many of her sister suffragettes, who regarded a jail sentence as a mark of honor; unlike Emily Davison, her tall, skinny, red-haired friend who had marched with her in the procession of more than a hundred women. "I yearn to suffer for the cause," Emily had confided intensely. "I'd even feel happy to die for it. . . ."

Dora had been impressed by her fervor. "You make me feel useless," she had said. "All I can do is march or work in the office. . . . I can't even risk arrest. . . ."

Strangely, Emily—despite the zeal that gave her the drawn, haggard look of a fakir—had not criticized her. "There's more than one way to serve," she had said as the long column of women entered Parliament Square.

Dora had been present only in a supportive role. She had planned to make no speeches, to do nothing to provoke the police. So how, she now agonized, had she ended up in a cell? The answer, she now realized, was that she had been in the wrong place at a critical moment. For at the time she had been near Emmeline Pethick-Lawrence and Annie Kenney, two of the WSPU stars.

The aim of the parade had been to exploit the first day of the new session of Parliament by demonstrating in the huge central lobby of the House of Commons. The police had stopped the column of suffragettes at the precincts of the Parliament buildings, but eventually permitted a group of twenty women to go inside—which was how Annie Kenney and the others had gained access. Dora had stayed outside with the rest, but she had heard later in vivid detail how suffragette after suffragette had stood up on a chair in different parts of that great marble-floored lobby and demanded the female vote.

The police had been ordered to eject them and had done so with such violence that battle had commenced outside, with many suffragettes trying to force their way back into the Commons. Both Annie

Kenney and Emmeline Pethick-Lawrence were knocked down in the fighting beside Dora—which was why, inactive though she had been, she had suddenly found herself lifted off the ground by great masculine arms. She was hustled, kicking and screaming, to a police van—to the frustrated fury of Emily, who saw her from some way away, having been parted from her in the melee. "Dora!" shrieked Emily. "Dora! You fortunate girl! Arrest *me*! Arrest *me*, you thugs!" But the police did not seem to hear her, and the last Dora saw of her, before she was thrust into the "Black Maria," was her pale, emaciated face and head of red hair bobbing up and down in the crowd as she tried to gain the attention of the custodians of the law.

Dora did not sleep and was still contemplating her dire situation as the dawn light began to appear at the barred window of her cell. For she knew that Thomas would be convinced that she had betrayed him *and* the family *and* the store—even though she had sent him a message.

At ten A.M. Dora was taken into court with the other detained WSPU members. After hearing the evidence, the magistrate sentenced them all to be fined and bound them over to keep the peace for six months. The others refused to be so bound and were ordered to jail. Only Dora accepted, and feeling as though she had betrayed them as well as Thomas, she stepped down from the dock. Sidney Baines appeared at her side and quietly paid the fine to the appropriate court official.

He had kept a hansom waiting, fearing there might be reporters present, so that they could escape from the court without delay. He had been wise. "What's your name, madam?" asked one of several gathered near the entrance. "Dora Smith," she said, and got into the cab.

For a few minutes, as the cab traveled through the streets of the City, she just sat back in the cab in silence. At last, she said, "Where are we going? The store, or—"

"The store," Sidney answered shortly.

"Am I to be flogged in public?"

Sidney tried to smile, for he was a decent man and he was sorry for her; but he was also an integral part of the store, and his facial muscles just refused to comply. "Hardly, Dora . . . but he does want to see you. . . . Naturally, he's very put out. . . ."

She nodded and said nothing for a minute or so. "If I'm to be taken before him like a criminal to explain myself, I must go home first, Sidney. . . . I must change, wash, have my maid do my hair . . ."

When she was ushered into Thomas' office an hour later, she no longer looked like a miscreant who had spent the night in a cell. She was wearing her best hat, heavily decorated with ostrich plumes, and a skirt and jacket of deep green.

Thomas was waiting for her, glaring, sitting stiffly upright with both arms lying on the desk in front of him, in the position of a sphinx. Ramsay was also behind the desk, standing rigidly at his father's side, a stern expression on his face.

As Dora entered the room, she stopped in the doorway, her head held high in challenge, but the comic aspect of the two grim men, facing her like statues of Retribution, suddenly struck her—and despite herself, she burst out laughing.

Thomas, already furious with her, was incensed. "Have you gone quite mad?" he demanded. "How dare you laugh after what you've done?"

"Pahpah . . ." she began, taking control of herself.

"This is no time to call me Pahpah," he snapped. "That is a name of affection, signifying loyalty to the family. No one could have been more disloyal than you. . . ."

Now it was she who was angry. "Pahpah," she insisted coldly, "I came to say I was sorry . . . but if I hadn't already been a keen member of the WSPU, the sight of you two men standing there as though it was the Day of Judgment would have sent me rushing off at once to join the movement."

"Dora, this has got to stop," said Ramsay.

"It will not stop," she insisted. "And as for loyalty, Pahpah, I was arrested in error. . . . Even so, if it hadn't been for you, if it hadn't been for your store, I'd have defied the court as all the others did. . . . I'd be in jail now for a cause I believe in."

Thomas was staring at her with disbelief. He found it difficult to credit that after what had happened, she could be displaying the same attitude that she had exhibited at luncheon on the day of the AGM. He tried to control his anger and reason with her. "Surely you understand now, Dora," he said, "that you must give up this SPU. . . ."

"No, Pahpah," she insisted.

"You promised you wouldn't be arrested."

"It was a mistake, I told you. . . ."

"There may be other mistakes. . . . I find it impossible to understand, after this narrow escape, how you still defy my wishes. . . . Dora, I insist you give up the movement."

"No, Pahpah."

"Dora," Ramsay said, "surely you realize—"

"No, Ramsay," she cried out, louder this time. ". . . *NO!* Not if they'll still have me!" Then she added in a quieter tone, "But I'll be even more careful. . . ."

Later, just before lunch, Ramsay walked through the Haberdashery in the hope of seeing Hannah. It was the fourth time he had passed through the department that morning, but she had never been at her usual place at the counter. At last, he stopped to have a word with Mr. Evans. "Where's Miss Redfield?" he asked at one moment.

"She's resigned," said Evans.

"Resigned?" queried Ramsay with astonishment.

"It was very sudden," Evans went on, "and quite irresponsible. . . . Not even a day's notice. . . . She just sent a note this morning. . . . Urgent personal reasons, she said. . . . Unavoidable, she said. . . . I was quite put out, I can tell you, Mr. Ramsay. . . . She was an excellent sales. . . ."

Ramsey was so shocked he could hardly speak. "Yes, Mr. Evans," he said quietly after a moment, "it's always a pity when we lose a good sales." And he walked on through the store trying to contain his turbulent emotions.

CHAPTER ELEVEN

February 1907

· I ·

"Come on!" she pleaded. "Come on, Tom . . . Spend, Tom . . ." He was out of breath from the exertion, and sweat was pouring from his body. "Spend, Tom . . . Please spend, dear Tom . . . Now, Tom . . . With me, Tom . . ."

He increased the speed and impact of his movements in response to her urging, and he felt the surge to climax rising like sap from deep within him.

She felt it too, and increased the vigor with which she was responding to him. "Spend, Tom . . . Dear Tom . . . Spend, Tom . . . Now . . . Now! . . . Oh!!" she cried out, "*what* an expenditure!!" And she laughed aloud with joy as he lay on her, heavy and still except for his panting. "Wasn't that marvelous?" she said. "Wasn't that absolutely marvelous?"

He smiled as he tried to regain his breath. "It didn't take as long as that when I was thirty," he grumbled after a moment.

"Who wants it to be quick?" she queried lightly. "I'm glad I didn't know you when you were thirty. . . . Oh, don't go yet!" she exclaimed in alarm as he began gently to move himself from her.

"I want to lie on my back with you in my arms," he said. "Is that not permitted?"

"I suppose so," she said reluctantly, and as he rolled off her, she turned to him, wriggling a little to fit herself to his contours, and lay with her head on his shoulder. "It's always a sadness, isn't it," she said—"the severing? . . ."

Lightly he ran his fingers over her body—her thighs, her pelvis, her belly, her breasts—marveling at the young, smooth softness of her skin. "You know, I love the way you use that quaint old word," he said. "Spend . . . It's what the early Victorians called it."

"It's a beautiful word," she murmured, barely audible because she was speaking into his armpit. ". . . The giving of everything that's there.

. . . Not of money . . . *that's* ordinary, nothing . . . but of the very essence of you . . . the essence of life . . ."

He chuckled softly, but her words had touched him. "You've a talent for expression. That was beautifully put."

"It was beautifully done," she whispered. "When are we moving into my little house?"

"Tomorrow, if you like." He said it casually, as though it were commonplace, laughing at her fast response, for she had sat up as though someone had given her an electric shock, her eyes shining like a ten-year-old's. "Tomorrow?" she exclaimed. "You never told me . . ."

"You never asked."

"Tom!" She scolded, delighted. "I thought it'd be weeks yet."

"Carpets and furniture went in last week."

"Why wasn't I there?"

"You'd have got in the way . . . changing your mind about things. . . . Anyway, I wanted the curtains up and the crockery and the glass installed and the maid employed, with the fires lit . . . I wanted it perfect for you when you saw it."

"You're unbelievable," she said. "Christmas-cracker material . . ." She kissed him gently on the mouth. "It must be costing you an awful lot. . . ."

He laughed. "The other sort of spending . . . the kind you said was ordinary, nothing . . . Don't you think you're worth it?"

"It's not a question of whether *I* think so . . ." She got out of bed, and he watched her walking out of the room, her naked back seeming to sway gracefully like long grass in a light wind. ". . . But whether *you* do." She was speaking beyond his range of vision. She returned, her breasts moved gently by the vibration of her strides, carrying a bottle of red wine and two glasses. "Are you certain," she asked, "that I'm worth so much?"

"Would I do it if I didn't? I'm a man of business—remember? . . . I've got a bargain. . . . At any price I'd have a bargain."

"That's a kind thing to say, Tom. . . . I think you've a talent for expression too. . . . When am I going to see the house?"

"I'll send the carriage for you at four tomorrow. Will that be convenient?"

"Oh, I think it might be possible to find a space in my list of engagements," she said.

She smiled happily and, placing the glasses on a table beside the bed, filled them both with wine and passed him one. She sat on the side of the mattress, with one leg doubled up beneath her, resting her glass on her bent knee, with the other foot touching the floor. Her hair was a tangled torrent falling over her shoulders. She lifted her glass to her lips, and he put his hand on her knee; then, almost absentmindedly, he reached out, enjoying the silk texture of her thigh toward her pubic curls. She smiled, her cheeks dimpling.

"It's a bit soon for that again just yet, isn't it?" she asked gently, adding, with a quiet affection, "My demon lover . . ."

"Your old demon lover."

"You don't feel old. . . ." He was caressing her lightly, idly, between her legs. "Anyway," she said, "it doesn't seem to get in the way much between us. . . . Does it worry you?"

"Sometimes a bit," he answered. "Just occasionally I wish I was twenty years younger—for you. . . . You've made a great difference to my life, Jenny."

Months had passed since he had first met her at the party to which Etherington had taken him after they had dined at the Reform Club. For Thomas, it had been an astonishing relationship that was utterly unlike any he had ever known before—mainly, of course, because of the huge contrast in their ages. The passion he had known with Eve Banbury had been that of a man and a woman who were roughly equal in emotion, and maturity. His feelings for Jenny were rooted in the fact that she was only just out of her teens—in the sheer enjoyment of her spontaneity; her quick humor; her beauty still not fully formed; her flowering personality, which, for all her easy chatter, was often hesitant, often vulnerable. In her lovemaking she was generous, eager to please him, but her capacities, her depths of feeling had not yet been reached. His love for her—and it *was* love, though of a fragile, delicate nature—was objective. In a sense, she was a toy, a possession. He liked to watch her, to touch her, to enjoy the immediacy of her responses, the immense range of expression that flashed through her eyes like those of a fawn.

She had, of course, had previous lovers, but that did not disturb him. In fact, by contrast to all he had asked of Eve, he demanded little of Jenny. Always, when he was with her, he would know a lightening of spirit, a temporary shedding of all his anxieties.

Gradually, she had become a part of his life—a splash of color. He had bought clothes for her—dictating, as it were, some of the color—and the odd piece of small jewelry. Then, soon after Christmas, as he had lain with her one day in bed in the rooms she shared with Angela, he had asked suddenly, "Would you like a little house . . . your own home?"

"A house, Tom!" she had exclaimed as if the thought had never crossed her mind, though he knew it must have, for the arrangement was not unusual. "Do you really mean it, Tom?"

So he had opened negotiations to buy a small terraced house in Pembroke Villas in Kensington, and for weeks there had been discussions about decorations and furnishings. "It's like a doll's house, isn't it?" she had said at one moment, adding with sudden sadness, "and I'm like a doll." The shadow had only been momentary, and within seconds she had been talking eagerly of her plans for the kitchen.

Their affair did not, of course, exist in isolation. He was drawn into the life she led with Angela, for he could not take her into his own world. He went with them to parties sometimes—and to the theater, the halls and restaurants. Even if he did not quite drink champagne out of anyone's slipper, it was a life of much laughter.

Naturally, he was often with Etherington, both in the twins' company and also in pursuit of the cause they had discussed in such detail at dinner. For Thomas, of course, it was still embarrassing to admit that a title was an aim to which he should address himself even for the store, hard to accept that Etherington's insistence that no title was ever granted, outside the service of the state, without championship was grounded in truth. "I don't understand your objections," Etherington argued. "I'm not asking you to rob the Bank of England. I'm urging you to play a positive role in causes that are in the national interest. What possible case can there be against that?"

There was none, of course—which was why Thomas, though suspecting that there was a flaw somewhere that he could not identify, agreed to meet a number of men to whom Etherington sought to introduce him. These meetings usually took place over lunch or dinner at the Reform, since Thomas had also agreed to stand for membership of the club, and Etherington had insisted that it was important to be there as often as possible. "There is," he said sadly, "still a lingering prejudice against men in trade in all the leading London clubs, although I'm sure that the sheer reputation of Kingstons will act as an adequate counterweight . . . but still, we need as much support for you among the members as possible."

So Thomas met and talked at length with a sample of Etherington's "acquaintances," which was how he came to be on the boards of a number of charities, of one or two artistic foundations, and of a medical research institute. As Etherington had predicted, he was warmly welcomed by his fellow governors, some of whom were eminent and titled, and with his long experience of business, he was able to contribute much, often suggesting ways of making economies or increasing revenue and even, in one case, detecting fraud. In fact, he so impressed his colleagues that very soon he began to receive invitations from other organizations, which delighted Etherington. He advised Thomas to accept only one or two of the more prestigious, since he could see that the snowball was rolling.

Under Etherington's urging, Thomas joined the Liberal Party and made a donation at a level that his adviser suggested should be "substantial without being speactacular." This involved no issue of conscience for Thomas, since he had, in fact, voted for the Liberals in the last election. Politically, he was of the center, and in the past each of the parties had won his support.

Now he found himself lunching with a number of Liberal politicians, including, on one occasion, a junor minister. All of them, like everyone to whom Etherington introduced him, offered to support his application.

In fact, the club's election ballots were held every Thursday while Parliament was sitting. The voting was secret, conducted by means of black or white balls, more than ten percent of black balls causing rejection. By halfway through February, Etherington had become confident that Thomas would have adequate backing and planned to put him up for election on the first Thursday in March.

By that late-February evening of 1907, therefore, when Thomas was lying in Jenny's bed sipping a glass of wine, his situation seemed good indeed. The store, after an excellent Christmas trading, was thriving as never before. He had a pretty young mistress and a life with her that was colorful and stimulating. With May, he enjoyed a social environment that was rewarding at its own level, and thanks to Etherington, as he had to concede, his own standing in the hierarchy of fashionable London appeared to be growing at a remarkable rate.

"What would you think if I was to become Sir Thomas Kingston, Baronet?" he asked Jenny.

She shrugged. "You'd still just be Tom to me," she answered shortly.

He laughed. "Come back to bed," he said, and drew her to him. But he knew that in his thoughts he had been tempting the Fates, and, as he kissed her, he reached out a hand to touch the wood of the table beside the bed.

By the time Angela got home, both Jenny and Thomas were dressed. They left with her almost immediately to go to a party, where they were joined by Etherington, who suggested that they go on to dinner at Verreys in Regent Street.

The proposal rang warning bells in Thomas' mind. He had always felt that there was a certain danger attached to his association with the twins and the social milieu in which they lived. It could hardly be said that they were not "respectable," for their circle included a number of highly distinguished people. Their youth was not exceptional in a segment of society that inevitably included young actors and actresses, writers and painters. And now that Thomas was a patron of the arts, he too had a place in this colorful new world.

There had, of course, been a little minor gossip. He had been seen with the twins a few times by people from the retail world, but always in large groups. One or two incidents had come to May's ears; but she had known that Etherington was involved, and reluctantly, she had now come to accept him as a kind of jester in Thomas' court. And even she conceded cautiously that he had provided a service.

To Thomas, however, there was a conflict between the two new social areas into which Etherington had introduced him. The twins were hardly in the same category as a governorship of the Lister Institute.

Etherington discounted Thomas' concern. "It's a question of discretion," he said. "Many eminent men have colorful friends, but they don't flaunt them . . . They don't take them to receptions at Holland House."

Verreys was busy that night, and both twins were in a particularly lively mood, often deploying their double act, switching their accents fast from Cockney to French, Italian to Chinese, German to Russian. At one moment, when they had both men shaking with laughter, Jenny had leaned forward excitedly to cap something Angela had said in a deep Carolinian drawl and placed her hand over Thomas', which lay on the table beside her. As it happened, her movement had not been deliberate, even though their fingers had become half entwined. It was not a conscious gesture of affection, because Jenny's attention was totally engrossed in the quip she was directing at her sister, but there was no question that it was intimate. Which was why it heightened the shock when Thomas' mood of relaxed bonhomie was shattered suddenly by the voice of Ramsay. "Good evening, Father. . . . Glad to see you're enjoying yourself."

All of them were stunned. Jenny did not even finish the word she was uttering. For a few seconds, Angela and Etherington just stared in astonishment at Ramsay, who was standing beside Thomas, one hand in his trouser pocket, with a bright, almost cherubic smile on a face that was flushed to a higher red than usual. "I say, did I give you all a shock?" he said—and it was then that Thomas noticed the slight slur in his words.

With an effort, Thomas tried to take control of the situation. "Oh . . . Ramsay . . . you quite surprised me. . . . Is Dora with you?"

"I'm here, Pahpah," she said, moving from behind him so that he could see her.

"Ah, yes," he said, and got to his feet. "Well, now . . . Ramsay, you've probably met Mr. Etherington, haven't you?—though I'm not sure about Dora. . . ."

"Not actually met, I don't think," Ramsay answered. "I recall his kind remarks at the AGM of course . . . and I've heard much about him since . . . though perhaps"—he tossed off the comment lightly with a glance at the twins—"I didn't realize the full extent of his services." Before Thomas could respond, Ramsay held out his hand to Etherington and said, "Delighted to meet you at last, sir. . . . Dora, my dear, may I introduce Mr. Etherington to you? . . . He's been the greatest help to Father. . . . And who are these beautiful young ladies, Father? . . . sisters, as they so obviously are."

For a moment Thomas was tempted to upbraid his son in front of them all for his rudeness to the girls; but the insult had been subtle, so Thomas controlled himself and tried to behave as though the situation were unexceptional. Somewhat hesitantly, still standing awkwardly, he introduced the twins formally—first to Dora and then to Ramsay, who bowed and shook his head slowly with open admiration. "They're a picture, Father . . . Quite devastating . . . I'd no idea you were acquainted with such exquisite young creatures. . . . Dora, did *you* know that Father was a dark horse?"

Dora, who was as embarrassed by her husband as was everyone else, smiled at Thomas with affection. "Ramsay," she said softly, "I don't think it's your place to comment . . . and if we stay here any longer, the others'll be wondering what's happened to us."

Ramsay did not appear to hear her. He surveyed Thomas with a broad grin, swaying very slightly. "I'm seeing my father in a role I've never witnessed before," he said.

Thomas was now livid. "You've said quite enough, Ramsay," he said shortly. "Now I suggest you join your party before you make matters any worse. . . . Good evening to you, Dora. . . ." And he sat down, jerked his chair angrily close to the table so that his back was toward them. "Is there any more champagne in that bottle, Etherington?" he demanded.

· 2 ·

Thomas was still very angry with his son when he stalked into his office at ten minutes past eight, having as usual watched the staff file in to work—and he sent for him immediately. Ramsay was suffering from the effects of too much alcohol and was relatively penitent. He apologized unreservedly, and it was only when Thomas refused to be mollified and insisted that his behavior had been "absolutely disgraceful" that Ramsay began to feel that his father was being a little over-censorious. "I was completely ashamed of you," Thomas raged at him.

"I wasn't exactly proud myself," Ramsay retorted calmly, "to find my father dining with two pretty little things, young enough to be his grandchildren . . . actresses, I suppose they were. . . ."

Ramsay had gone further than he intended, and he was mortified. Certainly, to Thomas, nothing could justify a son's speaking to his father in such a fashion. For a few seconds he looked down at his hands, which lay on his desk so tightly clasped that the skin at the base of his fingers was white. "How dare you?" he said softly.

"I'm sorry, Father," Ramsay apologized again, only to be disturbed by a sense of disloyalty to May. "I was a little concerned," he began, "as I'm sure you'll . . . Well, Father, I mean . . ."

"Concerned?" queried Thomas, glaring at him with cold anger. "You mean because I was entertaining two young friends of Mr. Etherington's?"

Ramsay stared with amazement at his father. "They were your friends too, Father," he corrected, conscious that they were treading strange emotional areas. "One of them even had her hand on yours. . . ."

"I think you were mistaken, Ramsay." Thomas was looking at him with eyes that bore an unusual emotional blankness. "You had, of course, had much to drink. . . ."

Ramsay could have conceded the point and shrugged his shoulders, but relations between a grown-up son and his father are complex, and suddenly he was overtaken by an angry irritation at Thomas' hypocrisy. "There was no mistake, Father, and it *was* in public, and a bit of an insult to Mother. . . ."

Ramsay knew his rebuke was pompous and exaggerated, but when he saw his father's fury as he echoed the word "insult," some primeval instinct moved him to goad him further. "The store too," he went on. "It can't have done the store much good. . . . Any customers who knew you—"

"The store!" Thomas shouted, leaping to his feet and striking the desk with his fist. "You dare instruct me what's good for my store?" he roared.

"It's my store too," Ramsay retorted. "I've worked in it for nearly twenty years. . . . Father, it's my store too, and . . ."

But he did not finish, because at that moment the door was flung open and they were facing events that were far more important than the question as to whether Thomas had been mildly indiscreet the previous evening. For Sidney Baines was standing there in the entrance, his face gray with anxiety. "I'm sorry to disturb you, Mr. Kingston," he said, "but there's a matter of the gravest urgency. . . . At this moment there are reporters in my office from the *Daily Mail*, the *Daily Mirror* and the *Westminster Gazette*. . . . Others 'ave been on the phone. . . ."

"Reporters?" queried Thomas with astonishment. "What's Dora been doing now?"

"It's not Dora," Sidney answered. "It's us . . . the store . . . We're under 'eavy attack. . . . In this morning's *Daily Chronicle* . . ." and he flourished a newspaper that he was carrying, ". . . the first of a series of articles . . ."

"I don't understand," said Thomas.

"The 'ole trade's under assault," Baines explained, "but we're one of those that have been singled out. . . . What's more, they've been informed of our plans, our policy, our strategy, all kinds of matters that only the directors can know. . . . I fear there's no doubt, Mr. Kingston . . . we've 'ad a spy."

Ramsay knew the truth then. His stomach tensed into spasm. He could feel the color draining from his cheeks. He hardly heard his father insist, "Don't be ridiculous, Sidney. There can't be a spy on the board. . . . Who wrote the article?"

"A lady named 'Annah Redfield."

"Redfield?" snapped Thomas. "That name sounds familiar. Do we know anything about her?"

"She worked 'ere for a while as a sales assistant," Sidney answered. "And other stores, too . . . Lewis' . . . Debenhams . . . Swan and Edgar . . . They're all named as well. So are others in the provinces and suburbs. . . . She's conducted a major investigation. . . ."

"Which department?" asked Thomas, his forehead creased as he tried to recall why he knew the name.

" 'Aberdashery. . . . I've spoken to Evans. . . . Apparently, she left very suddenly about three or four months ago . . . literally without any warning. . . ."

"Haberdashery?" Thomas repeated almost to himself. ". . . Redfield?" And then in a terrible cold moment the memory of the day when he had rebuked Ramsay for his familiarity with her came back into his mind. And he looked now at his son and saw the agony in his eyes, and there was a silence that both of them would remember for the rest of their lives. It was a silence of pain rather than rebuke, of sympathy and shock and horror and remorse and mutual concern for the store, their store, Thomas' and Ramsay's store—but certainly there was no hint that the accused of moments before was now in a position to charge his accuser. And because Thomas did not do this, or even appear to think this, as a smaller man might have done, Ramsay experienced a surge of gratitude and love for him so poignant that for a moment he was breathless.

"Well," said Thomas at last, "perhaps we'd better see what Miss Redfield has said about us. . . ." He sat down at his desk, and Sidney spread the paper in front of him on the top of it. Thomas gestured to his son. "You'd better read it too, Ramsay." Ramsay walked over behind the desk so that he could see over his father's shoulder the extent of Hannah's betrayal which was still scarcely believable to him.

Printed under the headline "The Disgraceful Life in Our Shops," Hannah's first article attacked the long periods that many stores were open for business; the poor wages; the hours that shop assistants had to spend on their feet; and in particular, the system of living-in, which, as organized by some firms, was a form of slavery, with prison-type rules, restriction on spare-time freedom, appalling food and the threat of instant dismissal without pay.

Hannah was campaigning with much justice but few ethics. The big central London stores, like Kingstons, were not her target, for they had long ago corrected these abuses, which were rooted in the history of the trade, but to make an impact, she had to smear the well-known names. She did this by deploying the old journalist's trick of association—by reporting an especially bad case of living-in conditions, for example, and following it with the information that "Kingstons, too, have a living-in system that, though conducted correctly, must by its nature share some of the unfortunate characteristics of an institution."

She castigated the big firms for their opposition to the union, of which, she emphasized, it was quite lawful for a shop assistant to be a member. "Some companies take their opposition to extraordinary lengths. I am informed that Thomas Kingston plans to force all new staff to sign an undertaking not to join the union and already practices a policy of dismissing any employee he discovers to be a member.

How this big store, to which our King has seen fit to grant the Royal Warrant to supply goods to the Palace, should be able to rob a man or woman of employment for an action that is lawful is something that deserves careful study."

"My God!" said Ramsay quietly when he read those words, but there was worse to come.

Hannah drew a vivid picture of the Kingston family's life-style— the estate in Buckinghamshire with the hunters grazing in the meadows, Thomas' big house in Cadogan Place, Ramsay's luxurious home in Montpelier Square, the carriages, the servants, the elegance of their wives, and even "the latest acquisition," as she put it—turning the knife for Ramsay in a wound that was already bleeding profusely—the Mercedes-Simplex. Then she compared this with the wages of thirty-two shillings a week that were paid to a Kingstons salesman. She did not add that these were the highest paid in any store in the country, but even if she had, it would only have given strength to the theme of the series.

As Ramsay read the words which Hannah had used to discredit both him and his father, and recalled the circumstances under which she obtained the information, he thought he was going to be sick.

"You'd better sit down for a moment, Ramsay," his father said, noticing his pallor, "while we decide what to do. . . ." Thomas leaned back heavily in his chair. "Well, one thing I do know," he said at last, "is that I'll still have nothing to do with the union. This is blackmail. . . . I've been blackmailed before. I don't suppose you knew that, Sidney, did you?"

Sidney glanced at him. "No, Mr. Kingston," he lied.

"Well, I didn't bow to it then and I'm damned if I'll bow to it now."

"Do we declare this as official policy?" Sidney asked. "The reporters in my office'll want to know. . . . There could be questions in the 'Ouse of Commons. One of these Labour Party Johnnies . . ."

"Damn it, Sidney, most firms have an antiunion policy. . . . The only way the unions get a company to agree to anything else is with strikes, if they can get enough people to strike. . . . I don't believe they can do that in Kingstons. We've a great store, and our staff are proud of it."

His telephone rang on his desk, and his clerk told him that Mr. Handfield was outside seeking an urgent interview. "Certainly not," he snapped. "If he was the last man in England I wouldn't see him."

He hung the receiver back on its hook, and Ramsay asked, "Are you still positive you're right, Father?"

"After *this*?" Thomas queried angrily, jabbing his finger at the newspaper on his desk. "The man's a scoundrel. . . ."

"Would you permit me to talk to him?"

"That'd be as bad as talking to him myself."

"It wouldn't," Sidney put in carefully, "if we didn't know about it. . . . An unofficial contact might 'ave advantages. . . ."

"I could say that you'd refused to let me see him," said Ramsay, "but I didn't agree with you. . . . We could talk in a pub. . . ."

Thomas thought for a moment. "I don't really like it . . . but after this . . ." Again he gestured at the newspaper. ". . . I'm not sure that the normal ethics apply any longer. . . . All right, Ramsay . . . but be careful."

"And the reporters in my office?" reminded Baines.

"I'm not going to be rushed on this, Sidney," said Thomas. "I want to see what happens—what other stores do, what other newspapers publish. . . . You can tell the reporters that the matter has to be considered by the Board."

When Sidney left, Ramsay lingered. Thomas smiled. "Put it behind you, Ramsay. . . . Just concentrate on how we can deal with the problem, see if there's not some way we can turn it to our advantage. There often is. . . . And at least we've bought a bit of time. . . ."

Ramsay had barely left his office, however, before Thomas was reminded sharply that the time he had bought was unlikely to be leisured. His clerk told him that Albert Brown was outside, requesting a brief interview.

Albert Brown, now a man of fifty-one, had not made the progress that Thomas had hoped. He had bought the Gentlemen's Hosiery for some years and was stuck in a rut that could end only with retirement. He was gray and bald and pernickety, and Thomas often found it hard to associate him with the errand boy who had caused the traumatic quarrel with David in 1870.

"I'm obliged to you for receiving me, Mr. Kingston," Brown said respectfully as he entered the office, but Thomas noticed that he seemed strangely nervous. "I presume, sir, you've seen today's *Chronicle*. . . ."

"You mean this scandalous article?" asked Thomas, tapping the newspaper on his desk.

"Well, sir, there are some who believe it reports what needs to be said. . . ."

"They think we merit attack?" queried Thomas. "I'd have thought you of all people'd agree we've always been thoughtful employers."

Brown nodded and studied his toe caps. "You were once very kind to me, Mr. Kingston . . . which is why this is hard for me . . . but there are things that are more important than personal feelings."

"Than loyalties, Albert? . . ." Thomas queried gently.

"Bigger things, Mr. Kingston, affecting thousands of men and women. . . . There's talk in the store today about your attitude to the union, as I suppose you'd expect . . . which is why I've . . . well, I've come to ask you a question. . . ." He broke off uneasily.

"Well, ask your question, Albert," Thomas urged quietly.

With an effort, Brown looked straight at him. "Is the article right, Mr. Kingston? Is it your policy to dismiss any union member?"

Until now, the policy had existed only in Thomas' spates of anger at Handfield's troublemaking. He had not sought to discover unionists on the staff and had taken no action in two instances where it had by chance come to his attention.

"Why do you ask?" Thomas questioned.

"Because," Brown answered, holding himself stiffly upright, "I'm a member of the union."

Thomas knew that Handfield had selected Brown as a test case because his sacking would make good material for depicting Thomas as a harsh exploiter of labor. "Do you really want to leave Kingstons, Albert?" he asked gently.

"It'd be easier if you'd call me Mr. Brown, sir. . . ."

Thomas shrugged. "All right, Mr. Brown . . . You've worked here almost as long as I have. . . . Do you really want to go?"

Brown found the question embarrassing. "Of course not, Mr. Kingston. . . ."

Because," Thomas went on, "I was just thinking it'd have been better if I'd not seen you this morning—as you'd have reported to Mr. Handfield. That'd have given us a chance to consider these very serious matters with the care they deserve. . . . Of course Mr. Handfield wants a battle—not with one of those appalling little stores that really do exploit their staff, but with a firm of repute . . . and you've been sent in to start it—you, Mr. Brown, who've worked with me since you were fourteen. . . ."

Again Thomas paused, watching Brown's troubled expression. "Well, *I* don't want you to start it, Mr. Brown. . . . I shall be answering your question in public in a few days' time, though at this moment I haven't quite decided how. . . . I need those days, Mr. Brown, and I'm asking you for them. . . . After all, I can always sack you then if there's really got to be a battle. . . . And with Miss Redfield's attack today, it wouldn't be surprising if my schedule was especially crowded, would it?"

Brown looked worried and uncertain. "No," he conceded. "I'd expect you to be pressed this morning, Mr. Kingston . . . and I doubt if a day or two'd make much difference, as you say. . . ."

"I'm sorry I haven't been able to spare the time to see you, Mr. Brown," said Thomas, and he began working on some documents on his desk as though there were no one in the room. When he looked up a minute later, Albert Brown had left.

· 3 ·

It was quite chilly in the hansom as May waited outside Number 2 Pembroke Villas soon after half past four in the afternoon of the same day. The dusk was beginning to settle, and soon it would be too dark for her to see the entrance of Number 33, which was the purpose of her vigil. She drew her fox cape closer around her, then sank her hands back into the warmth of her fur muff.

It was the sixth time she had driven down that little street since Number 33 Pembroke Villas had become an address of interest to her—through the simple fact of furniture she had not ordered being charged to her account in the store. An inquiry about it had elicited the delivery address and produced the information that Thomas had placed the order. Obviously, he had intended to settle the matter privately and the charge to the account had been in error.

Since her discovery, she had watched the furnishing and carpeting of the little house. And when, the previous day, the curtains had been up and smoke had been curling from the chimney, she had realized it was ready for its occupant.

Now, as she felt the damp cold of that winter afternoon, she wondered why she had not employed an agency for the purpose of this watch; but she knew the reason. She wanted to see the girl before her lawyers served the writ on Thomas.

May did not, of course, intend to divorce him—nor even sue for legal separation, which was an easier course for a wife. She had shared Thomas' life, his setbacks, his triumphs. She had helped him create the store. She loved him deeply. They had been married for some thirty-

seven years, and they had become merged, fired, each a part of a single
whole. But certainly she did not intend to permit him to keep a
mistress—especially, since she suspected she was one of the twins she
had heard about, a very young mistress.

She had endured her baptism of flame with Eve Banbury, although
that, for all the immense pain it had caused her, had been something
she could at least understand. It had been a very different matter from
a man of sixty's making an idiot of himself with a twenty-year-old—
not an idiot, by God, she repeated to herself angrily at the very
moment that the carriage, *their* carriage, turned into the road. He had
not even had the common decency to take a cab.

With cold rage she watched as the carriage drew to a halt before
Number 33 and saw her husband alight before handing down a young
girl with dark hair. For a few seconds the girl stood staring at the
house, almost like a child viewing for the first time a new toy. Then
she gave a little leap of pleasure and kissed Thomas impulsively on the
cheek.

"Cabby!" May snapped. "Thirty-four Cadogan Place!" And the
hansom moved off down the road past the waiting carriage with May
sitting hunched in the back, tears streaming down her fifty-seven-year-
old cheeks—tears that never came easily to May.

·4·

"I hate to say this, Mr. Kingston," Handfield insisted to Ramsay
when they met that evening in the noise and smoke of the George II,
"but your father's a stubborn man. Trade unionism is a force that's
growing all the time. . . . Men who take the attitude your father
does—and of course, there are many—only increase the strength of
that growth."

"Well, you won't change him with scurrilous articles like Miss
Redfield's in the *Chronicle*," answered Ramsay. "You know as well as
I do it was completely inaccurate."

"Not inaccurate, Mr. Kingston," insisted Handfield with a sly
smile. "Not one word was inaccurate."

"The impression was inaccurate—at least so far as Kingstons was
concerned . . . *and* Debenhams . . . *and* the other good stores. . . ."

Handfield sighed. "We're not playing a game of cricket, Mr.
Kingston. We're waging a desperate struggle . . . and I did try to warn
your father. Some of the unpleasantness might have been avoided if
only he'd been a bit more reasonable . . . like you are. . . ."

"If he'd traded, you mean?" said Ramsay. "Submitted to blackmail? . . ."

Handfield looked pained. "Not blackmail, Mr. Kingston . . . negotiations . . ."

"Pure semantics," Ramsay scorned. "You know, Mr. Handfield, I'm beginning to think my father's right in refusing to talk to you. . . ."

Handfield laughed. "Is anyone right in refusing to talk?" He changed the subject quickly, deliberately leaving the question in the air. "By the way," he said, "I've been entrusted with a letter for you. You can read it while I'm getting you a drink. . . . Brandy, wasn't it? . . ."

Ramsay looked at the blue envelope that Handfield held out to him with a shock of dismay. He had never seen her writing before, but it was characteristic—firm downstrokes combined with elaborate, even artistic curlicues at the ends of the characters. With fingers that he could not prevent from trembling, he drew the letter from the envelope. "Dear Ramsay," she had written, "Our position is strange. I don't expect quarter, for we're enemies, as I told you repeatedly. Yet I do want you to know that our meetings gave me deep pleasure. Many people would regard what happened between us as the ultimate a woman could give a man, would even suggest it was a compensation. Personally, I don't see it in this light, for the experience for me was overwhelming. They say that women in hindsight forget the sheer intensity of their pleasure at such moments, that the recollection becomes dulled, like the pain in childbirth. But Ramsay, I remember every shade, every nuance, every extreme of that intensity—and treasure it. I hope that despite everything, you'll remember it too, as I asked; that you'll understand that what lay ahead for me was a duty.

"I am, however, going to advise you—and you can betray me, just as I betrayed you, by showing this letter to Mr. Handfield. My articles will cause Kingstons and other stores to come under pressure from the union and the staff. Your father, I suspect, will invite a head-on clash. Don't let him, Ramsay. Times are changing, and he too must change. What he should do is to divert the attack. Let him defy the union if he wishes, but urge him with all the strength you can command to form a staff council—a council that must be more than a mere pawn in the hands of the directors, that must act as a true advocate for the staff, that is heeded by you and your father with genuine interest and sympathy, even if you do not always respond as its members would like.

"I don't have to tell you of the impact that this plan would have, both among your staff and in the press, for it would be novel. No store in Britain has ever before introduced such a scheme.

"And if you wonder why I urge this course, then you can either say it's cunning—as, in a sense it is, for in the end you'll recognize the union and the council will help that recognition—or you can say that all trade unionists are romantics, which they are, especially women trade unionists.

"I wish you well. Hannah."

By the time he had finished reading the letter, Ramsay's emotions were in turmoil. Her references to their last evening together had disturbed him deeply. Yet her suggestion for the staff council was exciting in the extreme. From almost every aspect, it was brilliant. It would be a powerful answer to the union, as she said; it would be timely, presenting Kingstons as a store that cared for the people who worked for it—and the staff in turn would be deeply impressed; yet the council would have no power—just influence, and the extent of that influence would stay completely in the hands of the directors.

Even so, as a concept it was revolutionary, and Ramsay was surprised, when he dined alone with his father later that evening at Cadogan Place, that he had no difficulty in persuading Thomas of its merits—dined alone because evidently May was not feeling well and had ordered supper on a tray in her bedroom. "And I know just the man to be the first chairman of our staff council," declared Thomas. "Albert Brown, the longest-serving employee on the payroll."

"Why, Father, that's a wonderful idea!" exclaimed Ramsay with enthusiasm. "What ever made you think of him?"

"Oh, I don't know," Thomas answered innocently. "Just occasionally, I too get a good idea."

He was refilling Ramsay's glass with port when Brandon came into the dining room to say that Mr. Etherington was in the drawing room and would appreciate it if he could spare him a few minutes on an urgent matter.

"Of course," said Thomas. "Ask him to join us here for a glass of port."

But Etherington, as he entered the room, declined the offer. "Thank you, Mr. Kingston, but I only have a moment. I thought, though, that I should come to you as soon as possible. . . . I've been speaking to a number of the members of the club. . . . This business in this morning's *Chronicle's* created an unfortunate impression, and the critical comment in the evening press has been no help. . . . I've been advised by the secretary that it'd be . . . well, tactful if you didn't stand for membership on Thursday as we planned."

Thomas was both surprised and disappointed. "Didn't stand? . . ." he queried incredulously.

"The article in the *Chronicle* suggested that conditions in stores were . . . well, scandalous. . . ."

"But not so far as we are concerned," insisted Thomas.

"Oh, I agree completely, as you know . . . but the implications were unfortunate—especially on the matter of living in."

"But our living-in arrangements are exemplary," Thomas insisted.

"I know that, Mr. Kingston, but everyone in the Reform does not. . . . There's really no doubt that it'd be wise to mark time for a few months. . . . Also, I find I have to go abroad unexpectedly, and naturally, as your proposer, I'd like to—"

"You mean—" Thomas cut in angrily.

"I mean," Etherington persisted, his voice suddenly hard, "that you'd almost certainly be blackballed."

· 5 ·

"And so, gentlemen," Thomas declared from the platform two days later to the representatives of the press, gathered in the large room where buyers' meetings and the AGMs were held, "we decided to make our policy clear. . . . We believe that Kingstons is one of the most important stores, if not *the* most important, in the world. . . . Our buyers search the globe for the finest-quality merchandise it's possible to acquire. . . . Our relations with our staff have always been excellent . . . which brings me to the reason we've invited you here today. . . ."

He paused, gripping the lapels of his frock coat with his hands, and surveyed his audience. "Now, gentlemen, we've been attacked recently in a newspaper on several counts, most of them patently untrue, but there's one which demands a clear statement of our policy. . . . We are opposed to the Shop Assistants' Union. There's no secret about this. . . . We do not knowingly employ members of the union. . . . However, we've decided that the time has come for the staff to have a greater voice in certain aspects of the business. We've always been a progressive house, of course . . . so you'll not be surprised to learn that the plan we're starting is utterly new, something that no store in this country has ever done before. . . . Gentlemen, it's my pleasure to announce the inauguration of Kingstons' staff council."

As he went on to outline the concept of the council as a body that would be independent of the management, he watched his audience eagerly scribbling notes and knew that his announcement was creating exactly the effect that he had hoped.

"The first chairman of the council has been appointed by me," Thomas went on, "because somebody had to start things going. However, I think that my choice will be popular in the store, which is why I made it. . . . Future chairmen will, of course, be elected by council members themselves, but for a year or two at least, I hope they'll vote for Mr. Brown . . ." Thomas smiled. ". . . for the thirty-eight years that I have known Albert, as I used to call him when he was fourteen and wore an apron, have taught me what a sound and honest man he is. . . ."

It was a triumph. When the meeting broke up, Thomas knew that the evening press would be publishing pictures of Brown. Already, the *Daily Mail* was planning an exclusive interview with him for the next morning's editions. The *Daily Mirror* was sending a man to see his wife. And *The Times*, which did not respond with the same kind of speed as the brash new popular press, was considering an article on the whole issue of staff councils for the following week.

Within the store, news of the council traveled fast. After the meeting was over, Ramsay encountered Handfield as he walked through the Linens. The union leader was clearly very angry. "That was clever, I admit, Mr. Kingston," he said with a scowl. "But don't you be sure it wasn't too clever by half. . . ."

Meanwhile, on the floor above, Thomas was involved with yet another crisis, this time one that was deeply personal. A visitor had been waiting for him in the outer office when he had returned to his room after the meeting—a short, sallow character with a soiled wing collar, baggy trousers and a bowler hat. He carried a letter that he had been instructed to hand only to Thomas in person. It was from a firm of London lawyers informing him that they had been instructed by his wife to institute proceedings for divorce.

"Good evening, Thomas," said May when he entered the sitting room that night, as though she knew of nothing untoward between them. Quite deliberately, he had not hurried home but had stayed working at his desk until the store closed. Partly, he had needed time to absorb the shock of those bald, formal words on the lawyers' notepaper and partly his tactical instincts had demanded an appearance, at least, of cool and measured response.

May's action in going to lawyers was out of character with the wife Thomas thought he knew. And now, by behaving as though everything between them were normal, she had skillfully grasped the initiative.

"Has it been a good day, my dear?" she asked, her eyes fixed for a few seconds on some embroidery she was working as she finished a stitch. Then she looked up at him again. "How did the meeting go with the press?"

He glared at her from the doorway. "I've had the letter from your lawyers," he said.

"Already?" she queried brightly. "They've been very quick for lawyers. . . . Lawyers are usually rather slow, aren't they? Obviously, they're a good firm."

Thomas strode across the room to the fireplace and stood with his back to it, staring grimly in front of him. "What are you playing at, May?" he said at last.

"Me?" May echoed, deliberately putting down her embroidery beside her. "It's not me that's playing at anything, Thomas. . . ."

The appearance she had prepared so carefully to receive him—the banter, the cool smile—was gone. Now there was a break in her voice and angry pain in her eyes. "Are you out of your mind, Thomas? Did you seriously believe I'd tolerate the Pembroke Villas situation? Do you think I don't care for you any longer, that I've no imagination, that I'm not haunted by vivid thoughts of you actually *with* her, of your hands fondling that young skin? . . . Is that what you think?"

He realized she was close to tears, which in another woman would not be strange, but in May was a rare indication of searing emotional wounds. "You're making far too much of it, May," he said. "It's something that's quite apart from us, something that's—"

"It's something that's going to stop," she said firmly, and stood up because, seated, she had felt at a disadvantage. "Otherwise I'll divorce you—or gain a legal separation. . . . It makes no odds . . . there'll be just as much notice of it taken in the press."

"The press?"

"It'll hardly go unobserved. . . . And don't think I won't go through with it, Thomas, because I will. . . . That's why I went straight to lawyers instead of having it out with you first. I wanted you to be certain I meant it. . . ." She had moved behind the chair she had been sitting on and was gripping the back of it, the fingers of both hands tensed.

"May," he said with a note in his voice that was almost patronizing, "your life as a divorced woman, as a separated woman—"

"I'd accept that, Thomas!" she challenged. "I'd accept everything that went with it. . . . I've told you: I'm not bluffing. . . . But in fact I won't have to accept it—will I, Thomas?"

"I'm not abandoning her, May," Thomas insisted quietly. "Please get that quite clear."

"You *are* abandoning her. . . . Do you know why I'm so sure you're abandoning her? . . ."

"Certainly your confidence has no grounds."

"Because of your store, Thomas. . . . It's not just her or me . . . it's her or the store. . . . Kingstons customers'd never accept a divorce. . . . If it was lower down the market, if it was an ordinary shop . . . well, perhaps you'd get away with it . . . but not Kingstons. . . . *You* know that. . . ."

Thomas shook his head at the thought. "I don't believe you'd do that much damage to the store, May. You've played too big a role in its creation. . . . Anyway, it's not necessary if you'll only—"

"Do that much damage to the store?" May cut in. "Thomas, you're so foolish sometimes I can barely believe it. . . . We're standing here speaking of divorce, of breaking a marriage of thirty-seven years, and you question whether I'd damage the store. . . ." Her eyes had suddenly filled with tears as she cried out suddenly, "Of *course* I'd damage the store, you dolt, you idiot, you fool. . . . A store's a *thing* . . . even your store's a thing. . . . All right, *our* store, for God knows, as you say, I've given it enough. . . . But people are more important than things. . . . So are marriages. . . . *I'd* certainly damage the store if I had to . . . but *you* wouldn't, Thomas, because to you it's the one thing in your life that *is* more important than people . . . *and* than our marriage. . . . You wouldn't let me damage it . . . certainly not for a little kitten like that, even if she has got her claws into a place where a man's particularly vulnerable . . . especially an old man. . . ."

She saw the flash of anger in his eyes as she referred to his age, was even conscious that temporarily she had lost ground with the taunt. For she had been aware that her distress had moved him to take her in his arms. Now she knew that he merely felt caged. He was standing quite still, his body rigid.

"It's not often you've seen me cry, is it? . . ." she said, touching her eyes with her handkerchief, "if ever . . . but it's all right now . . . I've taken control of myself. . . ."

For a moment he was silent. "I'm not giving up Jenny," he said firmly. "Your lawyers can take what action they like."

"You've no alternative, Thomas." Once more she was grasping the initiative, once again the woman who had greeted him so calmly when he had first returned home "You can be as generous as you like to her . . . I won't make conditions of that nature. . . ."

"Conditions?" he queried glaring at her. "Damn it, woman, you're in no position to make conditions! . . ."

"Oh, I am, Thomas, and you know I am. . . . Now go and tell her it's over."

Thomas stared at her with surging fury, not only because he did not want to lose Jenny, but also because he felt that her dictation of terms was degrading. "May," he said, "you can go to hell!"

He walked out of the house, stopped the first hansom for hire, and ordered the cabby to drive to Pembroke Villas. Jenny's face lit up with delight when he arrived, since she had not expected him, but it faded when she saw the grim expression on his face. "I want you, Jenny," he said. "I want you this very minute."

She looked at him anxiously for a second. "All right, Tom," she said quietly, and led the way up the narrow staircase to the bedroom.

His lovemaking was urgent, even violent at moments, but later he became relaxed and affectionate, drained of the extreme emotion—and he fell asleep.

When she awakened soon after six the next morning, he was already up and dressed. He combed his hair, straightened his tie; then, leaning down over the bed, he kissed her softly on the lips. "It's finished, Jenny," he said gently. "The marriage can't be broken. . . . I'm putting the house in your name and I'll make you an allowance to help you run it. . . . Thank you for everything. . . . I shall miss you very badly. . . ."

Without looking behind him, he walked out of the bedroom. As he strode down the little road in the morning darkness, he heard her call, "Tom!" He turned under one of the street lamps and saw her leaning out of the window, illuminated by the light in the bedroom behind her. "Not like this, Tom!" she pleaded.

"It's best like this, Jenny," he called back. He waved—and then walked on.

Three hours later, after the store had opened, he was told that a detective inspector named Jackson wished to see him. Welcoming any diversion in his unhappy state that morning, Thomas received him immediately. Jackson, a man in his late fifties, with gray hair and bushy moustache, was accompanied by a young, eager detective sergeant. "Apologize for troubling you, Mr. Kingston," said the inspector, "but we understand you're acquainted with a Mr. Maurice Etherington. . . ."

"That's correct," Thomas answered.

"Known him long, have you?" He had a strange way of making statements that were questions, as the French do.

"A few months," Thomas replied. "Am I permitted to know the reason for these questions, Inspector? ..."

"In a moment, Mr. Kingston. ... He's approached you for money ever, sir? A loan, perhaps ... or return for a service, possibly? ..."

Thomas shook his head. "He has indeed done me a continuing service. ... At the beginning I proposed a fee, but he refused, suggesting the matter should be left for a while."

The inspector gave his sergeant a knowing look. "Style, you see, Sergeant ... style. ... He was preparing you, sir," he told Thomas.

"I beg your pardon!" said Thomas, angry now at the innuendo.

"He was building up your trust, sir. ... After all, once you'd seen some results, the fee would have been far bigger, wouldn't it?"

"Are you aware, Inspector," Thomas asked coldly, "that Mr. Etherington's a prominent member of the Reform Club?"

"I am, of course, sir . . . like his father before him. . . . Very respectable gentleman . . . Colonial Service. . . . Introduced Mr. Maurice when he was very young . . . no trouble at all, naturally. The father was well liked. . . . Of course, Mr. Maurice's gambling did raise a few eyebrows. . . . Not really a gambling club, the Reform . . . not like Brooks or Whites. . . . Bit of a blade, but he was tolerated well enough. . . . Young, after all . . ."

"Inspector," Thomas cut in, "would you please come to your business."

"Of course, sir. . . . I was just explaining how he came to be short of money. . . . May I ask, sir, when you last saw him?"

"A couple of evenings ago. . . . He said he was going abroad."

"And he *went* abroad, sir." The inspector sighed. "I don't suppose he mentioned his ultimate destination?"

"No."

"I thought not. . . . Calais . . . that much we know, but it's not much help—not with the whole of Europe at his disposal. . . . Very aggravating, Mr. Kingston. . . . Somebody must have warned him . . . always did have good connections. . . . Sad . . . never got this close to him before. . . . We could charge him now, of course . . . all the evidence we need . . ."

"Charge him with what?" asked Thomas.

"Misrepresentation . . . fraud . . . whole range of things. . . . He was a confidence man, Mr. Kingston . . . made a speciality of offering to help gentlemen get titles. . . . Succeeded sometimes, too. . . . Knew a lot of people—mostly through his father of course. . . . Made a business of introductions, a kind of broker of people, you might say. Introduced supply to the market. . . . I presume he spoke of the matter of a title? . . ."

"Well, yes," Thomas replied, deeply embarrassed, "we did touch on the subject. . . ."

The inspector stood up. "If he contacts you at all, sir, even from abroad," he said, "would you please keep me informed." And he placed his visiting card on Thomas' desk.

For a few minutes after the two detectives had left, Thomas remained at his desk, deep in thought, conscious that this was one of those days that marked a change of course in his life. Not an important one. In fact, he mused, it was not so much a change in course as a resumption of the previous flow—as though for the past few months he had been traveling in a sidewater created by islands in a river, a very colorful sidewater featuring exotic foliage.

With a sigh, he got up and walked to the windows. He put his hands deep in his pockets. Low heavy gray clouds lay over London. It was raining, and the wheels of the vehicles were splashing through the water that lay in Sloane Street. On the pavements, people hurried, beneath open umbrellas held inclined toward the wind, or huddled within coats with collars up. It would not be a good day for trade, he thought. Suddenly for Thomas, life seemed almost unbearably dull.

CHAPTER TWELVE

April 1913

· I ·

When the Daimler turned into the yard, the lamps in the stables were still burning, even though dawn had broken and it was already quite light. In the boxes, there was movement as the first string was being prepared for the early-morning gallops.

The car door was opened by the chauffeur, and Thomas put aside the rug he and Robert had been sharing on the back seat and, taking the man's proffered arm, hauled himself heavily out of the vehicle. The heart attack he had suffered two years back had left its marks. He moved like an old man now, looked more than his age of sixty-eight. He needed a stick to walk. His mind, however, was as alert as ever—or almost, anyway—and even though he was in the store only three days a week, spending Friday to Monday at Quainton, he still retained a rigid control of the business by means of close contact by telephone.

Harry and Robert, who had got out of the Daimler by the other door, walked round the front of the car and joined him as Sam Jones, the trainer, came forward to meet him. "Good morning, Mr. Kingston," he said. He was an ex-jockey, as small as a child, with a raw face that was heavily lined. "It's a rare pleasure to welcome you here. . . ."

"Mutual, I can assure you, Mr. Jones," said Thomas. "I don't think you know my grandson, Robert. . . ."

"How do you do, sir?" said Robert, shaking hands. Although he was still only fourteen, he was already quite tall and towered above the little trainer.

"How's Meridian been since the Lincoln meeting?" asked Thomas.

"Excellent, Mr. Kingston . . . like working a different horse since last year. . . ."

"Think he's got a chance at Epsom?"

"He'll be a long shot, of course . . . but it's amazing what he can produce now when he wants to."

The stable lads began to bring them out for mounting, and when

Thomas saw his horse, he said, "He's looking very good, Mr. Jones. . . . I'm glad we kept him."

"Let's hope you'll be saying that on Derby Day, Father," commented Harry, who had been the advocate for retaining the colt, though he had never been able to explain quite why. He had been a good-looking, spirited foal, but no one could really judge a racehorse until he had seen him perform. "I've just got a feeling he's exceptional," he had said.

"No reason?" Thomas had queried. "The way he moves . . . conformation? . . ."

Harry had shrugged his shoulders with a smile. "Just a feeling, Father."

"Inspiration, Grandpapa," Robert had put in with a grin. He had been only eleven then, back from boarding school for the holidays as he was now, and ever since Thomas had first used the word on his seventh birthday, it had become a kind of private joke between them. Thomas had smiled at his grandson's teasing. "Robert," he had said, "you'll find people who'll be able to give you six sound reasons why a horse'll do well or a line of merchandise'll sell in the store—and somehow they'll still be wrong. . . . Feel, Robert, flair . . . that's what you've got to look for. . . ." He looked at him and winked. " 'Sprashun. . . . Well, your uncle's 'sprashun's pretty sound when it comes to horses. . . ."

So instead of selling him to run under someone else's colors, which had been the normal Quainton practice since Thomas had begun investing in top-class racing broodmares, they had kept him. Inevitably, he had been special, becoming almost like a household pet, and Thomas would often watch Robert and the other children playing with him in the meadow in front of the hall. Then, when the colt was old enough, Thomas had sent him to Sam Jones for training.

He had shown little form as a two-year-old, managing to be placed third in only one of the races in which he had run. "Slow developer," Harry had ruled confidently. Then, as a three-year-old, at the beginning of this season of 1913, he had suddenly surprised them by running a horse called Berkshire Lad so strong a finish over a mile at Kempton that it was obvious he would have won over a longer distance. But, when the 2,000 Guineas at Newmarket, one of the five top classics, also over a mile, was won by a colt whom Berkshire Lad himself had beaten, then it no longer seemed quite so absurd to think of Meridian for the Derby. For the Derby was a mile and a half, and the horse was now displaying all the signs that he was not only fast but a stayer.

A lad brought up Jones's mount, and the trainer vaulted into the saddle. "You'll join us on the heath, Mr. Kingston? . . ." he said. Thomas nodded and stood watching as the string went out the yard gate in single file, the lads sitting, shoulders hunched, as quiet as possible, riding short with their knees high. Then he climbed back into the Daimler.

Jones was running them in sets of three, and standing with Robert, Thomas watched the first group start off from the head of the gallop—not too fast, for gallops, despite the name, are not just for galloping, but for training. The horses were silhouetted against the flying clouds of the early morning sky, their riders hunched forward, the animals' heads seeming to bob with their movements. Thomas was watching intently as they approached, enjoying the sheer aesthetic pleasure of the scene, when he was astonished to hear beside him the voice of Ramsay, whom he thought to be in London.

"Good morning, Father," he said. "I say, that gray's going well. . . ."

"Good heavens, Ramsay," responded Thomas, without taking his eyes from the horses, "what's happened?"

"Nothing bad . . . it's just that A. J. Harris is up for a quick sale. . . . I think we should buy it, but others are after it and they want an answer today."

"Impossible," said Thomas.

"It's a good store . . . potential . . . our kind of potential. . . ."

"When did we adopt a policy of buying stores at all?" asked Thomas. The horses were close now, their feet pounding the turf.

"We've talked about it. . . . Logical extension of the business, you agreed the other day. . . . This'd be an ideal one to start with."

"When did you hear about it?"

"Last night at dinner. . . . I spoke to Harris later. . . . They want a hundred thousand. Profits are around twenty. . . . They'd prefer us to anyone else, he said."

The horses passed them, going at a strong controlled canter, and for the first time since Ramsay's arrival, Thomas turned to give his son his full attention. "You dined with Charles, I suppose?" he said.

"That's right."

"And he told you Selfridges were bidding?"

"Not exactly . . . he said they were interested. . . . But they will buy, of course. . . ."

"Unless we get there first." Thomas paused, a half-smile on his lips. "Exactly how far from Selfridges is the Harris store?"

"Three or four hundred yards," Ramsay answered. "I suppose there must be four buildings between the two stores. . . ."

"That's a long way for easy management," Thomas ruminated dubiously. "If it had been next door or even next-but-one . . ."

"The difference'll give them scope for varied policies. . . . That's why they want it, even though Charles does pretend the interest is only mild. . . ."

Jones cantered up to them. "They're starting now, Mr. Kingston," he said, positioning himself near Thomas. "I've told him to let him go but not to push him. . . ." He raised his arm as a signal.

Meridian was slow away, and the two other horses were ahead of him, running neck and neck. Then, after a few seconds, he was leading —and, as they began to tire, leaving them well behind. "By God, he's not even sweating!" Harry exclaimed as the horse flashed by them, his muscles rippling under his fine thoroughbred coat as he galloped.

"I'm impressed, Mr. Jones," Thomas told the trainer. "What's the distance?"

"Mile and a quarter," he answered.

"He finished very strongly. . . . I'd say he could manage a mile and a half . . . even at Epsom. . . ."

"I'd say so too," said the trainer, "especially since we've still got seven weeks. . . ."

Ramsay drove the Daimler back to Quainton, leaving Thomas' chauffeur to follow in the Hispano Suiza in which he had driven down from London. On the journey, Thomas studied the Harris balance sheet and accounts which Ramsay had brought with him.

Then he just leaned back against the soft cushions of the Daimler, watching the Buckinghamshire fields go past them. He found it hard to be enthusiastic about this type of expansion. It was the store, the single entity he had created, that really mattered to him. Ramsay, though, regarded the purchase of new businesses, or the launching of Kingstons branches, as essential to the company's progress, for there must be a limit to the trade that could be done from one site. Also, it would be his personal contribution to the enterprise his father had founded.

Thomas understood this need in his son and was fully alert to the enormous social developments that were in motion. He recognized that just as the future of shops when he had started lay in the great department stores that now existed, the direction of the trade might well be in large networks spanning the country.

Times were changing, he thought, at so many different levels. It was six years since that depressing morning in 1907 when he had left

Jenny's bed for the last time, to face the unflattering fact that his earlier suspicion that Etherington had merely been preparing him for fleecing had been sound. Not that he harbored any ill feelings. Etherington had taught him much, had directed his sights, as it were. He had perceived the potential of Kingstons' situation as a large and unique top-quality store, had known that because of it, Thomas would be welcomed into the prestigious areas to which he introduced him, despite the fact that he was in trade. And certainly, since his adviser's hasty departure, Thomas' role as a governor of charities and institutions, even as a philanthropist, had expanded and brought him to the edge of politics. His acquaintance with men and women of power and influence had broadened, even developed in some cases into genuine friendships. He had been consulted by the government on matters concerning the products of which Kingstons was so large a distributor —such as food, textiles, furniture—and had been asked sometimes to sit on official committees.

He had continued to make annual donations to the Liberal Party and at last, in response to pressure from his new friends, had become a member of the Reform.

His emerging role as a man concerned with national interests was not forced. What Etherington had done was accelerate a process that in time would have happened anyway. It was fanned, too, by external events. Thomas was a natural patriot, and the threat he saw behind Kaiser Wilhelm's military expansion had caused him to throw his energies behind the concept of the "citizen soldier," granting staff an extra week's holiday if they devoted this to training with the Territorial Army of reservists. Also, he had enlarged and promoted the Kingstons department that sold guns and military equipment.

However, the project closest to his heart was the scandal of the Crystal Palace. Thomas had been only six years old when he had accompanied his grandmother in 1851 on a visit to this huge and astonishing glass building, erected in Hyde Park to house Prince Albert's Great Exhibition, but he had never forgotten it. In fact, the memory of many little shops selling the products of different trades had later inspired in him his whole idea for an emporium, selling a range of merchandise.

When the exhibition had ended, the elegant palace had been rebuilt on a hill in South London, but it had now deteriorated because of neglect and was in danger of demolition. So Thomas had launched a subscription to buy and maintain the palace for the nation, offering ten shillings from his own pocket for every pound contributed by the public. The appeal had been popular, touching the country's imagination, and had provoked a strong response, not only in cash, but also in laudatory press comment. Etherington, in fact, would have thoroughly approved.

The Daimler passed Quainton Church, where, of course, generations of Kingstons lay buried—including Thomas' parents, poor Rose and, more recently, Edward, so that Harry and his sons now ran the farm. Thomas himself was fortunate not to be under the soil in the graveyard as well, he thought grimly as the car went by, for his heart attack had been a near thing. "It was a warning," the doctor had told him when he had recovered. "Mind you heed it. . . ." And, for all practical purposes, he had. He was still Managing Director of the store by title, but many of his duties now fell on Ramsay, with the help of Sidney Baines. Sidney, of course, was now sixty-four, but so far had avoided serious illness and despite his age, got on well with Ramsay. "I suppose" he had joked, "I've got accustomed to being a nanny."

They traveled on through the village and turned into the gates of the drive that led up to the hall, and as always, Thomas enjoyed the sight of his big house. Lillian was staying with them, recuperating from a bad bout of pneumonia in the late winter. She was sixty-eight too, of course, and like Thomas, had almost died. "We don't go that easily, do we?" she had whispered to him when she was recovering, but still weak, from the crisis. "With people like us, the Lord's got to be determined."

As the car came to a halt, May appeared in the front doorway and descended the entrance steps. "Hallo, my dear," Thomas greeted. "You should have come with us. . . . Meridian was a joy to watch."

"I fear I've taken a decision that I hope won't displease you," May said. "James is here. . . ."

"James?" queried Thomas.

"James Rawlings . . . Lillian's James . . ."

"I thought he was in America."

"He's come home to see his mother. . . . He telephoned from Paddington Station and asked permission to visit her."

Thomas grunted and began to climb the steps to the house. Sixteen years had now passed since the decision about James had been taken. Often, Thomas had wondered what David would have done about the affair had he still been alive. Would he have urged him to forgive James? In fact, Thomas *had* forgiven him, but so serious a matter could hardly be just shrugged off. So Lillian and Charles had decided he should be sent abroad, and since he had opted for America, he had been packed off in a ship to New York with his fare paid and five hundred pounds in his pocket.

Lillian had not received many letters from him, and those which had arrived had contained little real information and suggested that he was making little progress, drifting from job to job. One letter from San Francisco had announced his wedding, but the marriage had apparently broken up after a few months.

Still, Thomas noted as he walked into the drawing room and saw him standing beside his mother's chair, he looked a lot better now in his late thirties than he had as a youth, when he had been weedy and rather callow. He had filled out, and although he had begun to lose his hair, he was tanned, and the years of experience that had marked his face had matured him into quite a fine-looking man.

"This is a surprise, James," said Thomas, "but you're welcome." He held out his hand. "And I expect your mother's glad to see you."

"You'll be glad to hear, Thomas, that he's been doing very well for himself out there in America," Lillian interposed proudly.

"I am indeed glad to hear it," said Thomas, hoping his doubt of Lillian's statement was not obvious. "What have you been up to, then, James?"

"Stockbroking . . . in Chicago . . . branch of a New York firm. . . . Futures are my particular speciality."

"And how long have you been doing that?"

"Three years now. . . . It took me a little time to find the right niche . . . I did other things first. . . . The American continent's a stimulating place. . . . In fact, I started off in the Klondike."

"What? At the time of the gold rush?" asked Robert with sudden excitement.

"Of course, James," said Thomas, "you haven't met Ramsay's son, Robert, have you? . . ."

James smiled. "He wasn't born by the time I left . . . makes me realize how long ago it was . . . but yes, Robert, the gold rush was on . . . more or less, anyway." He turned back to Thomas. "I was in the Yukon a year. . . . After that I did all sorts of things . . . even worked with cattle for a few months in Texas. . . . Then I got caught up in the civil war in Mexico, going against Villa with Mandero's forces. . . ."

This was a new James, Thomas thought. America had done him good. "How in the world can you get *caught* up in a civil war?" he asked incredulously.

"I was working in Mexico City at the time. . . . I had a friend serving with Mandero and he suggested I go along. . . . They were a cruel lot, but efficient. In the mass executions, to save ammunition, they used to make the prisoners stand four deep so that each bullet killed more than one man. . . ."

"Good gracious," exclaimed May, "how horrible!"

"You've obviously had some varied experiences," Thomas commented.

"Sounds jolly exciting to me," said Robert.

"Perhaps . . ." remarked his grandfather with a note of rebuke in his voice that was not lost on James.

"I had some thinking to do, as I'm sure you'll understand, Mr. Kingston," he said.

Thomas nodded. James had certainly had some thinking to do. "I'm glad to hear you've settled down well. . . . I look forward to hearing more about the broking business, James, but just now Ramsay and I have to go to London. . . . I leave you in good hands, though. . . . Ramsay, if you're planning to drive me in that Hispano contraption of yours, I'll insist you don't go more than forty miles an hour. . . ."

· 2 ·

By midmorning Lillian was feeling tired and went to her room for a rest, and Robert suggested that James might like to go and see the horses. Ever since his arrival, the boy had been impatient for a chance to talk to this strange man, the younger brother of Uncle Charles— called "uncle," of course, out of respect to his parents' friend. Robert knew that years ago James had left the country suddenly under circumstances that presumably were not very admirable, since no one would ever speak of them. And now he had appeared without warning with a background that was as colorful as you could find in any boy's adventure book.

The light cloud that had marked the sky earlier had gone, and the sun was shining on the meadows, heightening the lush green of the young grass. As they walked down the entrance steps of the house, James inhaled deeply, enjoying the fresh air. "The English spring," he said. "There've been times when I've missed that, I can tell you, Robert. . . ."

"If you missed it so much," asked Robert, "why didn't you come back? . . . For that matter, why did you go away in the first place?"

James studied him for a moment. "They haven't told you, then? . . ."

"Told me what?" They were walking round the side of the house toward the stables at the rear.

"I had a disagreement with your grandfather," said James. "I thought they might have mentioned it. . . . I was working in the store at the time. . . ."

"You mean Grandpapa sacked you?" Robert asked, surprised.

"Not exactly," James answered. "I suppose you could say the parting was by mutual consent. . . ." He gave a short mirthless laugh.

"Couldn't you have gone to another London store—as Uncle Charles did?" Robert persisted. "Why did you have to leave England?" They had entered the stable yard—maintained, like everything else at Quainton Hall, in immaculate order.

"It seemed a good idea at the time. . . . Does the family ever speak of your Aunt Rose?"

"Occasionally. . . . She was killed in a hunting accident, wasn't she?"

James nodded. "It was a great shock for everyone. . . . She was quite young, of course . . . and delightful. . . ." For a moment, he was silent. Then he said, "I feel like some brisk exercise, Robert. I didn't get much on the ship. . . . What do you say to a walk down to the village?"

"I'm game," Robert answered with a smile. "The Klondike must have been quite an adventure. . . . Did you plan to go there before you left England?"

"I didn't plan anything."

"You mean you just got on a ship without any notion what you were going to do when you got to America? . . . What a wonderful thought . . . the whole New World beckoning you. . . . We'll go across the fields, shall we?" He opened the gate of one of the paddocks in front of the house. "What gave you the idea of the Klondike?"

"Chance," answered James. "There was a group of men traveling with me on the ship . . . Norwegians backed by an Oslo company. . . . They were a man short, since one had dropped out just before they'd left. . . . They discovered I hadn't any plans, so they asked me to take his place. It'd be hard going, they said, and dangerous as Hell, but the rewards could be enormous. . . . It was early on, of course . . . the first gold from the Yukon had only been brought into Seattle that summer . . . but there was a lot of it. Two ships had brought a thousand tons— all from Bonanza Creek, as they called it . . . and that was just one creek; there were many others."

"I don't suppose you took much persuading, did you?" Robert

asked, his eyes bright, vaulting over a stile on the footpath they were following across the fields.

James laughed. "Not the way I was feeling at the time. . . ." He clambered over the stile with somewhat less agility than the lithe four-teen-year-old. "The main trouble was getting there. . . . Dawson City's on a latitude of sixty-four degrees north. Well, the Arctic Circle's only sixty-seven. . . ."

"Whew!" Robert responded. "It must have been terribly cold. . . ."

"As low as fifty under in the winter sometimes. . . . It took us five months to reach Dawson from Seattle. . . ." And he went on to de-scribe the journey—the short sea voyage to Skagway on the Alaskan coast, the trek on foot to Dyea pulling sledges piled with their equip-ment of two thousand pounds per man, and then the awesome ascent to the Chilkoot Pass, which was so steep that even with ice creepers on their boots they could not haul the sledges; they had to carry the gear in two-hundred-fifty-pound loads, piling it up in forward camps while making repeated return trips for the remainder.

James described the journey after they had surmounted the Chil-koot. While waiting for the thaw, they made boats from the standing timber for the five-hundred-mile journey by water to Dawson—lakes and rivers that connected up with the stream of the Yukon. He ex-plained vividly how they had had to take these rough craft through the White Horse rapids—"an hour of white roaring water."

He spoke of Dawson City, the Yukon gold town. "I've never seen anywhere like it," he said. "Everyone seemed to have pokes of gold that looked like German sausages . . . some of them big, filled with several thousand dollars' worth of dust; some of them small, worth only a few hundred. Women even wore them in their hair. . . . In shops, people paid in gold dust, weighing it out on the counter. . . . I saw gamblers playing for fifty-dollar stakes when in any other Ameri-can town they'd be putting up fifty cents. Remember, this was 1898—fifteen years ago. . . ."

"And did you find a lot of gold?" Robert asked as they clambered over the last stile at the edge of the village.

"We didn't find *any* . . . we were too late. . . . On the very day we arrived in Dawson, one party brought in half a million dollars' worth of dust and nuggets from Eldorado Creek. Can you imagine how that made us feel after that long journey? Why, we were certain we'd all be rich in a few weeks. . . . But all the worthwhile claims were gone before we got there. Oh, we staked claims and worked as I'd never worked before . . . but we never panned an ounce. . . . There were tens of thousands like us. . . . Eventually we gave up, as most of them did, and went home. At least, the others did. . . ."

"Were you very disappointed?"

"A bit, of course, but really I'd been just riding along. It hadn't cost me anything to live. . . . I'd learned a bit about people . . . about greed in particular . . . I still had the five hundred pounds I'd taken to the States with me . . . and I'd had an experience that many men, working in safe jobs at home, would've given their eyeteeth for. . . . You know, I'd quite forgotten how pretty this village is. . . ."

They were walking along one side of Quainton Green. "You make me a bit envious," said Robert. "You've done so much that's . . . oh, I don't know . . . that's worth doing. . . ."

James laughed. "I don't think your grandfather took that view back at the house."

"Of course *he* wouldn't," said Robert. "All he'd admire would be building some business—preferably a store—or making money. . . ."

"He's got a point. He's achieved a great deal. . . . What have I achieved?"

"Is achievement so tremendously important?"

James glanced at the boy in surprise. "What a question! Of course it's important. Surely you think so too, don't you?"

"Well, it depends what you mean by achievement," said Robert. "Take a soldier, or a miner, or even one of the salesmen in the store. They don't achieve much in the sense that Grandpapa has, but they're vital. They contribute to the world they live in, just as you did when you went to the Yukon and Mexico or rode out on the range in Texas. . . . And there's another sort of achievement, isn't there? . . . within a man himself, I mean. You could argue that it's better, even more creative in one sense, to have a rich and colorful existence than to spend your whole life sitting in an office in London just making money —which is pretty limited, isn't it?"

"I've never heard such heresy," said James with a smile. "And you can't speak of building a great business, especially one like Kingstons which was new in concept, as just making money. It makes your grandfather sound like some kind of usurer. . . . No—I know," he said as Robert began to protest, "you didn't quite mean that. . . . Anyway, I suppose it's where *you're* destined—the store. . . . I take it you're Ramsay's eldest son. . . ."

"Only son."

"Then you'll inherit a great deal, won't you—including the Hall, presumably . . ." He jerked his head back in the direction of the big house behind them. ". . . And Cadogan Place . . . and the major holding in the Kingston stock. . . . Don't you want all that?"

"I suppose so," the boy answered. "I just wonder about it sometimes. . . . It's all being prepared for me. . . . Perhaps I won't want it to be easy. . . . I'd like to pit myself against the elements, as you have . . . or a herd of buffalo . . . or the enemy in a war. . . . Perhaps I need to prove myself."

"You'll prove yourself," James assured him. "I don't know where you've got the idea that running Kingstons'll be easy. . . . The bigger it gets, the bigger the enemies. You'll be up against opponents that'll be far more formidable than a herd of buffalo, I can tell you."

They were approaching the old church at the far end of the village, not so much by intention as because they had just walked on and on as they talked. "What about your sisters—and where are they, by the way?"

"In London with my mother. I just came down with Grandpapa to see our horse on the gallops and thought I'd stay a bit. . . . My sisters are all right, I suppose. . . . They're sisters. . . . Jane's a bit of a nuisance sometimes because she's older than me and jealous of all this talk of my destiny in the store. . . . Sometimes I'd hand it over to her happily."

"You mean that?"

Robert gave a short laugh. "Not really . . . I just fret about it at times. . . ."

"You're a bit of a mixture, aren't you, Robert?" James remarked. "In some ways you're very young and in others you're pretty old. . . . You think a lot, don't you?"

The boy concurred with a shrug, and although neither suggested it, they strolled through the cemetery, led by some mutual impulse, until they came to the Kingston graves—about twenty of them in all, ranged together at one end. Some of the older headstones had been eroded by the weather, partly cloaked by yellow moss, their lettering caked with dirt. Others had sunk in the earth at one end so that they stood crookedly, leaning toward their neighbors as though seeking affection. Robert stopped in front of one which was marked "John Henry Kingston 1801–1858." "That was my great grandfather," he said. "He died of consumption when Grandpapa was thirteen. It was because there was so little money that Grandpapa was sent to London to be indentured in the trade."

"Which is where he met my father," James reminded him.

"Of course. I forgot they were partners."

They moved to the next grave, which was that of Robert's great grandmother, and then, between her headstone and Edward's, was the one that James dreaded. "Oh," said Robert, "here's . . . " He broke off for a second before reading the words aloud: "In loving memory of Rose Alexandra Kingston, 24, tragically killed while riding to hounds August 25, 1897." He turned to James and, for the first time, noticed how pale he had become. "That was when you went to America, wasn't it, Uncle James . . . 1897?" James nodded, then turned away because there were tears in his eyes. "Was that why you went?" Robert asked gently. "Because Aunt Rose died? . . ."

"It had some bearing on my decision."

"But why did you quarrel with Grandpapa?"

"It's a complicated story. . . ." James turned back to him. "If we don't start back now, we'll be late for lunch."

· 3 ·

For a few minutes neither Thomas nor Ramsay had spoken as they drove through Amersham on the way to London. As they cleared the edge of the old town, Ramsay increased the pressure on the accelerator and the Hispano responded, its deep roar becoming louder. "Would you want to buy it if Selfridges didn't?" Thomas asked suddenly.

"Of course," answered Ramsay. "We've often talked of Oxford Street. . . . We could transform the Harris store, Father. . . . Already it does a fairly good fashion business. What it needs is the Kingston finish. I'd say we should raise the trading level a touch, bring in furs, possibly jewelry, overhaul the Fancy Goods and Haberdashery, give it a really good Lingerie section, perhaps introduce some household Soft Goods of the highest quality. . . . Essentially, it's a small store. What we need to do is to give it elegance, so that it's a worthy junior partner to Kingstons, trading a bit above Selfridges, letting him beat us on price but never on quality. . . . Selfridge always claims his appeal is directed at women. . . ."

"And you plan to steal some of those that have responded," said Thomas with a chuckle.

"You make me sound like a marauding pirate, Father."

"And so you are where Charles is concerned."

"All right," Ramsay conceded. " 'Tempt' is a better word than 'steal.' I intend to tempt the women with taste, with a flair for fashion, with a knowledge of fine things. . . . Harris' will become a store for the elite."

Thomas was looking ahead down the road, wondering if Ramsay was not driving a little too fast. "And you can't wait to see Charles's face when he discovers you've grabbed it from under his nose, can you?"

"I think sometimes, Father," Ramsay answered a touch suavely, "that you overestimate the competition between us. . . . I'd want that store even if Charles had never joined Selfridge."

"And if Selfridges wasn't there . . . ?" Thomas queried.

"How can you ask that, Father?" said Ramsay, easing his speed as they approached Gerrard's Cross. "Selfridge has changed everything."

He had, too. Thomas had just been provoking his son a bit mischievously. For Kingstons had been locked in combat with Selfridge ever since the American had opened his huge white stone store in March 1909—and challenged Thomas for the position of primacy, previously uncontested, in the British retail scene. His aim had been to create in the capital of the British Empire nothing less than the finest store in the world—which Thomas, of course, believed he himself was already directing in Sloane Street. Not only were Selfridge's ideas grandiose, even Olympian—"Is it to be a shop or a Greek temple?" inquired one investor on being shown the drawings for the building. with its 848-foot frontage of Ionic columns—but he also had the astonishing notion that the hard-sell techniques that had been so successful in Chicago would be effective in the sophisticated world of London.

His promotion campaign, before he even began to trade, was on a scale never seen before in London, with 104 full-page announcements in eighteen national newspapers, designed by noted artists.

The opening ceremony had featured all the showmanship that had made Selfridge famous in Chicago. From a position above the main entrance an army trumpeter had sounded a fanfare, and draped silk curtains, concealing the twenty-one windows, had parted to reveal a series of fashion displays presented against backcloths painted after the style of such romantics as Fragonard and Watteau.

The doors had opened, and the waiting crowd had rushed into an interior of soft lights, muted colors, banks of flowers and the strains of music from hidden violinists.

His sales techniques were even more dramatic than expected. He established a Cosmetics Counter near the entrance, openly selling rouge and lipsticks, which in other stores were provided only discreetly from under the counter in the Perfume Department. He sold men's collars in quarter sizes instead of the usual half fraction; he placed enormous orders for certain lines of merchandise so that he could, for example, in one promotion, offer stockings in three hundred different shades and guarantee to fit any foot. By skillful and elaborate display he created so big a demand for fancy jewelry, until then sold on the periphery of the Jewelry Section, that it soon merited its own department.

Charles, of course, had joined the Selfridge organization at an early stage. Instinctively, as he had discovered the plans for the new store, he had experienced the doubts that were being voiced by the whole trade. Would the British accept these methods? But he was soon won by Selfridge's confident enthusiasm.

From the start, Thomas was completely skeptical of his prospects. "I give him a year at the most," he forecast to Charles, knowing that the project would have to be an immediate success because Selfridge's financing was limited. Ramsay, however, believed the new competitor would be a serious threat to Kingstons and cause radical changes in the way the London stores were directed. He began to press Thomas to increase their budget for advertising, but gained only grudging minor concessions.

Charles's position was a strange one, for he was party to Selfridge's inner counsels at the same time as being the son of a substantial shareholder in Kingstons. What was more, he knew that Ramsay would not hesitate to exploit any information that he gained from him during their frequent social contact as close friends—as indeed happened in January when Ramsay cajoled Selfridge's exact opening date out of Charles in a moment at dinner when he was off his guard.

The next day, as Ramsay was lunching with his father, he asked, "We haven't actually settled the date for the celebration of Kingstons' birthday, have we, Father?" It was, of course, forty years since Thomas had opened the first shop in 1869, and plans to honor it had been under discussion for a long time.

"The date is September sixteenth," Thomas answered.

"I know, Father . . . I meant the date when our celebrations might start. . . . I suppose there's no reason why they shouldn't begin during the last week in March and continue through the year. . . ."

"The week that Selfridges opens?"

Ramsay nodded with a smile. "We could have our first concert then—one of a series, perhaps. . . ."

Thomas nodded ruminatively. "Well," he said cautiously, "our concerts have been quite popular in the past. . . ."

"I'm not speaking of string quartets, Father . . . or piano recitals . . . I mean a full orchestra, the best orchestra. . . . I'm talking of the London Symphony."

Thomas was astonished. "Ramsay, that'd be an enormous cost! Why, there must be eighty musicians in the London Symphony!"

"Exactly. . . . Then we'd need the best soloists—singers, pianists, violinists—names that would really attract the crowds. . . ."

Ramsay knew how to appeal to his father. Concerts—big, prestigious concerts—expensive though they might be, would strike at the newcomer in exactly the right way—emphasizing the wealth, dignity and taste of Kingstons without *appearing* to seek outright battle with an opponent who, though big, was in a different league.

When Charles saw the Kingstons announcements, which began appearing three weeks before the Selfridges opening, he just laughed. "What are you hoping to do," he mocked, "boost your sales of violins and oboes? You'll have to do more than that to hold off the competition."

"Competition?" queried Ramsay. "There *is* no competition!"

On Selfridge's opening day, Thomas called on him with Ramsay to wish him success. "I'm deeply impressed," he told him, "especially with your displays," as indeed he had been.

"But you don't think I'll make it, do you, Mr. Kingston?" asked Selfridge, smiling.

The directness of the question embarrassed Thomas. "I have some doubts that you've correctly assessed the nature of the people of London," he conceded.

"I'll prove you wrong, Mr. Kingston. . . . Within ten years, my sales and profits will be higher than yours."

Thomas was astonished. "Mr. Selfridge, I don't know what to say. I presume you saw our results announced last month. . . ."

"I did," said the American, looking at him with serious gray eyes behind the steel-rimmed spectacles. "Profits of just over two hundred thousand . . . sales of three million . . . No other store in Britain is near you—but *I* will be. Just give me a couple of years to get established and absorb our initial costs. . . ."

"But surely," said Thomas, "you don't think we'll be sitting still during that time. . . ."

"Oh, I'm positive you won't." He grinned slightly mischievously. "I'll tell you what, Mr. Kingston . . . We'll have a wager . . . a thousand pounds that my profits are more than half yours by 1915 . . . and if I've overtaken you by 1920, then you'll give me a model of my store in solid silver. If I haven't, then I'll present you with a silver model of yours. . . . How about that? Will you accept the bet?"

Thomas laughed. "You're certainly a character, Mr. Selfridge. . . . What's your view, Ramsay?"

"Well, Father," said Ramsay, "you can hardly refuse a challenge like that."

"All right, Mr. Selfridge," said Thomas. "We accept. . . . I only hope I'll still be alive to receive the model . . . *and* that your store'll still be trading to finance it."

"There's no doubt about that," Selfridge responded.

"I hope not," Thomas answered.

For months after that, Selfridge's confidence seemed ridiculous. He had taken an enormous gamble, needing to trade at very high levels from his opening day, which meant that he had to maintain his huge advertising costs. Other stores responded with cautious increases in their own budgets. Certainly the Kingstons sales did not appear to be suffering from the competition, and the concerts were a great success, attracting many customers to the store.

The strain on Selfridge's resources became evident very soon. He had to go to the London stock market for funds with a loan issue. His promotions became more elaborate, only confirming Thomas' view that his sales were below target, even though he conceded that some of his ideas were clever. At the end of July, for example, Louis Blériot became the first man to fly the English Channel. Within hours, Selfridge had astonished the whole of London by announcing that Blériot's aircraft was on view in the basement of his store. It attracted vast crowds and won the universal approval of the press, who knew a scoop when they saw one. "He's getting desperate," Thomas told Ramsay. "What in the world's this sort of thing got to do with selling merchandise or building a reputation?"

Thomas kept Kingstons' responses, when he made them, on a dignified, solid, even somber note. His favorite theme of the "citizen soldier," with its essentially English national message, was often featured in the store's advertising.

Certainly Selfridge did not fail in his first year, as Thomas had predicted, but his position was fragile. The price of the company's loan stock began to drop, reflecting the anxiety of investors. Angrily, Selfridge accused other store owners of deliberately talking the price down, even selling to add impetus to the fall—as Charles, who loyally shared his employer's defensive hostility, suddenly charged Ramsay one evening when they were all dining at Cadogan Place.

Thomas had never before been so angry with Charles. "Will you kindly repeat that abominable allegation, Charles?" he said, glaring.

Charles paled, but faced him out. "It's common knowledge, Mr.

Kingston, that our competitors believe Mr. Selfridge'll fail, even want him to fail. . . ."

"And you think *I* want him to fail . . . or would stoop to such actions if I did? . . . You believe *that*, Charles, after all the years you've known me?"

"No, of course he doesn't think that, Thomas," said Lillian.

"No, Mr. Kingston," Charles conceded after a moment, "I don't. . . ."

And, because Ramsay knew the reason for the hesitation, he asked lightly, with a gleam in his eye, "Surely you don't think *I* would, Charlie . . . ?"

Charles looked at him. "I think you're capable of it, Ramsay, which your father isn't, but I withdraw the charge. . . ." He turned back to Thomas. "I apologize, Mr. Kingston. . . ."

Selfridge did not change his methods, and despite the predictions of Thomas and his many other critics, he survived, though it was not until his third year, in 1912, that he managed at last to scramble into profit—less than £6,000 against Kingstons' £250,000.

However, by that April morning in 1913, one year later, when Thomas and Ramsay were driving to London, Selfridge had suddenly reported a great leap forward, with earnings of more than £104,000—which made the first stage of his wager that he would be at half Kingstons' figures by 1915 rather less of an absurdity, though they too had enjoyed a good year. On one point, too, there was no doubt whatever: Oxford Street had become a very different place as a trading area since Selfridge had opened, and there were opportunities to be exploited—which was why there was competition for the Harris store.

"This'd be a very big move," Thomas ruminated, "a very important change in policy. . . . It's not the sort of thing we should attempt in a hurry . . . certainly not with only a few hours' notice. . . . There'll be other stores, Ramsay. The end of the world won't come if we don't buy Harris'. . . ."

"No," said Ramsay with an angry shrug. "But Selfridge'll buy it."

"Does it matter that much if he does?"

"No," Ramsay answered, an almost petulant note in his voice. "It doesn't matter that much if we don't open a new department for which the time seems opportune. . . . It doesn't matter that much if we don't do many things . . . but if we go on not doing things because it doesn't matter that much, then we'll end up with a tired business. . . . You'd never have built Kingstons with such an attitude, would you?

You'd have stayed running a little shop until someone else with better methods and better merchandise took the cream off your trade." He paused, uncertain that his argument was having any impact on his father. "Like that poor old . . ." he began, intending to refer to White, who had committed suicide, but decided against it. "Like many old small shopkeepers," he said lamely.

"I'm glad your sense of discretion came to the fore," said Thomas a little grimly, for he still felt moments of guilt about White.

"Father," said Ramsay, changing to a lower gear as they approached Gerrard's Cross, "you often speak of the importance of hunch and feeling. . . . Well, I've got a very strong hunch about the Harris store."

"Your 'sprashun?" said Thomas with a smile. "Well, I'll grant you know exactly what you want to do with the store. . . . I suppose you realize how important this is—to *you*, I mean? If it fails, it'll be years before the board'd accept such a move again."

"It won't fail, Father."

"You've no doubts whatever?"

"None." He increased speed as they reached the open road and changed to top gear.

For a few moments Thomas was silent again. "At a hundred thousand the price is too high," he said, "even with the freehold. But if you could get it for eighty, perhaps eighty-five . . . then I suppose there's no real reason why you couldn't get agreement in principle with Harris today. . . ."

Ramsay was astonished. "You mean you'll back it, Father?" he said, looking at him with an incredulous smile on his face.

"Hey, watch where you're going!" exclaimed Thomas. "You won't be able to negotiate anything if we're both in hospital. . . . There'll be a lot of details to work out later . . . and you'll need board approval before you can sign a contract, of course. . . ."

"I've already asked Sidney to call an emergency meeting of the board for this afternoon."

Thomas laughed. "You haven't wasted any time, have you?"

Ramsay shook his head. "There was no time to waste," he said in a determined tone of voice.

With Thomas' support, Ramsay won the approval of the board at a short meeting held in the early afternoon. By four he was having tea with Harris. Within an hour Kingstons had bought its first subsidiary store—right in the heart of the territory of its big new rival.

He shook hands with Harris and left his office. He was, in fact, closing the door behind him when he saw Charles approaching along the corridor. A broad confident grin spread across Ramsay's face, and there was mockery in the way he shook his head at his rival. "You're too late, Charlie," he said. "I've just bought it."

"You have?" answered Charles with a light smile. "Well, I'm delighted. . . . I did hope you would."

Ramsay was taken aback. "What do you mean?" he demanded.

"Well, you know how Mr. Selfridge always welcomes competition . . . good competition. . . . He thinks it helps trade. When he heard that the Harris store was going up for sale, he remarked to me what a wonderful thing it'd be if Kingstons were to buy it . . . so I said I thought it was just possible I might be able to arrange that. . . ."

"You mean Selfridges wasn't in the market for it at all?" demanded Ramsay hotly.

"Good heavens, no. . . . Too far away for us. . . . Ramsay, old chap, may I offer you my congratulations. . . ." He held out his hand but Ramsay ignored it. "You rotter!" he declared, and walked past him angrily.

When he reached the end of the passage, he turned in fury to see Charles still watching him, a happy smile on his face. "By God, I'll get back at you for this, Charles," he said.

"Why?" asked Charles innocently. "Don't you want the store?"

"Of course! . . . I'm going to do great things with this store. . . . In a few months you won't recognize it."

"Then you should be grateful to me, shouldn't you?"

Ramsay hesitated. Then suddenly he smiled too. "Why, yes, Charlie, now I come to think of it . . . perhaps I should."

· 4 ·

Even to Dora, who was only thirty-seven, the music was alien. With that harsh blare of the saxophone, the stridency of the trumpet, the thumping of the bass, the fast beat of the drums, it induced in her a strange mixture of feelings. She found it stimulating. It made her want to leap to her feet and step, to that syncopated rag rhythm, into the Castle walk or the turkey trot or the zig-zag. But unlike younger women, she was not entirely happy about the correctness, even the morality, really, of this impulse. The music touched nerves in her that she was uncertain should be touched—nerves that were not stirred in the same way by the waltz or even such overactive dances as the polka. And if rag produced a reaction such as this in her, then what, she wondered, must it do to Thomas and May, whom she could now see

making their way toward her near the fast-moving dancers on the
floor?

The singer cut in again. "C'mon and hear! C'mon and hear! Alexander's Ragtime Band! C'mon and hear! C'mon and hear! It's the best
band in the land. . . ." Again the instrumentalists brayed in cacophonic
unison, the drummer and bass player seemed to increase the beat marginally and the dancers responded, all elbows, quickening their
movements.

It was a big charity ball, held in Selfridge's Palm Court restaurant,
promoted with all the panache that everyone had now come to expect
of him. It was inevitable that a jazz band should be among those
playing, for it was the newest thing, and no one could ever accuse
Gordon Selfridge of not being up to date. The occasion was fashionable, too. A number of women who were often pictured in the society
magazines were at the tables or on the dance floor. There were well-
known personalities from the worlds of entertainment, racing and even
politics. It was clear evidence, if any was needed, that Selfridge had
become accepted.

Thomas and May reached the table as the ragtime number reached
its peak. All the men in the party stood up, unable to make their
greetings heard above the crescendo. Then abruptly the number
ended, and the jazz band began to concede the dais to more traditional
musicians. "Quite a noise, eh, Dora?" said Thomas, sitting beside her.
"You been out there dancing it?"

"No, Pahpah. . . . I'm not quite sure about ragtime. Perhaps I'll get
used to it in time. . . ."

"I doubt if I will," he grunted, "but I suppose at my age that's
what you'd expect. . . . New music for a new era. . . . We live in
times of great challenge . . . strike after strike . . . The House of
Lords stripped of its powers—most of them, anyway . . . and your
suffragettes . . . setting fire to pillar-boxes, burning people's homes . . .
It's a revolution, isn't it? . . . a basic change in the framework and
values of society as we've known it. You're still connected with them,
I suppose, those suffragettes? . . ."

"Yes, Pahpah," she agreed quietly.

"That's always surprised me," he said. "I don't understand it . . .
certainly not now they're not even civilized any longer. . . ."

"It *is* more difficult now," she agreed.

He glanced at her suddenly. "Too much even for you to stomach?" he asked.

"I don't agree with extreme militancy," she said.

"You seem to have come round to your mother-in-law's view. . . .

Well, at least you've kept to your bargain . . . you haven't been arrested again. . . . Good gracious, they're actually playing a waltz. . . . Will you give me the pleasure?"

"Of course, Pahpah . . . I'd be delighted. . . ."

"I thought they'd probably be doing this tango thing," said Thomas as he escorted her to the floor. "Do you hold tango teas, Dora? That's the latest, isn't it?"

"No, but I expect I'll have to when Jane gets a bit older."

"There'll be something different by then. . . ." As they began to dance to the waltz music, Dora found it strangely comforting, not least because Thomas was still a good dancer, but mainly because it was familiar, and just at present, with the situation in the WSPU, she needed solid ground on which to stand. And Thomas, for all their occasional battles, was indisputably solid ground.

Over the past few months, the WSPU had been rent by a conflict that had been deeply disturbing to Dora. The leaders had split over the issue of violence, which was constantly escalating, and Mrs. Pankhurst and her fiery daughters had now won the struggle—which meant that there would be more of the arson, more of the acts of vandalism that Dora deplored.

She had considered resigning, but kept postponing a decision because her belief in the cause had not wavered. Strangely, she had remained friends with Emily Davison, who over the years had become even more passionately and ascetically militant than ever. She had now been in prison six times, endured forcible feeding to break her hunger strikes, but continued, on release, to set fire to houses and the contents of mailboxes. She had tried to die dramatically by throwing herself over the staircase of a Manchester prison, but though badly injured, had survived, with her hollow eyes and bright red hair, to continue the fight.

Her feelings about the need for martyrdom were coldly rational. "It'll create the necessary atmosphere for acceptance of the cause," she had assured Dora. "They couldn't stand a death . . . the public wouldn't let them. . . ."

"But martyrdoms have not always achieved their aim."

"This one would," she had insisted. "I'm positive of it."

"And you're willing to be that martyr?" Dora had queried, knowing that even the Pankhursts were opposed to so extreme a form of action.

"Not just willing," Emily had replied with great seriousness, "eager. . . . You don't understand that because you're not committed. For me the cause is everything, but it's not for you . . . there are other things in your life, more important things . . . your husband, your children, even your store. . . ." And as always when she talked with Emily, it made Dora feel ashamed.

The music stopped, and Dora returned to the table with Thomas. "That was enjoyable, Pahpah," she said.

"I found it so too," he answered, "but your thoughts were far away . . . with your suffragettes, no doubt. . . ."

She smiled. "Was it as obvious as all that?"

"I've never heard you express such doubts before," he answered. "It must be hard. . . . But I shouldn't worry too much. It'll be irrelevant soon . . . we'll have far bigger things to worry about."

"Bigger things, Pahpah?" she said, not understanding.

"There's going to be a war, Dora. . . ."

"Aren't you being a bit pessimistic?"

He shook his head. "There can't help being a war, Dora. All the great powers increasing their forces . . . There's us building our dreadnoughts . . . four this year, isn't it? . . . Germany trying to catch us up . . . And only in March, the Reichstag in Berlin voted to raise the annual intake of conscripts to three hundred forty thousand. That's almost twenty-five percent in one year. . . . There are people who think it'll be over quickly. I don't see how it can be with so many nations already joined by allegiances . . . Germany, Russia, Austria, France, us, Italy, and who knows what other countries'll be drawn in. . . . The available resources are immense. . . ."

He broke off with a desolate shrug, and she was silent for a moment. Then she said, "Thank God Robert's too young."

He nodded. "And Ramsay's too old. . . . Certainly we can't spare him. . . . It'll be the climax of all the changes we're witnessing. . . ."

"Good heavens, Kingston, I didn't expect to find you here. . . . Do you think Selfridge'll let you out alive?" They turned to see a smiling, impish face framed by a shock of gray hair. "Why, it's like finding Arthur Balfour in the Reform Club."

"My dear Chancellor," Thomas greeted him warmly, flattered to have been approached by a Cabinet Minister, and got to his feet. "What a pleasant surprise. May I please introduce you to my daughter-in-law, Mrs. Kingston. . . . Dora, this, of course, is Mr. Lloyd George. . . ."

"It's a great pleasure to meet you, Mrs. Kingston," he said with a warm smile. "What I've heard about you has in no way been overstated." Lloyd George was well known for his keen appreciation of women, but she was uncertain how to reply to him.

Charles rescued her. "Forgive me," he said to the two men, "but they're playing a tango, Dora. . . ."

The Chancellor excused her with a gesture of sad but resigned grace and turned to talk to May, who had left the other end of the table to join them. When he had moved on, May said, "I think, Thomas Kingston, that when the Chancellor of the Exchequer goes out of his way to seek your company on an occasion such as this . . . well, clearly he, at least, sees you as an important man. . . ."

"He's a good fellow," responded Thomas, as though unimpressed by the honor, "and a most amusing companion."

· 5 ·

When James returned to America in late May, he was driven to Waterloo in Thomas' Daimler. Since Harrow involved only a short detour, he told the chauffeur to stop at the school so that he could say goodbye to Robert, who was now back there for the summer term. They had found each other congenial company while staying at the Hall, often taking long walks or rides together.

Robert was pleased and flattered by James's visit. "You'll write to me, won't you, James?" he asked. By common consent he had dropped the "Uncle."

"Of course," James answered, "but they'll be pretty dull letters. Metal futures don't make the spirited reading of wars in Mexico or gold hunting in the Yukon. . . ."

"We've talked of much more than that," said Robert. "After all, it's not your surroundings that matter, is it? I mean, I may tell you about the cricket eleven and how I do in my exams . . . but it's what you think, what you read, what you believe that's important, isn't it?"

James laughed as he got into the car. "I'll try to conjure up some great thoughts to write to you . . . some suitable amateur philosophy. . . ."

Robert waved as the car moved off and wondered how many years it would be before he saw him again. In fact, it was not to be as long as he expected.

· 6 ·

"They're under starter's orders," reported Harry. He was studying the horses in the distance through his binoculars as they milled behind the starting line on the far side of Epsom Heath.

"I can't see Meridian," said Ramsay, also with binoculars to his eyes, as he searched among the jockeys for Thomas' colors, which, like those of the store, were blue and yellow.

"He's there," said Harry, "where he's drawn . . . number seven . . . moving forward quietly with the line. . . . They look all set to go. . . . Oh, God, that chestnut's turned right around. . . . The starter's ordered them back for a new approach to the line. . . ."

For a few seconds the tension eased in the box. All the men except Harry took their binoculars from their eyes. The jockeys would have to turn their excited horses and reposition them farther back before again moving forward slowly in as good a line as it was possible to persuade thirty-three highly strung thoroughbred racehorses to form.

It was a day that none of them would ever forget—the 131st Derby, the most grueling race in the British flat season, possibly in the world, and a horse bred at Quainton was among the runners. To May, it was still barely credible. In fact if anyone had told her on that day forty-four years ago when she had first set eyes on Thomas that he would ever own a horse running in the Derby, she would have thought him mad—*or* that they would be able to watch it cantering up the course with Anmer, whose jockey's colors of purple and scarlet indicated that he was owned by the King—*or* that Lord Rosenberry, one of the leading figures of the turf, would have passed Thomas in the paddock earlier with an "Afternoon, Kingston."

Dora, to whom Thomas had been a figure of stature ever since she had first known him, had thoughts of a different nature. She sipped her champagne as she stood with all those Kingstons—and Lillian and Charles, who were almost Kingstons—and surveyed the scene which, from her elevated position in the grandstand box, lay at her feet. She glanced below her at the gentlemen in their morning suits and toppers, with their ladies in the tight ankle-revealing silk skirts carrying their parasols—and then she looked across to the far side of the rich green turf of the course at the enormous crowd which, packed tight round the bookmakers' placards, reached fifty or sixty lines deep, toward the bend of Tattenham Corner. Beyond the crowd were row after row of motor buses, motor cabs and private motorcars, with here and there the odd wagon, carriage or four-in-hand coach. Higher on the heath was the traditional Derby Fair, with its caravans and tents and booths constructed round the central feature of the carousel.

The voice of that huge crowd was a loud hum, pierced by the hoarse yells of the bookmakers, still shouting the odds even at that late moment. There was music from a band near the grandstand, mingling with the brassy strains of the more distant carousel.

There was no day in Britain like Derby Day. It encompassed all sections of British life, from the highest rungs of the social scale to the lowest, from Cockneys to the King, who was, of course, present that afternoon to cheer on his own horse—although naturally the spectators were all ranged, on both sides of the course, in the areas that were proper to their station.

As Dora looked at the panorama of that vast sea of happy, excited faces, she found it hard to believe that Thomas' predictions at the Selfridges' Ball were soundly based. Where was the revolution? Where was the disintegration of the whole structure of society? How could there possibly be a war embracing all the major powers of Europe?

"They're almost there," reported Harry, his face taut as he watched intently through his binoculars as the horses moved forward once again toward the starting line. "As long as that chestnut . . ." he began anxiously. ". . . They're off!"

All the men in the box had binoculars to their eyes. "It's Aboyeur, isn't it?" asked Ramsay after a few seconds. "Mr. Cunliffe's colors are white with black, aren't they?"

"Aboyeur's among the leaders," agreed Harry. "I can see Shogun and Nimbus and Craganour and Day Comet. . . . There are about eight of them at the front, all racing close . . . then there's a gap . . ."

"Where's Meridian?" asked May eagerly, for the small mother-of-pearl glasses that she was using did not have the power of the men's binoculars.

"He's not far behind the leaders," answered Thomas. "I'm right, aren't I, Harry? . . . That is him, isn't it? . . . My sight's getting worse every day, May. . . ."

"Yes, Father . . . he's there behind the leading bunch . . . going well, though I'd like him a bit closer. . . . They're past the two-furlong post. . . . lengthening out now as the hill really tests them . . . I think it's still Aboyeur just in front. . . . Shogun's there still . . ."

"What about the King's horse?" asked Dora. At that distance it was hard to distinguish one jockey from another.

"Amner?" queried Harry. "He's way back in the field. . . . The pace's too hot for him . . . bound to be . . . he's not up to it. . . ."

"Where's Meridian now?" asked May.

"Lying about ten back. . . . He's moving forward a bit . . . about time, too . . ."

"Come on, Meridian!" shouted Robert, who had been given a day off from Harrow in view of the importance to the family of this year's Derby.

"I don't think he'll be able to hear you just yet, Robert," said Thomas with a smile.

Dora could see the horses more easily now as they raced down the hill toward Tattenham Corner. For a few seconds, as they reached the lower ground, all but the jockeys' heads were hidden for a moment by the crowd massed behind the rails. Then, as the leaders entered the straight, they came into full view again. "It's Aboyeur on the rails from Day Comet . . ." reported Harry. "He's being challenged hard. . . . There's a horse coming through. . . . It's Craganour . . . Craganour's coming through. . . ."

A deep roar was swelling from the crowd on both sides of the course at Tattenham Corner, growing in volume as the front group of six or seven horses cleared the bend and raced up the straight. Then suddenly there was a changed note in that great massed howl. Dora detected it through Harry's excited reporting of the battle between the leaders, through May's insistent demanding of the position of Meridian, through Robert's cries of encouragement, even through the crescendo-ing voice of the enormous human throng packed near the grandstand as the horses raced toward them. Harry must have sensed it too, or perhaps—experienced racegoer as he was—the unusual movements farther back caught his attention. "By God!" he exclaimed. "Someone's on the course. . . . A woman's on the course. . . . A horse is down! . . ."

Dora knew who it was. Even in the second before she had grabbed Ramsay's binoculars, knocking her hat awry because their short strap was still round his neck, she knew the horror of what had happened. She saw the three of them lying there on the course—the horse on his side, the jockey with his leg pinned under his mount, and the red-haired woman on her back, knees bent up double, arms outstretched in the position of crucifixion. She saw other runners, still racing, coming up behind, one animal having to swerve suddenly, seeming at that distance to cross his legs to avoid the obstructions. Then the fallen horse struggled to his feet and began to canter forward, the jockey hanging from the stirrup, where his boot was caught. Because he was so small and racing stirrups were strapped so high up the saddle, he was swinging without touching the ground, his blouse of the royal purple and scarlet outlined against the green of the turf. Then he fell clear and the horse galloped on.

It was almost as though Dora had two brains, one totally concentrated on the supine twisted figure with outstretched arms that she knew was Emily, the other absorbing everything else that was continu-

ing around her—the yelling of the crowd climaxing as the leading
horses raced past the grandstand in a flash of color, the comments of
the shocked people in the box. "It's the King's horse. . . . The jockey
must be dead. . . . Steward's inquiry . . ." Dora watched the police
surrounding Emily's body, waving back the public who had ducked
under the rails to gain a closer view of that macabre figure. . . . She saw
the riderless Anmer galloping by with saddlecloth flapping and stirrups
flying . . . the ambulance driving down the course . . . and then the
placard, held up above the heads of the dense crowd at Tattenham
Corner, worded "Votes for Women," which told everyone else in
Thomas' box what Dora already knew.

She found May looking at her with a face creased by shocked
pain. "Is there to be no end to it, Dora?" It was a question marked not
so much by criticism of Dora herself as by despair of human futility.

"No, Mother, I don't think so. . . ." Then she added quietly, "I
know her . . . she's a friend . . . mad, but a friend. . . ." She spoke of her
as though she still lived, though she doubted this. May just reached out
and squeezed her hand very tightly.

When Dora saw the ambulance return up the course, she went
down to the big courtyard behind the grandstand through which the
vehicle would pass to reach the road. Emily was not dead, a racecourse
official told her, but unconscious and severely injured.

Ramsay drove her at once to Epsom Cottage Hospital, but they
would not let her see her. They were, she was told, preparing to
operate.

Emily died two days later, and the funeral procession that passed
through streets packed tight with silent sympathizers would, Dora
knew, have met all her aspirations for it. It was a very long column
of mourning suffragettes, all wearing white, that walked four abreast
to St. George's Church in Hart Street for a memorial service before
proceeding to Kings Cross Station, from which the coffin was transported by train to Morpeth, Emily's family home in Northumberland.

For Dora, the impact of Emily's death was immense, but it did not
change her belief that it was a wasted death, that it would in no way
hasten the day when women would gain the vote. In fact, despite the
emotions it engendered in her, the funeral march crystallized Dora's
decision about the WSPU.

At Kings Cross, when the coffin had been laid in the train, Dora
departed alone. She called a cab and drove to the store, where she
asked to see Thomas. She stood in her white dress in the doorway of
his office. "Pahpah," she said. "At last, I'm going to obey your request
to me . . . I'm resigning from the Union."

Thomas stood up and smiled affectionately at her. "You mean I shan't have a rebel for a daughter-in-law any longer?"

She nodded, her expression serious. "It won't work this way, will it? . . . I think we've got to find some means of proving that we must have the vote, that it's intolerable for it to be denied us . . . by doing, by illustration, though I don't know how. . . ."

"I do," said Thomas. He moved round the desk and, knowing how near she was to tears, he put his arms round her and held her lightly. "When the war starts, a lot of men will go to fight . . . a lot more than most people think, I'm afraid. . . . That'll be your time, for women'll have to take their place. Then, women will be doing, illustrating . . ." Holding her by the shoulders, he moved her from him gently to the length of his arms and surveyed her, a tender expression in his eyes. "White suits you," he said. "You should wear it more often. . . ."

For a moment she did not speak. Then, with the emotion graveling her voice, she said, "Do you know what I was just thinking, Pah-pah? I suddenly remembered how terrified I was at the prospect of first meeting you. . . . I expected to find a stern, grim Victorian gentleman. . . ."

"Well, you found a stern, grim Victorian gentleman, didn't you?"

"Did I?" she queried. Then she leaned forward and, to his surprise, kissed him lightly on the lips. "I don't think I did." And she turned and left the office.

CHAPTER THIRTEEN

June 1915

· I ·

As usual, as they reached the store, the chauffeur slowed the Daimler to a crawl so that Thomas could study the twelve big windows they would pass before eventually halting in front of the central entrance. That morning he found them bright and well designed, which pleased him especially on that day of all days because there were likely to be visitors from other stores.

Ten months before, when war had broken out, Thomas had declared that the public would best be served by a policy of "business as usual"—to be reflected in particular, he insisted, in displays that should be as colorful as those in peacetime, as a contrast to the somber background of hostilities.

He had, of course, been one of the few people in those strangely blind, escapist prewar years who had seen the inevitability of the huge conflict that had now enveloped most of Europe, and from the moment the guns had started firing, he had been utterly skeptical of the common expectation that it would be over by Christmas. But even he had not predicted how grim that reality would be. He had not envisaged the sheer volume of casualties, listed daily in *The Times*, or the fact that already, after so short a time, most families would have been robbed of at least one loyal son, only too eager to rush to the front to fight for his country. And although he had spoken to Dora at the Selfridges' Ball of the enormous resources of the combatants, he had not foreseen for one moment that the force of 150,000 troops that General Sir John French had shipped so confidently across the English Channel in 1914 would soon have grown to more than a million men.

Nor had Thomas had any conception of the nature that the fighting would assume—the squalor of trench life, with its rats and slime and unburied corpses and, in recent weeks, the horror of those yellow-green clouds of chlorine gas that had drifted across No-Man's-Land at Ypres, to flood men's lungs with fluid by chemical reaction, so that they literally drowned.

As a family the Kingstons had been spared the toll of sacrifice, because all its menfolk were either too old or too young to answer the call—unless James, who was a Rawlings to everyone except Thomas and Lillian, was regarded as a Kingston. Certainly James's response to the war had been exemplary. As soon as hostilities had broken out, he had returned to Engand from Chicago to join the army, even though he had reached the ceiling age of thirty-eight, and within months he had been dispatched with his regiment to France.

The Kingstons were almost as proud of him as the Rawlingses, quite apart from Thomas' special reason for pride, for the two families had become closely meshed. They had shared much tragedy and sorrow and joy. June 3, 1915, however, would always stand out as a poignant, unique day in their joint histories.

Even breakfast at Cadogan Place was touched by a note of melancholy, although it should have been an occasion of considerable pleasure. For Thomas' name was there in the King's Birthday Honors List in the press that morning—as he had been informed it would be, which was how he had been able to make plans to hold a large celebratory dinner that evening in the Grand Restaurant, to be attended by family, friends and all buyers employed in Kingstons' two stores. At last he had been awarded the accolade, the baronetcy, that would crown his life of achievement. "What a wonderful thing for the store," May had teased when they had heard.

That morning, however, Robert had been the first person to acknowledge his grandfather's new station. "Good morning, Sir Thomas," he had said brightly with a broad grin as he arrived from Montpelier Square to join them for breakfast.

"Good morning, Robert," Thomas had responded. "However, despite my elevation, I give you leave to continue addressing me by your usual term of affection. . . ."

Even the boy, sixteen and excited, noticed that his grandfather was not as buoyant in mood as he would have expected. "I must say, Grandpapa, you don't seem to be all that pleased about it. . . ."

"Well, it's a sad day too, isn't it?" said Thomas. For that evening's reception had a second purpose: Thomas had decided to make it the occasion for his formal resignation as Managing Director in favor of Ramsay—which meant, of course, even though he would still be Chairman of the Board, that he would be giving up executive control of the company he had founded. He had considered the question for months, changing his mind constantly, but at last he had faced the basic unpleasant fact at its heart. He felt tired far too often. Stores did not thrive under the leadership of tired men.

"I'm afraid he's going to miss it," May remarked to Robert, "but I don't suppose your father'll be kept very short of his advice. . . ."

"You won't be able to understand just how hard it is, Robert," Thomas went on. "But I suppose you'll be doing the same yourself one day—handing over to *your* son. . . ."

Thomas watched his grandson tucking in with enthusiasm to a plateful of kidneys, sausages, bacon and eggs and felt a little happier. Robert was sound material.

He got up from the table. "Well, I suppose I'd better get on with my last day's duties as Managing Director," he said. He walked to the other end of the table and bent down to kiss May. She put her hand to his cheek affectionately and gave him a warm smile to indicate that she knew that this was no ordinary day for him, and with a salute-type wave at his grandson, he left the room.

A few minutes later the Daimler came to a halt at the main entrance of the store, and the commissionaire opened the door for Thomas to alight. "Good morning, Sir Thomas," she said with a bright smile—"she" because all the Kingston commissionaires were now women; and very smart they looked in their military-style blue tunics, skirts that reached to just above their ankles, and round wide-brimmed hats. "Good morning," he answered as he was helped from the car, adding in response to her use of his title, "I see you read the papers. . . ."

"Oh, we all know about it, of course," she said. "We're very proud. . . ."

As Thomas, leaning on his stick, went through the swing doors of the entrance, he found waiting for him a reception committee—alerted by phone of his departure from home. His entire senior management was lined up waiting to greet him, including Ramsay and Sidney, who now stepped forward.

"I'm claiming privilege," he declared, "as the director that's known you longest to give you our 'earty congratulations, Sir Thomas. . . . I'd add that we feel—and I know you'll want us to feel this—that it's not just a personal title vested in you alone . . . it's an honor for us all. . . ."

Thomas was so moved that he could do little but mumble his appreciation, and one by one, rather solemnly, he shook by the hand each man in the line, ending with Ramsay. Then, accompanied by Sidney and his son, he made his way through the crowd of sales staff who had gathered to watch his arrival, acknowledging their greetings by repeatedly nodding his head in their different directions. "We wouldn't appear to be doing much selling just at present," he grunted to Ramsay—then smiled suddenly to show he was jesting.

Even though it was not yet ten A.M. there were already quite a lot of customers in the store—a number of them, as usual, uniformed men on leave—as Thomas conducted a kind of morning round, but with the purpose this time not of commenting on what he saw but of showing himself to the staff, who so clearly wished to view him and express their congratulations. He was touched by how personally, and even possessively, so many of them really did seem to regard his title. "I feel as though I'm their own little baronet," he remarked to Sidney. "Perhaps I should be on display in the Toy Department, with a key in my back. . . ."

The impact of the war on the merchandise and even the layout had, of course, been enormous. There was, in fact, a big department for the "Requisites of War." Sections that in the 'eighties and 'nineties had been supplying officers serving in the colonies now occupied large areas where orders could be accepted for barrack-room furniture, tents and such necessities as haversacks, canteens and commode pails. The Gun Department was much expanded, and notices announced that there was a pistol range available to customers for target practice under the guidance of an ex-army instructor.

During the past weeks, the store had done a big trade in "respirators for bombs that emit poisonous gases"—partly because gas had now become a horrific new weapon at the front, but also because Zeppelin airships had just started bombing the eastern fringes of London and some of the coastal towns. Customers were buying the respirators both to send out to soldier sons, distrusting the army to issue adequate protection, and for home use; for although the Zeppelins had so far attacked only with explosives, gas-filled weapons were an obvious possibility.

At last Thomas reached his office and was about to read his morning mail when he was told that Dora would like to see him. She came in looking radiant, even though she had made every effort to appear severe, with her hair short, and a simple tailored costume. She had been working in the store ever since war had broken out and had now taken over the position, previously carried out by a man, supervising five of the Fashion departments—and, to the surprise of both Ramsay and Thomas, doing it very well. She approached Thomas and kissed him on the cheek in congratulation. "What am I supposed to call you now?" she asked, "Sir Pahpah? . . ." He laughed in response, and she went on

quickly: "I've come to see you on business. . . . I thought you'd be
interested in these. . . ." She placed a layout for a fashion advertisement
in front of him on his desk. "*Lady* magazine has decided to develop
the theme of 'Business as Usual' with a feature in its mid-July issue of
'Holidays as Usual' . . . We thought we'd run these summer dresses. . . .
We're well stocked. . . ."

"You mean you're consulting me?" asked Thomas. "I thought I
was being put out to grass."

"Not until tonight. . . . Anyway, I'll always have a nice hay bag
for you. . . ."

He laughed and took her hand as an old man's privilege. "I think
these are good," he said, studying the designs on the layout, "but then,
I find myself this morning in a rather uncritical mood. . . ."

There was a knock on the door and Ramsay came in. "Have you
time to receive a visitor from America, Father? *And* an emissary from
the opposition?"

Charles entered the room together with Leonard Mansfield, one of
Dora's brothers. It was almost twenty years since Leonard had first
entered Thomas' office with his father. He had now developed into a
large, broad-shouldered man in his early forties, with a clear loud
resemblance to Mansfield Senior. "I cannot tell you, Sir Thomas," he
boomed, advancing toward him with a heavy gait that reminded
Thomas of a buffalo, "what pleasure it gives me to have the privilege
of offering you the congratulations of the whole Mansfield family . . ."
And he shook Thomas' hand with a vigor that jarred his bone joints.

Leonard's arrival in London had been planned for several months.
Ramsay had, in fact, asked Charles to direct Harris' for him, hoping
that a degree of autonomy would remove his objections, but his friend
had just shaken his head. "I'm not reporting to you, Ramsay," he had
said. "Never!" So Ramsay had appointed a young man experienced in
high fashion, and he had done well, giving the store the ambience that
Ramsay had wanted. But he was only thirty and had felt the need to
answer the call to arms, which had made Ramsay think that Leonard
might like to become Harris' temporary chief until the end of the war.
Leonard had leaped at the chance.

Charles joined the big American at Thomas' desk and, with a
rather embarrassed grin, held out his hand too. "Can I add my good
wishes, Sir Thomas. . . . I have to confess it sounds strange . . ."

"It does to me too," said Thomas, "but I hope we'll all get accustomed to it in time."

"Charles thinks he's scored one off us this morning," Ramsay interposed. "I don't suppose you've had time to read the papers yet this morning. . . . Look at this. . . ." He laid an opened copy of the *Daily Mail* on Thomas' desk.

Strangely, the contest between the two men had been boosted, not curbed, by the war, since it had provided a new arena. Kingstons and Selfridges had joined battle to make ever-bigger contributions to the national cause. They provided facilities for all kinds of fund raising, and huge meetings of such organizations as the Sisterhood of Help or the Women's Emergency Corps were held almost daily in their restaurants. The two stores competed fiercely to acquire the most comforts, such as blankets and jerseys, for dispatch to the troops in the trenches —this being the special responsibility of May and a staff of twenty girls who had been given offices in the Kingstons basement. The Grand Restaurant, too, was often the scene of bandage rolling by large teams of female volunteers.

Each fostered special schemes. Selfridge set up a trained force of men from the staff who were too old for service at the front but young enough for useful spare-time support duties at home. During the Battle of the Marne, when Thomas learned there was a shortage of beds in France for the wounded—of whom there were far more, of course, than anyone had expected—Kingstons fitted out a whole base hospital in only three days!

Now, so it appeared from the *Daily Mail* on Thomas' desk, the newest field of contest lay in the sale of official fund-raising War Bonds for the government. Thomas had conceived the idea that Kingstons should sell the bonds and, as an incentive, conduct a lottery of the ticket numbers with a prize, contributed by the store, of fifteen hundred guineas—and it was not, of course, by chance that the announcement was made in the press the day before the Birthday Honors List was published.

But Charles had now capped the move by urging Selfridge to go one better. On this day of all days Selfridge had offered a lottery that was exactly the same as Kingstons' except for the prize, which was no less than five thousand pounds! "By God, Charles," Thomas exclaimed, "can't I even be honored with a title without your trying to steal my thunder?"

"I can assure you, Father," said Ramsay, "that the perfidy has not gone unanswered. This is the first edition of today's *Evening News*. . . ." He held up the newspaper so that they could all see the full-page Kingstons advertisement worded "Kingstons of Sloane Street are delighted to note that a certain rival store has followed their example in

the promotion of War Bonds. They hope that their competitor will
continue to tread the trail that they have blazed."

Before anyone could comment further, however, the telephone
rang on Thomas' desk, and after that there was no more jesting, no
mood remaining of amicable rivalry. For it was May with somber
news. James had been wounded, transported back to England, and was
now in the First London General Hospital at Camberwell. Lillian was
with her in Cadogan Place in a state of near collapse.

"In London already?" queried Thomas. "I'd have thought she'd
have heard from France first. . . ."

"I understand they're bringing them home quickly now," she
answered—"the ones that aren't going back to the trenches within a
few weeks. . . . They need the bed space out there. . . ."

"So he's pretty bad?"

"The telegram didn't say. . . . I phoned the hospital but couldn't
get anything out of them . . . a new convoy of wounded had just come
in and they were being run off their feet. . . . I've been trying to
contact Charles. He ought to go down there and find out exactly what
his condition is, but he isn't in his office. . . ."

"He's here with me now. . . . I'll break it to him," said Thomas.
"Tell Lillian how sorry I am. . . . I'm sure he'll be all right. . . ." He
replaced the receiver and told Charles what little he knew. "You'd
better get over to Cadogan Place to help comfort your mother. . . .
Then I should get down to the hospital at Camberwell just as quickly
as you can."

Charles hurried out of Thomas' room; but in fact, he would not
be the first member of the two families to visit James, for Robert, who
had been with his grandmother when his distraught Aunt Lillian had
arrived, was already on his way there. And, under those unhappy
circumstances it was some time before his absence was even noticed.

· 2 ·

It was a warm, clear day and Robert was particularly conscious of the
sunshine reflected on the river as the cab took him across Vauxhall
Bridge toward Camberwell. For all James's letters had been heavy
with dark winter. Even in the spring, in early May, which was the date
of his last letter, they had been marked by a bleak, bare cold. He had
written a lot about the sun, too, and more often still about the sunsets,
which, in Flanders, he said, were especially dramatic, often becoming
deep red before they faded into the night—but he had done so as a

contrast to a situation that could never be anything but inherently frigid. The beauty, he had explained, had made it worse. The birds still sang, as the sun still shone, over the barren wasteland of death and mutilation, with its constant gunfire; with its soon-learned knowledge that you had to stand completely still when they shot the flares into the sky because movement revealed you to the snipers; with its sensibilities which had become so brutalized that, as James had witnessed that day, men could joke and prank as they passed a dead comrade who had fallen into the trench with one arm outstretched. "How do you do," one had jested, shaking the hand of the corpse. Others, grinning as they went by, had adopted the same macabre theme: "Pleased to meet you, I'm sure. . . . Dr. Livingstone, I presume. . . . Haven't we met somewhere before? . . ."

Since James had called at Harrow before returning to Chicago, he had exchanged many letters with Robert. As he had warned, stockbroking could be dull stuff, especially futures, except just occasionally when the markets erupted. So he had written more about the books he read, his colleagues at work and the people who had rooms in the house where he lived. He had described his ideas and feelings and even made a mild attempt at the "amateur philosophy" he had joked about. He had explored in retrospect his short-lived marriage, his relations with his parents, the role of the store in his childhood—and especially that of Charles, his clever elder brother. He recalled some of what he referred to as his "adventure period"—how clear problems could seem when you were walking your horse quietly round the cattle at night under a starred cloudless sky, how strange he had found the first dead men he had seen in the Yukon because, since they had been buried in snow, the color had stayed in their faces.

Robert had responded with his own thoughts and ideas as, conscious of his lack of experience, he had tried to develop them. James had argued sometimes, though never in any patronizing way; had guided; had encouraged often. Strangely, the discussions in their letters had touched on areas of intimacy that they had never actually spoken of when they were together.

When James had returned to Europe they had seen quite a bit of each other and had continued with the kind of long discussions they had enjoyed at Quainton. James had fallen in love with a Canadian girl named Hazel he had met on the ship during the Atlantic crossing. Robert liked her, and she would join sometimes in their long talks. James had said they would probably marry after the war—"if I survive it," he had added.

To start with, after he had arrived in France, his letters had been marked with shock, for life in the trenches, he said, was in a category of human experience that it was impossible to imagine at second hand.

Toward the end of the winter, a note of quiet desperation had begun to appear in James's letters. He spoke a lot of the sight of the wounded men and of dismembered corpses; of the frogs and mice you could not help stepping on because they were trapped in the trenches; of the constant presence of the rats, which were more mobile; of a strange feeling of remoteness, almost as though the world outside the fighting had no reality. The spring, of course, he wrote, would be the time of the big pushes, the battles. It could happen anytime, of course. It happened often enough when things were quiet—"it," of course, being death or wounding. But obviously "it" was more likely in an attack, whether it was launched by the Allies or by the Germans.

Well, now, Robert realized as the cab rattled over the tramlines of Peckham, "it" had happened to Robert. The realization was strangely cautious, considering all the discussion that had preceded it. The human mind, Robert thought later, was evidently designed to cushion extreme experience, providing time for the impact to become absorbed. For although he had accepted the fact that James was wounded, he had not considered it in any detail. It was as though there were only one state of being wounded, and that state not very serious. It was only as they got to Camberwell High Street that Robert began to think consciously about how badly wounded James might be, to face the fact that the experience that lay before him might be harrowing.

"Sir . . . sir . . ." And Robert realized that the cabby had said the word several times. "This is it, sir, I think . . . the 'ospital. . . . We're 'ere, sir. . . ."

Robert shook himself from his deep thoughts. "Oh . . . sorry . . ." he said.

He got out of the cab and paid the fare—and then stood in a state of some bewilderment in the courtyard amid the bustling activity of arriving and departing taxis and cars, of ambulances parked in line, of blanketed, bandaged patients being borne on stretchers into the main building.

The First London Hospital had been adapted from a peacetime college, the extra bed space needed being provided by huts, erected in adjoining playing fields. It was to one of these huts that eventually, after much inquiry at a crowded reception desk, Robert was at last directed.

The experience was far worse even than anything he had imagined. The hut itself, even before he had found James, was a grotesque antiseptic-smelling bedlam. Gramophones screeched out from all sides of the ward, all playing different records, so that tunes such as "Don't Forget Your Soldier Laddie" competed with "When Irish Eyes Are Smiling." Men groaned in conscious pain, cried out in stupefied nightmare sleep, alerted nurses with such shouts as "He's being sick again, Nurse . . ." or, as one called, as Robert timorously passed the foot of his bed, "Better come and look at this one, Nurse. . . ." There was sudden laughter from another part of the hut that seemed to Robert to be unreal in that setting, to have a maniacal quality.

He never knew how he found him. He passed bed after bed containing men in bandages, often stained red and sometimes slightly green, legs often in traction, men lying still, eyes closed, breathing heavily. He was jostled constantly by rushing nurses and once by porters carrying an unconscious patient on a stretcher to an empty bed. He had a tube in his nose. It was, of course, a surgical ward.

If James had not raised a hand in signal as he passed, Robert would not have stopped. His head and half his face, including one eye, were concealed in bandages, as was one arm, bent at the elbow to his chest under his pajama jacket, so that the sleeve of it was empty. An arch of bedclothes over his legs indicated that one or both of them had suffered wounds.

"Robert . . ." It was a whisper, and he nodded at the boy as though to compensate for the lack of volume in his voice. He pointed with his good arm at a chair between his own bed and that of his neighbor.

"James!" Robert exclaimed, horror mixed with his relief at finding him, and sat down. James beckoned with his finger. "Not easy . . . talk . . ." he whispered.

As Robert moved his chair closer, James was gripped suddenly by a violent fit of hoarse coughing that shook his body and caused him to bow his head. He struggled to sit up to ease the attack, and Robert put his arms round his shoulders to help him. "Thanks . . ." he said, again in a whisper, when once more he could utter words. ". . . Lung . . . lucky one lung's 'lright . . . almost 'lright . . . not dead . . . Lot dead with the gas . . . on the Menin Road. . . . Went on too long . . . snouts are no good if it's long . . . cotton wool dries up . . ."

He was breathing heavily and stopped trying to speak for a moment and smiled—at least, Robert assumed he was smiling, for his lips moved and his one eye lightened. "Your eye . . ." Robert began.

James knew he meant the one covered by the bandage. ". . . 'lright . . . think . . . face bit hurt . . . flash . . . 't's all. . . . Arm, too . . . 'lright . . . leg trouble."

"Leg? . . ." echoed Robert, nerving himself.

"One gone . . . think other's 'lright . . . can't tell . . . feels still there. . . . They say that never stops . . . always feels there. . . ." Then again he was overtaken by a terrible bout of coughing, which obviously hurt him badly, for his one eye closed for a moment and his face was contorted.

This time, when the attack was over, James did not speak, but he nodded his thanks. A nurse came up. "Hope you're not making him talk. He oughtn't to be talking." She rushed off.

"I'll tell the family," said Robert, "explain you're all right. . . . Your mother'll be glad, and Eleanor. . . . Charles is sure to be down later. . . . I'll come back tomorrow."

James shook his head. "Few days . . ." he whispered, and pointed to his throat, then made a sign of writing with his hand. . . . "Letters . . ." Robert took his hand and squeezed it with what he hoped was a gesture of comfort. He was just letting go of it when James increased his grip and drew him toward him. "No Hazel . . . not here . . ."

"I'll tell her to write to you," said Robert, standing up and moving to the end of the bed, "until you're a bit better."

James nodded, lifted his hand a little off the bed in a movement of farewell. He tried to smile. Robert waved and stumbled off down the ward.

On the far side of the courtyard, he saw Charles getting out of a cab. He knew he should tell him where to find James, thus saving him the delays at the inquiry desk, but he could not at that moment bear to speak to him. He turned his back and strode swiftly out the entrance gates, hoping Charles would not see him.

Robert walked much of the way toward the river, trying to assemble his thoughts. At one stage he began to cry, so he ran, hoping that it would prevent anyone from noticing, until the tears stopped. At last, he jumped on a passing tram. As it crossed the river at Vauxhall, the sun was still shining. It had been shining all the time, of course, but it was the bridge over the water that made him think of it again. What would James's life be now? he wondered. What would be the future for any of those men? For any of all those men in all those other huts and all those other hospitals . . . and all those men who *would* soon be in huts like the one he had just seen, and were living meanwhile, with whole limbs, in the kind of wondering gray, cold fear that James had hinted at in his writings, the kind of fear that made letters dark and chill even when the sun was shining or its setting glorious.

The tram stopped at Victoria, and Robert walked the mile or so to the store. For a few minutes he did not enter it, as he had intended, but stood on the far side of the road looking at it, as he had seen his grandfather, and even his father, do so often. But his purpose was different from theirs. Their attention was always focused on the displays, on the effect of the merchandise, on selling. Robert just wanted to assure himself that any of it mattered. Strangely, he suddenly remembered his first talk with James at Quainton when he had questioned the importance of the store. And James had said that of course it was important. But would it really make any difference, Robert asked himself now, if that great terra-cotta building were not there—and if so, any difference to whom? To the family? To the customers? To James, who had lost a lung and a leg and burned his face and arm?

Robert tried to talk to his father first, but the Managing Director —which was what he was already, for all practical purposes—was busy. Robert told his clerk to tell him it was important and would only take a minute, but she returned to say it really was very difficult, but his father would see Robert with his mother for lunch. Several of the clerks were women now, only the older men still being at the desks of the outer office. "It's quarter past twelve already," she said when she saw the boy's agonized look. "Surely it can wait half an hour."

So he went straight to the office of his grandfather, whose clerk was away from his desk. He knocked on the door, which was half open, and peeped round the edge of it. Thomas was talking with a couple of buyers, but when he saw Robert he said immediately, "Hallo, Robert, come in."

"Are you very busy, Grandpapa?"

"Not too busy to see you . . . that's certain. . . . These two gentlemen were just leaving anyway. . . ."

The expression of amiable geniality faded a little from Thomas' face as the door closed behind them. "I've just had your grandmother on the phone. She's been wondering where you were. . . . You ought to have left a message with one of the servants. . . . I suppose you were in the store somewhere? . . ."

"No, Grandpapa," he answered. "I went to see James."

"James? . . ." echoed Thomas, realizing the probable impact on a boy of sixteen, sheltered as Robert had been. "Well," he went on cautiously, "how did you find him?"

"It was awful, Grandpapa. . . ." Briefly, Robert told his grandfather of his experience and the extent of James's wounds.

Thomas shook his head sadly. "This terrible war . . . I'm so sorry . . . It must have been a dreadful experience for you. . . ." And when Robert assented, with a brief nod, Thomas added, "We'll have to see what we can do to help him organize his life."

"Like you did before?" Robert demanded, suddenly angry. "You sacked him, didn't you? . . ."

Thomas was surprised and shocked by the vehemence of the boy's words, and for a second he did not reply. "Not exactly . . ." he answered at last. "Did *he* say he was sacked?"

"Not exactly," Robert said, a little sullenly, deliberately using the same words.

"We all thought it was best for him to leave."

"All, Grandpapa?"

Again Thomas paused. "I wouldn't normally allow you to question me on such a matter, Robert, but today, with the sadness of James . . . well, I suppose things are a bit different, aren't they? . . . When I said 'all,' I mean our two families . . ." He was speaking in a quiet, reasoned tone. ". . . But if the decision had been mine alone, it'd have been the same. . . . When you're sitting in my chair, you'll find you'll have to take decisions sometimes that are often hard and even unhappy. . . ."

"That's what I came to tell you, Grandpapa," Robert said in a voice so quiet it was almost a whisper: "I shan't be sitting in that chair. . . ."

Thomas did not react as strongly as Robert had expected. His hands were lying clasped in front of him on the desk, and the boy saw the fingers tauten. He noted the flash of hurt and wounded anger that came into his grandfather's eyes and then faded as he controlled himself.

"I can't believe you really mean that, Robert," he said, "but you've had a very bad shock at the hospital today, and—"

"It's not that, Grandpapa . . . that's just brought it to a head. . . . I've been thinking about it for a long time. . . ." He hesitated. "I knew it would offend you . . . that's why it's been very hard to say. . . . I know how important it's always been to you for me to follow my father. . . ."

"You've chosen a good day to raise the matter."

"I'm sorry about that too, Grandpapa. I thought about not saying

anything until tomorrow. . . . Believe me, the last thing I want to do is
to hurt you. . . . But I couldn't have sat there at the reception tonight
with you thinking of me in the future, even possibly speaking of it,
without . . . well, I'd have felt a fraud. . . ."

Thomas sat quite still for a moment, looking old, his jowls sagging.
For a second his eyes closed. "You've disappointed me, Robert . . . as
you knew you would. . . . I've watched you grow up. . . . You'd be
good . . . the store'd thrive under your leadership. You have the touch
. . . the . . ."

Robert knew he was tempted to say "sprashun," but the old man
resisted the urge, as his grandson realized gratefully, to avoid using
unfair weapons. "The feel," he said instead. "You've got the feel,
Robert. . . ." He paused for a moment. "I suppose," he went on, "I'm
permitted to ask why . . . why you should wish to abandon this great
opportunity? . . ."

"I don't think I'm cut out for commerce, Grandpapa."

"Commerce?" echoed Thomas as though the word were quite
inadequate to be applied to his store. He got up heavily and moved to
the window, as he did so often when faced with crisis, and looked
down on the people and traffic of Sloane Street. "If you're not cut out
for commerce, Robert," he asked with his back toward him, ". . . if
you're not cut out for the adventure of directing one of the greatest
merchant houses in the world, what *are* you cut out for?"

"I'm not completely sure, Grandpapa, but I think . . . I think I
want to be able to do something . . . try, at least . . . to make the world
a better place."

Thomas turned and, leaning gently back on the window frame,
began to swing his "Albert" on the end of his watch chain. "Strangely,
Robert," he said dryly, "that's what I thought *I'd* been doing for the last
forty-six years."

"Not like that, Grandpapa." Robert was standing a little awkwardly, not quite knowing what to do with his hands. Now he put
them in the pockets of his jacket. "Not on the surface, I mean . . . not
just in ladies' gowns and sets of china tea services and Persian rugs. . . ."

"Isn't that a public service?" The question was sharp. ". . . Supplying Persian rugs and china? . . . And we supply essentials, too—such
things as medicines, and farm machinery, and school clothes, and food
and . . . well you know the range as well as I do."

"Yes, Grandpapa, but don't you see? . . . It's trivial by comparison."

"Trivial!" Thomas snapped out the word with a fury that con-

trasted so sharply with the controlled calm with which he had so far
been speaking that Robert stepped back.

"Only by comparison, Grandpapa," he tried to explain. ". . . I
want to try to stop these awful wars. . . . I want to try to influence
events . . . world events. . . ."

"Oh," grunted Thomas, only slightly mollified. "Well, that sounds
like the Diplomatic Corps . . . or politics perhaps. . . ."

"Something like that," Robert agreed.

"Not that those professions have been very successful in stopping
this war that's had so great an impact on you . . . as well it should. God
knows it's had a great impact on us all."

"I'm sure they tried, Grandpapa," Robert persisted,

Thomas nodded gloomily. "Politics can be a shabby business,
Robert. So can diplomacy . . . all compromise, you see, of different
interests . . . trading . . . like merchants, really . . ."

"I don't think it's quite the same, is it?" said the boy. He had
recovered his courage now after the awesome moment that followed
his grandfather's reaction of insulted rage.

Thomas moved from the window and began to pace the room,
still swinging his "Albert," head bowed, deep in anxious thought. "You
know, Robert," he said, "your mother and I once had a quarrel about
this very situation. She challenged me, with those green eyes of hers
flashing with anger. . . . What, she demanded, would happen if you
didn't want to assume your place in the destiny of the family? I answered that it'd be your duty. . . ." He paused, still pacing. "I'm not
sure now that my argument was sound. . . . I'm not sure that anyone,
whoever he is, has the right to dictate to a man what he should do with
his life. . . . So perhaps, regardless of your inheritance, you must just
do the best you can with yours, deeply painful though I find it that
you don't wish to pursue the task that I began. . . ."

He sighed and looked at his watch, then put his arm round Robert's shoulder. "You'd better be getting on. . . . You're meeting your
mother and father for lunch, aren't you?"

Robert nodded, and managed a small smile. "Thank you for being
so understanding, Grandpapa," he said.

"I haven't been understanding, Robert. I don't understand . . . I
think you're quite mad. . . . But we live in mad times, so I haven't
given up hope." His features relaxed. "Off you go," he said.

When Robert had left, Thomas moved to his desk and leaned back
heavily in his chair, a desolate loneliness slowly encompassing him like
a black cloud. He found himself wondering if he had been too soft

with the boy, too undemanding. He had handled him like a horse that
had been exposed to a bad experience. No use whipping an upset horse.
And God knew, seeing James must have been devastating for him. . . .
Poor James, poor broken James. . . . How ironic, cruelly ironic, if James,
the product of that one evening with David's wife, should be the actual
cause of Robert's abandoning his destiny. . . . That really would be the
business of those malicious, grinning Fates of his. . . . But Robert
would change his mind, must change his mind. . . . Kingstons without a
Kingston? . . . He sighed and shook his head, overtaken suddenly by a
great weariness. He reached for the telephone and spoke to May: "I'm
rather tired, my dear. . . . I think I'll come home for lunch."

· 3 ·

That evening, no one could say that the Grand Restaurant was inaptly
named. The great chandeliers that hung from the ceiling were sparkling from recent cleaning. The dining tables were laid out in the
shape of an E, the decoration of flowers and silver pieces laid out in
exquisite design, the glass and cutlery glistening to a high shine. The
Kingstons orchestra played quietly from a small dais.

When Thomas had returned home at lunchtime, looking haggard
after his distressing scene with Robert, May had been concerned that
he might not be well enough to bear the strain of the evening, but he
had slept all afternoon, and when he had awoken he seemed to have
recovered his spirits. She had agreed that Thomas had responded to his
grandson in exactly the way he should have. The emotional impact on
so young a boy must have been immense. Even Charles, who had called
to see her after his visit to Camberwell, had been so deeply shocked
that he had decided not to return to work that day. As for Lillian,
there was clearly no question of her visiting the hospital just yet, and
everyone had assumed that she would not be attending the reception
that night. But despite James's tragic condition, he was not dead, and
although he had the deepest sympathies of everyone of both families, it
was not a case of mourning. At teatime, Lillian—displaying her capac-
ity for emotional recovery—had astonished her family by stating her
intention of celebrating Thomas' honor with him and declared that she
was sure that James would wish her to do so.

Robert had spent most of the afternoon walking in Hyde Park.
He was sorely troubled and confused, his resolution eroded. He would
have preferred his grandfather to have displayed outrage, demanded he

do his duty, ordered him from the room or at least threatened to disinherit him. At the same time, the reasons behind his decision not to go into the store still seemed sound.

He had returned home, his emotions still turbulent, to find a sympathetic but determined Dora sitting in her drawing room beside her sterling silver teapot. He was not quite sure, he had said, whether or not he would be attending the dinner that night. "*You* may not be," she had declared, "but I am. . . . It's an unhappy business, but you must now face the fact of it. . . . This evening's an extremely important occasion in the life of both your father and your grandfather. . . . So you'll be there, and you'll look as though you're proud to be there, as well you should. . . . Now, if I were you, I'd have a cup of tea. . . ."

All the family—and also the Rawlingses—were already waiting in the Grand Restaurant when Thomas and May arrived. It had been agreed that they should be there half an hour before the main reception started so that they could share a private toast before all the buyers and managers joined them. As they entered, Ramsay instinctively started clapping, which was immediately taken up by all the others.

"Thank you," said Thomas, beaming, adding, "What a lot of us there are, aren't there?"

There were twenty-five in fact, including the three Rawlingses, ten from Quainton—since, of course, Agnes and Letty still lived with Harry and Claire and their five children on the old farm—six from Montpelier Square and four of the Sidney Baines family, Ellen's grandchildren being too young to attend. Kate, Ramsay's youngest, was only fourteen, but two of Harry's were near her age.

Thomas moved straight over to Lillian and kissed her. "Thank you for coming," he said, and then all the others took turns to greet him. The champagne corks popped, the toast was drunk and he looked round at them—at Dora, now almost forty, wearing a shoulder-revealing dress of the inevitable dark green velvet, décolleté at both front and back; at Claire, who never looked anything off a horse; at his sister Mary and Lillian in simple black; at his sons and grandsons and Charles, who seemed almost a son, in their white ties and tails; at his granddaughters—the ones from Montpelier Square dressed to the fashion, as would be expected of Dora's children, the ones from Quainton looking as though their mother had made their gowns, which was also to be expected; and finally at May in a beautiful dress of dark brown silk, also décolleté like Dora's, but with the lace of the neckline extended to short sleeves that gave a flimsy covering to the upper arms of which elder women were so conscious. That night she looked magnificent, and he felt a great pride. As he watched her, she was actually congratulating the restaurant manager with that special grace of hers on the appearance of the room, but she sensed his eyes on her and turned and smiled.

Then the others started arriving, and Thomas and May took up their station near the entrance to greet their guests as they were announced. Some of the retired came too—including old Albert Brown, much younger, of course, than Thomas, but forced out to pasture by ill health; and even Emily, very frail now at eighty-five, but determined enough.

As the room filled, and the waitresses moved through the congestion with champagne, Charles approached Ramsay. "You know your father's bet with Mr. Selfridge . . . that we'd be over half your profits by 1915?"

"I was wondering when he'd be reporting," said Ramsay. "You're late this year."

"Staff shortage at the auditors'. . . . However, I know the figures now. They're being announced tomorrow. . . . Mr. Selfridge has given me permission to inform your father tonight."

"Who's won?" asked Ramsay. He suspected it was close since the previous year, Selfridges had attained £131,000 against Kingstons' £280,000. This year Kingstons had topped £300,000, which meant that Selfridges would have to go over the 150 mark. "Have we held our position?"

Charles grinned. "You can jolly well wait and hear like everyone else."

"We must have won. You wouldn't want to annnounce anything tonight that didn't please him. . . . How much by . . . ten . . . twenty? . . ."

"You're getting warm," Charles said. "Strangely, I'm glad. . . . Not very loyal to Mr. Selfridge, is it?"

"Most of us have conflicts among our loyalties. That one's yours—and that's only because you're so damned stubborn. . . ."

"Don't you forget that the bet's not over," Charles reminded him. "The important date is 1920 . . . for the silver model. . . . That gives us five whole years."

Ramsay shook his head at his friend with sorrowful affection. "We'll beat you then. . . . There's no store in the world like this one. There never will be. . . ."

The restaurant manager called for silence, banging on one of the tables with a silver hammer, to announce that dinner was served, and the evening proceeded.

They all assembled at their allotted places—all one hundred eighty of them—with May on Thomas' right and Dora on his left. After the meal, Sidney stood up and, for the second time that day, formally congratulated Thomas, on behalf of them all, and gave his best wishes to Ramsay on his new appointment as Managing Director. Then he announced the gift to Thomas from the buyers and managers of a bust of himself—which was no surprise to him, of course, since he had sat for it in the sculptor's studio; but it was a touching moment when the miniature curtains that had so far concealed it in its central position on the far wall were drawn back to reveal his head and shoulders, cast for posterity in bronze.

"It only remains," Sidney declared, "for me to ask you all to be upstanding and join me in drinking the health of our chairman, our founder, who has been our Managing Director for so long. . . . Ladies and gentlemen, I give you Sir Thomas Kingston, Baronet!"

Thomas, of course, stayed seated as all the others in the room stood up, with a scraping of chairs, and drank the toast. Then, when they had sat down again, he got very slowly to his feet.

"Ladies and gentlemen," he said, "I thank you for your good wishes and for your gift, which, naturally, has made me very proud. . . . It's a long time . . . nearly fifty years, in fact . . . since I first entered the shop from which this store has grown—to be joined, as you may know, by the young lady who has been my staunch companion and colleague in arms ever since. . . ." He paused for the clapping and smiled at May. "Since then," he went on, "we've seen many changes in the world, changes that have caused great stores like our own to emerge and thrive, but there has been no change that has approached what we are at present undergoing—the most terrible war in history, a war that has no doubt claimed victims from most of your families and, so I have learned today, has claimed one from mine—at least from a family that I regard as mine. . . .

"When it ends, this holocaust in which we are enmeshed, the world will be a very different place to the one we've known, to the world of the past in which I've had the task and pleasure of directing our business. . . . The future will be, must be, drastically different . . . but I will say this to my son—and to his son, if he chooses and shows himself fit to follow him, as I hope eventually he will: Kingstons must, of course, adapt to the new conditions, as it always has, but it is not by chance that it has won its unrivaled reputation. This, I'm convinced, has resulted directly from a definite policy, from certain principles, and from what I can only call a chemistry—a chemistry that even I, who mixed the early ingredients, do not entirely understand. Change that, I say to my son—not, I hasten to add, that he has ever suggested it—and you will do so at your peril, or at least, the peril of our store. . . ."

Thomas broke off again, conscious of the moments of total silence in that crowded room. "Already," he continued, "Kingstons has played a role of importance in the world. Our income is greater than that of several of our colonies and even of some small sovereign states. It is, therefore, with care that I choose my next words, ladies and gentlemen. . . ." He looked at Robert, who, knowing that his grandfather was speaking directly to him, kept his eyes fixed on the plate in front of him.

". . . The point I wish to make is that if the company continues to grow at its present rate, it will become very big . . . and as a direct consequence, the power exercised by its head and the duties arising from that power will become great indeed. . . . So both my son and, particularly, my grandson—for if it falls on his shoulders the burden will be extremely heavy—should ponder that fact well and consider its repercussions and obligations. . . ."

As Thomas paused, Robert steeled himself to face him. To his surprise, Thomas' expression was not marked by challenge or accusation. In fact, it softened as he saw Robert's response, and he almost smiled. Then he turned back to address the audience at large. "In any event, of course, that power will depend on the success of Kingstons . . . and that success will depend on all of you sitting here this evening. . . . I ask you, therefore, with all my heart to give my son, and his son, all the support that you have given me."

A wry smile came to his face. "The evening is young," he said, "and the orchestra will play for you to dance. . . . As for me, well I think it's time that I conceded my position as executive head of this company and retired to grass, like a horse that has won a few good races but can no longer maintain the speed. So Lady Kingston and I will leave you in Mr. Ramsay's capable hands. . . . Ladies and gentlemen, I thank you all."

As the burst of clapping broke out, May stood up beside him. The applause swelled, developed into cheering. They bowed in acknowledgment, then turned and walked together slowly toward the entrance. The restaurant manager held open one of the double doors as they approached, and Thomas nodded to him in appreciation. It had closed behind them by the time they heard the singing—one hundred and eighty voices raised in the rousing words "For he's a jolly good fellow . . . For he's a jolly good fellow . . . For he's a jolly good fel-low . . . And so say all of us . . . And so say all . . ." But they could hear no more because the lift was taking them down to the ground floor.

They passed through the store, only barely lit, with the counters covered by dust sheets, and out through the main entrance to the Daimler, which was waiting for them in the darkness—a darkness due partly to a light evening mist but mainly to the fact that, because of the Zeppelins, there were no lights on in the store windows or the street lamps.

Neither had spoken on their way down from the restaurant. They each knew what the other was feeling. Now as they sat in the back seat, Thomas took May's hand.

The car moved off from the dim outline of the store and traveled slowly up a Sloane Street that was still and obscured.

"Know what I was thinking, May? . . ." he said at last. "All those years ago . . . if I'd refused to employ you . . . what'd the situation have been tonight? . . ."

She did not reply at once. "Not much different," she said after a moment. "A different son, I suppose—and grandson . . ."

"You believe you've had no effect on the course of my life? . . ."

"I've given you comfort sometimes, I hope, and perhaps a little support when your resolve was faltering. . . . But you'd still have built your store. . . ."

Again there was a moment of silence. "I wonder . . ." he said.